Silver Destiny: From Chaos Begotten

Noel Priester

Copyright © 2023

All Rights Reserved

Table of Contents

Dedication i
Acknowledgements iii
About the Author v
Prologue vii
Shadows and Rainbows 1
Of War 7
Chaos 17
Heretical Zealotry 24
Tattooed Canvas 25
Anchor Hill 26
Before Bagmot 43
Eve of Bagmot 51
Dawn of Bagmot 60
Night of Bagmot 64
Continent Silver and the Machinations of Bounty Hunter 12 66
The Search for Immortality 74
Schemes Coming to Fruition 80
    Argon the Slayer 80
The Chronicles of Bounty Hunter 13 121
    The Birth of Bounty Hunter 13 121
    One Year Later 122
The Death of the Guardian: Run to Dust Child. 133
    Said Razor—Fang to the Dirt, Rise Up 135
    The Laughing Bull 136
    The Sheriff of the Pyramids 139
    The Mountain of Witch Fire 143
    The Diavonbry Rebellion 145
    Pyramids of Chombra 149
The Silveran Civil War 157
Silveran Civil War part 2 169
Paradox Fate 174
The Magus War 181
Enter the Red Rebellion and the Knight of Argent 190
The Gold Warrior and His Fate 197
The Hunter 200

Title	Page
In The Forest Of Lizard, Treachery Is Afoot	204
Raid on Grey: Who Is Slayerhammer	206
Raid on Black: Purple Fire of the Blackheart	209
The Demon vs. the Phantom	212
The Gold Warrior and His Fate	224
The Hunter	227
In The Forest Of Lizard, Treachery Is a Foot	231
Raid on Grey: Who Is Slayer Hammer?	233
Raid on Black: Purple Fire of the Blackheart	236
The Demon vs the Phantom	239
What Is a Hero	243
The Hunters	269
The Downfall of the Psycheos	293
Thirteen days ago, Planet Black	293
Twelve days ago, Planet Lizard	294
Twelve days ago, Stinalta	294
Eleven Days Ago, Planet Gold	295
Six days ago, Planet Metallic	297
One day ago	299
The Jump	308
Silver Destiny: The Invasions	371
The Invasion of Silver by Noamaiza	371
Succession	372
Under the Apple Tree	372
Scars That Remain	374
The March through Harsh Terrain	376
Escape to the Wasteland	379
Wandering Under the Moonlight	381
Lord Badger of the Inbetween	385
Winter	397
Hunters Journey	431
Invasion of Continent Silver by Continent Norvcryog	455
Age of the Hunt	455
The Forest's Revenge	459
The Horned Crowned King	466
Death of the Waster and the Warriors Grave	474

- At The Ruins a Wolf's Shattered Dream 478

Gods and Their Politics Part 1 481
- War, War Never changes 491

Rhapsody in Grey 501

Book of the Forgotten 504

Eden Tower 508

Death of Shogun Yu 512

Silver Destiny: Hunter Clan 524
- Legendary Hero: Sin Seeker Hunter 524
- Death of The Demon King Oda 528
- Death of The Assassin 529
- Sin Seeker's Rage 531
- Assault On Orkea 532
- Battle of Succession 534
- War In Central Komodo 535
- Introducing the Bear of Hizen 537
- The Folly of the Way of Peace 538
- The Usurper Falls 539
- The Hunters Blood 544
- Swordsmen in the Plains 545
- Smoke On the Water and Fire Burns the Horizon 551
- Dragon vs Wolf 559
- The Battle of the Big Bridge 563
- The Battle Without Justice 569
- Sanctuary of the Two Geniuses 571

Invasion of Silver by the Equus 575
- Reiga and The Dream Factory 597

Legend of Nightmare Hunter 605
- One Thousand Years Ago 613
- Seven Hundred Years Ago 619
- Current Day 619

The Hunter's Prize 623
- Gods and Politics Part 2 636

Silver Destiny Finale 657
- The Future of Bounty Hunter 13 Part 1 657
- Sucryog 662

- Equus Islands 668
- Komodo 673
- The Junk Heap 686
- Misogoke 692

The Hunter Clan is Reborn 696

The Arclands 737
- Noamaiza 740
- Olayazca 741
- Organos 743
- Diavonbre 745
- Irescotwel 749
- Norvcryog 750
- The Upper Depths 752
- Dragons Den Island 756

Silver Destiny 757
- Carzoka 762

Gods and Politics part 3 765

Dedication

Dedicated to my parents. Without you nurturing my creativity, this book may never have been written.

Acknowledgements

I give a hearty thank you to my mom and a regular thank you to my dad. I also thank all those that helped this book come to fruition. Lastly, I want to thank my friends for inspiring me with their friendship.

About the Author

Noel was adopted into a middle-class pastor and his wife's home. As a son of a pastor, he learned about religion. Growing up, he was always an imaginative boy. In high school, he wrote his first story. He found a creative outlet for his imagination. He was deeply interested in the mythology and folklore of other cultures. That melting pot allowed him to evolve his ideas.

Prologue

If a giant space Platypus exists in the milk of the space cow Bessy, who lays an egg that hatches the universe. There are openings for madness. However, there is one universally known rule; don't let the mouse that smashes on your shoulder, for he will only spout hate, and don't let the psycho fish cut through your thoughts too fast or you'll become like the mad monk Salim-Al-Jafar who thought the earth was trying to consume him because his feet would sink in the sand.

Well, afterall, the earth was trying to consume him.

-Attributed to Pliny the Mad BH 1320-1510

Shadows and Rainbows

"There once was as never before because if there wasn't, it wouldn't have been told there was a bird. The bird was forever alone. As the bird grew, a cow appeared. You see the white streak across the night sky?"

"Yes."

"That is the milk from her udders. Now amongst the milk swam a platypus. She laid an egg, which became the centre of this galaxy. The Eternals came next. They are the embodiments of life. And finally, from the writer, first of the Eternals, came the Psycho Fish.

"The Psycho Fish, Master?"

"How to describe the chaos of the primordial kind? Hmm, well, you know that violent fish you so enjoy. Psycho Fish is kind of like that. He is a betta fish like yours, but instead of two fins, he has one fin and a chainsaw. That is the Psycho Fish."

"Master Sidrodc, how were we created?"

"Well, my young apprentice, we were written. You see, there is an ancient being known as the writer. He wrote into existence his two siblings, Damsel Death and Azrael the Alpha. Azrael created the Triumvirate of Desire, Euphora, and Depression. His Sister created the Judge of Soul and the Judge of Flesh. Both were required for our creation. One takes the souls from the protector and deems them worthy or unworthy. While the other judges the body for the soul."

"Why is that?"

"Well, our bodies are just like armour without a form. The soul gives form and intelligence. Now, flip a coin to decide whether I continue this lesson or have you rest for tomorrow."

"Tails!"

"Heads, lady luck is with me today. It's time for bed." "Aww, but Master Sidrodc!"

"No buts. We have a long day of learning tomorrow. Good night, Thyne."

***

The night swam with many noises. There were howls from the Shadow Wolves and roars from the Moon Catz. There were screeches and squawks from any number of birds. The music of the universe enveloped him as Thyne of House Gragor floated, listening to these sounds, waiting for his new apprentice. His memory always returns to his master. The old man had disappeared a century ago.

Thyne was a Silveran. He had two large horns jutting from his temples. He had thick spikes on his upper arms with a smaller set below them. His legs were surrounded by numerous spikes that not only could be used for battle but the more elegant they were, the more great ways he had to attract mates or dance for dominance.

Thyne waited and then saw a pale elf walking towards him. He knew all the elven species, from the Shadow Elves under the mountains to the Sun Elves on top of the mountains. This fellow was neither Sylvanis, Shadow, or Sun. He finally sat and walked over to the elf. He walked around, examining this stranger from all sides. The boy had smooth ragged hair that was blue-black. It was the eyes of the boy that intrigued Thyne. The eyes were a pure orange and sent a shiver down Thyne's spine when he looked into them.

The stranger spoke, "Are you Thyne of House Gragor?"

Thyne nodded and motioned inside. "Welcome to my home. Are you Fringe of the walkers?"

"I am. My people travelled a long way over the rainbow bridge and through the void to get here. I am here to learn so that I may eventually help my people integrate into society."

"Well, I can certainly help you there. What's in the box?"

"My personal belongings. Ancient stones that remind me of my destroyed world."

"Rather morbid thing to carry around. Why weigh yourself down with the past."

"You wouldn't understand."

"Well, you'll have to trust me eventually. I am your teacher."

"Eventually…"

***

Thyne was looking forward to this day. Twenty years had passed since he had taken on Fringe as his apprentice. He was to be in combat for a bride. He floated to the arena. He looked over his opponents. Then he looked over his choices. He saw a pale elf woman who was around Fringe's age cowering in fear. He smiled at her.

The combat began. He advanced on his opponent and knocked leg spikes with him. Combat was a strong word for what was going on; dancing would better describe the scene. Thyne's hip bumped at his younger opponent, a boy barely half his age, knocking him to the ground due to his weight. He then spun like a top into the next, a stronger-looking fellow with red skin. The spin caught the man off guard and sent him to the ground as well. The crowd roared in appreciation. Points were based on style and strength. The more opponents knocked to the ground, the better the score. The tougher the opponent, the more points awarded. This was especially true when trying to take over as Patron or Czar of the Silverans.

He walked over to the young Pale Elf and hoisted her onto his back as he knocked six more to the ground with a swift thrust to the left, forward, back, around, and right. That was all for him and he walked away with the girl. He clotheslined his final opponent, who tried to attack while his back was turned. He floated out of the stadium and home, all while the girl whimpered pitifully in his arms. He got home and set her on one of his spare beds. He looked her over and treated some of her injuries. He then smiled as she got up and cowered in the corner. "Welcome home, young one. What is your name?"

"I… I… I am Tannid of the Walkers, sir. Or sh… should I call you husband?"

"You are too young for this old man. I chose you to save you from an unscrupulous fellow. Consider yourself my daughter. Welcome to House of Gragor!"

He walked over to a keg and filled a glass with an amber liquid that smelled of smoke. She fled and bumped into Fringe. She gasped in shock.

Fringe knelt and looked into her eyes, smiled and said, "Well, hello, cutie. Who are you?"

Tannid blushed, saying, "I am Tannid of the Walkers, sir and you?"

"Fringe. I probably led your parents over the rainbow bridge and through the Void."

"As in the Fringe!"

"Is there any other?"

***

Thyne sat listening to his friend Hunter Hawthorn yarn on about his woefully inadequate life. He was eyeing Fringe and Tannid as they schemed. It was downright worrisome, especially since he could feel them siphoning power into something at night.

"Pardon me, Hunter."

Hunter stopped mid-sentence as Thyne turned to look at Fringe, saying, "What are you two plotting over there? Come say hi to my old friend."

Fringe looked up, startled. "No, can't do pops. We are busy."

Thyne sighed and rolled his eyes. "So you were saying something about The Onyx Tower?"

"That's enough about that. Who's the new girl?"

"I adopted her twenty years ago. Her name's Tannid and my apprentice has been flirting with her. Now you were telling me about your son, Bonty, I believe."

"Ah, yes. Well, he blew up yesterday."

"Eh? What!"

"Yep, his pent-up psychic energy finally got released. Oh, don't worry, he's fine. However, our clan will never be the same again."

"Why?"

"Well, when he exploded, he also evolved. The energy changed him. He is almost eight feet tall now. His legs are very muscular and there are no spikes surrounding them."

"Where would God Silver put those spikes?"

"On his shoulders, elbows, and knees."

"Weird. Do you have any idea why Bonty was chosen to evolve?"

"None what-so-ever. I even went to the temple today and God Silver was mum about the whole ordeal. So I just have to trust there's a plan."

"If there's a plan..."

Both continued drinking and talking. Meanwhile, Fringe led Tannid to his lab. She picked up an orange stone and placed it on the table. The two began to polish it until it was rounded and smooth.

Thyne was sitting, meditating on the world. He had a strange feeling in the gut of his stomach that today was going to end badly.

"Now then, are you two practising what I taught you? Remember, anti-psychic energy is very volatile and reacts explosively with Dark Psychic, Mystic Psychic, and Regular Psychic energy. Are you even listening?"

Fringe was chatting with Thyne's adopted daughter, Tannid. He had grown to like her since she was a pale elf like him. She smiled and the two walked towards his room. Thyne grimaced. It had been sixty years since he began training the boy.

"Guess not. Was I this difficult to train? Oh great, I am talking to myself. The first sign of going mad[1], Thyne."

He had begun noticing this year that the boy was emitting a dark aura. He went back to focusing on his memories of the world and his psychic experiments. He was attempting to extend his life, but it was proving elusive.

Fringe and Tannid were looking at a group of twenty crystalline gems. Each gem was being imbued with a specific energy. Some represented the ten elements of fire, water, stone, plant, metal, ice, tornado, sandstorm, poison, and healing. These had already been imbued.

Two of them were opposites of each other, being holy and shadow, respectively. And eight held the energy to grant strange abilities. These had been stones that came with Fringe across the void. The last two needed imbuing. They both had to focus since shadow and holy were opposites.

As the two channeled psychic energy into these stones via the rune engraving on each one, an unforeseen side effect happened. Fringe saw into the future. He saw the Silveran species as four to six-armed beings looking more demonic than natural. He saw war and plague. That was when the energy siphoning into the shadow gem erupted. He had been using the Dark Psychic energy that Thyne taught him to use to imbue the gem. This anti-psychic energy was volatile to Regular Psychic energy and that caused an eruption in the PsyQi. He and Tannid were thrown back and both blacked out. The gems were flung into the time gash. They had been tainted by shadow.

Thyne felt the eruption and the wave made him lose focus. He felt excruciating pain and then nothing.

Fringe woke up to see an old man staring at him.

"You fool of a boy! You damaged the PsyQi. You destroyed my forest! You even caused an event that was never supposed to happen."

"Who are you, old man?"

"Who am I? I am God Silver. I am the third Silver and you, fool of a child, released my predecessor's predecessor. For your's and Tannid's atrocity, I hereby curse you with the mark of the dragon. Your souls are never welcome in the havens. I do applaud you, however. You accomplished a powerful thing even if it cost your master's life. His body was incinerated on

---

[1] Actually the first and last sign of going mad is when you see the Mad God Shegor. He appears with his table and tea set.

impact. Now go before I change my mind and erase you from existence."

Fringe lifted Tannid in his arms and walked off. Silver stood there staring at the crater in the centre of his once pristine forest, then vanished in smoke. A mismatched chimera popped into existence right where Silver had been standing. "Well, I did my duty to Silver since he could not make it by disguising myself as him. Now, what happened to my young apprentice Thyne?"

He walked over to a spot and lifted a leather book. He grimaced at the black book. "Well, old friend, it looks like you achieved immortality after all."

He then placed the book in his satchel and walked away, specifically towards the home of Bonty Hanter.

Fringe was near a cave system. He looked around and closed his eyes and smiled quietly.

"I may have lost my work, but I have eternity to find the gems again."

He opened his eyes and they had changed color from orange to swirling purple even his hair had changed to more smoke black. Tannid woke with a start. She looked at Fringe and whimpered.

She stood and backed away from him. "I refuse to join you in your search. We killed my father and I will never be able to see him again. Stay away."

She ran diving through a tear in time and it closed behind her. Fringe smirked and walked into the cave. He sat down and began meditation.

Of War

Bonty Hanter III placed the memory scroll back into its case. He shook his head slightly. This strange memory was more like something the gods would bestow their followers, but it was an artefact. Just not the artefact his people were looking for. They wanted ancient weapons, not mem-scrolls.

"The Red Elves are coming! Man your stations!"

Bonty looked up at the young scout and smiled. "No! Everyone hide and I will lure them into a false sense of security. Who leads them?"

"The queen of the Solar throne, sir!"

"Ah, the ambition of the young. When I give the signal, wipe them out."

The soldiers obeyed and retreated to the cave entrances. Bonty was sitting by himself as a legion of Red Elves surrounded him. Their queen was brought in and she looked at him disdainfully.

"You all alone, old man? We scared your soldiers into retreat. Hah, the Anubi were wrong your people are cowards."

Bonty stood slowly and smiled a dangerous grin. Before she could react, she was out cold on the ground from his haymaker. Her troops opened fire with their psychic projectiles. When the smoke cleared, Bonty stood unscathed with over three-fourths of the legion in smouldering heaps.

"Last chance to surrender."

The rest fled as Bonty sat back down, binding the queen in chains. His second in command, Warlord Sypher Thorne, walked out of the caves in awe.

"By the gods Bonty! You didn't even flinch."

Bonty looked at the crimson-haired youth. "Well, your lordship, I pride myself in my abilities. The fools did not even think that I may have a psychic barrier around myself. So they killed each other. But spread the word that it was more deadly than that. If we can scare the allies of the Anubi into submission, they will be forced to surrender."

"You are conniving, General. The king will most certainly be pleased with you."

"Please don't flatter me anymore. I would rather not be remembered as a mass murderer."

The two walked into the cave to collect their weapons, passing a statue of an elf deep in meditation. As they passed, the elf opened his eye, revealing a swirling purple abyss. The elf cracked a smile and closed his eye again. It wasn't the time yet.

That night Bonty stood in the centre of City Stříbro listening to Czar Artur Aurel exaggerate his accomplishment.

"We bestow the title of Armádní generál upon Bonty Hanter III for his act of subduing the Queen of the Solar throne. All accounts say that Bonty single-handedly fought off ninety-nine of the Sun Elves even while his men were trapped by the trickery of the red devils. When he was disarmed by a rather brutish Red Elf, he used his fists to force them back. Killing ninety more with his bare hands."

"Please, my Czar, that is enough. We don't want my ego to get too big. There are still legions of enemies. Let us leave the words for now and start the banquet."

"Yes, yes... What will you do with their queen? I say you should execute her."

"No, no, I will enslave her, for that will demoralize the elves. If we kill her, she becomes a martyr that they can rally behind. However, if she is a broken husk of her former self, that will force the elves to either flee or surrender. The more allies of the Anubi we can subdue, the more we weaken their force. The weaker they are, the stronger we are."

"Hear that, folks. Not only is he a great warrior, but he is also a deadly tactician, so tonight, we feast in honour of a great warrior."

***

"A hundred years have passed, my Czar. The Anubi have lost their strongest ally, but they are stubborn. Some, however, have seen that this war is going nowhere and have begun to build a continent. They're saying let the Silverans destroy this land with their war. For the land of the Anubi will be a land we can form ourselves. War only begets more war, for if you fight one battle, there is always another around the corner."

The Czar sighed, "Thank you for the update Zmatek. Now, my son, why are you here?"

The young prince stood in front of his father. He was a lad of one hundred. "Why do we fight this war, Father?"

The king was startled at this question, especially since it came from his son. "My boy, we fight to rid the land of Chaos. The Anubi worship Chaos gods!"

"But is not God Silver a Chaos god?"

"Who told you that?"

"Duke Bounty Hunter III, Father."

The adviser to the king was a dark and shady man. He always wore a dark robe with skulls of various animals on his belt and as shoulder pads. He decided to answer for the king since the king was soft, just like the Duke he so trusted.

"My young lord, it's true that we, too, worship a Chaos god. However, the Anubi are the enemy. We require fortifications. The Anubi are content to withhold land we require to survive. It is a war for survival."

"I see Zmatek. I still do not understand. Why fight them? The history books say we lived side by side with them for years. Why choose now?"

"Silence, child!" They turned to see Bounty Hunter III standing there with the former queen chained naked to his waist. "Some people may think you want to rise against your father."

"But General I…"

"No, no! We cannot risk showing a weakened front. Zlutohnedy, your father has tried to unite us against a common enemy. If it weren't for him, we would still be tribes warring against each other. The decision has been made. We must follow through on it."

"I... understand, General."

***

The world was falling apart, the Red Elves had fled. This war was going on its four hundredth year. The Anubi were being pushed back. Commander Ryna Colorwheel lay on the ground looking up at the pale sky. It was the middle of the warm season and the clouds were so dark that it looked like the heavens were angry. She shivered at the thought. She was leading a small group of guerrilla warriors. They were near the dark crater, hiding and waiting for the Silveran army led by Bounty Hunter III. She was odd for an Anubi. Her mane was multi-hued like the light through a prism. She had a twin sister named Prisma, who also had the same multi-hued mane. Both were Tuar commanders. She shifted uncomfortably as if the ground was too sharp for her.

Next to her was a huge muscular man who was a tank in battle and also one of the only warchiefs in this group. He was also very concerned. "Commander Colorwheel, why hide? Intelligence states that the grand commander only has two legions under his flag."

"I trust what the Bos says, but we cannot be too careful. The man known as Bounty Hunter III is devious. We cannot risk a full-on confrontation. The Anubi are down to ninety legions since most of our kind chose exile after the first hundred years. Do you understand Goldoak Onyxhide?"

"Yes, I suppose I do. After all, I am the only Bisonum in your ranks."

"Oh don't look so down, Goldy."

The two turned to see a lithe female standing there. She was the head of the Bos rangers and was herself a Bos. She had grey skin and bright gold eyes. Next to her stood an imposing elf with black armour and a helmet in the shape of a horse's head. What skin was seen was mysteriously pink. He looked around.

"I thought there'd be more. You sure this is all Taigan?"

"I wouldn't lie to you, Pie. You scare me."

Taigan stood there when all of a sudden, her ear twitched. She bolted and came upon her rangers lying dead from crossbow bolts. She had heard the chink of bolts hitting flesh now she knew why. She looked around and heard, much to her horror, the Silveran army coming. The trees were not as impassable as the Anubi thought.

She ran back as fast as she could.

"Commander! Warchief! They're here! By the horns of Coldharbor, we are in trouble."

Commander Colorwheel pulled out a large energy battle ax. "Goldoak, get ready."

Goaldoak sighed and stood. He had no weapons, so he traced runes over his body that would allow him to absorb the damage dished out. The second in command was a black Tuar by the name of Sal. She was preparing her cannon as the Silverans came into the clearing. They opened fire at the Anubi. Then a whole legion of Silveran Rangers undid their camouflage and began decimating the Anubi. Colorwheel hit the ground, bleeding profusely from twelve wounds. Her eyes were fuzzy, but what she saw did not please her. Her right arm was six feet away from the rest of her body. She saw her Tuarian second in command hit the ground with burns all over her body. She felt one of the Bos fall on her back, then nothing. She vaguely felt herself being lifted up and wondered if that was what it felt like to die.

Goaldoak charged into the Silveran army, scooping up Sal and then charging to the right and scooping up his commander and Taigan. The stupid Red elf had not bothered to help them at all. He ran until he got to a cave; he entered the cave and was promptly unconscious. Pie stood there with her helmet off. She had opened a portal to the future[2].

***

Bounty Hunter III stood near the dark crater. He looked around. He yanked on the chain of his slave, the former Solar Queen. She crawled forward.

"C… Can I help y... you m… m… master?"

Bounty looked down at her. She had grown into this position well. He smirked, saying, "Are you positive this is where Commander Colorwheel will camp?"

"Yes, my lord. She is skilled with tactical knowledge. She knows that your kind is large and would have trouble getting through the trees without making a lot of noise."

Bounty looked around and smiled, "Warlord Sypher Thorne. I need you and the rangers to camouflage yourselves and hide in plain sight or, at the very least, place tarps over yourselves."

The red and gray haired man nodded, "It will be done, General."

Bounty climbed on his steed, a gigantic equine with huge antlers, a pale white face, and claws on all four muscular legs. He lifted the former queen up and set her in front of him. She curled up in his arms and fell asleep whimpering. He rode off as Sypher began working.

Sypher quickly directed his troops to get into position. They did not have to wait long. He was lucky that Commander Colorwheel was lying right on top of him. It took all his will to stay still. She was heavy and was constantly grinding against him. He heard through his earpiece, "I see the Anubi rangers. Do I have permission to open fire, General?"

Sypher heard again, "Yes, Kalia Da'avi, annihilate them."

He saw one of the Bos go running off and then come back shouting. That was when the Anubi pulled out various weapons. He threw off his camouflage as his men opened fire. Colorwheel turned towards him and raised her energy ax as it embedded itself in the ground, he swung his sword and hacked off her arm. She cried out and fell. He saw one of the Anubi points a cannon at him and fires. The explosion threw him into one of the trees. He pulled himself off the tree and hit the ground, bleeding profusely. He passed out.

General Bounty Hunter III entered the clearing; he raised his shotgun and fired, blasting three

---

[2] This portal to the future is not metaphorical. Pie has the uncanny ability to jump through time. She transported them to a future time. Since they disappear in history. This time shock was the reason Goaldoak passed out.

Anubi to their god Coldharbour. He fired three more psychic rounds, killing what few Anubi remained. He saw one gigantic Anubi charge him. He quickly rolled out of the way. This was one of the Bisonum, and judging by the runes covering the brute's body, he was a Warchief. The Bisonum punched off one of Bonty's men's heads and then tore one of the women in two. The Bisonum rammed into another group that had surrounded his fallen comrades. He grabbed four of the Anubi and his leader and ran.

Bounty Hunter III heard behind him, "Well done, General. The Czar will be quite pleased with you."

Bounty responded icily, "Hello Zmatek."

"You don't sound happy to see me. I am hurt."

"Why are you here? I can handle things myself."

"Oh just checking up on your progress. The Czar is worried about you."

"Why, dare I ask?"

"You have not been giving updates like the other generals. We only fear you have failed."

"I cannot spare any soldier to bring orders to you. Since you have insisted, I take only one legion of warriors. The other generals get five to eight legions."

"You don't need the legions. You are a powerful man."

"That may be so, but it seems to me that you want me dead."

"No, no, dear General. Oh, and by the way, Warlord Netch requires half a legion of troops to replace the ones he lost in an ambush."

"Figures you would take them from me. Go ahead. But I keep Sypher. Do we have an understanding?"

"Certainly, General, I wouldn't dare try to take him from you."

One of the rangers came up and said, "Sir, we tracked the surviving Anubi to the cave of Doba."

Zmatek looked at Bounty, "You allowed some to escape?"

"More like their Warchief slammed into me trying to kill me."

Zmatek sneered, "So the high and mighty Bounty Hunter III is still prone to failure."

"Very well Zmatek you and I get to go hunting. The rest of you take care of the injured. We will take a break and rest up. Before moving on to pole květin krvavě červené."

Zmatek slunk behind Bounty and his pet. She was fidgeting with her chain. Zmatek smiled sinisterly. If he could get her to kill Bounty, his plans would be one step less. He saw the cave of Doba. He shrank back as a black armoured mare walked out; she held a sinewy sword and then vanished.

Bounty walked into the cave; there was an explosion and he came back out holding the former queen in one arm with blood on them both. "There you go, Zmatek. Problem solved. Or would you like to make sure I did the duty?"

"I trust your judgment."

"Good. Then let's go back to camp before we move on to the final battle."

"How do you know this is the end?"

"Well, there is only one Anubi stronghold left if the other generals are doing their duty. That would be the stronghold of Coldharbour. Their primary temple at pole květin krvavě červené."

"I see. How do you know that?"

"My dear Zmatek, you are not the only sneaky one in this army."

"Very well then on to pole květin krvavě červené."

It took only a day's march to the stronghold of Coldharbour; they would arrive just as the moons would rise. Bonty's men had more stamina than other troops since many of them had been hand selected by Bonty himself. They entered a massive field filled with deep crimson flowers. The air was filled with pollen and smelled of the deadly cinnamon.

Bonty spoke, "Men put your masks on. The air is full of pollen."

Bonty heard the sound of fighting and grimaced. He led his soldiers to the temple. The Anubi had already killed twelve generals and over three hundred thousand Silveran troops. Many looked bloated, meaning they had been poisoned. He saw the archers on the fortifications. He and his men crouched low. He motioned the archers to fire. The fortifications were on fire as more psychic energy projectiles slammed into the Anubi Archers. The light from the burning walls allowed the remaining Silverans to regroup.

Bonty stood and charged the Anubi ground forces. His sword voulge glistened in the moonlight. He whistled and his steed, Equinox, rammed into and through many of the ground Anubi. He did a swift jump and landed on Equinox's back. He rode up to the three generals remaining. "General Badger! General Hawthorne! General Wolf! Gods, it's good to see my cousins alive. Pull the troops back. The walls are en-runed. There is no easy way in."

General Hawthorne spoke, "And what, pray tell, will you do, General Hunter?"

"I will get in and open the gate for our troops to get in."

General Badger spoke, "Better hurry. It looks like they're getting over the confusion you caused, cousin."

Bonty dismounted and swiftly arrived at the gate. He looked around at the numerous runes and grimaced. He placed his hand on the gate and then injected a pale green liquid into his system since what he was about to do would hurt with the intensity of a billion suns. He focused his psychic energy into his hand and then punched the door. The explosion of psychic energy nearly blinded the other Silverans. They all put on their energy-dampener glasses.

General Wolf was the first to charge the now obliterated gate. As the Silveran army ran into the gate, they passed a smouldering General Hunter. The slaughter was quick and merciless. Only a few Anubi remained by the end of the night. The remaining were young and were loaded into prisoner transports. They would be exiled to the upper depths.

Bonty grimaced as a salve was slathered onto his charred body. He was then wrapped up in healing rune-encrusted gauze.

The nurse was thorough, "Tisk tisk, General. Why do you insist on being the one to get hurt instead of others?"

"Nurse Maberry, I have more psychic energy than others. It is better for me to get injured since I can heal faster. It also gives others a chance to show what they're capable of. Can you patch me through to Czar Žlutohnědý?"

"Yes, General."

As the screen in front of him glowed and shimmered, a face appeared. It was not Žlutohnědý's.

"Zmatek," Bonty growled. "Why are you on the Czar's private line?"

The icy tone that came from the screen chilled Bonty to his burnt, entombed bones.

"I am afraid the Czar will be unable to take calls from now on. His weakness only served to weaken you fools. I have disposed of him and his family. Welcome to the age of Chaos vile General. I am the all-powerful all-wise all..."

"Oh shut up, usurper."

"Oh, I wouldn't worry too much. You won't live very long now that your head is worth a billion silver sables."

Bonty saw the nurse pull out a knife and roll out of the way. She stabbed the bed and was thrown to the ground by the former Solar Queen. The girl grabbed at the nurse before a shot rang out. The nurse stood pushing the Red Elf off her, smiling. She grabbed the dagger from the bed and immediately fell without a head.

General Andrei Badger stood there, his blade bloody. Behind him stood General Storm Wolf and General Eindride Hawthorne. Next to them were two other generals that Bonty recognized as General Beatrix Hawthorn and General Sequoia Thorn, also his cousins.

Bonty lifted up the Red Elf as she rasped weakly. "Master... I... I... did good?"

Bonty smiled and closed her lifeless eyes, saying, "You did great, my dear."

Storm spoke "Theaym Sidroc uigde seul, theaym havens sunocme uigde seul."

The five of them conjured amber liquid in a glass and drank it. As her body burst into flames, Bonty stood and sighed, "I suppose you all are here to help me then."

A man came in with Sypher and a mysterious woman in green. The three greeted the others.

Sypher spoke, "Warlord Netch and General Silas Huntari Jr. have volunteered their skill to us along with May-Ling Shogun. Even though there are only ten of us, we should be able to stop this Lord Chaos."

Storm spoke, "How can we stop an immortal."

May-Ling Shogun grinned, "Well, we don't. He's not immortal. He's mortal like any of you. He was the first God Silver, but when he betrayed the gods, his immortality was removed and he was sent to the dark realm, or as it is better known, the havens for dead planets. He managed to break through over a million years ago. However, my clan pushed him back. Before he was trapped again, he had ten artefacts created; boots, gauntlets, pauldrons, greaves, a crown, a cuirass, an amulet, a sword, a shield, and a ring. If anyone found these artefacts, they would become the new Lord Chaos. In this case, it looks as if he's been hiding out as Zmatek."

Bonty nodded, saying, "So if we somehow imprisoned his body and removed the artefacts..."

Sequoia smiled, "We could hide the artefacts and make it so that Chaos is never reborn."

Silas spoke quietly, "How do we imprison him?"

Sypher Thorne spoke, "I may have learned a psionic spell, but it would require a sacrifice. Someone would need to kill the current body of Chaos. I will be the sacrifice since I am near dead anyway. We would need to assault soon. Once his soul inhabits my body, I will petrify myself. At which point you will take his armour off of me and hide it. Our souls will be imprisoned, but that is worth it to stop Chaos."

Bonty grimaced, "Very well, boy. We attack at dawn."

The others nodded and began plotting their assault. Dawn came quickly. As the ten of them neared Castle Silver, three heavily armoured royal guards stood in their way.

Storm Wolf spoke, "So this is either a badly planned last stand or a well-placed ambush." He sniffed the air with his snout. "I am confused. I only smell the three of them."

Bonty walked up to the three of them. "Are you hoping to die or are you here to help?"

The three bowed and one spoke, "General, Lauranna Księżyc. To my right is Darmok Halberd and Jalad Javelin. We wish to help. We failed in protecting Czar Žlutohnědý. Our failure must be rectified. Many guards have abandoned Zmatek; he still has a small group that seems to be his allies. We will escort you to the Cathedral of Chaos that he conjured."

Darmok and Jalad traded glances as the three led the way. Bonty noticed this and decided to keep an eye on them. The Cathedral of Chaos crackled with ancient magics. A bunch of disfigured armoured cloaked warriors were chanting in a dark tongue.

Darmok yelled, "Foul beasts taste the fury of God Silver!"

Both he and Jalad charged into the beings and began slaughtering them.

Chaos

"Professor, we all know what happens next."

"Oh, do tell, Ben."

"Well, Darmok and Jalad both died. Lord Wolf was poisoned by the chaos and vanished. May Ling Shogun is sent to the far reaches of the galaxy. The others are all expelled from the cathedral leaving only Bounty Hunter III and Sypher to face Zmatek."

"You are close there, Ben. However, you are off about the other being expelled from the cathedral. No, Zmatek was slain and absorbed by Sypher Thorne, who petrified himself, trapping both their souls in a stone statue. The others each took one artefact."

"Is it true, Professor, that the artefacts were stolen from the ten clans?"

"Yes, Harle, that is true. A pale elf by the name of Solan stole them and became Lord Chaos. He was slain by Bounty Hunter VII at the cost of Bounty Hunter III's life."

"Now we have Lord Chaos IV. Who will be the one to stop him?"

"That is only a rumour, Volk."

An explosion ripped through the school; fire was everywhere. Ben looked through the flames to see a large red-skinned Silveran with electric blue horns and silvery white hair. The demon sliced Professor's head off and walked through the flames killing anything that moved.

Ben struggled up and raised his hand. The fire became a funnel and then a twister as Ben absorbed it. He saw tripple when he was done and wobbled on his feet. The Red Silveran was gone. Ben felt arms support him and, through the blur, saw Harle and Volk. The two helped him to a bench, where he sat and fell into unconsciousness.

Ach, the chosen one, finally reveals himself. About time lad. I must say I did not expect a Silveran. Ach, you'll do. Bounty Hunter XI, it's time to wake up.

Ben opened his eyes to see Harle and Volk fending off chaos puppets. He grabbed a piece of rebar and smashed it into the puppets, seeing imaginary buttons as if he was playing one of his training games. After performing a spectacular combo, the rebar crumbled to dust. Ben stood there panting. Harle giggled and put away her pom poms that she had been cheering with.

***

It was dawn the seventh hour on the eighth day of the third week of the thirteenth month. Ben stood garbed in ritual armour. It had been ninety years since his school had been obliterated by a chaos demon. As the chime struck the time, several others also garbed in ritual armour entered the arena where he stood. Volk stood next to him, wearing ritual robes. Volk had taken the pacifist route but still needed to prove himself to the elders. His goal would be to avoid being attacked by the opponent. Ben saw Harle on the sideline with the other cheer squad girls. Their goal was to support their chosen warrior with dance and to generate excitement. Ben smiled. He had convinced Harle to support Volk. He did not need the support because he had full confidence in his fight.

All the warriors were garbed in ritual armour coloured by their clan crest. Ben's was just a vertical line with horns. The group lined up according to clan rank and each bowed to their opponent. The first round was always one on one. But the second round was an all-out brawl. The third round was an obstacle course. Ben looked at his opponent. The man was in green armour with the crest of Clan Halberd. He almost felt sorry for the man.

The Hunter clan had faded into obscurity after the death of his father, Bounty Hunter 10. This suited Ben just fine since it allowed him some anonymity. If he performed well, it would allow his clan to rise in rank, allowing some benefits. He would be allowed to buy servants and also get a wife. Of course, the opposite was true. If he somehow performed bad, his clan would suffer. They would be split up and doled out to the clans that performed well as servants. The points themselves were based on style and skill. The winning warriors were not declared until after round three, which was a triple bonus round. Everything was judged. Harle would be judged on her skill and style while cheering, Volk would be judged on his pacifistic nature, and Ben… well, he would be judged on his combat.

The chime rang again and each warrior began to combat their opponent. Volk was doing well, avoiding the attacks from a muscular fellow from Clan Hawthorne. The man was getting angrier and angrier, causing him to miss even easy openings. Volk seemed to be taunting him even though he really wasn't.

Ben smirked and blocked his opponent's sword. He then did a shield bash causing his opponent to lose balance. A leg sweeps and his opponent went down fully unconscious. The nurses came out and hauled the man away to the medical facility.

The announcer spoke, "Clan Halberd has been disqualified. Siam Halberd is no longer able to compete. Good luck to the rest of you. Round one is over. After a twenty-minute break, we move on to round two."

In the hydrating tent, the contestants sat. They were given a light meal followed by several cups of various liquids to keep them relaxed and hydrated. The big brawl was next. Everyone for themselves anything goes points here were rewarded for how many hits you took or gave. This would be the hardest for Volk since he was a pacifist and could not strike anyone. He would have to get very few hits to balance out the lack of hitting others. They all lined up again and the chime rang. There was a mad dash for any weapon to use against the others. As Ben suspected, the firearms were taken first. He picked up a large full-body shield and placed a rune on it to give it major defence against the small arms fire. A shield went up to protect the cheer squad and viewers from projectile attacks. He could also see the medical tent getting ready with healing tanks.

He charged into the fire and blocked the others from opening fire on Volk. When they reloaded, he took his opening and, in a flurry of strikes, incapacitated fifty per cent of them. The shield shattered on the head of the Hawthorne clan warrior. The muscular man hit the ground unconscious. He rolled and grabbed two swords that had not been picked up. He smiled a deadly smile that caused several to lose courage. The two blades lit aflame and he charged into the remaining warriors. Many fled and hid behind the various covered areas. Only one took his challenge, a man from Clan Hawthorn, his cousin Argento Hawthorn. Argento pointed his pike at Ben and the two clashed. During their clash, they each took out the rest of the warriors. The bell rang.

"Volk, Argento, Ben, Salim, and Chad move on to the final round. Nurses get these men to the healing tanks."

The judge in purple walked over to them. "Each of you gets this eyepiece so the crowd can see what you see. Remember, men, this is a triple bonus round. Good luck and may God Silver be with you."

The five were teleported into the gauntlet. Immediately something wrong happened; the people saw a tear in spacetime that sucked up Salim. They saw a muscular brown man, then fire then his eyepiece went to static.

As the four-remaining continued through the gauntlet, everything went foggy. The crowd watched as the camera on Chad suddenly landed on the ground and rolled only to focus on the body of Chad as it dropped without a head. They saw neon orange then the camera was cut so there would not be a bloody body to focus on.

Volk and Ben were walking through the fog when they came upon a wounded Argento. Argento was clutching his intestines, trying to hold them in. Volk grabbed Argento and then forfeited the match as he teleported out. Only Ben remained on edge. He saw neon orange and blocked a sword going for his head.

"Fuck! You again?"

The large red armoured man with blue horns and silver smoke-like hair smiled a fanged smile. His serpentine eyes blinked, adjusting to the light.

"You are Bounty Hunter 11, are you not?"

"I am. What are you?"

"I am your downfall, Scion of Chaos. I am one of his four horsemen. But you will be dead, so you cannot pass that information on."

Ben smiled and cracked his knuckles and neck. He took a fighting stance and energy blades shot from his gauntlets. "Bring it on, Chaos horseman."

The two clashed. Ben used his wind dragon style and the Scion of Chaos used brute strength and his flaming sword. Ben felt a searing pain as his arm went flying. He snarled and head-butted the Scion of Chaos. He collapsed and saw, through his blurry eyes, the Scion of Chaos raise his sword, ready to strike him down. *Pull yourself together, boy. I will not have my plans for you ruined.* Ben struggled to his feet. He howled in pain as a new metallic-looking arm instantly grew in place of the old one that had been sliced off. He became feral with rage and pain. Many vicious strikes later and the Scion of Chaos lay on the ground wheezing.

As Ben went in for the kill, the Scion of Chaos vanished. In place of the Scion of Chaos lay a female bound and gagged with blood seeping from her empty eye sockets. Ben stopped his swing an inch from her neck. He stood there as the fog lifted. He saw a med ship overhead and sent up a flare to alert them to his position. He removed her gag and lifted her up as she groaned in pain.

"Shh, It's okay. You are safe."

"Ben?"

"Yes, It is I."

"I foresaw this happening. The Scion of Chaos ripped out my eyes in retaliation for my prophesy."

"Alright, priestess, I will be handing you to some medical professionals. I will be right here next to you."

"You're a good boy Bounty Hunter 11. A little too good. Chaos will use that to his advantage. Never change and you will triumph."

The priestess went limp as the pain dampers took effect. The monitor showed her as stable. But she did have several injuries aside from her eyes being ripped out. She had several internal bruises and a broken jaw. Ben went to the judgement.

"The clan that did the worst was Clan Rivles. They will be passed among the different clans as servants. Say your farewells now. The second clan to be spread around is Clan Dal. Because Volk Dal quit in the final round, his clan will be passed around. Now Clan Hunter, a formerly unknown clan, made big waves. Ben Hunter, for your incredible display, has been granted a boon. What do you desire?"

"I could say many things, Lord Judge, but the only request I have is that you allow my clan to incorporate Clan Dal. And Clan Vental. Since Harle made a choice to cheer for Volk, I know her clan is to be passed around and removed as well."

"Very well, and how do you plan to oversee their lands?"

"My guards and siblings will take care of that."

As Volk and Harle were bound and passed over to Ben, Volk whispered, "Just how powerful is your clan if you have guards?"

"Very."

Many years passed and Ben Hunter was getting bored. Chaos had refused to show any signs of appearing and even the Chaos horseman was hiding. He looked at the small boy in front of him, who was Harle and Volk's son, Javelin.

"Now, Javelin, what have you learnt in school?"

"I learnt about the ancient theology of Silver."

"Theology? Aren't you a little young to be learning that?"

"I am fifty years old."

"My, how time flies. It seems like yesterday you were a baby in your mother's arms. Anyhow, tell me what you learned so I may see if it's correct."

"Well, we learned that God Silver once had a concubine who betrayed his trust and gave the knowledge of fire and mystic energy to the primitive Silverans."

"Sylar, correct?"

"Yep. Also, we learned she was imprisoned for her misdeed and the chains burned her so much she caused a massive earthquake."

"Partially true. Go on."

"Well, we also learned he had a son. This son was the one that allowed us to be immune to all disease and poison."

"Again, partially true. You are still young, so I cannot give you the true horrible details yet, but you are being taught correctly. So, what do you wish to eat?"

"Steak. When are Ma and Pa getting home?"

"Should be soon."

The door opened and a cloaked figure walked in. He tossed a body on the floor and Ben noticed it was Volk. *Poor bastard was still clinging to life.* Another walked in and tossed the critically injured Harle on the floor as well. And still another, this time a blood-soaked bag. Ben eyed them and frowned.

"Let me guess, Scion of Chaos and two other horsemen of Chaos?"

Javelin sneered as he transformed, "Partially true."

"Ah, all four of you. How many of my clan did you kill coming here?"

"Heh, see for yourself."

Ben looked at the bloody bag with disinterest. "So, what did you do with Javelin?"

"Don't know, don't care. Look in the goddamn bag. I want you to see your face. I want to see your light die."

The chaos Scion fell with a large hole in his chest. Ben stood behind him with a large gun drawn. He beheaded the Scion, then shot through his false image and killed another horseman before the two remaining realized what happened. He snarled and ripped the head off the third horseman. The fourth saw all three of its brethren dead and bolted. Bounty Hunter 11 roared in a fury and let out a mournful howl.

Ben gently lay Harle and Volk in the same medical tank. It would take time to heal them. He walked out into the storm and began to look for his family's bodies. As he found them, he teleported them to a large pyre. Three-fourths of his clan had died. He looked in the bag and grimaced at the over two hundred children's heads lying there. Aside from his family, the former clans of Dal and Vental also suffered heavy casualties. One-third of their clans had been slain. He looked at the pyre in pain, then shoved his feelings down.

"Thayme Sidrodc uigde het suol, Thayme havens sunocme het suol. Rest now, my blood ties. You will be in a better place soon. Watch over those of us still alive."

He raised an amber liquid-filled glass and downed it before tossing it on the pyre, causing the flames to burn brighter. His eyes glowed with the fire as he sat down weeping in the rain. He felt a heavy hand on his shoulder and looked up to see a large pure Silveran male.

"Let everything out, boy. Our clan has suffered, but we are not destroyed. Chaos failed in that regard."

"Brother, what shall we do? We can't risk revenge. Too many lie dead."

"We rebuild and wait. The time to strike will be soon."

***

Interlude: Musing the muse

Heretical Zealotry

The sun burns a path on this foggy mound of blues and purples that sits in the middle of the canyon. It sits blazing all alone in the middle of the canyon. There used to be a temple here to one of the many pagan gods. Now the mound sits forlorn and smouldering in dawn light. Zealots used to visit the mound; people used to pray here no more. Only religion here, the sky covered in smoky wispy clouds that balance the soul. A window into the mind surrounds this place. It is in the water in the sky and in the stones surrounding the mound.

This is the only cold place in the burning canyon. The ground boils in the sun, the clouds look smoky the stone is charred from the earth up to the sky. This is an anchor to the soul, to the living and to the sins skulking in the water. The mind is only temporary sanity dissolving in stone.

Three (skeletal) trees blacken the middle of this mound on Golgotha, the place of the mind of some men in cultist white drink of a red liquid poisoned with their gluttony greed sloth drinking out of lust, envy, hatred eating vice.

An altar to the gods burns gold in the dawn's light. An old man with one eye watches over the god's reflection in the stone water fire lightning the siblings.

Chronos leans on his hourglass, swirling the smoke creating worlds where religion forms a fountainhead of knowledge that becomes a mythical belief.

Monks meditate trying to achieve enlightenment, opening the chakras fountainhead swirls Hinduism, Buddhism, Jesusism swirl in the smelting pot of myth heretics disavowing paganism bring the soup to the dry ground and drop it into the water.

Three fish girls swim, luring sailors to their death. Their song is horrid to the ear, but their body tempting to the eyes as the sky hums.

I stand on the mound yelling why…

Tattooed Canvas

The fire smoulders against the dry grassy ground blazing a path of havoc. At night, the moon glows with the light of the sun on the forested mountain. The ink soaks up the blood and forms pretty colours as it opens a path. The world is still floating in an endless dream. The trees drip embers into the ocean of flames pain is only a temporary feeling.

This is the hottest place on the mountain. The fires of yesterday year are now ash, the snow is melted, revealing hard grey granite crystals of life glow in the sulfuric yellow-green sky. A storm brewing on the horizon aches for acceptance. This is an anchor for the body for the flesh and to the liquid waterfall flooding out of the mountain – the life forming a picture in the stone.

Three (petrified) trees bask in the hot glow of the embers on top of this mountain air sucks all oxygen from the flames that still burn without it, and the fire casts shadows that dance to an eerie tune. Only they can hear the music swells with each profound wave of fire swelling to unbearable heights and crashing into the deepest depths of the mountain, crashing an avalanche of ash and soot down the slopes. The red, warm flood washes away what had been the stone begging to be itself, only ends up looking like every other stone. The metal rings piercing the stony flesh burrowing into the ears, eyes and lips of this mortal canvas ink burns of fire and ice coursing through the canvas, locking up the mind with sensory overload. The pain bleeds into the teeth and head, smoke and music unheard shimmer in the cold air, a silent wind only the stone can hear, the fire coursing in the stone burns a path creating water from ice and then steam and nothing.

Here it is now, then, and soon to be a storm broiling the air, hating dreaming of what could be…

Anchor Hill

The moon glows a shallow phantasm on this grey-green hill rising up over the middle of the lake, sitting forlorn and by itself; only lovers slept on this hill now. They are gone, dreams sleep on it now, just minding their own business while blasphemies lurk in the water. The stars shimmer on the treetops like diamonds burning into the organic flesh. Nothing is still for long, nor will it ever be. This is the only warm place on the lake. The water is freezing. The sky is black ice souls seeking shelter float near trees. The hill is always there, an anchor for the dead, for the sleeping and for what lurks below the window of glassy water, the mind unfathomable, a heart beating under the floor.

Three [palm] trees stand in the middle of this hill. The hill is solitude, a place of the muse, a moon that isn't a moon. Elves dance on silvery water, smoke and fire fall with an old man searching for a prophesy, a king breathing his last on a broken table of stone chuckles ridiculously. Fellowship (of teens) soon to be broken a boy (dead) on the ground, a raven choked as a girl leapt down a hole, breaking her legs. Here is now standing on this anchor, bemusing the muse. Revelling in the depths of my mind, a black shroud covering me, the shadows of the past are soon dead, the shadows of the present soon to be I stand, dreaming…

Are these the steps to create God? I wonder…

***

The Machinations of Bounty Hunter 12

The Taur Island Upper Depths was a mechanical marvel. The Taur had gotten down to a science of how to engineer the flesh. Today one of the experiments they were working on would be born and change the world. To the Taur, he would be considered a traitor. To the Silverans, he would be considered a dangerous maverick. Today the Magic Melody of the Universe, he would eventually be torn asunder and reforged.

Deep in the Science Sector of The Upper Depths, two Taur stood side by side awaiting their child. One was a reborn Bounty Hunter 11 and the other his wife, Queen Ballona Slaughter. When they received their child, they were shocked. He was grey-skinned and grey-furred. His eyes were also grey, as were his horns.

Bounty Hunter 11 spoke, "I am not well versed in Taur physiology but should not the skin and fur be different colours?"

Ballona spoke, "Yes, husband, we Taur all have different skin colours than our fur. This should not be possible."

The scientist attending the reveal spoke, "We do not know what happened, but if you would prefer, we can get rid of this abomination."

Bounty looked into the child's eyes and spoke the words that would shake the universe. "No, he was born this way for a reason. We should let fate continue her scheme."

The scientist snorted, "If fate chose this form, I agree that in pure scientific inquiry, we should let it live. His sister was born with different colours, but she was also born with only one arm. I would strongly encourage you to be rid of her."

Ballona looked at Bounty, who shook his head. "No, I will take her and risk the ostracization. During the Chaos War, I saw too many of my children die. I would like for her to be given a chance at life."

"I understand, but if she proves worthless, you will be responsible for her elimination."

"I understand the Taur laws, Science Master Kalx Tamox. But I assure you she is of my genes and she will not be worthless."

"What will you name them?"

"The boy will take my name, making him the twelfth Bounty Hunter. She will be called Magenta Hunter due to her aura colour."

***

Bounty Hunter 12 sat with his sister, Magenta, listening to a story being told by their father. He had found this story while searching for a specific book. He was curious about an Onyx Tower he had stumbled upon while exploring the forest near his home.

***

The Story of the Onyx Tower

The air smelled of spring. The ground had finally thawed and the sixty-degree weather was refreshing. The wind blew through the silvery green leaves and caused dew to drop from some. The trees were sparkling in the sun and looked like giant thorns of thorns. Each tree was spike shaped in the trunk, but the branches were vine-like and had many spikes on them. Even some of the spikes on the vines had spikes on them. The trees moved in the wind as if dancing. The silver-grey bark was wet with the rain from the night before. The sun was reflecting off the bark and the feathery fey were dancing in the sunbeam. A large onyx stone sat in the middle of the ray. The grass, though soft, was spike shaped as well.

The forest was alive with sounds and smells. The forest moved every now and then since the trees got bored staying in one place. The only constants were the streams and stones and the giant mountains behind the forest. The Onyx stone was in the centre of the forest; you might call it the heart of the woods. It was the last piece of a great tower that once rose from the forest and the heart of a city long ago destroyed. There are many feral sentients in this forest, the primary of which was the Shadow Wolf and Moon Catz. Both were clan-based colonies. The Shadow Wolves were very dog-like and stood five feet tall. The Moon Catz was cat-like and stood six feet tall. Both had fur-like spikes that were good defence when they went to war. They usually fought other clans in their area, but sometimes they would fight against each other.

Back to the stone, the central point of this adventure. A tall demonic looking man sat on this stone. He was eight feet tall with two three feet curved horns upwards. He was wearing his armour, but the three spikes on his shoulders were not a part of this armour. Nor were the spikes on his upper arms and elbows a part of the armour. He had black eyebrows that looked like greasy black upside-down check marks, along with a black goatee. His hair was long and tied in a rogue knot. It reached his mid back and then wrapped around his waist. He also had some warlocks tied into the rouge knot. He wore silvery black sunglasses that obscured his eyes. If he were to open his mouth, he would have a sharp shark-like smile.

This story is not about him because he already has one. This story is about the phantoms of the past that he sees while sitting on this stone. The past is mysterious because one never knows whether what one sees is real or imaginary. Sometimes a powerful mind can see things differently than a weaker mind. And since this man has a very powerful mind, this story cannot be trusted.

There is a circle facing outward, towards a black abyss. Three people each see themselves as battle-hardened, years older, with the best equipment they can imagine. They're on the top of a black Onyx tower, probably twenty feet in diameter, with no visible bottom below the sheer sides. The sky is black all around, and the light to see seems to be coming from nowhere. Suddenly, reddish black clouds bellow, from all directions, with dark lightning cackling in them. Faces of slain men and women scream from below, illuminated darkly by the sinister lightning.

Their screams are felt more than heard. Many different faces, all with the same sinister grin, appear, at first just as forms in the evil clouds but slowly solidify into almost tangible forms. They all start laughing in the same voice, the same evil cackle. Then a light shines from within the group, and a princess is illuminated from within. However, the princess looked horrified and screamed out in pain. When she opens her mouth, a bright searing light shoots out of it, then it comes out of her eyes, and then goes out, letting the princess collapse, dead.

Then, one by one, each member of the group meets their demise, though all see each death as their own. Through others' eyes, one spontaneously combusts, turns to ash, and is blown off the tower. One rips apart at each joint, one sprout thorn bushes from their stomach, and is ripped apart by the aggressive growth of nature, and finally, each group member being last to die, flings themselves in horror off of the tower. Falling forever, they are all awakened at the same time, sitting up, sweat-drenched and terrified.

The three travellers awaken from this nightmare to see the princess they are guarding covered in blood. Many arrows protrude from the torn flesh. One of the travellers immediately traced many colourful symbols in the air. The symbols in the air surrounded the princess and the flesh began to mend. He is in a gold, red, and black robe and he looks like a knight. His face is covered by a helmet and he has a giant sword on his back. His skin is reddish and covered in symbols. In reality, the robe is the toughest armour known to the land. It is lightweight and made out of light but powerful metal. The other, a Gargoyle-like creature with huge golden Bat Wings and the emblem of a skull on his chest, flew up into the air to scout out of the area. The final, a spike and horned grey-skinned devilish-looking man stood with a large axe in his hands. The Gargoyle landed on one of the branches. His skin shone in the moon a golden colour.

He spoke in a harsh and scratchy voice, "There is a strange tower nearby that seems to be made out of Onyx. It is the size of a giant city."

"How Far off is it, Phoenix?" spoke the demonic man.

"These arrows," spoke the knight. "Is the rune crafted to seek out our princess? So I would not doubt that they came from that tower. But we still need to know the distance they flew from."

Phoenix spoke, "The tower is about a thousand yards away, so even a rune arrow cannot fly that far. I would think that a band of hunters may have done it. Probably emanating from the tower."

The three comrades stood waiting for the princess to awaken. Eventually, Phoenix and the knight dozed off. A tall, elegant woman walked into the clearing. She had long black flowing hair, blacker than night. Her lips were bright red and pierced and her eyes were bright green that glowed in the moonlight of the three moons. She wore very little, showing off her tattoos and piercings.

She said, "Well, we meet again, Master Hunter, but this time, I am not here for you. I want the princess."

Hunter spoke, "I think not Damsel Death. Tell your brother you failed to bring her in."

"I will have her. You cannot tell Death what to do!"

"I am not telling Death what to do. I am telling you what to do. You are not Death. Only the Reapers and Omega Reapers can collect souls. And last I heard, you were neither."

"I will have her soul and you cannot stop me."

At this, Damsel Death pulled out her sword and attacked. The sickle-shaped blade whistled through the air and cleaved at Hunter. It was blocked by a rune-covered hatchet. The two weapons were savagely gouging and tearing at each other. Damsel Death flew back as the hatchet embedded itself into her chest. She looked up at two red eyes glowing in the darkness. She gasped in terror and said, "You win Master Hunter. You may have the girl for now."

Damsel Death vanished and the princess awoke; gasping tears soaked her face. Hunter picked her up and cradled her whispering a song softly to lull her back to sleep. Morning came and the three men began to pack up while the princess ate. Phoenix rose into the air and flew off. Hunter picked up the, now full, princess and ran off, followed closely by the knight.

They came to the tower at about midday and rested. What they saw awed them. The tower reached through the clouds and was at least a hundred thousand meters tall. It was formed entirely out of Onyx and glowed with fiery runes.

The princess spoke, "That thing is multidimensional and the foul beast lives atop it plotting to conquer the world. So many imprisoned souls screaming out 'Kill us! Kill us! Free us! Free us!'."

Hunter looked at the princess and smiled softly, saying, "Don't worry, your people will be free if it takes all our life to find and kill that beast."

Phoenix spoke, "How noble of you! Do you even have a plan? Fuck, do you even know how many floors there are in that thing?"

Hunter turned to Phoenix and spoke, "If you do not want to help, leave. You have done your part. You can go too, Merlin Red."

The Red knight spoke, "I refuse to leave my friend behind. It is un-noble for a Redian to leave his brothers behind."

Phoenix growled softly as he looked up and said, "I have come this far, may as well go farther."

Merlin looked at the runes and spoke, "Gentlemen, I have a plan. Channel your mystic powers into Hunter since he is the strongest here, and then Hunter, you will trace each of those runes backwards. They are runes of binding. Without them, the tower will collapse. It will cause critical casualties and may release The Alpha Reaper, but I think it is worth it."

The three went into a meditation stance and channelled their power into Hunter. He raised his finger and began tracing all the runes backwards. As the last rune went out, the tower began crumbling. The stone became black dust and boulders crashed into the city below. The trees had moved away and were far from the city. Many screams echoed from the ruble and soon died out.

Only a few stones were left; the remaining one was a large stone shaped like a throne. The other stones were moved to different parts of the world while the throne stayed in the centre of the forest.

Hunter looked at the princess. He looked up as Merlin Red took off his helmet, revealing a sharp face with two purple eyes and maroon hair. Merlin smiled a sharp smile bearing pearly white fangs. Then he placed his helmet on and vanished.

Phoenix spoke, "Well, it's been fun. Feel free not to call me when you need help. I have hatchlings to take care of." He, too, vanished, leaving only the princess leaning against Hunter, who smiled as the other two left for their home planets.

As Hunter and the princess left, the true Onyx Tower stood, piercing the moonlight.

Azrael, the Alpha Reaper, stood on top of the tower. He was once again free. He stretched and vanished as the moons glowed red.

***

Bounty Hunter 12 spoke as his sister lifted her head from under his jacket. "What was the True Onyx Tower?"

"That is not something I can give information on. It is a Druidic secret. Frankly I do not particularly care about towers and circles, nor should you. This story is merely fiction. Did you have a reason for wanting this story to be read to you?"

"Yes, father, I have seen the Onyx Tower and was curious about it."

"Hmm, push that curiosity from your mind. It will only lead to catastrophe."

"But father, is it not scientific curiosity that allowed us Taur to survive the war with the Silverans?"

"While there is some merit to scientific curiosity. We are talking about the core concepts of this planet. Concepts that should remain the way they are and not be disturbed. This planet should not exist. We have three moons that change colour. We have day and night but no sun that can be seen. The plants and animals can all speak. Our species have two hearts, six lungs and can walk in the cold vastness of space without protection. Our world is strange and when one begins to meddle trying to make sense of that strangeness, terrible things can happen."

"I understand." *I will need more information. Father is hiding something. I will not be idle on this information.*

Magenta whispered, "Brother, relax your mind and muscles. I think we have had our fun for today. The night will soon be here. I yearn for bed."

Bounty sighed, "Father, who was Master Hunter?"

"Ha! Crafty ones, aren't you? You saw that, yes? Master Hunter, Master Red, and Master Wing were the first of a long and prosperous alliance between Planet Silver, Planet Red, and Planet Gold. Many of the species of Silver can trace their genetic family tree back to the first alliance when Planet Silver was strong. We had conquered most of the galaxy. Sowed our seeds and waited for the ensuing crop. Our clan supposedly descends from Master Hunter and the princess."

"So, it's not fiction?"

"It's a fictional telling of the first alliance. Understand this Bounty, the past is an extremely sensitive subject to many beings on this planet. There are things that get brought up that many species would consider Taboo. As a Taur, you will run into many roadblocks. The past is a sore subject. Ignore stories like this. Focus on the here and now."

"But how can we gain knowledge if we do not look in the past?"

"Not now, Bounty. Go get ready for bed."

"Just tell me!"

"I can't."

Bounty Hunter 12 huffed and snorted in disdain before leaving. He glared at his father. No, the man who was keeping knowledge from him. He and his father had a stare-down. He could see the fire in his father's eyes and shuddered before turning away. *I must know more.*

He entered his private chambers. He saw a book that was not there before. A book about the past. It was a journal.

***

It is chilly here, but I have grown used to it. In the back of my mind, I hear the queen giving orders to the mindless drones. I also hear about the brutal human slaughtering of our kind. Those damnable war-like Homo Indomitus have been a thorn in the queen's side for far too long. I am one of the few who the queen does not order. She needs my mind to be my own. She only has a few others out of her control. The others that are free are the CEO of Fleshway, the Hacker, our tech expert, and various scientific minds.

The Hacker is free because he works with the scientists to create better strains of our serum. He was once known as Andy, but when the queen cured him, he began tirelessly working on things. He was able to create many strains of the cure and thus created new drones for the queen. He eventually made himself into a cybernetic organic. This was because the cure caused him to decay at an increased rate. He is also a technology expert. He is able to pinpoint weaknesses in human machines and he also has been able to hack into security systems and other electronics with ease. His skills are devoted to creating stronger drones and then breaking the security of humans so that the CEO can collect his products.

The CEO is free because he was once a smarmy businessman named Peter. He was cured along with Andy and me. His skills involved creating a business around selling flesh and brains. He created what is now known as Fleshway. We, the collective, require his products so that we may strive on with diligence. The queen only keeps him informed like she does with me and the Hacker.

The reason I am free from the collective is because I need to be impartial to the story. I am a historian, a chronicler, a writer, a spy, and a mutagen. The queen uses my unique blend of skills to infect and minimize the humans.

Speaking of the queen she was the first cured by humans. She was an experiment with immortality. She found a way to control the recently cured using a primitive form of psychic energy. She cured four other girls who were going to be replacement hosts in the event that she died. This has not happened yet because she has a whole army of cryogenically frozen females cloned from her. The four girls were nicknamed Red, Brunette, Blond, and Raven. They all represent something. Red is a fierce warrior and the bodyguard of the CEO. Blond is promiscuous and sexual because she is also a cure bearer but also the queen's personal pet. Brunette is a scientist who helps the Hacker with his job.

Raven, Raven, is different. Raven holds untold power because she has somehow gained the ability to regenerate constantly. This regenerative process allows her flesh to constantly renew. You see, the side effect of being cured is that the flesh cannot keep up with the metabolism of the body. Therefore, it begins rotting.

The only other person free from the queen's control is a child. This child is an enlightened one. He/she sees and hears all. He/she has untapped power that all of us fear. He/she is stuck as a child even though he/she is as old as the queen, about three hundred-plus years. He/she was somehow related to animating lifeless objects. That is the other reason he/she is free from the queen, he/she is not a human.

I am currently keeping my eye on the sleeping woman known as Raven. The queen wishes me to scout out the man who has been killing her drones. I walk over to the bed and take my eye off the nightstand. I pop it back into its socket and walk out the door. The humidity hits me and my body becomes sluggish. I activate the cooling system in my regulation suit. A dome covers my head and fogs up slightly. A small camera appears on my shoulder and transmits what it sees to my helmet and then to the queen. I scratch my wrist and some of my flesh peels away. I slip the fallen flesh into a small dart tube and it liquefies.

My suit keeps my body from falling apart in the humid air. It also keeps my body from freezing in cold temperatures. I keep myself from getting mauled by hungry animals, unlike the drones. The animals fear me; therefore, they would rather hunt down and devour the drones than someone like me.

I see a man who is at least eight feet tall. His armour looks heavy, but he seems comfortable in it. He has a gauntlet that holds a chainsaw. On his back are a golf club, a sword, a bat, and a gun. He also has a gun by his side and on his other gauntlet. He is assisting a group of humans. I am told to infect a few of them. I chose the second in command. She is a fierce looking being. Her wild hair is blue and green. She has many tattoos and piercings. She is dressed in revealing armour, but I am told by the hacker that the weak point is just above her shoulders at the clavicle and spine.

I aimed my dart thrower and fired. It hits her and she slaps her neck and curses about bugs. The dart is in her system. It will take a full day to dissolve and cure her.

During this process, I am able to track the hero using her eyes. Soon the others would be cured and would join the collective. The queen tells me that the girl will be mine when she is cured. I sneak back to my lair. They are awfully close to my mountain fortress. But in the event that they step inside, I have a complex array of mazes and traps that will dissuade them from coming further.

Through my special drone eyes, I see a blond seducing a few of the men. She looked to be in perfect condition. I am told by the hacker that he has developed a strain that allows regeneration under certain conditions and that blond is the test monkey. Blond plays with the hair of one of the younger men and pulls him into my cave system.

I turn on my system and see her playing with her food. She is having sex with the young man. When she goes in for a blow, she rips off his manhood with her teeth and swallows it whole. She then digs her nails into his flesh and rips and tears until he is no more. The moment her hunger fulfils, she slinks through my door and collapses onto my bed.

I watch as the small group enters my labyrinth, looking for the kid. I smile. It was almost time for the cure to take place. I had pulled myself from the mind of the woman she had secretly infected several of the survivors. As they changed, I pulled my new guard into my secret room. She also changed and was then forth my personal slave. I look on as the man slays the infected and then I am told to interfere again. I release a toxin into the area of the caves that the small group is in and they crystallize in their own blood. The man survives and I walk out in my suit and point a sword at his eye.

I speak, "Eye for an eye, dear boy." I then stab his eye with my sword.

He had once fought me and had been infected, but he had somehow become immune to the toxins in his system. He was immune to all my toxins. I look at him holding his face and walk away.

I feel a dagger enter my flesh and pull it out and throw it to the ground. "My job isn't done yet. You cannot kill me, nor can I kill you. Welcome to hell, dear boy and use your rage to your advantage."

He snarled, "Why do you torment me?"

I look over my shoulder using the camera. He is still holding his eye. I smile under the fog of my helmet. He will be okay. He has the same regenerative ability as Raven. I walk through the wall releasing a freezing mist throughout the labyrinth. He cannot see me. I look over at the sleeping Raven and place my eye back on the nightstand. I am told by the queen to assist the hacker with the human population near his facility.

It is the night when I arrive at the facility. I see another heavily armed human sneaking around. This one looks more feminine to me and I see her leading a small army towards the secret entrance. I push a button on my suit and a large beam strikes the ground around the small army. This beam draws the Zomborgs to the group. It would soon be a feeding frenzy. I enter the facility and encounter Brunette. She is sitting near a Zomborg, tinkering with the equipment.

She looks up at me and then says, "I think I figured out how to use the Zomborgs effectively. I have upgraded them with a serum made from nanomachines that effectively animate even the most grotesquely maimed drone. These machines could effectively pull together a dismembered body to create even more drones that can be used as shock troopers. What do you think? Will it work?"

I look at her and say, "Only one way to find out. I will take a test tube and inject it into the dead bodies that the Zomborgs just stopped from entering your secret entrance. By the way, what did you need help with Hacker?"

A large dome descended from the ceiling. "I require you to permanently remove that heavily armed chick. She has been getting the humans to band together. Humanity is stubborn and unruly. They do not realize their time is over and the reign of the Undying is soon to be a reality."

I looked at the pink fleshy orb floating in a metal skull. And smiled again, saying, "Good to see you have upgraded yourself even further. If this works, I may have a design for you."

I walked out with Hacker's evil laugh. I saw the woman lying against a large metal wall. She was panting. I pulled out my sword and pointed it at her, saying, "Do you value your life?"

She looked up at me and gasped. She got up and her gauntlet became a drill and her other gauntlet became an energy shield. I raised what was left of my eyebrow. If my regulation suit was damaged, I would begin decaying. But I also saw something that worried me. She had many cuts that should have changed her by now. She was still human, just like the young man.

I blocked her attack and rolled out of the way. I landed near the Zomborgs and dismembered bodies. I injected the nanomachines into the dead flesh. Lightning struck the ground near the flesh and an unexpected thing happened. Not only did the flesh begin pulling together, but it began fusing the various parts together. The mass of goo then covered the destroyed Zomborgs. Energy lanced out and struck the metal. Soon a sparking construct made of flesh and metal rose twenty feet into the air. The gargantuan looked around and lumbered off.

The woman could have killed me while this process was happening, but she had fled. I growled and spoke into the gauntlet, "Hacker, we have a problem. I think you need to work on your nanomachines. Not only did they pull together the flesh, but when exposed to the energy, they became a goo-pile that absorbed the destroyed Zomborgs. In a more favourable light, you now have a twenty-foot-tall Zomborg on the rampage."

The hacker spoke, "Yeah, I can see it. I have been trying to tame it. So far, my ability is working. I have instructed it to stay guard and also use its large size to help me with my satellite. I hope to expand my Zomborgs ability to roam. So far, they are only confined to this facility because my link stops near the human colony in the jungle. That is as far as my control goes."

I walked out of the facility tracking the girl. I followed her scent until the jungle. I then relied on scanning with my suit. I found her hiding out in a cave near my headquarters. I entered the cave and saw her wrapping her wounds. She had slain more of the drones on her way here. I stayed in the shadows watching her. Then I heard heavy steps and the other heavily armed human walked in. He now had a patch over his empty eye socket. He looked even more dishevelled than the last time I encountered him about a week ago.

He took off his armour and spoke, "Well, sweetie, I think we are safe for now. I still have not been able to find your mother."

The girl looked up and said, "I sense her presence near here. Is there any cave system around here she might be in, Daddy?"

I slid quickly out and entered my facility. I uploaded all I had recorded in the past week to my computer. I soon cleared out more space on the camera's hard drive. I growled and looked at the sleeping form of Raven.

I spoke to her unconscious body, "So more has been revealed. This is just great. No wonder you are in a coma."

I looked at my new pet. I walked over to her and said, "I need your savagery. There is a small colony of humans nearby that I want you to destroy. Here you can use my spare suit."

The tattooed woman looked up at me and I saw in her eyes fear and loathing. She had retained her humanity but was now a drone under my command. She bowed and hurried off.

Within a few minutes, I saw a distress signal from her. I muttered under my breath and walked back out into the humidity. I entered the demolished city and saw her sitting in a pool of blood.

I said, "Your distress beacon went off. Where are your troubles?"

She looked at me and then spoke, something very uncommon in drones, "Those slackers, I eat punks like those for breakfast. Speaking of which, would you like some breakfast?"

She held out an arm to me and I shook my head no. I looked around and said, "Then why in the world would the distress beacon go off?"

I heard a whirring and turned to see the duo standing there. The tattooed woman stood up and smiled, showing her red teeth.

She looked at me and then lunged for me. "You turned me into this. Now with my mind back, I will kill you again!"

I growled and stepped aside as she bolted past. I caught her by the leg and threw her in an arc towards the two. She crashed into them.

I growled and said, "How are you not a mindless drone?"

She looked angrily at me and said, "Because, like my brother and niece, I inherited a trait of regeneration. All toxins get expelled from the system in an amber teardrop."

I saw the daughter activate her drill and charge me. I rolled out of the way but slipped on the gore. I fell into a crater nearby. The crater had been from when one of the human satellite drones crashed into the jungle before the cure happened. It was how scientists discovered the cure. I hid in the green crater using my camouflage technology. I sent a small spider camera after them. It followed them into my lair. They entered and dismembered blond. I then saw them with the eye that I had left on the bedtable. I saw them wake her. She looked around bewildered.

I heard her through the camera say, "Jarex, Liz, Maya! How did you find me?"

The man spoke, "Alice, my love, it was merely by chance. If that monster had not infected Maya, we never would have found you. Now we are together. I have been searching for you for years and raising our daughter Liz."

Raven looked at them again and then saw my eye; she gasped, "he knows. We must get out fast. He is watching us."

The four hurried out and I slipped back in and collapsed on my regenerative bed. Before I shut down, I sent all of the blond's body parts to Hacker. As I regenerated, I felt the queen's rage. She was fuming because now there were four humans immune to the cure. She wanted to destroy them. I mentally calmed her and spoke of an idea I had that may work or it may end up going horribly wrong. She connected me to Hacker's brain and I began to describe a ship that could send these immune humans off our planet or else they could pose a serious problem.

The hacker began working on it with the help of his construct. The satellite was ready and this ship could easily be the way to get it off the planet.

My job was to lure the immune humans to the ship and send them away. It would be the riskiest thing I have done, but I was tired of immortality. I selected a few encrypted files and placed them on a gauntlet. I placed the gauntlet in a small box, which would only open to the touch of Jerax. I smiled and fell into hibernation to reserve energy. The building would take at least a year and that was how long I would hibernate.

I awoke a year later and caught up on things. I found those immune humans easily. My spider had stayed with them. I donned my suit and walked out into the unbearable heat. My skin had become even more sensitive. I amped my suit to the max and hunted down the five immune humans. The man was holding a child. I slipped the box into his carrier.

I then revealed myself and said, "I challenge you lot to fight me!"

The man spoke, "I will accept this challenge."

I smiled, then ran off yelling, "Catch me if you can, boy. Use that anger at me to charge you up."

The five ran after me and I lured them into the hacker's facility. He had called off his drones to their regenerative pods. He had turned his entire facility into a ship. His brain was linked to the central computer. Only one-fourth of it would be used to remove the immune humans. The queen even had sent three of her mortal clones to stasis pods with no memories, just blank.

When I arrived, Jerax was there. He was standing with his sword raised. Next to him stood his daughter and sister. Both were in heavy armour like his. They attacked me, breaking open my containment suit. I stumbled back, purposely pulling my toxins away from them. They ran into the cave as I opened fire. The cave was actually their ship. The hacker lifted them off and sent them to Aries.

He had equipped their small pod with terraforming machines. My cam beeped and I saw Jerax open the box and watched him touch the gauntlet. A holographic me appeared. He leapt back in shock.

The hologram spoke, "If you are listening to this, I thank you. You have freed me from my body. I, in a former life, had a son. He was a fierce warrior. When I was caught by the undead, I volunteered myself to keep my son and daughter safe. Their mother was dead. And it was up to me to defend them. Yes, Jerax, this son of mine was you. When you first fought me, I was testing you. And you passed by, cutting my eye out. I knew I had found a catalyst. Your mother was dead, but somehow her genes were immune to all toxins. Even the cure. I decided to discover what it was that allowed this. So I sent the black-haired girl to you. Her regeneration and your genes created the perfect body. When I fought your daughter, she was better and had succeeded in causing my body to decay faster than normal. It was then I began discussing with the queen how to get the immunities off this planet. We succeeded, you see, the queen was your mother's daughter in her first marriage. Your mother was a scientist working on the immortality serum. She perfected it while the MK 1 was used to create the zombies. Mk 2 was perfect in every way. That is why I sacrificed myself to keep you safe. You have passed my expectations, son. And this gauntlet has all my memories and knowledge. This should help you in repopulating your people. Go and never return to this blasted Earth. Sanit out."

My charred body looked up into the sky and crumbled. I was free.

***

Bounty looked at the book and smiled. *So that was the past of Tarah Aert. But how did Tarah Aert become the cyborg planet it is now? And how did Tarah Aert lead us? Questions have been answered, leading to more questions. Father won't tell me. I can't trust Magenta not to tell father my secrets. So, where shall I go from here?*

A voice cut through his thoughts. "I would start, Boyo, by researching your genetic history. Where does the Hunter clan come from? Why did you gain your father's name? Who was Bounty Hunter 1?"

"Who's there? How did you get into my private sanctum?"

"Look down, Boyo. You're holding me."

"The book?"

"Indeed, Boyo. I am the memories of Lord Sanit of Aries. Well, what remains of his memories? As he died, his soul became one with the stars. He ascended, unlike his kindred. He was deemed too vital to pass away. His memories were bound into a codex that can take on many forms. I decided to take on a book since you, strange one, like your books."

"Uh, why choose me?"

"You have a curious mind and I can help you expand upon your desires. Lord Sanit knew many things. These things can help you, but first, I encourage you to look to the past of the Hunter clan."

"Where?"

"Your question was about Tarah-Aert, no? Seek out the book titled Before Bagmot."

"How would a book about the Silveran Apocalypse help me?"

"You are talking to a sentient book boyo. I think you already have nothing to argue with."

"I see. So a secret, maybe?"

"I see the wheels in your head turning. That is good."

***

Bounty Hunter 11 smiled, Ah youth. Believing a book can talk. He thinks I did not know about his private room. A simple bug, the teleporter, my private stash of books that I can copy instantly, and his desire for knowledge and his path is set. Oh, don't get your panties in a knot God Silver you and I both know how this ends. Now, what should I do about Magenta?

***

Many years had passed now Bounty Hunter 11 lay on his bed. He was old and grey and his time would soon be up. He smiled, Magenta had left for Diavonbre to forge her own story. Bounty, however, had stayed to study some more. He could tell the boy was frustrated.

"Bounty, you have stayed in this home for many years, seeking what knowledge you could. Why have you not forged your path yet?"

Bounty looked down. "I still seek one elusive bit of knowledge."

"Ah, you seek the Book of Bagmot. Did you really think I would not know what you were up to? I have been helping you along this entire time. A talking book, who'd of thunk it? Anyway, since I was forbidden from sharing what you seek by God Silver and Lord Anubis, I found a loophole. Go back to your sanctum and you will find what you seek. I hope you don't do anything rash, but things are now in motion that cannot be undone. May the Havens forgive me. Be strong, boy. I leave you now."

***

Bounty Hunter 11 closed his eyes for the last time and ceased to breathe. The Taur nurse who was at the bed waiting anointed his body and placed it in a stone coffin. Many runes were carved into the coffin and then it was dumped into the sea. By chance, it washed ashore on Dragons Den Island. The Great Silver dragon smiled and placed the coffin with the others he had collected. He breathed silver fire into the coffin incinerating the body inside. No sense in letting the Taur know their dead were burned like tradition dictates. The tradition that The Great Silver Dragon made up.

***

Bounty Hunter 12 stared at the red and gold book on his desk. In bright silver letters on the cover, he read ApocalypseBagmot.

He opened it and the words filled his brain

Before Bagmot

When the Satyr opened the third seal, I heard the third Beast say, "Come!" I looked, and there before me was a black horse! Its rider was holding a pair of scales in his hand." – Bagmot Revelation 6 verse 5

The sky is starting to darken and rain begins falling. The night sky is swiftly overtaking the day. The night is soon upon the caravan. The sky is a sickly green from the smog in the air. The ground is an ashen grey colour. Ash golems and a few fire rabbits that taste really good are lurking in the forest nearby. A gust of ashy wind picks up. One of the scouts reports a nearby cave system. They had sent scouts out ahead of them to scan the surroundings; the scout that had given the report was sent to the cyclopean mountains. The leader of this caravan seems rather anxious. As if he is waiting for someone. He looks up just as a flying siege tank-like object drifts overhead; this is what he had been waiting for. He nods approvingly and looks back at the caravan, especially at the freaks he had killed a freak show for. He had been working for the boss when he did this.

The caravan began to speed up so they could make it to the caverns before the ashy winds picked up. They make it in time, for the wind has taken a turn for the worst and is blowing huge clouds of ash and smog outside. This lightning cuts the sky like massive scars and burns the air searing it with pale blue energy. The clouds catch on fire because of the chemicals in them and small bits of rain become fiery streaks hitting the ground.

The caravan is now settling down in the caverns, which smell of sickly death with the overpowering stench of rot. The caravan gathers together and huddles down. We see here that a young writer who has been travelling in the caravan is quickly moving his fingers across a blank book. As he moves his fingers, seemingly on an invisible keyboard, elegant writing begins to appear. The leader of the caravan sees this and quickly picks up a piece of leather near him and beats the boy unconscious. He hates this boy because of his power.

There is a young yet beautiful girl who is dictating over two marionettes and controlling them. She is practising her play that she is putting on for the caravan. After all, she is the only thing entertaining for them. Near her is a thin man who has started to paint a strangely surreal image. The painting is of two octopus-headed women fighting over a man of the same species. The background is the caravan that he is travelling in. The tattooed woman next to him sees the painting and looks out along the cavern walls, but she cannot see the creatures he has drawn, so she shrugs and goes back to her duties.

As the caravan huddles together, a scraping of paws is heard and a slight hissing noise. Some of the caravan light fires reveal more of the cave as they do so. The girl dictating the marionettes in motion looks up; she lets out an audible gasp and says, "Look!" The people obey almost unwillingly; they see a huge cave big enough to fit many gigantic beings. She directs their attention to the pillars that hold up the ceiling. They are huge dragons with strange octopus-shaped heads. The stone that these dragons are made of sparkles like crystals in the fire. The cave glitters with untold crystalline objects. The painter is the only one who notices that in the middle of the cave, a black onyx monolith sits. And that all the dragons are facing it.

As the writer regains consciousness, he groans in pain. The sting of the leather strap still marks his skull, revealing some bone. Outside the cave, however, the grass burns with an intensity that causes the strange fire rabbits to get near it and begin to dance around it. As the rabbits dance, the fire grows in energy, threatening to consume the trees. The trees are swaying in the wind and as they sway, they seem to be getting farther from the growing fire. The writer has been watching this strange and cult-like dance and has started to bring it to life in his book. He smiles, for he knows what is to come.

The fire rabbits continue their dance as the mighty grey ash-covered gem-powered golems, the ash golems, saunter toward them. The golems are very interested in the dance. One of the fire rabbits seems to collect the fire around it to form the shape of a woman. The rabbit controls the fire and grabs hold of one of the golems and the two begin to waltz to an inaudible tune. The other rabbits do the same and soon, there is a large masquerade going on. The trees sway in the heavy wind while the writer watches them. He vaguely hears music on the wind that seems to match the sway of the trees. He continues writing. He catches a glimpse of three figures, two seemed rather demonic and the other was a feminine form in all red. They seem to realize they are being watched and disappear.

After the awe of the girl has passed, the people hear that the hissing and scrabbling of claws are louder now. And the light seems to cast strange shadows on the wall of the cave. The howling wind outside brings flights of fancy to the eyes of the caravan. They begin to think they see the movement of a wolf in the dark. Their fear is audible since many were whimpering, but most try to forget about it as they slowly drift into unsettling sleep. The boy who was painting begins having a strange, surreal dream. He has had dreams like this before.

In his dream, he is walking along a four-pronged path. He is next to the man who writes all the time and the girl who seems to have the power to control with her voice.

The images are blurring together and he vaguely sees a giant wolf with a giant snake for a tail. The creature is mauling and killing the caravan. It is devouring the corpses and then he sees the statues that he was sleeping under move and the monolith is activated and glows blood red.

As he wakes, he expects to see the worst because the dream seemed so real, but instead, the caravan was still sleeping the scrabbling was no longer audible. It was morning and the storm had finished. The grey, murky sky was as hazy as ever and it had gotten colder. This was to be expected because usually, the smog gets in the way of the sun. However, this was a cold that seemed unusual. A cold they were not used to. The elder noticed as he peeked outside a woman in red walking towards them. In his head, he heard her voice. He motioned the caravan to move out of the cave.

The caravan went outside to see a woman in red standing there. She seemed interested in the leader. She smiles at him and speaks in a very strange language to him. "Hello, do you have any intelligent and powerful, in a weird way, humans? Mainly the ones I sent you to find. I am seeking people of the Wyrd." He understood it, however, and brought the writer, puppeteer, painter and tattooed girl to her.

He spoke, "My lady Luci Fer I present to you our prize entertainers; Elion seems to have a precognitive ability and…" He finished snidely, "loves to write about us." He mirthlessly shoved the writer forward and then continued. "Our favourite entertainer since he does nothing but draw, I present Raka. There is one downside to him and that is he sees strange things and paints those things very vividly. They usually consist of tall octopus-headed things that provoke vomiting and sickness in the clan. He is very odd as well, too quiet for our tastes. But he gets us money and we need that." He gently prodded the painter forward and scowled.

Luci murmured something as she scanned the boy, she smiled softly and went over to him. She whispered, "I know what you see. The Thullhuid have been here for many millennia. They are our omens to when the world ends because they will be the first to leave the world."

She snuck a small triangular-shelled insect-like creature called a trilobite onto his head.

 The leader then turned to the two girls and spoke again, "My lady, these two are the most terrifying of our entire caravan. Liju controls with her voice. She has marionettes that she uses. But she can also control people. It might be the reason you're here. And the one next to her is

Lexa; she has the ability to use her pheromones to induce desire in anybody. She can also cause those tattoos on her body to become runes. I believe you know what runes are. Both these women would do well as your bodyguards besides those two creatures behind you."

Luci looked at him and bared her teeth, causing the elder to flinch. He spoke again, "I am sorry, mistress, I forgot. Runes are a mystical craft that only certain heavily powered people can use. All those tattoos on her body represent an element or power she likes to play with. The main one is fire. She loves fire to the extent that it turns her on whenever she uses the rune. She seems to be the one that requires training the most."

Luci spoke in a soft voice, "I thank you for showing me these children. If what you say is true. I am afraid I will have to take them all, thus closing your travelling freak show." She motioned to the two giants behind her and said, "Take these four younglings."

The two giant men with grey skin, black hair, spikes, and horns lumbered over; they easily grabbed the four kids and walked onboard the siege tank they had come in. Luci turned around and walked back to the elder.

She said, "You have done your duty to the world, but I am afraid that your usefulness is over." With that, strange vines emitted from her hand and stabbed him, poisoning him and killing him.

Luci followed close behind her bodyguards to the siege tank. She looked at the four as they were sat down by the two men. She smiled at each one. She then spoke, "Do you know where you are headed?"

Lexa sneered and spoke, "Yes, you are taking us to your gulag in the Grand Canyon. I have been there before, so don't think you can scare me. The last time I was there, they treated me like an animal. So if you even dare to put me back, I will maul you and your guards."

She sneered, saying, "Your pheromones are strong. You seem to be the most useful out of these others. Yes, I believe I know who will be the winner. I just hope you refrain from going berserk. I do hate having to fix my canyon. I have high hopes for you. The rest of you, however, not so much."

Raka spoke, "I do not understand, but what are these creatures you call Thullhuid? And why am I able to see them, but nobody else can?"

Luci smiled and spoke, "Here's a history lesson for you. It is the year 3113, right after the election of the new president. The Casimeras are preparing for war. The whole Earth is riled up.

In 2012 the sea revolted and a giant behemoth squid-like creature attacked the coastal cities of both Napja and Casimera. Both thought it was the other who had sent the beast. The beast was immune to conventional weapons and sank many warships. Finally, all the countries fired their nukes at the monster and it went back into hiding. That was the aquatic god that the Thullhid obeyed and worshipped. Because of the massive firing of nuclear missiles, the atmosphere became charred but not severely. It healed up and pollution took hold, suffocating many of the plants. It also made disease run rampant. Over three-fourths of Terra-Aert's population had died by the year 3000."

Raka looked confused and said, "That explains nothing!"

He was immediately smacked by one of the guards. Luci motioned the guard to stop, then spoke to Raka, "You, however, seem to have the ability to see the creatures that worship the Aquatic Beast. Which means you are a half-breed. Somewhere in your family line, one of your ancestors or even parental units has married a Thullhuid. Even more possible is the fact you were an avatar, meaning god human, of said aquatic beast." She smiled, looking at the computer she put on the breaks.

Luci spoke, "We are here, toss them out and let the test begin." She turned to the four and smiled. "I expect only one of you to survive; that one will become my new general. You four have very special powers, so it will be an even match. I will be seeing the winner at the gigantic organic tower covered in vines. My base of operations… here anyway. See, it is almost a day's walk ahead. Tata dearies."

The four were savagely thrown out of the vehicle in the middle of a dense dark craggy forest inside the Grand Canyon. Elion looked around and began to jot down all the descriptors he could find. The canyon was approximately 300 miles long. He looked up to the sky to judge the distance down they were. He estimated that the width of it was almost 30 miles wide. He looked from one distance to the other and judged that he was down at least a mile. He saw that, at one point, there had been a river here. No longer, the volcano nearby had completely covered the river. He touched the ground and felt it rumble. He simply smiled. He now knew where to drill for water.

He heard a voice in his head, "You know, brother, being the writer, you could always escape now."

He mentally spoke, "I cannot, that would be a paradox. As fate, I cannot mess with fate."

"Yes, I understand. Damsel is worried. There are at least five of our siblings down there." "I'll find them. Do not worry, brother, nor you, sister."

The painter shook his head in awe at the surroundings and saw two of the Thullhuid advancing to them. He saw both were brandishing machetes and a smaller group of the creatures followed close behind. They were conversing among themselves. He began painting them as they approached him.

Liju spoke, "I hear water, but I don't see water. I'm thirsty; someone get me a drink."

The writer turned to her and spoke, "Liju shut up! We have been here only a minute and you begin to demand things. Play with your dolls."

She looked hurt and began tearing up. "They aren't just marionettes; they are my friends. Why do you have to be so mean?"

Elion glared at her and then turned and walked off. By now, the Thullhuid had walked past, but they were forever on canvases because Raka had done a quick sketch and paint while he listened to Liju and Elion.

Elion came back with a dead rabbit and a bucket of water. He set them down, causing Liju to gasp in awe. The rabbit was the size of a normal human and was cooked to a tender brown. Lexa purred and attempted to seduce Elion, with her pheromones, into giving her the largest piece of the rabbit steak. Her pheromones did not work on him, just like the commanding voice of Liju. He glared at her and handed the largest portion to Liju then the second largest to Raka and then he handed a medium piece to Lexa and finally gave himself the smallest piece. He smiled and finished it off and then went to bed.

He wrote in the book *Need Water and Food*. The objects appeared in front of him. He smiled and began roasting the meat all night long. He could smell desire in the air. It was not Lexa's pheromones that were causing this scent to burn his nose. Even through the oxygen mask he could smell it. He looked around and noticed Raka and Liju were playfully talking and flirting with each other. He smiled and saw Lexa shivering. He summoned blankets from his book and brought two to Raka and Liju and walked over to Lexa.

He sat down and said, "Here, you look cold."

She looked blankly at him as he handed her the blanket but ended up accepting it and snuggling up next to him. She was purring in his lap like a small feline. He looked to the sky and saw some mountains lift off. Their bottoms were glowing with strange shapes and colours. He opened his book and looked in it. In the book, he saw Raka and Liju get taken up into one of the mountains while he had his back turned. He also saw Lexa throwing fire at him. He nodded approvingly and dozed off.

When morning came, he noticed that Liju and Raka had snuggled up together for warmth. He saw Lexa nowhere, however, he could smell her. He noticed a gleaming metal something in the distance. And judging by the sun, it was about noon.

He walked over and gently prodded Raka and Liju awake. They woke and he smelled the pheromones of sex on both of them. She was partially nude and he was completely naked. They both woke up and were startled by him. She quickly pulled her clothing on. Raka motioned her to eat and she did.

Raka stretched and spoke, "Well, how about that. How much did you see?"

Elion smiled and patted him on the shoulder, saying, "I was asleep the entire night and I saw nothing when she got dressed. Go eat, I am not hungry."

Raka joined Liju in the small feast. Elion looked up and rubbed his eyes. He swore he saw the sky fill with mountains. He shook his head and looked over to Raka and Liju but they were gone. He looked up to see the last of the mountains ascend. And then felt something crawl up his leg. He looked down to see a trilobite. He reached down and it attached itself to his hand. He felt all the emotion and could see all the memories it held. He looked down at his hand to see that the trilobite had become fused to him thus creating a small shield for him.

He started to become overwhelmed with the scent of Lexa. He summoned, by writing in his book, an air mask that shielded his face from the pheromones. He could see Lexa, but it was near impossible to get a good look because one of her runes was glowing. It was the speed rune. It increased her speed and movement to superhuman levels. He knew instinctively that she was after the trilobite because it held important memories inside it, especially of the strange creatures, the Thullhuid. They had been hiding something about the creature that had attacked the coastal cities in 2012.

He became distracted as the Siege tank shot overhead and opened fire upon the two of them. He rolled out of the way but began hacking because his oxygen mask had fallen off. He struggled to reach it and succeeded, only to see in his hazy state another rune glow on Lexa; it was the rune for fire.

He saw nothing as a fireball engulfed him. Lexa smiled, saying, "That will show you! You freak writer. No one says no to me, NO ONE!"

She smiled as Luci's ship dropped into the canyon.

Luci walked out and said, "So it seems you remain. Good, I was hoping it would be you. You're cuter than the others. The mountains have disappeared. It means the end is near. You, my new general, will help the end come swiftly."

As the tank rose back into the air, the fire had died down. Elion stood now clothed in a black robe holding his book. His hair had gone back to its natural white hue and he had aged slightly.

He growled and spoke, "I hate that woman."

He opened his book to a page with a woman dressed in red connected to the Earth by large spiked vines. The ground was broken. He also saw a large army of those grey-skinned men that Luci had as bodyguards. He began his trek out of the canyon and saw as he reached the top of the mountains large masses of vines and thorns littered the ground. He saw a large group of people in the distance and walked toward them.

As he neared, a boy ran up to him and said, "Hey, old man get out of the way or the boss'll run you over."

He stepped aside as a large truck hovered into view; it was the caravan he had started out in. He stopped the driver and was directed to the new leader. He saw her. She was dressed in army fatigues and had a very soft look about her. She had long black hair and strange symbols painted on her cheek. Her eyeliner was a green hue that emphasized her looks.

She looked at him and said, "What do you want, old man?"

He said, "I require a lift to the next city. Would you mind taking me?"

She looked at him and chuckled, motioning him to get on board one of the trucks; he did so.

In the distance stood a city covered in smoke with a vine-covered wall. He smiled and began counting down the days till Bagmot.

Eve of Bagmot

When the Satyr opened the second seal, I heard the second Beast say, "Come!" Then another horse came out, a fiery red one. Its rider was given power to take peace from the Earth and to make men slay each other. He was given a large sword. – Bagmot Revelation 6 verse 3-4

An elderly-looking man stood on a large tower reading a book. Inside the book, he was looking at two large tanks hovering on the battlefield. It was a gloomy and rainy day. The green sky was really hazy on a day like today. The clouds smouldered with lightning and fire. There were two armies on the dry and burning plains of Naitirb. This continent had once been a powerful empire led by a queen of renown. But Luci had taken over by force. Her army had ravaged the land killing all who stood in her way. There was only one being that had survived her wrath. This species was what Luci's army would call savage beasts. These beasts, as they were called, had been foiling The Teal Force of the Oreganos Empire for ten years. It had all come down to this burning region of Naitirb.

One army was in green armour and the other was in crimson armour. The crimson-armoured ones were very odd looking because they all had bull-like heads. They were also only in upper body armour because their legs were animal-like with hoofs. They had no need for oxygen masks because this was what evolution had allowed them in this environment. These were The Taur of Naitirb and they knew things that the "superior" Teal Force did not.

The other army was well-equipped with high-tech weapons. They all worked for Luci Fer's Oreganos Empire. These men and women had been through the most horrid training ever and those that would survive were given armour and sent to various battlefields to take cities in the name of the Oreganos Empire. This was the fearsome Teal Force. This army was led by a grey-skinned man with long horns and wicked-looking spikes that jutted out from his body. He seemed to be able to breathe in this air, as well. They were opening fire upon these beasts, but the beasts kept coming.

The leader of the Bull men stood over, seeing the battle. He looked at the enemy and his bull lips curved up in a smirk. He bellowed out orders and the first flank moved forward in a charge. He knew his army would be protected by the mystic runes that covered his soldiers' armour. This is why his army could take the punishment of the Oreganos army.

The Oreganos army was firing everything at this unstoppable foe that was now charging them. The enemy had breached the outer defences because the barrier that had been erected was now rubble and the front-line men were all either crushed or cut open. One of the bull men was now using his sword to carve through their ranks. He had cut a swath through flanks two through four. The general was nervous, but he was prepared to sacrifice himself for the empress. The bull general bellowed out more orders and the soldiers began using makeshift catapults to hurl large deposits of iron at the enemy.

The Oreganos army was struggling now that there were massive metal chunks falling from the sky. More men and women were crushed under the chunks. The battlefield on the side of the Oreganos army was now pocked with craters. Only the general and six of his men were standing. He had lost almost all of his soldiers attacking these worthless beasts. They dropped their weapons and surrendered. It was better to live to fight another day than die in an unwinnable war. The old man smiled and waved his hand over the book. He was selecting those that would survive Bagmot.

***

The old man turned the page to see that a few miles away, another army made of Dwarves and their Bane Bear mounts were fighting to protect their cavernous cities. The Oreganos Elite Crimson Legion of Luci Fer had attacked at night when they were least expected. The Dwarf leader growled savagely as he cleaved open an attacker with his war axe. His men were outnumbered.

A Shadow Elf female was eying this battle. Her people had heard that the war was going on and had sent her as a scout or spy, whichever it came down to. She was recording the battle on a special stone that the scouts used to communicate with. Her queen could see what she was seeing. And her queen was quite displeased. First, the Dwarves had taken this massive cave from the Shadow Elf ancestors and now an army of upper-dwelling elves was trying to take it. Upper Elves do not belong underground.

The Dwarven army was taking a massive beating from these technologically superior Elves. They had withdrawn behind the wall and were resorting to the inferior rock hurling to hold back the invaders. The King of Dwarves was pissed he had lost too many good warriors in the preliminary attack. He walked into his barracks and growled as he saw the piece of paper on the table. He looked down at the map of the battlefield, then angrily crumpled it up and threw it in the fireplace. It burst into grey flames and then crumpled as it was devoured.

The general of the Crimson Legion was a very tall man with dark steel-grey skin. He had two jagged horns jutting out of his temples. He was in full body armour of Crimson and held a gigantic meat cleaver. He quickly crushed a Dwarf under it and instantly executed the freak. He was the most violent of all Luci's Generals and was nicknamed as the butcher. To his right was a portly man with tusks who was also brutally killing the Dwarves. He was not using weaponry; he was using his hands to rip apart the enemy. The two knew they would win.

The Dwarf king walked outside and angrily hurled his spear at the pork man and saw it pierce something. A squealing most hideous echoed through the caverns. When it subsided, the pork man was gone and in his place was a pool of blood. He saw the other general on a rock outcropping and realized that the blood was not ordinary. He saw the bodies of his men get vaporized as the pool expanded. Then there was so much fire.

The butcher smiled as he leapt out of the way of the spear. He landed on an outcropping as the spear split the portly man's skull. He again smiled as the blood overcame the dead bodies, vaporizing them. He ordered one of his men to fire a flamethrower at the blood. It burst into flame and began to cut the barrier to the remaining Dwarfs. That was when the ceiling lit up with runes and his men began falling from strange beams that the ceiling shot at them. He looked up at an athletic female with white hair and ash-black skin dropped upon him. She pulled out two sinewy swords and attacked him. He stumbled and managed to roll to the side and strike her, but she seemed unfazed by the attack. She cut off two soldiers' heads and the blades cut into him.

The dwarves were hiding under their rune-protected shelters as the flaming beams killed all that were on the battlefield. When the light show died down, the dwarves peered out to see a Shadow Elf army standing there, surrounding a horned man. He was bound by Shadow Elf chains and was unconscious. The Shadow Elf queen stepped forward and motioned the Dwarf King to emerge. He did shakily and she lithely slinked over to him and shook his hand. He motioned her to the mead hall. The old man turned the page.

***

On the ocean, a dragon ship floated, facing off against a gigantic metal atrocity. The metal ship was piloted by the one called Captain Juno. Juno was a smart man; he had come here with the invasion force even though he was not a Silveran. He glanced up as his female counterpart walked in. She was in full admiral regalia. She nodded to him and he could not help but stare at her horns. She was a Silveran female and also one of the highest-ranking Silveran females he had seen. She looked at the dragon ship and gave him permission. He opened fire; the laser fire burned holes in the ship and it sank.

Three Thullhuid lurked under the water; they could see the metal boat floating above them. Strange rune-like markings appeared around them and one gigantic Thullhuid made of water rose from the water. It screeched something horrible and began lashing out at the boat.

Juno gulped and tried to manoeuvre ineffectively. He saw three shadowy forms in the aquatic beast as the large spiked tendril slammed into the ship.

The large Oregano's ship sank. Juno and the female were the only survivors. They floated on the driftwood of the dragon ship and landed on a sandy beach. It twinkled in the sun. They looked around and saw a road. Off in the distance was a large tower made of vines. They were near the Oreganos Stronghold of Carrotte. The old man, Elion, vanished from the tower with his book. He appeared on top of a hover truck.

***

On the way to the city of Carrotte, Elion, a writer of fate, stood on top of a large hover truck. He was eying the leader of this caravan. She seemed familiar to him. He muttered and swayed heavily as the trucks came to a stop. He leapt off fairly acrobatically for an old man. His white hair blew in the wind. Off in the distance, he saw a large army blockading the road.

The general, a tall, elegant man dressed in skin-tight garb, stood there. The man walked forward and spoke to the woman. Elion could not hear what he said, but he saw the look of alarm in her eyes. The man extended two laser claws from his gauntlets and sliced open the truck. Inside was a small one-man tank. The caravan suddenly opened fire on the army.

As the energy lanced out, the ground in front of the army burst into flame and chunks flew up and struck the enemy. Between the energy lances and flying dirt, Elion could see the elegant general was evading all attacks very skillfully. He decided that it was time to help. But he stopped as the leader of the caravan stepped down wearing a gauntlet with two twenty-sided dice in it. She pressed a button and the dice rolled. She rolled a 29 and the air fogged up and a misty creature rose from the fog and attacked the army. Within seconds the army was dead, but the creature turned on the caravan. Elion and the leader struggled against the creature and it was prevailing. Within minutes they had to flee and the caravan was destroyed. Those two and the elegant general were the only survivors. He fled and they continued on. As Elion and Gem, the leader of the caravan, reached the Oregano's stronghold of Carrotte they had to set up camp outside the city limits. Elion summoned a temporary portal and the two entered it. Inside the portal was a nice little inn. The creature behind the counter was tall, sinewy and had purple energy tentacles surrounding it. He/she, the gender was hard to tell, offered the two a room for the small price of ten Obsidian Six Dollar Bits (in mortal terms, twenty credits or, in layman's terms, five hundred dollars). Elion paid up and the two retired to separate beds. Elion looked in his book and smiled as he watched the female Silveran and her partner.

Juno and his admiral, Beatrice, arrived at the stronghold that night. They also arrived at an inopportune time. As they entered the city, the ground split open. The only light was from the moon and a half and that was all that Juno needed to see. What he saw was the ground caving in and an army of Shadow Elves and Dwarves riding massive bear-badger mole things. He heard the dwarf king order his Bane Bear Cavalry to charge. Elion turned the page.

The Minotaur King looked down at his prisoners and growled that he had stolen their ship and was about to land at the stronghold of Carrotte. The ship thudded and the Minotaur King and his army charged out. They saw the dwarves of the Celtic caves charging the surprised army. The king, Minotaur, sent runes of protection around each of the Dwarven soldiers. He felt something wisp by him and looked down to see a Shadow Elf general slide through the shadows into the stronghold. He sent his rune crafters forward and they cut into the stronghold and out the other side. They would bathe in the blood of their enemies tonight. Elion nodded approvingly and turned the page.

Juno went to help his allies but was held back by Beatrice. She shook her head and pointed up. He looked and saw a mountain bottom covered in ethereal silver symbols. The mountain landed and opened up, revealing a tall man with a little scruff. The man looked around and smiled. Behind him was a ten-foot-tall Thullhuid with sharp blade-like tentacles in the shape of wings. He gulped, but the admiral remained unperturbed. He heard the name, Huntari, in low-frequency colours. He paled as the man walked out. His features were more prominent now. He was missing an eye and his hair looked dishevelled. The woman next to him had two dolls hanging off her shoulders. She moved them surreally and Juno was dragged into the mountain. Beatrice Huntari smiled and walked aboard.

The Minotaur leader walked out of the vine tower and saw the mountain ship. He bellowed and his army walked out. They were drenched with the gore of their enemy. And they were still unharmed due to the Tuarian runes on their armour. As they moved forward, they were stopped by a general in skin-tight clothing that looked vaguely dancer-like. The general ignited his energy claws and attacked. He did not land a blow because the Minotaur King stood in front of him, holding him aloft with his blade. The leader grabbed the general and pulled him off the sword. The general's corpse splurted on the ground with a sickly squelch and the Minotaur clan stepped over it as they moved to the mountainous ship. They walked on, followed by the Shadow Elves, which had convinced the Dwarves to board.

Elion looked down at his book on the next page and released the prisoners of the Minotaur. The prisoners tried to flee, but their ship was grabbed by pinkish energy tendrils and dragged into the mountain. The mountain lifted off and Elion closed the book. He did not see The Butcher break his Shadow Elf bonds and leave the caverns.

Nor did he see The butcher board a ship and head to the continent he was on. He did not see an old man with long white hair and a long sinewy moustache walk into the city. He did not need to see this in his book, for he saw it in his mind. He smirked and began to meditate.

Deep under the sea, The Thullhuid leader Thull Thanos floated, watching his people board the undersea mountains. There were many of them, they had all awakened from their slumber. He would remain on the planet until Bagmot, when he and his child would leave. She floated next to him. Her cuttlefish body had just begun to sprout more features. She was still drowsy, but soon she would be fully awake and fully grown. His facial tentacles twisted up in his species version of a smile.

Elion rose the next morning and saw Gem practising with her armament. She was also stretching and exercising her acrobatics. He watched her for a moment, slightly entranced by her moves, but he turned away as a form emerged from the forest. It was the man in white he had seen in his head. He smiled and welcomed the man to join them. The three sat down for breakfast. A ship shot overhead, a ship filled with reinforcements.

The ship landed and a woman with extraordinarily long red hair exited. The woman was covered from head to toe in tattoos that she had carved into herself. They were all symbols of certain abilities she could activate. She walked out to survey the destruction. She did not notice the mountain was still there, not the same mountain as before but a different one. She looked around angrily and ordered her troops to search for survivors. As they began creating a perimeter, the sky went pitch black, with only the two moons glowing feebly. This was an unnatural darkness, a darkness that was as mysterious as it was deadly.

The mountain had opened up, but it was not producing the inky mist that was surrounding the troops. The Shadow Elf queen stood on the ramp alongside the Dwarf king. Both seemed to be humming in low-frequency colour. The troops began to feel sick and keeled over, vomiting. The humming grew louder and a mysterious streak plummeted toward them. It crashed into the Earth and split or, as the owner would say, hatched.

Thousands of orb-like beasts emerged from the egg pod. This was what it looked like to the onlookers, mostly Oreganos soldiers. The creatures floated but, in reality, were actually walking on the tenth colour of the psychic spectrum. That is, if one were to view this through the PsyQi. They would also see that the orbs were actually foot-tall creatures with flat tails and very round bodies with swirls of colour. They had webbed feet that were covered with soft-looking orbs of fur that helped them balance. They also had eyeballs for a head. Most would say that these things were actually adorable were it not for the fact that they could implode people. That is if you could see them.

The creatures hovered over and surrounded the troops. A soldier screamed and caved in on himself; his energy was absorbed by the Fluff/puff balls. The usually brave troops were thrown into confusion and began opening fire. The orbs floated easily around the energy blasts and bullets. Nineteen more troops imploded. And that was when the ground began shaking and all hell broke loose.

The ground burst open as many bane bears (part badger, part mole, part bear, all business) stormed out. On top of these beasts was another dwarven army. The orbs hovered over and attached themselves to the dwarfs.

The refortified walls caved as the shadow army broke through them. The hover tanks that were in the armoury were brought out and opened fire. One exploded as a very large Minotaur smashed it. This Minotaur was four times the size of an elf and wielded a wicked-looking ball and chain that glowed red in the PsyQi. Red glow usually means that the weapon was made by a species in the galaxy known as Hellions. The giant Minotaur smashed the ball and chain into the tower. Or at least what was left of the tower. The tanks opened fire on this beast and it merely lifted one up, causing the soldier inside to jump out and parachute to the ground. The Minotaur tested the tank on his teeth and then tossed it to the ground. He smashed a building and the rubble fell, revealing a huge vine-like structure that was hidden inside it. The monster stomped, causing a shock wave to lift the tanks several feet in the air and fall, destroying them. The reinforcements fled to the inner sanctum as the vine tower began to writhe. It was sending out a message to Queen Luci Fer. Elion cleared his head and began moving faster.

As Elion entered the city, an overwhelming scent of fear and blood pervaded his sinuses. He looked up at the Minotaur as it shrank down to eight feet and nodded at the Shadow Elf queen, who glared smugly at him. He raised his hand and the tower lit up like a kindle and Luci's screams could be heard through the crackling. A vague shadow of her could be seen screaming.

The Minotaurs were guarding any conceivable exit. The troops came out with their hands up, their general had fled. The Minotaur herded the troops onto the mountain ship along with the Bane Bear army and the Fluffy Puffies. Elion looked in the distance as if seeing something far off that no one else could.

Havold Hawthorne and his daughter, Heather Hawthorne, walked towards the burning tower to see if they could help any survivors. These two were more natural looking than any species on this continent. They had been travelling on the road for some time now and also were hoping to get some warm food and a change of clothes from the troops. The leader of the Crimson Guard, Butcher, appeared covered in burns and shadowy chains. The butcher lunged at the two with his cleaver. He was intercepted by an old man with giant tarot cards. The old man was easily blocking the cleaver with his cards as if there was no effort.

Havold turned as his daughter screamed in terror; what he could perceive made him throw up a little in his mouth. The vague form of a creature from the deep sea had his daughter. He felt a hand on his shoulder and looked around and heard a grunt. He looked up at a very tall Minotaur who motioned him to follow. He did so uneasily because the creature had his daughter.

Elion smiled as another two would be saved from the upcoming Bagmot. He jumped down and sent an energy wave that tossed the butcher aside like a rag doll. Gem stood testing her rolls and pulled out a shifty weapon. This was again one of her specialities, the blade of Chaos.

Elion knew what would happen now that all those that were deemed too powerful for the Oreganos Empire were gone. His eyes focused on the future.

In the citadel of the Oreganos Empire, Luci and her advisor, a tall devilish man nicknamed as the dragon, looked at their plans for conquest. Now that the powerful foes were gone, they needed to crush what was left of the rebellion.

Deep under the sea, Thul Thanos floats, meditating, waiting for his children to awaken. Many have already woken and moved into the mountains. He watches as many more swims into his sight. The next mountain had just been finished with the runes that were needed to move it. It opened and the school of ocean dwellers entered.

The sea was getting empty. That meant the end was near. Thull Thanos smiled a squid-like smile and went back to calling his children to awaken. Three more ships lifted off. The end was near at hand and it was good.

Dawn of Bagmot

I watched as the Satyr opened the first of the seven seals. Then I heard one of the four Eldritch Beasts say in a voice like thunder, "Come!" I looked, and there before me was a white horse! Its rider held a bow, and he was given a crown, and he rode out as a conqueror bent on conquest. – Bagmot Revelation 6 verse 1-2

The sky was a sickly reddish green. It was the dawn of the year, BH 80. The clouds were heavy with poisoned rain. It was not a good day for General Lexa Noir. She had just left her army to be destroyed by the scum that was the rebellion. This was also not a good day because she had been assigned a new partner, a male by the codename butcher. She hated all men and deemed them lower than the scum on the bottom of amoebas. She now had to turn around to rescue him.

She saw him with her enhanced eyesight and was very displeased. He was currently surrounded by two strange people and one she thought she vaguely recognised. This left an unpleasant taste in her head. She charged down the hill throwing fire at the mysterious warriors attacking her partner.

Elion heard the screaming and ducked as fire grazed his hood. He put it out and waved his hand holding the fireballs in place. He spoke, "Gem, stranger, it's time to move Lexa here. Let's retreat for now."

The two backed away and fled into a blue/purple/black folder, with Elion diving into it as it closed.

Lexa stood there glaring murderously at the butcher. Her displeasure radiated from her. She looked toward the city of Charlotte, or what was left of it, which was smoldering ruins. She watched as the mountain near the city lifted off. Her eyes glimmered with newfound energy. Those freaks that caused trouble were gone. She would be receiving orders soon and she was right. Her wrist beeped and she raised it to face level. Out of her watch, a hologram of a woman in red armor appeared.

The woman spoke, "Lexa, I have a job for you and your new partner. There is a small city near you with a very powerful woman. I want the woman captured alive. No incinerations. She is five feet tall with blond hair and red eyes. She is a threat to me and therefore, she is to be imprisoned within the onyx tower. Go, do not disappoint me. If you succeed, I will give you more troops." The hologram immediately disappeared.

Lexa's nose wrinkled up in a sneer. She looked despairingly at the butcher. She really hated men.

***

In the city of Mellone, a purple folder appeared. It became bigger until it opened, allowing three beings to emerge. One had long white hair and a sinewy mustache, one was a female with fatigues on; she had purple hair and green eyeshadow, and the last was a man in a multi-colored shirt with brown eyes and a mullet and beard combo. The three looked around. The old man spoke, "It seems we are in the city of Mellone."

The mulleted man nodded. "I managed to get us here in one piece."

The woman looked him over and shook her head. "Changed form again, have you, old man?"

"Yes, since we are in the city of sin. I figure I may as well look like one of the many tourists. Remember, we are looking for a red-cloaked girl. She also has red eyes. We must find her before Luci."

The white-haired man spoke, "Why do we need to find this girl? Hell, why do I need to help? Who are you people and why did you help me?"

The girl nodded. "He brings up a good point, old man. Why do I need to help you? What is so special about this girl?"

"This girl is the leader of the rebellion. Luci wants to imprison her in the Onyx Tower. Neither of you has to help me. I would like the help, but it's not necessary. Gem Hologram, you will be hunted by the empress if you go off by yourself. You have power and Luci hates those with power. As for you, Crane of Tarot, you are already being hunted. The butcher does not like to leave survivors. When I pulled you in with us, he tagged you. He will be here soon. If you wish to face him by yourself, go ahead. I personally wouldn't recommend it. As for as who I am—I am The Writer. I was sent here to save those deemed worthy from the coming apocalypse. Bagmot will soon be upon us and my brother, Azrael, is still missing."

Gem looked at him quizzically. She grimaced, shrugged and rolled her dice. It rolled fourteen. The sun began setting and an army of shadows appeared. Gem spoke, "Find me every girl with red eyes and bring them to me."

Crane spoke, "That's not going to work. It's too simple."

The shadows brought back four girls and forced them to the ground. The Writer looked them over and smirked. He waved his hands as the ground thundered and a beam of light engulfed the girls and they vanished. He created a lifeless replica of the leader and was suddenly stabbed through the back with an energy sword. He fell to the ground in a heap. The shadows were suddenly incinerated by a wave of fire.

***

Gem rolled to the side as Lexa stabbed at her. The blades meant for her instead went into the old man. She grabbed Crane and yanked him down. He pulled out a black deck of cards and flung them into Lexa.

Lexa gasped as the cards sliced through her skin. She rolled as elemental energy flew out of Crane's hands. She grabbed the replica and vanished as the butcher charged into the fray. His meat cleaver swung wildly. Elion got up off the ground and a wave of energy sliced through the butcher. He fell in half.

"That was annoying. So why did you need a lifeless replica of those girls?"

"Well, Crane, it's to trick Luci into a false sense of security. The Crimson Hood is a vigilante group of quadruplets. They all wear the same outfit so as to make their enemies think the same woman is in four places at once."

"To fall for a replica? Hmm, do you truly believe Luci Fer is that stupid?"

"No, but she will pass it off. They always do."

Gem spoke, "So what was that beam of energy?"

"Look up."

The two looked up and saw a large flying mountain with its hatch open. The hatch closed and it vanished.

Gem spoke, "Okay, well, I can't say I'll ever get used to that. So why are the Mountains flying now?"

Elion smiled, "They are evacuating the planet. When the Mountains fly, you will know our time is at an end. A small prophecy was written by the ancients on a stone clock they hid away in a temple to Quetzalcoatl."

"So this world is really dying then?"

Crane spoke, "Yes, Luci Fer is the herald of destruction. She is but a pawn in the long game. Her advisor is a shifty fellow. I am positive he is testing a theory."

Elion nodded, "I am sure you know what that theory is. However, we must keep going. I have many more to save from Bagmot."

Luci Fer watched in glee as her army took city after city. In each conquered city, a tower was being erected by the citizens of the city. Each tower housed a bit of her. She was using this power to control the people's hearts and minds. They obeyed willingly; they were her thralls.

The Dragon spoke to the gathered generals, "We must pick up the pace. We must find death before the end. We have already captured Euphoria, Lust, and Innocence."

Night of Bagmot

When Satyr opened the fourth seal, I heard the voice of the fourth Beast say, "Come!" I looked, and there before me was a pale horse! Its rider was named death, and Hades was following close behind him. They were given power over a fourth of the Earth to kill by sword, famine and plague and by the wild beasts of the Earth. – Bagmot Revelation 6 verse 7-8

The Writer sat on an outcropping studying the burnt moonlight. Gem was sleeping in a tent. He noticed the Fire Rabbits sniffing around a large altar. Now, this intrigued him. They sniffed and then began dancing a strange dance. This dance seemed to conjure fire. He saw the Earth move as stone golems rose from the burnt hearth.

The Fire Rabbits continue their dance as the mighty gray ash-covered gem-powered golems, the ash golems, saunter toward them. The golems are very interested in the dance. One of the fire rabbits seems to collect the fire around it to form the shape of a woman. The rabbit controls the fire and grabs hold of one of the golems and the two begin to waltz to an inaudible tune. The other rabbits do the same and soon, there is a large masquerade going on. The trees sway in the heavy wind while The Writer watches them. He vaguely hears music on the wind that seems to match the sway of the trees. He continues writing.

A large man emerges from the forest. His hair is wild with the wind. His eyes were like embers burning in the night. This was War and he was amused. His master, Devastation, was currently imprisoned in the land where dead planets go to die. This planet would not be joining them. This planet had a future. He looked up at the sky as acid rain began to fall.

The Writer moved many off the soon-to-be-destroyed planet. They were given vague recollections of their home. These would become the catalyst for rebuilding the world after Bagmot. The Fire Rabbits and Ash Golems had finished their dance and were being escorted onto a large mountain. The Writer smiled.

Luci Fer looked upon her army. Death had not yet been found. "Lexa! Find the old man and artistic woman. Kill them. They are to be destroyed. Do this and you will be greatly rewarded."

Lexa bowed and walked out with a small contingent of soldiers. They did not get far. A massive thirteen-foot-tall man stood before them, this was The Bodyguard of the Eternals. The sky cracked with purple lightning. His black, Silver, and red armor glinted malevolently in the purple lightning. He looked like the beings Luci had brought with her, but his horns were curved down. His battle-ax cleaved through all of the soldiers. They died and were incinerated instantly. Lexa backed away only to glow as all her runes lit up simultaneously. She cried out in agony as she was cooked alive from the inside. The man closed his fist and her corpse hit the ground. He opened his fist, revealing a glowing gem.

He continued into the large tower. Those that tried to stop him were slain and incinerated. He found the prison section. He saw the lifeless puppet of the red-cloaked girl. He removed her and smashed open the containment cells containing Euphoria, Lust, and Innocence. He also gathered the other prisoners and vanished.

Luci Fer sat on her throne. Her vines had hollowed out the planet. Bagmot was upon the lands. Her prisoners had been freed, but she smiled since death was here. The greasy man she called The Dragon stood nearby. Before them stood the woman, the old card master, and Elion. The Dragon vanished, leaving Luci to her fate.

Deep beneath the waves, Thul Thanos loaded up the last ship. All his sleeping children were now aboard. His cuttlefish daughter is still dreaming in her tank. The last mountain left Tara Aerht. The planet shattered behind them. As they flew through the great Star Vale, a curious thing took place. Somehow they were hurtled back through time. When the great mountain landed, they were on a strange planet inhabited by dragons. A massive Silver serpentine Dragon with small spikes on all of his scales seemed to rise from the water. He spoke, "Ah Thul Thanos, keeper of the sea. This was when you arrived. How pleasant. It's a pleasure to meet you for the first time. Welcome to Planet Silver."

***

Bounty Hunter 12 gasped as she awoke. A weathered man stared down at him.

The man spoke, "Ah, you are alive. What a pity! So you are the one to usher in a change. Heh… good!"

"Who are you and how did you get into my private sanctum?"

"I am Sidrodc the mad and as for how I got into your sanctum, well, I am Sidrodc the mad."

"I have never heard of you."

"Haha! Nor should you have. You Taur are scientific and do not particularly believe in the

Gods. However, you still pay lip service to Lord Anubis. I love it. So you now know what your father knew. Tarah-Aert and Silver are connected. Circles within circles, how I loathe circles. Ah, sorry about that. Anyway, I am or once was a seeker of knowledge. Time has a way of changing one's perspective. You can start your path on continent Silver. However, you may want to pass yourself off as a Silveran. They still have some racism towards your kind."

"Thank you for your help."

"Ah, think nothing of it, little mortal. I look forward to what you sow."

"Should I be concerned that you are excited?" All that he heard was mad laughter followed by silence. He shook his head, but now he knew where to start. He would create a God. It was the only way to be remembered.

Continent Silver and the Machinations of Bounty Hunter 12

Bounty Looked at the desolate fortress. This was gifted to him in his father's will.

Why does Father have a fortress on Continent Silver? Who was Father?"

Bounty examined the dusty fortress and then felt something on the back of his neck. He followed his feeling to a large room with a strange-looking orb in the middle of it. He touched the orb despite all senses telling him not to.

The room lit up and he saw a holographic woman appear. She spoke, "Oh, hello. I am the Artificial Intelligence of this home. You have Hunter clan DNA. Are you the new owner of this palace?"

"I am. My name is Bounty Hunter 12."

"Ooo, hello, boss. Good to see you. Shall I clean up the house?"

"Yes, please."

"You're the boss."

He left the core and as he emerged from the path he took, he could see the living area was fully furnished and clean. He could see tiny little robots cleaning up the dust and cobwebs.

Hmm, must find a source of income to make it seem like I can afford this place.

"Computer, find me a job."

The screen lit up and a wanted poster appeared. It was a Marauder Chief that had been terrorizing the Rising Falls area of Continent Silver. He smiled. "Computer, can you please pull up the map of Continent Silver? I wish to know more about these Marauder attacks."

The screen shimmered and a large map of Continent Silver appeared next to the picture of the Marauder chief. He studied the map. He looked at the mountains and nodded. He touched the mountain range and a layout of the caverns that may or may not still exist appeared.

"Computer, do we have any weapons?"

"I can provide most bladed weaponry. Anything with moving parts, like a gun, would not be in my database to manufacture. Your clan believed in close combat. Any guns were considered worthless."

"That is fine. I would not know how to shoot anyway. I'll take a glaive since I am well versed in spear combat."

***

Three men stood on a sun deck on top of a massive skyscraper in the city of Angela's Grove. They watched as another hero battle tore past them. A fourth walked into the sun, then hissed and returned to the shadows of the building.

The first man was a blond-haired blue-skinned gray Silveran. He spoke with a southern Silver accent. "Why do we wait? The city is ripe for burning."

The second man spoke with a thick irescotwel accent, "Ay, that is correct; however, our machines are not yet ready to take this city."

The one who hissed at the sun spoke while his green ember eyes glinted malevolently from the shadows. "The wealthy elite are here. I have taken the liberty of beginning the plan. The wine and beer have been spiked. They will rip each other to shreds."

That night a party was held for all the upper-class elite. The three men stepped outside and an hour later, they re-entered the room. A small girl was giddily playing with the gore of the dead.

The Silveran spoke, "How in the thirteen hells did you survive?"

The girl grinned, bearing her sharp goblin-like teeth. "I drank the vodka, not the fancy stuff."

"Ah, that would explain it, but why are you playing in the gore?"

"It's fun. Gooey and warm. Tastes good too."

"Okay, then, have fun."

***

"I do not like those men. Do you know what they did to me?"

"Calm yourself, Underking. They will get theirs. Old Silver will see to that."

"Hades, I do not trust him. He may be gleeful that those three will attempt to conquer that city."

"Underking… when has Old Man Silver ever let us down?"

"Ugh, you are correct. He has never once let his allies suffer. Still, I am forgotten while you and the other underworld gods are strong. I fear even Old Man Silver has forgotten me."

A fiery bass voice cut through the air, "I have not forgotten you, brother. My predecessors may have ignored you, but I am not them."

The two turned to see a very old Silveran male being wheeled in on a chair by an Angelus nurse.

"What happened to you?"

"Good seeing you too, Hades. How is Persephone?"

"She is fine, but seriously what happened to you?"

"Too many gods feel they would be better at controlling planet Silver. That is what I get for allowing so many different gods to exist on Silver. The fool of an Oni God, Sol, I think his name was, tried to poison me with a nasty concoction. He no longer exists. The ass tried to absorb all the souls of the Oni in his battle with me. Needless to say, he did not last long."

"Wow… remind me never to get on your bad side."

Silver smiled. "I have a plan to help those that have been forgotten. It's not a safe plan, but it is a plan."

"Pray tell what this plan entails?"

"You will soon see, Underking. Very soon, I grow weary. Please, take me back to my resting place."

The Angelus nurse nodded and the two vanished.

"Hades, should I be concerned he seemed almost giddy?"

"I wouldn't put too much thought into it. He is a dangerous friend sometimes but clearly far more dangerous as an enemy."

***

Two men stood on the deck of the building, watching black smoke rise from a massive crater in the middle of the city.

The man wearing a trenchcoat spoke, "You… you just murdered two-hundred-thousand people. You will fry for this."

The blue-skinned man grinned evilly, "Will I? No, I do apologise, Inspector Argent Bubbles. Our time has come to an end. Enjoy the fall!"

The inspector felt cold steel against his neck and tried to jab his assailant but was stabbed through the back. He looked down at the cold steel exiting his stomach and his body was kicked off the sky platform.

The shadowy man snorted as he looked over the railing. "You sure that was a good idea, Zon?"

"Of course, it was, Andrew, with him out of the way, our next step is complete. Petran has completed the machines. We will conquer the city within the month."

"I do hope you are correct. Or our plan to conquer the world is fucked."

Petran walked out covered in grease and various welts. "They will work as promised. I must warn you the girl has taken a liking to one of the drill tankers. I have assigned it to her as a guardian of sorts. I would heavily encourage you not to take her guardian from her. She has a nasty left hook."

"The suggestion has been noted. Why not let her paint it her favorite color so we can tell the difference between it and the others."

***

Bounty Hunter 12 sat in his study. He had managed to create a viable fetus to experiment with. It was floating in a large tube. "I have successfully created life, but I am not certain this is the right way my path should go."

The computer spoke, "Ah, but you know how to create life. So the first step is complete, is it not?"

"That is an astute observation. Yes, that would be correct."

"Oh, you have a call about your secondary services."

"Do I, now? Okay, patch it through."

He looked at the gray-skinned Pure Silveran. "You are calling about my mercenary work?"

The man spoke, "Yes, I am. I am Tsar Zarikon Ankara. I would like you to escort my son Zenthin Ankara to help the city of Angela's Grove. They are under siege from some very powerful robots."

"And your offer?"

"I am willing to pay six hundred thousand commons to keep my boy safe. Add in an extra two hundred thousand common to bring back a robot so that we can understand the technology. Something that can stand up to various super-powered beings is of great interest to me."

"Very good. Am I to pick him up or meet him somewhere specific?"

"Do you have something to pick him up in?"

"I do; however, it's not exactly discrete."

"That will be fine. Is it weaponised?"

"My lord, you are talking to one of the top of the line mercenaries. Of course, it's weaponised."

"Good. He will meet you at the gates of City Silver."

Bounty smirked and walked to his ship port. He looked at the large cobbled-together scrap ship he had relieved those marauders of. Everything worked well. He had been updating it so he could use it as his personal warship. Soon it would be space worthy. He drove it to the gates of City Silver and opened the hatch before stepping out.

He saw a man his age. The man had a dark aura about him. Bounty spoke, "You must be Zenthin Ankara."

The man snorted, "And you are the lowlife who is my bodyguard."

"Lowlife, huh? And who is this lovely beacon of light?"

The woman snorted, "I am Queen Maitaiga Moth of the Rising Falls. You will refer to me as such. Do we really have to deal with this scruffy Balkath farmer?"

"Father wants us protected. I don't see how this man who can't even afford a proper ship can protect us."

"Oh, I am going to love the two of you. Get on; next stop is Angela's Grove."

The two scoffed and walked on, only to come face to face with many auto turrets and a large weapon rack with many blades. Hanging from the ceiling was a very large shotgun.

Bounty spoke, "Touch Becca at your own peril. She's got a hair trigger and likes only my touch."

They saw it emblazoned in fiery silver calligraphy on the side of the Shotgun Becca. When they arrived at Angela's Grove, they saw a large phalanx of robots driving back the heroes.

***

The three men were sitting on their sun deck, watching the chaos down below. Petroth spoke, "Damn Ice users. Should have installed the cold-proof technology in those assassin shadow bots. Ah well, the tankers seem to be doing really well."

The large golems with one massive drill arm and one regular arm were tearing through some of the lesser heroes. However, there seemed to be several invulnerable heroes that were making quick work of the golems. The golems with guns for hands were laying down extreme walls of covering fire.

That was when an entire phalanx was destroyed by gunfire from the air. A large scrap ship was floating over the towers of Angela's Grove. As it cleared the area, it landed and three people stepped out. All three were Pure Silverans. One cocked his shotgun, braced himself and pulled the trigger sending out an explosive rocket that destroyed even more of the golems.

The man with the shotgun smiled a fanged smile and then blew up the control towers. The golems stopped moving.

***

Bounty looked at these golems and snorted. They looked like what Elves would use to dive underwater. Dive suits with drills or guns, depending on the model. He could also see some that were thinner with blades instead of hands. He marked one of each model and caused them to vanish onto his ship in storage. He finished off what he identified as the control towers for the robots, then looked up and saw three dark men.

"My Lord, if you will destroy the rest of these robots. I will make sure no more can be made."

"Hmph! Easy enough, I may have underestimated you." "Battle is not over yet, my lord…"

He stepped in front of the two of them as a bullet hit his left horn, cracking it. He then ignited his hand via the PsyQi and threw a fireball back at the location where the bullet had come from. One of the three men combusted in a cry of terror.

He grunted and shook his head to clear his vision before grabbing one of the heroes. He spoke gruffly, "See those two. If they get hurt, it's your head, got it?"

The kid shook his head in acknowledgement. Bounty leapt and grabbed ahold of one of the flying heroes only to leap off of them, sending them to the ground in a crater and landing on the sun deck with a thunderous bang. He rolled and sliced through one man, then grunted as a knife entered his side. He beheaded the knife wielder. As he advanced on the girl, she backed up in fear. A large drill tanker golem stepped in his way, with the drill whirring threateningly.

Bounty looked at the Golem and then smirked as he put away his pike.

The girl jumped up on the Golem's shoulder and sat cross-legged on its head. She spoke maniacally, "Come, Mr Bubbles, let's go home."

The Golem grunted and stepped onto a platform with a few other golems before the platform vanished in a strange pink and purple portal.

Bounty heard from the portal as he swore he saw a sinister smile with glowing eyes. "Ah, Alice, welcome home." He shook his head to clear it, passing it off as an aftershock from his horns getting struck.

He heard a ticking and leapt off the building as it exploded. He landed with a grunt near the prince and smiled.

The prince looked at him. "Your reputation is not exaggerated. I do like that. I may need your strength soon, Bounty Hunter 12."

"Of course, Prince Zenthin Ankara."

***

Underking looked at the three men before him and let out a dark menacing laugh, "You pathetic mortals thought you could renege on our agreement by destroying me. I am a god. Now you get to suffer… enjoy!"

A pit opened up under them as they were dropped into black and gold fire. As the pit sealed, Underking sat back and sighed contently.

"Feeling better?"

"I am feeling amazing, Silver. I do not know what you did."

God Silver, who spoke while smiling, "I am glad you are feeling better. My chosen has excess power to spare, so he siphons his power to the forgotten gods."

"Is that what you mean by your plan? Well, Old Man Silver, I suppose his name is now."

"All us Silvers are the same, so his plan, my plan, all the same."

"Hah, well, little brother, I thank you for your help."

Silver smiled and vanished in a gout of silver fire.

***

Bounty Hunter 12 sighed and looked at the fetus before him. It was floating in the mechanical womb he created. "This is not working! Why?"

His computer chimed in, "Maybe you need to have a physical womb. Impregnate some female with the specialised sperm you created."

"Hmm, I see what you are saying. The power I seek needs to be natural, not unnatural. Well, at least I know my experiment is stable. Place her in suspended animation. She may have some use yet."

"Of course, sir."

Bounty left the lab and sealed it behind him. He would not need to use the lab. He now had a better idea of what he needed to do.

The Search for Immortality

Bounty Hunter 12 grimaced as he held his side where he had been stabbed. *How had I not known Zenthin would steal from me? I knew he wanted me dead, but I did not know he was so bold as to take my data and create his own child after my experiments.*

As Bounty fell to the floor, bleeding out his purplish green blood, he remembered how it came to this.

***

Bounty was currently kneeling before the new Tzar. His friend Zenthin Ankara had usurped the throne from his father. He had also sentenced his father's allies to death alongside their families. His thought was to keep any dissent from forming. He had already shown his brutality. He had subjugated all the non-Silverans and enslaved them to his allies. Bounty was currently in possession of twenty non-Silverans, including a Felis that he had plans for.

"My Tsar, you are truly the most powerful man now. By showing your strength, you have quelled many uprisings that could have happened. I appreciate these slaves."

"As you should, my loyal friend. Due to your exemplary work in helping me achieve my goals, I would like to offer my sister's hand to you. This will cement our two clans as one."

"And I gladly accept your offer. I look forward to our prolonged unity."

***

Zenthin sat in his war room. His sister, Mia, was sitting next to him. He spoke to her, "Mia… I require you for a plan."

"As always, Zen, I obey."

"I wish for you to wed that man."

"Who Bounty Hunter 12?"

"Yes, he is scheming something and I need a spy I can trust in his home to keep an eye on him."

"Oh… hmm. Very well, Zen, I will wed him. You will be able to keep your eye on him. I will slit his throat personally if he ends up being a traitor."

"Thank you for taking a burden off of my mind. However, should you feel you are at risk, please do not hesitate to return to me and I will annul the marriage."

***

Bounty Hunter 12 sat looking out across the forest that surrounded his house. His disguise as a Half Pure Silveran had dropped due to the immense Psy storm his son had conjured up at birth. The three moons were red and the constellation of the Hunter was in the sky. As his son came from the womb, the halberd of the warrior and the chains of the prisoner appeared. His bull face winced as the Psy storm increased. He was a Taur in reality. His grey fur bristled as thunder ripped through the sky. There was wailing from inside the home. When the Psy storm calmed and he was able to replace his disguise, he re-entered his home. Laying on the bed was his wife. His computer had been able to spare her, but she would not survive another birth like this. His eldest daughter Mar-Ra Looked over at him.

"Father, there are six of them. Three boys and three girls. Father meets Chain, Marla, Mia, Deirdre, Chaos, and the final is unnamed. We await to hear it from you. Is this the prophesied thirteenth Hunter?"

Bounty looked down at the boy. His intelligent eyes stared back. They sent a chill down his spine. And in his cowardice, he did something he would regret until his death. "No, he does not match the prophecy. Get rid of him. I care not how."

She bowed and vanished. Leaving his elder son, Gawain, to shake his head in disappointment.

***

On Continent Diavonbre, two brown-skinned boys were being cleaned up from the afterbirth. The woman cleaning them smiled sweetly, then handed them to a large Arachnetaur.

He looked them over and then smiled. "Yes, they are perfect. I do feel bad your wife had to die in labour, Lord Wulf."

"Do not worry about it, old friend. She is now at peace. Can you tell which one Efreet has chosen?"

"Both, but one will fail the test. I look forward to their training."

"It shall truly be glorious. I am just concerned that something will be wrong with them. Did you see how the moons went blood red?"

"I did, Lord Wulf. That just means they are special."

"If you say so, Anansi. In Silveran culture, when the moons glow red, that means the planet will consume blood. Back in the old days, when we were still warring tribes, we would sacrifice our prisoners to the woods to keep them at bay. It is not a good thingwhen the moons glow red."

"Ah, but you are not as fine-tuned to the Magic Melody of the Universe as I am. They are special since last night, a very dangerous being was born on Silver. So strong as to be deemed a god but not a god."

"So, a change then? Well, that bodes ill."

***

Bounty Hunter 12 lay in bed with his new wife. After the difficult birth several years ago, his wife, Mia Ankara, had begged her brother to annul their marriage. Zenthin had happily obliged. However, this new wife was Zenthin's own daughter. Mar-La was even better for his plan. She was young, powerful, and a skilled warrior. He fondly remembered her chopping off his horn during their fight.

"Lightning flash rumble of the thunder death on those who hunted you. Behold the Thunderer Helm and Gauntlets. The sound of rage roars in the wind, behold Dragons boots, arms and scales. As your wrath like water rushes to drown the treacherous, behold Cloak of Wind and Water. Rise Nightmare beast arises with the amulet of thorns."

"Are you done yet, Mar-la? Or should I attack you now?"

"Wait, you were just standing there?"

"Yeah, I don't think it would count if I were to strike you while you were enchanting yourself."

"Uh, then prepare to fall on my blade!" "Sure."

Bounty prepped his pike as she charged him.

She had desired him to prove himself and he did. Her cybernetic arm attests to his strength.

***

In the city of Silver, among the dark back alleys of the city, a girl lay in the muck, her tattered pink dress torn. Blood was coming from her vagina, where she had been brutally raped. Her eye was black where the man had punched her. She was crying, begging for help, but no one could hear her. Well, no one except a man overlooking the city on one of the roofs of a building. He saw her originally as prey, but his heart softened when he got closer and saw the state she was in.

He gently picked her up and wrapped her in a warm towel. He held her in his arms as she cried. He searched her mind seeking out why she was out there. He learned she was from clan Lughnasadh and she had fled from her home because of dark forces. That was how he read it; her mind was just saying her family was acting weird. He followed the directions in her mind to her home. It was a modest-sized home with a dog house out front which currently had a girl chained to it on a leash.

He grimaced and walked toward the girl. She let out a feral growl and then collapsed. He saw she was emaciated from lack of food and nutrition. He hid as a woman walked out and tossed some scraps on the ground causing the girl to hungrily gnaw at the bones. He cloaked himself and entered the home to see the woman from before riding an older man while an older woman watched them.

The woman climaxed as the man filled her up. He then struck the older woman and forced her to eat out their daughter. Bounty saw that the man was actually a Kytanmatriarch. He grimaced. *I thought the Kytan had been wiped out due to their parasitic nature.*

The girl he was holding looked up at him with a pleading look. He nodded and stroked her until she dozed off and then stabbed the man, swiftly revealing his body its true self. A small wave washed through the house, snapping the rest of the family back to normal. The mother, however, was broken. Her mind was only able to be subservient and enslaved. He grimaced.

He spoke into his com, "Mar-La, I am putting you in 3d mode. I found something that may interest you. I had originally been hunting a weakling for prey but have since changed my mind. The woman you see before you used to be a great warrior and was mind raped by a Kytan and can no longer function as the family matriarch. I would like to take her in as a secondary wife so that her family, who were all mind raped by this Kytan, can survive. Though I am not sure, it's such a good idea."

"She seems useless. That is fine, husband. Place a collar on her and she will be my pet. I will accept her children as my own."

"Thank you for easing my troubled mind Mar-La."

"Sure, whatever."

When he brought them to his home, he immediately began training them. His current children helped. Mar-a, Chain, and Biran worked hard to train the girls in self-defense and other useful skills. Chain could tell his father was troubled by something, but he did not know what.

***

The night was calm, all three moons were full and there wasn't a cloud in the sky. The rocky terrain was foreboding but not difficult. Two men stood side by side on the cliff outside a small cottage. One was significantly older than the other. He had a wizened grey beard and wore a robe of blood red. His hair was long and bleached white by age. The other was a demon of a man with two horns jutting out of his temples. They were small but sharp. He wore pale green armour that accented his black fu manchu. On his head was a bronzed circlet that wrapped around his coarse black hair.

The older man spoke, "So, Bonty, what is troubling you?"

The younger man replied, "Crane, my wife is pregnant with septuplets. She will not survive the night of their birth. I have also been summoned to the King of City Silver's Throne. I have a feeling Zen Ankara wants me dead. If he executed me, I need you and The Dragon to assist with the birth of my children. They must survive. It took decades for my father, Bounty Hunter 11, to bring our clan back to the glory it held. My father died protecting me so that the Hunter clan would prosper. Now on the cusp of glory, I, too, will be snuffed out. Promise me, Crane, you will try to get along with your fellow immortal to make sure my children grow strong."

Crane, the older man, smiled. "General Twelve, I give you my word that your children will live to avenge your death, should it come to that."

"I am afraid it will, my friend. Zenthin Ankara is my father-in-law. He has been deceived by darkness. He has already slain many of the Clans in opposition to him. He has replaced the governing body with his supporters and family members. I am the last of the five great clans. My death is assured."

"That is not necessarily true. Your wife actually has octuplets."

"Then he is not the one. I forsook my previous son because he did not fit the prophecy. I was a fool."

"I agree about the fool part, but Braid may have been the chosen one if given a chance. He was not. However, The one that is to be born from your wife is the one because you forsook your first powerhouse of a son fate had to fuck around and create this one. But because it was a last-minute thing. He was quickly added to the ones already in your wife's womb. Fear, not Bounty. For the one that will be the Thirteenth Hunter is the one to be born from your current wife."

"That gives me a glimmer of hope, Crane, but not much."

"As my word as a former God Silver, I can assure you. Things are now in motion. The Thirteenth Hunter will be born. Now I believe you have a meeting to attend to."

***

Bounty looked up at the boy who had wounded him. Zen had called him Bonestorm. "You think you are the best. No, I am sorry to say the data your father created you from was only a prototype. You will die. Maybe not by hand but by another's. And you, Zen, I thought you were the one to lead Silver to greatness. No! In one hundred years, you will learn the folly of your ways. Goodbye, old friend. May Lady Luck always be in your way."

He let out a hearty laugh as his disguise gave way. He slumped to the ground. His body vanished as soon as Bonestorm went to slice his head off. All the two heard was dark menacing laughter. Bounty Hunter 12 was no more.

Schemes Coming to Fruition

Argon the Slayer

The wind seared my lungs as I stumbled out of my pod. I have no recollection of this place. I have no recollection of what I am. I look at the wreckage and see myself lying there. I help the doppelganger up and we get some ways away when an explosion has destroyed the strange wreckage. I hear voices as darkness overcomes me.

I woke up, who knows how long later in a white room that smells of pine. The first thing I see is three very well-endowed women with red hair and white skirts. All three had a large red plus sign on their chests which were covered by spandex. I am surprised by their looks and one turns to me. She is startled that I am awake. She gulps, visibly disturbed.

I asked, "Where am I and why do you look so disturbed?"

The woman said, "Well, you are on Neo-Earth, the only techno-organic planet in this galaxy. My sisters and I are disturbed because…"

"Because," said one of the others. "You were prophesied by our lord protector Darien Marr."

The third gulped and said, "Emily, we shouldn't have told him that." Emily snarled at the girl, who whimpered and fled the room.

The one who was talking to me smiled weakly and said, "My sister is a little grumpy. We have been healing the wounded non-stop since this God's Forsaken War. I am Liz and I am taking care of you and your comrade Scott."

I looked at my doppelganger and realised it was a twin I was looking at. I finally realised my stomach was groaning in pain.

I struggled up and said, "Where can I get some nutrients?"

"Our adopted sister will escort you to the armoury and then to the food."

I then noticed a beautiful blue-skinned red-haired girl walk in and she was stark naked. She looked at me and grinned lustfully.

Emily snarled, "Stop it, Ami. You are no longer a sex slave from Murcurose. Get that into your small brain and stand up for yourself."

Ami stood straight and led me to a huge room full of weapons. I saw a Red skinned man with a goatee standing defiantly. Ami spoke, "Cristobel Sultan Retseirp get ready to fit this man in lord's armour. He is attending a banquet in the main room."

The man walked over to me and lisped, "Well, he sure is a fine specimen. I know just the armour."

He pranced to a wall and pushed a button and a large suit of armour appeared from nowhere. The armour had spikes on the shoulder pads, knee braces, and elbow braces. It also had two gauntlets covered in large spikes that curved up. The boots were black and looked like leather until one got up close, revealing it was metal. I tried it on and it bonded to my body. It was tight until I moved my arm and found it quite comfortable. It was also lightweight and I had to ask, "What is this made of?"

Cristobel said, "I built it with a combination of steel, titanium, Silver, gold, and iron. It is the toughest metal known to Elvin kind."

Ami smiled and looked at me, saying, "Now for the food; if you just follow me, I will take you to his lord's table. You, like me, are part of his lord's guardians. We protect Prince Silas Horon-Mon."

We walked into the huge room and I saw many strange species. First, I noticed more red-skinned men like Cristobel Sultan. Then I saw strange, almost blurry multicoloured men. Next, I saw small aliens with huge heads.

I turned to Ami and asked, "What are they?"

Ami spoke happily, "Those are called Big Heads. They are all scientists."

The building suddenly squealed and Jason spoke, "That would be our next stop, Africa. We are on his majesty's Behemoth class land vehicle." The door opened and seven tall, dark-skinned elf men walked in, their hair tied in warlocks. The head man walked over to the prince and talked to him.

While another man, this one huge and burly, slid up to Ami and spoke, "Oh, the prince knows how to pick worthless Murcurosians."

Ami whimpered as the man fondled her. I stood and snarled, "Leave her alone."

The man turned to me and struck me, saying, "Whelp! Speak when spoken to." I slammed into him.

He stumbled back and then charged at me. Scott intercepted him and threw him out of the way.

I smiled and said, "Thanks, bro." He smiled and we both tackled the man as he got up.

Soon the whole food room was in a fight. One tried to pull out his massive axe but was tackled by a copper-haired man, a bronze-haired man, and a metallic green-haired man. I was sidetracked as I rolled to avoid the man's fist. Scott leapt on the man's back as I kicked his legs out from under him. Suddenly a huge screech filled the room and bounced off the walls. Everyone fell to the ground writhing in pain, except me because I had sensed it somehow.

The prince stood and yelled, "Who started this and why?"

I raised my hand and said, "I did. I was standing up for a comrade, little Ami."

The big guy profanely touched and spoke to her. The prince looked at me and smiled, saying, "Well, Argon, you have done something no one else would to an ally. And for that, I commend you. So does Blood Gulch, the leader of these warriors."

The huge man that had been speaking to the prince smiled and said, "Your comrades are very fierce and I commend them for their bravery. Axel couldn't even pull out his huge broad axe and attack. We will be happy to aid you." The HQ continued on its way until a massive explosion caused us to halt.

As all the men pulled out a gun, I felt my side and realised I had no gun. I silently growled and muttered, "Stupid effeminate man."

We walked out wary and suddenly, the whole first flank was cut down by a hail of bullets.

One of the generals yelled, "Men take cover!" Half the troop dove into the bushes. I looked around while in hiding and saw shadows in the trees. The trees were massive and scraped the sky.

I leaned over to Jason and said, "Get me up there and I will be able to help… Cristobel Sultan did not get me a gun."

Jason whispered something to Batholomew and I was handed a grappling gun. I fired it up and into the trees. It wrapped around a branch and I was launched upwards. I saw twenty shadows in each tree and smiled. I climbed up and started throwing tan, red-haired elven beings from the tree. I got up to the top and jumped to the next one. I continued tossing the soldiers off one by one, finally clearing the trees.

I climbed down the tree and met Jason and the Prince. Jason spoke, "My goodness, that was amazing. How did you do that?"

I shrugged my shoulders and spoke, "I just trusted my instincts and they did not fail me."

Jason smiled and grabbed a soldier saying, "Alright, where are the rest of your soldiers?"

The woman snarled, "I will not tell you anything, imperial scum."

The general from before walked over and said, "Leslie, what have you learned?"

A man grunted and got up. "Well, I learned falling one hundred stories hurts like hell."

"No, about the rebels."

"Oh and I refuse to talk in front of the traitors."

Jason turned to the prince and said, "What is he talking about?"

Horon Mon gulps and then walks inside the HQ, his shoulders sagging. Jason turned to go in when Teal shouted, "I could use a little help here."

The African warriors look to see their leader wounded, so they rush him inside. Jason yelled, "Drill you and the others get inside and protect the prince Bat and I will aid Teal."

I saw the copper-haired man rush inside along with the rest of the protectors. Jason pulled out a sword and said, "These would be the berserkers we were told to watch out for. We had better hurry before Teal dies."

The three of us rushed to the open plains and saw a half of Teal's troops dead and the other half wounded. They had managed to kill forty per cent of the berserkers. Teal was still fighting. I picked up massive swords called claymores, according to Jason, and charged into battle.

I didn't quite remember what happened next, but I woke up in the Med bay a week later. Ami was watching over me diligently. It looked like she had nothing to eat in days.

She was startled when I opened my eyes and yelled, "Liz, he's okay. The experiment worked." I saw Liz rush over and push a button. I felt a searing pain and then a slight numbness in my arm.

I was then helped up by Teal, who said, "Thanks, man, I was almost killed out there. My troops and I thank you, but we are now retired because all of us sustained major injuries."

"Well, what exactly did I do? I don't quite remember clearly."

Jason walked in and spoke, "Well, we saw you easily lift up two claymores and charge into the Irescottway berserkers. After that, we saw limbs and other parts flying as if in a circle around a central point. This continued until a huge bloody whirlwind whipped up. When we looked again, only you stood there, both arms completely shattered, with one terrified red-haired girl who looked as if she had wet herself. It looked as if you had stopped right before you beheaded her. As if she reminded you of someone. She is now in Area 100, a prison facility developed by the empire."

"What was the experiment you performed on me?"

Liz smiled and said, "Well, it was a Nanite injection that healed up your bones. We did not expect you to make a full recovery, that's why Ami was so astonished that you woke."

Jason said, "Nanites?"

Teal responded, "Well, Nanites are small semi-organic machines that basically assist us and cause us to heal fast. Almost every Neo-Earthian has them except a few select ones and those are the prince's bodyguards. Like the lot of you."

Jason smiled and said, "The funny thing about this all is that your armour had no blood on it whatsoever."

Teal spoke, "Wow, that came out a whole lot different than I thought it would. I thought you were going to say that those of us with nanites sure are dying more than those of you without them."

The prince rushed in and said, "Sorry to break up this happy-go-lucky party, but we are all wanted criminals by my father. He has declared us traitors to the empire. And he has sent his personal army to kill us. In fact, they are already here."

I said, "I will hold them off until you all get to safety. Go into space or whatever."

I walked out the door without hearing the response from the group and was face-to-face with a huge army. I smiled and pulled out my swords. I then charged into them and soon, I saw a huge bloody whirlwind pick up and suck in more troops. I stopped and saw six men staring in awe. I wiped my swords off and sheathed them. I then struck a fighting move pose and motioned them to attack.

They blindly charged in. I lightly stepped out of the way of their fists and lashed out smoothly, gouging the eyes out of one while swinging around and knocking two to the ground by taking out their knees. I avoided another blow as I slammed my fists into the stomachs of the two I knocked down. I then did a forward rebound and landed behind another one, which I struck on the neck. The other two were terrified and fled. I then noticed a huge burly man with massive muscles who walked into view holding the two cowards by the seat of their pants. He set them down and roared at me. He slammed his fist into me and I passed out.

I wake up in a cell with a red-haired girl and a strange lizard being. The lizard walks over and said, "Welcome to area 100. I am Don Demarco and this small fleshling is Ray Firehawk. Our third cellmate is somewhere… ah, here they bring 'im'." I looked and saw a blue-haired man being dragged.

They opened the cell and threw him in. He groaned and saw me. He said, "Nice to see a friendly face. I'm Raiden Scarabaeldae. My brother sent me here after hereplaced the prince in the emperor's eyes."

Raiden then passed out from the pain. Don lifted him up and placed him on the bed and spoke, "Well, he won't wake for a while. Crap, here they come." The guards opened the cell door and grabbed the girl.

I grappled one of the guards and twisted his neck, killing him. The other guard pulled out an energy rod and lunged at me. I pulled the rod from him and impaled him with it. His smouldering body hit the floor with a thud.

Two guards in black suits walked over. One was bald and had a tattoo of a skull on his head. The other was thinner and had red hair with black streaks. Both werewielding electrically-charged rod-like weapons like the one I had fried. They attacked in unison and grappled me and dragged me to a large grey room with torture devices—all looked deadly. I was tied to the ceiling and my feet were tied to a crank.

The bald man spoke, "I hope this will teach you to mind your matters." He turned the crank and I felt several of my bones pop. I smiled and said, "Thanks, I've been trying to get that kink out for days."

The red-haired man snarled and said, "HeyRondohesasmartaleckainthe."

The bald man sighed and said, "Excalibur, how many times must I tell you to stop talking so fast."

Excalibur smiled and said, "Let'storturehimagainitsfun."

I rolled my eyes and said, "Are you two ladies done talking yet or should I go back to my cell?" That comment earned me a hit in the stomach and then it devolved into me being a punching bag for the two of them.

I awoke in the cell again and groaned as I got up.

Don spoke as if reading my mind, "You've been out for a week."

I cracked my neck and shivered. I viciously punched the bars and they shattered. The two men rushed to our cell and I viciously slammed into them, causing Rondo to sag to the ground unconscious and then I kicked Excalibur, who passed out from the force of the landing. The two lay unconscious and I sat down, causing Don's jaw to drop.

He spoke, "I'm getting outta here."

I stopped him. "Do you really want to face those guard drones right now?"

He looked up and spoke, "Oh, I forgot about those beasts. Well, just go destroy them. You took out the heads of this facility. Oh wait, the smaller guards fuck."

I smiled and said, "Hey, we have prisoners trying to escape." The entire group of soldiers rushed to our cell. Don smiled and created an energy sword from nowhere. He cleaved through all of the soldiers mercilessly.

He then picked up a gun and tossed it to Ray, saying, "You know how to use one of these?" She picked it up and opened fire, destroying the drones. The two of them hoisted up Raiden and hurried to the docking bay.

I sighed and continued to free prisoners. All were soon freed except for a room that said WARNING. I broke into the room and saw a young man in stasis. I slammed into it, causing the facility to begin to self-destruct. I got all the personnel out, along with the two who were just beginning to come. The station exploded as I covered the young man with my body.

I woke up in an energy cell. The young man stood, he looked dumbfounded and said, "Well, thanks for saving me. You have been out for a year, which was worrying us."

I groaned and said, "I only see you. Who else is here?"

The kid helped me up, proving he was much stronger than he looked. I saw a man with grey hair standing with a small big head on his shoulder. I then noticed a furry woman with no clothing and big breasts.

I saw a Lionman who was dressed in full armour and he was standing next to a man in grey. I groaned and muttered, "What a nightmare."

The Lionman laughed. "This ain't no nightmare and believe me, I know nightmares."

The kid smiled and said, "These guys heard about your valiant escape and how that cowardly lizard fled, leaving you behind. We wish to help bust out of this joint."

I walked forward and looked out of the cell. Suddenly I felt really heavy and asked, "Why do my legs feel sluggish?"

The kid said, "Well when you saved me, both of your legs were destroyed. So the scientists gave you cybernetic implants that allow you to walk but will keep you slow, so you don't escape again."

I asked, "While we're on the subject, who the hell are you guys?"

The kid smiled. " Well, the grey-haired man is an enigma. He is from planet grey, that I know. The big head is Ami, the Venusian. I don't know where Goldenrod, Greydenrod, and Zed are. Also around here is the White master. I am Cheleon and the catgirl is Cleo."

I smiled and said, "Why are we in such a strong cell?"

The kid looked at me and then placed his hand on his chin as if contemplating something. He then said, "Well, I assume it's because you have escaped once already and they want you kept in one place. I think they may be afraid of you."

I laughed and sneered at the guard, "You women are afraid of a teenager? Pitiful!" The guard pushed a button and entered in with nine others.

I sneered, "You women wish to play, so be it…"

I slammed into the first one causing him to slump. The others attacked. I was soon piled upon but launched up, causing them to fly into the various walls around me.

I sat down and waited for the mega guards to show up. They did and I was hauled away to the prison torture area. I saw the energy core and smiled. The lead guard walked in. He was holding a large bomb, he just smiled and said, "Get the welder."

I saw the female guard walk in with another prisoner and lay her on the table. She flicked a switch on her gauntlet and the bighead screamed as her body was welded together. My eyes glowed darkly as my anger resurfaced. The guards used me as a punching bag and then welded the bomb to me. They set me in the cell and I noticedthe grey-haired man. He was fiddling with something. He smiled and stepped back, revealing Ami the Venusian curled up happily in a warm blanket and wrapped in a cradle that the man then placed on his back. The kid walked over to me and looked at the bomb.

He traced strange markings in the air and the bomb floated off. He smiled, saying, "We have three hours to escape before this place is destroyed."

The lion man walked through the cell and said to me, "Tell the kid that the guards are immobilised. And have been removed from the facility."

I spoke, "My spirit guide has told me the guards are immobilised so we can start freeing the prisoners. I will handle the head of this blasted prison. If I am not back in one hour, get out. I am a soldier of honour and will not stand for what these prisons stand for. Especially what these prisons stand for and who created them. I can now see why they were awed by me. They called me the chosen one. Now I see what I can do to help them. I am Argon the Slayer."

The kid raised his eyebrow and walked out. He said, "See you then. Good luck with your quest, but please hurry and destroy this place."

The kid led the prisoners to the ships and I went to find the head of this facility. I came across a tall, elegant man. He was dressed in a skintight, very feminine dress. He turned to me and smiled as two energy claws extended from his gauntlets. He coed happily and attacked.

I dodged his first swing, but then he began glowing and sped up swipe after swipe struck me. Blood was beginning to seep from my gashes. I fell, gasping; suddenly, a shot rang out and the effeminate man fell with half his face blown off. I felt a furry paw help me up and a purring. Cleo got me out right before the station exploded.

When I woke up, I was in a white chamber. A nurse walked in and handed a sinister man a small compact bomb.

The sinister man spoke, "I have no more use for you, Tara Talon. We captured you six years ago. Your time is up. Soon so will Amelia Goth's, your lover, I believe."

He then turned to me and said, "Argon Retseirp, I will now show you the power of the Magus." He electrocuted the nurse, who fell smouldering.

He laughed and said, "You are now a full Android. If you try anything funny, all I have to do is push a button and you die."

He then turned to a female guard and said, "Take them away and place them in the cell with the ferals."

The girl obeyed and ruthlessly threw me in and gently placed the nurse on the bed. She yelped and fled. I looked around and said, "Oh this is really starting to piss me off."

A wolfish man growled and said, "Tell me about it, this is the third time I've been here. Oh, and since we know who you are, I will introduce you to the crew. I am Will W. Wolf. My comrades are Aladdin Ien, just call him Al Ien, Shadow Scar Hunter, also known as Shadow S. Hunter. My good friends Judas Bloodsong and Toreno. We have escaped from this facility three times. This is

Area 300."

The radio blared, "In today's news, both Area 400 and 500 have been destroyed by a huge ship that is rumoured to belong to the Rebel prince Horon Mon."

Will Wolf howled happily, as did all of the prisoners. I chuckled and looked at the wall. I saw an indent and pulled it open, seeing tons of wires. I laughed and said, "Ah poor simple fools forgot to learn about Androids when they recreated me to contain me. Increased strength, no tiredness and unfortunately, no sex organ."

I lifted the wires and pulled them from the wall viciously. The entire station went into a blackout and I walked through the station. I soon released all the prisoners who got to their ships. I heard gunfire and screaming and a bloodthirsty howl.

I then heard ships lifting off. I bumped into the female guard and spoke after jabbing her in the side, "Take me to the core and don't try any funny shit."

The frightened soldier led me to the core and said, "Are you going to kill me?"

I smiled and said, "Why would I kill you? I only wish to destroy this facility."

The green glow of the room pulsed as I opened my chest and pulled out the bomb. I placed the bomb in the core and closed my chest. I walked with the wounded guard out and heard a scream of terror. I went back in and encountered the mage torturing a young woman.

Al was unconscious in the corner. I yelled, "Hey monster, I was the one who freed her. It is me you want. Bring it on." The mage attacked in a rage.

He lunged at me and then jumped back, his body swirled with energy and he began firing energy at me. I rolled towards him and launched up, hitting him in the chest. He roared in agony. As he fell, I saw in the dim light a hole in his chest. He laughed weakly and pulled out the control. I rolled and grabbed Al and the girl as the station exploded.

I awoke in a cell made of some type of energy. I felt a strange energy as a tall, elegant lizard-like being very much unlike Don.

I looked at him and said, "Are you imaginary?"

The lizard laughed and said, "No, Argon, I am your rescuer. The prince is here and waiting for me to bust you out."

The lizard traced more lines and said, "See you on the other side."

The alarms went off and I saw millions of aliens flee into the docking bay while killing guards left and right. I saw a wounded werecat trying to protect her kittens. I ran

to her and realised all aliens were gone except for her and I. I covered her as the station exploded. I burst out of the rubble in agony.

I looked down and saw spikes on my torso and legs. There were spikes on my arms and I groaned. I helped the catgirl up along with her kittens. She purred and nuzzled me and then ran off carrying her kittens.

***

A small girl ran over to me and whimpered, "Supreme General Blade is right outside with three men. He's found us!"

I patted her on the head and walked out. I saw a huge man with two thick horns jutting from the sides of his head. All of his spikes were tipped with grey and his cape fluttered in the invisible wind.

He sneered, "So Silver was right. You are here. The great Argon the Slayer is rumoured to be the strongest in all of Silveran history. What the twins of Mick Mack didnot accomplish, I will. You are dealing with a man who genetically altered his body so he can shoot energy spikes from his body. Prepare to meet God Silver."

I looked at him and smiled. "I see you heard of me." I struck my dragon-style pose and motioned him to attack. He laughed and pulled out his sword and lunged at me. I swiftly dodged and rolled behind him and punched him in the mid-back. He reeled and spun, nearly decapitating me. I pretended to trip and caught myself with my hands. I then transferred my weight to my legs and kicked him, with both of them, in the stomach. He stumbled and fell. As I went in for my finishing move, he raised his sword and stabbed me in the stomach.

I stumbled and then stood. The sword was all the way through my abdomen. I looked down and saw small sparks flitting from the gash. I chuckled and said, "Obviously, you haven't heard it all."

Blade stepped back and blanched. He threw off his cape. I saw the three men dive for cover. I felt an increase in power and saw his body glow oddly. And out of the blue, spikes fired from his body. I put my arms up to cover my face and felt an odd presence.

When I looked, I saw Enigma standing with Amy. The two both had their hands out and blade was on the ground writhing. Enigma walked over to me and pulled the sword from my body. Amy took a vile of fluid and poured it into my body. As if something awoke, I felt energy coursing through my body.

Amy smiled and spoke quietly, "Your nanites are back. They now work in harmony with your body. If you fear death, place the little guys back into this fluid and then when you reincarnate, place them back into your body. They contain all memories and genetic enhancements you had up until the point of death."

I looked at Amy and smiled my thanks. I looked down and saw the cut seal. I then turned to Blade as Amy and Enigma disappeared.

Two men bowed before me. I looked at them and said, "Very well, I accept."

I turned to blade and knelt down. I placed my palm on him and smiled. I easily lifted him up and brought him into the sick bay of my new home. I attached him to the heart monitor and had the computer scan him. I saw, in the scan, a strange object embedded into his shoulder. I gently picked up a knife and sliced open his shoulder. A blood-red crystal fell out. I picked it up and it glowed and then rolled up into my arm. Blade awoke as I sewed him up. I stood over him, still holding the knife I was using. He yelled and tried to escape.

I held him down and calmly said, "You need to rest and recuperate. Relax, I am not here to kill you. If I was, you'd be dead already." He looked at me as I left and then passed out.

***

I looked around and said, "We may as well rest here tonight. Get some sleep so we can attack the city tomorrow."

The troops and my allies, except Monohorn, walked into the destroyed base. I sat down as night fell and looked across the valley. I saw a huge fire burning in the city and saw two figures running away from the fire into the woods with two bodies. I sensed an ominous presence that I had felt before I got knocked unconscious and before every explosion I caused in the areas. I turned around to see two women standing there, both were naked and one was holding the other. I recognised the girl from the underwater pass. The other was unknown to me. The taller one with black hair cut open her breast and a crystal dropped and rolled over to me. The other one healed her and a flash of energy showed a tall Pure Silveran Silhouette covered in writhing shadows. The figure vanished and a tall three-fourths pure appeared. The two girls stepped aside and the man walked forward.

"So you are the loner who challenges my master. I am Javelin Blade. Prepare to die!" I looked at Javelin and pulled out my sword. He pulled out his as well. We clashed while lightning flashed and thunder rumbled. The stone was soaked in blood and rain. Monohorn charged in like an enraged rhino. The two girls attacked him, holding him off. I saw a huge winged man with many horns land and help out Monohorn. I jumped back as a sword sliced past me. Suddenly Javelin slipped and fell. He tumbled and I caught him before he fell off the cliff.

I hauled him back up and he lay wounded on the ground. The two girls ran over

to him. The grey-haired one quickly healed him, but he was bleeding out fast. Monohorn walked over and traced odd runes in the air. The runes surrounded Javelin and he and the two girls disappeared.

Monohorn spoke, "Well, that was interesting. What do you make of it, Teal?"

The winged man walked into sight and spoke, "Well, I think they went back to Spike tower. You did good, Monohorn. He has been purified from his curse. Zarbon will be quite happy to have his student back."

The two walked off and I looked towards the city. The fire had died down and only smoke was simmering in the air. The sun rose and I saw a massive charred husk of a building. I smiled and stood.

Monohorn helped me up and said, "Here, kid, let me help you. You really need a break."

I said, "No, I cannot take a break until my father's death is avenged. He was murdered by Zen Aka."

Monohorn shook his head and said, "Kid, take a breather. We have a long way to go until we get to the city."

***

I walked to the spike tower to talk to Enigma to see if he could handle the students some more. I entered the newly rebuilt spike tower's door. Enigma walked out with Ami the Venusian on his shoulder.

He smiled and said, "I take it you need more time something has come up?"

I smiled and said, "Well, I found a magus who was born from Leon von Blackheart's blood and supposedly mine. I will personally invade the magus stronghold on Golgotha, but since I will be passing myself off as a master, I need a temporary apprentice."

Ami smiled and said, "We have one. She has been unruly, but to get her, you must demonstrate how to get through the Leviathan, our holographic training grounds. Please follow William."

A tall wolf-man walked out with Cleo clinging to him and a strange furrymonkey-like being. He led me to a large door and spoke mentally to me, "Walk through the door and show us how it's done."

I opened the door and was on a huge stone bridge hovering over lava with many chains dangling from the ceiling. I began walking across the bridge and was suddenly attacked by Androids. I was thrown off the bridge but caught myself on a chain. I swung back and knocked the Androids off the bridge. I then swung from chain to chain and landed on the other side.

I opened the next door and appeared in a windy wasteland. The wind whipped up, but I pushed through as the wind got stronger. I closed my eyes and summoned a counterwind that caused the wind to neutralise. A door appeared and I walked through.

I appeared in a valley of solid stone. I scanned the area and was ambushed. I pulled out my sword and attacked, the ambushes became more frequent and I dispatched all Androids. Another door appeared over a cave and I entered only to appear in a giant plain of ice. I skated forward and showed off a bit until the Androids attacked. I dispatched them and showed off more until a door appeared.

I entered the door and was on a small stone island surrounded by water. I summoned stone steps since the door was high above me. As I carefully jumped from stone to stone, the water formed figures that leapt at me, trying to knock me off. As I neared, the huge top waves destroyed the stones. I caught the water in my hand and then pole-vaulted off the last stone to land on the platform. I opened the door.

I appeared in a massive Jungle. I growled softly and spoke, "Stop recording. Something has malfunctioned."

Enigma responded, "The malfunction happened within the ice area. We cannot stop recording, for it is a part of the Leviathan. I growled as a tall man in Black Armor emerged from one of the trees. Lord Psycheo and I will kill you."

The figure vanished and everything went dark except for a blue moon in the sky. I leapt from tree to tree and finally found a door. I opened it and came upon a throne room. I went to a computer and saw twelve symbols appear:

I looked at them carefully and smiled. I typed in the second half of the sector. Stinalta, Volcano, Ice, Techno, Lizard, Casualty Station. The computer pulled up a map of the galaxy and highlighted the silver sector. Then I typed in Silver, Red, Gold, Copper, Bronze, and Metallic.

The planets formed and the map zoomed in on Silver. A ton of symbols appeared and a door hissed open. I entered and saw a young boy resting in a tube along with five other kids. A mist covered the room and the six tubes opened. The kids stumbled out and collapsed on the floor in agony. Their bodies drastically changed into adulthood. They all had small horns and small spikes like my siblings. When the change had finished, the six kids lay naked I lifted them all up telekinetically and walked back into the Leviathan.

Enigma stood there and saw them. He baulked and immediately ordered the nurses to get working on the kids.

He looked at me and Ami said, "We lost sign of you when the night forest appeared. We were worried, especially when the power failed temporarily. We thought you were trapped in here."

Enigma said, "What happened?"

I said, "I leapt from the trees hoping to find a door. I did find a door and came upon a throne room with a computer. Several runes appeared on the computer that matched the astral signs of the planets in this sector. I matched the sign with the planet and a door opened. I entered the door and saw six young children in six tubes. A fog covered the room and the kids fell on the floor in agony as they hit puberty rather fast. I brought them from the room."

***

As I meditated on this semi-organic world, I felt two different strands of energy envelop me. One was mechanical in nature and the other spiritual in nature. I also felt a tug of anger. I finished meditating and followed the anger.

I began my journey through the forest of Neo Earth. It was the same one I had shattered both my arms in. The trees were different and more metallic in nature. I had not noticed this before. The trail I was walking on went through a lake. The lake was glistening with the sunlight. It had been two days since I landed. The lake was crystal clear and I could see the bottom with my enhanced eyesight. The bottom of this lake was filled with large monolithic stones that had darkened runes on them. I sent these pictures to my computer via a nanite signal. I saw movement in the depths of this lake. It was a strange creature. The creature walked on two legs and had bladed fins on its forearms. The creature also had what looked to be ancient jet engines on its hammer-like head. It had thick scales that glowed eerily with the same runes on the monoliths. But this thing was clearly organic, with a shark fin and tail. Unlike the monoliths, which were clearly nonorganic.

I finished documenting this creature and its habitat and continued on the path. As I exited the forest, I came upon a strange factory. The factory was not in operational order and looked as if it had been bombed.

The metal definitely was rusted and old. I entered warily and was soon confronted by a female that glistened like metal.

She spoke, "Why do you intrude upon my lord's resting place? If you do not remove yourself, I will remove you."

I smiled and walked past her. She turned and fired a gun at me. The bullet fell and clunked on the ground. I continued walking as the Android kept firing. She finally ran out of bullets and attacked with hand-to-hand attacks.

Her fists flew like lightning and struck like a semi. I finally got tired of her hitting me and launched my swords from the wrist. They embedded themselves in her and she fell sparking. I called my swords back to their place. She screamed in agony and finally quieted.

I looked at the still body and spoke into my gauntlet. "Computer, teleport this body to my ship and then tell the ship to come to Neo-Earth and await me."

The body vanished and I continued down the hallway. As I exited, another girl appeared; this one was more sexual in nature. She rubbed against me and moaned softly. I pushed a button on my gauntlet and she vanished. I chuckled lightly and continued on. I was finally confronted by a tall darker Android female.

She looked down at me and growled. I smiled and walked past her. She stopped me and spoke, "No one gets past me." I shrugged my shoulders and continued past her. She snarled and grabbed me. Then lifted me up into the air only to slam me into the ground over and over. I extended my blades and stabbed into her metal skin. It split, revealing a shapely Android female stark naked and a foot smaller than myself. Her eyes blinked and she desperately tried to get away. Instead, she was dragged by a tendril into a large room.

I followed the tendril and came upon a room full of metal junk heaps. A voice more robotic than menacing spoke, "Why do you come here? I thought you were imprisoned."

I chuckled and said, "Well, you have been out of it for a while. I escaped the areas almost a thousand years ago."

The voice spoke, "How has it been one thousand years?"

I rolled my eyes and said, "Sorry, I am still going by my planetary time. Twenty years have passed here. But that is still a long time."

The voice growled and pulled out the female I had followed. She squirmed unsuccessfully. I spoke, "My morals cannot let you hurt her. Let us make a deal. I am guessing you want a body. I can get you one, but in return, you must give me your female Androids. Do we have a deal or not?"

The voice spoke, "I want your body instead of some generic crap body you may come up with."

I smiled and went over to the control panel and browsed through the bodies it had and I combined the features of all the differing bodies. I made the data under an X-10 model of Android. I uploaded it to the network and the junk began smelting into a nearly humanoid form. The exoskeleton was very humanoid, except it had bladed long spiky hair. The inner parts were of blades and strange rune-covered gems. Soon the body had materialised and formed a nearly identical form to me. The body was holding the Android female by the leg and it dropped her. It began laughing in a voice I recognised from my previous time on Neo Earth. It was Vincent Scarabaeldae, the crown prince, who killed his father and placed a warrant for Horon Mon's arrest and destruction of Horon Mon's forces.

It laughed and said, "I live again. Thanks to you, a fool of a Silveran. Who are you so I may rightfully take your place?"

I said, "There will be no taking of places I am…"

He said, "I shall name myself… X-10. In honour of my resurrection, I will now end your life."

An explosion ripped through the building. I shielded the female and when the dust cleared, I had a sword embedded in me but no arm to go with it.

I chuckled and said, "So he can shoot blades. This is going to be fun." I stood to see cannons pointed at me and… X-10… X-10 smiled sinisterly and lit up his fist. He punched the first tank and absorbed it. He lifted another tank and slammed it into the rest of the tanks. All of them blew up and he absorbed the pieces of the tanks and of the building. He smiled and lunged at me. I grappled him and threw him into the ground. I pulled the blade from my back using the psyche. Grabbing it from the air, I embedded it into the ground, impaling… X-10.

He vanished cackling and I heard a voice behind me saying, "How the hell did he escape? I imprisoned his soul in that bunker of trash. He should never have been able to recreate himself."

I turned to see a large man in heavy armour. He wore a helmet with one horn and his armour looked like it was shaped like a face. I said, "That would be my fault."

He turned to me and yelled, "What!" He growled and said, "Who the hell do you think you are…!"

I spoke, "Now, why would you say that?"

The man spoke, saying, "Only…. would be dimwitted enough to release my brother Vincent Scarabaeldae. It took me twenty years to track that son of my father down and kill him. It took me twenty years to make sure he was dead and still five more years to create this bunker and imprison his soul in it, then destroy it. You freed him."

I spoke snidely, "Wow, you are old." Even though I knew that the time difference between Silver and Neo-Earth was almost a hundred years, the man walked over to me and examined me. He then pulled out his large axe.

The girl I had saved stood immediately and said, "Maester Monohorn, this man saved me. Your brother in that pile of trash tried to smelt me."

Monohorn spoke, "Sonya, did Vincent not realise you are organic and his step-sister?"

***

Argon woke up with a start; he was still on Planet Zircon, still in his tent resting.

He gasped in pain and clutched his head. *I wonder what that dream was. Ugh... I wonder if it has something to do with my heritage...*

He looked at the woman resting next to him. This was Harmony Green of the Mystics. She was currently topless, allowing her bra-covered breasts to be exposed to the cool night air.

Argon sighed and walked outside; he was still in his pants and shirt. He heard a voice in his head. *Argon still lives, huh... guess I need to step up my plans. You are not supposed to be in this time period. Do not worry. Death is warm. I don't plan on dying yet, old man. My life is my own. Is it? Well, we will see, won't we? Yes we will, God Silver, yes we will.* He sat down on a fallen tree and allowed the world to engulf him. *Even if I fight this fate, I will fail, but I will not go down without a fight. Send what you want at me. I will beat them all. Ah there's the bravado I was hoping for. Good, you were always a stubborn man. If you can pass the trials, I may still have plans for you. And what would happen to my companion? She is lost and not very welcome back in the land of Strawgoh. I will make sure she is safe and well cared for. If you think you can feel me, Silver, I will prove you wrong as I always have.*

***

Argon stirred from his meditation to see harmony filling up a bowl of the soup he had made. She was now fully clothed in what almost looked to be a school uniform. He shook his head. He heard a commotion and reached for his blade.

"Whoa, hold up! I'm friendly."

Argon relaxed as he saw a black stone-covered man standing there with gold highlights on his rocky skin. "Hello, Berylin. We have been here for a few days waiting for you."

"Yeah, sorry about that. Ran into some trouble with some Magus trying to dig on sacred land. Had to dispose of them."

"Well, as long as you are safe, my friend, we can find the temple I was searching for."

"Yeah, about that… before I allow you to enter the forgotten temple, I need to know what you are trying to accomplish."

"God Silver and I are butting heads. I am proving myself capable to him by finding his lost blades and returning them to him."

"Lost blades?"

"Yeah, you know how the gods are. Mysterious and full of riddles wrapped in conundrums and squashed between enigmas."

Harmony chimed in, "I do suppose since the Silverans once ruled the galaxy and many species can trace their DNA back to Silverans, God Silver has many lost or forgotten temples."

Berylin nodded. "And, of course, he would want whatever's inside those temples to regain his power, so to speak."

Argon sighed. "Yeah, I think that is it. However, I can't help but think that by doing this, I am only hastening my end."

Berylin chuckled, "I can see God Silver being that petty. He is afterall, a god and many of the

Gods are very petty."

***

God Silver sat in his wheeled chair. His hair had become dull grey from the poison coursing through his system, thanks to that young idiot Oni Invictus. But he also realised many of his rivals had taken this opportunity to increase their power while he was weak from the poison and the spite the other gods had for him. His council of Silvers were doing their best to keep Planet Silver from devolving into chaos. But he knew it was only a matter of time before the many species of Silver would go to war with each other.

His son Zarkanus walked in and spoke, "I do not know what you are scheming, Father, but I think it's vile of you to trick that mortal Argon the Slayer."

"The trick is necessary. I do not like being the schemer trickster god, but this is necessary. Not just for me to regain energy and purge this poison but also for Planet Silver. Things must change for the planet to thrive."

"And what will happen to those mortals?"

"Do not worry, Zarkanus. They will live on, maybe in a different form, but they will live."

"Do you really think this will work?"

"Zarkanus… I do not know… I see glimpses of the future, but my power is no longer firm. My blades need to be freed, that is a fact. Even my allies on Silver do not particularly like me. They help me because I helped them, but if I get any weaker, they may very well choose to cut off the dead branch, so to speak."

"Father… ugh… I will do what I can to help, but you must promise me to assist your brother."

"Fine, I will help The Under King."

***

Argon looked at the liquid mercury door as it shimmered ethereally.

Berylin spoke, "Lad, you better hurry up. I can't keep this door open forever." "Sorry… is it safe?"

"Is anything really safe? Just hurry up."

Argon walked through the door with Harmony right behind him. As she exited the door, she was nude and covered in the silvery liquid, making her seem like a spirit. She looked down and tried to cover herself up. Argon rinsed her off with a short burst of warm rain, then dried her off with a burst of wind. He then removed his jacket and placed it around her.

"Thanks, Argon. I am guessing this is a perverse god?"

"Or because your clothing was enchanted, it was destroyed by the door." "So, no magical clothing, got it? Is your outlaw duster normally gray?"

"Yes, I change the color via illusion spells. Gray gets dull after a while."

The two entered the main chamber only to see a vast graveyard of bones. The images on the wall portrayed a vicious god flaying his subjects with prickly pear cacti and ripping out the hearts of children to feast upon. Then it showed a battle between the bloodthirsty god and a hawk-headed man holding a sword that had rays coming off of it. It then showed the hawk-headed man slice the cannibal god's head off. It then showed the god being pulled into the hawk-headed man's sword.

God Silver spoke through the statue of the cannibal god, "Ah, there you be, Boyo. Smash this statue of my former blade, Goranchacha. He was too ambitious for his own good. He was a cruel tyrant and even had a tailed elf as his advisor. Nothing wrong with the Elf, just Goranchacha. He was justly slain by Bloodhawk the Destroyer. By destroying his statue, you release his power so that I may appoint a new blade to take his place."

"What will happen to the tomb?"

"Oh, it will be destroyed. Do not worry, Boyo. You and your bonnie lass will be spared from the explosion. And the story of Goranchacha will be placed in the lost tomb in the ancient Spike Tower of Silver at the vast end of Spike Canyon. I enjoy legacy as much as you."

"How do I destroy this statue?" "Push it over and I will do the rest."

Argon struck the statue with a fireball causing the entire temple to vanish in a gout of fire, leaving himself and Harmony in the middle of a vast field.

Berylin stood there with his arms crossed. "That God, Silver is awfully showy. You had best get out of here before my people come to investigate the pillar of flame that appeared."

"Thank you for your help, Lord Wraithbone. I do not think I would have been able to find this place otherwise."

"Of course, my friend. I wish you the best on your journey and may we meet again under better circumstances."

"Thank you. I hope you will excel in the coming conflict."

"The Magus are slowly encroaching the inner circle, as you well know. While I do not like their methods, at least I can have some semblance of control of what happens to my planet as long as I am a Lord of the Magus."

"With any luck, they will be able to achieve unity among the planets, but I have no hope for that. Their methods are extreme, which is why I left the order."

"I won't say anything in that regard. Just stay safe, my friend." "Goodbye, Berylin."

The ship lifted off. Harmony looked at Argon and then spoke, "So you made that seem final."

"It was. He and I both know my time is coming to an end. I forsook the Magus oath and that means the Magus will want me dead, but it's not just that. I have seen my death. Also, God Silver and I are at odds. He wants me dead as well for some scheme of his."

***

Sonya had a look of worry on her face. This was when my ship landed and Tallon walked out. She was being supported by Jubilate. I looked at her and said, "What happened to her?"

Jubilate looked helplessly at me and tried to speak but still could not form words. I hurried over to Tallon and saw a sword wound that cut diagonally across her torso. I placed my hand on her forehead and saw a long-haired man wearing a Silveran wolf-bear skin. He had steel-colored skin like all Silverans, but he had no horns. The young man's eyes were a teal color. I saw him, through Tallon's eyes, take out his sword and strike her with it.

I mended her and as she opened her eyes, I saw a look of fear in them. She gasped, startled and said, "Who, what, where?" While she did this, she was frantically looking around. I placed my hand on her and said, "Relax, you are on Neo-Earth being supported by Jubilate. It will be okay."

She spoke, "The Silver Knight has been swaying people to his side. He is trying to usurp the king. He calls himself The Silver Knight. He is helped out by two men. One calls himself Aries Wolf and the other calls himself Clowd Windsong. They have been creating a rebellion of the Pure Silverans who claim to want the throne back from Half Pure scum."

I stroked her hair and said, "Relax, relax, the ordeal is over and I will take care of it

I climbed aboard the ship and Rino lifted off. We arrived at Planet Silver in prompt order. Sure enough, a small war was going on. I landed at my home in the woods and jogged off to see Blu. As I entered the city, I saw the Sol clan fighting against another group of people I did not recognize. I noticed Shang Zhan fighting a fierce-looking tigress (cat-girl/woman) who was getting aided by these two small girls. Both were wielding bladed fans while she was wielding two bladed rings. The three were agile and seemed to almost dance around the tigress. The tigress was quite displeased and tried to cut at Shang Zhan, but the two girls intercepted and slashed at her. She collapsed in exhaustion because she could not break the three girls' attack. Shang Zhan positioned her blades against the tigress and said, "I could kill you, but that would be an affront to what... 13 would do."

She then turned to the two girls and said, "Let's bind her and get out of here." They did and then fled the battlefield. During the girls' dance, I was also getting to watch Sol Jia and what looked to be his two sons fighting along with their friends. First, I will get what seems to be the elder son down.

The elder son was fighting with these two bladed tonfa or billie clubs, I could not tell which. He was with a tall, handsome man and another tall man covered in armor. They were combating a tall beasty that looked like a mix between an octopus, a bat, and some sort of amphibian. The creature itself was very tall and towered above the three. The only thing that kept it from crushing them was how slow that thing seemed to be on land. Within mere minutes it was on the ground, out cold. The three bolted as well.

The younger son was combating a snake-man, a bear-man, and an ape-man all at once with a man in black armor and a boy with two daggers that combined into one sword. The three were an even match for the strange bestial men and it seemed to be a stalemate until an explosion flung the ape-man and snake-man up in the air and caused the two to pass out from shock.

I heard a voice, "Sorry bout that boy. This old man couldn't help but throw a few grenades." The three overpowered the remaining one and then bound it and fled the battle.

Sol Jia was leaning against a tree and said while avoiding the last being's attacks, "Kid, just give up, your friends are out of action. Don't be a fool in front of your brother."

The being spoke, "I have no siblings!"

Sol Jia spoke, "...Would you come down from that tree and say hello to your younger sibling?"

I jumped down and landed near Sol, who stepped aside saying, "...Meet Bonty. You are the... he is the fourteenth. Nothing special, just born from a different mother, same father."

I looked down at the boy and saw he had two red wings and was wearing a strange gold armor with blades built into the gauntlets. He also had very large talons on both his hands and feet. His face was bird-like in appearance, except for the two horns that curved up from his forehead.

Sol Jia turned to me and said, "He and his friends, The Coalition of Silveran Species, have been aiding The Silver Knight because your son, Moonstalker, convinced them to."

I scratched my head and then said, "Oh right, the one who had a Felis mother, so I totally forgot about her. Yeesh!"

Sol Jia smiled and stroked his chin. He finally spoke, "So boy, do you give up or will you continue this pointless struggle?"

"I am a warrior and I will not be defeated. It would bring shame to my birthright."

I spoke, "Very well, how about I make you a deal? I challenge you to a duel. If you win, you're free to go with your friends. But if I win, you surrender and take me to this so-called Silver Knight. As the Sol clan as my witness, I promise to this."

The boy spoke snidely, "I will agree to your terms only because I know I will win."

He flew up in the air and began firing at me with his gun. I rolled aside and caused lightning to flare up out of the sky. I then began firing firebolts at him. He was agile in the air, but when I caused a large windstorm to swirl around him. He was buffeted around like a rag doll. He plummeted to the ground and stood swaying, then shot forward at me using his bone-like forearms to pummel me. I smiled and grabbed his arm and twisted it, hearing a snap. I kneed him in the gut. He hit the ground and then struggled up. I felt a knife enter my abdomen and turned around to see a black-haired amber-skinned female holding a very large sword. I growled and struck her to the ground. My back suddenly lit up like fire. And I turned to see the boy standing there holding fire in his hands. He threw more at me and then collapsed in pain. I was behind him and had shocked him with more energy. He lay on the ground smoldering. I then put a healing cocoon around him and looked at the girl. She gulped and fell to her knees.

"Please don't eat me. I'm too chewy!"

I smiled, showing my fangs. "Take me to the Silver Knight and I will not sauté you." She got up and motioned me to follow her and led me to a cave and pointed inside, then fled. I entered and saw an eight-foot-tall, well-muscled man sitting by a fire.

He looked up and sneered. "If it isn't the great... 13. Come to kill me, have you? Did that dog Blu Silver send you?"

I looked down at him and spoke, "Why have you incited a rebellion? What makes you think that the Pure Silverans would be better than Blu Silver, who has brought this continent to a golden age?"

"How easy weaklings are swayed to the plans of the puppeteer." A mechanical yet deep voice spoke. A form walked into the light.

"X-10," I growled.

"Yes, fool Silveran, it is I... X-10, the strongest of all. You have fallen right into my trap like the animal you are. I planned this to weaken the Silverans so that my robot army can wipe you out."

***

Argon sighed as he was once again woken by dreams. He was on his ship still.

Are these dreams portents or are they just dreams?

Harmony wrapped her arms around him. "Relax, Argon. Your body is so tense." "I'm sorry for waking you. Just some bad dreams, is all. We will be arriving at

Blood Ocean soon. We will have to convince Blood de Gulch to help us. I hope he is as eager to help an old friend as Berylin was."

Harmony smiled, "I suspect he will be. Though what would happen if he wasn't?" "I would have to fight him. He was always better than me in combat."

The two were teleported to the Moon Blood Ocean of Planet Blood Gulch. Argon looked around and was kicked in the face by a red boot. He staggered back and blocked the secondary attack. As the crimson-skinned man went in for a punch, he was frozen in mid-air by an ice crystal. Harmony stood there with her staff drawn and glowing.

She walked over to the man and thawed his face. "Hi, there, Blood… we need your help. Then we will be out of your hair."

Blood de Gulch snarled, "The traitor relies on help to face me. I refuse."

"Then we will just leave you there. Hope there are no nocturnal predators out to eat."

"Er… uhh… fine, let me down and I will help you."

Argon waved his hand and the ice shattered. Blood choked out, "Ow, that actually hurt. What kind of ice is this?" "It's not ice. It is a level twenty burst called Diamond Dust. It freezes you and then shatters the ice while you are frozen. Usually kills instantly, but it can't kill what is already dead, isn't that right, Blood?"

"When did you notice?"

"When I saw your foot coming at my face. You are still fast but not as fast as you used to be, where you could not even be seen."

"Yes, I was slain by the new Lord of Blood Ocean, Lord Bladesong. It was my punishment for being your friend."

"Then why attack? If you help us, we can send you on to the havens even if your body was not given the proper rites."

"You and I were always rivals. Very well, Argon, I will help you."

The three came upon a large vine-covered city ruin. There were ancient

Silveran runs on all the walls. Argon looked around and saw a large pillar and on top of the pillar was a statue.

As he placed his hand on the pillar, the entire ruin started to glow silver and gray. There was a sound of a hurricane and the ruin vanished, leaving a perturbed Argon in its wake.

Harmony looked at him with concern. "As soon as you touched the pillar, Blood Gulch vanished as if his soul had been claimed. I heard the wind but could not see you. What happened?"

"I saw my death. It was not pleasant. Ugh, anyway, we are done here, better leave before the Magus come and see us."

***

The moon shone a bright blue through the irradiated sky. The wasteland glowed with its cold fullness. A lone man was walking the long dusty road. He wore a black trench coat over brown leather armor. On his head, he wore a fedora to keep his unkempt hair out of his line of sight. The full moon shone brightly, making the night like day. He heard a noise and instinctively went for his gun. A blue rabbit crossed the road.

He relaxed slightly. From the darkness of the nearby ruined house leapt a glowing two-headed hound. The hound tore into the moon rabbit and then turned towards him. He grabbed the shotgun on his back and fired a round into the wolf. The wolf sagged to the ground without a head. He fired with his smaller gun, killing the wounded beast. He heard howling and immediately ran.

"Figures there'd be more," he muttered as he ran through the woods.

As he ran toward his destination, the wolves caught up to him. He grimaced as they surrounded him.

"Guess two heads are better than one."

Then the night sky lit up with fire. Six heavily armored Tech Paladins were firing on the beasts with their giant flamethrowers.

The man jumped over the nearby wolf and into a ditch. The Paladins were soon done with their work. He stuck his head up over the ridge only to see a light-armored woman with two guns pointing at him.

She spoke through her tech helmet, "Get up, you're under arrest for the murder of King Oberon III."

He smirked and put his hands up, thinking, *excellent, they are taking me where I want to go.* He spoke, "Lead the way, General Kalsis."

"It's been too long, Stranger. 'Bout time we caught you."

She took his two guns and cuffed him. The guards loaded him into their hover truck. His eyes adjusted to the darkness of the covered truck and he saw three other prisoners. There was noise and then nothing. He woke in a magna-locked cell with the three others.

"About time you woke up, dude." A young woman with a platinum blue streak in her greasy black hair spoke.

He got a good look at his fellow prisoners. The girl with the weird hair was in a black, purple, and pink top with numerous tattoos on her arms. She wore a weird necklace with a charm of a rainbow-maned unicorn. He saw the other prisoners, a man with no unique features and another man with dark glasses.

"So what're you guys in for?" he asked.

The girl smiled smugly, "I killed nineteen Ascendancy Tech Knights."

The man in dark glasses spoke, "Why does it matter? You are to be executed as well as us. Welcome to LLeh, the end of the road for us criminals."

Stranger smirked, "We'll see."

The three were quickly brought into an Antechamber where a headsman was waiting. The people loved the executions and wanted them to be as visceral as possible. The Ascendancy had tried humane ways, but in the wasteland, people get bored and boredom leads to violence. You can only do so much with drugs. So they brought back the ancient ways.

General Kalsis spoke, "First prisoner, Doctor Felinus Feral, the only remaining scientist from the failed Nuclear genetics program."

The no discernable features man was brought forward and shoved mercilessly onto the block. The headsman lifted his electro ax and cleaved the man in two, then sliced off the head. Stranger looked around the chamber, noticing various cameras. *So they were doing this live. Excellent!*

"Next, the killer of kings."

Stranger was brought forward. He kept his face stoic so as not to alert the General to his plan. The wall was blown up and several Coterie of the Titanium Knights entered, guns blazing. Stranger got up and headbutted the headsman.

"Come on, you two. We don't have much time."

The girl and man shrugged and followed him. They came to the armory and Stranger kicked the guard to the ground taking his keycard. He opened the door and tossed a few weapons at the two and then grabbed his shotgun and ray gun. He stuffed some grenades into his coat and picked up what looked to be a small ammo box coated in crimson and gold glyphs. He pocketed it. He then led the two out of the facility. He placed a cube on the Titanium knights' tank unnoticed.

As they entered the forest, the dark glasses man spoke, "What the hell was that? You nearly got me killed, Stranger."

"Sorry, Wenceslas, I needed to get in. But things worked perfectly when that woman arrested me."

The girl spoke, "So you two know each other?" Both spoke at the same time, "Yes, unfortunately."

She looked at them both warily. "Well, I had better be going."

Stranger placed his hand on her shoulder. "No, you aren't… there were cameras everywhere. You're stuck with us. May as well tell us your name."

"Mayhem de la Sol."

"Welcome to the club, Mayhem. Try not to get yourself killed."

Back at the Facility, General Kalsis rose from the rubble. She grabbed the headsman's ax and then quickly ducked into hiding as the Titanium Knights walked past her and into their troop tank. The tank exploded, sending shrapnel everywhere. A large chunk embedded itself into the wall above Kalsis' head. She looked up at it and sighed in relief.

***

Stranger was building a campfire while Wenceslas slept. Mayhem was staring at the irradiated sky. She saw the full moon and shivered.

"Mayhem, do you need anything to eat?"

"I do not, Stranger. I am unsure if we should be in the open, especially since the moon is so bright."

Stranger heard something and saw a moon rabbit sniffing around the ground. He looked through the darkness and activated his cybernetic eye. There was nothing except the rabbit. He shrugged and continued to stir the soup.

***

Argon finished writing his premonition down. Something told him that the dream he had just had was a vision of the future. Mayhem de la Sol would be a nasty piece of work, but he did not know why.

Argon sighed as he beamed down to planet Teal. Lord Teal would not be hard to sway since Lord Teal was his first master. *Speak of the devil and he shall appear.*

Lord Teal was a tall man with spikes on his shoulders and large bull-like horns on his head. His skin was teal in color and he wore heavy teal power armor with blade-like wings on the back of it. He had his blade drawn in his clawed hand, but sheathed it as soon as he saw who it was. "Ah, Argon, I see you and your lady friend came to visit."

"Hello, Lord Teal. I see there was some trouble."

"The bodies? Nah, no trouble. My allies assisted me. My rival did not make it, though. He was a fool to think he could beat a former mystic in Psy combat."

"Can you take us where we need to go?"

"Of course, I can. Let my allies and I clear you a path."

The three came upon a large temple with many Magus studying it. When they saw Teal, they fled all except for a lanky fellow who wielded a pike.

Lord Teal spoke, "Braid, you wish to challenge me?"

Braid snorted. "No, I wish to face Argon. Silver wishes to test him in combat since Gilgamesh and Enkidu are together in this temple. The power we give off while fighting will allow them to be free."

Teal stepped aside and had Harmony stand next to him.

Braid looked to be a boy of about one hundred. However, his soul felt ancient. Argon was nearly blinded by the overpowering gray he saw. He spoke, "You are quite powerful. Well, this will be fun."

Braid struck fast and hard. He was using both psy elemental attacks and striking with his pike. Argon was easily keeping up with him. He could tell the boy was angry. He was uncertain why. But he could feel the anger in every strike and every elemental burst. He could also tell Braid was slowing down.

His blade stopped short of Braid's neck and he spoke, "You strike with fury, boy. That could cost you in the end. Do not let anger cloud your attack. Otherwise, you will die. I dub you Deathseeker. And as long as you remain angry, that shall be your name."

Braid shakily stood and leaned on his pike. "I will gladly accept that name. My birth father threw me away, deeming me worthless for his scheme. He seeks to replace me. I truly hate the man and my replacement."

Argon nodded, "Just do not let that hatred blind you. I see great things will come of you. Stay on your path and you will achieve greatness."

Deathseeker smiled and vanished in a gout of white fire alongside the temple complex and the dead bodies that lay strewn about.

Argon spoke, "Lord Teal, I wish you well. I hope that the Magus empire will not attack you."

"Even if they did, the Tealians would repel them. We are as strong as, if not stronger than, the Silverans of Silver and the Mysticans of Myst. And the magus has yet to take those planets. If they can't beat a Silveran, what hope do they have against a Tealian?"

Argon smiled and teleported back to his ship alongside Harmony.

Harmony spoke, "You have been pushing yourself hard. Let me take care of the temple in Angro. You need your rest."

"I don't think you understand very well what you are getting into."

"I understand you have been dreading Planet Angro. You are tired, Argon. As your wife, it is my duty to help you."

"Very well then. Harmony, I leave Planet Angro to you. I have to do something on Planet Hollow anyway."

***

Argon arrived on Planet Hollow, also known as Moon. This was a land of Wyrdwolves, Vampires, Golems, and other undead monstrosities. This was also his home. The Living had been purged by the great Stone Vampire clan Bloodsong. However, the Bloodsong clan was no more; there was only one survivor, a man by the name of Judas. *I am not looking forward to this. Old Judas is the kinslayer. He slew my mother and siblings, but it has to be done.*

Argon arrived at a mist-filled ruin. He could see the Fog Wraiths doing their job of collecting souls for the Reapers. He readied his blade. A large Fog Wraith in black armor and a crown over his hood stood before the status Argon was looking for.

Ah, Argon, the so-called slayer, I see you are here for your daughter. Well you will have to face me.

"Yes… yes; I know the process, old man."

The two of them tapped the ground with their blades and then bowed to each other. They struck blades and they flashed in and out of existence with each strike and parry since the mists and fog were so thick. Finally, the fog wraith kneeled on one leg.

Ah, Argon you truly are a magnificent fighter. I release her soul from this statue and give you my word she will be allowed to reincarnate with a loving family.

"Thank you, Toreno. I hope to meet you again someday."

The statue vanished alongside Toreno. Argon sighed and walked out of the ruins to find himself in a vast wooded land. He knew these lands well. The large claw mark that was on his face lit up in the moonlight alongside a large scar that bisected his chest. His body changed slightly to become more bestial. However, he retained his form. He shook his head and downed a reddish liquid from his flask.

"I see you still drink Blood Whisky."

Argon smirked as he saw the shadowy wolf being, "That I do, William. I see you are still stalking the forest."

"The Wyrdwolves worship me as some sort of forest god. I am also a guardian of this land. In the event any non-undead beings wander through. I protect them from the horrors lurking just beyond the veil. I see the mauling you received that caused me to donate some of my blood to you still burns in the moon."

"Yes, and still hurts even after all of these years. You, Toreno and Judas saved my life. I do not understand why, among all of the mortals, you all saved me."

"Call it luck or the scheming of the gods. You have surpassed many of the Gods' expectations of you. Many fear you, but there are those who wish to use you for their own schemes. However, the one who is most interested in you is God Silver. You interest him because of your status as a former Magus. His plans for you will be interesting, to say the least. Well, my mortal friend, here we are at the edge of the forest. I am guessing you are off to see Judas Bloodsong next."

"That I am, thank you for your assistance, Will. I hope to meet again under different circumstances."

***

Harmony leaned on her staff. It was as if she had been struck by something. She heard a voice, "You are the one to insist on coming here. Our memories were erased of this place and replaced by false memories of a long-dead girl."

"Who's there?"

"I am you… well, who you were. My name was Fury Noirthought, the Magus Lord in charge of Planet Angro. However, I was captured by a man named Henry Hawthorn. He tore apart my mind so he could have his lost girlfriend back. I was the eighteenth he had done this to."

"So you wish to regain your body?"

"No… that desire is long gone. However, we can't achieve unity in my mind and your mind. One of us must fall."

"So a fight then."

"Yes, and I have taken over this statue of Brinn, the Skin changer. She was the one you were here to release. If you can't beat me, your task will fail."

"Clever. Very well, Fury, you and I will duel."

***

Argon looked upon the large castle with many statues out front. The fog wraiths avoided this place, but the fog was still thick. He saw Judas on one of the towers and vanished. He reappeared on top of the tower.

"Hello, Kinslayer."

"Hello, Argon. I felt the release of your daughter. You will not claim your mother."

"Someday I will, Judas, but I am here for my previous wife. I require to release

her so that God Silver's scheme can continue."

"Ah, very well, she is here. I release her soul. I hope Silver chokes on it." "Thank you. I leave you to your solitude, old man."

***

Harmony stood over Fury, who lay there breathing weakly. She closed her eyes and then knelt down. She climbed on top of Fury and kissed her. The two minds then became one. Harmony Green was now Harmony Noirthought. Her outfit even changed as well. She still had her skirt, but her top was now a black belt buckle that just covered her nipples. She was also now wearing thigh-high boots and a fishnet body stocking.

Brinn, the Skin changer's statue, was now gone. Harmony vanished and reappeared on the ship. Argon stood waiting for her.

"Ah, you found unity. That is good. You look great."

"You look worse for wear. What did you do? I told you to rest."

"I took a walk down memory lane. I did rest my mind and body."

***

I looked at the screen and my friends all looked grave, except for Sylverado, who had his helmet on.

Death Knight spoke, "My spies have traversed throughout. Black, I think they may have found where these beasts that you told us were in your dream were created. You may want to get to Black quickly."

The computer teleported me to Casualty Station and Death Knight sent me down to Black. I was standing in front of a black stone building. The stone felt alive and glowed from the inside with plum. I felt a malevolent presence and I immediately became aware. The trees were skeletal and I smelled bloodshed. I pulled out my sword and entered the lab. The first thing I saw was a head on a pike and then I noticed arms and legs not with their torsos and heads missing from their shoulders. The floor was slick with blood and guts and squished under my boots.

I entered the main room and saw twelve broken tubes with a thirteenth still in one piece. I saw a fetus growing in the thirteenth one and heard a voice. I turned to see a silver-haired girl with green eyes. Her aura swirled and looked like fog to the psychic eye. She was wearing a lab coat and she was glaring at me.

I spoke, "Hello, small one. How did you survive the destruction?"

The girl snarled and leapt at me. I dodged and then slipped on the floor. I hit the ground hard and rolled my mechanic parts whirred as I struggled up. The girl snarled again and bone-like claws extended from her hands. There were four of them and they all had a metallic glint to them. I avoided her attack as she leapt at me.

I caught her and grabbed her, saying, "Relax, small one, I am a friend. I am not one of your enemies."

The girl calmed and whimpered. I took pity on her and gently stroked her hair. She then broke into tears. She could not speak properly, so all I heard were mumblings about how the scientists tortured her after her brothers escaped. I carried her to the computer and hacked into the data files. What I saw did not please me at all.

Thirteen large pots were boiling. The pots were cooled by liquid nitrogen and the coagulation of the liquid was poured into tubes. I watched as small bubbles formed and then a fetus developed and grew until it was a full-grown being. One of them was the creature that I had seen on Black when I had first ventured there during the magus suppression. I then saw the creatures escape due to the machinations of a hell-like wizard. The girl I was holding was captured and the thirteenth creature was still developing. I then witnessed the girl gets thrown in a cell and tortured. After a few minutes, she broke out and killed all of the scientists.

I downloaded the data to my gauntlet and spoke, "Death Knight, I have a challenge for you. I need you to teleport an unborn fetus in a test tube to Casualty Station and keep it stable."

Death Knight spoke, "I will try to." I saw the tube vanish and heard Death Knight say, "It's stable. My scientists will take good care of it."

I opened up my satchel and planted several bombs. I then walked out of the lab and it blew up behind me. I chuckled and stroked the girl sleeping in my arms. I said, "I will name you Jubilate."

I then heard a shuffling in the bushes behind me. I turned and saw a shadowy figure. Tallon leapt at me and then hugged me.

I looked at her and spoke, "What are you doing here?"

She smiled happily and said, "I followed you when you teleported." She then clambered up my arm and sat on my shoulder. She was about five feet, while I was almost nine feet tall. I walked to City Black and entered the castle.

I bowed to King Blackheart and spoke, "I need information from you."

Blackheart spoke, "How can I help you, young man?"

I looked at him and then said, "Who are the Psycheos?"

He paused, then looked at me and motioned me to follow him. I followed him to a room with eleven Statues. He spoke, "These were my friends. They died along with me when the Psycheos attacked us because we were the secondary donors. We were a mighty guild called the Blackhearts. We were hired by a man named Lucifer to give blood to an experiment to create the perfect soldier. He lied to us. We gave our blood and he gave us money and then had us killed by his experiments."

I spoke, "You only have ten friends. Who was the eleventh I saw?"

Leon shook his head and spoke, "Are you an idiot? Your friend Techno 100 is a robot. Lucifer created a massive techno-morpher. He called Tonk to be the opponent to your friend Techno 100."

I nodded my head and smiled, saying, "Thank you, your highness. That was all I needed to know. Just one question, Did Lord Psycheo tell you who his allies are?"

Leon looked solemnly at me and said, "No, he did not give me the honor of a long speech."

I bowed again and spoke into my gauntlet, "Death Knight, Do you read me? I need a teleport."

King Blackheart spoke, "Don't you want to know who the girl your holding was and the unborn was?"

I looked at him and said, "You're going to tell me anyway."

Blackheart smiled and said, "My daughter, Tallon, was the donor of her along with a man named Badger. The other one, I have no idea about. But I fear it may be a duplicate of that bastard

Lord Psycheo."

I smiled and thanked him as the teleport happened. I appeared in Casualty Station and saw a small gray and black-haired boy in the arms of Death Knight.

He handed the boy to me and said, "Get him a good home on Silver. I called him Brovone, it means brave in black."

I saw the test tube was empty and I picked the boy up and set him next to the girl and we were teleported back to Silver. I looked through the clan books and saw the family name of Bjorn. I lay the girl down and told Tallon to wait and watch over the girl. I went to the home of the Bjorn clan and gave them the boy calling him an orphan I found. The woman thanked me and carried the boy inside. I walked back to my house. It was dark and I suddenly felt a chill and turned to see the monster.

He spoke, "I have finally got you alone... 13. I, Lord Psycheo, will finally get my kill."

I pulled out my sword and saw the man pull out a massive axe. We clashed and fought for what seemed like hours. Finally, he swung and sliced my arm off. I stumbled and stabbed him as I fell, and he vanished while cackling evilly. I picked up my arm and sealed it to my shoulder.

I walked back home and got my arm fixed. It was a few months of quiet. The New Year was coming up fast. I looked outside as it snowed most, if not all, the clans were south where it was warm.

I stayed at my home, keeping vigilance over the city. I heard a call over my com, "We need help. The Psycheos, as you call them, are attacking City Black. Get your ass here now!"

***

Argon grunted as he awoke from this latest dream. The bags under his eyes were getting darker due to these many sleepless nights. More questions than answers were swimming in his head. It also didn't help that God Silver just chuckled whenever he brought it up.

They had just reached Planet Silver and needed to find a Gatekeeper to open the path through the Star Vale. His next stop was planet Ares. The Gatekeepers of Silver were a secretive bunch. They had no headquarters on Planet Silver nor any of the Moons of Silver. They also had no space station like the Gatekeepers of Planet White and Oblivion Station. It was downright impossible to find them unless you knew where to look. He knew where to look. *Look for the Hunter Constellation. Between the Warrior Constellation. Seek out the Chains of the Prisoner. The third loop is where the Gatekeepers exist.*

He looked at the ripple in space and sent his ship through. The ship arrived in a vast canyon filled with statues and trees. At the far end of the canyon was a massive waterfall that echoed through the canon like a song. He could see sky and land but nothing that would indicate a building. Harmony was looking around the canyon as well, then raised her staff and the waterfall parted, revealing a very high-tech-looking building with a ship bay. He landed in the bay and as he exited, thirteen people materialized.

The one that wore silver armor spoke, "We are the Hunters thirteen. I am the Thirteenth Hunter. I speak on behalf of the others. Why do you seek access to the First Sector?"

"I am on a mission from God Silver to release his sacred blades. Two of which are hidden in the First Sector."

"I see very well, then. I will open a rift. Be warned time works differently in the First Sector. It is slower than here. Do not disturb the people. While they are technologically advanced they are not as advanced as this side of the Star Veil."

Argon piloted his ship through the rift. It was spat out in the vast emptiness of space. He saw his computer update with star charts. He set a course to Planet Ares. When he arrived, he beamed down to the planet, allowing Harmony to rest. She would be needed on Tuatha de Danann but not here. A man appeared, "Oi, laddy, glad ye could make it. Glad te see you."

"Good to see you as well, Leslie, so what happens now?"

"You get to attend a masquerade slash orgy. I have the mask that you will wear."

"Orgy?"

"Ay, an orgy. While the Ares of this Planet is not the Ares you are releasing, the orgy is held in the old temple. Since Ares of Silver was the predecessor to this Ares, by joining in the orgy, you will be able to release the Silveran God of Hedonism, Debauchery, Alcohol, and Parties."

"A demon mask? Interesting choice."

"Yeah, it just called to me for some reason. Anyway, enjoy yerself, laddie. When you are done, I'll just be waiting on your ship for you."

Argon entered the temple and was immediately grabbed by a bare naked woman wearing an owl mask. She spoke in a raspy, almost masculine voice, "Darling, so good to see you. I understand you were summoned by Ares himself. Come enjoy the fun. Don't worry about protection since as long as you are in these halls, you are sterile, as is everyone. Thanks to the priestess' magic."

The two danced throughout the night, both vertically and horizontally. When the sun rose the next morning, Argon was inside his ship with several claw marks on his back. The ship lifted off.

"You are driving the ship, Leslie?"

"That I am, lad. Harmony is still sleeping; she seems just as exhausted as you."

"Ugh, we are doomed to die as sacrifices to God Silver's schemes and it's starting to affect us both."

"Hoo boy, that sounds great. What is God Silver scheming?" "Who knows what the old man thinks."

***

The computer teleported me to Black and I appeared in a carnage. I saw two dead Minotaurs and a demon that was dead. I also saw two bug-like things dead. I saw Death Knight facing off against a gray armored man and I also saw Stingray facing off against a giant shark. All dove out of the way as a huge tank-like robot hit the ground. I heard metal clashing above me and rolled as Bat Wing was slammed into the ground by a robed demon.

The demon sky dove and tried to kill Bat Wing but was beheaded. I was tossed into a building by a red armored body. I got up and saw my arm was missing and I sighed, pulling out my sword with my other arm. I charged into the fray.

I saw a skeletal man vanish in a cloud of red smoke and the bodies did as well. I helped my friends to their healing vats and got my arm. I placed it back on and teleported to my bed. The computer fixed me up again. I went to Spike Tower and began training students. One was a young Blackian who stood out because he had curved horns and red eyes. They all knew how to fight. They had been watching me traverse through the Leviathan.

***

Enigma walked over and said, "We need more trainers, sir. We have too many students." I smiled and left a message on my allies' computers saying trainers are needed for the psychic academy. They came to Spike Tower and began training certain students. The only ones who did not come were Sting Ray, Drill Bit, Wampanor, and Lava because they all live on inhospitable planets and would be unable to stand certain temperatures of Silver, plus they need to heal still.

The days went well and the nights were better. I forget all that I trained them with, but as the year grew on, I began noticing my mechanical parts were starting to wear. I trained them to the best of my extent. I finally placed my nanites in their jar with their fluid and placed a piece of elven metal with dwarven runes in the goo so they could feed.

Six months passed and I was getting news that Magus were on the rise again. They had been joined by Vera and Aerick-Starr and were on the way to confront the psychics. They were led by a new emperor. I learned from my allies, who had gone into hiding, that the Magus had taken all of the Silver sectors. My mechanical parts were screaming in agony now. I leaned on the staff I had taken from the tombs. The kids were removed to a secret location. My close allies, Sylverado and Bat Wing, stayed while all the others went into hiding.

I even had to order the temporary masters, Monohorn, Enigma, Ami, Cheleon, and the enigmatic Blood Neon, to go with the students and get more masters. As the temporary masters entered the portal, the door caved in.

For the first hour, it was only Sylverado and Bat Wing cleaving through the frontal attack. Anyone that got past them was killed by me, but soon, we were overwhelmed and dragged to the central room where Lord Psycheo stood. He walked over to Sylverado and beheaded him, then cut Bat Wing in half. He smiled evilly and raised his axe to kill me. The room suddenly filled with fog.

***

Argon and Harmony appeared in a vast temple. On the walls were pictures of bulls, phoenixes, dragons, saber-toothed cats, and wolves. Before them stood a man dressed in black and Silver armor with a red scarab on the chest piece. He stood holding a great axe or headsman cleaver. Argon could not tell which it was.

"Argon of Teirinos I am Lord Leon Psycheo. You are to die by my hands just as you once slew me."

"So you wish to fight? I think you are a bit outnumbered. Two to one."

"Ha, you think that will stop me? Come, my brother, face me. Only one of us will survive."

The three clashed, but Lord Psycheo proved to be the stronger he immediately focused his attack on Harmony. She was soon bleeding profusely from a wound that cut across her chest. As she faded, her eyes opened to see an Oni-Ettin weaving magic from his flaming bell staff. He had just finished overseeing the birth of a Half-Oni girl.

Her mother lay panting from the difficult birth, but she survived thanks to the energy the Oni infused her with. The girl, however, was marked. During her birth, the sky had become a raging thunderstorm. The moons had also turned red. She was destined for great things. Her elder sister stared at her burning orange eyes and saw eternity.

***

Master 13 stood surrounded by six figures that I did not recognize. The six had turned the Magus army to crystal and were now feeding their power into Master 13. Master 13 attacked with brutal ferocity, but as he struck the weird man in black armour, his bad arm fell off. The bad man took this opportunity to behead my master. But he did not stop there; he cleaved through the waist and up the other arm, but out of spite, he just embedded his axe into the torso. A bright light filled the room and when it vanished, the mean man was smoldering. He vanished and the spirit of Mr. 13 appointed Master Sorbane Woften to supreme master of the Psychics. I was terrified and ran to my master's body. His spirit touched my hair and then spoke, "Go to my house and tell the computer my body has been destroyed. She'll have you bring a new body. Also, tell her to contact King Technos. He will come and help create three bodies. I knew this would happen and I knew how this would happen. Go now!" I obeyed my master and the computer created three schematics. Technos and a strange man that looked like a rhino helped. They brought the three bodies to Spike Tower.

***

Argon burned Harmony's body as he defended himself against the furious assault from the dark spirit before him.

"Hear me and obey. God Silver, I accept my fate in your scheme. However, you must release my soul when your scheme comes to fruition. The same as you must do for Harmony."

"Oh, very well, Argon. I will give you my promise, for whatever it's worth, that you and Harmony will be released when my scheme is complete. Do not worry. I will also make sure your daughter is released as well. She will be reborn and find you in the body of my chosen mortal. Even if she does not know it, she will be with her father."

Lord Psycheo beheaded Argon only to find a black blade embedded into his chest and he vanished in rage. He would find his brother's soul and destroy it.

***

I went to neo earth first because I knew instinctively that was where Psycheo was. He was the last Psycheo, besides Skull, left. I found him in a cave, trying to absorb the powers of three mystic children. He was smoldering with energy, but as I walked in, he looked up and snarled, "The weakling comes back for more. I will kill you for certain this time."

He charged me with the black energy enveloping him. I saw a strange crystal formation as I rolled away. I activated my arm blades and swung, slicing and dicing Psycheo like he did me. When I finished, his armour fell, revealing two souls, one silvery and one ink-black. I raised the crystal and it glowed and pulled in the dark soul. The light soul vanished and I freed the children. I left the cave and went to a good place in the forest. I began meditating and resting.

***

Argon opened his eyes to see an old man staring down at him. He seemed to hear, "By the gods, look at his eyes. They have no pupils. He is blind. Please tell me this isn't who I fear, it is Chain?"

Chain chuckled at her dramatics, "I am afraid so, Marla. Meet Bounty Hunter 13, our most powerful and therefore cursed brother. I really would hate to live his life."

Argon's mind faded; he had failed to beat God Silver. Now all he would wait for is God Silver's promise that he would hold him to.

The Chronicles of Bounty Hunter 13

The Birth of Bounty Hunter 13

The thirteenth Hunter will be a powerful warrior. His power will be unmatched. When the three moons glow red and the constellation of the hunter is visible in the night sky he will be born. He will have six siblings. A coward, a chaos spawn, a dark girl, a boy with the eyes of an eagle, and conjoined twins. His power will be unmatched by even the gods. He will be hated, he will be feared, his destiny is not death. You will know him by his eyes.

-The Mad Monk Salim al-Jafar (right before he died when the ground swallowed him up.)

The night was calm, all three moons were full and there wasn't a cloud in the sky. The rocky terrain was foreboding but not difficult. Two men stood side by side on the cliff outside a small cottage. One was significantly older than the other. He had a wizened gray beard and wore a robe of blood red. His hair was long and bleached white by age.

The other was a demon of a man with two horns jutting out of his temples. They were small but sharp. He wore pale green armor that accented his black fu manchu. On his head was a bronzed circlet that wrapped around his coarse black hair.

The older man spoke, "So, Bonty, what is troubling you?"

The younger man replied, "Crane, my wife is pregnant with septuplets. She will not survive the night of their birth. I have also been summoned to the King of City Silver's Throne. I have a feeling Zen Ankara wants me dead. Should he execute me, I need you and The Dragon to assist with the birth of my children. They must survive. It took decades for my father, Bounty Hunter 11, to bring our clan back to the glory it held. My father died protecting me so that the Hunter clan would prosper. Now on the cusp of glory, I, too, will be snuffed out. Promise me, Crane, you will try to get along with your fellow immortal to make sure my children grow strong."

Crane, the older man, smiled, "General Twelve, I give you my word that your children will live to avenge your death, should it come to that."

"I am afraid it will, my friend. Zenthin Ankara is my father-in-law. He has been deceived by darkness. He has already slain many of the clans in opposition to him. He has replaced the governing body with his supporters and family members. I am the last of the five great clans. My death is assured."

"That is not necessarily true. Your wife actually has octuplets."

"Then he is not the one. I forsook my previous son because he did not fit the prophecy. I was a fool."

"I agree about the fool part, but Braid may have been the chosen one if given a chance. He was not. However, the one that is to be born from your wife is the one. Because you forsook your first powerhouse of a son, fate had to fuck around and create this one, but because it was a last-minute thing. He was quickly added to the ones already in your wife's womb. Fear, not Bounty. For the one that will be the Thirteenth Hunter is the one to be born from your current wife."

"That gives me a glimmer of hope, Crane, but not much."

"As my word as a former God Silver, I can assure you. Things are now in motion. The Thirteenth Hunter will be born. Now I believe you have a meeting to attend to."

One Year Later

The Magic Melody of the Universe echoed through the souls of the living. Tonight the melody would change. Whether for better or worse depends on who is speaking. Two men, both very old looking, stood inside a mansion. They had a window open to release some of the reek. It smelled like blood, shit, and sulfur. In front of them was an elvish girl of the mountains, an elvish male wrapped in bandages, and a woman panting in agony as a small head was pushed out of her body. That was where the stink was wafting from. The head was followed by a body and was lifted into a bowl of water, where the elvish girl cleaned it.

The elvish girl spoke, "It's a boy. His eyes are like a Syrien's. What should his name be, Chain?"

The bandaged man looked at the child and saw it smile as a storm blew in. He nodded his head and spoke, "This looks like the one Father wanted to be named Corvus, which means that the girl that will be breached next is Trinity."

The man helping with the birth looked at the child that was in his arms and then spoke, "You sure this is a female?"

Chain looked over the child and seeing the penis, grimaced, "Yes, I am positive. She will be raised by The Dragon and his wife. This is what Father foresaw and so it shall be."

The man tending to the pregnant woman spoke, "Too bad, Dragon. We promised we would follow through with Bounty Hunter 12's wishes or would you forsake the oath?"

The old man lowered his head. "No! I suppose I must." He then turned and opened his purple eyes and smiled an evil looking smile. *The child will be perfect for my designs. I will need to plan this carefully.*

The other old man yelled, "That whelp wants me to raise a mutant child? How dare he?"

The next two came in quick succession. One male, the other female, a huge blast of thunder shook the room, causing the boy to scream and cry in terror. Chain rolled his eyes, "Yep, figured that's why. He shall be named Myst for his cowardice which makes him the fourth in our family to be named such. The girl is Eris or, in common, Erin."

The elf girl brought both over to the bowl and bathed them, soothing the boy until he fell asleep. She handed them over to the next servant girl, who soon found herself being sucked on by the girl.

Everyone in the room suddenly clutched their heads in pain as the woman screamed really loud. The storm outside suddenly became much worse than before. The sky was shredded by lightning and the house shook, trying to be torn apart. The only thing visible was the constellation of the Hunter. There was also a surprise as the Halberd of the warrior appeared. No one saw the Prisoner's Chains appear as well. The moons took on an ominous red color and the forest awoke. It would be a bloody night. Many huge sigils and runes suddenly lit up the home. Outside, numerous puffballs floated up the mountain, searching for the energy the runes blocked. Inside, the smell of gore was replaced by the smell of cinnamon. Dragon spoke between bouts of head pain, "Whichever child is next is a powerful one. Svētais sūdi! His psychic energy is tearing open the sky, causing a psychic storm. Good thing we're on a mountain with no living things outside, or we'd be in trouble."

As the child was breached, the girl spoke, "By the gods, look at his eyes. They have no pupils. He is blind. Please tell me this isn't who I fear—it is Chain?"

Chain chuckled at her dramatics, "I am afraid so, Marla. Meet Bounty Hunter 13, our most powerful and therefore cursed brother. I really would hate to live his life."

The one helping with the birth spoke, "If that's Bounty Hunter 13, then... quick, get me the knives and anesthetics. We're going to have to cut her open."

A voice echoed through the air, "Ah ah ah... you forget one old friend."

Chain looked at the girl who had just been breached. She seemed awfully calm and was staring at them with curiosity.

Marla picked her up and brought her to the bowl. "Do we have a name for her?"

"We do not, but I think I like the name Amari. If I was able to have children, that would have been the name of my daughter."

Crane sighed, "Let's go with that name, then. But for now, I need you two as second hands. The two that are going to be born next will likely be the ones to kill their mother. I need you to help with the surgery."

The two were suddenly drafted into surgery. Dragon anaesthetised the mother while Crane began brushing some strange-smelling liquid on her stomach. Then he pulled out a serrated knife. He used the sharp, not serrated side to cut a small line across her womb.

Dragon yelled, "She's going into cardiac arrest and hurry it up. We both know she's going to die, use the jagged edge."

Crane shook his head. "Ah ah ah... we wouldn't want to harm the conjoined ones now, would we?"

Crane tossed the knife behind him and it landed perfectly in the sink. He dug both hands into the cut he made and then tore open the womb pulling out two very small, very bloody children. He handed them to the dragon, who waved his hands, causing three runes to appear. There was a sound not unlike the tearing of paper as the two were separated.

One quick surgery later and two children lay side by side on another operating table. Their mother lay dead from the energy she had expelled while giving birth. Dragon was sewing her up to make her look presentable before her funeral.

He brought the body outside and placed it on the ground. As it was engulfed by mystical fire, Dragon saw a horned shadow in flames. It was eight feet tall, had two large horns jutting from the side of its head, and four medium-sized spikes on its shoulders. He raised a glass of amber liquid in a mocking fashion. "Theaym Sidroc uigde seul. Theaym Havens Sunocme uigde seul." He tossed the liquid on the fire and walked back inside as the pyre consumed the dead. Silently he was vowing that he would destroy the Clan Hunter.

He kicked aside the metal arm that was all that remained of the woman. He scoffed and walked away.

***

The next morning, Dragon sat near the cliff with Crane. Both were looking out across the land. Crane spoke, "Amazing what a little light can do to lift your spirits. The Island of Order and Chaos sure looks pristine. I wonder if any felt what happened last night."

Dragon was bouncing his daughter on his knee and she was giggling. His voice was weary with immortality. "If they did, we're in trouble."

Crane nodded, "So now we need to decide how these will be raised. I think we need Mick Mack to take Bonty, Amari, Myst, Eris, and Corvus to their home on Silver. I suppose you will be heading back to Angel's Grove with Trinity?"

Dragon looked at the little one on his lap and said, "Yes, my wife will need to get accustomed to her. But what should we do with the conjoined ones Erick-Starr and Vera?"

A mechanically enhanced voice spoke, "I will take them since I suppose we need to keep them separate so that Zenthin cannot find them?"

Both turned to see a cybernetic man; his labored breathing could be heard through the respirator he wore. It sounded mechanical and yet had a warmth to it that no mechanical voice could recreate. Crane nodded his head, "Yes, Warlord Scarabaeidae, that would be excellent. Is Mick Mack behind you?"

"I am here, pale one." This one's voice sounded like the rumble of thunder as a storm made itself known. The three turned to see a man with leathery wings and a crown of horns standing there. He had pale gray skin and a skull and crossbones on his vest.

Crane looked him over and said, "So do you know the plan?"

Mick Mack smiled, "Yes, I will be raising the four along with my adopted daughter Elena. When King Zen Ankara sends Maester Zarbon's two children after us, Chain is to take Corvus, Elena, Myst, Amari, and Bounty Hunter 13 to Diavonbry. While Marla convinces the two to spare her and Eris only to convince Ankara to adopt Eris and send her to Noamaiza."

Dragon grimaced, "You know Maester Zarbon's kids will probably kill you, right?"

Mick Mack tilted his head and smirked, "We Daemus do not die. We merely return to

Chaos' Purity and regenerate. I do not know the term *Death*."

Crane looked out across the land again. "Good, you both know your orders. Have fun, they will be difficult."

Dragon watched as the sky filled with shooting stars. *Good, all things are according to plan. Scarabaeidae will die on the way to Metallic and Mick Mack will take many years to recover. If only Tannid could see me now. But she is displaced. Her replacement, Lonava, will have to suffice. Now to convince young Knight Stynarii to rebel against The Psychics. I think I still have Grigori Rasputin's mysteries. Yes, he will eat those volumes up. God Silver will rue the day he crossed me.*

***

On Continent Organos, a woman who bore a striking similarity to the woman from the night before used up the rest of her strength to give birth to six girls. She vanished in a glowing blue flame as her body burned up from the inside. Four men stood there. One was Lord Hawthorn, one was Lord Wolf, one was Lord Huntari, and the final was Lord Ursa. Lord Wolf and Lord Ursa were core beings of the Organos Pantheon. Lord Hawthorn was of the Taur and Lord Huntari was of the Oni.

Lord Wolf spoke in a soft wind-like voice, "So Lord Shadow's daughter passes from this world. Lord Shadow's time is coming to a close. So why would she bequeath the universe with these six girls?"

Lord Ursa spoke in a deep rumble, "I sense the melody of the universe, the very fabric that makes this universe this universe, has been rewritten. Ah, Bounty Hunter 12, you strike again. Why should I be so surprised?"

Wolf huffed, "Of course, that bastard has his hoof prints all over this. Lord Hawthorn, one of the blond girls, will be yours to take care of."

"What has my cousin done?"

"Your cousin has succeeded in his experiment. However, he may not know it. Both His plan A and plan B are prepared. And now I just felt a shift. He had a plan C and D as well, that conniving schemer. And while plan B, C, and D are with Mick Mack of the Daemus, we must split up plan B's siblings."

"I see, so that is why the moons turned red on an off-season. Ugh, this does not bode well. How many lives were altered because of cousin's hubris?"

Lord Ursa looked up at the stars as if figuring out something. "Six plus the fourth that happened many decades ago."

Lord Huntari snorted in disdain, "And the world will quake at his coming. The sky will bow down to his greatness. He will be the Avenging demon. The death of the gods."

A large Taur walked into the clearing with a Gargoyle dressed in black "Somehow, I don't think it will come to that, my friend. The gods will not die by Bounty Hunter 13's hand. They will however, despise him. He will become like them. And when he does, Bounty Hunter 12 will become something else."

Hawthorn smirked, "Well, well, well, Taro Greyhull, I heard you were on Planet Myst?"

"I was recently freed from my prison. Bounty Hunter 12 has succeeded where no

Silveran or Taur has. He has created a God."

Wolf scoffed, "Regardless, I am glad you are here, Taro. You will take the dark girl. She has a shadow taint on her. She is strong, perfect for somebody of your tutelage."

Taro blew steam from his nose with a scoff and a smirk, "My brother Zenthin's taint will be on her for her entire life. Pity. I will do what I can for her."

Huntari looked at his fingernails and picked at them. "I will take one of the blond girls. She will be safe with The Oni of the Bell. Hmm, why are there now only five girls? What happened?"

Wolf spoke, "There were always five, weren't there?"

Ursa grumbled, "She has been forgotten; her name is in the book. Come the time when the book is opened and all those written in it are remembered, she will return to our minds. Thank you for that, Lord Cossak."

The black Gargoyle with wings like the night sky smiled and he, too, vanished.

Lord Wolf picked up the final girl. "We must keep them safe as long as we can. They must not know of their heritage. I fear they may try to find Plan B if they do learn of it."

Lord Hawthorn picked up the girl he was given and vanished into a portal of pure Mag. This was his second adopted child. Lord Wolf wrapped the girl he had in a pouch and bounded off. Lord Silas sighed and walked away with his girl. Taro Greyhull stroked the dark girl and vanished in a wave of gray. Lord Ursa eyed the final girl. He shook his head and scooped her up in his large hand. She grabbed his finger to gnaw on. He chuckled and brought her to his village. She gurgled as a boisterous woman collected her and fed her. She could see the Music in the air and gurgled happily.

***

On a space station near the start of the Meteor sector, seven people stood worried. They had to rush here since their mysterious companion had just gone into labor. The doctor helping with the birth came out of the surgery center. He shuddered, then cleared his head.

The burly man spoke, "Doc, what happened in there?"

"Well... good news, the birth was successful and the children are healthy. Bad news... well... it's hard to say because of how confusing it was, but she died midway through and her body just vanished, leaving behind her mechanical arm. So I am uncertain what you wish to do for her seven children. She was unable to even name them."

The woman wearing a catsuit spoke, "We should be the ones to raise them. We were her closest companions."

The burly man shook his head in worry, then nodded, "I agree, Rogue, but should we really split the children up like that?"

The winged man spoke, "Yes, we should. I have scryed out and deciphered all there was to know about our mysterious companion. She was the daughter of a devious man by the name of Lord Shadow. She was married to another devious man by the name of Bounty Hunter 12. If you knew anything about those two men, you would want to split the siblings up."

The man in heavy armor spoke, "I see. Yes, I do get it now. We should raise them separately, but every few years, we should bring them together. I feel bad about ripping apart siblings."

The winged man smiled, "I agree, Lord Steel. Let us take our leave for now. Each of us should take one child. Name them how we wish and we will meet up on Meteor in ten years."

The small group disbanded, thus ending the Blackheart Mercenary Guild and starting the Blackheart Guardians.

***

On the forgotten Continent Fantasy, a third woman who looked exactly similar to the other two mentioned shuddered. Her birth had been hard, but with the help of three witches, she had survived. She felt her doppelganger return to her but could not feel the second one. She had the unique ability to separate her body multiple times. She had done this because she had felt how many children she was to bear and knew it would rip her apart if she did give birth to that many. Curse Bounty Hunter 12 crossed the line. I understand wanting power, but to have three backup plans to gain that power is; fuck him and I hope he can never return to the mortal world.

The younger witch spoke, "Hecate has heard your plea. You are free of the wretched man you cursed so loudly."

The middle-aged woman spoke, "You have given birth to some strong beings. However, because this is a forgotten continent, they will be forgotten until the world is ready to remember them."

"That is fine with me. I am happy that my family thinks I have died. I can start a new. I will raise these children and give them something their other siblings will never have—a Mother."

***

Meanwhile, across the ocean on the continent Komodo. Two large bearded men sat watching the sunset. One was Lord Badger, while the other was Lord Oda. Badger was holding a small bundle. They were watching as another cloaked female burned the corpse of a woman.

Oda spoke, "Lord Badger, was it necessary for my wife to die in childbirth?"

Badger sighed as he blew green smoke from his mouth and sucked in the burning reed he had in his mouth.

Oda growled, "Mysterious as always. What is the point of her anyway?"

The cloaked woman walked over and lowered her hood, revealing a very pale face with glowing green eyes. "The girl was born the same way a cursed boy was. On the same day, no less. She is a contingency plan in the event my former lover, Dragon, wins."

"I see. I will go along with this fool plan of yours, Lady Wyvern. I still have my other children."

Badger spoke, "It will all work out, Lord Oda. You will see. She has not steered us wrong yet, now has she?"

Oda let out a dark and menacing laugh. "No, I suppose she has not."

Badger looked at the horizon with dread. He saw fire and saw large war machines marching on cities. He saw anger and pain. He saw a burned man holding a flaming halberd. He sighed and finished his drink. Oda looked at him with concern, then shrugged and finished his wine as well.

On the outskirts of the Komodo Orkea region, An Oni-Ettin sat weaving magic from his flaming bell staff. He had just finished overseeing the birth of a Half-Oni girl. Her mother lay panting from the difficult birth, but she survived thanks to the energy the Oni infused her with. The girl, however, was marked. During her birth, the sky had become a raging thunderstorm. The moons had also turned red. She was destined for great things. Her elder sister stared at her burning orange eyes and saw eternity.

***

On Continent Misogoke. There was a wailing cry that came from an alleyway. A woman lay in a pool of blood. She was an outcast, so she was relegated to the slums where no professional help was. She had died from an impromptu c-section. Her daughter was being cleaned up by a priestess. The priestess wore a fishnet body stocking and nothing else. All Electranikka priestesses wore barely anything or nothing. Next to the priestess was a hermaphrodite. The man/woman was stroking the child to try and get her to sleep.

"Lucifer, did you see the sky?"

The hermaphrodite nodded, "Yes, she is destined for things even I cannot fathom."

"I will take her in. She is an orphan that will get around the rules of being an outcast. We, in the temple, will raise her, but she is most definitely an outcast—a Nephilim Outcast. She was born with male and female genitals. Though I have a feeling you have something to do with that."

"Maybe I do, maybe I don't. My lips are sealed. Name her how you wish, but like her mother, she should be named Darkspeed."

***

The large Taur looked down at the scientist. "Are you telling me that my son is an abomination?"

"Not an abomination per say. He came out of the tube when the sky changed. He is touched. The three moons went red. There was a huge Psy storm that erupted from an island far away. He was also born with unique coloring. Look at him, he's gray-furred but blue-skinned. You know that this coloring has not been seen in centuries."

"Yes, the traitor to our people was born with that coloring, but why would Anubis allow such an abomination to exist?"

A deep rumbling voice echoed forth from an Icon of Anubis. "Because he is not to

be my champion. My champion will come from the womb of Magenta Hunter, the traitor's sister. No, he is Coldharbour's chosen. While I dread that fact, it is what it is. He is to be the champion of the Taur since he was born under the same set of circumstances as a cursed boy from Silver."

"I see… very well, Anubis. I will send him to live with my brother on Diavonbre. What shall his name be?"

"Gunner Rhapsody."

***

On Continent Irescotwell near Norvcryog, a woman sat on a boat just after giving birth. It had come on unexpectedly while she was hunting for food. Luckily her shieldmaiden had been there to help. The boy had ethereal green eyes that seemed to stare deeply into her soul.

"Lady Djinnai, what shall the young prince's name be?"

"I don't quite know. Hmm, QiKong meaning waterbirth, sounds about right. I am just concerned since the moons went red. Especially since they broke through the aurora, he is destined for great or terrible things. It scares me."

"Then would you rather I drown him?"

"No, Kyrie, it's going to be fine. With the right training, he will be set on the right path."

***

On an unnamed island in the south quadrant of planet Silver the tribe of Maui danced around a massive pyre. They were celebrating the birth of Maui in one of their many ceremonies. A tattooed woman lay watching them, her bulging belly ready to pop any day. She was pregnant, her three breasts full of milk, eager to be set free. As the moons burst forth behind the smoke, they became crimson. The woman cried out as she gave birth.

The child was born strangely. She had two tones of skin on either side of her body. One half was gray and the other was the usual bronzed that the sea people had. Even the fine hair on her head was dual-colored. One side was blue and the other side was red with a small streak of purple between them. Her eyes opened, revealing one green cat eye and the other brown.

The shaman muttered some prayers and then spoke, "Welcome to the tribe Hunapo."

***

On the continent Diavonbre in the far north, the Great Dragon Bahamut, first son of the Great Silver Dragon, first of the gods, looked down curiously at the bright platinum pink dragon. She had just hatched and was looking up at him with curiosity mixed with fear.

He spoke softly, "Do not fear, little one. You are unique. You hatched during the great blood moons on an off-season, no less. You are touched. I am guessing the old goat Sidrodc may have had a hand in your change."

He reached a claw down and tickled her belly, causing her to let out a giggle and grab playfully at her father's claw.

***

There was an ear-splitting howl that echoed across the wastes of Norvcryog. A small wolf rose from the bloody ice. His small body was weak and in need of sustenance. He saw a half-frozen corpse and dug into it, feasting on the frostbitten meat. There were many corpses here. They would be his only source of food. His icy fur bristled. He was not alone. He turned to see two icy eyes staring at him. He then saw the Midwinter Dragon rise from her nest. He backed away in fear. But her large claw stopped him.

"Hello, little wolf. No... no... Dread Wolf. Yes, that shalt be your name. Come closer, I will not bite. You will be warm. Yes... warm... in my nest."

The Dread Wolf blinked, then begrudgingly curled up under her wing. She smiled a dark smile. Dreams of fire and rage echoed in her head. She saw fire. She saw mad rage. The Dread Wolf was free.

The Death of the Guardian: Run to Dust Child.

An old-looking elf stood by as four, barely seventeen children played outside. He had his gun holstered by his side and a sword on his back. A bandaged man walked in. "Mick Mack, you know what today is?"

"Yes, these little ones turn eighteen today."

They both watched as one of the boys bumped his head on a chair. He was crawling because he had yet to reach walking age.

"Where's Eris?"

"She's inside playing with Marla."

Both heard gunfire and crashing. Chain nodded his head and herded the four children onto a small ship. He closed it and stood by it with his guns drawn. He saw Mick Mack rush the home and then get thrown out the window. Two heavily armored people walked out. The more feminine looking one fired nine rounds into Mick Mack's head. She then stomped on the remaining bit and ground it into the dirt.

Chain spoke while clapping, "Oh, congratulations, you killed an old man. You must feel so very proud of yourselves. Now let's see how you do against someone who can disappear at will."

As he vanished from sight, the masculine one spoke, "Jay, take our prisoners to the boss. I will handle the freak."

The woman nodded, "Just be careful Jayzon. That freak has ten years more experience. We got lucky with the old man."

As she hurried away, the small ship lifted off and Jayzon suddenly felt weightless. He looked around for the bandaged man before he was suddenly slammed into a spiked tree. Had he not worn such thick armour, the tree would have killed him. As he dropped, several stone pillars slammed into him. His armour shattered. He stood, his pale skin shining with sweat. He hefted his minigun and looked around. The stone had withdrawn to the earth. He opened fire on the pod only to see it explode. He smiled, turned, and then dropped his gun. He fell on one knee as a blade jettisoned from his sternum. As the world went dark, he heard an ominous laughter.

The girls that Bounty Hunter 12 had adopted looked around from the catastrophe. The eldest sister looked at her wounded siblings. She shuddered and had the computer bring them to the medical bay.

Mar spoke, "Laura be not afraid too much. You and your sisters have been through quite a bit. Father cared for you as much as he did us. Mother… hard to tell, but as long as you live, you are welcome to stay in this home. I will do what I can to be a mother-like figure to your little sisters."

"Thanks, Mar. Do you think we did well defending our home?"

"You managed to kill everybody besides Jay and Jayzon. So yeah, I'd say you and your siblings put Father's training to good use."

***

Chain was surfing the pod that he made to look like it blew up. He smiled as the ocean waves crashed under the pod's hover jets. He seemingly melted into the hull and arrived in the nursery. In here, he began to accelerate their growth. He saw his blind brother fiddling with some pieces of metal. He walked over. "Bonty Hanter XIII! What are you doing?"

The little boy held up a tin soldier. "Made this for you, big broder."

Chain blinked in surprise. "Well, you continue to surprise me, Bonty."

Then he felt a small hand tug at him and he looked down at Elena, who had tears in her eyes. "Grampa's dead!"

Corvus hobbled over and embraced her, patting her reassuringly on the back. He had yet to speak, which worried Chain slightly. Even Myst had spoken. Chain had not been too thrilled with the first word from Myst's mouth, but that was the past. The mysterious girl, Amari, was sitting and reading a book that she should not have been able to comprehend but seemed to understand perfectly.

A computerized voice followed a small chime, "Continent Diavonbry. Home of the Black Silverans and the Brown Elves. Where would you like me to land?"

Chain looked at the map he had then he typed in the coordinates. The ship hummed as it landed.

He was outside his uncle's home. The shack wasn't much, but it would do. "Hello, Uncle Tynamus."

A man with black and gray hair stood brewing tea. He looked up to see a bandaged man followed by four toddlers. He shook his head and sat down, smiling as he sipped his tea.

"So, Chain, who are your friends?"

"My little siblings and your niece and nephews. Tynamus, may I present to you Myst, Corvus, Amari, Bonty, and Elena."

Tynamus smiled, "Welcome to Diavonbre, home of the worst sleazebags the world has to offer."

Said Razor—Fang to the Dirt, Rise Up

It had been seventy years. Tynamus had died in battle and his second oath brother had sent his son, Axel, to keep an eye on Chain. Axel was the same age as Chain. It turned out he was born on the same day as well. The Black Silveran had proven quite useful around the home and had even sworn an oath of brothership with Chain. That had been around the time Myst had wandered off and been captured by slavers. Chain sighed as he stirred the soup. They had never found Myst.

He poured the soup into bowls for Bounty, Corvus, Elena, and Axel. He went to give a bowl to Amari. She was in her little bunker reading some more books. She smiled and took it.

"Thanks, Papa."

"Uh, you're welcome, kiddo, but I am not your father." "You act like one to us, so why aren't you?"

"I am your older brother. It is my duty to take care of you."

"There is a fine line between those two words. Are you not a Father in tempore? You took care of us after your uncle passed away, so, therefore, it's only right that you be called papa."

"Amari, there is another reason why this is shocking to me."

"Oh yes, I heard you after I was born. You are unable to have children."

"Oh, you understood that well. You certainly are a special one. I knew that was the case. Excellent. Very well, you may call me Papa."

He then looked outside. He saw two huge green eyes staring at the shack from the shadows of the mountain. He walked outside with his gun held ready. "Who's there? I'm warning you, I know three hundred fifty ways to kill a man."

A voice that sounded like the earth had opened up spoke, "I am no man."

Chain dropped his guns as a massive copper dragon rose from the earth. On his back was a whole ecosystem of trees and stones and animals. His jagged tail lashed against the mountain, causing an avalanche.

Axel walked out. "Morning, Razorfang!"

Dragon smiled a wide toothy predatory smile. "Axel, my boy! And a good morning to you."

Chain spoke, "I have never seen a Turtle Earth Dragon up close. Is it true that you are siblings with the great Silver Dragon"

"I am the second eldest. Not only is he my brother, but I also know the ruler of the tides and the ancient god of the seas, Thul Thanos of the Thulhuid."

"I would be honored if you could train me."

"It shall be so. I have already been training Axel."

The Laughing Bull

Axel was with Corvus. They had been sent north to find some specific herbs. Corvus had just turned one hundred eighty. Bounty, his brother, had come down with a rare strain of Psy buildup nicknamed Psy-Cancer. It was eating away his insides but there was a rare nectar that could relieve his buildup that is why Corvus found himself walking down the road with Axel. Corvus was one hundred Axel was two hundred fifty. Axel stopped Corvus in his path.

"Be careful we are entering the territory of the Hyaenidae. They are fierce warriors. They are not to be trifled with. Let me do the talking."

Corvus raised his eyebrow at Axel then signed (As if I could talk anyway. What do I need to look out for?)

Axel processed the hand motions and then nodded, "If you hear giggling or see shattered bones a Hyaenidae is near. They use bone weapons and their powerful jaws to take down their enemy. As long as we prove we are non hostile they will not attack us. This means do not help anyone who has fallen prey to them."

Corvus nodded as they proceeded deeper into the savanna. Loud laughter suddenly bombarded them as they were setting camp for the night. Nine pairs of eyes gazed hostilly from the large grass. One pair moved forward and a massive barrel chested Hyaenidae emerged grinning wickedly. The eight others had disappeared.

The Hyaenidae stood on its back legs and spoke in a scratchy yet feminine voice, "You stand in the presence of Shenzi Fang, little prey. My pack will make your death swift."

Axel stood, he only reached her chest. He spoke, "I have done nothing to earn your ire. Why do you desire to attack me?"

Instead of replying she attacked her large paw like claw smashed into Axel sending him into the grass where he was set upon by her pack. Corvus avoided her attack causing her to stumble. He took advantage of the opening and struck her with the palm of his hand. Sending a shockwave from his palm into her solar plexus. She coughed and went limp as her body rolled with the shockwave she landed weakly on all fours and shook herself before vomiting. Her pack mates were thrown from the grass into her and all nine lay in a heap. She stared at Corvus and saw blood running from a claw mark across his chest. She grinned and giggled.

"You won't live long prey. That wound looks deep. As soon as you fall, my pack will feast."

Corvus looked down at the wound and shrugged. He began to build a fire as a wounded Axel emerged from the grass. Flames were shooting off of him but not burning anything.

Corvus signed (What the hell are you?)

"I am an Efreet of the fire variety. Her pack did a number on me, looks like she got you good."

(Not really. I am a follower of Nevermore and was marked by him around the time Myst disappeared. These gashes are actually his mark. When the moon rises you will see it more clearly.)

The three moons rose in the sky. One was full, one was a waxing gibbous, and the other a waxing crescent. The full moon's light happened to hit the mark on Corvus' chest, lighting it up a neon purple. Revealing more than just four claw marks. There was a hawk skull and large bony wings behind the skull. The claw marks looked to be scar tissue while the rest was like a smoky tattoo.

"How did you get blessed by him?"

(Took on a Felis raider with my bare hands. He cut me good with his claws but Nevermore healed me. What about you? You don't look like an Efreet.)

"As a Black Silveran I was born into the black Silveran community of Onegansa in the north along with my twin brother. However I was chosen to have an Efreet inhabit my body while he was not. This caused a rift between us since he had been training with the village shaman to be the one chosen by an Efreet. My father encouraged me to find my story and I left the village. Soon after I was taken in by Lord Tyran, the sworn brother of your uncle Tynamus. He trained me then told me to seek out Razorfang and also to keep an eye on the children Tynamus took in."

Shenzi stared in awe at the two warriors. Her pack was still unconscious. She wriggled out from under them and crawled towards the fire. She felt crazy weak. Corvus was watching her. The one known as Axel was stirring something in a pot. She crawled closer and collapsed near his feet and a bowl was placed in front of her. She eyed it warily.

Axel spoke, "Eat up you survived the palm of Lenore. You need your energy."

"What of my pack?"

"As soon as they awake they will find raw meat waiting for them. Now eat."

"No! I cannot eat like a common dog."

Corvus walked over to her and rolled her over on her back. He pressed three areas of her torso, she gasped and her pseudo penis became erect. He hefted her into his lap and began to feed her. She hungrily accepted his help. She didn't feel weak anymore.

Axel spoke, "He just performed the Tale Telling Heart technique on you. It is the counter to the Palm of Lenore. Your strength should begin to return shortly. How do you feel?"

"I feel better. Where are you heading so I may alert the other packs that you are not food."

"North. We are looking for a certain herb that is supposed to increase the immune system and blood flow. My friend's brother is in a feverish state and requires that herb to heal."

"Ah you seek the golden nectar of the Drakonis tree. As soon as my pack is full I will send them out to alert the other packs. You want to head to the dragon lands, but first, you must pass through the lands of the Anubi. I will aid you to the best of my ability as soon as my pack is sent out."

"Do not worry about helping me as I have traveled these roads many times."

"No, I insist. You bested my pack. We were known as the Golden Stalkers. The third best pack among my kind. Undefeated until now."

"I see so I have no say in this matter. Your pack sees me as an alpha."

"Correct, which means I must mate with you to make our pack stronger. I will follow until you and I mate."

"Oh Goody. Very well as soon as your pack is full and sent out we will head out."

"Yes, my alpha!"

"First thing's first don't call me that. My name is Axel, memorize it. Secondly I have no desire to be your alpha. Your kind are meant to be a matriarchal society. I will not have you sully your pack by being submissive to a male. Act like you were before you were beaten."

"Er, very well, Lord Axel."

"That will have to do. I guess. Come get some rest."

She wrapped herself around Axel and Corvus and let out a throaty giggle then snored.

The Sheriff of the Pyramids

As the sun rose, the Golden Stalker pack awoke from their sound thrashing. They cowered at the sight of Axel looking down upon them. They scrambled to untangle themselves. When they did, they saw a large pile of raw meat. The eight tore into the pile, forgetting that they had been scared a minute ago. When they had eaten their fill, Shenzi barked orders in their language and they rushed off, disappearing into the wilds. She stood on all fours.

"My lord, would you like to ride me?"

"No, Corvus and I can keep up with your pace. We are only in cloth and leather, not our usual armour. You would be surprised how fast Silverans can move."

"Suit yourself."

Shenzi vanished into the grass, rushing off, but when she stopped near the border marker and looked back, Corvus was standing there, his gray eyes piercing her very soul. Axel caught up.

Corvus tilted his head and then moved his hands quickly. Shenzi was curious; it seemed he was trying to speak with his hands.

She heard Axel say, "Hold on, you're talking too fast. What? No, I am just out of shape. It's been a long time since I trekked five hundred miles in a day. Yes, we are at the border of the Tuar lands. Keep your eyes out, you know how well Silverans and Taur get along."

Corvus moved his hands again. Shenzi spoke, "What is he doing?"

Axel smiled, "Corvus here is mute. He is using sign language to speak. It takes a while to get used to. I don't expect you to learn it. He just answered my statement with like oil and water."

"I take it that something big happened between your species and the Tuar?"

"Oh yes, we threw them from their ancestral lands and shipped them off to other continents and the Mechanical Island of Upper Depths. After banishing them, we took their lands as our own. But that was ages ago, back when the Silveran Capital was on Western Silver. Now it's on Eastern Silver since Western Silver is a desolate wasteland because of a Nuclear Psy Bomb. But my kind have lived on Diavonbre before that. Corvus' kind, the Grey Silverans, lived on Continent Silver. Oh, hold on, Shenzi. I'd like for you to get behind me."

She obeyed as a small crater about a hand long appeared right where she had been standing. She looked around and wrinkled her muzzle in disgust as the smell of ozone filled her nostrils.

A voice spoke, "Y'all varmints better skedaddle. We don't want your kind 'ere. Next shot won't miss."

Corvus waved his hand, causing a portion of the cliff nearby to crumble. When the dust cleared, a golden-furred Tuar lay in front of them holding a tri-barrelled quad firing Ultra Shotgun. Each of the three barrels had four holes with a different elemental symbol on it. She was unconscious. Corvus lifted her easily and slung her over his shoulder. He passed the checkpoint and pulled up a shield of black feathers. When the firing died down, he waved his hand and the black feathers shot forward, injuring the platoon of soldiers that had been hiding in the cliffs. The injuries were nonlife-threatening but certainly incapacitating.

A booming voice echoed from his mouth, "I am the High Druid Priest of Nevermore. You will allow us passage through your lands. We are going north. If you make attempts on our lives, I will call down the wrath of Nevermore upon you."

A magenta-skinned bull walked out; she had a black scarab on her armour. She pointed her jagged cyber blade at Corvus.

She spoke, "I am the High Druid Priestess of Anubis. Pray, tell me why you think you can order us what to do?"

"Do not test me, Anubis. You and I are both Death gods. Remember what happened last time? Two Death Gods butted heads."

"Very well, but you had best keep out of trouble. Why north?"

Corvus staggered back and Axel spoke, "We are heading into the dragon lands to look for an herb that will help my friend's brother."

"Hmm, very well. I know you are listening, Jackie. Go with them and make sure that they stay away from all populated areas."

Jackie's tail swished in annoyance, but she made no sound.

Corvus eyed the bull, then signed (good to see you, Aunt Magenta. Glad you are still kicking).

She eyed him, then smiled and signed back (I knew I recognized your scent, child. I see my brother succeeded. Pity. I really wish he had listened to me).

After they left the lands of Anubis, they stopped by a small cave. Corvus unceremoniously set Jackie down and leaned against the wall of the cave.

He signed (I need a break to replenish my psy; using Nevermore's voice drains me).

Axel nodded and motioned Shenzi to watch the entrance to the cave. She obeyed eagerly.

"So, Jackie, was it? Why did you fire on us before stopping us?"

"I ain't talkin to you. Your kind is filth beneath my hooves."

"You are talking now. I get the animosity. I come from a Brown Elf village. Like your kind, they don't like my kind. They only keep us around because we make good protectors. My brother and I are three-fourths elves. The only reason I look more like a Silveran is due to Efreet."

She was startled. "You worship the fire, Jinn? But we are nowhere near Komodo."

"While true, Efreet came to Diavonbre when the dragons came. Along with the God Ramuh. I see you are a follower of Ramuh."

"Not a follower. I was found by a tree that attracts lightning. The Ramuh Druids built their grove around this tree. I am an unknown. I am three-fourths positive I was left there to die of exposure. See my cybernetic arms? I was born without arms. The Druid Priest of Anubis forged new arms that grew with me."

"Are you hungry? It could be a full day for Corvus to recover."

"Why does he need to recover?"

"He used the voice of Nevermore. He himself is mute, so when you and the Druid Priest of Anubis challenged us, he tried to settle things without violence. But your tactic of shooting the first question later forced his hand. So are you hungry?"

"I guess I could eat something"

"Alright, I'll start the stew."

Night came quickly and Jackie fell asleep. Her sleep was interrupted by a screeching howl. She bolted awake with her shotgun charged and ready. A hand forced her down. She looked up to see Corvus's glowing gray eyes. He held his finger to his lip, telling her to be quiet. He had a small handgun out. There was another screeching howl as the Hyeanidae was thrown into the cave by an unknown assailant. The Black Silveran, Axel, was holding up a fiery shield in the doorway. He had smoke coming off him as if something was trying to get out. She could vaguely see a boar-headed and bull-horned fire jinn in the smoke. She shuddered. Corvus created a rune out of feathers which caused a barrier to appear. The phantom feather barrier made her drowsy to look at it. She dozed back off.

With the dawn came blood. Axel lay against the wall of the cave, wounded from a spear in his shoulder. There were Elf corpses all over the cave and outside. It looked like a whole raiding party. Corvus was carrying the bodies to a pile. Shenzi lay wrapped up tightly in bloody bandages. She was sulking. It looked like the Elves had overpowered her by sheer numbers. The spear was pulled out of Axel by an invisible force. If one looked closely, they might have been able to spot a glint of a red hooded Serpenti. A watery form appeared and assisted Corvus in moving the bodies. It looked squid-like in appearance, with fin protrusions on its arms and legs surrounded by tentacles that were assisting it.

Several small puffballs floated around inside the cave and also outside the cave. Jackie eyed the small floating things with fear.

She spoke, "Uhg, what happened last night?"

Axel snorted, "A Brown Elf raiding party. Don't particularly know what the reason they attacked was, but I have a feeling and have sent out my spies to confirm."

A hissing voice spoke, "Information has come back. As sssoon as this mess is clean, I would sssuggest moving into the dragon lands via the mountainsss."

"So, it was true my brother has split from the clan due to his anger at not being chosen as an Efreet."

"Yesss, he has sssent out his elite unit of Red Guardsss to find you and eradicate you and anyone you are with."

Jackie watched as the puffballs floated out and disappeared into the aether. Axel watched the puffball go and shook his head. He finished helping clean up the bodies and lit them on fire.

"Thayme Sidrodc ugde het seul. Thame Havens sunocem het seul."

Jackie looked at the amber drink that had appeared in her hand during the prayer. She saw it in everyone else's hand, including one that seemed to float in mid-air.

All the glasses were downed and tossed on the fire. The small group left the cave. None saw a fat dwarf with metal forearms watching them. He looked at the small band and shook his head. He disappeared underground.

The Mountain of Witch Fire

Axel pressed his palm to a hidden door. It hissed open and he motioned everyone inside. The hallway was large and hummed with psy energy. He led them to a large pillar that seemed to cut into the mountain high above them. He typed in a code and a door clanged open, revealing a massive lift capable of lifting an interplanetary jumper. They entered the lift and it hummed to life, soon opening on a snow-covered peak. They saw a tall woman wearing nothing over her pale gray and shimmering skin. She had six arms and void black hair. She eyed them curiously.

Axel stepped out of the lift. She tackled him full force. He heard Shenzi snarl in anger. He spoke, "Good to see you too, Archera. Be careful, I still have a hole from a spear in my left shoulder."

"You must tell me the tale."

"Yes, yes, I'll tell you while we walk. We must get to the Witchfire by moon up."

"Oh, heading to the dragon lands, are we? Why?"

"That is where the story begins."

Many hours of walking through waist-deep snow later. They arrived at a massive crater with many smaller craters near it. Each crater was filled with a black viscous substance. The larger one had an altar and many benches facing the altar. Behind the altar was a platinum-pink lizard girl with dark pink hair on her head. She had deep pink eyes and an unsettling grin.

"I have been waiting for you, Axel."

"Hello, Jinxi. As you can see, I gathered an eclectic group."

"Why, though?"

"They followed. I led."

"I must examine each one. The nectar can only be given to a certain type."

"Even though only I or my sworn brother are the ones that require it?"

"Even that, yes. Sorry. The nectar is very sensitive."

"Do try not to injure them or scare them too much."

The pink one smiled before fire exploded out of the pits as she transformed into a platinum pink dragon. She stared down at them with a predatory grin. She then breathed fire. Shenzi snarled and challenged the much bigger Jinxi. Her fur stood on end, trying to embiggen herself. Jinxi giggled and bounced up and down.

"I like her, but the nectar likes tall, dark and spooky."

"You mean Corvus?"

"Yeah, big guy with curly black horns and a green bushy beard."

"Uhh, sure, we'll go with that. Corvus, it seems that the dragon nectar has chosen you to receive it and return it to Bounty."

(What's the catch?)

"You must retrieve it from her tail fork. Good luck."

Corvus vanished and reappeared in a gout of smoky feathers holding a vial of gold liquid. (We done here?)

Axel looked surprised but smiled, "Yeah, I think we are."

Jinxi giggled and returned to her normal size; she then weaved an elaborate rune that sent all of them back to their homes. The only one that returned to a different home was Shenzi. She arrived at Axel's home with Corvus and Axel. Corvus hurried inside and administered the Nectar to Bounty. Unfortunately, because it had taken them longer to get the antidote than they had hoped, he developed a lame leg. The woman they had hired to keep an eye on him had been naked on top of him when Corvus had entered.

Axel spoke to her, "Thank you for your assistance, Vicky. I hope you enjoyed yourself?"

The red-haired and green-eyed girl smiled, "Oh, I very much did. Thank you, now pay up."

"Here is your fee plus a little extra for the child you carry."

"Can I get rid of the child?"

"Frankly, Vicky, I don't give a damn what you do as soon as you leave home. If you feel more comfortable aborting it, do so, but If you want to keep it, we can set you up with a cushy trust fund to provide for yourself."

"Hmm, I may be in touch."

She kissed Axel on the lips and left. He shook his head and began cooking some soup. He grimaced as he foresaw a war.

The Diavonbry Rebellion

An old crone stood on a cliffside as the moons became full. "Three times called the Moon Catz Roar."

A middle-aged woman walked up the hill. "Three calls, the horn blower sounds."

A young woman followed. "It's time, it's time." This was Lucifer Ankara

The crone uncovered a large pot and croaked, "Dancing round the cauldron sing. Throw in the entrails three. Frozen toad and eye of the storm. Sweltering venom and sleeping charm boil first in this charmed pot."

The three danced around the pot. "Double, double, toil and trouble; let the pot burn and bubble."

The middle-aged woman spoke, "Fillet of snake thrown in the cauldron to bake. Newts eye and toads toe, bat's fur and hounds throat, the sting of rain and lizard fork, Owl wing on cardboard cork. With the Hell-broth bubble and brew a charm of powerful trouble."

The three danced around the pot. "Double, double toil and trouble; let the pot burn and bubble."

The girl sang, " Scale of a dragon. Tooth of a wolf. Jaw of a shark torn from his maw. Root of hemlock found in the dark. Silvered in the full moon's view, a pirate's gal torn by a ewe. Nose from a beggar, birth strangled babe, foot of a storm shrew baked in our cauldron. Summon Hecate to our domain."

The three danced around the pot. "Double, double, toil and trouble; let the pot burn and bubble."

The cauldron exploded and a shadowy form rose from the smoke. "Oh, well done, my girls. This soup will make a fine dinner. You did well for your first time performing my ritual, young Lucifer Ankara."

The young girl smiled and bowed. The crone spoke, "Hold my lady at the knocking of the thrush. Hide us in the shadows of the brush. By the pricking of my thumbs, something wicked this way comes."

The four watched as four men walked past them. One was dressed in black feathers with a purple scar that glowed in the moonlight, the other had mechanical augments on his limbs, and the fourth laboriously walked with a cane, each step causing him pain as his malformed body floated through the moonlight.

The four shuddered as the malformed one looked directly at them and smirked. It was the year One Hunter. Fort Ironsides, the main hub of the Diavonbry

Rebellion was under siege. Their Auto-Cannons and psych-armour had been destroyed by some traitors. The massive titanium gates were about to be destroyed. The outer wall had been destroyed by the enemy's Camazotz class siege breaker ships. The Bugbear class mech troops were almost through the gate. The giant Roc class ships were spitting out numerous Cockatrice class hovercraft. The twenty dozen rebels still alive were struggling against Aka's robo-shock troops. In the distance, General Scarabaeus Hercules could see a Behemoth class land tank lumbering up to finish them off. His one eye squinted as he thought he saw three figures on the nearby cliff.

That was when one of the four Roc class ships suddenly took a nosedive and smashed into the Behemoth tank. The other four ships soon followed. The Cockatrice class hovercraft began to smash into each other, causing it to rain fire and shrapnel. Only a legion of soldiers remained.

Scarabaeus spoke, "Alright, troops, let's push them back, use the wreckage as cover and finish off the rest."

The remaining legion of soldiers were quickly annihilated. Scarabaeus smiled a tusked toothy smile. He pulled out his sword as a large horned man landed. The man scoffed before turning to the three newcomers.

He spoke, "I have shown you the rebellion. Now leave me alone."

A thin, scrawny-looking Silveran with a black feathered cloak clapped his hands together and then shook the older man's hand.

The other scrawny-looking Silveran spoke, "Thank you for your help. We appreciate it."

"I suppose that will be good enough, Mister Hunter. Keep an eye on my student."

"I will. The tide of battle has changed."

Scarabaeus spoke, "Who in the thirteen hells are you?"

A third limped forward, shifting as much weight to his Kyber Cane. His body was a mess. One arm looked shorter than the other. While one leg looked malformed, he wore a blindfold over his eyes. Each step seemed to cause him pain.

This third spoke in a raspy whisper, "General Scarabaeus, I am Dutch Hunter. This is my brother, Myst Hunter, and my other brother, Corvus Hunter. We have come to offer our service to you. We heard from master Infernus that you were struggling."

Lieutenant Quezal Qotal walked over with a large brown Silveran. He spoke, "What can a blind malformed mutant, a mute imbecile, and a scrawny sack of meat do for us?"

The brown Silveran with the fiery orange hair tied in seven battle braids spoke, "Trust me, looks can be deceiving. Corvus Hunter is my sworn brother's brother. I know what he can do. And you just witnessed what Dutch Hunter can do."

The three looked at the devastation around them and then back at Dutch. The grin on his face was unsettling.

Scarabaeus smiled, "Well, you may join us if you can get us through Gorgon pass."

Dutch bowed before turning around and limped towards Gorgon Pass. Corvus took this time to vanish in a gout of feathers. He had business to attend to. This left the uncomfortable Myst with Axel.

Gorgon Pass was a small canyon with unused turrets and statues standing in grotesque horror against the walls of the canyon. The dust whipped up as several serpentine women slithered towards Dutch.

Their stone gaze was ineffective against him. He took off his blindfold, causing them to scream in pain.

His voice rasped, "I will release you from this pain if you allow my allies to pass. They will be through in a few days."

Dutch continued on through the pass. Mapping it out and threatening the other Gorgons into compliance. A woman with a large sword landed, her brown duster whipping in the wind. Three others landed as well.

One was a short male Dwarv Silveran, his blood-red beard was smoldering from his forge. He absentmindedly scratched his eyepatch while his piercing green eye narrowed. His forearms were solid metal fused to his upper arms at the elbow.

The next was a tall large breasted green Orkean Silveran. She had straps covering her nipples but nothing else. Around her neck were large prayer beads. On her legs was cybernetically enhanced war armour.

Dutch looked at the third. "A Gnomish Silveran!"

The small creature with a sniper rifle strapped to her back bared her fangs. "Yous gots a problem wit dat?"

"Hardly. Your kind is very rare above ground. Just surprising to see one." There was a thud. Dutch turned around to come face to face with a White Silveran with electric blue hair. Circling her were various discs that she placed on a summoned disk jockey table with ethereal speakers attached to her clear armour.

She smiled and lifted her shaded glasses, revealing deep red eyes. Her blue-painted lips curved up in a sneer.

"And now a bard enters into play. Judging from your conjuring, you are an electro-bard. And from your eyes and hair, most likely a Misogoke Silveran, so how is this going to play out?"

The woman with the big sword pointed it at Dutch. "We protect this pass so no Gorgons can slip into Chombra!"

"So mercenaries. Oookay, well, either you let me pass or you die."

The Gnomish Silveran gasped, "Did your voice just get deeper?"

Dutch smiled a violent smile sending chills down their spines. "Care for a demonstration. Kneel!"

She dropped into a submissive position as Dutch pulled out a blade and ignited it with fire.

The woman with the big sword suddenly gasped, "We surrender, you may pass."

The bard snarled, "What! You can't be serious, Elena."

Dutch spoke, "So that is where you disappeared to after Myst's rescue. Now we're on two different sides of this battle."

"I said we surrender. You may pass. Please release Tam Tam."

Dutch limped past them and into the city. Elena stared at him with terror in her eyes. The bard and monk looked at Elena with curiosity while Tam Tam lay on the ground gasping for air.

Tam Tam whispered weakly, "That was hot."

They were being watched by a gray-skinned woman with red glasses on. She watched with curiosity as the malformed male limped into the city.

She spoke to her hooded companion, "That is the cursed one that you told me about, is he not?"

The hooded female nodded and whispered, "You have the same curse."

"Hmpf... whatever. He looks worthless. I can see why you need me."

A Pure Silveran walked up the hill behind them. "Looks can be deceiving, Dai Luong. If you reach out with the PsiQi, you will feel what I mean."

She did and gasped in shock.

Pyramids of Chombra

The bard followed Dutch into the city. He stood wincing in pain and suddenly collapsed against the nearby wall. He caught his cane before it could clatter to the ground.

"If you are done gawking, be a dear and assist me in removing the guards. They are female, so I suspect you will enjoy yourself."

"What are you paying?"

"I can give you half a million common currency."

"You have a deal. They were only paying me a quarter of that price to guard the pass."

She slunk off, allowing Dutch to rest. He pushed himself off the wall, nearly buckling in pain from the sudden weight on his bad leg. Elena watched him with curiosity.

She spoke, "Tam Tam get up on the hill and keep an eye on the pyramids. Ram, I need you to prevent the rebellion from entering the Pyramid area. Non-lethally, please. Gilda, where are you going?"

The Green Orkean female spoke, "I am curious about that man. You seem afraid of him. I wish to investigate why you would be afraid of a weakling."

A green-skinned tiny female with a large head spoke, "Looks can be deceiving, love. There is much power boiling under the surface of that man."

"I am not scared, Buttercup. In fact, I will relish the fight."

Buttercup walked with Gilda over to Dutch, who was still resting. They could see nothing through his blindfold. They then saw a silver light as one of his eyes opened. Gilda stepped back and Amy gulped.

"How can Dutch help you ladies?"

"What is your plan?"

"Fire."

Flames erupted all around the buildings. There were screams of terror as the soldiers fled the city. Those that remained were reduced to ash in seconds. All except a tiny pyramid where the bard had seduced many female guards. She was lying in a pile of naked women erect.

Scarabaeidae walked into the now-empty city along with Ram. His soldiers looked around in fear. Dutch was leaning against one of the pyramids with what looked to be an opium and cloves cigar in between his lips.

Scarabaeidae spoke, "We saw smoke and were stopped by a Dwarv. He put up a fight before allowing us through. You wouldn't happen to know anything about that, would you?"

Dutch smiled a fanged smile. "I must apologize for the mercenary I hired. She and her team's motto is there's no kill like overkill. I hope he didn't cause too much trouble for you."

"Your brother fought him."

Axel and his team went through the main pyramid to mop up any survivors. No one noticed a Pure Silveran watching from the cliffs. He was tall with blue horns and coarse black hair with a tint of blue. His eyes were a deep blue. He was watching the pyramids with interest. This was Zenthin Ankara jr. son of the Shadow Lord Zenthin Ankara. He had been feeling displeased with his father lately and had been doing recon on the various Rebel cells. He heard a click and evaporated into shadow.

He reappeared behind Tam Tam with a serrated knife. "What do you think you're doing?"

"I was going spy hunting."

"Hmm, well, be more careful. I may attack next time."

"Who are you?"

"Hmm, well, that is a difficult question. You may call me Blu Silver."

"Well, mister Silver, you seem different from the other Pure Silverans. I'll let you off easy. See you around."

***

Dai Luong looked at the mercenary that had nearly stumbled upon them. Had it not been for the misdirection aura that Lady Wyvern had, she would have been found out.

Dai Luong grimaced as she watched the conversation. A voice in her head spoke, "Beatrix, my love, that is your rival. He is of God Silver while you are of me."

***

Many weeks passed as the Diavonbre rebels rebuilt and refortified the pyramids. Axel had been lenient with the captured guards and they were well taken care of. The sun was hot and Dutch was resting by the river outside the walls of Chombra.

Gilda was standing under the shade of a nearby tree when a pure Silveran male with a large scar across his face and armour that looked like bone attacked her.

Dutch caught Gilda as she fell wounded. He set her down and picked up her very heavy sword. He dragged it behind him. This man glowed fiery gray in the PsyQi, causing Bounty to wince. The man attacked him; however, Bounty stumbled and rolled. The man was barely able to catch himself before he fell. It didn't matter, though. He looked down to see the blade in his stomach.

Dutch spoke in a dark menacing voice that was not his. "Goodbye, Bonestorm. And good riddance."

Dutch was resting in the medical facility. He had shattered his deformed arm fending off Bonestorm Ankara, according to Gilda.

The nurse stood over him with a needle. "This may hurt a bit, but it should help your healing. They are experimental nanomachines. They will repair your bones, muscles, skin, and really anything that needs repairing. Just going to inject them, you may also get a cold tingling sensation that is normal."

Night fell on Moon's Day sixty-four Hunter. The sky glowed red from the Hunter's Blood Moon.

Scarabaeus spoke, "The sky bodes ill and the night grows long."

One of the soldiers spoke, "Sir, we have reports coming in that a massive armada is coming to destroy us. Over fifty Roc class destroyers are arriving by hluboká noc. There's only three hundred of us, sir. We are going to be destroyed."

Dutch smiled a dark and sinister smile. "Fear not! It's Noční lov. The ground begs for sacrifice. It will drink its fill by noční konec."

"I worry that you forget that when three moons are red many must be sacrificed."

"That is true, General, but many will die tonight. I recommend getting the guns primed and ready. Keep firing until we're out of bullets. Leave the defense of the pyramids to me."

Elena spoke quietly, "General, the main keep must be protected. Have your remaining troops stick to the main pyramid and the three next to it. The outer pyramids are nonessential. They are only barracks and mess halls. This will be a tough fight. I overheard one of the generals state that

Diavonbre is a necessity to hold. They will be throwing everything they can at us. Dutch is very skilled, but he must have no distractions."

Quetzal Qotal sneered, "We don't take orders from you. Nor your freak of a boss."

Scarabaeus glared at Quetzal. "I do agree with Quetzal on this. What makes you think that Dutch can hold off the entirety of the Diavonbre Aka-ites?"

Dutch rasped, "It's alright, Elena, let them make plans and I can work with what they decide."

Scarabaeidae nodded. "Have Axel and Kim stay in reserve to keep an eye on Dutch. I would like the guns up and operational before the fleet gets here. Have Ankh Shaka and his troops patrol the outer ring. Have the Anubis guards patrol the inner circle. Quetzal, you and your troops will guard the central pyramid. You mercenaries and Dutch can stay here, please do not interfere with our defensive positions."

Dutch nodded and sat down in a meditative position. "We have a stealth-cloaked assassin here. Watch out. He's currently behind you, Lieutenant. Please duck."

Quetzal sneered and scoffed before his throat was slit and he fell gurgling. Dutch raised his hand and clenched it. There was a sound of shattering armour and a slender, robotically enhanced female appeared on the ground gasping for air. Dutch waved his hand and her shattered armour reforged around her head and her mechanical breathing could be heard. Dutch used the rest of her armour as shackles to pin her to the wall. Scarabaeidae stood slack-jawed.

A female general dressed in jackal armour rushed in. "Sir, the Anubis guards have been routed. I am the only survivor."

Dutch smiled, "Okay, if you are the only survivor of the Jackals, where are your fallen allies' tags? I know the Anubis guard will pick up their fallen allies' tags."

She started to back away when she was forcefully shoved to the ground by Axel, who had a sword through his chest. It melted as his body started to become like fire. Scarabaeidae pushed him outside as a large roar shook the building. That was when the bombs dropped.

Dutch raised his eyebrow. "That was an Efreet. That was also the roar of a Bahamut. Now that is interesting. How many do you have?"

"Twelve that we know of."

"Good makes my job easier."

The large gray and blue Taur next to scarabaeus spoke, "Uncle, are you not concerned about what just transpired?"

"I am not, Commander Rhapsody. We should count ourselves lucky he was here."

***

King Admiral Fel Ankara stood on the viewing deck of her airship. She was watching the battle with interest. Next to her stood Brawl Ankara. It appeared to her that the bombs were detonated before they even hit the pyramids. She had also watched as her fleet was being torn apart by the guns that she had disabled before retreating from the pyramids.

She spoke, "I swear on my left breast that I dismantled those guns, Lord Ankara."

Brawl combed back his inky green hair and placed his hand over his right eye. "I believe you, cousin. The right eye of the Ankara clan sees all. You have nothing to fear from me."

Twelve large dragons had suddenly formed out of nowhere. There were also reports on the ground of Fire Spirits helping the enemy. Other reports say that the sand was alive and hungry for blood. Three of the dragons had been slain before a fourth, rather pink one had ripped through the airship. While that one tore apart her ships, she saw two more falls before a nine-foot-tall black bipedal dragon with ethereal laser wings rose into the air. The wings glowed and she saw numerous lasers fire at her fleet. Within seconds her armada was scrapped.

Commander Valence spoke, "Boss, none of our attacks are doing anything. What should we do?"

Fel sighed, "Release the bastard."

"Boss, that would irradiate the entirety of Diavonbre."

"If we cannot hold Diavonbre, then no one should be able to."

"We are prepping the bastard now."

***

Dutch sat there meditating; he could feel each explosion of the bombs on his psionic shield he was projecting around the pyramids. He felt a large psybomb heading towards his shield. When it impacted, his body drastically changed. His image disguise failed him as he absorbed the psybomb into his being. Half of his body took on a burned look. He shoved Scarabaeidae and the others out as he exploded. When the dust cleared from the collapse, he rose from the rubble. His body was no longer mangled-looking. He still looked thin, but he had become toned. Aside from the massive burn on the left side of his body, he looked healthy. Flames were everywhere as his body tried to regulate his psychic energy. This was a venting process. The Aka-ite shock troops descended into the inferno and started to massacre the defenders. Dutch's eyes glowed as a fiery spiked demonic-looking dragon formed from the fire. Half of its body was black, while the other half was the silvery fire.

Within minutes the Aka-ite troops were nothing but ash. The fiery dragon turned towards the airships.

Six men stood on the nearby cliff.

The man in a red coat with a pirate's cap on his head spoke, "Uh Groll… this is where you said we should go to assist our brother Luke Darkfaith."

The man with wolf-like features but skin that glistened like Nymodium spoke, "Yes, Blood Gulch, this is where he said he was requesting aid. Why?"

A gruff voice spoke, "Do you see what I see, Nymodiumian? Or are you as blind as they say you are?"

Groll scoffed, "I see flames, that is it! Is there something else I should see, oh mighty Zenoth?"

A soft voice spoke, "How about a giant flaming dragon made of darkness and fire? Since that is what we see."

Groll looked over to the kendo-wearing man with skin that glittered like Osmium. "Hmph, if you say so, Sashar."

Two more stood smoking a strange-looking reed. The one with Steel-like skin spoke, "Groll only sees what he desires to see. To him, this is just a raging inferno. To us who are inexperienced with this world, we see a dragon made of flames."

The man with rainbow skin spoke, "Vagrant is right. I have been on this planet enough to be unsurprised by this, but I, too, see a Dragon. Hmm… ah! I see now… The Wrath of God Silver made flesh. I see great and terrible things will come of this war. When the flames die down, I suggest we go and find our brother."

Blood Gulch spoke of that we can agree, Aragnok of the Leifsoul tribe.

***

Fel Ankara stared in horror as the bastard was absorbed by some sort of Psy Shield. She was even more surprised when a massive dragon formed out of the fire. She grabbed Valence and dove off the side of her airship as a fiery claw took it out. She watched from the ground as her entire fleet was destroyed by the demon.

Valence whispered, "The wrath of God Silver taken form. He is displeased with our actions. Who holds his wrath inside them?"

Fel looked around and saw a young Silveran male standing atop slag and glass. He seemed to be the center of the vortex. She advanced on him with her chain sword drawn. He pulled a blade from the scabbard on his back and fire covered it. She grinned maniacally and charged him.

***

Dutch sidestepped the furious Silveran female charging him. He kicked her in the back as she went past. She hit the ground hard. She wiped the blood from her face and slashed at him. He blocked the attack and pulled out another sword from his belt, slicing through her wrist. He caught her as she fell towards him. He struck her horns, causing her to cry out in ecstasy. He saw another female charge him, but she was pinned by Gilda.

Gilda spoke, "Alright, who the hell are you?"

Dutch smiled, "I am Bounty Hunter 13."

She backed away. "That name holds ancient power. Why do I suddenly fear you?"

Elena landed nearby. "Bonty, I need you to pull back your psychic energy. The ground is becoming glass."

"I'll do my best, Elena, but no guarantees. Shit!"

Brawl landed on the ground with a thud. He rose from the shattered earth, his muscles pulsating with power. He roared in rage and charged Bounty. He smashed his fist into Bounty's chest and proceeded to pummel him. As he went for the finishing blow, he vanished. Bounty hissed in pain, "That should keep him busy."

Bounty walked over to the dazed Fel Ankara.

***

Fel Ankara felt herself get lifted up and she saw Valence through the fog of lust. She looked around her at the devastation that one man, no demon, caused. She looked into the gray fire of the demon's eyes and passed out. She awoke in a medical facility. There was no demon, only an incredibly sexy well, muscled Pure Silveran male with dark glasses on.

He spoke, "Welcome to my home. The war is over. King Blu Silver sits on the throne. I had to put you in cryo stasis while you healed. Your girlfriend is waiting for you."

She was given a robe and escorted into a vaulted living room, where she saw Valence. Valence hugged her and the two were then brought to their own living area.

The man spoke, "Take it easy for a while. Your body needs to adjust to the time skip. If you need anything, ask my computer to create it for you."

Fel Ankara lay her head against Valence, but her rest was fitful; she could see the fiery gray eyes whenever she closed her own.

***

Bounty Hunter 13 stood near a dock that was being loaded with supplies to bring to the Silver Rebellion. He was studying himself in the polished metal of the ship. He sighed in frustration as he touched the burned skin. His soul had been scorched and he would forever look like this, even if he got reincarnated.

Axel walked over to him. "Corvus has come back from his journey. He does not seem happy with what he discovered. I brought you this mask forged by Razorfang. It should help conceal your burn and also suppress your power. I must say Bahamut Prime is scared of you. I have never seen her so afraid. I must ask you, do you know what you are going to do?"

"I will be joining the Silver Rebellion. Likely going to have trouble with that." He boarded the ship heading to Silver with Corvus and Myst as it set off to Continent Silver. Amari stared at him. She set down her book as he boarded the ship.

She shrugged. "Hey bro, did you have a good war?"

"Bounty looked startled and then saw who was speaking. He smiled, "For the most part, Amari. Got a little banged up."

"I see that."

***

Dai Luong, now calling herself Beatrix, stood on the deck of the supply ship as she watched Bounty Hunter 13 examine himself. She looked upon the icon of Goddess Silver that she held. She rubbed its chest and whispered, "I can see why you need me. With power like his, God Silver has no equal."

The Silveran Civil War

A dark-skinned mohawked Silveran woman stood leaning against a wall in the rebel compound. She had painted her two short horns red. She also wore bright orange war paint. Her hair was dyed neon blue. Her armour was bestial in nature, with random fanged mouths on her shoulders, knees, collar, elbows, and breasts. She watched with disgust as two half-pure Silveran men walked up to her. One was in feathered furs, the other in a silk-type uniform. She looked disdainfully at them and bared her fangs, hoping to scare them away.

The shorter one in silk spoke with a mechanically altered voice, "Commander, my brother and I were told to join your unit. Private Myst Hunter reporting."

She growled and cursed. "He sends me men to work with. You weaklings had the best leave before I rip you open."

Myst paled slightly and looked over to his brother, "Told you we were unwanted."

The one in furs smiled a dark smile as his brother sighed in defeat. "Well, Commander, I suggest you take it up with the superior."

She snarled and shoved them out of the way. She stormed off towards the Armandi General's office. When she arrived, she kicked down the door. The Armandi General was unfazed.

He looked up at her and saw the two men behind her smirking as he spoke, "Is there a problem, Commander Storm?"

"You fucking damn know well what my problem is!"

"I am sorry, Paradox, but all units must have at least one of the opposite sex. The other commanders obey this rule. Why can't you?"

"You know damn well why."

"How about this? These two came in with their brother, who is blind. You can take the brother and I'll assign these two to Commander Colorprism."

"Fine! But I will not allow him to be a soldier."

A young, pure Silveran male sat on a chair outside the office. He had a severe burn covering half his body. His pure gray eyes swirled with ancient energy. He placed a half mask on the burned side and wrapped the black cloth around his eyes as she stormed over to him.

The Armandi General spoke, "Paradox, this is Bounty Hunter 13. He is blind. He is also now your new private. You are to take him with you against Zenthin Ankara, the third in the forest."

"Fine! Bounty Hunter 13, welcome to the Storm you will be helping cook."

She grabbed him by the arm and yanked him away with her. Myst stood smirking. He spoke, "Corvus, I do believe she's bit off more than she could chew."

The man in furs smiled darkly.

***

It was night when Commander Paradox Storm and her army finally rested. It was in the middle of a large clearing with a large flat black stone in the middle of a small pond. The women set up camp while their unit cook worked with a Pure Silveran male.

He spoke, "Madam Maungirtha, the soup is ready. Shall I begin passing it out?"

The woman next to him had greenish-gray skin with six war braids tied into one large one. She was wearing a dirty blue jumpsuit. She had very intelligent eyes and always had some sort of meat cleaver on her hip.

She spoke in a dingy rough voice, "No 'oung'in. I 'ant you to start cleaning the odher pans."

"Yes, madam."

As she started to pass out the soup, Bounty began to clean. He was scrubbing a pan when all of a sudden, he tuned in on the wind. His delicate hearing picked up the creaking of branches. The wind was not strong enough to cause branches to creak. He heard a soft thump and swung. The pan slammed into the skull of a psionic armoured pure Silveran man. The man lay there unmoving. That was when fifty black psionic armoured men attacked from the trees. The women were thrown into confusion. Bounty untied his blindfold. He folded it up and placed it in his shirt pocket. Psychic energy flooded his senses and he could see what was going on. He waded into the fray with the pan bludgeoning any Aka-ite he came across.

He found Commander Storm surrounded by five men. She had several injuries, but none were life-threatening. She was unarmed but managed to kill all five with well-placed blows. Bounty walked away from her and into another woman finishing off nine men while protecting seven of her comrades in arms who were critically injured. He purposely bumped into her, knocking her out of the way of a throwing dagger. He caught the dagger in mid-air and sent it back. He heard a feminine yelp, then a thud as she hit the ground. The Aka army had been defeated. The few survivors fled. The injured girl struggled to move, but her Achilles tendons had been cut, so she was unable to. She feebly crawled but was grabbed by Bounty before she could get too far.

Commander Paradox Storm stood panting. "Alright, get the wounded to the transporter. Tell Chastity Sinner and Ithula to begin their duties. I want a casualty report on my desk ASAP! Jasmine Doomshroud interrogates the prisoner. Ivy Florareaper! I want you and Violet Ragnarok to secure the area."

She turned towards Bounty and looked at the damaged pan in his hand. She blinked, confused to see blood dripping off of it. She looked at a few of the dead Aka-ites only to see their heads bashed in.

She muttered, "By the Chaos Jester, what is he?"

Bounty got off the girl he had fallen on when he saw a purple-haired woman with numerous tattoos and scars walk into view.

She spoke, "Is this the prisoner?"

Bounty replied, "She is a prisoner."

"Are you being smart with me, boy?"

"No, ma'am. I am simply stating she is the only prisoner I know of. There could have been a few other injured survivors."

"Doubtful. In this unit, we kill all who oppose us."

Bounty looked down at the wounded girl and grinned sinisterly. He opened one of his vials and rubbed his hands with the liquid. He placed his hand on her back and she let out an unearthly yowl.

He whispered in her ear, "Tell us where your base is."

She gasped, "Never. I will never tell you anything."

He moved his hand up and she screamed in agony again.

"F... fine, I'll talk. General Ankara is near the spike valley. The others are near Silver Pass, the falls, and Dragon's Den Island. Please, no more!"

Bounty removed his hands and was thrown back by a fiery blast that knocked Jasmine away as well. Another woman landed from the tree. She grabbed her partner and fled."

Bounty got up and dusted himself off. Jasmine backed away from him. He smiled and washed his hands off.

Jasmine looked at him and then dragged him with her to go see Paradox. When they arrived, Paradox glared daggers at Bounty. Jasmine shoved him in front of her.

She spoke, "He interrogated the prisoner. She said that there was one general in spike pass, one near the falls, and several near Crystal pass. Not to mention the ones we know about in City Silver, Capital City Frozen Tundra of Norcryog, and the Prime city of Noamaiza."

Paradox grimaced, "Okay, Boy! Why did you do Jasmine's Job for her?"

"I used a special tracking oil. The reason she was in pain was because I hit certain pressure points with my hand. She was lying to us. The oil will allow us to trace her movements. Therefore we can ambush the ambushers."

"How do you know all these techniques?"

"I was in the rebellion on Diavonbry. My sworn siblings, siblings, and I slew The suppressing General Fel Ankara."

"How can you be sure she lied?"

"It's hard to explain. Let's just call it a gut feeling. I was ambushed by Aka-ites on Diavonbry when I was lied to by an enemy I interrogated."

Jasmine spoke, "So how do we ambush someone who wants to ambush us?"

Paradox said, "How about we call the leaders together." She then turned to Bounty, "You stay out of our business. We don't need a man's help."

Bounty shrugged and walked back to the wash. He repaired the pan and continued to wash it. Maungirtha looked at him and smiled.

She spoke quietly in his ear, "Dehr youngn's eyes are showing. Don't you worry bout da, Commander? She has difficulty dealing with da men."

Bounty replaced his blindfold. He smirked and thought quietly, *so the commander hates men. This could pose a problem for me. No wonder I have been detecting dangerous thoughts from her. I better watch my back.*

Commander Storm sat in her tent, thinking quietly. *That boy is dangerous. I must find a way to get rid of him. I can not have my unit tainted, so aha... I will make him the distraction so the girls can ambush those Aka-ites. Then if he somehow survives that I will place him at the front, hoping he gets himself killed. Maybe I can have him do a suicide mission. Yes, that is a great idea.*

Her troops were resting for the night. She looked outside at the black onyx stone in the center of the pond. She watched as Bounty easily walked over to the stone and sat down on it. The water had to have been six feet deep, but he was not even wet. The moons glittered off his clothing. He looked almost ghostly. She shivered with fear and closed her eyes, allowing her head to rest on her desk. Her last thought of the night was he must die.

Bounty rested under the moonlight. He had felt the hate towards him vanish, so he knew Commander Storm had fallen asleep. He smiled and began his meditation ritual.

Morning came quickly and Bounty was summoned to Commander Storm's Tent. He entered to see her with two others. These two looked weak and smelled weak. He raised his left eyebrow.

Commander Storm spoke, "I want you three to lure the Aka-ites out. You are to march towards the spike valley. The rest of the army will be in hiding. You are to lead them towards us."

The two girls nodded and saluted while Bounty bowed slightly to the commander. "So the woman wants us dead. I did my best to protect these two to the best of my ability."

The pink-haired girl looked at Bounty as they walked towards the valley. She spoke, "Why does the commander want us dead?"

Bounty looked at her. "We are weak in her eyes. I am blind, your sister is mute, and you are chaotic. And the two following us, I suppose, are your little sisters. Meaning they are weak in her eyes as well."

She looked at Bounty and sighed, "Feldspar, Jade, Travertine, and I, Kimberlite, are weak in the commander's eyes, so she wants us dead?"

"Essentially."

"Damn, I knew we shouldn't have joined the army."

"Ah, don't worry about it. She hates me more than you and I will keep you safe."

"How can someone blind keep us safe?"

"Magic."

The four of them were ambushed by a man in black armour with his spikes and horns painted red. This was Zenthin Ankara 3; he was a near replica of his grandfather Zenthin Ankara, the shadow lord. He sneered and attacked the four of them. His army of conjured shadow ninjas dropped down from the foliage. Bounty smiled and removed his blindfold. His hands lit up with psychic energy and he waved his hand, blasting a curtain of energy at the army. Those that were caught off guard were killed instantly. Bounty then reached into his satchel and pulled out a large Gatling Gun. He grinned as the gun glowed with runes and opened fire. Psionic bolts fired rapidly at the enemy, destroying them and leaving only Zen Ankara III, who growled in rage and lunged only to find Bounty's arm shoved into his sternum. Bounty twisted his hand and a sharp crack was heard. Blood spilled out of his mouth and he fell dead. Jade stared at him, slack-jawed. Bounty removed his hand and washed his arm with psychic water. The gun had vanished by this point back into his satchel. He replaced his blindfold and continued walking.

He spoke, "Kimberlite, you and your sisters are free to go. I will tell the commander, you died."

Kimberlite looked at him and said, "Wait, why don't you come with us for a second? We have been staying in an abandoned mansion nearby. Since our home is being foreclosed, which is why we joined the rebellion. It's the least we could do to repay you."

Bounty followed them to an old building. He saw a shadow move and a man in bandages appeared.

The bandaged man spoke, "About damn time you showed up, Bounty. Father's home was bequeathed to you in his will."

Bounty smiled, "Hello, Chain! It's been a while. Not since the surgery."

Chain nodded his head. "How are you feeling, little bro?"

"Tired. These four girls are giving me a tour of their living place."

Feldspar spoke quietly and monotonously, "So you own this place? Does that mean my sisters and I have no place to live?"

Chain looked at them and then at Bounty, who spoke, "Yes, you do. I will not be kicking you out. I won't even require you to pay for an apartment. Let's just go in the house, shall we?"

The four followed him as Chain vanished into the shadows. They entered the home and Bounty felt a presence. He followed the feeling to a massive room with what looked to be a giant orb in the middle. He touched the orb and the house came alive.

A holographic woman appeared and spoke, "Are you my new master?"

Bounty smiled warmly, "Yes, I am Bonty Hanter XIII. My father bequeathed unto me this home in his will."

"Oh yes, I remember you. The blind one that the old man was always doting on. I went into hibernation after the attack. My, you've grown well."

Bounty gently hugged the hologram, who seemed to snuggle into his embrace. She then vanished and his gauntlet lit up. He walked out as the wall was sealed behind him. He looked at Jade, who was resting in her sister's embrace. The four were sitting on a couch.

The smallest of the four spoke, "Are we being kicked out?"

Feldspar whispered, "No, Travertine. Mr. Hunter here is allowing us to stay. Get some rest."

Travertine and her twin Kimberlite curled up on the floor. Bounty looked them over and spoke, "Computer, can you make room for these girls? They will be staying indefinitely."

The computer hummed a tune and a wall vanished only to be replaced by a large pillar. The pillar hissed open and the four were led into an immense room. The room was covered in a field of stones and a medium-sized home sat in the middle of the field. The girls walked into it and looked around. A large screen came to life with many words on it.

The computer spoke, "Okay, girls, you can arrange the house however you like and I will make the adjustments. You can also tell me what kinds of food you would like and I can cook for you. If you want, I can also get clothing for you as well."

Kimberlite began bouncing with joy as Travertine and Jade began exploring the home. Bounty smiled and walked out of the home. He spoke, "I'll be back in a few days. Computer, please keep those girls safe."

"Will do, boss."

As he exited the home, he heard a soft whump. He turned to see Chain standing there. "Something wrong, Shadow?"

"Those girls were meant to die today."

"So?"

"Bounty, Fate has a way of righting what is wrong."

"Fate is Equus crap. I will do everything I can to protect them."

"We will see the demon. We will see." He then vanished in a puff of smoke.

Bounty typed something into his gauntlet and a listing popped up. It was for an old quarry under foreclosure. Since the Stoen family had a rough year, he quickly used all his savings and bought it. It would be the start of his new business, Hunter Corporations. He smiled deviously and began his trek toward where he last knew of Paradox Storm's army location. He arrived to find nobody. He typed in his gauntlet again.

Bounty shook his head and walked towards the ocean, where a ping was telling him where his commander was. He came across her and the rest of the army. She saw him and sneered, "So only one survived. Ha, I knew they were pathetic."

Bounty spoke evenly, "Commander Storm, I was able to slay King General Zenthin Ankara 3. However, the Stoen sisters were slain. What are your orders."

"I want you to go blow up that camp down there." She wrapped a vest around him, which was filled with explosives. "I don't want you to survive. Go and die."

Bounty shrugged his shoulders and walked towards the camp. He entered the camp and removed his vest. He dove into the water as it exploded. He sank to the bottom of the shore and watched as Commander Storm and her army walked to a ship. Maungirtha looked in his direction and saw him in the water and smiled with relief. Bounty swam to Dragon's Den Island. He watched in awe as the grand army of Zen Aka was decimated by Dragons, speedy blurs that he figured were the Serpenti and Lizardfolk. He smirked as they finished off the army and disappeared into the night. He walked out of the water to see a young man in blue and green armour. The boy looked at him and removed his armour. His nude body lay still as Bounty walked over to him.

Bounty sat next to him, saying, "you are the only survivor, King General Fenix Ankara. Why do you strip before me?"

Fenix sobbed, "Please just use me and get it over with."

Bounty sat down and put his arm around the boy. He stroked the boy's hair until he fell asleep. Bounty waited an hour. He saw a fog roll in. He could see cloaked beings move in the fog. He saw a woman his age, barely alive, struggling. He went over and mended her body. In the dark, her face almost looked like his. He was confused for a second but ignored the feeling marking it off as a trick of the light. He felt cold and saw a wraith with a crown over its hood. The wraith stood pointing a serpentine fire sword at him.

The wraith spoke, "You interfere with death. You must face me. I win the girl's soul. You win the girl's soul."

Bounty smiled and picked up a discarded sword. He saw other Wraiths collecting the souls of the dead. He lunged at the king of wraiths. He soon had the upper hand and the king collapsed to one knee, breathing raspily.

The Wraith King spoke, "Know the name Toreno for you have earned my respect and the respect of all Fog Wraiths. Should you require to save another soul from us, we will gladly face you in battle."

The fog vanished and Fenix Ankara woke up. "Please, why have you not raped me yet?"

"Why would I rape you?"

"That's what everyone else did. My own troops turned on me and used me. We were instantly routed. Please just get it over with."

He raised his bruised and used butt to Bounty and waited. Bounty did a swift strike knocking the boy out. He entered Fenix's mind and locked the pain away. He whispered into Fenix's mind your name is Fenix, you are a survivor of a shipwreck. Your family was slain by the wreck. You have no place to call home.

He then placed Fenix on the boat he had created from thin air. He then prayed to God Silver to protect the boy and guide him to a place where he could start anew. He then dove back into the water and guided the ship to a strong current going away from the continent Silver. He released the boat and watched as the current swept it away. He did the same for the girl.

He swam towards Mt Silver and surfaced in the Underwater Caverns. He saw several corpses and burned them. He donned some discarded armour that was red. He walked up the stairs and looked at the guard. He smiled as he saw his brother's face looking back at him.

His brother saluted, "Sir, are you here for the site inspection?"

Bounty examined the stolen armour. "Yes, Commander, I am Protector Argon Slayer. I hear you have managed to repel numerous rebel attacks."

"Yes, sir, we just repelled a bunch of women. Those that survived the attack were captured and are in cells to be broken. We need new slaves, after all."

"Well, then, boyo, let us see these new toys."

Bounty was led to Commander Storm's cell. She was with two others. She was also stark naked. He recognized Jasmine and Ivy. He saw that Maungirtha was being tortured. She didn't seem to feel the electricity curling through her body. She almost seemed to be enjoying herself. In the next cell, he saw Ithula shivering as a group of girls were being tortured.

Bounty turned to his brother. "Well, I think I would like to see the armoury. Just to inspect the guns and such."

"Right this way, Protector."

As they entered the armoury, Bounty pulled his brother aside. "How long have you all been in hiding?"

"We raided this place six weeks ago. Around the same time as you were sent against Ankara's grandson. Don't worry, quite a few got away. We just had to detain the ones you saw since we knew there was a site inspection today. By one King Admiral Javelin."

"Well, then, let us free the girls."

"Not recommended. Commander Storm is well known as a man-killer."

"Allow me to speak with her, Myst."

"It's your funeral, you piece of shit."

Bounty sauntered into Paradox's cell. Maungirtha eyed him, then bared her fangs in a devilish smile. Paradox attacked in a fury. Bounty deftly blocked each of her precise strikes. Then his hands became engulfed in flame. He punched Storm in the chest, causing her to stumble back and hit the wall. She glared daggers and lunged again. This time Bounty caught her and lifted her over his shoulder only to slam her into back body drop. She lay there stunned. He got up and dusted himself off.

Maungirtha smiled, "Vell I be. Youse done verr' good der chil' I never seen de commander loose. May as well reveal yer self der chil'."

Bounty removed his helmet and tossed it at Commander Storm. Paradox looked up and gasped.

She weakly spoke, "No! Impossible! You! How did you survive?"

Bounty knelt down and whispered in her ear, "Shoulda tied the bomb tighter. I am a very scrawny man."

She lay there just staring blankly at him. Jasmine walked over and gently stroked her hair. Jasmine looked up at Bounty and sighed.

She whispered, "Why are you torturing us?"

Myst walked in. "To keep up appearances. Unfortunately, we were hoping to ambush King Admiral Javelin, but he hasn't shown up yet."

A youthful girl ran in, "Bounty! Myst! Javelin is right outside on the pass. He has a whole army with him. Even King Generals Jenara Ankara and Fenara Ankara are out there. He must have caught on somehow. We gotta evacuate."

A very dark-skinned Silveran male walked in and eyed Paradox Storm. He spoke, "We cannot escape Jinxi. The chamber is flooded. We would have to hold out until the tide retreats."

Bounty rubbed his temples. "Well, we just fight. I mean, we faced worse at the Pyramids of Chombra and we still came out on top."

Myst spoke, "Yes, I suppose. Alright, I'll have the men hold up here and provide cover fire. While you oh hated one, Jinxi and Axel distract the Aka-ites. Corvus and I will sneak behind them and launch a pincer attack. It'll be like the siege of Fort Ironside all over again."

Bounty smiled and walked outside, which followed was a series of loud explosions and screams of the dying.

Myst waited until the noise ended before saying, "Or we could do that."

Axel and Jinxi peered outside to see Bounty squaring off with Javelin. They then saw Javelin bow to him, hand him something, and vanish with Jenara and Fenara. Axel shrugged and walked out with Myst and Jinxi. They saw Corvus finish off one of the near-dead soldiers. Only to vanish in a burst of feathers and reappear near them in a burst of feathers.

Axel looked at Corvus. "How many did you kill?" Corvus held up all twelve of his fingers.

Axel smiled. "That many, huh? How many did Bounty kill?"

Corvus waved his hand over Crystal Pass, showing all the dead, including some that had been impaled on the crystal spikes. Bounty was dragging the dead into a pile.

"I see, I don't see your usual craft among the dead. What happened to yours?'

Corvus clapped his hands together and mimicked a large explosion. Axel blinked in confusion as Corvus shrugged. Jinxi was bouncing up and down. She then vanished in a blur and all the dead were in a pile. Axel and Myst walked over and Corvus teleported over.

Bounty was placing the last body on the pile. Several crystalline glasses filled with amber liquid appeared in the hands of Axel, Myst, Corvus, Bounty, and Jinxi.

Bounty spoke, "Theaym Sidrodc uigde het seul, theayme havens sunocme het seul"

A raging inferno engulfed the bodies as the rain poured down from the psychic storm Bounty had caused. Bounty replaced his blindfold and put on a circlet that caused the storm to weaken. He then downed the amber liquid and the glass vanished.

Commander Paradox Storm charged out, "Why do you honor those scumbags?"

Bounty was about to speak when Corvus spoke up in a deep bass voice that rumbled like thunder, "It's the warrior's code. We honor those who fight and die. It is an ancient tradition. You dare think that those who die that are your enemies deserve no respect."

"Yes, I dare think that. They work for the enemy. They deserve nothing."

"Then know this, Commander, when you die in combat. You will not be honored. Your soul will not be welcome in the havens, so speaks Nevermore."

A fiery bird engulfed Paradox and vanished, leaving behind a black marking that looked like a thunderbird. Paradox lunged at Corvus and was knocked to the ground by Bounty, who had hang-manned her. She lay there twitching in anger.

Bounty removed his foot from her chest and spoke, "Do not think to harm my siblings. I may not be so generous next time. Focus your anger on me. I am the one making a fool of you."

Jasmine helped Paradox up after Bounty had removed his foot. Bounty walked over to a broken crystal and lifted it up. He walked over to the lava flow from Mt.Silver and leapt onto it with the crystal and surfed down the mountain. As he vanished in the distance, Axel peered over the edge and kicked the side, causing a slope to appear as he, Jinxi, Myst, and Corvus walked down it. It vanished behind them, leaving Commander Paradox Storm, Her commandos, and Myst's team behind. Myst's commander chuckled and pulled out a pack of reeds. He opened the pack and lit one of the reeds. He scratched the scruff of a rainbow beard and leaned against a crystal. Paradox sat there despondent. Jasmine was sitting next to her, humming a sad tune.

Silveran Civil War part 2

Near City Silver, a large ship descended. This was the mercenary ship of Luke Darkfaith, the Death Knight of Casualty Station. He had been asked politely by Bounty to infiltrate the city in repayment for saving his life at the battle of Fort Ironside. As he walked out, he was accompanied by a man in all red and a gargoyle-looking creature. Both of these men had been saved by Bounty Hunter 13 and were repaying their debt to him.

***

Bounty launched off a sloped stone and was thrown through a wall a mile away from where he had launched. His crystal was embedded in the wall along with a corpse that it had impaled. A young woman with red hair was being assaulted by two people in armour. One smelled male, the other female. They had been caught with their pants down. Bounty cleaved up, slicing through the male's genitals with ease. The girl they had been about to rape now had blood on her. She yelped and rolled away as Bounty finished off the male with a flourish.

The female yelled in anger and violently attacked Bounty with her serrated chain blade. Bounty blocked her attacks and leapt into the rafters as gunfire immolated the west wall of the home. The woman who had been attacking fell to the ground as a bunch of red armoured warriors walked in. A gray and black-haired man walked in his orange tiger eyes flitted around the room. He proceeded to stab the woman, finishing her off. Bonty then saw in the PsyQi two children walking away with their hands held by an old man Bonty recognized as Zarbon the Doombringer.

The older man with tiger eyes looked up at Bounty and spoke, "Thank you for saving my daughter Shang Shang. May I ask who you are?"

Bounty landed. "I am private Bounty Hunter 13, sir. And you?"

"I am Sol Jia, the Tiger of the Eastern Falls."

Bounty bowed slightly. "I have heard of the exploits of the mighty clan Sol. If you don't mind me asking, why help the rebels? Are you not a Pure Silveran?"

Sol Jia smiled warmly, "My cousin asked us to assist in the early years of the war. We were never really fond of the laws and regulations of Zenthin Ankara. Especially once he betrayed and executed his closest friend and General Bounty Hunter 12."

Bounty smiled and said, "Mind if I get a lift to City Silver? All of Zenthin's army has been routed except for the ones in the city. I do believe this war has gone on long enough."

Sol Jia nodded and led Bounty to his ship. Bounty boarded and sat down before snapping his fingers and causing the home to be engulfed in flames. He was sitting across from an old mohawked man with scars all over his body and muscles that could crush a hovercycle. The man looked up and offered a bottle of Fire Ruby Whisky to Bounty. Bounty took a swig of it and passed it back to the man, who downed the rest in one long gulp.

The man spoke in a gruff voice, "Never seen anyone else aside from Master Sol Seh who can handle the fire."

Bounty raised his eyebrow. "Well, it may have something to do with the fact I have no taste receptors. I also process heavy whisky differently than normal people. It was actually a very sweet taste for me."

"Hah, Ha! I like you, kid. You have a fire inside you. I hope you never lose sight of it."

The Sol ship landed near the meeting point and the Sol Army walked out. Bounty followed them and saw Myst, Corvus, Jinxi, and Axel talking to a blond-haired Silveran woman, he walked over. Only noticing the mercenaries, she worked with standing in the back.

The woman was saying, "Well, the city is heavily fortified and locked down. If you are looking to assault the castle, we would need to go around."

Myst gave her a hug. "It's good to see you're safe, Elena."

She smiled softly and ruffled his hair. "You know me bro. I am always safe."

Bounty rolled his eyes under his blindfold. He walked up to the gate with the army looking on in horror. He walked over to a black-haired man in an eyepatch with gray and black camo on.

"Hello, Luke. You ready?"

"As I'll ever be. I got my payment. Try not to destroy the city. It's a nice city."

He stepped aside as the gate opened. Bounty tossed him a green and black crystal. Luke caught it and vanished behind a smoke bomb. Halfway through the city, a bunch of red armoured elves stopped Bounty and the army. Bounty held his hand to stop the rebels.

"Hello, Argentorado, are the guards taken care of?"

"Yes, they are, Bounty, and now for my payment."

Bounty rummaged through his satchel and pulled out an ancient-looking bag and handed it over. Argentorado looked into it, smiled and walked past the rebels with his army. The high commander's jaw was open. His second-in-command looked unfazed. They soon arrived at the castle gates. A twelve-foot-tall golden gargoyle-like creature with a mane like a lion's stood there, his massive wings unfurled. He stood holding a large battle axe that showed crimson in the light of the one full and two half-moons.

Bounty walked up to him. "Bat! It's good to see you made a recovery. How's the wing?"

The creature grunted. Bounty nodded and rummaged through his satchel again, this time pulling out a gilded dagger and a long chain. The bat-like man took it and flapped his wings once to rocket into the air.

The Grand Commander spoke, "How have you planned for everything? I thought you were just some blind kid looking to help out a cause."

Bounty turned and kicked the gate down. "I'll explain later. Right now, we have a king to usurp."

The rebels walked into the main area and were greeted by a massive muscular man with acid-green hair and deep green eyes. He was standing next to a woman with sickly blue hair and a man with red and orange hair. Myst held Bounty back.

He sized up the man. "Careful bastard, that is Brawl Ankara. He is the adopted son of Zenthin. He is also a part demon. Rumors say he has acidic blood and can increase his muscle mass."

Bounty eyed the man in the PsiQi and smiled, "Very well, I will handle Brawl. The rest of you attack the two others."

Bounty leapt at Brawl, catching him with a grapple and threw him through the door. He only then realized the door that he had thrown Brawl through was the throne room door. Brawl gave a dark chuckle as Zenthin rose from his throne. Bounty grimaced and swallowed a green liquid he had conjured. He then created a psionic blade that he proceeded to stab into Brawl. He followed that up with a pure energy explosion. Brawl vanished in a blinding white curtain. When the smoke cleared, Bounty stood singed beyond recognition. King Zenthin Ankara sneered, "So Hunter's spawn thinks he can defeat me. You are a fool like your father."

"Am I now?"

Bounty tossed a silver ball of energy that evaporated the shadows around Ankara. He roared in agony as his body was torn asunder. He left behind two gems, a pitch-black one and a crystalline one. The crystal one vanished. Bounty placed a ward around the black one and placed it in a box. He collapsed soon after. Bounty woke in a sterile room, his sworn brother was standing over him.

Axel spoke in his deep baritone, "You had us worried. Jinxi's beside herself."

"Only you two came to see me?"

"Myst would have been here, but he was sent to Norvcryog to deal with the Aka-ites there. Elena and her mercenaries led Commander Storm and her army to Noamaiza to help the rebels there. Corvus vanished soon after we found you. He said something about needing to remove a box from this plane of existence."

"And who is the new king?"

"That would be Blu Silver, the High Commander's second in command."

Bounty faded back into sleep only to wake when he felt a presence near him. He cracked open an eye to see Jinxi bouncing up and down.

"By Bahamut, you are okay. Yay! We were so worried, but now you're all better."

Bounty reached out and patted her head. He saw a large puppy in the corner looking at him. He smiled. It was good to be home.

"Who's the mutt?"

Axel chuckled, "That would be Lunatic Moonshadow. We found him curled up on the couch."

The dog creature's ears perked up as a monotone voice rang out, "Loony, where are you?"

Lunatic bored and Feldspar walked into the med bay. Her eyes widened and she rushed out and returned with her three sisters.

Kimberlite looked at Jinxie, then squealed in joy, "I have a twin!"

Both began making silly faces at each other and mimicking each other. Feldspar smiled as Jade examined Bounty. Her eyes were narrowed, finally resulting in her undoing some bandages and pressing on his chest, causing a loud crack to be heard. She then bowed and hid behind her sister.

Travertine rolled her one visible eye. "She just fixed your ribcage. You had nine broken ribs, one of which was a centimeter from your lungs."

"Thank you for the assist, small one. I do appreciate the help."

When they had left, Axel, standing alone, turned to Bounty. "You want a smoke?"

Bounty sighed in relief as the mint and clove reed did its work. He blew out a green smoke before saying, "The pain is getting worse. How much longer do I have?"

"Twelve years. The magus somehow retrieved a sample of your blood. A clone has been made of you, sorta. They had to mix your blood with an unidentified female to stabilize it. She has been seen on Diavonbry looking for a passage to Noamaiza."

"Lovely. Not like I will be missed. When will you be heading back to Chombra?"

"Soon as Jinxie is done playing. Ram will be joining us since he cannot go to Noamaiza. Thanks to Goddess Silver's rules."

"Since when have the Efreet-Bahamut alliance been concerned with rules?"

"Since Goddess Silver can obliterate us."

"Fair enough. Can you help me up so I can walk outside?"

"Yes."

The two walked out the door and Bounty looked up at the three moons and smiled. He could feel his aches go away.

"How does death feel?"

"It's not bad, rather warm, actually."

Paradox Fate

A dark-skinned mohawked Silveran woman was fake sleeping in a cave. She had painted her two short horns red. She also wore bright orange war paint. Her hair was dyed neon blue. Her armour was bestial in nature, with random fanged mouths on her shoulders, knees, collar, elbows, and breasts.

She had fled to this cave in rage. Here her mind wandered to what brought her to this goddess-forsaken continent.

***

"Sir, you expect me to help Aka-ites rebel?"

Her commanding officer stood there sternly. "Yes, I believe it's a fitting punishment for trying to kill your own allies."

"What do you mean, sir?"

"The entire army is talking about how you sent a blind boy into the enemy camp strapped to a bomb. Frankly, you should be safer on Noamaiza. Many are displeased with you. Even his new lordship Blu Silver is debating whether to discharge you dishonourably."

"Fine! Who am I to go with?"

"Lady Elena Mack, daughter of the great warrior Mik Mack. Whose father died while protecting his friend's family."

"Who gives a damn what an old man did?"

"Everyone gives a damn. Even Zenthin Ankara honoured him and they were enemies. Just for that, I should demote you."

"No! You can't demote me. Please, I worked hard for this position," he sighed. "I said I should not will."

"And what would you do if I refuse to help those scum?"

"Blu Silver has given me permission to bind you to Elena. You would be forced to obey."

Fear entered her eyes. "I'll do it, but don't expect any miracles."

"Fair enough."

Their ship had arrived at a secret inlet twelve days later. The ship slowly entered into a hidden cave where Elena disembarked with the freakish mercenaries that Elena worked with. She had followed with her small army that chose to stay with her. Jasmine was her most loyal ally. She, Chastity, and Ivy had accompanied her. The traitorous Maungirtha had chosen to stay behind along with Ithula. They had chosen to help the blind boy she hated with a passion. She looked around and saw that the Aka army only consisted of about a hundred women. She saw their leader, who was a pale elf dressed in black armour and wearing a purple cloak. Her face was covered by a concealing mask. She also saw a small woman with two tiny horns on her head. The woman had red eyes and pale grey skin. She looked partially blind but seemed to need no help.

She growled and whispered to herself, "Another weakling."

Elena was near her and heard the snide comment. She smirked and walked away. She followed Elena and was soon face to mask with Scorpi Ankara. Skorpi looked her over, then stepped aside and deftly punched Paradox in the chest, sending her down.

Paradox got up and growled, "What the hell was that for?"

Elena spoke, "She's testing you. She wants to see if you can match her."

Paradox smiled sinisterly as she grabbed the small girl and held a knife to her neck, saying, "If you continue to attack me, she will get the knife. I always go for the weakest link."

The small girl smirked and vanished with a shower of confetti. She smashed Paradox's foot and then elbowed her in the stomach. As Paradox fell to the ground, the small girl kicked her up and piledrove her into the floor. She then stepped on her back, pinning her.

Scorpi walked over. "You thought that Eris was the weakest, why?"

Paradox spoke muffled, "She's blind."

Scorpi turned to Eris and nodded as Eris stepped off, she offered her hand to Paradox, "Eris is my bodyguard. She's actually the strongest link in this army. The weakest link is those who underestimate her. She's taken down six enemy generals so far. But you've proven your moxie. Welcome to the army of the Scorpion."

Paradox shoved Scorpi's hadaway, then looked over at Eris and grimaced.

***

Paradox lay in the cave waiting. She looked around and thought she saw movement. "Who's there?

The shadows whispered, causing Paradox to look around, nearly in a panic. That was when the cave shook. Some dust fell on the ground along with pebbles. She peeked outside and saw an armoured man with a massive axe fighting an unarmored woman who wielded dual-bladed daggers. The woman was enjoying herself.

The woman vanished and reappeared behind the man. "Gotcha, sis!"

The armoured man chuckled and took off her helmet. The armour retracted into a shapely bodysuit that accentuated her assets. "That was a good sparring session Llere. Is Leca coming soon?"

A small form appeared, giggling, "Silly Leon, I am already here. While you two were sparring, I was examining our surroundings."

Llere looked at her quizzically. "And?"

"I found a peeping Lisa!" With that, she pointed towards the cave that Paradox was in.

Paradox snorted in anger, "So what. Whatever you dish out, I can do double!"

The girl known as Leon looked at her and then spoke, as she prodded the snake armour, "Why do you wear armour that brands you as a traitor?"

"I am a warrior. I was cast out of my clan for killing our chieftain and a rival chieftain. I started a war between six clans."

"Why?"

"They looked down on me and treated me like dirt. No one looks down on me. Especially men."

One of the others with black and purple hair looked at her. "Lies, I saw you behead the queen, then turn on your allies. Your savagery was a sight to behold. Why then did you kill your lover Jasmine?"

"She got in my way."

The small girl, Ller, spoke, "That's awfully cold of you. I like it."

The one known as Leon smiled. "If you would like to join us, we could use your help. We are hunting a man named Bounty Hunter 13. The Magus emperor wants him dead."

"I would be honoured to help you. I can even lead you to him. But we need a hostage to lure him out."

Leon spoke, "Well, if you could bring his sister to us, that would be of extreme help. He seems to care deeply for any of his siblings and would go to great lengths to save them."

"No problem, she has been aching to fight me ever since my treachery."

***

Paradox Storm stood on the beach of continent Silver. The plan had gone off without a hitch. But it had not been Bounty Hunter 13 who had come to save Eris. It had been his brother, Mist.

She sighed as she stood looking at the ocean. Her eyes glowed with rage. She let out a howl and smashed her axe into the ground.

"You done yet, or shall I wait? You made a mistake, General. You threatened my siblings. That is why you are here. I teleported you to face me. Not only have you betrayed your leader, Skorpi Ankara, but you have also betrayed the world. The Magus empire seeks to erase life on Silver. We are the last bastion before the Star Vale. If they breach the Star Vale, they will have access to the first planets, where all life came from."

"Shut the fuck up, boy. I fought in many wars before you. Then you came along and ruined me."

"Ruined you! You tried to kill me! You made it your mission in life to destroy me. Well, here we are! A one on one duel. Isn't that what you wanted? Your exact thoughts were If I had him alone, I could take him. Well, here we are. Pick your axe up and fight me like the warrior you claim to be."

Paradox violently grabbed her axe and hurled it at Bounty Hunter 13. He sidestepped as it went flying past him. He ducked as she punched at him. He grabbed her arm and twisted. She cried out as her arm snapped. She kneed his groin. Startled that he didn't seem to feel her attack, she was caught off guard and he slammed her into the ground. Her armour dug into her skin, causing blood to dribble out. She watched him turn around and saw her axe sticking out of his back.

"How do you not feel pain?"

"I have nanites in my blood given to me after the assault on the pyramids of Chombra."

"You fought at Chombra?"

"I am the reason General Axel and his soldiers survived."

"Three hundred versus thousands. That was what the reports stated."

"Did the reports also tell of how a fiery dragon obliterated the fleet of King Admiral Fel Aka?"

"Yes. A massive inferno blazed from the firebombing then, from that fire, a dragon with large spikes on its shoulders appeared. Many called it the Avatar of God Silver."

Bounty Hunter 13 laughed darkly before fire exploded around them, much of the top sand became crystal and she saw the fiery dragon. Her eyes widened in terror as she scrambled back, only to stop when her armour touched the flames.

She started to whimper as a sense of overpowering dread engulfed her. The axe was pulled out of his back and thrown at her feet. The flames vanished and he stood before her.

She was cowering in fear. "Please don't kill me. Oh, goddess, please protect me."

"There you are Paradox. I followed the trail of the psionic teleport. Well, Pie did."

Bounty Hunter 13 looked at the newcomers. One was a menacing horse-headed man with pink skin. The other was a short female with long hair pulled into pigtails. And the final was a woman who looked exactly like Bounty Hunter 13 but her horns curved downwards. He could feel the power radiating off of her.

"Well you must be this timeline's version of Lord Psycheo. Also known as Leon Psycheo. So today is the day. Very well, girl. Come complete your destiny."

Psycheo smiled and lifted Paradox's axe in her hands and swung at Bounty. He blocked with his dual khanda zweihanders. He smiled a fanged smile as he was pushed back. He sliced at her neck, but she ducked, throwing him off balance and cleaving him upwards, she sliced through his arm, sending it and one sword flying.

He smirked, took a needle out, and injected his body with the fluid inside. He then put the needle away before releasing a large amount of power, sending her tumbling. She flipped and landed on her feet, sliced again, but this time a burst of energy sliced into Bounty. He gasped and fell with his legs and arms sliced off. She stood over him, grinning. Paradox got over her fear and shoulder-decked Psycheo to the ground, she picked up her ax and cleaved Bounty's head from his shoulders.

Lady Psycheo smiled at the bloodthirsty display. "Welcome to the team Paradox. We have many things to accomplish together."

Paradox cried out as the shadows overpowered her.

She was back in Noamaiza with the Scorpion army attacking the city of Amazonia. As they entered the main castle, she watched as Ivy and Chastity were cut down along with several of the soldiers. She watched as Jasmine and Eris slaughtered the gunners. She charged into the throne room with Scorpi Ankara cleaving the queen's head from her shoulders. She turned her bloody axe on the army of the Scorpion. Many fell, yet she was only stopped when she killed Jasmine.

Scorpi and Eris tied her down, removing all her armour and clothes before whipping her. Eris then dragged her to a cave. She threw her bloody body into the cave and told her to think on her sins. That was when an old man in green appeared. He placed the armour she wore on the ground. He then materialised an axe out of thin air. And gave it to her. He had called himself The Dragon and had given her a green and red tome.

As she came to, she was standing over the wounded form of Leon Psycheo. She had severed Leon's legs. Pie stood there with a gun drawn and pointing at her.

She stood grinning madly as the shadows wrapped around her. "I am Lord Psycheo now. You foolish peasants thought the shadows would die. We have become stronger. This one's rage and treachery fed us. Now we join the Magus as Phantom. Thank you for your help."

Paradox vanished and Leon heard an ethereal clapping and looked around. She saw the soul of Bounty Hunter 13 standing there.

He spoke, "Congratulations, the Magus now have the ability to break through the Star Vale and gain the power they seek. I hope you are happy. But to show you no hard feelings for my death, I mend your body. You are revitalised. Now get out of my sight."

Leon whimpered and looked down. She could see her legs along with black streaks running through her left foot. She had been cursed. Her left foot would now forever be her weakest part. If it were hit, she would be defeated. She looked at the spirit pleading for forgiveness.

"You will earn my forgiveness. I suggest going to the planet Mythic and meditating. Think about where you go from here. The Magus have no need of you, they have Phantom. Goodbye and good luck."

He vanished as his body burst into flames. She saw a feathery-cloaked man standing there, along with a woman in a brown duster and a cybernetic man. She felt Pie lift her and the two appeared on Noamaiza. She saw her sisters bleeding out and cried out in fear. The hunting party came upon her and she saw the look in Queen Scorpi Ankara's eyes. She blubbered, begging her. The look vanished only to be replaced by pity. She was bound and her sisters were brought aboard a hover command centre. It hummed and trundled off to Amazonia.

Bounty Hunter 13 stood there sighing before appearing again in the havens. "Your first death. How was it?"

"Expected and painful, Toreno. Thank you for allowing me to see my siblings. I doubt it will be a short while till I am reincarnated."

"That all depends on how the Judges decide."

***

The spectacle had been viewed by Beatrix Badger-Oda. She was puffing on one of Bounty's Peppermint, opium, and clove cigarettes. She looked around and shuddered. The demon of God Silver had struck again. She saw his corpse on the ground smouldering and eventually, she approached the headless form. She moved her hand and a rune took form on the ground. She dragged the corpse over the rune and looked around until she found his head. She grimaced and removed the half mask it wore. She was unaware of the three watching her. She drew two more runes and the body burst into flames. She turned away after bowing to it and walked off.

Beatrix felt a presence behind her and quickly drew her blade. She stopped her swing before it connected to the massive sword held by a blond woman in a brown duster.

The woman spoke, "Beatrix Badger-Oda, a harbinger of Goddess Silver, you hold something that belongs to me. My brother's mask. Please hand it to me."

Beatrix nodded, after seeing a druid, a woman wearing robes holding a book open with fire in her hand, and a cyborg.

She handed her the half mask. "Why do you support such an insidious being?"

"If I don't, no one will. He needs allies since he is so powerful. He was also cursed at birth. The same curse I sense on you. I could be your ally too."

"I am Beatrix the Great and Powerful. I need no allies... but thank you."

Beatrix vanished, leaving behind the cyborg, the mage, the druid, and the woman.

The Magus War

Bounty Hunter 13 stood in line, waiting for his soul to be judged. He could see the golden-skinned man behind the desk of judgement. The man had a crown-like structure on his head, but they were his horns. He had Sanguine eyes that could see all the wicked deeds a person had done. The guards surrounding the room were the fabled Angelus and Daemus. His keen eyesight noticed a commotion. One of the Angelus was bisected in half by a purple sword. The one wielding the blade was a bird-headed man. The man killed several more Angelus and lunged for The Judge of Souls. Bounty picked up one of the fallen Angelus' black blades and blocked the purple blade. The Bird looked shocked and screeched at him.

Bounty sliced through the beast's legs. It roared in a savage display and continued to try and kill the Judge of Soul. Bounty shook his head and cut off his arm. The creature grabbed its sword with its other arm and still tried to kill the Judge of Soul. Bounty finally cut through the beast's head. The four pieces fell through the floor and vanished. He stumbled and hit the floor with one knee. He held his burned side where the purple blade had cut him. One of the female Angelus began to tend to his wound. She looked terrified.

Bounty spoke, "Don't worry about the burn. Heal what you can."

"It's not the burn I worry about, mortal. That was Bloodhawk the Destroyer."

A massive Silveran man made of pure muscle walked in. The large assembly on his back constantly billowed psionic steam as if his body nor spirit could contain his Psy energy. He hefted a massive black blade onto his shoulder and looked around.

The Judge of Souls spoke in an umber voice, "You are late to the party WARDEN."

"Bastard killed my entire guard, not to mention the former WARDEN. He let the most violent offenders out. I just finished rounding them up. So cut me a wee bit o'slack here. Now would someone be kind enough to remove the axe from my back, it itches."

One of the Daemus floated over and removed a large jagged axe made of scrap from the WARDEN's back."

"Thank ye kindly, wee lad. Now, where's Bloodhawk?"

Bounty snorted, "Dead. Fell through the floor. Don't quite know what that means?"

WARDEN looked at Bounty with a crooked fanged grin, "Tain't nothin', good boyo. Means he has formed now."

"Four different forms, I presume, since I beheaded him, de-legged him, and dismembered his arm."

"Well, that gives the galaxy extra time, I suppose."

The Judge of Souls growled before waving his hand, causing the floor to open and drop Bounty through. As Bounty fell, his soul took on bone and organs, blood and nerve vessels, muscle, then, finally, flesh. His skin took on a bluish-grey colour and his eyes became fiery silver.

As the ground rushed up towards Bounty, he muttered, "Well, this is going to hurt."

***

Elena stood staring up at the night sky. There was a meteor shower tonight, along with the aurora. It made the sky bright. There was a cacophonous explosion behind her as several hooded Magus attacked the civilian centre she was near. She pulled out her sword and turned towards the enemy. The ground erupted in front of her, sending her into shock with several stone shards in her body. Gilda sliced through one of the Magus before another set her on fire. Ram managed to kill two more before his arm went flying from a berserker magus in heavy red armour. The civilians had evacuated aside from the wounded or dead. There was fire everywhere. Amongst the rubble, a woman in vibrant orange cut through several Magus. She flipped her hair back from her face before cutting through the lead Magus. The other Magus backed off as a heavy object impacted the ground. There was a groan from it and a ten-foot-tall, incredibly muscular male pure Silveran with four-foot horns rose from it. His skin was blue and sweaty.

He looked around before speaking in a deep earthy voice, "You made a wrong move coming here."

The fire took on a nuclear green glow as the man charged forward. He picked up a halberd from one of the fallen guards and began cutting through the Magus. The red-armoured Berserker vanished along with the woman in a red leather catsuit. The man finished and stood leaning on his halberd atop a pile of gore. He summoned rain that put the flames out and walked over to the injured. He got the stones out of Elena and used some scrap to forge a new arm for Ram. Gilda vanished as he snapped his fingers. He then proceeded to pile the dead together away from the Magus. He set the dead Magus afire, then healed some of the wounded civilians. Buttercup, the bighead, waddled over to Elena with Vinyl Darkspeed. She started stroking Elena's hair and held her head while she whimpered.

Up on one of the roofs, Tam Tam stared through her scope. She had noticed something dangling near the man's thigh. Four spiked balls attached to a two-foot-long ribbed shaft that ended in a flat rounded object. It soon dawned on her the man was naked and she had just spent the last ten minutes staring at his penis. A deep blue blush appeared on her cheeks as she licked her lips.

Buttercup looked at the man. "Can you at least put some clothes on? I am in heat and the water rivulets on your muscles are very distracting."

The man looked at her and then smirked before flames and steam erupted around him as he vanished. Fluttering in his wake was a business card. The medevac came blaring sirens. Ram had picked up the card and his face paled considerably. He brought it over to Buttercup and Vinyl, both looked it over as Tam Tam landed near them, adjusting her sombrero to hide her cheeks.

Vinyl spoke, "Okay, so… who is Argon the Slayer and why does he scare me so."

Ram spoke, "It's not so much the name as it is his mark. And if I understand marks, we are dealing with a dead man."

Vinyl raised her eyebrow. "Okay, so what's a dead man doing fighting Magus?"

Buttercup shook her head in disdain. "A good question for a later time. Elena needs to get to a hospital. And we need to find where the hell Gilda disappeared to."

***

The Blue-grey skinned man appeared in his home. He was confronted by a man wearing a cloak of feathers. Next to the man was a girl in a neon yellow trench coat with a venom green jumpsuit underneath. Her eyes were hidden behind red-tinted psychic dampening glasses.

The man signed, "Well, Bounty, it looks like you easily adjusted to your new form. I would like you to meet Tallon Blackhart. She is to be your partner in hunting down the Magus. You are to be disguised as a Mystic Maester and she is your student, but first put some clothes on."

"That was why I am here, Corvus. Also, to check up on my patient who got burned alive by dark fire. Follow if you wish otherwise, I will be right out."

Corvus rolled his eyes and led Tallon in. They saw four well-toned women sitting on the couch. The vibrant one jumped up as Bounty walked in.

"Oh, my goodness, look at you. You're alive!" Bounty raised his eyebrow.

The busty gray-skinned Feldspar spoke in a monotone, "She has been eager to meet you ever since she felt your resurrection."

With a purr, she continued, "I can see why. Look at you."

Bounty smirked and vanished. He appeared in his private chambers and saw what he was looking for. He picked up the vial with purple-blue liquid. He pulled the liquid into a needle and injected himself with it. He vanished again and reappeared in the living area with a trenchcoat on and nano-adamantine fibre pants. He had clawed boots on and his hands were covered in spiked gloves. In a holster on his side was a gun and a satchel was on the other.

Feldspar pushed herself against Bounty. He eyed her and sighed, "You are in season, aren't you? Oh, very well, I'll humour you. Corvus, I will be out within the hour. Can you check on my patient?"

Corvus shook his head, then motioned Tallon to follow him to the med bay. She looked curiously at Feldspar, then quickly followed Corvus. The vibrant girl dragged her two sisters with her as they followed Feldspar. Corvus looked in the med bay and saw three patients.

Tallon spoke, "Boss, which one was burned by dark fire? There are three of them in here."

They heard feminine moaning and panting, then the bored-sounding voice of Bounty, "Gilda is the one you want. She's the Green Orkean Silveran. The other two are in stasis until such a time I deem them harmless."

"I see her. She's pulled out the IV and is struggling to undo the straps."

Corvus shook his head again before walking over to Gilda. He placed his hand on her to stop her struggling. His deep purple eyes scanned her readout and he motioned Tallon to grab a vial. She did and he poured the vial down Gilda's throat and forced her to swallow. She immediately went limp. Corvus then traced a rune in the air and the dark fire burns glowed before a stream of energy was drawn into a small crystal that Corvus held out. The burns vanished.

He then handed the crystal to Tallon and signed, "This is now a dark fire bomb. Try not to drop it."

She placed the bomb in a box with others like it. There were numerous bombs ranging from poison to healing. She then placed her box in her satchel. Her stomach growled and Corvus smiled, leading her to the kitchen.

He whispered, "Computer one gargant steak for the girl. I will have a glass of shadow rum and a ventari burger."

The computer hummed a jovial tune and the two meals appeared on the table. She also placed a glass of Amber Mellon juice on the table for Tallon.

Talon spoke, "Why did he sound so bored? He has four hot chicks fucking him?"

He has nanites in his blood. He feels nothing because of how experimental they were. He cannot even feel pain. Hence why his body is so scarred up.

***

Bounty lifted the sperm-covered Feldspar into a bath and cleaned her up before placing her unconscious form in his freshly made bed and covering her up. He did the same to her sisters. The four snuggled deeply together.

"Sleep tight little ones. I will try not to get killed this time."

***

Bounty looked on as the large stingray ship docked with the Grand Silver Station. It was a few days later. He had just finished redoing his clan's holdings. The Prism clan had tried to overthrow Blu Silver. Since Bounty and his siblings had defended Blue Silver along with some of his cousins, the Prism clan was forced to submit to the Hunter Clan. This was like the old ways. Which was one of the many changes Blu Silver had reinstated when he took the throne. He had also calmed his cousins since they felt they had been jipped because the holdings of the Prism clan near them were smaller than the Holdings of the prism clan near Bounty's lands. He had to explain that it was only the Main Stronghold of the Prism clan he received. They had received far more holdings than he. That had calmed them considerably. He was also worried Benyerxo Hunter 11 looked very ill. He would have to check in on his cousin after his mission.

Tallon was standing next to him in a fishnet undershirt with a yellow trench coat over it and ripped jean shorts. She still had her rose psychic dampening glasses on. Her jaw was hanging open. The boarding ramp opened up and an amber-skinned woman with leather straps all over her body walked out. She had bone-white hair from a military cut that showed off the jagged claw scar on the right side of her face.

Bounty snorted, "I see you still like big things, huh! Pain?"

Pain looked him over and scoffed, "Looks like you still overcompensate. Who you trying to impress? We all know you're a wuss. Who's the new meat?"

"Pain, meet Tallon. Tallon, this is my associate Pain. She is the best pilot in this sector of the galaxy. Are the others aboard? We have some issues that need going over."

"Nope, still waiting on the mercenaries."

"We are here, dark one."

Bounty turned to see Elena and her mercenary group. She still had bandages on from the shrapnel wounds. He also saw a slightly burned Gilda with them. Then there was an amazon woman wearing rune-inscribed orange leather armour. A large grey taur stood near Elena. But he was not one of her mercenaries. The mercenaries and the stranger boarded the ship.

A timid voice stammered, "Is this the Stinger One?"

Pain looked around while Bounty looked down. He saw a two-foot-tall mouse girl with glasses and an unkempt look about her. Her tail swished nervously.

Bounty sighed, "And you are?"

"I am Guri 123 and Admiral Javelin sent me here as a scribe."

"So you're his eyes on the field. So to speak. Very well, stay out of trouble and welcome aboard."

Bounty entered Stinger One and smirked as he saw Guri 123's eyes widen in awe. "It's bigger on the inside!"

"That's because the outside is a hard light hologram. It's meant to deceive the enemy. We are a warship disguised as a cargo ship. And now that you know, I will have to kill you."

Bounty spoke to the large muscular shark man, "Chill out, Sting, before you make her wet herself. And here we go."

Guri yelped and whimpered as she curled up in terror, "Oh, goddess, I'm sorry. Please don't eat me!"

"Sorry about that. That is how Stingora's people greet each other. Don't let his looks fool you. He is actually really nice." He scooped her up and placed her on his shoulder. "We had better get you acclimated to the Nuclear Seven."

He brought her into the lounge area where the four others sat. He set her down and put his hand on her shoulder. "These are the Nuclear Seven. The red armoured Knight is Argentorado Red 100, hailing from the planet Red; he is the noblest. Next to him is the violent Rex-Lizardian Scarr

Lizard. In front of you is Deathknight of Casualty Station. Also, somewhere is Talicon of Metallic and the copilot beside Pain is Azolas Dul of Bronze. Finally is Bat of the Golden Wings. He is a monk of God Gold just don't piss him off and he'll be nice to you. You will be working with us and my sister Elena's mercenary team. Did Javelin ever give you information on what the goal of this operation is?"

"No, he did not. I am just a scribe."

Elena spoke, "Actually, you were kind of withholding that information when you hired us. What is our goal?"

Bounty hit a button and a hologram of the middle section of Galaxy Silver appeared. "You see these red planets. They are all held by the iron fist of the Magus empire. Our goal is to free the allied planets of Red, Gold, Copper, Lizard, Stinalta, and Metallic. Along the way, we will be eradicating the Magus strongholds at Black and Grey. This will all lead up to an assault on the primary Magus Stronghold Golgatha at Mellone. We will have to split into groups. Tallon and I will be infiltrating Golgatha after I assist at Metallic since I am the only one here who can breathe Nitrogen. We will be splitting our forces Deathknight will take Pain, Elena, and Guri 123 to help out Black and Grey. Scarr will take Gilda, Grimm, and Ami to Lizard. Argentorado will take Vinyl, the stranger, and Tam Tam to Red. Though it looks like I will have to lend a hand on Gold and Stinalta."

Pain spoke over the speakers, "Boss, we're coming up on Copper. I am opening the viewports and entering the atmosphere."

Bounty smiled a sad smile as he watched the faces of his allies upon viewing the planet Copper.

Guri 123 whimpered, "What happened to the planet?"

"Planet Iron was once a thriving galactic heavy hitter. This is where all metals and ships were built before being shipped out. This was a hub of activity. During the first Magus War, the Magus dropped 24 psionic nuclear bombs on Iron, turning it into the vast wasteland you see before you. The Magus also erased all information on Planet Iron. So when it was rediscovered, the ones who discovered it called it Copper. Nothing can survive here. Well, nothing organic."

Elena spoke, "Then why are we here?"

"You'll see soon enough."

Pain yelled, "Boss, we have incoming."

"Open hailing frequency Ig 379az Ben."

A mechanical voice spoke, "Greetings, Bounty Hunter 13. I am Drill Bit of Copper, formally King Alkaline of Iron. Designated Mining unit Dexal 700. My general Vexis Ten-Twenty will escort you to the Magus. Please make sure to remove their bleight entirely."

"Will do Drill Bit. Please make sure all your units are away from their area. I suspect heavy seismic activity."

Drill Bit buzzed and beeped some orders before. "Acknowledged all units retreat from sector Veltan. What do you mean not all units can retreat? Zeta unit has been captured and used by the Magus. Those bastards."

"I'll handle it. Drill Bit, some seismic activity could occur but not as bad as plan A."

"Good luck, please try to rescue Zeta unit before anything. Vexis lead them to the Magus."

The smaller craft flipped around and shot off Stinger One followed. They arrived and Vexis made a loop and fled as several giant mechs opened fire on it.

"Boss, what the hell are those?"

"The reason we are here is each of those mechas is equipped with a psionic nuclear warhead, this is where the Magus has been producing them. You all stay up here. Pain, drop me."

"Boss, if I drop you, no Magus can survive. We need to keep you a secret."

"I know, Pain. Now drop me."

The floor opened up and Bounty hurtled to the ground. They watched as fire erupted everywhere and one of the mechs was cleaved vertically in half.

"Pain, I found Zeta unit open teleporters on my location. Make sure they're sent to docking bay twelve."

Bounty watched as the smaller mining robots vanished. He cleaved the head off of the overseer. He then proceeded to slaughter any and all Magus that got in his way. He put a virus in their computer system that caused a cascade of failure and erasure of all data. Secretly making a backup on his computer. He finished his slaughter and proceeded to walk through the facility, making sure there were no survivors.

"My job is done here, beam me up to my chambers so I can clean up. Drop off the Zeta unit at the great hole. Drill Bit will be happy to have them back. Did Vexis make it out?"

"It did, boss. I made sure to move the ship into position to cover Vexis' escape."

As Stinger One left the atmosphere, Bounty grunted in pain. One of the Magus had severely wounded him. It would take months for his Nanites to repair the wound.

"Boss, we are coming up on Red. How do you want to proceed?'

"Teleport Argentorado, Vinyl, Tam-Tam, and our mysterious guest from Noamaiza down. I am positive that once Argentorado cleans up the infestation, he will find a way to get them off the planet."

A few hours later, pain spoke, "Planet Gold is right below us. Are you and Bat ready to teleport?"

The golden Gargoyle-like man spoke in a rasp, "I am ready if you are Demon." Bounty nodded and the two vanished. Pain quickly arrived at Lizard and dropped

Scarr, Gilda, Amy and Grimm off. Then arrived at her destination of Gray.

"Azdul, please keep an eye on the ship while Luke and I investigate Grey."

The bronze-skinned man smirked and leaned back in his chair, "Sure thing."

Enter the Red Rebellion and the Knight of Argent

Amidst the deep red jungle, Argentorado stood waiting for his allies to stop throwing up. The only one who seemed unaffected by the rapid change in gravity was the Noamaizan.

"If I may ask, girl, what is your name?"

"I am Beatrix Badger. I am a priestess of Goddess Silver. Why are we helping you?"

"The Cult of Scarlet, the chaos Goddess of Red, allied with the Magus Empire and helped them conquer Red. We are to assist my family in taking back our home. As you know, I am Argentorado Red, the 100th. There are many in my family named Argentorado, so from here on out, you have my permission to call me Jason. But only temporarily, that is the name Bounty gave me when he met me and it kind of stuck."

Vinyl coughed, spat, and then spoke, "Well, it looks as if we have company."

Tam-Tam was tossed into the foliage by a heavy man wearing red armour and a pirate hat. She threw up some blood and passed out. Several tendrils converged on her and wrapped her up.

Jason grimaced, "Hello, brother. Been a while. I see you finally betrayed the clan and joined Lady Scarlet."

"You are the only traitor, brother. All of our glorious clans submitted to Scarlet. You are not allowed to wear the noble armour of Red. Now remove your garments or face execution."

Jason raised his axe and swung it at his brother. "No, I do not think so, Buccaneer."

"It's not like you have a choice in the matter. Your little friend is being raped by the carnivorous violet fern. The pale girl is struggling against my magus allies and that Silveran female you were talking to is getting her ass handed to her by Jay."

Jason sighed and pressed a button. His armour opened up, revealing his pale red skin. He stepped out and Buccaneer saw a massive scar across his elder brother's chest.

"What happened?"

"Oh, don't pretend you care. Now have your allies release Vinyl and tell Jay to back off from Beatrix."

Jay walked out of the forest dragging Beatrix by the hair. She was dressed in a red leather leotard. She tossed Beatrix in front of her bare-chested brother.

She spoke giddily, "For your treachery, dear brother, the pale bitch has been taken to become one with Scarlet. She will make a great priestess."

Jason snarled but picked up Beatrix and his axe and jumped into the forest to rescue Tam-Tam. He saw her unconscious, naked form dangling above one of the Violet Fern maws as it was using its vines to stimulate her. He looked around at all the emaciated women who were being consumed by the plant. He snarled and sliced through the tentacles and caught the bloody and stamen-covered Tam-Tam before flipping back and lifting up Beatrix as well. Fire exploded, destroying the small fern andits victims. He got the two to a safe cave. He then left the two there while he went to grab some healing herbs.

He returned to the cave as Beatrix was waking up. She groaned, "What hit me?"

"My sister Jay, she caught you off guard and used her wind style on you."

"Why are you mostly naked?"

"I had to relinquish my armour to save you and Tam-Tam."

She saw a blood-red skull on his back. "What is with the mark on your back."

He sighed, "I have been branded an outcast since I have allowed an outsider to see my skin."

"I'm sorry we caused you such pain."

"Oh, this was not from you. I do not blame you for my predicament. This mark was from when I was violently raped by Slavers. Bounty rescued me from them and I owe him greatly."

He walked over to a stone basin and placed the herbs into it. He stirred and then placed Tam-Tam into the basin with her head resting on the side of it.

"Rest up, Beatrix. We have a long day ahead of us tomorrow. I just hope Vinyl can withstand Scarlet."

"Shouldn't we go after them?"

"No, the little one needs constant attention so she can heal. Even if Vinyl succumbs, I have a way to free her. Which will be even better once the Magus are dealt with."

Beatrix nodded and closed her eyes. Jason waited before going over to a statue of God Red and kneeling on one knee. "Your Templar awaits your orders, oh holy one."

The statue moved. "Some templar you turned out to be. I expected more fromyou."

"I highly doubt that."

"You are correct. You have actually surpassed my expectations. Thus I give you this boon. Since you forsook your family armour I will now clad you in the Armor of God Red. Wear it well Templar."

The sun rose on the jungle of Red. The crimson trees dropped their dew and the ruby flowers and Violet ferns opened wide to accept the sun. Jason sat outside smoking a thin stick that smelled oddly like mint. Beatrix walked out with Tam-Tam clinging feverishly to her back in a carrying bag. Jason got up and felt Tam-Tam's head before placing the thin stick in her mouth and forcing her to inhale the mint fumes. She coughed but looked much stronger than before.

"Come along, we have a long walk to the Chaos Temple, formerly the Temple to God Red. I just hope we can free everyone from the control of Scarlet."

An orange-haired kilt clad warrior dropped from the trees. His freckled face and intelligent green eyes stood out.

He spoke, "There you be, laddie. I've been looking everywhere for ye. Sorry I couldn't contact you aboot the ambush. I got ambushed myself."

"It's alright, Leslie. I am fine. We just have to rescue an outsider from the clutches of Scarlet. Oh, ladies, this is my companion Leslie Torque. Leslie, Beatrix and Tam-Tam."

Beatrix raised her eyebrow. "So you two are in a committed relationship?"

"Let's just say that Leslie and I have a history and leave it at that."

"We met as slaves. What they did to us...?"

"Sorry, I brought it up."

"You're alright, girl. You should know since we're aboot to hit the grove of memories. It is a magus trap designed to torture their enemies by forcing them to relive all their bad memories. We will see your bad memories and you will see ours. If we can make it through, we will be at the Crimson temple. The stronghold of the Magus."

As they entered the grove, they saw two naked young boys chained together. The two were forced to perform numerous sexual acts on each other and on the vicious raider-looking men. One was frail looking with orange hair and the other was a red-skinned muscular boy.

Suddenly the images changed to that of a tiny girl being viciously beaten by her elders and tossed out of a cave system with an older girl. The tiny one was forced to hide as her companion was brutally mauled by an elf with sharp teeth. She then watched as the feral elf was put down and several number-skinned elves walked into her line of sight. One put her friend out of her misery and another captured her. They watched as the elves experimented on her before she fled. They watched as she sold her body to pay for food. Beaten and emaciated and hungry, she wandered the streets.

The final image was on fire. It was a home that was burning as many heavily armoured women attacked it. The scene switched to the inside and they saw a female trying to fight the warriors off. She was beheaded by one of the women; five other girls were brought out and executed. They only noticed a sixth under the corpse of the one beheaded, but the other women did not notice her. Beatrix screamed and the grove of memories became fire. She burned it to the ground. She stood there panting in fear and anger.

Jason placed his hands on her. "Relax, Beatrix. It's over, you are safe."

"Never safe. I want to kill. Give me blood and vengeance."

"Woah there! Shit, how did that encounter end?"

"Killed them all. Slaughtered them like animals. Made them pay for what they did to my siblings and mother."

"It's over. It's over. That was the past; this is now. Calm yourself and regain control." She panted and collapsed in tears. She curled up in the fetal crying position.

Tam-Tam stroked her hair, trying her best to comfort her.

Jason carried Beatrix away from the now-destroyed grove. Her tears had dried now she was shaking from adrenaline withdrawal.

Jason looked at Tam-Tam. "How did you survive?"

Tam-Tam grinned sheepishly, "Elena found me covered in spunk, clinging to what little money I had gotten. She brought me to her home and cleaned me up. She taught me how to defend myself and then taught me how to be a sniper. I owe her my life and intend to repay my debt to her somehow. What about you two?"

Leslie looked up at the night sky. "Bounty Hunter 13 found us. He had apparently been hunting down the slavers that had taken his brother. And sowed a path of destruction against all slavers in his wake. When the slavers refused to sell us to him, he slaughtered them all. He showed no mercy even when one of the younger ones lay there begging for his life. It was kind of hot to witness. I have never left Jason's side since then. I keep him out of trouble and he keeps me safe. From others and myself."

"Enough of the past, we are here. Ladies, this is the Temple of God Red, now infested with Magus and Chaos worshipers. We need a plan."

The temple was a red stone stepped pyramid-like structure. It was covered in rubies and runes that kept it protected. Thunder shook the sky as a wild storm struck.

Tam-Tam jumped up a tree and took up a sniper position. "We have twelve guards and I think I see Vinyl. She looks different, though. I think we arrived too late to save her."

Jason shook his head. "Beatrix, can you try to cause a distraction? I need Buccaneer and Jay distracted while Leslie and I sneak in. Tam-Tam, think you can kill the guards silently?"

"I have no bullets. They all fell out when that plant used me. I do have a box of sleeping darts, however. I just need to get through the armour."

"Aim for their neck seam. It should be the best way to get the dart into the skin. None of our armour is airtight unless we are off-world, where we do not allow our skin to be seen ever."

As Beatrix walked out, she watched the guards all fall to the ground. "I challenge Jay Red and Buccaneer Red to a duel. Unless they are cowards."

The two warriors walked out. The voluptuous Jay sneered, "You could not even handle me. What makes you think you can handle the two of us?"

Beatrix pulled out a serrated blade. "I'm armed now. I was caught unaware by you, but now we are on an even footing."

Jay vanished and began her pummeling whirlwind attack. Beatrix became dizzy trying to defend herself and stumbled back right as lightning hit the ground. It ignited Jay even though there was rain. Jay screamed and began thrashing, trying to tear herclothes off. They were too slick, she was sobbing now. Beatrix knelt down and summoned a geyser of water that put the flames out. She was then slammed into by Buccaneer. The two went careening into a tree that splintered under the force of the hit. Buccaneer began to viciously beat Beatrix until she was a bloody, mangled mess. Beatrix passed out.

Jason stood as a woman in a red fishnet body stocking walked down from the temple. Buccaneer walked over to her and bowed before tossing the mangled form of Beatrix at Jason's feet. The woman stroked Buccaneer's face and then shooed him away. He collected the smouldering form of Jay and walked back into the temple.

She spoke in a silky voice, "Ooo, the great paladin of that little bitch, Red, comes to challenge me. But I have no time for you. Darkspeed, please eliminate the rebels."

A woman wearing nothing but leather boots appeared with a dark giggle and threw Tam-Tam into Leslie, who was knocked off his feet. Her large penis and breasts jiggled as she rushed Jason. It soon became erect from the adrenalin. She grinned a fanged smile. Jason deftly dodged her. He snorted as she rushed him again. This time he struck her from behind. He grappled her and grabbed her penis from behind. He pulled and she cried out.

"Move any more and I'll rip your dick off. Understand?"

She whimpered and nodded. Tam-Tam climbed off of Leslie and placed her gun against Darkspeed's balls. Jason let go. He walked towards the temple. Crimson fire and maroon smoke soon engulfed the complex. There was an unnatural howl that echoed through the air. The flames and smoke vanished. Two men in deep red armour walked over and grabbed Darkspeed. They took her into the temple complex. Two more carried Beatrix in on a stretcher. Leslie hefted Tam-Tam up and walked in. Jason stoodthere in prayer to God Red. Goddess Crimson's statue was on the ground as if it had been knocked over, which was impossible unless the Goddess had lost her powers.

Beatrix awoke in a white room with Vinyl standing over her. Vinyl grinned a sinister smile.

"Darkspeed, step back from my patient, please."

Vinyl frowned and stepped back, revealing Jason, who looked shocked. Beatrix noticed Jay in some kind of healing tank. The burns on her body looked to be healing.

"How in the nine hells did you fully heal after two days? You were a mess three-fourths of your bones were shattered, including three ribs that had punctured your lungs. One of your horns was unsavable and we fitted you with a prosthetic horn."

"Does it matter?"

"No, I guess not. Anyway, while you were out, the Magus were forced to flee when I caused Goddess Scarlet to submit to God Red. I was able to free my people from whatever mind control they were under. Unfortunately, Vinyl was broken to Scarlet's will. She is now called Darkspeed."

"I was not broken. I am a manifestation of Vinyl's will that protects her from harm. I am the persona she takes on when she performs at raves. I was formed from her abuse at the hands of her family for being born different."

"I see. So you were just playing the part of thrall."

"Heh, um... no... That was… not an act. She actually had me as her prisoner. I apologize for my actions."

As those two talked, Beatrix slipped out and entered a cafeteria. She saw Leslie talking to three girls. One was tall, voluptuous, and blond. The other was a brunette in punk-style clothing, and the last was a young girl holding a book of spells with midnight purple and black hair.

"Ah, lass, you're awake. Come meet my half-sisters on my father's side."

Beatrix sat down and the blond spoke, "I saw the tail end of your fight. Kinda surprised you are fully healed from that berserk beating you received. Regardless, I am Alina Torque. My little sister is Aluna Torque and my dark sister is Aluci Torque. Sorry, we got here so late. We ran into some Magus that tried to capture us."

Jason walked out and smiled, "Good news Beatrix. I did manage to get you a ship off the planet. I see you have already met the pilot. Good luck. I suspect Bounty will want to rendezvous with you at Mellon."

A large brutish man with muscles and gold eyes watched from the far end of the dining hall. He frowned into his drink and combed back his neon-red hair. This will be an interesting challenge. He is strong, but I am stronger.

The Gold Warrior and His Fate

About five hours from when Argentorado was dropped off at Red, Stinger One was over the Jungle planet of Gold.

Bounty, Tallon, and Bat dropped "Have the auto pilot pick Tallon and I up as soon as you are done with Dropping Scarr on Lizard and Death Knight at Casualty Station."

"Will do Boss. Be careful you're going to be a father soon." "Yes, I know. I already promised Feldspar I would survive."

Bounty reappeared on a floating dock that was hovering above the Gold forest. Bat looked around and saw a little calico furred fox girl with wings.

She ran to him "Uncle Wing you're back. Woah I knew aliens existed but I thought they were little and green."

"Rusty where's your mother?"

The girl pointed out across the forest where a group of dragon winged humanoids were facing off against numerous rocket packed Magus.

"I see the Magus got smart."

"Yeah they're led by some chick calling herself Arch Magus Ching. She is a master of Technomancy. At least that's what mom yelled over the inercoms."

"Ah that's why there are so many of our kind over there. Bounty are you ready togo?"

"Tallon, get on my back. I will show you how to avoid the forest."

"Why?"

"Planet Gold hates when sapient beings touch her sacred soil. She will sick theforest on them. The only reason Bat and his people survived so long is because they built these flying Aeries."

Bounty lifted off the landing platform and shot off towards the battle. Tallon clung tightly to Bounty's shoulder spikes. Bat Wing caught up quickly and opened fire on the Magus with his canon.

Bounty handed Tallon off to Bat "Here hold her I will finish this off. Pull the soldiers back to Aerie Twelve. Also activate force fields over the forest."

The Magus converged on Bounty with Lady Ching mocking him "You are a fool to stand against my might. Who do you think you are?"

Bounty drew two swords and flew forward bisecting three Magus and incinerating them before they hit the forcefield. He then spun and drew the Magus into his blades by using wind. As the wind became a tornado he spun with the vortex. There were screams of terror as the vortex became bloody. Then the fire started and the bloody vortex became an inferno. Lady Ching cried out as her arm was vaporized and her rocket pack shorted out causing her clothes to catch fire. As she plummeted towards the forest the forcefield shorted out and Bounty grabbed her by the rocket pack and caused a rain storm to put her out. He placed her on the platform to Aerie Twelve.

He saw the shocked expressions on the faces of Bat Wing's clan. He dusted himself off and picked up Tallon. He noticed the warriors pull out their guns as he quickly was teleported out along with Lady Ching and Tallon.

"I think you pissed them off Boss."

"As long as Bat doesn't try to defend me he should be fine. I hope."

On the Aerie Bat stood surrounded by his family they had him pinned to the floor by heavy ropes.

"You brought a demon to our sacred land, Therefore you must pay." "I did not realize he was a Demon. He deceived me. I was tricked."

"You know the rules brother. Regardless of your innocence your wings are to be severed and you are to be thrown into the forest."

"Very well I revoke my name of Wing. Mark me a traitor."

Rusty cried out "You can't do that. He has been off planet for years. Has he not earned a bit of leeway? That rule was made three years ago when the Magus Razorwing summoned a demon to destroy us. He was stripped of his life."

"Rusty do not soil your good name by defending me. Rules are rules no matterwhat."

Rusty watched as her mother took a large blade and heated it up. She swungand Bat's wings were sliced from his back in one fluid motion. She then took a large flat piece of metal and welded it to the stumps so they could not regrow.

"Consider yourself warned brother. If you disobey our rules the forest will have you as a feast. You are hereby banished from all Aeries, leave before I change my mind."

"Mother, can I at least help him to the mountains."

Bat smiled a sad smile and snapped the ropes and back flipped off the platform. No one had noticed him grab a chain and axe head. Rusty cried out and looked over the edge to see if she could see him. She started crying. Her mother looked away and walked off followed by the rest of the clan. Rusty tied her wings to her back and jumped. Bat saw her plummeting form pulled his axe from the beast he had slain jumped and caught her.

"Damn fool of a girl, what'd you do that for?" "I need you uncle. I can't lose you as well."

Rusty's mother had witnessed her daughter's suicide and grimaced. She lay her head down on her bed and wept. In the shadows of the aerie two blue eyes glowed with malevolence they blinked then a shadowy winged wolf slid over the side and into the darkness of the forest below.

The Hunter

Bounty looked over the toxic atmosphere of Metallic. "I have to do this alone. Tallon, stay up here. You are not equipped to handle the toxic gas of Metallic."

He teleported to the ground and felt his third set of lungs, the space lungs, kick in to begin filtering the atmosphere into breathable air for him.

A mechanical voice spoke, "I figured we would encounter you here, brother. Your friend Metalicon lies dead. We killed him."

"Hello, Vera. Hello Aerick-Starr. What do I owe the pleasure of this encounter."

"Silence, fiend. You will not win against us. Why are you hunting down theMagus?"

"You are a threat to the Star Vale."

Aerick-Starr's bass-augmented voice spoke, "How do you know our plans?"

"They're the same plans the first Magus War was waged to prevent. Seriously,does Grand Emperor Magus Belphegor not know the history of the Magus."

"It's not Belphegor anymore. She calls herself Psycho Phantom."

"Figures. Anyway, why are you two in Mandelic armor?"

"Don't pretend you care, Bonty."

"Very well, stop me if I am wrong. Your lungs were scorched when you attempted to defend Belphegor from Psycho Phantom. She wiped the floor with you and the elite guard. You were the only two to survive. Hence your exile here. So my head will be your ticket back into her good graces."

Vera charged him and sliced at him with her serrated sword. He heard a revving as Aerick-Starr activated his chain sword. He smashed into Vera and she was knocked unconscious. Aerick-Starr roared in anger and slashed at him multiple times. He fell with a chain sword through his chest as Metalicon struggled to his feet.

"Bout damn time you show up. I almost bled out."

"Well, you're healed now. Thanks for the assist." As Metalicon was teleported to the ship, Bounty lit a fire that exploded due to the gas in the air. It vaporizedAerick-Starr and Vera. Bounty quickly put it out before it could spread. He winced and spoke, "Thayme Sidrodc uigde het seul.

Thayme havens sunocme het seul." Downing the amber liquid conjured during the prayer, he teleported out.

As he arrived on his ship, Metalicon spoke, "Sorry about killing your brother. I am sure you wanted to spare him."

"I am not too worried. Stay still, I don't want you to scorch your lungs from my atmosphere."

"You seem awfully unconcerned that he is dead."

"I may have ended up killing him, anyway. He wanted my head as a trophy."

Bounty helped him to a healing stasis chamber. He put a bubble around them and the atmosphere changed to be something that Metalicon could breathe. Bounty helped him out of his suit and lay the frail, pale metallic green body in the healing tube. He wiped up some of the yellow blood and set the healing to two months. He looked over the power armour and sighed. It was severely damaged. He put it on his list of things to do. His ship was soon at Stinalta. He walked over to the large tank and pressed a button.

"We are here, Sting. Are you ready to be sent home?"

"I am very eager to see how things have changed. Will we be hunting for those Magus?"

"Let's get you home first, then we can decide what to do from there."

Bounty hefted Sting into a smaller drop jet, then took the pilot's chair. As the two entered Stinalta bounty, saw many small Islands that were uninhabited. Each Island marked a school of Stinaltans. They splashed down near some wreckage. Bounty sent the smaller ship back and sank into the water. Due to how heavy he was, he sank fast before summoning runes that made him more bouyant. His water lungs began filtering water so he could breathe.

Sting looked around. "Looks like we missed the fun. I see the Magus stronghold still stands. Let us head out then. Come demon, let me show you how we do things down under."

Bounty followed and the two soon came upon the Magus stronghold. It was under attack by many different aquatic beings. He saw Thulhuids, Shark men, Merpeople, a massive whale-like being, and numerous smaller fish people. He even noticed a strange amalgamation of technology and biology. The hammerhead shark beings had jet engines attached to their skulls and large blades on their arms. The Magus were outmatched but were intent on holding their fortress despite how many casualties there were.

A feminine Ray girl shot over to them and embraced Sting. She spoke "Father we have been trying to destroy a wall, so we have access to their facility to wipe them out. Now that the siege breaker is here, can you lead the attack?"

Sting smiled. "All forces converge on Whalgolith. Defend him while we shatter the walls of these abominations."

All the forces formed up around the giant whale-like being. Bounty noticed Whalgolith had a strange formation of metal on its head. The metal glowed with many runes and Whalgolith slammed into one of the walls that had cracks on it. It shattered, allowing the water to rush in and drown many Magus. Unfortunately, the doors sealed off, preventing more loss of life. As Whalgolith charged up for another run the Magus in their diving suits began throwing lightning. Several smaller fish people were fried instantly. Bounty drew his two blades and began to slaughter the bolt throwers. By the time he was done, another wall was destroyed.

Inside the facility, several Magus were finishing loading their escape ship. The leader looked at all the work they had completed but could not save and spoke, "Withdraw all surviving forces and lure the enemy into the facility. I will stay behind and take as many enemies with me as I can."

Outside, the aquatic warriors cheered as the Magus withdrew. They were about to charge when Sting held up his hand to stop them. "All forces, we have won this battle. Do not be foolish enough to charge a retreating enemy that has obviously withdrawn to lure us like common fish. General Octabull, what is the scrying saying."

A large muscular green and yellow Thulhuid spoke, "There are self-destruct runes enabled."

"Then we have victory. All forces we are free. Go home and celebrate our victory here today."

The aquatic forces split, leaving Bounty and Sting behind. "Stay out here, Sting. I will finish this off."

"Don't be a fool, Bounty. They will kill you."

"Don't you worry about me? I have a plan."

Sting shook his head and swam off. Bounty entered the facility and immediately downloaded all the data the facility had to offer. He entered the main lab and saw a scaled woman waiting for him. He looked around at all the test tubes and shook his head. He typed in a command and his ship teleported all the experiments out. The woman looked shocked and then snarled. That was when the stronghold exploded. Bounty stood there floating in the water while across from him, the female was unconscious. A psychic bubble vanished and Bounty went back to breathing water while he teleported the female to the med bay of his ship. She was put into stasis. Tallon looked at Bounty curiously as he reappeared on the command deck, dripping with water.

"Are you prepared, girl? We are heading to Mellon."

In The Forest Of Lizard, Treachery Is Afoot

Grim, Scarr-ed, Vinyl, Gilda, and Buttercup appeared in a swamp and Gilda immediately became aware. They looked around and heard a sloshing sound. They looked around and saw some robed figures with guns running through the swamp. They got over to dryer land. They stood in the shadows of a massive fern. The soldiers marched past them and suddenly, they were attacked by nine huge Alligator men with tree trunk thick legs and near-impenetrable scales. Their heads looked like logs and theireyes were crimson. They had foot-long claws that dripped with the swamp. The Gator's men mercilessly slaughtered the Magus. They then began rolling in the gore, gurgling sickening laughter. It sounded like a laugh but one that was mixed with gravel and ash. It was so guttural it sent shivers down Gilda's spikes. She saw a green-scaled lizard man walk out of the nearby cave and sit down, just smirking as his comrades played in the blood. The Alligator men then noticed her crew. They charged forward, causing them to scatter.

Grimm Chaosforge stood looking around for his allies. They had gotten separated when they had been attacked by Gatormen. Scarr was next to him with his sword drawn. There were Magus surrounding them. That was when Gilda burst through the jungle and sliced through several of the Magus. Buttercup was flying behind her and began to speed around, beating the Magus up. They saw a feathered Raptorian girl perched on the tree, her blue-black feathers glinted in the setting sun.

Scarr hissed, "Raven Deathcrow, why have you allied with the Magus?"

"I am no longer Raven of clan Deathcrow. You may refer to me by my Magus name of Blue."

"Ha, as if! No, I will continue to refer to you as Raven."

As the last of the Magus were slain, Scarr led Grim, Buttercup, and Gilda in chasing Raven down. They arrived at a cave entrance and Gilda hung back.

"Why are you stopping Gilda?"

"Buttercup, Something doesn't smell right."

Grim had overheard and nodded. The three entered the cave. Grimm and Gilda both activated their Inferno vision to see in the dark.

"Of course, It's a trap."

Light flared, nearly blinding both Gilda and Grimm; they were surrounded by many Magus.

That was when Scarr walked over to them. He kicked them to the ground and his body changed into that of a green-skinned male with numerous scars jutting across his torso like lightning.

"Too easy. Blindly following me in here. Oh, before you ask, I know all of Bounty Hunter 13's plans and have passed them to Psycho Phantom. Your little revolution was finished the moment Pain let me aboard your ship."

He stopped talking and wheezed as he saw a large jagged blade sticking from his sternum. Gilda walked past his falling corpse and grinned. She began assaulting the remaining Magus as Buttercup finished helping Grimm up. He quickly shielded her as a Magus threw a fireball in her direction. He grunted as his body caught on fire.

"Girls grab the Magus known as Blue. I will end this."

Gilda looked at his burning form and nodded. She grabbed Buttercup and Blue and fled as the cave suddenly became a volcano. The Chaos energy swirled around the new volcano in a violent fashion that could be seen from miles away. The Chaos then spread its tendrils and began engulfing numerous Magus strongholds. Blue watched in slack-jawed horror as the cataclysm continued. It continued for days by the time itended, Gilda had found where the Magus had imprisoned the people of Lizard.

The real Scarr looked her over and snorted, "Sorry for your loss, but you had best leave the planet. Your dead friend has caused us untold amounts of trouble. Usually, thiswould call for execution. However, you can't execute a dead man. And I will be lenient since you did help destroy the Magus, but please leave our planet."

"Uhm, the slight difficulty there. We were dropped off and our ship left."

"Well, in that case. Use one of the Magus' ships. Oh, you can leave Blue here for punishment."

Buttercup nodded and was picked up by Gilda as the two went ship searching. They found a small interplanetary burster fully fueled and they left Lizard. Gilda set a course for Mellon, hoping the fuel would last. She felt something touching her nethers and saw Buttercup trying to feel her up. She smiled and gently stripped the heavily aroused Big Head. She allowed her access and Buttercup eagerly went at it, fully consumed by her lust.

Raid on Grey: Who Is Slayerhammer

Pain landed the ship on Planet Gray at the hub, which was Planet Gray's main spaceport.

"Azdul, please keep an eye on the ship while Luke and I investigate Grey."

The bronze-skinned man smirked and leaned back in his chair. "Sure thing."

Right away, she could see Magus foot soldiers guarding the hub. It was still open to the public, but all were carefully examined and scanned for hidden weapons.

Deathknight spoke, "This looks fun. Wonder why they're being so benevolent."

A young woman with raven black hair, pale skin, and large breasts walked over to them. She looked them over and handed Deathknight a card. He looked at it and nodded.

"Well, girls, it looks like we are going to a bar."

They entered the bar called Nox Inferno and ordered some drinks. The busty woman sat down across from Deathknight. He saw several patrons get up and leave. Leaving behind a small group of heavily armed miscreants. One of the miscreants was a man from planet Brown. His brown skin rippled with muscle as he picked up a large keg in one hand and drained it. He crushed it against his skull as the miscreants cheered.

The raven-haired girl spoke, "Barlotet, stop showing off. I hired some Mercenaries to help us. Introduce the plan and what's going on."

Barlotet smirked and spoke in a heavy accent, "Well, well, well, more mercenaries. I have already recruited the former RAVAGER to our cause. Clowd Windsong. Who arethese?"

Deathknight smiled, "I am Deathknight. This is Pain. We are from the Alliance of Allied Planets. We were told there were Magus here, but as far as I can tell, they are not cruel or violent like all other Magus."

The girl smirked, "They are being nice because they're afraid of ZinnRa, a global conglomerate that has been sucking our planet's life force to create power. Many have already suffered because of it. Magus are just cashing in. I am Tanya and you three will be working with us. Over there is Jessie, James, Bob, and Will, who are some of our founding members. I hired you and, to a greater extent, Clowd to help us. We are known as Earthquake the, according to ZinnRa, the terrorist group."

Bartolet spoke, "Like Tanya said ZinnRa is sucking our planet dry. We are going to raid their main factory. Sector 5G is the one closest to us. We will infiltrate there and blow it up, followed by 6G. Any questions?"

The small group shook their heads no. Deathknight lit a cigar and placed it to his lips. He inhaled the toxic fumes and blew out red smoke. Elena looked him over and saw concern in Pain's red eyes. Guri 123 sat writing things down. The next evening arrived and Earthquake snuck onto a train that was heading towards sector 5G. They arrived at the power plant and quickly killed the guards. Clowd and Bartolet went to the reactor level. Within two minutes, they came running back out.

Bartolet yelled, "Get moving. She's about to blow."

Elena spoke, "What the hell is that thing?"

The small force turned to see a massive mecha wasp descend from the sky. It began firing lasers from its stinger. The reactor exploded, but the Mecha was unharmed. Clowd jumped into the air. His blade took on six sizes and he sliced down, causing the Mecha to split in half and explode. His blade returned to normal as he landed. He turned and walked off.

Deathknight watched him as Pain spoke, "We are not needed here. They have everything under control. We should leave. I don't like the vibe that Clowd gives off. He's too dangerous."

"We have a job to do after G6 falls, we can leave."

"Alright, but you promise, right?"

"Yes, I promise we will leave and charter a ship to Black."

The next day was the same as the first. They boarded a train to get to the sector 6G power plant. Clowd and Bartolet went in along with Tanya. It took far longer for them to leave. There was no explosion this time. Instead, there was shouting and an army of Zinn-Ra guards appeared. They opened fire on the small group. Guri was hit in the shoulder and flung by the impact. Elena caught her and mended the wound to the best of her ability. She saw Jessie fall with numerous bullet holes. Her empty eyes stared off into the sky. Elena rushed her. She quickly felt for a pulse. Then Jessie vanished and she felt a warm presence. She could have sworn she saw a man in a horned badger mask pick Jessie up, but she didn't have time for that. A grenade landed near her. She rolled away as it exploded. She saw Bigus and Will fall next due to another grenade throw. A large war mech descended from the sky. It sprouted its legs and crunched the pavement under its feet. Two large gatling lasers extended from the side and opened fire. James leapt up the war mech and pulled the pilot out, tossing him to the ground. He marched the mech towards the reactor core as it was being fired upon by the Zinn-Ra guards. Bartolet, Clowd, and Tanya were struggling against a large tank-like mech. James opened fire and pushed the two mechs towards the core. Bartolet grabbed Tanya and rushed off while Clowd followed close behind. The two tanks exploded, sending Clowd plummeting towards the lower level, with Tanya crying out for him. The two arrived as Deathknight jumped into the air and spun around, firing on the guards and finishing them off.

He landed hard and Pain supported him. She was covered in blood, not her own. He turned and snarled. "I hope it was worth the death of your close allies. Regardless, my crew is done here. Keep the money you owe us. Goodbye"

Elena scooped up Guri and followed after bisecting a boulder with her blade in rage. Her fiery eyes focused on the dead. "Give your dead proper burial. Sorry, we couldn't help you more."

Raid on Black: Purple Fire of the Blackheart

Deathknight, Elena, The Taur, and Pain arrived at Casualty Station, which circled around Planet Black. Guri 123 was resting in a cryogenic pod in the med sector. The Taur had promised her she would keep track of what happened on Black. Elena stared out the view pane waiting for the shuttle to take them to Black. There was a large storm roiling over Black as the shuttle departed. When the shuttle landed, Pain stayed back tentatively.

Deathknight smiled warmly, "It's alright, Pain. The lightning won't touch you as long as you stay by my side."

"I'm scared. I don't like the feel of this land."

"I know. It takes some getting used to."

A voice spoke up, "Luke Darkfaith, what the hell are you doing down here?" Deathknight turned after grabbing Pain by the hand and leading her off the ship.

Before him stood an imposing black armoured figure. With two large horns on his head curving down. His shoulder spikes glistened purple in the glow of Black. Jagged purple lightning shattered the sky, followed by an explosion of thunder. Pain jumped and whimpered, falling to the ground in a fetal position. Deathknight sat down next to her and wrapped his arm around her comfortingly. She curled into him.

He looked at the armoured man and spoke, "Lord Blackheart, what a pleasant surprise. I heard you died."

"I did. I am currently inhabiting this armour until my mission is complete."

"And what pray tell is your mission?"

"To pass on this message and to protect Planet Black."

"What message?"

"Purple fire graces the horizon. Dark beings emerge. A blasphemy against science and mystic energies. Beware your mirror..."

Purple lightning scorched the sky again and Blackheart vanished. Deathknight sighed. He looked to the horizon and saw a purple wildfire. He shook his head and walked towards it. Elena easily lifted Pain up and carried her with them. The Taur followed close behind, looking around for any danger. They arrived to see a very large compex burning brightly in the dark gloom of

Black. Deathknight huffed and sat down, watching the fire burn. Then a deluge of rain hit them. The fire was immediately snuffed out. The skeletal remains of the complex glowed with the lightning. Deathknight walked into the rubble and saw gore everywhere.

There were heads missing their bodies, legs missing their torsos, arms missing their torsos, and standing before him was a man as large as Bounty Hunter 13. He wielded an axe that hummed with dark energy. He almost looked exactly like Bounty Hunter 13 except that his body was not burned, nor were his horns curved up. The horns were curved down and his shoulders were covered in a shell-like structure. He still had shoulder spikes, but they were jagged instead of smooth. He looked up at Deathknight. His glowing red eyes twinkled with bloodlust.

"Luke Darkfaith. You are unworthy to face me. Where is my donor?"

"Who is your donor?"

"Bounty Hunter 13! Ah, I see he is on Mellone. Come forth, Reaver. The Darkfaith has arrived. Die well, Luke, goodbye."

The creature vanished. A muscular, pale-skinned man walked out of the shadows. He wore ragged armour and wielded two pistols.

He rasped, "My donor appears. I will enjoy drinking your blood."

Deathknight smirked, "Let's see what you got. Elena and Mr. Bull, get as much information as you can from the computer. I will handle ash face here."

Elena, still carrying Pain, hurried off further into the ruins. She came upon a large room with many shattered test tubes. On the floor lay a woman wearing a lab coat. She was breathing but not well. Elena teleported her to Casualty Station. She gave orders to keep her confined until she could check up on her. The Taur began downloading all the data on the computer while wiping it in the process. Pain was stable now and guarding their backs. Deathknight limped in, holding his palm to his eye. He was bloody from several bullet wounds.

Pain looked worried. Deathknight grinned, "You should see the other guy. Never duel a Deathknight by yourself."

Pain rushed him and hugged him. "You idiot, don't scare me like that."

"Oh, Pain, you know it'll take more than a few bullets to take me down. The Magus thought to clone me, but you cannot clone training. That's why he's dead and I amliving."

Elena spoke, "So the readouts don't lie. The Magus cloned Bounty Hunter 13, Argentorado, some guy named Talicon, and you."

The wall hissed open, revealing an intact test tube. Inside this tube was a fetus. The three stared at the fetus.

Deathknight spoke into his comm, "This is Luke Darkfaith Deathknight of sector Nine. Calling the Science sector."

"This is Science sector Doctor Amil Felca speaking. How may I assist you, Deathknight of sector Nine?"

"I need a medevac. Also, need to bring an unborn fetus in a test tube up intact."

"Doable one moment."

The test tube vanished. Deathknight soon followed along with Elena, the Bull, and Pain.

The Demon vs. the Phantom

Bounty Hunter 13 docked at Golgotha. Two Magus walked out to greet him. One was a neon blue woman with electric blue hair dressed only in a fishnet catsuit. The other is a red-haired woman with a green tube top and jeans.

"I am Argon the Slayer. This is my apprentice Fang. I received word you were searching for a new Baron."

The blue girl smiled, "Welcome, Argon the Slayer. I am Ember Hawthorn and this is Vicki Huntari. We wish to welcome you to Golgotha. You are lucky in that the new Overlord wishes to test you herself. Follow, please."

Bounty Hunter 13 followed after giving Tallon instructions to meet up with Gilda and the others when they arrived. He also instructed her to take the ship out of the docking bay. He followed the two to the throne room. He saw Psycho Phantom sitting there in her serpent armour. He could feel the soul of Paradox Storm crying out in rage. He could also feel the shadows that possessed Paradox. He looked at Psycho Phantom, who was picking at her fingernails.

She looked up and grinned a grin that sent chills down Bounty's back. "Hello, Bounty Hunter 13. I've been waiting for you to show up. Girls scramble the fighter ships and purge his allies."

The two bowed and vanished. Psycho Phantom pulled out a blood-red blade. She grinned maniacally. Bounty pulled out his halberd. He blocked her attack and the two clashed. Out in space, Gilda avoided several blasts from the enemy ships. Her jump ship was running on fumes. She gulped and dive-bombed the citadel. She ejected with Buttercup and clutched the little bighead tight as she plummeted towards the ground. She was caught by the mystery woman in orange leather armour and pulled into a large ship shaped like a sword. Beatrix set Gilda and Buttercup in the infirmary.

Beatrix spoke, "Alina, how are the defences holding?"

"Not good the smaller fighters are too much and too many."

"Teleport me to Golgotha and then get out of here. Get to Casualty Station. That's where we'd meet up with Deathknight."

"Alright. Good luck."

Beatrix appeared outside the throne room as Bounty was thrown through the wall next to her.

He stood up and dusted himself off before leaping over the rubble and continuing his attack. She saw two swords flashing instead of his halberd. Beatrix joined in and found she was outmatched by the Magus leader. As the leader's red blade severed through her sword, the wall exploded inwards as Gilda's jump ship smashed through, impacting the Magus leader. She snarled in rage and threw the small ship at Beatrix. Beatrix yelped. The ship crushed her into the wall and she blacked out. Bounty Hunter 13 took this time to stab Psycho Phantom in the back. She cried out as the energy blade severed the shadows from her. The shadowy woman snarled and lunged at Bounty, who pulled out a cane.

"No! How did you come to own the Cane of Shadows?"

"Your previous host Zenthin Ankara had it on him when I killed him. I took it so as to keep it out of the hands of those that would misuse it. Now return to the darkness."

The shadows roared and vanished. Paradox lay on the ground, placing pressure against her wound. She stared in shock as Bounty walked over to her. He sheathed his blades and they vanished. He knelt down to heal her wound.

"Piss off, demon. I don't need a man to help me."

"You know what, Paradox. I give up. I'm trying to be nice to you and all I ever did was help you and your army only to get shit. The only one who cared about me was Maungirtha. So go ahead and die."

He walked away and Paradox whimpered. Bounty extracted Beatrix from thewall.

"Wait! I'm scared of death. Please, I'll let you heal me."

Bounty looked over at her, shook his head, then snapped his fingers. "Thereyou're healed. Get out of my sight."

"I need a lift off the planet."

"Fine, I'll drop you off at Casualty Station. Tallon, please bring the ship back and get the med bay prepped."

"Hang on, boss. Gotta get past the hawk class bolter ships first."

The ship landed and Bounty carried the two into the ship and it lifted off, shooting off towards Casualty Station. Bounty saw the two Magus who tricked him into sleeping in healing pods and smirked. They soon arrived at Casualty Station. Elena met up with them. Deathknight walked in, supported by the Taur, with bandages on his torso.

Elena spoke, "You are supposed to be in bed resting. Why are you here?"

Bounty smirked, "What happened to you, Luke?"

"I got injured facing my clone."

Elena sighed, "Men and their stupid pride. Anyways I am surprised your clone didn't show up. He vanished as soon as he saw us calling us unworthy. Before you ask, here's all the information I could collect."

Bounty looked it over. "I see, so not only will I have to contend with Clowd Windsong but also my clone. Beautiful. Regardless we had best collect the others. It's time to go home."

The ship flew off towards Casualty Station. He studied the tube that Ember was in. He raised his eyebrow and shook his head. *There is something off about you, but I can't figure out what it is. How annoying. Your skin and hair are way too neon. Ah well, I can study you later. Now to let Paradox Storm decide her own fate. At least she isn't trying to kill me anymore. Ugh, should have had some extra hands. Too many got injured. I also need to do better. How did I not discern Scarr was a fake?*

They arrived at Casualty Station and disembarked only to be greeted by a tall, lean muscled tannish red-skinned man. Behind that man was a large boxy robot with a gear on his back and a bronze-skinned man with a mask over his mouth and a large double voulge with chainsaws on each end.

The tannish red-skinned man spoke, "Sorry, I was having a hell of a time trying to get your message. I assume the war is over?"

"Yes and no, but I am glad to see you Swift-Fang-Coyote of the Onyx Ursa tribe. I see that Rob O'Techno 100 and Berylin Wraithbone are with you as well."

Yeah, funnily enough, I had to pick them up. They responded to your call, but nobody ever arrived. Almost as if they were forgotten."

Bounty looked down at his readout. "Oh look, nine missed messages. Sorry guys, I dropped the ball on that one."

Swift Fang chuckled, "Oh, kimosabe, you never cease to inspire us. In this case, I am in awe of your stupidity."

"Yeah yeah, laugh it up. I am in need of a good failure every now and then, but this one had too many failures added up. My head was elsewhere."

"Well, my friend, you are in luck. With the Magus Empire crushed, we will be at peace for some time. How about we all get a drink? I will tell you how we eliminated the Magus on our planets."

"I would like that. A good war story always invigorates the blood."

What is a Hero? Many years after the Magus war, Bounty Hunter 13 sat meditating in a secluded pond-filled glade. He had discovered this place many years ago during the Silveran Civil War. He sat on the onyx boulder, deep in meditation. The Magic Melody of the Universe enveloped him. He felt the tune shift, becoming darker and more invigorating. The glade was medium-sized with a pebble-bottomed pond. In the far corner, he had erected a statue of God Silver along with a small Hunter family altar. Thanks to a recent Firebug mating season, the spike trees had closed in closer to the glade.

He was deep in meditation when he felt something snuffling against his crotch. He looked down to see a Kitsune licking her lips and nuzzling him.

The statue of God Silver he had erected spoke, "Bonty, I would like for you to impregnate her."

"Why?"

"I have plans for the future of my people. Many of the Silveran species have died out or moved off-world to New Silver and Silver Two. She is in heat. Obey your God, please."

"Very well, God Silver, but you owe me greatly for this."

"Yes, yes, I'll put it on the list of things I owe myself for."

"You know I get no pleasure from this."

"I do, which is why I am asking you to fuck her silly. It's just business."

Bounty commanded his nanites to harden his penis as he undid his pants. He saw the little Kitsune's eyes widen in shock. She began whimpering and trying to flee.

"See, Silver, she doesn't want to. I will not force her."

His necklace glowed and a small Succubus emerged from it. She quickly dove into the Kitsune and took over. Inside the Kitsune's mind, the Succubus scratched behind the Kitsune's ears. Smiling gently and relaxing the small mental projection of her mind. Outside was different, however, the Kitsune was writhing with ecstasy as she was impaled on Bounty's penis. She was panting and letting out small gasps and moans. Her eyes rolled back as her womb was filled with the seed of the next generation. Bounty pulled out and immediately, the Succubus shot from the Kitsune and wrapped her lips around his shaft as he finished ejaculating.

He watched as the Kitsune vanished. He shook his head disapprovingly. He then sighed and patted the succubus' head. She cooed happily and snuggled against him before going back into her gem. He went back to meditation. There was a light stirring in the trees and a female Felis walked out.

She cooed, "Ooo, Bounty Hunter 13. You will make a great mate. Please use me."

Bounty sighed and motioned the felis to sit on his lap. He penetrated her drawing a small amount of blood into his testes. His semen shifted into Felis-compatible semen. She was climaxing right as he ejaculated into her womb. Here a small change took place. She would give birth to three Canis boys and two Felis girls. Thus paving the way for God Silver's Nu Silverans. When Felis was done, she fell asleep and Bounty placed her near the statue of God Silver.

He heard shouting and opened his psychic sight to the world. He saw a small, barely one-hundred-year-old girl being rushed by men wearing metal plates strapped together by leather. He wrapped the girl in his psychic aura and hid her in his cloak. The men had Hunter Corporation guns that Bounty quickly dismantled thanks to hismechanus psy powers. It didn't hurt that he had designed and built the weapons himself. They looked confused as their guns fell apart in their hands.

Bounty spoke, "Who disturbs my slumber and why?"

One of the men snarled, "Where you hidin' that little brat? She escaped right as she was getting sold."

"I know of no little beings near me, but as it stands, I am grumpy from being woken. Goodbye, little slaver."

The three men were slain and immolated. Bounty uncovered the brown-skinned girl. He noticed she had spiked ridges on her head and frowned. She was a Brown Silveran from the south. He typed into his gauntlet for missing children. He saw

Rona-Alexandra pops up as a missing Brown Silveran child. Her picture looked exactly like the girl that was cowering before him.

"Let's get you home, little one."

"Wait! Aren't you going to rape me or beat me or do other horrible things?"

"Now, why would I do that?"

"That's what they did."

"Well, I am not like them. I am going to take you home."

"Can't you do something about the rest of them?"

Bounty opened up his armour and placed her inside it. The hum of the armour made her drowsy and she fell asleep as the armour closed. *I think I will go for a walk.*

Bounty walked through the forest and came upon the slaver camp. It was a large stone ruin from the old days. He could see the head slaver on a computer and he also saw a large transport heading away. He pushed a button on his gauntlet and a small insect popped up and buzzed off. It attached itself to the truck and burrowed into the metal hull.

Bounty walked in with several other buyers. He had wrapped his cloak around him. The cloak made him look like a monk of sorts. The guard eyed him and shrugged, allowing him in.

Bounty looked around the auction hall and he could see all the people the slavers were selling. He frowned, then smirked evilly. As the auction began, he locked the doors. He put protective runes over the slaves and waited. A thin female was brought out. Her body had whip marks and she looked well used. No one bid on her.

Bounty spoke, "Two hundred common."

The crowd laughed and the auctioneer spoke, "Two hundred for number seven sixty eight. Since you're the only one wanting a worn-out bitch like this, I won't even slam the gavel."

"Seethrassa thanks you but Seethrassa has other ideas."

A large wind whipped up and became sand. The moment it touched the flesh of the buyers, they petrified and dissolved into dust as well. Soon there was a raging sandstorm that broke through the fort. Within the hour, no living thing remained except the slaves and one buyer.

"Seethrassa wonders why you live. You should have died by Seethrassa's power."

The man looked at Bounty and smirked, "Lower the disguise Bonty."

"Seethrassa knows not this Bonty. Seethrassa is Seethrassa."

"We're doing this, fine. You stand before Mistic Hunter the fourth. I felt your scan earlier and tweaked it to only kill those buying the slaves for a cruel reason. I was purchasing them to free them."

"Seethrassa just saved you thousands of currency. You should be happy."

"Hmpf, seriously, asshole. Can't even acknowledge your brother."

"Seethrassa believes you should look behind you. Seethrassa sees fourcameras. Seethrassa thinks that you should get the slaves out of here and bring them back to their homes. Seethrassa has some data to take care of."

Mist glanced behind and saw the cameras and growled, "I just revealed myself. Dammit, Mist, how stupid are you."

Bounty downloaded all the data the slaver crew had, then deleted it. He saw their primary hub was on Misogoke. He reappeared near a small city near the water of the river Granen. The sign said the city of Devani. He walked to the police station and asked for the address of the family of the girl. He also showed the lost girl poster. They gave him the family's new address, which happened to be in the city of Grove of Angels. He would have to wait. He gently placed Rona-Alexandra in a cryotube and froze her in suspended animation. He went home and saw Feldspar nursing their child. The girl was small and premature. He smiled and wrapped his hand around her.

"She's getting bigger. What have you been feeding her?"

"All natural milk."

He kissed Feldspar on the forehead. "I have some children I need to rescue. I promise I will return and we can discuss our future."

"Take your time, love. I am going nowhere."

As he exited his home, he felt a dark presence and turned to see a large man with a metallic green beard and swirly horns.

"Ah, Corvus, you usually never come this close to the Hunter Clan Fortress," he spoke using Nevermore's voice. "Bounty, I have some grave news."

Corvus handed Bounty Hunter 13 a readout. Bounty looked it over, then frowned. "What do you mean four extra twins to us? That is impossible."

"Not according to this. Maybe you should send out your spies. To investigate further."

"I don't like having followers."

"Brother, those that worship the Shadow Lord are quite useful. I understand your reluctance to be worshipped. But they don't worship you. They worship the Shadow Lord of which you have mantled. You and he are separate beings, still. And for the time being, those that live under the shadows of day-to-day living are a utility you currently can't afford to neglect. I heard about the whole Magus Empire fiasco. Had you listened to the shadows, you would not have been caught so off guard."

"Thank you, Corvus. You have eased my mind a bit."

"But seriously, if this document doesn't lie, that means I was father's plan B. I don't feel comfortable being you."

"I hear you. I don't feel comfortable being father's Plan A."

"Sorry, I brought it up."

"You're alright, girl. You should know since we're aboot to hit the grove of memories. It is a magus trap designed to torture their enemies by forcing them to relive all their bad memories. We will see your bad memories and you will see ours. If we can make it through, we will be at the Crimson Temple. The stronghold of the Magus."

They saw two naked young boys chained together as they entered the grove. The two were forced to perform numerous sexual acts on each other and on the vicious raider-looking men. One was frail looking with orange hair and the other was a red-skinned muscular boy.

Suddenly the images changed to that of a tiny girl being viciously beaten by her elders and tossed out of a cave system with an older girl. The tiny one was forced to hide as her companion was brutally mauled by an elf with sharp teeth. She then watched as the feral elf was put down and several number-skinned elves walked into her line of sight. One put her friend out of her misery and another captured her. They watched as the elves experimented on her before she fled. They watched as she sold her body to pay for food. Beaten and emaciated and hungry, she wandered the streets.

The final image was on fire. It was a home that was burning as many heavily armoured women attacked it. The scene switched to the inside and they saw a female trying to fight the warriors off. She was beheaded by one of the women; five other girls were brought out and executed. They only noticed a sixth under the corpse of the one beheaded, but the other women did not notice her. Beatrix screamed and the grove of memories became fire. She burned it to the ground. She stood there panting in fear and anger.

Jason placed his hands on her. "Relax, Beatrix. It's over. You are safe."

"Never safe. I want to kill. Give me blood and vengeance."

"Woah there! Shit, how did that encounter end?"

"Killed them all. Slaughtered them like animals. Made them pay for what they did to my siblings and mother."

"It's over. It's over, that was the past, this is now. Calm yourself and regain control." She panted and collapsed in tears. She curled up in the fetal position crying.

Tam-Tam stroked her hair, trying her best to comfort her.

Jason carried Beatrix away from the now-destroyed grove. Her tears had dried now she was shaking from adrenaline withdrawal.

Jason looked at Tam-Tam. "How did you survive?"

Tam-Tam grinned sheepishly, "Elena found me covered in spunk, clinging to what little money I had gotten. She brought me to her home and cleaned me up. She taught me how to defend myself and then taught me how to be a sniper. I owe her my life and intend to repay my debt to her somehow. What about you two?"

Leslie looked up at the night sky. "Bounty Hunter 13 found us. He had apparently been hunting down the slavers that had taken his brother. And sowed a path of destruction against all slavers in his wake. When the slavers refused to sell us to him, he slaughtered them all. He showed no mercy even when one of the younger ones lay there begging for his life. It was kind of hot to witness. I have never left Jason's side since then. I keep him out of trouble and he keeps me safe. From others and myself."

"Enough of the past, we are here. Ladies, this is the Temple of God Red, now infested with Magus and Chaos worshipers. We need a plan."

The temple was a red stone stepped pyramid-like structure. It was covered in rubies and runes that kept it protected. Thunder shook the sky as a wild storm struck.

Tam Tam jumped up a tree and took up a sniper position. "We have twelve guards and I think I see Vinyl. She looks different, though. I think we arrived too late to save her."

Jason shook his head. "Beatrix, can you try to cause a distraction? I need Buccaneer and Jay distracted while Leslie and I sneak in. Tam-Tam, think you can kill the guards silently?"

"I have no bullets. They all fell out when that plant used me. I do have a box of sleeping darts, however. I just need to get through the armour."

"Aim for their neck seam. It should be the best way to get the dart into the skin. None of our armour is airtight unless we are off-world, where we do not allow our skin to be seen ever."

As Beatrix walked out, she watched the guards all fall to the ground. "I challenge Jay Red and Buccaneer Red to a duel. Unless they are cowards."

The two warriors walked out. The voluptuous Jay sneered, "You could not even handle me. What makes you think you can handle the two of us."

Beatrix pulled out a serrated blade. "I'm armed now. I was caught unaware by you, but now we are on an even footing."

Jay vanished and began her pummeling whirlwind attack. Beatrix became dizzy trying to defend herself and stumbled back right as lightning hit the ground. It ignited Jay even though there was rain. Jay screamed and began thrashing, trying to tear her clothes off. They were too slick; she was sobbing now. Beatrix knelt down and summoned a geyser of water that put the flames out. She was then slammed into by Buccaneer. The two went careening into a tree that splintered under the force of the hit. Buccaneer began to viciously beat Beatrix until she was a bloody mangled mess. Beatrix passed out.

Jason stood as a woman in a red fishnet body stocking walked down from the temple. Buccaneer walked over to her and bowed before tossing the mangled form of Beatrix at Jason's feet. The woman stroked Buccaneer's face and then shooed him away. He collected the smouldering form of Jay and walked back into the temple.

She spoke in a silky voice, "Ooo, the great paladin of that little bitch, Red, comes to challenge me, but I have no time for you. Darkspeed, please eliminate the rebels."

A woman wearing nothing but leather boots appeared with a dark giggle and threw Tam Tam into Leslie, who was knocked off his feet. Her large penis and breasts jiggled as she rushed Jason. It soon became erect from the adrenalin. She grinned a fanged smile. Jason deftly dodged her. He snorted as she rushed him again. This time he struck her from behind. He grappled her and grabbed her penis from behind. He pulled and she cried out, "Move any more and I'll rip your dick off. Understand?"

She whimpered and nodded. Tam Tam climbed off of Leslie and placed her gun again

Darkspeed's balls. Jason let go. He walked towards the temple. Crimson fire and maroon smoke soon engulfed the complex. There was an unnatural howl that echoed through the air. The flames and smoke vanished. Two men in deep red armour walked over and grabbed Darkspeed. They took her into the temple complex. Two more carried Beatrix in on a stretcher. Leslie hefted Tam Tam up and walked in. Jason stood there in prayer to God Red. Goddess Crimson's statue was on the ground as if it had been knocked over, which was impossible unless the Goddess had lost her powers.

Beatrix awoke in a white room with Vinyl standing over her. Vinyl grinned a sinister smile.

"Darkspeed, step back from my patient, please."

Vinyl frowned and stepped back, revealing Jason, who looked shocked. Beatrix noticed Jay in some kind of healing tank. The burns on her body looked to be healing.

"How in the nine hells did you fully heal after two days? You were a mess. Three-fourths of your bones were shattered, including three ribs that had punctured your lungs. One of your horns was unsavable and we fitted you with a prosthetic horn."

"Does it matter?"

"No, I guess not. Anyway, while you were out, the Magus were forced to flee when I caused Goddess Scarlet to submit to God Red. I was able to free my people from whatever mind control they were under. Unfortunately, Vinyl was broken to Scarlet's will. She is now called Darkspeed."

"I was not broken. I am a manifestation of Vinyl's will that protects her from harm. I am the persona she takes on when she performs at raves. I was formed from her abuse at the hands of her family for being born different."

"I see. So you were just playing the part of thrall."

"Heh, um... no... that was... not an act. She actually had me as her prisoner. I apologize for my actions."

As those two talked, Beatrix slipped out and entered a cafeteria. She saw Leslie talking to three girls. One was tall, voluptuous, and blond. The other was a brunette in punk-style clothing, and the last was a young girl holding a book of spells with midnight purple and black hair.

"Alas, you're awake. Come meet my half-sisters on my father's side."

Beatrix sat down and the blond spoke, "I saw the tail end of your fight. Kinda surprised you are fully healed from that berserk beating you received. Regardless, I am Alina Torque. My little sister is Aluna Torque and my dark sister is Aluci Torque. Sorry, we got here so late. We ran into some Magus that tried to capture us."

Jason walked out and smiled, "Good news Beatrix. I did manage to get you a ship off the planet. I see you have already met the pilot. Good luck. I suspect Bounty will want to rendezvous with you at Mellon."

A large brutish man with muscles and gold eyes watched from the far end of the dining hall. He frowned into his drink and combed back his neon-red hair. *This will be an interesting challenge. He is strong, but I am stronger.*

The Gold Warrior and His Fate

About five hours from when Argentorado was dropped off at Red, Stinger One was over the Jungle planet of Gold.

Bounty, Tallon, and Bat dropped, "Have the autopilot pick Tallon and I up as soon as you are done with Dropping Scarr on Lizard and Death Knight at Casualty Station."

"Will do, Boss. Be careful. You're going to be a father soon."

"Yes, I know. I already promised Feldspar I would survive."

Bounty reappeared on a floating dock that was hovering above the Gold forest. Bat looked around and saw a little calico-furred fox girl with wings.

She ran to him, "Uncle Wing, you're back. Woah, I knew aliens existed, but I thought they were little and green."

"Rusty, where's your mother?"

The girl pointed out across the forest where a group of dragon-winged humanoids were facing off against numerous rocket-packed Magus.

"I see the Magus got smart."

"Yeah, they're led by some chick calling herself Arch Magus Ching. She is a master of Technomancy. At least that's what mom yelled over the intercom."

"Ah, that's why there are so many of our kind over there. Bounty, are you ready to go?"

"Tallon, get on my back. I will show you how to avoid the forest."

"Why?"

"Planet Gold hates when sapient beings touch her sacred soil. She will sick the forest on them. The only reason Bat and his people survived so long is because they built these flying Aeries."

Bounty lifted off the landing platform and shot off towards the battle. Tallon clung tightly to Bounty's shoulder spikes. Bat Wing caught up quickly and opened fire on the Magus with his canon.

Bounty handed Tallon off to Bat. "Here, hold her. I will finish this off. Pull the soldiers back to Aerie Twelve. Also, activate force fields over the forest."

The Magus converged on Bounty with Lady Ching mocking him, "You are a fool to stand against my might. Who do you think you are?"

Bounty drew two swords and flew forward, bisecting three Magus and incinerating them before they hit the forcefield. He then spun and drew the Magus into his blades by using wind. As the wind became a tornado, he spun with the vortex. There were screams of terror as the vortex became bloody. Then the fire started and the bloody vortex became an inferno. Lady Ching cried out as her arm was vaporized and her rocket pack shorted out, causing her clothes to catch fire. As she plummeted towards the forest, the forcefield shorted out and Bounty grabbed her by the rocket pack and caused a rain storm to put her out. He placed her on the platform to Aerie Twelve.

He saw the shocked expressions on the faces of Bat Wing's clan. He dusted himself off and picked up Tallon. He noticed the warriors pull out their guns as he was quickly teleported out along with Lady Ching and Tallon.

"I think you pissed them off, Boss."

"As long as Bat doesn't try to defend me, he should be fine. I hope."

On the Aerie, Bat stood surrounded by his family. They had him pinned to the floor by heavy ropes.

"You brought a demon to our sacred land, therefore, you must pay."

"I did not realize he was a Demon. He deceived me. I was tricked."

"You know the rules, Brother. Regardless of your innocence, your wings are to be severed and you are to be thrown into the forest."

"Very well, I revoke my name of Wing. Mark me a traitor."

Rusty cried out, "You can't do that. He has been off the planet for years. Has he not earned a bit of leeway? That rule was made three years ago when the Magus Razorwing summoned a demon to destroy us. He was stripped of his life."

"Rusty, do not soil your good name by defending me. Rules are rules no matter what."

Rusty watched as her mother took a large blade and heated it up. She swung and Bat's wings were sliced from his back in one fluid motion. She then took a large flat piece of metal and welded it to the stumps so they could not regrow.

"Consider yourself warned, Brother. If you disobey our rules, the forest will have you as a feast. You are hereby banished from all Aeries. Leave before I change my mind."

"Mother, can I at least help him to the mountains."

Bat smiled a sad smile and snapped the ropes and backflipped off the platform. No one had noticed him grab a chain and axe head. Rusty cried out and looked over the edge to see if she could see him. She started crying. Her mother looked away and walked off, followed by the rest of the clan. Rusty tied her wings to her back and jumped. Bat saw her plummeting form pulled his axe from the beast he had slain, jumped and caught her.

"Damn fool of a girl, what'd you do that for?"

"I need you, Uncle. I can't lose you as well."

Rusty's mother had witnessed her daughter's suicide and grimaced. She lay her head down on her bed and wept. In the shadows of the aerie, two blue eyes glowed with malevolence. They blinked then a shadowy winged wolf slid over the side and into the darkness of the forest below.

The Hunter

Bounty looked over the toxic atmosphere of Metallic. "I have to do this alone. Tallon, stay up here. You are not equipped to handle the toxic gas of Metallic."

He teleported to the ground and felt his third set of lungs, the space lungs, kick in to begin filtering the atmosphere into breathable air for him.

A mechanical voice spoke, "I figured we would encounter you here, Brother. Your friend Metalicon lies dead. We killed him."

"Hello, Vera. Hello Aerick-Starr. What do I owe the pleasure of this encounter."

"Silence, fiend. You will not win against us. Why are you hunting down the Magus?"

"You are a threat to the Star Vale."

Aerick-Starr's bass-augmented voice spoke, "How do you know our plans?"

"They're the same plans the first Magus War was waged to prevent. Seriously, does Grand Emperor Magus Belphegor not know the history of the Magus."

"It's not Belphegor anymore. She calls herself Psycho Phantom."

"Figures. Anyway, why are you two in Mandelic Armour?"

"Don't pretend you care, Bonty."

"Very well, stop me if I am wrong. Your lungs were scorched when you attempted to defend Belphegor from Psycho Phantom. She wiped the floor with you and the elite guard. You were the only two to survive. Hence your exile here. So my head will be your ticket back into her good graces."

Vera charged him and sliced at him with her serrated sword. He heard a revving as Aerick-Starr activated his chain sword. He smashed into Vera and she was knocked unconscious. Aerick-Starr roared in anger and slashed at him multiple times. He fell with a chain sword through his chest as Metalicon struggled to his feet.

"Bout damn time you show up. I almost bled out."

"Well, you're healed now. Thanks for the assist."

As Metalicon was teleported to the ship, Bounty lit a fire that exploded due to the gas in the air. It vaporized Aerick-Starr and Vera. Bounty quickly put it out before it could spread. He winced and spoke "Thayme Sidrodc uigde het seul. Thayme havens sunocme het seul." Downing the amber liquid conjured during the prayer, he teleported out.

As he arrived on his ship, Metalicon spoke, "Sorry about killing your brother. I am sure you wanted to spare him."

"I am not too worried. Stay still. I don't want you to scorch your lungs from my atmosphere."

"You seem awfully unconcerned that he is dead."

"I may have ended up killing him any way he wanted my head as a trophy."

Bounty helped him to a healing stasis chamber. He put a bubble around them and the atmosphere changed to be something that Metalicon could breathe. Bounty helped him out of his suit and lay the frail, pale metallic green body in the healing tube. He wiped up some of the yellow blood and set the healing to two months. He looked over the power armour and sighed. It was severely damaged. He put it on his list of things to do. His ship was soon at Stinalta. He walked over to the large tank and pressed a button.

"We are here, Sting. Are you ready to be sent home?"

"I am very eager to see how things have changed. Will we be hunting for those Magus?"

"Let's get you home first, then we can decide what to do from there."

Bounty hefted Sting into a smaller drop jet, then took the pilot's chair. As the two entered Stinalta bounty, saw many small Islands that were uninhabited. Each Island marked a school of Stinaltans. They splashed down near some wreckage. Bounty sent the smaller ship back and sank into the water. Due to how heavy he was, he sank fast before summoning runes that made him more buoyant. His water lungs began filtering water so he could breathe.

Sting looked around. "Looks like we missed the fun. I see the Magus stronghold still stands. Let us head out then. Come demon, let me show you how we do things down under."

Bounty followed and the two soon came upon the Magus stronghold. It was under attack by many different aquatic beings. He saw Thulhuids, Shark men, Merpeople, a massive whale-like being, and numerous smaller fish people. He even noticed a strange amalgamation of technology and biology. The hammerhead shark beings had jet engines attached to their skulls and large blades on their arms. The Magus were outmatched but were intent on holding their fortress despite how many casualties there were.

A feminine Ray girl shot over to them and embraced Sting. She spoke, "Father, we have been trying to destroy a wall, so we have access to their facility to wipe them out. Now that the siege breaker is here, can you lead the attack?"

Sting smiled, "All forces converge on Whalgolith. Defend him while we shatter the walls of these abominations."

All the forces formed around the giant whale-like being. Bounty noticed Whalgolith had a strange formation of metal on its head. The metal glowed with many runes and Whalgolith slammed into one of the walls that had cracks on it. It shattered, allowing the water to rush in and drown many Magus. Unfortunately, the doors were sealed off, preventing more loss of life. As Whalgolith charged up for another run, the Magus in their diving suits began throwing lightning. Several smaller fish people were fried instantly. Bounty drew his two blades and began to slaughter the bolt throwers. By the time he was done, another wall was destroyed.

Inside the facility, several Magus were finishing loading their escape ship. The leader looked at all the work they had completed but could not save and spoke, "Withdraw all surviving forces and lure the enemy into the facility. I will stay behind and take as many enemies with me as I can."

Outside, the aquatic warriors cheered as the Magus withdrew. They were about to charge when Sting held up his hand to stop them. "All forces, we have won this battle. Do not be foolish enough to charge a retreating enemy that has obviously withdrawn to lure us like common fish. General Octabull, what is the scrying saying?"

A large muscular green and yellow Thulhuid spoke, "There are self-destruct runes enabled."

"Then we have victory. All forces we are free. Go home and celebrate our victory here today."

The aquatic forces split, leaving Bounty and Sting behind. "Stay out here, Sting. I will finish this off."

"Don't be a fool, Bounty. They will kill you."

"Don't you worry about me! I have a plan."

Sting shook his head and swam off. Bounty entered the facility and immediately downloaded all the data the facility had to offer. He entered the main lab and saw a scaled woman waiting for him. He looked around at all the test tubes and shook his head. He typed in a command and his ship teleported all the experiments out. The woman looked shocked and then snarled. That was when the stronghold exploded. Bounty stood there floating in the water across from him. The female was unconscious. A psychic bubble vanished and Bounty went back to breathing water while he teleported the female to the med bay of his ship. She was put into stasis. Tallon looked at Bounty curiously as he reappeared on the command deck. Dripping with water.

"Are you prepared, girl? We are heading to Mellon."

In The Forest Of Lizard, Treachery Is a Foot

Grim, Scarr-ed, Vinyl, Gilda, and Buttercup appeared in a swamp and Gilda immediately became aware. They looked around and heard a sloshing sound. They looked around and saw some robed figures with guns running through the swamp. They got over to dryer land. They stood in the shadows of a massive fern. The soldiers marched past them and suddenly, they were attacked by nine huge alligator men with tree trunk thick legs and near-impenetrable scales. Their heads looked like logs and their eyes were crimson. They had foot-long claws that dripped with the swamp. The gator's men mercilessly slaughtered the Magus. They then began rolling in the gore, gurgling sickening laughter. It sounded like a laugh but one that was mixed with gravel and ash. It was so guttural it sent shivers down Gilda's spikes. She saw a green-scaled lizard man walk out of the nearby cave and sit down, just smirking as his comrades played in the blood. The alligator men then noticed her crew. They charged forward, causing them to scatter.

Grimm Chaosforge stood looking around for his allies. They had gotten separated when they had been attacked by Gatormen. Scarr was next to him with his sword drawn. There were Magus surrounding them. That was when Gilda burst through the jungle and sliced through several of the Magus. Buttercup was flying behind her and began to speed around, beating the Magus up. They saw a feathered Raptorian girl perched on the tree, her blue-black feathers glinted in the setting sun.

Scarr hissed, "Raven Deathcrow, why have you allied with the Magus?"

"I am no longer Raven of clan Deathcrow. You may refer to me by my Magus name of Blue."

"Ha! As if. No, I will continue to refer to you as Raven."

As the last of the Magus were slain, Scarr led Grim, Buttercup, and Gilda in chasing Raven down. They arrived at a cave entrance and Gilda hung back.

"Why are you stopping Gilda?"

"Buttercup, Something doesn't smell right."

Grim had overheard and nodded. The three entered the cave. Grimm and Gilda both activated their Inferno vision to see in the dark.

"Of course, It's a trap."

Light flared, nearly blinding both Gilda and Grimm; they were surrounded by many Magus.

That was when Scarr walked over to them. He kicked them to the ground and his body changed into that of a green-skinned male with numerous scars jutting across his torso like lightning.

"Too easy. Blindly following me in here. Oh, before you ask, I know all of Bounty Hunter 13's plans and have passed them to Psycho Phantom. Your little revolution was finished the moment Pain let me aboard your ship."

He stopped talking and wheezed as he saw a large jagged blade sticking from his sternum. Gilda walked past his falling corpse and grinned. She began assaulting the remaining Magus as Buttercup finished helping Grimm up. He quickly shielded her as a Magus threw a fireball in her direction. He grunted as his body caught on fire.

"Girls grab the Magus known as Blue. I will end this."

Gilda looked at his burning form and nodded. She grabbed Buttercup and Blue and fled as the cave suddenly became a volcano. The Chaos energy swirled around the new volcano in a violent fashion that could be seen from miles away. The Chaos then spread its tendrils and began engulfing numerous Magus strongholds. Blue watched in slack-jawed horror as the cataclysm continued. It continued for days. By the time it ended, Gilda had found where the Magus had imprisoned the people of Lizard.

The real Scarr looked her over and snorted. "Sorry for your loss. But you had best leave the planet. Your dead friend has caused us untold amounts of trouble. Usually, this would call for execution. However, you can't execute a dead man. And I will be lenient since you did help destroy the Magus. But please leave our planet."

"Uhm, the slight difficulty there. We were dropped off and our ship left."

"Well, in that case. Use one of the Magus' ships. Oh, you can leave Blue here for punishment."

Buttercup nodded and was picked up by Gilda as the two went ship searching. They found a small interplanetary burster fully fueled and they left Lizard. Gilda set a course for Mellon, hoping the fuel would last. She felt something touching her nethers and saw Buttercup trying to feel her up. She smiled and gently stripped the heavily aroused Big Head. She allowed her access and Buttercup eagerly went at it, fully consumed by her lust.

Raid on Grey: Who Is Slayer Hammer?

Pain landed the ship on Planet Gray at the hub, which was Planet Gray's main spaceport.

"Azdul, please keep an eye on the ship while Luke and I investigate Grey. The bronze-skinned man smirked and leaned back in his chair. "Sure thing."

Right away, she could see Magus foot soldiers guarding the hub. It was still open to the public, but all were carefully examined and scanned for hidden weapons.

Deathknight spoke, "This looks fun. Wonder why they're being so benevolent."

A young woman with raven black hair, pale skin, and large breasts walked over to them. She looked them over and handed Deathknight a card. He looked at it and nodded.

"Well, girls, it looks like we are going to a bar."

They entered the bar called Nox Inferno and ordered some drinks. The busty woman sat down across from Deathknight. He saw several patrons get up and leave. Leaving behind a small group of heavily armed miscreants. One of the miscreants was a man from planet Brown. His brown skin rippled with muscle as he picked up a large keg in one hand and drained it. He crushed it against his skull as the miscreants cheered.

The raven-haired girl spoke, "Barlotet, stop showing off. I hired some Mercenaries to help us. Introduce the plan and what's going on."

Barlotet smirked and spoke in a heavy accent, "Well, well, well, more mercenaries. I have already recruited the former RAVAGER to our cause. Clowd Windsong. Who are these?"

Deathknight smiled, "I am Deathknight. This is Pain. We are from the Alliance of Allied Planets. We were told there were Magus here, but as far as I can tell, they are not cruel or violent like all other Magus."

The girl smirked, "They are being nice because they're afraid of ZinnRa, a global conglomerate that has been sucking our planet's life force to create power. Many have already suffered because of it. The Magus are just cashing in. I am Tanya and you three will be working with us. Over there is Jessie, James, Bob, and Will. They are some of our founding members. I hired you and, to a greater extent, Clowd to help us. We are known as Earthquake the, according to ZinnRa, the terrorist group."

Bartolet spoke, "Like Tanya said ZinnRa is sucking our planet dry. We are going to raid their main factory. Sector 5G is the one closest to us. We will infiltrate there and blow it up, followed by 6G. Any questions?"

The small group shook their heads no. Deathknight lit a cigar and placed it to his lips. He inhaled the toxic fumes and blew out red smoke. Elena looked him over and saw concern in Pain's red eyes. Guri 123 sat writing things down. The next evening arrived and Earthquake snuck onto a train that was heading towards sector 5G. They arrived at the power plant and quickly killed the guards. Clowd and Bartolet went to the reactor level. Within two minutes, they came running back out.

Bartolet yelled, "Get moving. She's about to blow."

Elena spoke, "What the hell is that thing?"

The small force turned to see a massive mecha wasp descend from the sky. It began firing lasers from its stinger. The reactor exploded, but the mecha was unharmed. Clowd jumped into the air, his blade took on six sizes and he sliced down, causing the mecha to split in half and explode. His blade returned to normal as he landed. He turned and walked off.

Deathknight watched him as Pain spoke, "We are not needed here. They have everything under control. We should leave. I don't like the vibe that Clowd gives off. He's too dangerous."

"We have a job to do after G6 falls, we can leave."

"Alright, but you promise, right?"

"Yes, I promise we will leave and charter a ship to Black."

The next day was the same as the first. They boarded a train to get to the sector 6G power plant. Clowd and Bartolet went in along with Tanya. It took far longer for them to leave. There was no explosion this time. Instead, there was shouting and an army of Zinn-Ra guards appeared. They opened fire on the small group. Guri was hit in the shoulder and flung by the impact. Elena caught her and mended the wound to the best of her ability. She saw Jessie fall with numerous bullet holes. Her empty eyes stared off into the sky. Elena rushed her and quickly felt for a pulse. Then Jessie vanished and she felt a warm presence. She could have sworn she saw a man in a horned badger mask pick Jessie up, but she didn't have time for that. A grenade landed near her. She rolled away as it exploded. She saw Bigus and Will fall next due to another grenade throw. A large war mech descended from the sky. It sprouted its legs and crunched the pavement under its feet. Two large Gatling lasers extended from the side and opened fire. James leapt up the war mech and pulled the pilot out, tossing him to the ground. He marched the mech towards the reactor core as it was being fired upon by the Zinn-Ra guards. Bartolet, Clowd, and Tanya were struggling against a large tank-like mech. James opened fire and pushed the two mechs towards the core. Bartolet grabbed Tanya and rushed off while Clowd followed close behind. The two tanks exploded, sending Clowd plummeting towards the lower level, with Tanya crying out for him. The two arrived as Deathknight jumped into the air and spun around, firing on the guards and finishing them off.

He landed hard and Pain supported him. She was covered in blood, not her own. He turned and snarled, "I hope it was worth the death of your close allies. Regardless, my crew is done here. Keep the money you owe us. Goodbye"

Elena scooped up Guri and followed after bisecting a boulder with her blade in rage. Her fiery eyes focused on the dead. "Give your proper dead burial. Sorry, we couldn't help you more."

Raid on Black: Purple Fire of the Blackheart

Deathknight, Elena, The Taur, and Pain arrived at Casualty Station, which circled around Planet Black. Guri 123 was resting in a cryogenic pod in the med sector. The Taur had promised her she would keep track of what happened on Black. Elena stared out the view pane waiting for the shuttle to take them to Black. There was a large storm roiling over Black as the shuttle departed. When the shuttle landed, Pain stayed back tentatively.

Deathknight smiled warmly, "It's alright, Pain. The lightning won't touch you as long as you stay by my side."

"I'm scared. I don't like the feel of this land."

"I know. It takes some getting used to."

A voice spoke up, "Luke Darkfaith, what the hell are you doing down here?" Deathknight turned after grabbing Pain by the hand and leading her off the ship.

Before him stood an imposing black armoured figure. With two large horns on his head curving down. His shoulder spikes glistened purple in the glow of Black. Jagged purple lightning shattered the sky, followed by an explosion of thunder. Pain jumped and whimpered, falling to the ground in a fetal position. Deathknight sat down next to her and wrapped his arm around her comfortingly. She curled into him.

He looked at the armoured man and spoke, "Lord Blackheart, what a pleasant surprise. I heard you died."

"I did. I am currently inhabiting this armour until my mission is complete."

"And what pray tell is your mission?"

"To pass on this message and to protect Planet Black."

"What message?"

"Purple fire graces the horizon. Dark beings emerge. A blasphemy against science and mystic energies. Beware your mirror.."

Purple lightning scorched the sky again and Blackheart vanished. Deathknight sighed. He looked to the horizon and saw a purple wildfire. He shook his head and walked towards it. Elena easily lifted Pain up and carried her with them. The Taur followed close behind, looking around for any danger. They arrived to see a very large complex burning brightly in the dark gloom of

Black. Deathknight huffed and sat down, watching the fire burn. Then a deluge of rain hit them. The fire was immediately snuffed out. The skeletal remains of the complex glowed with the lightning. Deathknight walked into the rubble and saw gore everywhere.

There were heads missing their bodies, legs missing their torsos, arms missing their torsos, and standing before him was a man as large as Bounty Hunter 13. He wielded an axe that hummed with dark energy. He almost looked exactly like Bounty Hunter 13 except that his body was not burned, nor were his horns curved up. The horns were curved down and his shoulders were covered in a shell-like structure. He still had shoulder spikes, but they were jagged instead of smooth. He looked up at Deathknight. His glowing red eyes twinkled with bloodlust.

"Luke Darkfaith. You are unworthy to face me. Where is my donor?"

"Who is your donor?"

"Bounty Hunter 13. Ah, I see he is on Mellone. Come forth, Reaver. The Darkfaith has arrived. Die well, Luke, goodbye."

The creature vanished. A muscular, pale-skinned man walked out of the shadows. He wore ragged armour and wielded two pistols.

He rasped, "My donor appears. I will enjoy drinking your blood."

Deathknight smirked, "Let's see what you got. Elena and Mr. Bull, get as much information as you can from the computer. I will handle ash face here."

Elena, still carrying Pain, hurried off further into the ruins. She came upon a large room with many shattered test tubes. On the floor lay a woman wearing a lab coat. She was breathing but not well. Elena teleported her to Casualty Station. She gave orders to keep her confined until she could check up on her. The Taur began downloading all the data on the computer while wiping it in the process. Pain was stable now and guarding their backs. Deathknight limped in, holding his palm to his eye. He was bloody from several bullet wounds.

Pain looked worried Deathknight grinned, "You should see the other guy. Never duel a Deathknight by yourself."

Pain rushed him and hugged him. "You idiot, don't scare me like that."

"Oh, Pain, you know it'll take more than a few bullets to take me down. The Magus thought to clone me, but you cannot clone training. That's why he's dead and I am living."

Elena spoke, "So the readouts don't lie. The Magus cloned Bounty Hunter 13, Argentorado, some guy named Talicon, and you."

The wall hissed open, revealing an intact test tube. Inside this tube was a fetus. The three stared at the fetus.

Deathknight spoke into his comm, "This is Luke Darkfaith Deathknight of sector Nine. Calling the Science sector."

"This is Science sector Doctor Amil Felca speaking. How may I assist you, Deathknight of sector Nine?"

"I need a medevac. Also, need to bring an unborn fetus in a test tube up intact."

"Doable one moment."

The test tube vanished. Deathknight soon followed along with Elena, the Bull, and Pain.

The Demon vs the Phantom

Bounty Hunter 13 docked at Golgotha. Two Magus walked out to greet him. One was a neon blue woman with electric blue hair dressed only in a fishnet catsuit. The other is a red-haired woman with a green tube top and jeans.

"I am Argon the Slayer. This is my apprentice, Fang. I received word you were searching for a new Baron."

The blue girl smiled, "Welcome, Argon the Slayer. I am Ember Hawthorn and this is Vicki Huntari. We wish to welcome you to Golgotha. You are lucky in that the new Overlord wishes to test you herself. Follow, please."

Bounty Hunter 13 followed after giving Tallon instructions to meet up with Gilda and the others when they arrived. He also instructed her to take the ship out of the docking bay. He followed the two to the throne room. He saw Psycho Phantom sitting there in her serpent armour. He could feel the soul of Paradox Storm crying out in rage. He could also feel the shadows that possessed Paradox. He looked at Psycho Phantom, who was picking at her fingernails.

She looked up and grinned a grin that sent chills down Bounty's back. "Hello, Bounty Hunter 13. I've been waiting for you to show up. Girls scramble the fighter ships and purge his allies."

The two bowed and vanished. Psycho Phantom pulled out a blood-red blade. She grinned maniacally. Bounty pulled out his halberd. He blocked her attack and the two clashed. Out in space, Gilda avoided several blasts from the enemy ships. Her jump ship was running on fumes. She gulped and dive-bombed the citadel. She ejected with Buttercup and clutched the little Bighead tight as she plummeted towards the ground. She was caught by the mystery woman in orange leather armour and pulled into a large ship shaped like a sword. Beatrix set Gilda and Buttercup in the infirmary.

Beatrix spoke, "Alina, how are the defences holding?"

"Not good the smaller fighters are too much and too many."

"Teleport me to Golgotha and then get out of here. Get to Casualty Station. That's where we'd meet up with Deathknight."

"Alright. Good luck."

Beatrix appeared outside the throne room as Bounty was thrown through the wall next to her.

He stood up and dusted himself off before leaping over the rubble and continuing his attack. She saw two swords flashing instead of his halberd. Beatrix joined in and found she was outmatched by the Magus leader. As the leader's red blade severed through her sword, the wall exploded inwards as Gilda's jump ship smashed through, impacting the Magus leader. She snarled in rage and threw the small ship at Beatrix. Beatrix yelped. The ship crushed her into the wall and she blacked out. Bounty Hunter 13 took this time to stab Psycho Phantom in the back. She cried out as the energy blade severed the shadows from her. The shadowy woman snarled and lunged at Bounty, who pulled out a cane.

"No! How did you come to own the Cane of Shadows?"

"Your previous host Zenthin Ankara had it on him when I killed him. I took it so as to keep it out of the hands of those that would misuse it. Now return to the darkness."

The shadows roared and vanished. Paradox lay on the ground, placing pressure against her wound. She stared in shock as Bounty walked over to her. He sheathed his blades and they vanished. He knelt down to heal her wound.

"Piss off, demon. I don't need a man to help me."

"You know what, Paradox. I give up. I'm trying to be nice to you and all I ever did was help you and your army only to get shit. The only one who cared about me was Maungirtha. So go ahead and die."

He walked away and Paradox whimpered. Bounty extracted Beatrix from the wall.

"Wait! I'm scared of death. Please, I'll let you heal me."

Bounty looked over at her, shook his head, then snapped his fingers. "There you're healed. Get out of my sight."

"I need a lift off the planet."

"Fine, I'll drop you off at Casualty Station. Tallon, please bring the ship back and get the med bay prepped."

"Hang on, boss. Gotta get past the hawk class bolter ships first."

The ship landed and Bounty carried the two into the ship and it lifted off, shooting off towards Casualty Station. Bounty saw the two Magus who tricked him into sleeping in healing pods and smirked. They soon arrived at Casualty Station. Elena met up with them. Deathknight walked in, supported by the Taur, with bandages on his torso.

Elena spoke, "You are supposed to be in bed resting. Why are you here?"

Bounty smirked, "What happened to you, Luke?"

"I got injured facing my clone."

Elena sighed, "Men and their stupid pride. Anyways I am surprised your clone didn't show up. He vanished as soon as he saw us calling us unworthy. Before you ask, here's all the information I could collect."

Bounty looked it over. "I see. So not only will I have to contend with Clowd Windsong but also my clone. Beautiful. Regardless we had best collect the others. It's time to go home."

The ship flew off towards Casualty Station. He studied the tube that Ember was in. He raised his eyebrow and shook his head. There is something off about you. But I can't figure out what it is. How annoying! Your skin and hair are way too neon. Ah well, I can study with you later. Now to let Paradox Storm decide her own fate. At least she isn't trying to kill me anymore. Ugh, should have had some extra hands. Too many got injured. I also need to do better. How did I not discern Scarr was a fake?

They arrived at Casualty Station and disembarked only to be greeted by a tall, lean muscled tannish red-skinned man. Behind that man was a large boxy robot with a gear on his back and a bronze-skinned man with a mask over his mouth and a large double voulge with chainsaws on each end.

The tannish red-skinned man spoke, "Sorry, I was having a hell of a time trying to get your message. I assume the war is over?"

"Yes and no. But I am glad to see you Swift-Fang-Coyote of the Onyx Ursa tribe. I see that Rob O'Techno 100 and Berylin Wraithbone are with you as well."

"Yeah, funnily enough, I had to pick them up. They responded to your call, but nobody ever arrived. Almost as if they were forgotten."

Bounty looked down at his readout. "Oh look, nine missed messages. Sorry guys, I dropped the ball on that one."

Swift Fang chuckled. "Oh, kimosabe, you never cease to inspire awe. In this case, I am in awe of your stupidity."

"Yeah yeah, laugh it up. I am in need of a good failure every now and then, but this one had too many failures added up. My head was elsewhere."

"Well, my friend, you are in luck. With the Magus Empire crushed, we will be at peace for some time. How about we all get a drink? I will tell you how we eliminated the Magus on our planets."

"I would like that. A good war story always invigorates the blood."

What Is a Hero

Many years after the Magus war, Bounty Hunter 13 sat meditating in a secluded pond filled the glade. He discovered this place many years ago during the Silveran Civil War. He sat on the onyx boulder, deep in meditation. The Magic Melody of the Universe enveloped him. He felt the tune shift, becoming darker and more invigorating. The glade was medium-sized with a pebble-bottomed pond. In the far corner, he had erected a statue of God Silver along with a small Hunter family altar. The spike trees had closed in closer to the glade thanks to a recent Firebug mating season.

He was deep in meditation when he felt something snuffling against his crotch. He looked down to see a Kitsune licking her lips and nuzzling him.

The statue of God Silver he had erected spoke, "Bonty, I would like for you to impregnate her."

"Why?"

"I have plans for the future of my people. Many of the Silveran species have died out or moved off-world to New Silver and Silver Two. She is in heat. Obey your God, please."

"Very well, God Silver, but you owe me greatly for this."

"Yes, yes, I'll put it on the list of things I owe myself for."

"You know I get no pleasure from this."

"I do. Which is why I am asking you to fuck her, silly. It's just business."

Bounty commanded his Nanites to harden his penis as he undid his pants. He saw the little Kitsune's eyes widen in shock. She began whimpering and trying to flee.

"See, Silver, she doesn't want to. I will not force her."

His necklace glowed and a small Succubus emerged from it. She quickly dove into the Kitsune and took over. Inside the Kitsune's mind, the Succubus scratched behind the Kitsune's ears. Smiling gently and relaxing the small mental projection of her mind. Outside was different, however, the Kitsune was writhing with ecstasy as she was impaled on Bounty's penis. She was panting and letting out small gasps and moans. Her eyes rolled back as her womb was filled with the seed of the next generation. Bounty pulled out and immediately, the Succubus shot from the Kitsune and wrapped her lips around his shaft as he finished ejaculating.

He watched as the Kitsune vanished. He shook his head disapprovingly. He then sighed and patted the succubus' head. She cooed happily and snuggled against him before going back into her gem. He went back to meditation. There was a light stirring in the trees and a female Felis walked out.

She cooed, "Ooo, Bounty Hunter 13. You will make a great mate. Please use me."

Bounty sighed and motioned the Felis to sit on his lap. He penetrated her drawing a small amount of blood into his testes. His semen shifted into Felis compatible semen. She was climaxing right as he ejaculated into her womb. Here a small change took place. She would give birth to three Canis boys and two Felis girls. Thus paving the way for God Silver's Nu Silverans. When Felis was done, she fell asleep and Bounty placed her near the statue of God Silver.

He heard shouting and opened his psychic sight to the world. He saw a small, barely one-hundred-year-old girl being rushed by men wearing metal plates strapped together by leather. He wrapped the girl in his psychic aura and hid her in his cloak. The men had Hunter Corporation guns that Bounty quickly dismantled, thanks to his mechanus psy powers. It didn't hurt that he had designed and built the weapons himself. They looked confused as their guns fell apart in their hands.

Bounty spoke, "Who disturbs my slumber and why?"

One of the men snarled, "Where you hidin' that little brat? She escaped right as she was getting sold."

"I know of no little beings near me. But as it stands, I am grumpy from being woken. Goodbye, little slaver."

The three men were slain and immolated. Bounty uncovered the brown-skinned girl. He noticed she had spiked ridges on her head and frowned. She was a Brown Silveran from the south. He typed into his gauntlet for missing children. He saw Rona-Alexandra pop up as a missing Brown Silveran child. Her picture looked exactly like the girl that was cowering before him.

"Let's get you home, little one."

"Wait! Aren't you going to rape me or beat me or do other horrible things?"

"Now, why would I do that?"

"That's what they did."

"Well, I am not like them. I am going to take you home."

"Can't you do something about the rest of them?"

Bounty opened up his armour and placed her inside it. The hum of the armour made her drowsy and she fell asleep as the armour closed.

I think I will go for a walk. Bounty walked through the forest and came upon the slaver camp. It was a large stone ruin from the old days. He could see the head slaver on a computer and he also saw a large transport heading away. He pushed a button on his gauntlet and a small insect popped up and buzzed off. It attached itself to the truck and burrowed into the metal hull.

Bounty walked in with several other buyers. He had wrapped his cloak around him. The cloak made him look like a monk of sorts. The guard eyed him and shrugged, allowing him in.

Bounty looked around the auction hall and he could see all the people the slavers were selling. He frowned, then smirked evilly. As the auction began, he locked the doors. He put protective runes over the slaves and waited. A thin female was brought out. Her body had whip marks and she looked well used. No one bid on her.

Bounty spoke, "Two hundred common."

The crowd laughed and the auctioneer spoke, "Two hundred for number seven sixty-eight. Since you're the only one wanting a worn-out bitch like this, I won't even slam the gavel."

"Seethrassa thanks you but Seethrassa has other ideas."

A large wind whipped up and became sand. The moment it touched the flesh of the buyers, they petrified and dissolved into dust as well. Soon there was a raging sandstorm that broke through the fort. Within the hour, no living thing remained except the slaves and one buyer.

"Seethrassa wonders why you live. You should have died by Seethrassa's power."

The man looked at Bounty and smirked, "Lower the disguise Bonty."

"Seethrassa knows not this Bonty. Seethrassa is Seethrassa."

"We're doing this, fine. You stand before Mistic Hunter the fourth. I felt your scan earlier and tweaked it to only kill those buying the slaves for a cruel reason. I was purchasing them to free them."

"Seethrassa just saved you thousands of currency. You should be happy."

"Hmpf, seriously, asshole. Can't even acknowledge your brother."

"Seethrassa believes you should look behind you. Seethrassa sees four cameras. Seethrassa thinks that you should get the slaves out of here and bring them back to their homes. Seethrassa has some data to take care of."

Mist glanced behind and saw the cameras and growled, "I just revealed myself."

"Dammit, Mist, how stupid you are!"

Bounty downloaded all the data the slaver crew had, then deleted it. He saw their primary hub was on Misogoke. He reappeared near a small city near the water of the river Granen. The sign said the city of Devani. He walked to the police station and asked for the address of the family of the girl. He also showed the lost girl poster. They gave him the family's new address, which happened to be in the city of Grove of Angels. He would have to wait. He gently placed Rona-Alexandra in a cryotube and froze her in suspended animation. He went home and saw Feldspar nursing their child. The girl was small and premature. He smiled and wrapped his hand around her.

"She's getting bigger. What have you been feeding her?"

"All natural milk."

He kissed Feldspar on the forehead. "I have some children I need to rescue. I promise I will return and we can discuss our future."

"Take your time, love. I am going nowhere."

As he exited his home, he felt a dark presence and turned to see a large man with a metallic green beard and swirly horns.

"Ah, Corvus, you usually never come this close to the Hunter Clan Fortress," he spoke using Nevermore's voice. "Bounty, I have some grave news."

Corvus handed Bounty Hunter 13 a readout. Bounty looked it over, then frowned. "What do you mean four extra twins to us? That is impossible."

"Not according to this. Maybe you should send out your spies. To investigate further."

"I don't like having followers."

"Brother, those that worship the Shadow Lord are quite useful. I understand your reluctance to be worshipped. But they don't worship you. They worship the Shadow Lord of which you have mantled. You and he are separate beings, still. And for the time being, those that live under the shadows of day-to-day living are a utility you currently can't afford to neglect. I heard about the whole Magus Empire fiasco. Had you listened to the shadows, you would not have been caught so off guard."

"Thank you, Corvus. You have eased my mind a bit."

"But seriously, if this document doesn't lie, that means I was Father's plan B. I don't feel comfortable being you."

"I hear you. I don't feel comfortable being Father's Plan A."

***

Bounty stood on the deck of his hover ship as it soared across the ocean. He was heading towards Misogoke, a volcanic continent surrounded by rings on which the people lived. The inner two rings were closest to the currently dormant volcano. He would need to use his space lungs if the slavers were there. The volcano still spat out occasional ash clouds so that ash, smoke, and soot covered the inner two rings. The middle two were where middle-class citizens lived. It was primarily inhabited by the Silverans. The outer ring was where the wealthy lived; it was also where the docking was. Then a train would take you where you needed to go. Bounty was not looking forward to it. Misogoke has a reputation as a wild continent. Even the wealthy are considered uncivilised by the rest of the world. And that was coming from a Silveran who themselves are considered brutish, violent, and uncivilised.

It had been the witching hour when Bounty had entered the chambers of his cousin, Benyerxo Hunter 11. It had been as Bounty had feared Benyerxo was dying. He could see Benyerxo's two concubines he had from the Prism clan. The twins were worried and scared. The male twin was injecting Benyerxo with pain medication to keep him happy. The girl twin was clutching his hand and crying on his chest. Bounty weaved a spell that put them to sleep. He saw Benyerxo's eyes open.

He smiled, "I had hoped to do this while you slept so it would be a surprise come morning."

His sickly body could barely whisper, "What are you talking about, Cousin Bounty?"

Bounty placed his hand on Benyerxo and ripped psy cancer from his body and placed it into his own. His Nanites went into overdrive, attempting to destroy the cancer cells. He would be weak for some time.

"Enjoy your revived body, Cousin. You have many years ahead of you now. Use them wisely."

"Why would you shorten your lifespan to increase mine?"

"My fate has been sealed, Benyerxo. I will die fighting my clone. I do not know the hour or day when. But to give the poor bastard a fighting chance, I am weakening my body. In return, I am giving you new life. May I suggest looking into Nanomachines? They helped me repair my body. They might be able to keep you from ever having psy cancer again."

Before Benyerxo could respond, Bounty vanished with a shadowy chuckle.

Bounty snapped out of his remembrance when the boat landed with a thunk. Bounty opened his eyes and was greeted with a familiar sight. A pale-skinned female with electric blue hair dressed in clear power armour that had two large speakers for pauldrons. Because the armour was clear, he could see her naked body, including her penis was shiny with sweat. She stood there smoking a cigarette that spewed pink smoke. Her crimson eyes were hidden behind rose-coloured glasses. Her black-painted lips turned up in a smirk.

"Hey, boss, I knew you were coming."

"Hello, Vinyl, what is the honour I receive for getting a priestess of Elektranikka to meet me in person?"

"No honour, just two friends. Also, I've been eager to feel you again."

"I'm here for business, not pleasure. Though what happens, happens."

"Elektranikka said you were here to purchase children. I guess she wants me to accompany you. Probably to make sure there are no incidents."

"I guarantee nothing."

The two boarded the train. It shot off and entered inner ring two. The two got off on ring one and Vinyl put on a breather mask. The soot was heavy today and as thick as the first snowfall. The two walked until they came upon the coordinates Bounty stole from the slavers on Silver.

"This whole section needs a cleansing."

"No incidents, please, boss."

"If I give you what you want, will you look the other way?"

"I... I mean, the goddess sees all. She won't be happy. Especially if I am a part of it."

Bounty smiled a dark smile and walked up behind Vinyl. He placed his hand on her hip and she whimpered eagerly. She pushed a button and her armour retracted. Bounty took that time to enter from behind. She let out a spastic moan and arched her back eagerly. His armour enveloped her and he became a shadowy figure with white specks making him look like the night sky.

He entered into the facility after showing his invite to the guard. A slender, scarred female walked up in scrap armour. "You must be the VIP that was looking for a large purchase. I am Scorge, the leader of these mongrels. What specifically are you looking for?"

"I need children. Preferably ones that know each other. The threat of their sibling being tortured makes them work harder. Also, they are easy to manipulate."

"You, sir, are in luck. We received a family of twelve about a year ago. It didn't take long to break them. We have just been struggling to find buyers for them."

"You probably did too good of a job breaking them. Also, most buyers don't want used children. They want them fresh. The first time raping a child is their thrill. Since I am not looking for sexual conquests, just workers, they will do fine. May I see them note what state they're in so I know how to implement them?"

"Roit this way."

Bounty looked at the sad state of affairs. There were many children and women. There was one heavily scarred child that was chained up. She looked like she had tried to break free multiple times. She lunged at him only to be struck by Scorge, sending her reeling. She snarled and tried again.

Bounty caught her by the throat. "Bad dog, sit."

She whimpered and obeyed, leaving Scorge impressed. "How did you do that? That bitch never obeys so quickly."

"You have to have power behind your words. Show who the alpha is. You can beat her all you want. She smells weakness on your men. She smells hidden strength in you, but you don't act on it."

"I'm impressed. Who are you?"

"Call me Onyx. Onyx Void."

"Well, Mr Void, here are the children."

Bounty looked at the kids. He smirked and walked over to one. The boy was eyeing his sisters like a predator eyes prey. He saw one of the girls had a bulge in her pants and another smelled of sulfur. He raised his eyebrow and shook his head.

"They look awfully scrawny, but here is the promised amount. I'll also throw in a little extra for that feral girl."

"Pleasure doing business with you, Mr Void. Please remember Scorge as your go-to slave purchasing place."

"Yes, I will."

Bounty smirked and shadows enveloped the entire compound. Screams of the dying echoed around and when the shadows vanished, only Scorge remained, along with all the slaves. Bounty waved his hand and Scorge, who was unconscious, became stone and the slaves vanished. He snarled and the volcano began to erupt. He had tagged all those worthy of being saved and had evacuated them to the third ring. The fury of the molten fire and stone melted in a circle one and two. A protective barrier enveloped circles three, four and five. Then a large storm riled up, turning the area not enveloped by protection into a massive waterspout. Inside this vortex, Bounty stood smoking his cigar. When it quieted down, the volcano lay dormant yet again. Bounty appeared on ring three and released Vinyl from her orgasmic state. She collapsed to the ground panting.

"What the hell was that place?"

"That is my own private hammerspace. Think of my armour as a wearable bag of holding. Usually, those that enter are put into a sleeping stasis so as not to be affected by the sights. You only saw through a euphoric state since we were fucking."

She looked at the large space now filled with rubble and massive spikes of stone where rings one and two had been. "What happened and why are we on ring three?"

"Don't worry about it. You had nothing to do with it."

Time slowed and then stopped as a woman wearing only a neon fishnet body stocking walked over to Bounty. Her eyes glowed with ancient fury. "You fucking asshole. You killed so many of my people. I should smite you right now."

Dark laughter echoed throughout the air as a man wearing a gold and black trench coat with a red fedora walked into existence. "You need to relax, Elektranikka. He only killed those who dared to rape, imprison, and enslave children. They are mine to play with now."

"Lucifer, how dare you. Urgh, fine, I'm still pissed."

"If you want them, come on down, it's going to be a fun time."

"Maybe later. I kinda do want to see if their suffering is enough. You are off the hook, Demon of Silver, but don't do it again. I would hate having to change my allegiance because of you."

Bounty sighed, "I will not hold back on slavers and those that would harm the innocent. Even if it means alienating the Gods."

"Thanks for giving my girl what she wanted. That's all I'll say at this junction."

"You're welcome."

Time went back to normal as Bounty exhaled orange smoke. Vinyl looked at him with curiosity.

"She spoke to you, didn't she?"

"Yes, she's pleased with you."

"Oh good, I was getting worried."

"I shall leave you now, Vinyl. I must get these children to their homes safely and without incident. Good fortune to you."

"I suppose I should thank you. Hmph, whatever, old man. Get going."

Bounty walked off and boarded his hover ship. He landed outside the city of Angela's Grove. The city was a massive three-tiered maze of streets and buildings. The land was also in the centre of a large lake with swamplands nearby. Also, a small section is dedicated to immigrants from Komodo and another to immigrants from Olayazca. He looked into the children's minds to see where each lived. He soon returned many children. He kept those that had been sold by their parents in a callous display of money grabbing. He finally found Rona-Alexandra's family and rang the doorbell. They were in Little Olayazca of Angela's Grove. A buxom and big-hipped teenager opened the door. Her mascara was dripping as if she had been crying.

She spoke in broken common, "Hello, how may I help you?"

"Is this the residence of the Vulpe clan?"

"Sí, I am Carlotta Vulpe. You must forgive my appearance, my little cousin has been missing for over a year now. It's the anniversary of her disappearance."

She started crying again. Bounty sighed, "Will you and your family come with me? I have her, but she needs to wake up to a friendly face. I, a scarred old man, would likely freak her out if I woke her now."

"Don't get our hopes up, please. She was kidnapped by slave traders on behalf of the cartel. Her family couldn't pay the protection money, so they took her and killed her father. My aunt then fled here."

"I am telling the truth. You just have to trust me."

"No!"

"Er, very well. I will bring her here."

He walked into his truck and floated out of the cryo chamber. Carlotta gasped and spoke in Olayazkan to her family and they rushed out. They stared in awe at the cryotube where Rona-Alexandra rested.

The mother, or who he assumed was the mother spoke. "You have her. Please, I'll do anything for my little girl back. I will even take her place, please."

"I am not a slaver and have no desire to keep her."

He pushed a button and the cryotube hissed open and Rona-Alexandra staggered out. Her mother caught her. Bounty smiled and vanished along with his truck. He appeared in the upper tier of the city near a small home. Bounty looked at the home and shrugged. He walked up to the door and rang the bell. A muscular woman opened the door with her husband near her holding a Hunter Corporation cryo-shotgun. Bounty looked at them and shook his head.

"I'm guessing you are Mr and Mrs Cacophony?"

The muscular half-pure Silveran woman cracked her knuckles and flexed in a display of dominance. "We are, what's it to ya?"

"I am here on a tip that you were looking for someone to find your children."

She growled and her Elvish husband cocked the shotgun. Bounty raised his hands to show he was unarmed. "I take that as a yes. First, you must trust me, I mean no harm. I just want information."

Many things happened at once. First, a baby started crying then the shotgun went off. Bounty was hit by the cryo burst and then by a nail board that embedded into his back as he stumbled back. He steadied himself and lit his cigar, releasing a purple smoke from his mouth. He inhaled the smoke and sighed, "I will ignore the fact you just tried to kill me. And wait for you to give me the description of your children so I may look for them."

The man stood there shocked. His wife spoke, "If he was able to withstand that attack, there is nothing we can do to prevent him from taking Leila. Please come in, sir. Is there anything we can get you to drink?"

"I suppose rum is out of the question, so what do you have to drink?"

"Orange, amber, and red juice, milk, and fizzy drink of any flavour."

"Just a red juice, please."

She shakily handed him a small box filled with the juice he requested. He looked at the tiny box, shrugged and stuck the straw in as gently as he could. The husband handed him a frame of the family photo with all their children. Bounty smiled and finished off the box. He stood and motioned them to follow him. They tentatively did. He opened the back of his truck and motioned them in. They saw their children malnourished and sipping on soup.

"What? How?"

Bounty smiled, "I am very skilled with what I do. Also, I wanted them to be taken by a friendly face. Mine is not very friendly."

"Is there anything we can do to repay you?"

He saw her unbuttoning her shirt. He shook his head no. "It's alright. I can see you have your hands full as it is. Here is my card. If you need any help whatsoever, give me a call. I have children of my own, so I know how it is. Good luck."

He drove his truck into the dark underbelly of Angela's Grove. He was looking for a bar. This part of the city was very dark due to the industrial portion where the many smokestacks belched out fire and smoke. What a hellish place. *And yet I still somehow stand out, oof.* He parked and climbed out of his truck and began walking to the nearby bar. The air was heavy and Bounty felt like he was being watched. The people were looking at him with worry in their eyes. The tension was thick enough to cut with a knife. He heard a whoosh and something sliced into his arm. He frowned and then felt a kick to his back. He turned swiftly and gave a haymaker to a man dressed up as a gargoyle. The man rolled across the ground unconscious.

A car painted in circus colours tried to run the gargoyle-like man over but instead hit Bounty full-on. He saw a woman in a leotard leap from the window as it shattered and flipped multiple times with a large mallet-like hammer. She smashed the ground sending a fissure out from the impact. She grinned maniacally and lunged towards the man, ready to smash his head in. Bounty caught the hammer and tossed her aside. He felt a splat against his chest and looked down to see a small cupcake which promptly exploded. He staggered from the hit.

Several playing cards sliced into him as a man dressed as a clown walked from the shadows. He had a rictus grin on his face. Several police vehicles showed up, along with another man dressed in black and gold spandex. The man rushed over to the man on the ground and dragged him away from the street. The cops pulled many weapons out and aimed at the rictus-grinning man. He twisted his head towards them before chucking a windup box at them, which played a tune before opening and releasing a smaller rictus-grinning puppet. The puppet opened fire before exploding. Bounty watched as the grinning man vanished and the female leapt up an apartment complex.

The police were dazed and injured, so Bounty began to work on healing those that he could. He ignored his pain and focused on the task at hand. He heard ambulances and climbed into his truck before flying off, leaving the scene of the attack.

A feminine voice spoke, "So you are the one causing a ruckus. I'd be careful if I were you. You look like a villain, therefore, you are to be treated as such by the more paranoid like a gargoyle."

Bounty lit his cigar as he turned to see a Silveran woman with his facial features in Noamaizan armour. She wore yellow, pink, white, and purple armour with a small metal band that wrapped around her head in the shape of wings. Strapped to her back were a sword and a shield. On her side, there was a whip curled up. Her piercing green eyes were intelligent and youthful. *So is this female, also my sister. But if so, how? She does smell like a Hunter clan member. Ugh questions can wait...* "Why am I not surprised someone snuck aboard? Who in the Thirteen Hells are you?"

"I am Princess Galatea of Thyme. You may call me Wondra."

"Alright, Wondra, what are you doing here?"

"You are an invader in the City of Garkon. You took out Garkon's protector, gargoyle. I want to know what threat you pose."

"I pose no threat. I was returning many children to their homes. The five that remained were sold by their parents to slavers. If you do not believe me speak to the Cacophony family. Your ally, gargoyle, attacked me first. I only defended myself. Then, of course, those two painted buffoons tried to kill him and, in the process, did this to me."

He removed his coat, revealing a hole that was stitching itself up. Wondra looked at it and turned green.

"How are you still alive?'

"I have experimental Nanites from Diavonbre that were put there during the first Silveran Civil War between the half pure and the pure. Or as I refer to it in my memoirs, The War Against the

Shadow Lord."

"You are him, Bounty Hunter 13, the Demon of God Silver."

"Correct."

She unsheathed her blade and swung at him. He sighed and placed the truck in park. He pulled out his blade and blocked her second attack. He kicked her out of the truck so as not to harm the children. Her blade struck his face dislodging his half-mask. He let it fall, revealing his heavily burned features and missing eye. This caused Wondra to gasp as his image disguise dropped. He now stood before her in his full thirteen-foot height, with half of his body burned and the other half scarred up. He snorted and kicked her down before pulling out his gun.

"If you value your life, sheathe the blade. I do not wish to kill you, but I will if you continue to attack. I am old and tired. I have been through the hell of war three times so far. I am the Demon of Silver. So shedding your blood will be nothing to me."

She whimpered and Bounty holstered his gun. He was thrown from her by a speeding fist. He heard and felt his chest crunch. He climbed out of the crater he had produced when landing at much speed. He shook himself off, snapped his finger and his truck vanished. He had teleported it back to his home. He saw Mr Cacophony rushing him. He shook his head. He jumped in front of a beam burst that would have hit Mr Cacophony. His chest was now smouldering and his arm was scorched.

"You assholes almost hit a civilian. Watch your fire. You should be ashamed of yourselves. Look at this mess."

A muscular man in leather armour floated down from the sky. He spoke in a deep baritone, "Your kind are not welcome in my city."

"My kind. You have Silverans all over the place! Look, there's one now, crossing the street."

"You are not a Silveran. You are a demon of the thirteenth hell."

"Gods above, aside, and below! My title is The Demon of God Silver. I didn't fight in the war to be smashed into the pavement. Just because I look evil doesn't make me evil. You wouldn't understand that, though, would you, Ultra Magnus."

Ultra Magnus was taken aback. "Get out of my city, beast."

"Fine. I'm gone." Bounty vanished with Mr Cacophony and reappeared in a smouldering ruin. He saw the Cacophony family sitting on the curb. Looking dejected.

He looked around. "What happened? I wasn't even out of the city yet."

The pale black-haired girl spoke, "It's my fault I was trying to place protection runes up and misspelt one with explosive results."

"Ah, I see. Well, I can fund your new home, but it will take a while for Hunter Corporation construction workers to get here. In the meantime, why don't I get you somewhere with a roof over your heads? Best make your mind up quickly. The heroes of this place are on high alert and looking for me."

There was a crack and a man in blue and gold appeared, another in green and red landed with his crossbow trained on Bounty. Two more appeared, both had large wings on their back with hawk-like helmets on their head. Both brandished Void metal weapons. There was a flash of grey and a man in white, black and grey appeared. His bracer glowed with the same colour as his suit.

"And here they are."

Another voice spoke up, "Bounty Hunter 13. It's been a long time since I saw you."

Bounty turned to see a team of six dressed in a rainbow of colours. They were led by a man with long white hair and piercing, almost evil purple eyes. "Lord Dragon, I thought you passed from this world?"

"I did not. I was busy."

"Ah, I see you have the resurrected Zarbon twins in your ranks now. Are you here to attack me like these heroes?"

"Hardly, I just felt your presence and wished to see you. Whatever tiff you have with the Heroes of Angela's Grove is nothing compared to what my team faces daily. Speaking of, I heard a monster alarm go off in this area, but I can see it was a miscast spell. False alarm, kids. We had best get back to the command centre."

The team of six teleported out, leaving Bounty with the Heroes. He snapped his fingers and a barrier appeared around the Cacophony family.

"Since you heroes have no regard for civilians when fighting, they are protected by God Silver. Bring it if you wish to join your friend Gargoyle in the hospital."

Ultra Magnus landed with Wondra. She had her sword brandished and he cracked his knuckles. A large ship descended from the factory moon White Gold. It had the logo of the Hunter Corporation on it. It landed and a dark-skinned man with white hair, golden eyes and glasses walked out in a purple business suit.

He spoke, "Am I interrupting something?"

Bounty smiled, "Hardly, Nox Tarot, The barrier should be safe for you and your men to walk through. Just a little disagreement with the local heroes."

"Right, okay, men, let's get to work constructing a new home for these people."

The barrier opened, allowing the construction machines, crew, and Nox Tarot to enter. Bounty turned back to the heroes and lit his cigar. He unholstered his gun and twirled it in his hand. Glaring at them. Waiting to see if they would attack him. The hawk-helmed man charged in first. He tried to strike Bounty with his void metal mace. Bounty caught the mace in his hand and twisted, causing a snap that shattered the man's arm. Bounty followed it up by throwing him into the woman dressed like him. Both their wings crumpled, causing them to cry out.

A water spear impaled Bounty and exploded, ripping his already burned skin open. He gasped in pain and staggered back. He fired his gun at the water user, causing him to twitch and collapse as the electrical burst did its work. He holstered his gun and a flurry of blows by the black and gold sonic speedster crushed into him. He wheezed as it finished, then blew fire from his mouth. The speedster cried out in shock as he became a flambe. Bounty grimaced before causing a rainstorm to appear, putting the speedster's fire out. The man with the glowing bracelet fired several concussive bursts, each one impacting Bounty and exploding, knocking him back. He staggered as the final blast struck him but steadied himself, only to be flung into the air by Ultra Magnus.

"Oh, you are starting to piss me off."

Ultra Magnus smashed into Bounty and flung him at much speed towards the ground. Bounty snarled and adjusted his flight flipping up and landing on his feet, causing a massive wall of fire to shoot up. The flames surrounded the heroes and Bounty whipped up a whirlwind. He landed in the centre of the vortex and watched impassively as the heroes were tossed like toys. Ultra Magnus tried to rescue them but was unable to, thanks to the powerful psychic energy that he was weak too.

Bounty stopped his assault and the heroes dropped to the ground. He walked over to Wondra and picked up his half mask, placing it back on his face and causing his scars and burn to disappear. He snorted as Ultra Magnus launched at him. Ultra Magnus stopped dead in the air as a mechanically enhanced being appeared. The being was breathing through a respirator and spoke in a mechanical voice.

"Enough, Ultra Magnus. Bounty Hunter 13 is not our enemy. If anything, he is a maverick. There is no need to continue this pathetic display. Unless you want a sword in your chest."

Bounty spoke as he summoned a cane to lean on, "Al Ian, you know these jerks?"

"That I do, Demon of Silver. I apologise on their behalf. You just look so evil. It doesn't help that all stories of you are exaggerated to the point where it makes you the bad guy."

"Nothing, I am not familiar with Al. After all, in many eyes, I am the villain which is why I wrote my own book so that people see it from my eyes. Not that it matters. I am cursed to be the most hated man on Silver. Probably why these poor fools attacked me on sight."

Ultra Magnus growled, "I thought I told you to get the hell out of my city."

"Language! There are young ears present. They can hear everything through the barrier. They just won't get harmed since you don't know how to control yourself around civvies."

"Get out of my city. You demons aren't welcome here."

"Firstly, Hunter Corporations are here to rebuild like they always do. Secondly, You have Silverans all over your city. They are obviously allowed to live here. Thirdly I am a Silveran and this is not just your city. There are hundreds of heroes here and millions of civilians. My title and rank in the Silveran army is Demon of God Silver. Finally, I came to this city to return many slaves back to their homes. Slaves who were kidnapped under your heroes' watchful eyes. You did nothing to stop the kidnapping nor attack the slavers doing it. So don't get all high and mighty with me. Your civilians go missing and you sit back and wait for a supervillain to attack. You have the powers of a god. Yet you let slavers get away scot-free."

"Enough! Spawn of the thirteen hells, leave my city or you will be forcefully ejected."

Bounty smiled darkly, "I will leave when I am ready to. My crew is here rebuilding a home for a nice and lovely family. I am the one paying them at the end of their day. Once they are done, I will leave."

"You will leave now!"

Ultra Magnus tossed Al Ian away and stopped short as a blade ejected from his sternum. Bounty pulled his sword out and wiped the blood off of it. The barrier lowered and Bounty walked over to Nox Tarot.

"Here is the payment for the crew. Make sure they get it. I am not wanted here. Also, make sure the family is well provided for. Oh and make sure Ultra Magnus doesn't die."

"Will do, boss. Get going before they recover."

Ultra Magnus lay on the ground, his breath shallow. He could feel his life fading from him. Then he felt invigorated and opened his eyes to see the brown-skinned man with golden eyes and white hair.

Nox spoke, "Oh good, you're alive. Nearly lost you there. I'd be careful from here on out by calling fifty per cent of the city's population demons. You alienated many potential allies."

"Don't threaten me. I could crush your head in."

"Oh, you truly believe that, hmm. I am a level fifty-six Grim Reaper. You are not immortal. Watch your tongue."

Ultra Magnus gulped and nodded. Nox Tarot boarded the construction ship and it lifted off. Ultra Magnus watched it go, then turned and left. The other Heroes had already recovered from their brutal beating and had gone their separate ways to lick their wounds. Al stood there shaking his head in disappointment. He, too, teleported back to The Space Station, which was the main hub of the Justice Daevas.

Bounty wheezed as he entered the door of his home. His body was still trying to recover from his near-death experience. Feldspar stood holding a toddler, her eyes wide with concern.

"It's okay, Feldspar. I just need to be stitched up."

"It's not you, I am worried about. We have a guest."

A man in heavy armour walked out. He was heavily armed. He spoke, "Demon of God Silver, I am Maester Ren Greene of the Mystics. I have a proposition for you."

"I am busy, Ren. Can it wait while I recover?"

"You think I care about your recovery? No, If you do not help me, your little girl and wife will die."

"Don't threaten me, Ren. What do the Mystics want with me?"

"You killed Psycho Phantom, head of the Magus. We wish for you to do the same to the Head of the Psykikx."

"Ah, you wish to repurpose the remaining Magus and Psykikx to bring them back into the fold of the Mystics. They severed from you for a reason."

"You don't have a choice. Your wife and child are on the line."

"Fine, Ren, but don't expect the Psykikx to join you willingly."

"That is no problem. We are Mystics, after all."

Bounty Pushed a button and Ren vanished, his communicator crackled with many swears and curses.

Bounty smiled, "Hello, asshole. I will do as you request but stay away from my family, or else the Psykikx and Magus will not be the only ones without a leader."

He disabled the explosive runes on Feldspar, her sisters, his daughter, and all the servants and patients and even his house. He snorted and walked out after kissing Feldspar on the lips and Cherry, his daughter, on the head.

Bounty arrived at the Rising Falls. The large crystals that protected the Rising Falls glowed with ancient energy. There were floating stone pathways leading to many small home-sized islands. In the centre, at the very top of the pathways, was a large mansion. The King of the Rising Falls was the one he was after. What he would do next would change the dynamic of the Moth family drastically. He entered the mansion in the centre of the town. He saw Lord Frederick Moth smoking a pipe. He also saw Lord Moth's young daughter Mysy. She would not be next in line. Only her father knew of her relationship with a mutate and he protected her from the wrath of the family.

"Ah, the assassin comes. So do I get the pleasure of knowing who wants me dead?"

"Lord Moth, Wizard Green of the Mystics, wants you dead. He threatens my home with my family and all those I take care of. I do not wish to kill you, but he has eyes everywhere."

"I understand Bounty Hunter 13. Make it swift, but may I request you kill him for me? And take my daughter from this land to be with her soon-to-be husband."

"Your request has been noted. I will keep your daughter safe."

Lord Moth smiled as his pipe dropped. It hit the floor and rolled towards Bounty's feet. His last breath was taken with his eyes closed. Bounty scooped up Mysy and vanished with her and the pipe. He purposely set off the alarm so the guards would find their leader dead. He arrived at a cave where a massive red-skinned Grey Silveran with six eyes sat. The man snorted as Bounty placed Mysy in his lap.

"You two will be protected by the power of God Silver. Make sure you wear this charm at all times."

Mysy spoke, "Why?"

"Your father wished for your protection in death. I am honour bound to provide that protection. You, however, will no longer be accepted in the Rising Falls. Simply because they fear the outcasts and you are married to the outcast leader."

"I see. Will you honour my father's request?"

"Oh, oh, oh, you bet I will. Ren Greene pissed me off good."

"Thank you. That is all I ask."

"Here is your father's pipe. It is yours now and mister Gronathis, take care of her. She loves you dearly."

The large six-eyed man nodded his head in confirmation. Bounty vanished and reappeared near the Spike Tower in the deserts of Western Silver. This was where Ren Greene and the Mystics would be trying to mind control the Psykikx as they attempted for the remaining Magus. The Magus had broken free of the control and, from the reports he heard, killed many Mystics in the process. Many more would die today.

Ren Greene appeared with twenty high-level Mystics. Bounty stood there leaning against the door, smoking his cigar.

"What are you doing here?"

"Ren Greene, I have been paid fifty million commons to kill you."

"Then you are a fool." He pushed a button that would have detonated Bounty's home, but he had not deactivated the runes. "What! Why is this not working?"

"I took the liberty to deactivate your explosives when I teleported you out to the swamp. You pissed me off by threatening my family. Even more so when you act like slavers."

Ren snarled, "If you stand in my way, I will kill you. You are nothing compared to my power."

Bounty smiled an evil smile, "So be it."

"Kill him!"

The other Mystics opened fire. They used high-level abilities like Magic Meteor, Explosive Fire, Kristallnacht, and Bursting Earth. Bounty just stood there smoking as the chaos engulfed him.

That was when their spells turned on them. Bounty had his psy-damper glasses off. His pupilless grey eye glowed with unearthly power. Within seconds the twenty Mystics had been killed. He ignited his blade with psychic fire and swung at Ren. Ren blocked with his own blade. Ren tried to stab Bounty with a knife, but it melted as it tried to get through Bounty's aura.

"You are an imbecile, Ren. I am The Demon of Silver, Bounty Hunter 13. Now die!"

Bounty impaled Ren on his blade and immolated him and the other dead Mystics. He collapsed against the tower and blacked out.

***

It had been one year ago. Bounty was in his father's laboratory. He heard a chime and turned on the computer screen. Old Blu Silver was on the screen. "You are a hard man to get a hold of, Demon. I need you to represent me in a duel. Clan Prisma has tried to assassinate me six times. The first three were amusing to me, but now it's annoying. I have told the head of the Prisma clan that if he wishes to claim my throne for himself, he must face my challenge. He does not know he will be facing you."

"Very well, Blu Silver, I will do this for you, especially since we are family. Isn't that right, Zenthin Ankara jr.?"

"When did you figure it out?"

"Soon as I heard, you took the throne. I have no animosity towards your clan, so don't give me that look. I will gladly represent you. I am guessing it's at the Great Spike Canyon Colosseum. See you there."

The Colosseum was a massive mechanical structure built during the Chaos War. It was multi-tiered and split between either side of the canyon. One side had the fighting pit, but there were four collapsible walls within the fighting pit. One led to a corridor that led to an underground acid pit. Not real acid, of course. Nothing was meant to kill in this colosseum, just injure. It was a strike-based system of winning. Whoever had the most strikes on their opponent was the winner. Also, if one was unable to continue fighting, they would be disqualified and declared the loser even if they had more strikes on their opponent. Another wall led to the massive ever-changing bridge that filled the gap between either side of Spike Canyon. This bridge could alternate between stairs leading down to the canyon or a maze-like structure above the canon. The other side of the canyon held the other part of the colosseum, a razor-sharp spike-covered wall was covering the walls of this section. The final two walls that collapsed were unique and both represented instant loss. One collapsed into an oil-covered pit and the other collapsed to the outside of the colosseum.

Bounty stood smoking his cigar, waiting for his opponent. He was leaning on his halberd lazily. He eyed his opponent, a boy of barely ninety. The boy was staring up at him with terror in his eyes. He could see Lord Prism sitting, looking smug as the bell rang. The boy charged Bounty only to find himself in midair. Before he could react, he was face down in the dirt. He tried to get up but was sent into one of the walls. He tried to focus on Bounty, only to see six of him. He cried out in terror as he was yanked from the wall and sent into one of the collapsible walls. This dropped him down into the oil pit and he lay there hearing the announcement he was defeated. He sighed in relief and was lifted out of the pit and forced to kneel in front of Tsar Silver.

Blu Silver spoke, "Lord Prism, you thought you could win against me with this boy, why?"

Lord Prism snorted and pushed a button, only to frown. Bounty stood there holding a crushed bomb in his hand.

"My Tsar, he was hoping his son would lose to blow you up. I removed the bomb with my first strike."

"Thank you, Bounty. Seeing you fight truly reinforced my choice to call you a Demon. As you are the winner, Clan Prism will now be split up according to the Old Laws. Their holdings are now clan Hunter's holdings."

"The Old Laws! Ooo boy! Ah, well, can't be helped. As Lord Prism is a cheating coward, I leave his fate to you and I shall take his eldest as my concubine. My cousins, the Northern Hunters, will get all the holdings to the north and my family will claim all the eastern holdings."

"And how will you guard them?"

"My cousins, the Northern Hunters, have plenty of guards for theirs. I will purchase guards from you to watch my holdings."

"Very well. I will send a unit of guards to the main holding of the Prism clan."

"Oof, Cousin is not going to like this. Ah well, thank you, my Tsar."

Bounty oversaw the updating of his holdings. He looked at his total ownership.

He had received the main centre of the Prism clan as his. The rest of the Prism clan had happened to be north of the main hub. Since many of the Prism clan under him were traders and smugglers, he decided he would use them as the beginning of his new business—Hunter

Corporations. Now he would not only be working on medicine and pornography, but numerous other things could be gained from this happy accident. The only thing that made him frown were the thousand Goblinoid slaves he now owned.

***

He woke up in a tube. He looked around and saw he was in the Spike Tower. A naked blue-skinned woman stood there with a lab coat on. *Oh, interesting, a Murcurosian. Why did they bring me here?* She was studying him. She jumped when he turned towards her. She quickly pushed a button and several Psykikx Maesters teleported into the room. They all had their weapons trained on him. The tube lowered and Bounty staggered out.

One of the men in green with grey skin spoke, "Demon of Silver, why did we find you outside our sanctuary?"

One in red spoke, "Especially since we heard the Mystics were coming."

Bounty summoned a black onyx cane and leaned on it. "The Mystics pissed me off and I was only fulfilling your Grand Maester's dying wish after I killed him on behalf of Wizard Ren Greene, who threatened my family and home."

The woman in black spoke, "So it is true. Supreme Grand Maester Frederik Moth is dead."

"Yes, he is."

The one in red spoke, "Then you are under arrest for his murder."

"No, I'm not. I have places to be, so goodbye."

The woman in black snarled, "I call upon the unholy clouds of Zarothec." This blocked his teleport, causing a resonance cascade that blew up the medical bay. When the dust cleared, Bounty stood there, holding everyone in a protective bubble.

"Don't be an idiot, girl! I am surprised that you even blocked me. You're lucky to be alive. Are you alive?"

She floated there limply with empty eyes. Bounty snorted and electricity fired from his gun, sending the girl in black into convulsions. She jolted awake, gasping for air. Bounty set her down as she coughed. She looked at him weakly.

"You are strong in the PsyQi. Who are you?"

"I am Bounty Hunter 13."

"Fuck! Please don't kill us."

"Muahahaha, please, you are not worth the wasted energy."

"Okay, creepy. Stop it or I may have a panic attack."

"Sorry, I always wanted to do that. You know who I am, but who are you to be able to block me?"

"I am Raven Triagonal, also known as Lady Pegasus."

"I have heard of you. You took out a Greater Abbolith single-handedly. Something even I would have had extreme difficulty with."

"Yeah, that was me. I am the reason for the Veltan Scarr."

"Don't be sorry. You saved numerous people. You should be proud."

"Yeah, but what about those I couldn't save?"

"Girl… if I worried about all those I didn't save during my wartime feats, I would never have been able to get out of bed in the morning. Focus on those you saved. As long as the proper procedure was taken in regards to those that died, they will move on happily to the heavens."

"Thanks, I guess. It's just so hard that I keep replaying the encounter in my mind. If I only did it differently, then I may have saved others."

Bounty smiled, "That is a part of life. I can tell you it never gets easier. Just keep on going. Do your best to save as many as you can. Just don't go overboard because that will wear on you. You cannot save everyone."

She smiled sadly. Bounty sat next to her, waiting for the others to wake. "Why haven't you run?"

"Simply put, I don't want another incident. Technically I could easily incapacitate you and escape, but I am intrigued by your dark one. No one in my lifetime has been able to block my teleport."

"I am an Enigma even to the other Maesters. They only know me as Lady Pegasus, the one who killed a Greater Abbolith. Some even know me as the one who created the Psy Scarr of Veltan Pass. I only told my real name to you. I don't know why."

"Kindred spirits, most likely."

The other maesters slowly awoke. They looked at the destruction and the large Hunter

Corporation Ship descending from the sky. They prepped their weapons.

"Don't be shooting the construction crew. They are here to rebuild this wing of the tower since it was obliterated. They are not here to free me."

One of the men in grey spoke, "Yeah, like we trust you."

"Ah, but if you fire upon them, you will have the wrath of a reaper to deal with. Nox Tarot is the overseer of the construction crew. Also, if I had wanted to escape, I would have. You have been sleeping off a psionic resonance cascade for the past twelve hours. I am still here. So lower the weapons and let the construction crew do their job."

"Gah! Fine!"

"Nox Tarot, you have permission to proceed. I have calmed the trigger, happy Maesters."

"Thank you, boss. I need them to leave with you, though. Some of the equipment we are using cannot be used around those sensitive to psionic abilities."

The Maesters escorted Bounty out and to a large room where his trial would be as if he'd get a fair one.

A grand Maester in purple sat upon the judgment seat. He would be the one overseeing the trial. He spoke, "Bounty Hunter 13, you stand accused of murdering Lord Moth. I also wish to know what happened to Wizard Greene, who was coming to meet with us."

"Wizard Ren Greene threatened my household and family if I did not kill Moth. He insinuated he would try to enslave your people like the Mystics did to the Magus after I killed Lord Psycho Phantom. I killed Moth, he was expecting an assassin. He made no attempt to defend himself and only requested that I kill Ren Greene. I obliged the dying wish, so do your worst."

"I find no issue with you. Lord Moth was already suffering from a heart condition and would never have been able to stand up to an assassin. Especially one of your calibre. You also prevented the treachery of Ren Greene. You are free to go, but we will call upon your help later. You are obliged to assist us when the time comes."

"I agree to the terms Grand Maester QiKong Djinnai."

A Maester in blue jumped down. "You bastard. Beasts like him should be executed. Those with me, raise your arms against the fools."

Half of the Maesters pulled out weapons and attacked the other half. "You proud of yourself, Wizard Gre Bluee?"

"You have lost, Demon! Once my followers crush the Maesters, the Psykikx will be ours. Just like the Magus."

Bounty sighed and beheaded Gre Bluee. He pulled out his gun and opened fire on the traitors. Within minutes they all lay dead. The Maesters that survived began to pile the dead in separate corners. One for the Loyal and one for the traitors. Grand Maester Djinnai sighed as he lay his head back and winced. Bounty walked over to him and saw the blood-soaked robe. He found the wound and began mending it.

"Relax QiKong, there is no need for another Grand Maester to die. You'll be good as new in a few minutes."

"Thank you, Bounty. I underestimated the level of infiltration the Mystics had. I hope the rest of the school still holds together after this."

"I have no doubt it will. I will be sending my cousins, the Huntari, to assist you in bolstering the Psykikx forces. Do not let them fool you. They are incredibly skilled and will be a good asset to train your students."

His communicator pulsed against his wrist. "This is Bounty Hunter 13. How may I help you?"

A woman's face appeared. "Hello, I believe we met. You returned my family to me. Well, we would like to know if you can find us a new home. Not that the one you built for us isn't great. It's just after witnessing what the heroes did to those that look different than them, we can no longer in good conscious stay in Angela's Grove anymore."

"I can house you at my home until we build a home in City Silver for you."

"Thank you, but will you have enough room for eleven children plus us?"

"Definitely. My home is in the forest. If a man in a feathered robe comes to greet you at the edge of the forest, he can lead you there. I'll be home in a few days. Until then, you will be provided for."

After the woman hung up, his communicator pulsed again and a young male appeared in the projection.

He spoke, "Cousin, why did you call us?"

"Ah, hello, Tim. I need you and your family to help out at the Spike Tower."

"Why us?"

"Well, I can't call upon my siblings. Amari has been studying and practising in her little bunker, Corvus has his Druid grove, and Eris is on Noamaiza. Elena and her mercenaries are busy. I refuse to talk to the Hawthorns after what the Mystics tried to do. Your clan has numerous powerful Psykikx in it. You all have trained here, so logic concludes that you are the best choice."

"Even after what Vicki did to you?"

"Ha! I'm blind. One eye doesn't matter in the long run."

"Very well, Bonty, I will talk to the clan and we will send some help to the Spike Tower."

Bounty arrived at his home at dusk. He entered and saw the Cacophony family talking with Feldspar and her sisters while Tallon played with Leila and Cherry. The great Shadow Wolf Moon Catz hybrid, Lunatic Moonshadow, sat staring curiously at the group. He plodded over and lay his head on Feldspar's lap and she scratched his ear. Bounty smiled.

The Hunters

Bounty Hunter 13 sat in his dining room. *My, how time flies!* Three hundred years ago, this family moved in. *Ugh never would have seen me as a family man, but they have taken a liking to me. I don't know why, especially since my real daughter despises me.* He was currently eating a Gargant steak and enjoying the company of the Cacophony family. The kids had basically adopted him as their second father. Their mother was still in her uniform from her role as Tits MaBoobs, the pornographic heroine, Titanium. She was currently discussing with her second eldest daughter what the title of the next movie Titanium would be in's name.

It has been three years since Feldspar was slain by our daughter, Cherry. Ugh, I should have seen it coming. Shit! Also, poor Lica is still in a medically induced coma from the attack.

Bounty got a notification that there was something at the door. He excused himself and walked to the door. Opening the door, he saw a grey-skinned woman with deep blue, almost black hair, purple eyes, black lipstick and eyeshadow, wearing a simple fishnet stocking and skirt combo. Her skirt was blue and black and she had piercings. She looked uncomfortable.

"Hello there, how may I help you?"

She stammered out, "You are Demon of Silver, yes?"

"I am. What's wrong? Woah, what are you doing?"

She had her skirt lifted and was pulling out a canister from her vagina. She licked it off and opened it, revealing a holo video.

"Ah, Demon of Silver, I see you have received my gift and down payment."

"Down Payment?"

"Yes, she is one of many I will reward you with if you can take care of a little problem."

"Alright, Green Silver, I'll bite. What is it you need me to do?"

"There is a group of hoodlums causing havoc in the city. They call themselves the Knights of Silver. I would like you to take care of them."

"I'll do my best, your lordship."

"Regardless, this girl is your down payment. Please do not fail me."

"I'm not sure I like your tone, your highness. At least your father, Blu Silver, was respectful towards me. Regardless, I don't plan on failing."

He crushed the portable screen and tossed it in his junk pile. Bounty brought the girl inside, she was shaking. He probed her mind and saw the anomaly. He carefully removed the mind control device and laid her in a warm bed. He sighed and sat down at the table. He would enjoy his family's presence before he had to go fight.

***

Several moons rises later, Bounty stood on the outskirts of City Wintersplunge, the capital of Northern Silver. He was by a campfire he had set up to cook some stew before he faced the Knights of Silver. He knew they were nearby. He saw movement and went for his gun.

"Whoa, dher grey skin. I am friend."

Bounty turned to see a Goblin. "Are you? What's your name… friend?"

Roughly translated in Silveran, "I am She who devours-the-cock-of-her-enemy-and-crushes-heads-with-her-legs."

"Ah, Alexandra! Hello. I am guessing you are the one Elena sent me to find?"

"Yes, Elena, friend. Choose life out here. Very tired."

"If you lead me to where the Knights of Silver usually are, I'll find you a nice warm bed."

"Very well, de grey skins are dis way."

She waddled off quickly, forcing Bounty to jog to catch up to her. He was soon set upon by a bird-like Silveran. He defended himself but was soon on the defensive as the red-skinned bird-like man sped up. He was thrown back by a large muscular wolf-like Canis and a Felis who tried to tear into him with her claws.

"Hello, old man. Do you like the friends I have?"

"I am not pleased with the welcoming committee, Cherry."

Cherry walked out with a dagger against the Goblin's neck. The little creature struggled in vain. Bounty rolled to avoid a thrown dagger.

"Release Alexandra, please. Your beef is with me."

"Just for that old man, she dies."

Bounty snapped his fingers and Alexandra vanished along with Cherry's hand. Bounty winced. He looked down to see a blue metal sword sticking through his sternum. He chuckled, then laughed.

"Oh, it's been way too long since I've been stabbed. Why so shocked, Brovone Bjorn? Did Cherry not tell you about me?"

"She explained you were her father and that was it."

"Firstly, get your sword out before my blood eats it. Secondly, I am a cyborg, so your stabbing is as ineffective as this surprise attack."

Cherry collapsed from blood loss. Her allies quickly got her away. Brovone Bjorn stayed behind.

"So tell me, boyo, why do you terrorise Wintersplunge?"

"Who told you that? Was it the King? Feh! He is a tyrant and dictator. He has been kidnapping women and children and forcing their fathers and husbands to be in his army. And he still has the audacity to turn some of those girls and children into mindless puppets for some unknown reasons."

"Well, kid, you're looking at the reason. He seems to think he can buy me off with slaves, which is why I am here. Now hold before you say anything. I had suspicions when he gave one to me as a down payment. I am here to investigate my suspicions. If I find them true, you are off the hook. If they are false, I will see you again."

"I don't think you'll be seeing us again. Come on, guys let's join up with Cherry and the others."

The small team hurried off. Bounty sighed, remembering the second reason he was here. It had been at midnight when the Hunter's Blood Moon glowed ominously above the forest. He had gotten word his home was under attack. He quickly got the Cacophony family to safety, even though three wanted to join his defence. He found the disturbance and his wife's bloody corpse on the ground.

He got snapped out of his reverie by the raspy voice of Alexandra, "Hey, you okay dher grey skin? You got awfully quiet and radiated cold."

"No, I am not okay, little one. My wife was murdered by the Knights of Silver. I shouldn't even be here. I want to exact vengeance on them."

"That is why you are here, then. Likely why his lordship sent you."

"You are perceptive, especially since you've been out here for years."

"My mission is my own, just like yours is your own."

Bounty nodded and looked to Wintersplunge. "Well, come along, Alexandra. You may as well ride on my shoulder since we are going to the same place. That is your mission, is it not? To keep an eye on me?"

"You are a terrifying individual, grey skin. I accept your offer."

She clambered up Bounty and wrapped her small arms around his shoulder spike and got comfortable. He entered the lift station to take them down the canyon. Wintersplunge was right in the middle of this snowy canyon. The lift hummed and stopped at substation 2. Then a hover bus brought them over to Lift Station 3, which brought them up to the entrance of Wintersplunge.

***

Beatrix Badger-Oda stood in a semi-organic world. She looked around and sighed. This world was Neo Tarah-Aert. Once populated by beings known as Homo Indomitus now populated by what her people called Elves. She knew of the round ears thanks to a museum that she had been to long ago. She went back to meditating. She could feel the two halves of this world. The Techn half and the spiritual half, much like her. She felt an odd tug. There was fury and rage and darkness. She opened her eyes and stood up. She climbed aboard her hovercycle. It lit up with runes and psionic energy and roared off. She stopped by the river to recharge her reserves. Being this far from Silver meant she had to be careful with her PsyQi energy. Having to traverse long distances with her cycle did not help matters.

She looked around and grimaced. This is the same forest I shattered my arms in, thanks to those warzerkers. Thank the gods, Ami was able to patch me up. Even if that meant using experimental nanomachines, now I cannot feel pain or any sensation on my skin, nor can I get aroused. But I live, so that is good.

The metal-like trees glistened in the noonday sun. Beatrix lay against one of them, resting. She felt a presence near her and opened her eyes. "Impossible! You are just a figment of my imagination. I saw you die."

The naked blue-skinned girl with orange hair and pink eyes smiled. "I did die, Beatrix, but was recently reincarnated. Good to see you, big sis."

"I don't believe you. Re-incarnation doesn't take this short of a time."

"It's been seven hundred years. You've been gone a long time."

"Right, different time scales. Damn, Neo Terra-Aert year cycles, so you are real."

"As real as the sun in the sky and the Mecha-Gabit Sharks in the river."

Beatrix looked into the pristine waters. She could see the ancient monoliths of the moor people. Among these monoliths was a herd of large bipedal shark men. They swam lazily among the ancient jet engines that fuzed their heads and helped to propel them through the waters. Every now and then, their blade-like fins cut through the weed, sending it to the surface where it floated lazily down the river.

"Where's your guardian?"

"Enigma's around, probably fishing or something. He took a liking to sit by the water and fishing."

There was a large crash sending the cyber birds streaking into the sky, their techno bass shrieks echoing through the still air. Ami and Beatrix hurried over to where the crash originated and saw Enigma lying there with blood on his chest. He stirred as his wound healed and grunted.

Ami spoke, "Hey, big guy, what happened?"

"Cyborg girl jumped me. Said something about the scrap heap and fled." Beatrix blinked in confusion. "What junk heap?"

Ami pointed off in the distance, where Beatrix could barely make out a massive pile of metal. "That Scrap Heap. Mono-Horn created it to trap something. It's kinda off limits."

"Yet something has clearly escaped from it. We should investigate."

She pointed to her neck where a collar was. "You do what you want, sis. I gotta obey the king."

"What did Mono-Horn do to you?"

"Not Mono-Horn. He's not the king. His son is. It's also my fault. When I reincarnated, I was inducted by brainwashing into some crazy cult. I had no memories of my past life and attempted to kill the king on their behalf. Enigma here stopped me. But my punishment is this collar. I have to be a good girl for three more years, then I get it removed, so you go have fun. Just remember, it's off-limits for a reason."

"Right, I will investigate."

Enigma spoke, "If you see this android, spare her. She seemed conflicted when she attacked me."

Beatrix nodded and walked off, soon arriving at the massive junk pile. She could feel the malevolent energy coming from within. She entered into the forbidden pile.

***

Bounty Hunter 13 entered the city of Wintersplunge and enveloped himself in shadows to remain unseen. He soon found the place he was looking for. It was a factory. He entered the factory and created an aura of misleading deception. This allowed him to slip past the guards and cameras. He arrived in the reprogramming room and saw many young children and teen females. He also saw his face on a large screen with hypnotic rays emitting from it. He snorted in disdain. He continued through the reprogramming room and entered the reprocessing room. Here he saw girls being dipped in a vat of pink sludge. Their bodies underwent a change. Their breasts grew larger, as did their butts. If they were tall, this looked natural, but if they were a child or of similar size to a child, this looked unnatural. He let out a growl that nearly revealed his location to a guard.

He felt a hand over his mouth and a mental command to zip it. He sighed and continued on. Entering the processing room, he saw a large ursine girl chained up along with other species.

One of the guards spoke, "His lordship wants these girls untouched but will still need them to go to the reprogramming centre. Take them there now."

The other guard saluted and his team led the girls off. The only girl remaining was a blond girl that looked very familiar to Bounty. He looked through his missing children's report and saw her. His pseudo-daughter, Lodi Cacophony.

"Now, I am pissed off! Screw this!"

Flames erupted everywhere. The guards were incinerated instantly. Bounty stalked through the factory with the flames following him. He teleported the prisoners to his ship. Soon the entire facility was on fire. He slid into the shadows as he exited the facility holding Lida Cacophony. Her body had been exposed to the reprocessing ooze.

***

Beatrix looked around the scrap hallway she was in. She snorted and walked through. There were no traps nor sentries. She arrived in a large room where a massive robot stood. It turned to her and tilted its head in curiosity.

It spoke in a feminine voice, "Intruder! How... interesting. I apologise, but I must stop you. Master would not like to be disturbed at this point."

The robot stepped forward, but Beatrix had already cleaved it in two. The robot crumbled, revealing a smaller android girl who scrambled back in terror. Two female-shaped robots emerged from the ground. One had a flaming sword in its right hand and a laser gun in its left. The other had two Gatling lasers on its arms. Both opened fire with a beam from their heads. Beatrix yelped and rolled away. "You singed my coat. Alright, let's have some fun."

Twenty minutes later, she exited the room. She dusted herself off. The robots and the android had been teleported to her ship. She looked at the door in front of her. She saw the smaller android that had attacked Enigma standing by the door. She smiled and walked forward, only to have the girl vanish. She looked down to see blood dribbling down her chest from a slice in her neck. She caught the girl as she went for another pass. Shattering both her arms and one of her legs. The small android let out a cry of pain. Beatrix huffed in annoyance and the girl vanished. She kicked down the door and saw a large pile of wires and scrap.

A voice spoke from the pile, "Ah, how quaint a mortal comes to be processed."

"Sorry, beast, the only one being processed here is you."

"Oh, the bullheadedness of a warrior. It's been too long since I dealt with one of you. As soon as I kill you, I will be your new master."

"Done talking? Show yourself and face me like a man."

"Man! Man! I am no man. Not anymore. My wretched brother Scarabaeus Monohorn imprisoned me here after disposing of my body. I think I have an Idea. If you so desire to face me, give me a body. There is a computer over there somewhere. Use it to design me a robotic body then I will face you."

"If the king trapped you here, why should I help you?"

"You don't have a choice in the matter. See how many adventurers I have imprisoned. I can immediately make them robots if you do not do as I say."

"Fine, I'll give you a body."

She found the computer fairly easily and began searching for the weakest robot body she could make. She found a robot schematic that was called the X-10.

"Hurry it up, warrior. I am very trigger-happy."

"I'm going... I'm going. This should suffice. Now how do I start the transfer?"

"Processing schematic. Ooo fun. Beginning assembly."

The Junk Heap rattled and began to melt. Soon only a forge and assembly line remained. A ten-foot robot was soon assembled. Energy lanced through the robot as it came to life. Two orange eyes glowed from behind a spiky mask. Electric yellow fibres emerged from behind the skull area, forming waist-length spiky hair. He had spiked forearms and two small cannons on each shoulder. He looked at his new body.

"Very nice warrior. You chose well. Who are you so that I may repay you by killing all those you care about."

"Hmpf, I am B. Hunter. Now face me like a man."

"Heh, Heh, no, I want to watch you suffer. Goodbye, B Hunter of Silver. Next, we meet your family and friends will lie dead before me."

He vanished as a large hover tank came into view. Beatrix snarled, "Lousy weasel!"

***

Bounty saw Brovone Bjorn waiting for him. He sighed, "Figures... you wanted me to see for myself, but you knew what was going on. You truly are my clone."

"Ha! Me, a clone of you? No, no, I am a clone of Belith Blackheart. Your friend Deathknight showed me that. But yes, I did want you to see for yourself. So what do you say, Demon of Silver? Am I in the right?"

"No, but neither is the Duke of Wintersplunge. Your little rebellion is causing weakness among the Silveran people. Something we cannot afford at this time. Especially with the canis uprising and the taur looking to invade us."

"My way is justice, old man! I am the hero these people need."

"Your way, maybe. But do you want to know the true reason I am here? I seek my own justice. My wife, her two sisters, and several of my staff were killed by my daughter Cherry. She, along with the help of her little brother Moonstalker slaughtered them. They also maimed my wife's little sister and one of their siblings. I am very, very, very, extremely unhappy with her."

"I see. So you believe there is justice in revenge?"

"I believe there is revenge in revenge. I need her to face me and explain why. Why would she do that to a woman who cared deeply for her and only wanted her to be happy."

"You will get to speak with her. Whether she'll speak to you is up for debate. You did sever her hand."

"Enjoy your rebellion, Brovone Bjorn. Just know if I hear you have caused more rebellions to ignite, I will make an example of you and your Knights. Goodbye for now. I have places to be and people to return to their homes. If they have homes to return to."

As he walked off, he heard his brother's words echo in his head fate always has a way of fixing what is wrong. *Sure, you protected them this time but what about next time?*

***

Beatrix raised her hands up as Scarabaeus Mono-horn exited from his tank. He was shaking his head in annoyance. "Why does this not surprise me? As soon as I heard from Ami that you had come here, I knew you'd pull some stupid stunt or another. Did not expect you, however, to release my little brother from his imprisonment. I am very disappointed in you. The least you could have done is blow him up. Where is he anyway?"

"I gave him the wrong name to trick him. He took it as a challenge and vanished. Probably back to planet Silver. I hope he doesn't do too much damage."

"Silver, huh? Well, what's done is done. Why are you here anyway?"

"I came to claim an artefact on behalf of my goddess. She desires the Cube of Chaos and sent me to retrieve it."

"We'll you're on the wrong continent. You want the Arklands, not the Firstlands."

"I see. Uh, can you find somebody to give me a lift to these Arklands?"

"Well, you did free my brother, but you also got rid of him. Eh, I'll see what I can do."

***

Bounty stood on the outskirts of The Rising Falls. He lit his cigar and inhaled deeply. Next to him stood Alexandra the Goblin and Gilda the green Orkean Silveran. "I would question why you're here, Gilda, but I suspect I know the answer."

"I was hired as extra security. And since Tam Tam is no longer among the living, I brought Alexandra along with me."

"Are you the only ones here?"

A rough female voice spoke from atop the wall, "What do you think, old man?"

"Hello, Vinyl. Let me guess, Elena's with you?"

"I am, brother. Why are you here?"

"King Moth hired me to try to negotiate peace with the Canis."

Elena jumped down and landed, her brown duster opened in front, allowing her ample breasts to hang out. "He thinks you have the skills to negotiate with savages?"

"Now, Elena, what did I tell you about your attitude towards other species?"

"Be nice to them. Their general calls himself the Savage Fang."

"Oh well, that makes racism all better, then."

"Don't get sarcastic with me, brother. As if you are any better."

"And on that note, I am off to go negotiate peace with Duke Abner and the King of the Canis, Blood Razer."

Bounty arrived at the meeting area as Duke Abner, in his leather muscle jacket and Electro Webbing Jeans walked into the clearing along with his bodyguard, a very massive woman named Gronta. King Blood Razer walked into the clearing, followed by several emaciated Canis and two guards.

"Do you see why I fight for land Demon of Silver?"

Bounty exhaled green smoke. "I can see you trying to tug at my heart by showing me children you probably starved to get pity."

"They are not children, they are full-fledged adults. The land near the Rising Falls is rich in nutrients that we need. The game around here is hard because of it, but the King of the Rising Falls hoards these resources."

"I know not what you speak of Blood Razer. He has stated he would willingly let you live here as long as you don't hurt his people."

"Really, the machine man said he would never give up his land."

The duke spoke, "Machine man? The king has no allies that are machine-like. Here you go, your lordship, a recording made by my king saying the same thing as The Demon said," he said.

"Hmm, have I been misled?"

Elena walked into view. "You couldn't leave well enough alone, could you, brother? Now I will make sure this war continues."

She pulled out her sword and attacked the king. Bounty stepped in front of him and saw Elena's eyes. They looked like computer screens portraying binary. Bounty hissed, mind control, *who would dare?* He pushed Elena away. Grinning darkly, he caught her by her throat and slammed her into the ground. He electrocuted her, causing her to scream and pass out. Smoke came off the back of her neck and a small circle dropped off. Bounty picked it up and placed it in containment.

"I do apologize for my sister's attitude. She's been extremely stressed out lately. Please come with me and we can formally allow your usage of this land. King Moth must sign the treaty as well. Gilda, I know you're there, have the emaciated ones lead you back to their fort. Keep an eye on things, something is trying to increase tensions with the varying species."

"How do you know you can trust me?"

"Come now, Gilda, you and I both know you are bull-headed. Just like me. Little too hard for a mind control machine to take control."

"You callin' me an idiot?"

"No, I'm calling you stubborn and unyielding. Two things that mind control devices cannot break through."

She snorted and the emaciated Canis led her to their fort. Alexandra followed and nodded at bounty Hunter 13.

She's planning something, but what? Why are Goblins so hard to read? Bounty escorted King Blood Razer and Duke Abner to the Rising Falls. King Moth was waiting for him.

"Ah, you return successfully. We will be allying with the Canis to make our land thrive. I thank you for this. Here is your reward. Now before you say anything, I know you don't like flesh as a reward, but these kids have caused so much trouble they are on death row. I believe you would be a more suitable punishment for them than death. And it also appeases the populace by getting rid of them. Just non-lethally."

"I will accept them. Thank you, your highness. Remember, if you have any more trouble, you know who to call."

"I will keep that in mind. Do you know who was behind the misinformation?"

"I do not, but believe me when I say I will find them and make sure this never happens again."

***

A man wearing a blank mask walked into the snowstorm. He had encountered a vicious man in black and silver armour that smelled like a woman, with horns that curved down instead of up. The man that smelled like a woman had come from this direction. The snowstorm let up suddenly and without warning. The man looked at the oasis in front of him and huffed in a mechanical voice. "Sneaky sneaky. A fake snowstorm hides a steamy oasis. What is being hidden, though, and why?"

His companion, a massive white-furred Ursar, spoke, "I would say we are in the unknown lands. Norvcryog holds many secrets that even we Ursar do not know. Look in the distance, my friend and tell me what you see?"

"I see a large facility. A lab, maybe. Now, why would a lab be out here? Hidden from the world. I don't like it. We may need backup."

"I don't think it will come to that. Just stay low. Walk slow and we will remain unnoticed."

"Wampanor, there is no foliage to hide ourselves with. What makes you think we won't be seen?"

"The Sky Mother and Earth Father protect us and keeps us safe. Also, I have a scout."

"Always one step ahead. You would like my twin brother. He always seems to be one step ahead of everyone."

"This the same brother who is called The Demon of Silver?"

"I see you already know him."

"Not really, but I have heard of him. Everyone has heard of The Demon of Silver. A mass murderer and violent rogue. He follows no one and no one follows him."

"Yes, he does do a lot of overkill. I can see why he would be called a mass murderer. We're here. It's awfully empty."

"Yes, as it should be, this place has been abandoned for many years. But something is still around. I smell trouble."

Three women appeared. One of which was the horned being from earlier. The masked man pulled out a gun axe and readied it.

The horned girl from earlier spoke, "Whoa there! We don't mean any harm. We come in peace. My name is Leon Psycheo. These are my siblings, Llere and Lecca."

Lecca purred, "Ooo, I like this one, big sis. He's feisty."

Llere spoke, "Keep it in your pants, girl. He is the one we've been waiting for."

Wampanor eyed the women suspiciously. Then turned his head as if listening to something. If one were to look very closely, they'd see a serpentine female with gold scales. He nodded his head.

He spoke, "So you are Bounty Hunter 13's female clone. As are your sisters, I suppose. Why have you been waiting for my friend here?"

Leon spoke, "Aside from the fact this is our home and where we were created before the Magus left. There is something I need Mr Mask to do."

The masked man sighed, "And will you tell me what that is?"

"Go deeper into the facility. There you will see. Follow the screams in the PsyQi."

"Why me?"

"Because I know your true Identity. I know that you will do what is right."

"And what of you? You cannot survive out here by yourselves."

"My girlfriend has a way of getting us off the planet. I really don't want to be around for what's coming."

Wampanor and the masked man walked off. A portal appeared and Leon and her sisters walked through. Wampanor huffed as he was hit with a PsyQi shockwave.

"You go ahead. I'll stay back here. Whatever is beyond those doors is insanely powerful. Right up your alley."

"Ha! I wonder what it is?"

He entered the doors to see two pods glowing with grey light. He frowned under his mask. I recognize this energy. More clones of my brother. He walked towards the pods and they cracked open, the energy spilling forth knocked him off his feet. He forced his way through the psionic energy and managed to throw his cloak over the two children that lay there. He huffed in pain as his skin burned from the onslaught. He made sure they were wrapped well.

"Wampanor, can you hear me? I'm going to need a medevac."

"I'm coming in. Since I no longer feel the outpouring of PsyQi energy."

Wampanor entered to see a nearly passed-out from holding a bundle in his arms. He sighed and lifted the man up along with his mask that had fallen off. The scars on his back glowed ominously. He walked back through the snowstorm as his spy drove a med truck into view. He placed the man on a table and looked at the intelligent eyes of the male child. He grimaced and vanished in a rush of ice.

***

Bounty Hunter 13 was assisting Rona Cacophony in fitting Lodi for the role of Tits MaBoobs, aka Titanium, the pornographic superhero. Thanks in part to the ooze she had been tainted by, she now fit the role perfectly. The next film would be about her taking the mask from her mother. Though in this case, her mentor. He heard a beep and turned towards a screen.

"Who the hell are you?"

The massive white bear spoke, "I am King Wampanor of Northern Norvcryog. My associate was unable to deliver these children to you. So I did in his place."

"Computer let our guest in. Show him the seating area. I apologize, I'll be right up."

"Take your time. I'm in no rush."

"I can hear your sarcasm. I'll be up immediately."

Bounty finished the design and gave it to Llodi to help flair it up a bit. He teleported to the living area and looked over the massive Ursar. He only reached the bear's chest. He shook his head.

"What can I do for you, your highness?"

"You seem much more impressive in stories. Anyway, my friend and I came upon these two children in a Magus cloning facility. My friend was severely injured in retrieving them due to their immense power. He feels that you are the only one capable of keeping them safe."

"Hmm... follow me, please. I need to see this for myself. Computer prep the fallout shelter."

"Do try not to destroy it. It's only a prototype."

"I'll do my best."

He entered the chamber and numerous runes began glowing on the wall. Soon the walls were completely covered in ancient Silveran runes. Bounty unwrapped the two bundles and was immediately pushed back by the overwhelming power of the Gray. So much so that his image disguise failed him and his true thirteen-foot form was revealed. Wampanor snorted, "still unimpressive."

"I see, alright." He began weaving a powerful spell. It enveloped the two children and dissipated. "That should hold them. You said you found them in a cloning facility?"

"Yes, I suspect they are clones of you."

"Of course, Leon was only a prototype, along with her siblings, but why would they abandon something this powerful?"

"My idea is that they had to quickly abandon the facility and move off-world before they drew attention to themselves."

"That would make sense since they moved to Black. Thank you, Wampanor. If you need my help with anything, here's my number, give me a call. I'll do my best to assist you."

"Thank you, Demon. I'll keep that in mind. Goodbye." He vanished in a cascade of ice.

Bounty looked down at the two now toddler children. "Well, this is interesting. I think you will be called Devon Hunter and you will be called Bounty Hunter 26. Welcome to the family."

A feminine voice spoke, "Dad, can I speak with you?"

Bounty turned to see Llodi Cacophony standing there. He saw her hair was spiked and her eyes were draconic. "I see. What is wrong, sweetie?"

"Why does it hurt? Why did my siblings have to die?"

"They didn't have to die, but it hurts because you love them. I apologize. I should have realized sooner."

"Lica is in critical condition, Lade has been cremated, and Loni is soon to be cremated. Lunatik and Samara have run off together. I just saw what happened to Lida. And Lucy has been trying to seduce Lude. Luckily he's oblivious to her advances. He's more focused on Jordyyne, Stella Nova, and Rona-Alexandra, but I fear for her fragile psyche. She did try to summon me after all."

"Yes and we saw how well that worked out. You got fused with her sister and now are permanently stuck since you are not classified as a succubus anymore."

"I care for them, Father. Why does this hurt so much."

"You have all of Llodi's memories. Sure, her soul is fused with you, but you care because she cares. However, you may be pleasantly surprised. Lica may well make a full recovery."

"She was mutilated, Father. How can she survive?"

"Her intellect is terrifying. I suspect she wanted to get mutilated so she could try out an experiment, but you have something to look forward to. Llodi, I would like you to meet your new siblings, Bounty Hunter 26 and Devon."

"Woa."

"I know right! They have intense power and intelligence. You can see it in their eyes. They are studying us to see how to form words."

"They're awfully cute."

"Babies usually are. Until the first sleepless night of bodily functions."

***

Beatrix Badger-Oda stood staring at the massive complex made of onyx. Her companion next to her was a woman in plate armour her height and face showed her as 120. She is not even old enough to be in her first cycle on Silver. Here she commanded a large army. Though at this point, it was just her and Beatrix.

"So Joan, was it? This is the correct place?"

"Yes, can you not feel the chaos energy coming off of the cathedral?"

"No, I cannot. But that may be more due to my goddess's nature than a fault of my own."

"Hmm, oh well. Let's keep moving less. I am forced to suffer through this the better off I am."

The two walked in to see a large dark-skinned man with a steel hammer swatting away at small onyx spiders. Beatrix sent forth a whirlwind that sent the bugs scattering. He turned to them.

"You kill stealers. I was gaining xp on these things."

Beatrix spoke, "Are you mad? This is not a video game. This is real life!"

"Nuh uh, I've been killed multiple times and respawned at the entrance again. This is totes a video game."

Joan spoke, "Are you in some sort of Avatar? You are clearly a black man, but you sound like some valley girl."

"I don't know what you're talking about."

Beatrix continued walking. "Alright, just going to ignore you now. Have fun gaining xp or whatever you call it."

"Woa! Hey, wait up! Can I join up with your team?"

Beatrix shrugged. "Sure, why not just keep up? We are trying to retrieve an ancient chaos crystal for a goddess."

The three continued on, "So you guys are adventurers like myself?"

"Beatrix here is more of a mercenary. I myself am a paladin of Joan d'Arc. I was tasked by my queen's friend, Scarabaeus Monohorn, to keep her out of trouble."

"So cool! I am Lexi Steel. I'm here with my siblings, but unfortunately, I'm not so good at this game."

The three rounded the corner to see a small campfire with a female bard sprawled out snoring. Standing guard was a pale-haired male with a five o'clock shadow on his face. He looked tired. Next to him, snoring and drooling on his shoulder, was a witch dressed in all black. Perched up on a pillar was a girl dressed only in a loincloth. On her back was a lizard curled up in a sleeping pouch.

The man looked at them and spoke, "Well, well, look who finally made it to the camp."

Lexi cringed slightly. "Sorry, bro, bro, I'm not so good at this game."

The witch spoke in a monotone, "Hey, Lexi, who's your friends?"

"Don't know they watched my back, though."

"Let's get you out of that form and into your normal one."

The witch caused a large rune to appear and it wrapped around Lexi, causing the masculine form to melt away, revealing a blond girl with horns and a tail. She was dressed in a teal belly shirt with a teal booty skirt and plain white knee-high boots.

"There, that's the Lexi I know. So you two are adventurers like us?" Joan sighed.

"Not adventurers. Why would you come here anyway?"

The boy spoke, "We can talk in the safety of the bonfire. Not here."

The five walked into the small alcove. Joan grimaced at the chaotic energy that cascaded over her. "The sooner we find the cube, the better off I am. I hate this place."

The girl in the loin cloth jumped down from her perch and spoke, "You're looking for the Chaos cube as well? Cool, maybe we can team up."

The man sighed, "I don't think that is a good idea, Lana. We don't even know what their plan for the cube is."

***

Corvus stood in the forest looking at the man in red. His voice reverbed as if using another's vocal chords, "Why are you here, Argon? We had a deal. Stay away from my grove and I leave you and that ridiculous summoner you protect alone."

"Your grove protects a Daeva that Uni needs to speak with. The Daeva of the Crow."

"Ugh, as long as she doesn't bring that hyper girl with her, she can come in. I will accept one guard to accompany her. That guard cannot be you."

"Deal! I would rather avoid the other world for now."

The man in red walked off into the forest. The girl in yellow power armour with a tiger helmet standing next to him spoke, "So who was that? One of your conquests?"

"Ha! No, Argon the Slayer is an old rival of mine. He's a warrior monk of God Silver. He died a few years back. Went up against a powerful Daeva who proceeded to smush him into a fine paste."

"Then what is he doing alive?"

"No, not alive. Angry. He saw his summoner sacrifice everything and his other friend and fellow guard became like the Daeva. The Final Daeva, so to speak."

"I have no idea what any of that is."

"Nor should you. The Daeva are nature spirits. They are used by Summoners to fight. As a Druid, I protect the Daeva. We, Druids, guard the Daeva while the Summoners seek to use them."

"Then why allow a Summoner to speak with your Daeva?"

"Well, Trinity, Uni is an interesting girl. She is naive to the world. Her main passion is dancing."

"That is how she summons. I see great things for her. She will be the one to create great peace. A time when Summoners are no longer needed, but with that peace will come war. I see giant machines and atomic fire. I see death and devastation. I see our brother defiant and enraged. Fury incarnates his blade glistening with godly blood. I see his ascension immortal."

"I know, Corvus, I have seen the same thing. Why, then will you allow this?"

"Morbid curiosity. Also, the Crow Daeva is eager to speak with Uni."

"I do not want my brother to be gaining power."

"I understand that. But, Trinity, understand this. The Demon of Silver was born strong. He will only get stronger. I know the Grey is the Pure Land's rival in the trinity."

"How do you know of the Trinity?"

"When you talk to a Daeva, you learn things. Things mortals are not meant to know, but also Druids are a part of the Grey as well. Even though we lean more towards the In-between."

"Sometimes you scare me more than Bounty does, Corvus."

"As well I should. I was Plan B. Now I have visitors coming. I am tired of using Nevermore's voice. Please vanish back to Angela's Grove."

"You can't get rid of me that easy, brother." She saw his eyes gleam menacingly. Before she was teleported away, she appeared five feet above The Lucky Raccoon, one of Angela's Grove's tallest towers. She dropped and quickly ignited her boosters to slow her fall. She lightly touched down. She snarled, "Damn it, I should have struck first."

As Corvus began to walk to shut the gate to the Druid Grove, a small furry badger demon ran up and slammed into his legs.

"You have to help her. She is in pain, please!"

Corvus looked at the creature and then sighed. He closed the gate behind him and followed the creature to his owner. An Elf lay bloody on the ground, but the blood was not hers. It was coming from an Olayazcan Elf that she was holding.

He cleared his throat and spoke with Nevermore's voice, "The Strigidae needs help. So why should the Crow help her?"

"She is my apprentice. I did this and I can't heal her. Please, you must help."

"Oh very well, Ava Ursa, I will help."

He hefted the girl up and walked back to his Druid grove. Ava followed him. As he arrived, he saw five women standing there. Two were blond, with dark grey skin, green eyes, large breasts, well muscled, and horns that looked to be on fire. One of the girls was pure blond and the other had tri-coloured hair. The pure blond girl was wearing teal clothing, while the tri-coloured one wore green. The one in green hair was blond, red and black. One was a very pale silver with black hair and teal horns that curved past the back of her head. The other was a dark grey-skinned red-haired girl with black combat armour and orange horns that curved behind her ears. The final one was a very strange-looking girl. She had metallic blue skin. She also had tri-coloured hair like the blond in green. In her case, it was black, purple, and blue. Her horns were purple and curved behind her ears as well. He grimaced. Using Nevermore's voice, he spoke, "Ladies, I must tend to this child first, then we can discuss why you are here. I hope one of you is fluent in sign language because I can't keep using Nevermore's voice."

The blond one in teal smiled, "I can understand it. Hello, brother."

Corvus shook his head and went over to a hut. He opened the door and disappeared inside.

***

Beatrix stood in front of an altar. On this altar was an abnormally large cube. Lexi and her family stood near her. Joan lay unconscious due to Lucy Steel and Selene Steel doing what they called a combo move on her when she tried to kill Beatrix.

Victor Steel, the brother, spoke, "Be careful! A large open room like this usually means a boss battle."

Beatrix struggled not to roll her eyes and touched the cube. The room violently shook. All over Neo Tarrah-Aert, maps suddenly showed the Arklands vanish. Monohorn stared at the map he was looking at and sighed, "Again?"

Beatrix and the Steel family appeared over empty land that had once been the chaos cathedral. The cube had shrunk. Beatrix caught the falling form of Joan and created a crater as she landed. She also quickly caught the Steel family.

An armoured figure walked out of the mists. Beatrix bowed and said, "Lady Silver, why are you on Neo-Tarrah-Aehrt?"

"My dear, you are on Silver. Also, thank you for retrieving the cube for me. Please hand it over so that I may gain knowledge from it."

"Here you are, Goddess Silver."

"Hahahaha! You fool of a girl, Goddess Silver lies dead. I killed her. I am Athena."

"No! Why?"

Another armoured woman walked out of the fog. "I am Artemis. Thank you for bringing us this land. We will enjoy sacrificing you to appease the gods of this land so that they may join us in our crusade against God Silver."

Beatrix snapped her fingers, causing the Steel family to vanish. She pulled out her sword and sliced through Artemis. Athena snarled and stabbed her in the back. She ignited her sword and vaporized Beatrix.

A wizard walked into the clearing and looked at the two women. "So we are on planet Silver. Hmm... you must be Athena and Artemis. Where is your third?"

"We don't speak to men."

He became massive, dwarfing them and became like fire. "You will speak to me. I was the head of this pantheon. I am Merwyn. You speak now!"

Athena gulped, "I am Athena of Noamaiza. My battle sisters and I would like your pantheon to join us in our crusade against the top God of Planet Silver."

"Why would I want to go against God Silver? Regardless I will discuss it with the others and if we decide to join you, Joan d'Arc will be in contact with you."

***

Bounty Hunter 13 shuddered. He quickly teleported, catching a bunch of falling children in his psychic bubble. He looked down at them and sighed. He brought them to his home and placed them in observation. He let out a throaty growl that caused Llodi Cacophony to appear and try to calm him.

"Dad, what's wrong?"

"An intrusion to this world. My female counterpart Beatrix Badger died violently five minutes ago. Since she is as powerful as I am, I felt it."

"You are saying this world is in danger?"

"I don't know, Llodi, but I suggest you make as much time as you can to be with your siblings."

***

In Angela's grove, Trinity collapsed in the middle of a fight with Gold Wing and Scorpi Aka. The girl in pink power armour defended her to the best of her ability until she hit the emergency transport that sent them back to their HQ. Zarbon, the Green's head, floated in his tube with Lord Dragon monitoring the events.

Lord Dragon spoke in his harsh whisper, "You recalled too soon, Kimber. Why?"

"Trinity collapsed in battle. She is always the last to stand."

"Hmm, not good, not good at all. Very well. Get her to central healing and out of her power armour. Make sure she is attached to her life support system before you do."

Zarbon spoke, "Did you feel it, Dragon? The world has gained a new pantheon. How will your plan work now?"

"I have no secrets, Zarbon."

"Sure and I'm not a head floating in a tube because his body is out of phase with reality."

"I assure you, Zarbon, I have no plans."

"If you say so, Dragon. Do you think they will side with or against God Silver?"

"Against? They are too orderly, while Silver is Chaotic. The only one who may remain neutral is Merlin. He seems to be a bit chaotic."

***

Deep in the woods where Corvus had his Druid grove, Corvus leaned heavily against the statue to Nevermore. He was holding his chest as if he had suffered a severe heart attack. Inside one of the homes that called this land home Ava Ursa the Strigidae also collapsed in agony.

Uni came out of the planemeld with The Crow Daeva to see Corvus like this. "Lulluz, quick, get a health tonic. He's having a heart attack."

The tall ethereal woman clothed only in belts rummaged in her cleavage and pulled out a green and gold tonic that smelled of berries. Corvus went limp as his body hovered in the air. The Crow Daeva appeared and spoke, "Do not worry, little one. He is fine. A massive shift in the balance between Grey, In-between, Shadow Realm, and Pure Lands caused him to experience Psyonic whiplash. He will come within the day. We have spoken. I have given you a small piece of my power. Now go do your duty."

Uni looked pained as Corvus floated into the large tree nearby. Lulluz stroked her and led her off. "There is nothing we can do for him. Let Daeva handle it. We have the second Daeva. Now we must go to Diavonbre to ask God Bahamut for his blessing."

***

The masked man stopped dead in his tracks. Wampanor spoke, "You felt it as well. Are you able to continue or should we clear out the nearby cave for you to recover in?"

"What happened?"

"Aside from Beatrix Badger-Oda, your brother's female counterpart, dying?"

"Yes, aside from that."

"Old One-Eye has a new ally."

"So a new pantheon that will be against Silver has appeared. Of course. Things will progress much more quickly now. I think I'll be fine, Wampanor. Let us move on."

***

Gilda blocked the fiery attack from the android in red armour. He was blasted back by a wave of sound coming from Vinyl's speakers. He flipped in mid-air and used his rocket feet to launch at Vinyl. She dodged his attack, but a fist entered her sternum she gasped. The armoured man pulled his fist out of her and turned towards Gilda and Alexandra. Gilda snarled. Alexandra smiled devilishly and Gilda vanished. She pulled out her serrated knife.

"So Bounty Hunter X-10, you have successfully killed Elena Hunter, Vinyl Darkspeed, and soon myself. Why?"

"I owe you no explanation."

"Oki doki." She sliced through his neck and planted a bomb into it. As his body healed up, he was vaporized along with the bodies of Elena, Vinyl, and Alexandra.

His spirit appeared as his body began to reform. "Damn it! Damn it! All to the thirteen hells! It'll take years for my body to reform. But when it does. Mark my words I will find you, Bounty Hunter 13 and I will kill you."

Bounty walked into the clearing. "Pity I was too late. So you are the puppetmaster. See you in a few centuries." He walked off, leaving X-10 to scream at the sky. He whispered a blessing under his breath. Now all that is left is the Psycheos. *My death comes nearer and nearer. I will relish the time I have.*

A grey-skinned and grey-furred Taur appeared and walked over. "So this is where the disturbance came from. Hello, Bounty Hunter 13. I do not know if you remember me."

"You are commander Rhapsody, yes?"

"Grand general now, but yes."

"Why are you here?

"I came to investigate and also pass on the news that Axel passed away this morning. He died in the company of your sister, Amari. His wife was soon after. She did not want to live without him."

"I see, thank you for telling me. Now I have a question for you. I know you were Scarabaeus' nephew. But what is a Taur doing working with Silverans? I thought your kind hated my kind."

"My full name is Gunnar Rhapsody. I was born under three red moons. My father considered me a failure and an abomination. He sent me to live in Diavonbre with my uncle. He marked me as a failed Taur, so my only hope now is to live out the rest of my life as a Silveran."

"Shit man, that's rough!"

"It's not so bad. I am surprised you think it is."

"I just know when a Taur declares themselves a Silveran, they are giving up."

"Hah! Well, you are not entirely wrong, but as I was born different from other Taur, my mindset is different as well. May the Grey protect you, Demon of Silver. I can sense your time is coming to an end."

The Downfall of the Psycheos

"The drums of fate are beating, Bounty Hunter 13. Will you survive the coming battle or will you die? What do the drums say?"

"Shaman, it matters little what the beat says. Every Bounty Hunter 13 must go through some milestones. These milestones are written in the book of fate written by The Writer. The first is the milestone of death. He will be killed by Lord Psycheo. While I have already gone through that milestone, it didn't count because I was slain not by Lord Leon Psycheo but by Psycho Phantom. Leon Psycheo must slay me himself. The second milestone is, of course, the birth of my daughter, Cherry, who grows to despise me and tries to kill me on many occasions. That has already happened. The third is me becoming a scrap haulier and becoming the most hated man on the planet. The final is becoming immortal and never experiencing the havens. For even the gods will fear me. Their hatred will force me to stay in the realm of mortals."

"Is that truly what you believe? Anything The Writer writes can be erased. You are not imprisoned by fate's beat."

"While I agree with your sentiment, Shaman Triagonal, it never turns out well when a Bounty Hunter 13 tries to go against his fate."

"The drums still beat. What is your next move?"

Bounty pulled his halberd out and blocked a man armoured in black and silver's axe. Raven Triagonal smiled and vanished. Several men walked into the cathedral.

Bounty smiled, "So Lord Psycheo needs his cronies to attack an old man. Pathetic."

"Your team lies dead and only you remain. I look forward to seeing the life bleed from your eyes."

Thirteen days ago, Planet Black

Lord Psycheo looked at the rotting corpse of Reaver The Black. He snorted and vaporized it. He looked up at the artificial moon Casualty Station. He vanished and appeared near a pale man with two guns and an amber-skinned woman with a scar on her face. The woman barely let out a cry before her head fell to the ground. The man turned only to have the axe connect with his shoulder. He hissed in pain and fired several shots; one hit the alarm. Lord Psycheo finished him off and held his side where blood dripped from a hollow point bullet. A portal opened and he walked through it. "Tallon mark Reaver the Black off as dead. His donor killed him. I killed his donor and his donor's bodyguard. I'll be sealing my wound in the medical bay. Alert me when we are ready to march on Bounty Hunter 13."

"Yes, sir."

Twelve days ago, Planet Lizard

A muscular Oruc stalked through the forest of Lizard. He was a mercenary hired to slay one Scarr-ed Lizard. He had been hunting this prey for six days straight. He had to avoid all manner of beast and leather hides. The dark green Lizard with one blind eye was currently sleeping at a camp stone.

The man crept up on his prey. His prey opened his eye. "Ah, there you are, Gore from Ash. I've been waiting."

Gore from Ash was thrown into a tree by his prey. He saw the sleeping form vanish. He was taken aback, which cost him his life. Scarr-ed Lizard ripped open his jugular with his claws. He then exhaled fire from his mouth, incinerating Gor. He blinked his inner eyelid and then his outer eyelid. He then lay back down. "Bounty can deal with it. He probably already knows."

Twelve days ago, Stinalta

A large Tuar-Anubi rowed his scrap boat. He was waiting for his moment to strike. He had been given a suggestion by a horned demon in black and silver to kill a shark by the name of Sting Ray. He had no idea where this Sting Ray was, nor did he have a plan. It seemed to him, however, that his scrap boat knew where to go. The boat stalled near an Island where a nine-foot-tall Shark man stood holding a trident. The bull climbed off his boat.

"You must be Sting Ray. I am Bull Dozer. I will be the one to kill you."

"So be it, Bull Dozer. Be prepared; I will not hold back."

"Nor will I."

A magical mist enshrouded the island. Bull Dozer felt invigorated by this strange phenomenon. It took many hours, but he soon killed his opponent. He tossed Sting Ray into the water and watched as he evaporated. His boat was destroyed and a large water elemental shaped like Sting Ray formed. It smashed its fist down, paralyzing Bull Dozer. A portal opened and Bull Dozer was pulled through by a blue-furred arm. He appeared face-to-face with Goddess Prisma.

"I see you have returned to the land. I am eager to see what you offer. I hope you can kill the scourge that is Bounty Hunter 13. Allow me to send you to the man who contacted you."

He looked around the deck of the ship. He could see his home of Silver out the window. So close yet so far away. He looked at the woman glaring at him and writing something down.

She spoke, "You are the only one to come back uninjured. I approve."

"No one asked your opinion, girl."

"And that deducts points. Ah well! The others have yet to arrive; the boss is in the med centre if you wish to speak with him."

Eleven Days Ago, Planet Gold

Wing Blade stood staring down a shadowy phantom-like wolf. She smiled, "You can help me find Gold Wing and take my revenge for the death of my daughter?"

The wolf nodded.

"Then I accept your offer. Join with me and I will help your friends defeat the demon who ruined my life."

The wolf let out a sinister howl and plunged into his willing host. She let out a moan of ecstasy and flew off. The two soon found Bat Wing sitting with his axe meditating. Wing Blade could feel the shadow wolf's bloodlust. She attacked Bat Wing and ripped out his jugular. His eyes opened and he snarled. As he bled he threw her into a blue portal. He took off his fake neck and shook his head. A small leather-winged girl looked at him from the tree.

She spoke, "Uncle, is my mother dead?"

"She will be soon. I am sorry little one. She succumbed to her hatred and fused with The Flying Shadow Wolf of Dark Essence. She is more of a feral now. My companion will end her suffering. It is best I do not."

"I understand, uncle. What will happen to us?"

"We will be fine, Rusty. Everything is fine. Come, it's time for lunch."

Wing Blade appeared in a containment field. The woman at the controls looked at her and sighed, "Hello, Shadow Wolf. I see you found someone to help us."

A shadowy wolf rose from the floor. "Yes, this is Wing Blade. She is the sister of Bat Wing. She just finished feasting on his jugular, so I doubt he will be able to interfere."

"Good, it is almost time to attack. Soon Bluud De Gulch will be joining us."

***

Argentorado Red 100 stood next to a horned being dressed in green with a red helmet. He looked over his foe. He smirked, then motioned his opponent to follow.

"You must be the one known as Bluud de Gulch. Come follow. Don't you worry! You'll get to strike me down eventually, but we must go to a ritual site first. Until we reach the site, you will be unable to kill me no matter what you try."

"Lead the way, donor. My blade can wait to sample your blood."

"So you are my clone yet at the same time, not a full clone. Who was your second donor that was used to stabilize your genetic sludge?"

"You, Bounty Hunter 13, and a fellow by the name Judas Bloodsong."

"I see, of course, a Stone Vampire's blood would be stable enough to fuse two vastly different genetic structures. Perfect, we are here. Let us wait until nightfall. You will see why this place was chosen."

"I waited this long, why not wait a bit more."

As the moon rose to prominence, the stars lit up the sky. There was a red and gold aurora Bluud gasped.

"Isn't it something? My dear boy, you may strike me down now. Fulfil what was meant for you. Then one day, you too will be here awaiting your death. And on that day, you will truly be an Argentorado."

Bluud stabbed swiftly and as the old Redian fell, he vanished in a gout of fire. A spirit stood in his place. The spirit turned towards Bluud and smiled before vanishing.

Bluud walked through the portal that had been sent to his location. He looked back through the portal as it closed and sighed.

Tallon looked at him and smiled, "Welcome back, Bluud. I see you succeed. And with no injury."

"He died willingly. I am unable to process that right now. I will be in my chambers resting. Notify me when we march."

"Rest up, Bluud. All we need to do is wait. We will meet up with a King shortly."

Six days ago, Planet Metallic

"Reaver? Oh, Little Reaver? There you are, you pesky clone."

Talicon struck a stone, shattering it and revealing a terrified boy in heavy Mandelic Armor. This was Deathskull Slaughter.

Deathskull fled. "Leave me alone. I don't want to die."

"You should have thought of that before attempting to stab me. Get over here and your death will be painless."

"Never!"

"Damn coward! You show no respect for your genetics. Run! If I see you again, I will end you!"

"You are too hard on the boy."

"Oh goody, his lordship graces my presence."

The old and wrinkly metallic green male with electric sapphire eyes behind him spoke, "You know, Talicon, I distinctly remember you fleeing in terror after you failed when you were young."

"God Metal, that was then."

"Of course. Maybe you are so wrathful towards him because he reminds you of you?"

"And what let him kill me to boost his morale?"

"No, just be a little less terrifying."

"Everybody needs a mentor."

"You're using my own words against me. Argh! Fine. Reaver, I will not kill you. I only wish to talk."

The boy poked his head out from behind a tree. "You promise?"

"I promise."

***

On Planet Silver, the massive Ursar King Wampanor of northern Norvcryog stood facing a smaller Ursar. The runt had the Audacity to challenge Wampanor to a duel after wounding Wampanor's companion.

"You injure my guest and challenge me for leadership of the North. Who are you so I may etch your foolishness on your gravestone?"

"I am Ice Mage of Doom."

"Oh, ho! What are you ten? Trying to be an edge lord or whatever the kids call it. Very well, Ice Mage of Doom. The snow will be red with your blood."

"You talk the talk, old man, but can you walk the walk? Icy Spear of Black Fangs!" Wampanor sidestepped the Black Icicle spear that launched at him. He scoffed. His massive battle axe cleaved into Ice Mage of Doom's shoulder. Smashing through bone and muscle. Ice Mage of Doom's top half severed from his lower as his guts flew out and bathed the snow in his brackish red blood. His lifeless corpse hit the ground with a splat as his body hit his guts. Wampanor walked over to his fallen companion. He hoisted him up and walked off.

His companion weakly spoke, "Bounty is in danger. He needs help."

Wampanor scoffed, "Somehow, I doubt that. I suspect he is waiting for his death. He seemed very tired when I last saw him."

"He is too important."

"Mystic, my boy, relax. Your injuries are more severe. The Demon can handle himself. You should know that by now."

"You don't understand Wampanor. If he dies today, his destiny is set."

"Rest now, Mystic. Let me tend to your injuries. If by the time you are healed and your brother still needs help, I will go. My concern is you."

"You are too good to me."

"Yes, well, when you find a boy barely alive in the wastes with the mark of Lucky Seven cut into his body, you change your ways a bit."

"Please promise me you will help my brother."

As Wampanor put Mystic into stasis healing, he sighed, "I promise I will help your brother."

The Golden serpenti next to him tilted her head. "I notice you did not specify which brother."

"He focuses on Bounty too much. That is the one I'll help with, but I suspect he is already dead. Destiny always has a way of righting what is wrong. If I help Bounty survive this, another Lord Psycheo will kill him. His path was set for him the moment he absorbed the psionic nuclear bomb into his being."

***

Two green-haired, green-eyed men stood facing each other. Both were over ten feet tall. Both were also very muscular. One had a cigar in his mouth and was holding a glaive with the hunter clan crest on it. His aura was a murky blue and sparked with psionic bursts that smelled vaguely of rot. The other looked slightly younger but had a large scar that bisected him from the right shoulder to the left hip. His aura was murky red and smelled vaguely of sulfur.

The younger spoke, "Braid Deathseeker, you donated your sperm to the infernal mistress Null. I am her child with you and Zenthin Ankara. I am here to kill you."

The older one with the cigar smirked, "Are you? Well, Brawl Ankara, I wish you the best. But I would have thought you would want to kill Bounty Hunter 13. He is, after all, the one who killed your siblings, sans Scorpion."

"Hmm, you are right. My father despised you, though, so I feel I need you dead."

"Then come, boy! Strike me down if you can."

The two clashed. Brawl increased his muscle size by ten and struck angrily. Braid blocked the attack with his glaive. However, the glaive was shattered by the force of Brawl's punch. Braid scoffed and as Brawl charged him with a haymaker, he stabbed Brawl through the stomach with his hidden arm blades. As Brawl fell, he smiled. Braid Deathseeker incinerated his fallen foe's body.

"Rest easy, boy. Everything works out in the end."

One day ago

As the dark ship landed, Lord Psycheo waited. He walked out only to see the corpse of the one they were supposed to meet. He cocked his head and saw a massive Ursar standing with a fierce and jagged axe watching him.

The bear spoke, "You must be Lord Psycheo. Your little friend there thought he could challenge the God of Winter. He lies dead. Will you join him or will you leave and go on your way to fight The Demon of Silver?"

"I have no need of weaklings. He died, so be it. My goal has always been Bounty Hunter 13. I also have no need to prove anything to the likes of you. I will be leaving."

"Then go. Know, however, if I see you anywhere near my kingdom again, I will kill you."

"I expect nothing less. Goodbye, King Icefang of the North. May we never meet again."

"Feelings mutual."

Psycheo walked back onto his ship and it lifted off. Wampanor Icefang, King of the North, watched him go. He scoffed and went back towards his ship back to Norvcryog. He put up an ice wall as Lord Psycheo's ship opened fire on him. He threw his axe and it sliced through the engine with ease. The ship careened out of control and hit somewhere near Black Witch's Mountain.

Lord Psycheo exited the wreckage. He dusted himself off and looked around. Tallon followed soon after she looked green.

Leon Psycheo looked down at her, then sighed, "Casualty report."

She struggled to her feet. "The only one dead is the bull. Not that I feel bad for his death. He was an asshole. Bluud is well, but I think Wing Blade is wounded."

Wing Blade threw off some scrap metal. "I am not injured small prey. Who the hell opened fire."

Leon looked at the wreckage. "I suspect Bull Dozer did. I knew the Tuar had bad blood with the other species of Silver, but by ignoring orders not to strike, he got what he deserved. It is a pity Reaver Deathskull was never found. Could definitely use his extra hands right now."

Talon spoke, "Do you fear Bounty Hunter 13 that much to need so much backup? I thought you were created as his equal?"

"I do not fear him. I just know he is strong. I may be able to handle him myself, but backup is always welcome."

"Regardless, let us use the wreck as shelter. This is Black Witch's Peak. The second-highest point in the Silver Mountain range. The first being Mount Silver, so it gets insanely cold up here."

"We have no need of shelter. We landed near a defunct bunker. Likely it leads down to the forest below us as long as we can get it functional. We can press on."

Bluud opened the bunker door and it fell off into the snow. He looked down at it and snorted. His cloak flowed with a sudden burst of wind as the pressure inside the bunker became the pressure outside the bunker. He looked around with his sword drawn.

"Nothing but bones of some long forgotten culture. I see the lift, but it looks like it fell during some long-past cataclysm. Luckily the destruction left a path for us to get down. Watch your step."

The small group climbed down except for Wing Blade, who used her leathery wings to flap down. Talon was hanging on her grappling hook as it lowered her down. She sighed, "It would be so easy to kill them now. They killed my pappa. But the Demon wants a battle. I just need to fake my death. The forest should do nicely."

She sent a quick message to Corvus Hunter. After a few hours, the group finally reached the bottom. Lord Psycheo kicked open the lower door and coughed as corpse dust entered his helmet. The lower floor was covered in bones. It looked like a large number of people had swarmed the bunker and fought each other to get into the lift.

Talon snarled, "These people killed each other like animals. If I can't survive, you won't survive either. Ugh, so much anger and wrath in the air. My Lord, watch out!"

She stepped in front of Lord Psycheo as a large piece of rebar stabbed through her. It was embedded into the wall. Psycheo scoffed and waved his hand and everything went still.

"So this is the power of the Blood clan. Ha ha. Worthless. Leave us be and I will not exorcize you."

A shadowy form rose from the corpses. It had glowing red eyes and rotting grey skin. "I acknowledge your power, Lord Psycheo. You are welcome to join us."

"No, thank you. I have my own scheme. I do, however, thank you for getting rid of that little traitor for me. Saves me the trouble of killing her myself."

"Well then, thank you for releasing us from this prison we created for ourselves. We can now find hosts."

The corpses vanished in a black and bloody wind leaving Tallon pinned to the wall with a large gash across her face. Lord Psycheo pulled the piece of rebar out of the wall and caught her corpse. As they continued through the forest, he saw feathers. He set the corpse down.

"I have no quarrel with the Forest King. Here is your spy. She was slain by the Blood clan. My only quarrel is with your brother, the Demon of SIlver."

A large man with spiral horns walked out of the trees. He looked down at Lord Psycheo. "Very well, Pawn of Fate, I leave you to it. Good luck. The Demon awaits you at the Cathedral of Chaos."

Lord Psycheo entered the Cathedral to see an Amber skinned elf with long brown hair, terrifying green eyes, and a well-groomed beard sitting on one of the pews watching the entrance.

"Are you the final challenge before my donor, Maester QiKong Djinnai?"

QiKong spoke in a stern yet quiet voice, "Hardly worth my time. You are here to face Bounty Hunter 13. I am here to watch. That is all. I observe before deciding to act."

Psycheo walked past Maester Djinnai and deeper into the cathedral.

***

Bounty kicked the shadowy wolf as it tried to bite his ankles. He threw his halberd and it severed Wing Blade's head from her shoulders. She dropped and the Shadowy Wolf of Dark Essence howled in rage. It lunged again but was sliced it two by a sword that Bounty Hunter 13 had pulled out. He blocked the attack by Bluud de Gulch, purposely leaving his flank open for an attack by Lord Psycheo. He took the bait but was disarmed by another blade. He looked down at his bloody stump of an arm and gasped. He staggered back. Catching himself on one of the pews. He grabbed Bounty Hunter 13's fallen halberd.

Bounty smiled a sly smile and jumped back as Bluud swung at him again. He threw Bluud into the wall and followed up by pinning him with nine stone benches. He turned to Lord Psycheo.

"Come, my pernickety clone, you knew eventually. It would be just you and I facing each other."

"Yes, but I thought that they could wear you down. I see even fate has me by the balls."

The two clashed. Lord Psycheo was failing, however. His blood gushed from his injury and soon, he would bleed out. He pressed the attack. Eventually, he succeeded in slicing through one of Bounty's legs. As Bounty fell, his head was removed from his torso. Lord Psycheo stood triumphant. Then he fell. His blood fully drained from his body. Bluud de Gulch stood in awe. He saw the massive Bear from earlier, along with a huge Lizard man and Wing Blade's brother, walk into the cathedral. The three stood there. The Elf from the entrance stood up and bowed as the feathered man from the forest walked in; he specifically walked over to Bluud. He pulled the benches away from him.

Bluud kneeled. "Please spare me my life. I have yet to see the promised aurora."

The man chuckled a warm chuckle. "I have no plans to kill you, nor do any of these men. You are the only Psycheo to survive. I admire that. I will charter you back to Red. Think about your life and change your ways, but first, we must perform the sacred duty. Come help us pile the dead near the statue."

When the dead were laid out, the horned man began to chant in the tongue of the forest. Eventually, a large fire blossomed into existence. Bat Wing, Wampanor, and Scarr-ed spoke all together, "Thayme Sidrodc uigde het seul. Thayme Havens Sunocme het seul."

The flames grew brighter and five glasses of an amber liquid appeared, one in each of the men's hands. Bluud stared at it curiously.

The horned man chuckled again, "Don't think too hard about it. Just drink and throw the glass on the fire."

Bluud nodded and opened his helmet, revealing a youthful red face with a green beard and ruby eyes. He downed the glass and closed his helmet again. He tossed the glass on the fire along with the others. The fire exploded and then vanished, leaving nothing behind. Even the statue was gone. Wampanor nodded and vanished in a cascade of ice. Bat Wing knelt down and picked up the half mask on the floor. He handed it to the horned man and walked off.

Scarr-ed hissed, "Well, Corvus Hunter, this was fun. Please never summon me again. The less I see of that wretched man, the better off I am."

"Scarr-ed Lizard, don't worry, you will see him again. He likely will come to cleanse your planet of the chaos energies released during the Magus War."

"Oh, goody." Scarr-ed Lizard vanished with a smile.

Corvus Hunter sighed and looked over at Bluud, "Well, come along. Let's find you a ship to Red. I wish for you to find your promised Aurora."

The two walked off and the Cathedral vanished behind them. Raven Triagonal stood watching them walk off. She looked up at the stars. She shuddered as a cold wind struck her, but it was not the wind that made her shiver. She saw death. Fire billowing from a ruined city, a petrified man standing in a fury against the havens, an old Demon torn to shreds. The drums kept beating as she walked off.

***

Corvus dropped Bluud off at the station after talking with a Blackheart captain under the employ of Hunter Corp. Captain Oneida would make sure Bluud got back to Red in one piece. He entered the Druid Grove of Nevermore and sat down at a table with five women. Ada Ursa was tending to her apprentice.

He sighed, "So I understand the fact you are my twin sisters. What I don't understand is why show your face now?"

The woman in teal spoke, "I wanted to meet you. I found my sisters after we all were split up to hide from Tzar Ankara. We then learned of you and your siblings. We all agreed we wanted to meet them."

He sighed in response, "Well, you are a pinch too late. Myst has vanished, as has Amari, Bounty lies dead along with Aerick-Star and Vera, Eris is being tortured by the rebels who slew Scorpion Ankara and dismantled the Order of Mysteries of Goddess Silver, and Trinity is in Angela's Grove under the tutelage of the great deceiver."

"We don't particularly care about them. We truly only desired to meet you. Bounty Hunter 13 is an enemy of all of the clans that adopted us. I would prefer not to meet him. Myst is… unstable. You are the only one who has a calm demeanour and has more chill than any of the others."

My dear Rani. Amari is far calmer than I am. Father wanted a backup. I, unfortunately, am that back up. His desire to attain fame caused him to push the boundaries of what the PsyQi could do. It caused him to treat everybody like an experiment which is what led to his assassination by Lord Shadow's hand. Zenthin Ankara and him were close. Zen gave him the hand of his sister and his daughter with that sister's hand in marriage. By all accounts, the two were close. However, Zen was learning from him, stealing his ideas. Manipulating them to match his ideals. In the end, he killed his friend, but Bounty Hunter 12 deserved it by all accounts. Two men who wanted to do things their own way butting heads for that length of time did not end up well for either of them.

"I do not need a lecture about what power does to somebody. I just want to see you with my own eyes."

"So why stay? You have clearly seen me. Go home, ignore the Hunter clan, live your life."

"I don't know, something is keeping me here."

"It is the innate desire in all Hunter clans descended from Bounty Hunter 12. Learn the forbidden, the unknown, the taboo, a desire for knowledge. A desire for power and I am giving that knowledge to you."

"Ugh, I don't understand any of this, but I am glad to see you. After all of these years separated, I yearn to understand what our father's grand plan was."

"What about yourselves? Mayari, why do you stay? Kori, why do you? Lucy, what makes you stay? Lulu, how about you?"

The woman in a black cloak spoke, "Corvus, I desire to know more about the Hunter Ankara history. Grandfather was a very powerful man. He learned dark things and I, too, desire to know those things."

"Lucina, that is not a path you should walk. The shadows will eat you alive."

"I know, but something had to have created us. I desire to know that. How that power can be translated."

"I can pass you to somebody who knows, but that is something I can't teach. He lives here in this grove."

A tall thin, sickly-looking man walked out, he was covered head to toe in bandages. And it looked like he was on fire, but it wasn't fire, it was smoke. It wasn't smoke either it was shadows that bled off of him thanks to what he had tried to do.

He spoke, "I heard my name mentioned."

"Hello, Chain, I am glad to see you up and moving."

"Who are these girls?"

"My twin sisters."

"Excuse you, what?"

"Yes, due to some time-space continuum bull, I have five new twin sisters. Lucy, this is our elder brother, Chain. He can train you in the ways of darkness."

"Does she understand what she is getting into?"

"I assume so, but why not gauge her willingness to learn when training her."

"Young Lucy, was it? I will take you to my nook. I will have you pour over all my tomes and if you still desire to learn from me after what I show you, I will teach you."

"That is acceptable."

"Then follow."

Lucy walked off with Chain. Corvus looked at the woman in black combat armour. She gulped.

"And what of you, Lulu? What do you desire by coming here?"

"I overheard the Canaries I work with talking about this place and how you were a master of death. I would like to learn from you."

"Ah, now that is interesting. I follow Nevermore, a God of Death and the Gothic. We can teach, but first, you must subject yourself to the Psalm of Poh. If you survive, I have much to teach you."

"Woah, wait!" She vanished before she could say anymore. Corvus smiled. She will survive. She is a Canary.

"And that leaves you, Mayari and Kori."

Mayari, the woman dressed up as a punk rocker with her Guitar on her back, spoke, "I heard the Melody of the Universe call me. I wanted to understand why I would be called here. Especially now."

"While I am not a Bard, I believe I know the reason."

"Will you tell me the reason?"

"After I speak with Lori. Have patience, my dear."

"Ugh, annoying."

"It won't be long, Mayari. I am here because I want to meet my long-lost twin sisters. I met them, then I discovered you. Now I have met you. I still have this gut feeling I am missing somebody, but when the time comes, I am sure I will meet her. I am going back home to my husband. I will keep in touch, Mayari. Have a good day, Corvus."

Corvus spoke with Nevermore's voice, "I wish you the best, Lady Sanchez. If you happen to see the Adamorte clan tell them, they chose a good helper."

"So why was I called here by the Melody of the Universe?"

"To keep you safe. Bounty Hunter 12 had a plan B in the event of his plan A being a bust. Since Plan A is currently dead, along with most of his siblings, Plan B must be kept safe. I am plan B. As you are my twin sisters, you also must be kept safe. Well, you are Corvus' twin sisters. As he is using my voice to tell you this, I am temporarily your brother."

"I see, so somehow Bounty Hunter 12 warped the very fabric of the universe to create his magnum opus, so to speak."

"Yes, he did, which is why he is dead. And why he is considered a traitor to both the Silveran species and his true form, that of a Taur."

"Very well, I suppose I have nothing else to do."

"I must relieve Corvus of the burden of using my voice. I look forward to seeing what you and your sisters can do."

Corvus slumped forward and burst into a cloud of black feathers, only to be reborn in a younger, more rejuvenated form.

He shuddered, "That was unexpected, but I feel much healthier now."

Lori spoke, "Uh, what was that? That won't happen to us, will it?"

"That was me dying and being reborn. And no, it will not be happening to you. You have already been reincarnated."

The Jump

"There are four key concepts of the thirteenth Hunter. One, they will be blind but will see perfectly due to their immense strength in the PsiQi. Two, they will become the most hated being in the galaxy. Three, as their power grows, the gods will become resentful of them. Four, their DNA will become the basis for the next generation of Silverans. This is all I know. This is all I can tell you," said Zora Von Skuellenheim of the temple to God Silver

Deep in the heart of Galaxy Silver, past the Star Vale and circling a grey planet known as Silver, floats a space station. In this station, a group of cadets waits for their test. This test shows the higher-ups what rank to give them and where they will be placed. With these cadets was a young man. This man was furious he had been reborn into the body of a teenager instead of his adult body. Adding insult to injury, he was still blind and his body had taken on his younger form. He limped on his shorter and more frail leg past a few older students who were having a laugh at his expense.

"Burned blind mutated Dutch thinks he can join the Spacewalkers." One tripped him and he fell. "Look at him, he can't even see where he's going, much less the console of a ship."

Dutch Hunter snorted, got up and adjusted his cadet uniform. He made sure his half-mask was still on and tightened the blindfold he used to cover his eyes. He entered the exam room as his name was called.

He heard a familiar voice. "Fuck, not you again. This is your thirteenth time here. How did you even get past admissions?"

"I proved myself to them, Galifon. Now, are you going to give me the test or not?"

"Oh, I'll give you the test. First up is the physical test. How well can you handle yourself in a boarding scenario? Your ship is under attack and the enemy has broken the hull. You have only your 44 and combat knife. Show me what you got."

Dutch smiled, he had picked up the foam knife and stunner. These were the stand-in for real weapons. Afterall, he was against real opponents. He sensed them.

Three opponents to his left, five to his right and ten in front of him. He also sensed two of his injured allies behind him. He emptied his gun and tossed it aside as he dodged an attack from his left. He stepped on his weak leg and stumbled under their gunfire. He regained balance and stabbed one, then slit the throat of the other. He blocked the attack from one of the assailants aiming for his ally. Unfortunately, the attack disarmed him. He weaved under the knife thrust of one of the assailants before hitting them hard. He stepped back and twisted one over his shoulder. He hefted another up and tossed them into the rest. He picked up his two allies and rushed them to a safe area. The hallway was now filled with enemies. Dutch smirked as he locked the hull door behind him so no help could get to him. He also shut down the entire hallway where the enemies were. It was just them and him.

Galifon watched in annoyance. He had put Dutch Hunter at zero odds of survival, but Dutch still stood. He would have to call off this portion of the test before anyone got seriously injured. And there it was, a student who now had a broken arm. He sighed, "Physical test is over. Dutch Hunter, please take a seat for the tactics test. You are the navigator, the ship has just encountered a massive enemy fleet. Your captain lies dead his second has declared a retreat."

"First off, Galifon, how many ships account for an enemy fleet? Anything over ten is considered suicide regardless of fleeing."

"There are twenty ships, one of which is a command ship."

Dutch smiled again, baring his fangs. He looked over to where the second in-command seat was. "Commander, I must apologize for what I am about to do. We are doomed regardless of whether we flee or not. Better to die fighting than as a coward."

"We still have a chance of survival. Don't do anything rash and listen to me. Turn this ship around."

Dutch sighed and pushed several buttons. An explosion noise sounded and he heard the communications office say, "Shields are down and the jump engine is damaged. One more hit and we cease to exist."

"What are you doing, Dutch? Stay at your station."

Dutch socked the second in command and typed in order. The ship turned around and Dutch took control of it. He pushed a button and the ship jumped and blew up in a fiery explosion taking the command ship with it. That was when several allied ships appeared and destroyed the enemy fleet.

Dutch spoke, "Their victory would not have been possible without the command ship destroyed. Like I said, better to go out fighting than a coward."

Galifon snarled, "You disobeyed a direct order. You are not fit for the Spacewalkers. Do not make me call security."

Another more feminine voice spoke, "Supreme Admiral Galifon. I like this kid and I want him for my ship."

All of the captains in the room turned to the voice. She was a Draconic Silveran. Her scales were exposed and the downy spikes on her skin had been smoothed out. She wore a black uniform with an insignia of sun with two swords crossed on it.

Galifon looked at the obscene woman with fire in his eyes. She returned his stare with cold, calculating eyes. He snarled again, "Fine, but if you take him, you are not allowed back on base as long as I live. The same goes for all those under your command."

"Considering the mission that I was given. That is fine with me. Dutch Hunter, I will see you at docking bay thirteen."

Dutch arrived at docking bay thirteen. He was dressed in his cadet uniform, but he now had on a long black duster. His boots had back-of-heel spikes and toe spikes that made them look demonic. He also had replaced his blindfold with dark-covered psy-dampening glasses. His right side was horribly burned, so he had covered his hands with gunslinger gloves. He still limped because of his leg, but at least he looked vaguely intimidating.

He saw who he would be dealing with for however long they were out. He saw a Red Silveran locking lips with a Black Silveran while a Gigas Silveran sharpened his Bal-Heth blade while glaring at the others. He saw an orange-skinned teen with blue tendrils on her head that were connected to two white crescent-shaped dermal spines. She looked nervous and kept smoothing her cadet uniform. He saw one of the wolf like Nu silverans in a medic coat along with one of the red-haired Irescotwel Silverans talking. He also saw a Qwn with six horns and then, much to his surprise, he saw a pale woman with electric blue hair talking to a green-skinned woman with Oni heritage. Next to them was a Brown Silveran with smoke coming off his body. He raised his eyebrow when he saw a haggard-looking grey Taur talking with an Amber skinned elf with terrifying green eyes. He also noticed, even though she was trying to hide, a bighead in a science officer uniform. The captain walked into the docking bay and looked at her crew. Of course, this wasn't all of them. She still had a bunch of red shirts and various other crew. She smiled, "Ah, the people I will be working closely with. Allow me to give you your assignments. Dutch Hunter, I want you as my second so that I may keep a close eye on you. Also on the main deck will be Wulf as the head of security, Gilda as navigations, Ashka as my pilot, and Vinyl as communications. In the medical and science bay, I want William Wolf as Chief Medical officer and Solan as Chief Science officer. In engineering, I want Leslie. Kimberly is the counsellor, while Feldspar will be operating. Please get acquainted with your crew members. Once we reach a decent distance, I will announce our mission. You all are dismissed."

The group entered the ship and placed their belongings in their private quarters. Dutch looked his room over. He saw the food dispenser in the corner near a large spacious desk. On the desk were a Hunter Corporation computer and several containers that were fuzed with the desk so they would not come tumbling down. He hung his coat up along with his shirt. It was far too warm on this ship, but he figured it had to do with the many species involved. Of course, the waste disposal was connected to the jump core. It's heat vaporizing anything and also giving the core energy due to the waste. He snorted and took out a cigar and lit it. These were clove cigars laced with opium and other spices that dulled Dutch's pain. He blew out purple smoke that smelled like mulled cider.

"I see you still smoke those things."

Dutch turned towards the door he had not heard open. He saw the Brown Silveran, Wulf, standing there. He blew out some more purple smoke and spoke, "I'm sorry, do I know you?"

"Not surprising since I never gave my last name when we last met. It's me, Axel."

"Ah, so I wasn't hallucinating when I heard Leslie, Vinyl and Gilda. What made you decide to join the Spacewalkers?"

"Boredom and the fact I was just reincarnated a few years ago. Still can't believe you go by that stupid pseudonym of Dutch."

"Keeps my identity safe. Also makes people underestimate me. My real name comes with a sense of dread. Something that Dutch doesn't have."

"Well, we best get going. I'm sure the captain is waiting for you. I have met the many red shirts and my officers. They'll do nicely with plenty of cannon fodder. Just wish we didn't have so much cannon fodder."

"Well, we most likely will go through them fast. Got to have plenty of backups. I suspect we also have a bunch in cryostasis in the unforeseen event of death of all current grunts."

"You have no idea."

The two laughed as Dutch snuffed out his cigar and put it away. They soon arrived on the main deck. The captain shifted her tail as she sat down. She looked out the view screen and spoke into the shipwide transmitter, "Our mission is to explore the uncharted territory past planet AcidGreen. This is a twenty-year mission. Our first off-ship will be Casualty Station. I expect you to do well and not make Spacewalker look dim and stupid."

***

"Captain's log AH 221000 Wodansday fifteen hundred hours, we have arrived at Casualty Station. The crew is getting ready to depart for a week of relaxation. Then on to Plasma Station, where we will restock. The only thing of note was some pirate ships looking for easy pickings. They avoided us, we avoided them. Just hope Casualty Station will be as uneventful. This is Captain Bela Le Foe signing off."

Dutch Hunter stood smoking his cigar, staring out at the empty void of space. Had he been on the other side of the station, he would see the Planet Black. He heard a noise behind him and reached for his gun.

"Woa chillax boss, it's just me."

"Vinyl?"

"Yeah, dude. I just want to talk."

"Alright, I'm listening."

"Cool, so why did you join up with the Spacewalkers? It is you, right? There are very few people with the name Dutch Hunter."

"It's me, alright. I joined up because I am a young man again. Need to learn something new. Also, I am not exactly wanted on Silver right now. There is a golden age going on and I bring war."

"I won't deny that war seems to follow you. Alright, so what are your plans?"

"I plan to go to a bar and see what happens."

"Sounds fun. I'll join you. I heard there's a great bar called Ravager on deck nine. All the others we know are heading up there."

"I will see you there. I have some stuff to take care of here first."

Dutch smiled as she walked away in a flirty manner. He saw who he was waiting for. A young man walked into view wearing the uniform of a Deathknight. He noticed Bounty and shook his head.

"You, old devil. What are you doing on my station?"

"Well, Luke, it seems my first stop as a Spacewalker was here."

"Look at you looking young. If I were a woman, I'd be trying to jump on you."

"Look at you. Hell, the same can be said of you. I figured Pain would be nearby."

A rough female's voice rang out, "Who says I'm not."

Dutch looked up to see a woman wearing just belts hanging upside down from the ceiling. Her gravimag boots hum. Her amber skin shone with sweat. And her face had a large scar down one side of it. She wore an eyepatch over the eye with the scar.

"Don't tell me you got into another fight, girl?"

"Yeah, no thanks to the previous Deathknight."

"Shit, well, you still look good."

"Aw, you big flirt. Bite me."

"Come down here."

"No thanks. What are you doing here?"

"First stop as a Silveran Spacewalker. Heading over to the Ravager bar. When do you two get off patrol?"

"Ten minutes. We'll see you there, most likely. Most officers of Casualty Station hang there after work."

Dutch smiled as the two walked away. He began walking towards the elevator. He hit floor nine and leaned back against the wall. He got off the elevator and headed towards Ravager Bar. He arrived and was about to enter when the owner of the bar walked out.

"A Hunter clan freak. Gods damn it. Stay away from my bar."

"Oh goody, Hello cousin Stalker."

"Which bastard are you?"

"Dutch Hunter at your service."

"Fuck off, go taint someone else's bar."

Luke walked around the corner and said, "Mr Stalker, what is going on here?"

Bounty shrugged. "Don't worry about it, Deathknight, just a small disagreement between cousins. If you see a bright blue-haired woman in there, tell her I decided against going to Ravager."

"Sure thing, Dutch."

Dutch walked across from Ravager to a bar called Blackhearts Machine Shed.

He entered the dimly lit bar that smelled strongly of oil and heavy machinery. It was lit by many bars of neon light. He saw the bartender. The man was large and bulky. He had a rhino head and looked almost like a cyborg, with many tubes feeding through the metal plates he had on. He looked at Dutch.

"What can I do for ya?"

"What beverages do you have here?"

"Hard liquor and Toxic liquor."

"I would like a Silveran Fire whiskey with a shot of iron gut."

"Ha, that stuff is weak. Try Blackheart's Tiamut. That'll put a fire in your belly."

"Alright, I'll have one of those. What's up with this place?"

"Well, boyo, this is Rino Von Rhino's bar. Former captain of the Blackheart Pirate fleet. We retired early while we still had our lives. Space got too dangerous, especially once you hit the Junk Belt. It's also a machine shop since all of us are cyborgs from Seaborgium. Retired due to the various United Allied Planet ships, Federation of Allied Planet's ships, and now apparently Silveran Spacewalker ships. It's not a good time to be a pirate."

"So you went into the bar business?"

"Not just bar business but also mechanics, loaders, security, and legit trade."

Dutch's communicator chirped. He opened it to reveal Vinyl's face. "Yo Dutch, some dude just tol' us you decided not to go to Ravagers. Woa, where are you?'

"I am across the way at Blackhearts Machine Shed. They serve extremely toxic liquor, so I would not recommend drinking here. Especially since you are already drunk."

"Ha, we have a week off, man. I'm coming over."

Dutch looked at the bartender. "Hope you have enough room. Knowing Vinyl, she'll drag the rest of the crew with her."

"Ha ha, well, the more, the merrier. My boys are still working; they won't be off for two hours still. And many are still out and about as shipping crew. I'm sure you noticed the various pirate ships on your way here. Those are ma boys."

Bela La Foe walked into the bar with Vinyl trailing her. "You're Rino von Rhino, the notorious pirate."

"Not a pirate anymore, lass. Just a bartender."

"Can I get your autograph?"

"Wha? Why?"

"I collect all Blackheart memorabilia. Trading cards, action figures, model ships, hell, even replica weapons."

"Ha ha, well, I can't say no to an avid fan of the Blackheart fleet."

She took off her shirt and handed him a tattoo pen. "Right here on my shoulder."

Axel spoke, "Uh, Dutch, why do you have a knife sticking out of your back?"

"Do I? That sneaky little... anyway, can you pull it out, please?"

Axel smiled and did. He wiped the bloody knife off and handed it to Dutch. "Here you go."

Dutch walked out of the bar temporarily. He walked over to Ravager, "Cousin Seeker, you left something behind."

"Keep it, you asshole."

Dutch shrugged and walked back inside. He folded the knife back up and put it in his pocket.

Dutch sat in his hotel room meditating. While the others worked out, he rested. He couldn't work out even if he tried, thanks to this leg. He was tempted to inject himself with his nanites but decided against it for now. He was aware of his surroundings and felt a dangerous presence lurking in the shadows. He rolled away as a blade came down towards his head. He felt the bones on his mutated leg break. He groaned as the assassin took her opening. The long blade ejected from Dutch's back. He coughed up purple blood and went limp. The assassin walked away after stabbing her blade that was still in Dutch's chest into the wall. She suddenly keeled over as if having been punched in the stomach. Dutch stood there with a large gaping hole in his chest. She rolled and saw her blade in the wall, but there was nobody attached to it.

"So, little assassin, who sent you? Was that you trying to puncture your fake tooth to kill yourself? Pity I already disabled that tooth. Now answer me."

She struggled to stand, but Dutch kicked her into the wall. He clenched his fist and the wall enveloped her, leaving only her helmet exposed. He gripped the helmet and took it off her head. He exposed a heavily scarred woman with a small band circling her head. She had deep silver eyes and dark red hair. Her eyebrow was pierced, as was her nose. He saw terror in her eyes. He grinned, exposing his sharp teeth to her. He was the predator, she was his prey. He smelled something awful as she peed her pants.

His nose wrinkled in disgust. "If you don't tell me, I will rip it from your mind in the most painful fashion."

She shook her head, keeping her mouth shut. Dutch sighed and placed his hand against her face. He felt her take a chunk out of his hand. He got the information he needed and vanished. He reappeared in the workout facility to see the crew already dealing with the assassins. He looked around and vanished again, this time appearing in his captain's room. She was naked, struggling against three assassins. She looked like she had just gotten out of the shower. He walked forward and let out a roar that caused the three to turn toward him. He bared his fangs in a display of dominance and lunged at them. He grabbed two and smashed them together, causing both to slump. The third tried to commit suicide but was instead knocked unconscious as well. He stood there panting.

Bela la Foe spoke, "What the hell are you?"

Dutch looked down at his chest, still seeing the gaping hole he had created by pulling himself off that sword. That, combined with the wild hair from all the wind, made him look unsettling. He looked at her and vanished. He reappeared in his room and injected himself with his nanites. His wound slowly began to heal. By morning only memory would be left. He cleaned the sword of his blood and, for good measure, lit it aflame. The fire burned what little of his DNA remained on the blade.

He sat down as his door caved in. Several Casualty Station officers rushed in with their guns drawn. A very large cybernetically enhanced Ursar walked in. His metal parts bore the mark of a Deathknight. He looked around and saw the burning sword impaled in the wall and the assassin trapped by the metal wall as well. He looked at the bloody man in front of him and shuddered.

"It seems you have everything under control. Unlike some of your crew. You are number one, right?"

Dutch looked up at the Ursar. "I am. Captain La Foe sent you?"

"She did. But so did the security chief Axel Wulf. The other Deathknights are dealing with the others on your ship. Let's get you to the hospital. Men take that assassin into custody. Take the sword as well."

By now, the sword had become unlit. Dutch clenched his fist again and the wall released the assassin. She slumped to the ground, shivering. The Ursar Deathknight called for a medical robot. It took a few minutes, but it appeared via teleportation. It looked over Dutch and deciding he was stable enough for the teleporter, the two vanished. Dutch reappeared in a hospital room and the robot began to hook him to the various machines. Dutch rolled his eyes and let the robot work. He knew he would have a clean bill of health come morning.

Bela Le Foe paced restlessly. Axel rolled his eyes in annoyance. "Relax, Captain things will work out fine. We suffered zero casualties, just some injuries. The doctors here are very skilled. They will all have a clean bill of health by morning."

"You don't understand, Mr Wulf. When I saw Dutch Hunter, he had a gaping hole in his chest. I could see through him. How is he still alive?"

"Ah, I see. Don't fret about him. The old devil likes to play games."

"Old devil? You speak as if you know him. Also, he can't be that old. He looks to be just under two hundred."

An alarm went off and all the nurses fled. The rooms went into lockdown mode except for one which suddenly and explosively ejected its door. Bela kneeled in pain as her head felt like it would explode. Suddenly the pressure let off and she collapsed. She looked up as a very tall and very muscular Pure Silveran with one half of his body grey skinned while the other half was a charred and scarred mess. He waved away the smoke. He shook himself off and raised his hands in the air as many Casualty Station guards busted in. They were led by Luke Darkfaith, who wore a mischievous grin.

"You, old devil, what are you doing wrecking my station?"

"Sorry, it came on rather suddenly. I didn't have time to eject into space. Bill the damages to my account."

"Tell me you at least kept the robot in one piece?"

"It's fine."

"Stand down, men. This is a common occurrence with him. Thank you for your swift response."

The troops filed out and Dutch took a cigar from his coat and lit it. He blew out green smoke and cleared the air from his transformation. He saw Axel looking unimpressed and Bela clutching her head in a fetal position. Axel shook his head disapprovingly. Dutch sighed and pulled even more of his Psychic energy into himself. Bela gasped for air.

Axel spoke, "You interrupted my little talk with the captain."

"Sorry, Axel, you know how it is. Spontaneous and annoying always at inopportune times."

"Regardless, I think you owe her an explanation of who you really are."

Bela shook her head. "I would rather not know. It'll help me sleep better at night. But how are you still alive?"

"Nanites, thanks to that assassin, I had to inject them."

Axel sighed, "Experimental nanites from continent Diavonbre. Back when they were still new. Hence why we call him the old devil."

"We?"

"Vinyl, Feldspar, Leslie, Gilda, Gunnar, and myself. Plus The Deathknight who came in here and his second."

Bela stared at Dutch, then at Axel. She shook her head and left. Dutch waited until Axel followed before collapsing.

He lay there on his face as he heard, "You are a total pain in the ass, you know that?"

"QiKong, is that you?"

"Yes. You know this will make her distrust you?"

"As it should be."

"Whatever, let's get you back to your room before anybody finds you here like this."

***

Dutch stood on the command deck, watching the warp go by. They would arrive at Acid/Green in a few days. After the incident at Casualty Station, the rest of the week had gone by uneventfully. Especially since he slept for three days straight, as they exited warp, an impact struck the shields.

The view screen was opened and they saw a Killgrethin Warbird.

Bela la Foe spoke, "Vinyl open hailing frequencies." Vinyl did as Bela continued, "This is Grand Admiral Bela le Foe of the Silveran Spacewalkers. We are on a peaceful mission. Please stop firing and let us pass."

A heavily scarred face appeared on the screen. He had a thick ridge coated in some kind of metal across his forehead and on the front section of his head. He sneered, "No passing. This is Killgrethin space. All who cross it are subjugated; you are surrounded."

Several other Killgrethin Warbirds popped into existence.

Ashka spoke frightened, "I em detectin' a large amount of powa coming from dhe ships. Dey are chargin' dher laza weapons."

"Axel, how are the shields?"

"Holding strong captain. Hold on, I am detecting interference in sector nine."

An amber face appeared on comm channel 3. "Captain, there are many Killgrethin warriors that just materialized. They are heavily armed and two men just got vaporized."

Axel vanished to assist Djinnai in sector nine.

The Killgrethin captain growled, "You see, I am Captain Gorphazon of The Killgrethin. We are unstoppable, your ship is ours."

Bela snarled, "Fat chance of that."

Dutch massaged his forehead. "Captain Gorphazon of the Killgrethin fleet. This ship is a Leviathan class nineteen Starhopper. While we may be on a diplomatic mission, we do have the firepower to wipe your fleet out. Your men on board our ship have already been eliminated. Do you wish to risk more?"

"Ha, I don't believe you."

Dutch spoke, "Axel, please produce the severed head of the boarding commander."

"Sure, which one is the boarding commander?"

Bela looked back to see Axel holding a sack with a bluish stain spreading through the bag.

Dutch spoke, "The one that has the most scarring is the likely candidate."

Axel pulled out a grizzly head with several scars and an eyepatch. Dutch watched the look of horror cross both Captain Bela and Gorphazon's faces.

"May I suggest you let us go and we'll forget all about this. Your dead have been sent over to your ship, their heads are right behind. If you do not let us go, all your ships will be wiped out. As your readout can tell you, our autocannons are locked on and ready to fire."

"Grr, you have made an enemy of the Killgrethin Empire. What is your name so we may mark your name down?"

"I am Dutch Hunter, the Demon of Silver."

The Killgrethin ships cloaked and Gorphazn turned off the screen. Ashka punched it and the ship sped off. They reached Acid/Green in record time. The Station Venom stood surrounded by a large belt of stones surrounding the mega planet Acid/Green. Bela gasped as she stared at Acid/Green. The planet, if you could call it that, was split in two. A cataclysmic force had smashed planets Acid and Green together, binding the two in the destruction. One half was toxic green and yellow looking, while the other half was a lush jungle planet. The ship docked and Bela walked out to be confronted by a green-skinned man with one side of his hair yellow and the other green. He wore a lab coat but also had several others with him. They all looked alike.

Dutch stared at the men with his hand resting on his holster. Behind him was Axel, also ready to fight if needed. The men had laser rifles trained on them.

Bela spoke, "I am Captain Bela Le Foe. We are here to replenish supplies and offload many of our dead crew."

The leader spoke, "You must go through a process to step foot on our station. My men will lead each of you to the cleansing station. Where you will be subjected to various tests to make sure you are clean. We do not want contaminants on our station."

Dutch nodded and lowered his hand, taking a relaxed pose. "Well, then, Science commander, who will take care of our dead?"

"We have a process that we must subject your ship to as well. By the time you are done with your tests, the ship will have been thoroughly cleansed of both contaminants and dead. At which point we will begin loading supplies for you."

"Very good I expect none of my crew to be harmed. Do we have an understanding?"

"We do, First Mate Dutch Hunter."

Dutch snorted and followed the scientist that would be testing him and cleansing any toxins from his body.

Bela gulped and told her crew the issue. She then turned towards Axel. "Is he always like this?"

"Dutch Hunter is an interesting person, but you must also realize he has dealt with this shit before. You have not, which is why he took the lead."

"How? He's no more than two hundred."

"Currently, he has had several lives before this, just like me, Gunnar, Gilda, and Vinyl."

"I see. Should I be concerned that he will usurp my authority?"

"Long as you don't piss him off, he'll follow just fine."

Bela looked out across the void. The next stop would be Oblivion Station. That was at the farthest reaches of known space. Then they would be hitting unknown territory. She sat in the purifying chamber as the scientists scurried around like ants. The needle they used shattered as it tried to enter her skin. The scientist looked at it in surprise. Dutch was in a different room and the scientists were in a panic.

"Boss, this thing has strange readings. There is something alive and moving around inside of him."

Dutch sighed, knowing this would happen. "As long as you all have loaded the ship, I can remain sequestered in the ship in my quarters. Don't bother answering."

Dutch vanished, leaving behind a mystified group. Dutch reappeared in his private quarters aboard the ship. He sat back in his chair and began to meditate.

"Excuse me, the green people sent me back to the ship due to my mutations. What is it you are doing?"

Dutch looked at the Red Silveran. "Meditating. What mutation you look fine to me?"

"They said something about my blood."

"I get it. I'm guessing Feldspar sent you here to collect me?" "She did. She did not tell me why, though."

"I'm an old friend of hers."

"She is in her room if you'd like to follow me."

"Lead the way."

The two arrived at Feldspar's room. They entered to see her lying seductively on the floor. The Red silveran gulped and loosened her collar.

Dutch spoke, "So Feldspar, you wanted to talk?"

"Talk? No, I wanted to dance the horizontal Tango."

Music started and Dutch raised his eyebrow as the Red Silveran stripped. "Ah, I see. Let me make a guess here and you tell me if I am wrong. You want a baby with Kimberly here. But since neither of you has a penis, you need me."

Feldspar smiled seductively and pounced, "You're wrong."

Kimberly giggled and pounced as well. Both girls began kissing him.

Bela le Foe sat waiting for the all-clear. She had been placed in the same room as Gilda, Vinyl, and Axel. They were laughing. She sighed.

Axel looked over. "What's wrong, Captain?"

"You all seem well-skilled. Why did you join my crew?"

Vinyl chuckled, "I wanted entertainment. Gilda here also was bored with the way things are on Silver."

Gilda nodded. "Just wish the Acid-Greenans would let us smoke. Boss' cigars taste so good. I need the numbing of them."

Axel spoke, "Still have issues from the Magus war?"

Gilda nodded, "Every year, I feel the dark fire burns on the day it happened even though I was healed fully from them."

Axel smiled sadly, "Those will never heal. But to answer your question, Captain, I joined because I am no longer arthritic. Now that I am young again, I want to get off the planet and experience the galaxy. Been fun so far."

Bela nodded. "But why me?"

Axel spoke, "You are a silveran like us. Gilda is a green Silveran, I am a Brown silveran, Vinyl is a Neon Silveran."

"Not quite Axel. I am actually a Fog Nephilim outcast. My hair is a dead giveaway. All of us outcasts have Neon hair. The only reason I am not as reviled because I am a priestess of Elektranikka."

"Ah, I see. Good to know. In the event, we need a holy person." Bela closed her eyes. "Who else knows you?"

"Aside from Dutch? Well, Feldspar was at one point Dutch's wife before her daughter killed her. And that Leslie fellow seems to know him. The big Grey Taur also knows him. Other than that, no one else."

"I see. That is good to know. The other question, though I fear the answer is, Who is Dutch Hunter?"

Vinyl spoke, "He's a demon forged from the very lands itself. Calls himself the wrath of God Silver made flesh."

Gilda snorted, "Most call him a demon. He certainly acts like one."

Axel frowned, "An old man struggling to cope with fate's hand."

The others looked at Axel in shock. "What? He is..."

Gilda spoke quietly, "That is the nicest anyone has said anything about him."

Bela sighed, "Not what I wanted to hear. I need to know his real name."

Vinyl spoke, "One does not speak the real name of the Demon of Silver unless they are willing to face the danger it brings."

Bela looked worried now, but Axel calmed her fears. "Remember what I told you. As long as you stay on his good side, he will remain loyal. He will not hurt you anyway. You took him when no one else would, so he owes you."

The rest of the stay at Venom station was uneventful. Soon all manners of tests had been run and the ship was scoured of all contaminants. The loading process began. Bela watched with curiosity. Axel sat meditating until one of the scientists walked over to them.

She was smaller than the others, almost stunted. She spoke, "Excuse me, which of you is the security chief?"

Axel opened his eyes and spoke, "That would be me. What's wrong?"

"The one called Ashka was kidnapped by one of the scientists and dragged down to planet Acid. He was always touched, but no one expected him to do this."

Axel spoke into his comm, "Dutch Hunter, meet me at the landing pad of Acid one. Ashka's been taken."

Bela spoke, "I'm coming too. Ashka's my responsibility. Gilda, please keep an eye on the loading process. Vinyl, continue the security sweep."

Axel spoke, "I am not sure that is a good idea, Captain, as you command."

Vinyl began meditating while Gilda looked at the loaders. The small scientist led them to a small short-range jump ship. She climbed into the pilot seat and motioned for Axel and Bela to sit behind her. They landed on the Acid side of Planet Acid/Green Dutch Hunter stood waiting for them. He handed a breathing apparatus to Bela and Axel. They put them on the right as a harsh wind struck them. Bela grunted. Dutch took off his coat and handed it to her.

"Put this on. It'll protect you from the acidic winds."

"What about you?"

He motioned to his burned side. "Ha, I have no need for it. Look at me, I am already messed up as it is."

They followed Ashka's tracker through acidic swamps that Dutch floated Axel and Bela over past a large stone pillar with many runes on it, marking where the natives lived. Dutch hurried past the pillar.

"We don't want to encounter the natives. They are not very nice towards outsiders."

They soon arrived where the tracker was. The marker pointed to a cave. They entered. Bela gagged as she saw mutilated corpses. Dutch blew blue smoke from his nose. They entered the main area and saw numerous scientists running tests on corpses. Ashka was bound tightly to a table with many saws above it. She looked dead. Bela saw many of her red shirts and a few of the other people being dissected.

Several of the guards finally saw them and went to intercept them. Dutch roared, "What is the meaning of this? Kidnapping and killing representatives of a different planet. Do you want to start a war you can't win?"

A scratchy voice spoke over the speakers, "Welcome to my little lair. We will be honoured to kill and dissect you. The fools on that station think they can gather the data we need by just running tests. No! How do your organs work? We don't know unless you die. This glorious cavern will allow us to learn about any species we encounter."

Dutch beheaded the guards that came at them, his fury unabated. "You made the wrong choice to kidnap our people. You made an enemy of me."

"Whoopty-fucking-doo-dah. You're nothing."

Several guards opened fire, one hitting Dutch's mask, causing it to dislodge. One also pierced his eye with a bullet. The mask dropped to the ground allowing Dutch's burned and scarred face to be revealed.

"Nothing! I am the Demon of Silver, Bounty Hunter 13. You are the ones who are nothing!"

Fire erupted everywhere. Bela yelped and took cover behind a rock. She fumbled for her blaster. She saw several beams of lasers hit Axel, who staggered back. His body then took on flames and he became a fiery wolf demon with tusks and horns. She holstered her weapon and decided to wait out the carnage. She grabbed the mask that had dropped and looked it over. She was shaking by the time the flames vanished.

Dutch Hunter stood supporting the wounded Axel and holding Ashka. She was breathing laboriously. He had a tube connecting her directly to his chest and seemed to be giving her the use of his lungs. He hefted Axel onto his shoulder and walked over to Bela.

"That takes care of that. I will have a report ready on our losses. I will also take full responsibility for the murder of the fifty Acid/Greenans. Let us get moving."

The two walked out of the cave and Dutch snapped his fingers, teleporting them to the landing pad of Acid One. The smaller girl gulped when she saw them.

Bela spoke, "I'm going to need a medical evac for my crew. Can you please call one down?"

The little one spoke, "I will call one, but I need to know what is needed."

Bela looked to Bounty. He sighed and spoke, "I will need a life support unit for the girl who had her lungs cut out and a healing unit for the man on my shoulder who suffered from multiple laser shot wounds."

She paged it in and a larger, more ornate drop ship landed. It had the markings of a Medical ship. Several med-scientists rushed out with the two units.

Bounty spoke, "You may remove one of my air lungs for the girl. You will also need to inject this vial into her to prevent her from rejecting the lung."

He walked into the ship with the med-scientists. As Bela climbed into the jump ship, they came down to the planet.

She sat in her command chair sullen. *Why can't I shake this feeling of doom? What was that I saw back at the cave? So many questions!*

Bela spoke into the intercom, "I need to speak with Gilda, QiKong, Gunnar, Feldspar and Vinyl. Will you five meet me in conference room nine?"

She soon arrived in conference room nine and saw Vinyl with her legs up on the table, casually leaning back. She sighed, "Show some decorum, please."

Vinyl smirked, then saw that Bela was serious and quickly adjusted her uniform and sat up straight. "Captain, if I may speak freely. What the hell happened? You look like you saw the jaws of the under realm open up."

"Because I did. Tell me, who is Bounty Hunter 13 and Axel Wulf?"

Gilda frowned but spoke, "Axel is a follower and avatar of Eefreet. Bounty Hunter 13 is the Demon of God Silver. His only goal is to rip those who would harm others apart and kill all who oppose him. The only person able to reign in his fury was his wife. When she was killed by her and his daughter, he went on a rampage. Nearly killed the girl. I was able to get him to some semblance of normality."

Vinyl shook her head. "Axel Wulf, on the other hand, is a great guy. He only takes on avatar form if he is nearly slain in battle. I'm sure you heard of the Pyramids of Chombra. It's in every historical document."

Bela blinked. "I have. All the texts state that there were one hundred survivors from the holding force of ten thousand. They also state that during the battle, nine fire demons appeared along with six Bahamut. At the climax of the battle, a massive fiery dragon with one side made of darkness rose up and consumed the flying fortresses of the Aka-ites."

"Axel was one of those Fire Djinni. An assassin stabbed him in the chest. His flames melted the sword."

Gilda spoke quietly, "The dragon that appeared was claimed to be the Wrath of God Silver incarnate. In reality, it was Bounty Hunter 13 absorbing a vast quantity of Psionic Nuclear energy. That was the venting process since he absorbed so much energy it had to vent. He is now permanently disfigured because of it."

Feldspar smiled, "But the man has a soft side. What did he do to make you ask all these questions?"

"Some treachery from the Acid-Greenans killed ten per cent of our crew. He killed them and managed to save one of the one hundred. I hope."

Feldspar looked at her, smiled, then spoke, "Did he take full responsibility for the deaths?"

"He did."

"Oh, Bounty Hunter 13, you must stop trying to make people hate you."

"What do you mean by that?"

Gilda looked at Feldspar curiously, along with Vinyl. "Gotta agree with boss here. What do you mean by that?"

QiKong spoke, "If you do not mind my interruption Feldspar." Feldspar was startled but nodded. "The old devil told me about his family curse. The thirteenth Hunter will be on par with the gods but at a price. He will be the most hated Hunter and will be a war bringer…"

Bounty walked in. "Ha! Best part is I wasn't even supposed to be the Thirteenth Hunter. My father manipulated events leading to me being the Thirteenth. He exiled my elder brother. The one that was originally Bounty Hunter 13. Claimed he didn't fit the prophecy. Since he only had Chain, Mar, and D as his twin siblings. Supposedly the Thirteenth Bounty Hunter was to have six twin siblings. I never met the man, but Chain states he was as strong as the gods, just like me."

Bela looked at Bounty. "How is Ashka?"

"Stable and will be able to be brought aboard the Doom Shroud in two days. Will still need to be in the medical centre for a week but will then be able to return to normal duties. In the meantime, I suggest Axel take over as communications. Due to his injuries, he is no longer fit to be head of security, at least for a year."

"And you?"

"I've had worse happen to me. This is nothing."

"So we are currently down a security chief."

"Maybe."

"Maybe?"

"Correct. If you don't mind, the planet Hollow/Moon is nearby. William Wolf and I would like to go there. He has been getting troubling news from his family. That many young girls are disappearing from the many villages dotting Hollow/Moon. I have an inkling of who's behind the disappearances."

"We'll go there after we get Ashka back."

"Very good. Back to my vigil."

He vanished, leaving Bela baffled.

Gilda shook her head. "He does like to appear randomly. Honestly, I don't think he was even here. He does have the ability to astral project."

Feldspar smiled. "So, are we done here? Or do you need to know more?"

"We are done. I will learn more from the historical texts now that I know who I'm dealing with."

Gunnar spoke in his deep earthy voice, "Just remember the texts do not show him in a good light. Those that wrote those texts had a feud with him. Thus they put him in a bad light. Most people consider Bounty a boogeyman because of them."

Several weeks later, via black hole travel, the Doomshroud circled the planet Hollow/Moon. Bounty stood in full battle garb, including his eponymous grey duster. The duster was singed and ragged at the bottom and was patched in various parts. He stood next to a large wolf-like being. There were two red shirts with them.

The Wolf spoke, "Honestly, I can't believe the entire cryogenic facility got destroyed. It's utterly ridiculous. How inconsiderate of them. How did that explosion happen anyway?"

Bounty rubbed his temples. "Malfunction in the cryo system also when you have so many expendable things in one place it tends to get messy. Sorry, you two, we shouldn't be commenting on the deaths of your fellow redshirts."

"Uh, since we are the last two, should we be here with you?"

"Don't worry about it, so William, where is your village?"

"We are inside the borders. I know not why it's a ruin."

"You two do a scan of the area. I have an old friend to visit. Mr Wolf, take care not to get our last two redshirts killed."

"Iye iye, sir."

Bounty walked down the dusty road. He was heading towards a castle in the distance. The dust swirled around his feet and rose into the air via the wind. That was when the fog rolled in. Bounty saw black cloaks moving about the fog. He sighed. He entered the castle and looked around to see many statues frozen in sensual poses. All were naked. Bounty shook his head.

"Judas Bloodsong, get your ass down here right now! I wish to speak with you."

"Rude! Didn't your mother teach you to be nice to people?"

"My mother died because of you. Now I am not in the mood to be nice. Reveal yourself."

A pale red-haired man appeared with blood-red eyes and armour with a swirling cloak made of blood billowing behind him. Bounty snorted.

"You look near death. Did you consume all your prey too fast?"

"I did no such thing. I only pick out the most beautiful girls to feast upon."

"So what killed the population of the Wolf Village nearby?"

"Not me."

"Oh, right, I forgot that Stone Vampyres cannot affect Were folk."

"But you are right; I have exhausted my food supply."

"I can provide you with Blood Whisky in exchange, you will provide your security expertise."

"Why?"

"Oh Judas, do I need a reason or will you do it? It's either that or starve."

"Ugh, fine, you win like always, Bounty. I submit."

"Good. Let's go and let the wraiths do their job."

The two left the castle open and the fog seemed to flow into the castle like a flood. They arrived at the village to see William facing off against a man wearing a brown trenchcoat and pirate hat. His yellow eyes had a wolf-like quality about them and his fangs looked vampiric in nature. He howled in rage and swiped at William. The two redshirts lay on the ground with claw marks across their chests. Bounty shook his head. Judas stepped back and contemplated running for it. A sharp look from Bounty quelled that thought.

Bounty stepped in and gave a fierce haymaker to the Lycanpyre. The boy stumbled but shook himself off and charged in again. Bounty slammed his shoulder into the boy, causing blood to spill out onto the ground from him, getting impaled on Bounty's shoulder spike. The boy struggled but eventually succumbed to sleep, which is what Lycanpyres do when they are critically injured.

A voice spoke, "Release my son, you foul monsters."

Bounty looked up. "Cedric Von Hellsong, what are you doing here? Shouldn't you be on the planet Myth?"

Cedric blinked in confusion. "You know me?"

"Of course, I know the great Von Hellsong, slayer of a thousand Magus destroyer of Fantas

Six. You are the one who bares his fangs at god. The Magus fear you and rightfully so. But your son did destroy a village of innocents. He also attacked my crew. I cannot afford to lose these two redshirts, so I bid you adieu. Here's your son. Teach him restraint. This is Commander Dutch Hunter to bridge. I have four to beam up. Have two med tanks ready."

"This is Axel Wulf to Dutch Hunter, which four? There are six of you."

"How about now?"

"I see you. Leslie Torque is beaming you up now."

Bounty stood in the medical bay. The scientists who had survived the cryo facility explosion lay there, along with the two redshirts and Ashka.

Bela lay in her bed shivering. Everything was going to hell. They hadn't even reached Oblivion Station yet. She was worried about their future. Her door chirped. She looked at it and sighed, "Come in." Bounty Hunter 13 stood there. She lay there and groaned, "Why you?"

Bounty looked down at her and sighed, "Captain, the crew is worried about you. You have been here almost a month. I cannot keep deflecting. Especially since we are nearing Omega Station."

"Just leave me alone. I should never have taken you. You're bad luck."

"Very well, Captain. At least show your face to the crew. Moral is plummeting without Captain Bela le Foe."

"Just leave me alone." She threw her sidearm at him. "Get away from me, you wretched beast."

Bounty walked out and shook his head. Axel was walking with a cane towards him. Bounty smiled, "Just the man I was looking for."

"Whatever it is, can it wait? We are being hailed by the grand admiral of Omega Station. He needs to speak with Captain Le Foe."

"You can try rousing her, but she doesn't seem to want to do her job."

"Uhg, fine. I'm guessing you already tried?"

"Yes, I did, which is part of the reason I wish to speak with you."

"No time." He banged heavily on the door. "Captain, I don't care how you are feeling. You are being hailed by Grand Admiral Thorn of Omega Station."

"Just send him to my personal phone."

"Axel hurried back to the bridge."

Bounty sighed and went to the bridge as well. He slumped into his chair. And looked at the starfield. He saw Omega Station, an imposing forge station, in the distance. And beyond that was the Junk Belt. The Junk Belt existed because nine planets hated each other. They waged interplanetary war and ended up wiping each other out. The planets were destroyed in the conflict. Only the destroyed ships remained. Any ship caught unawares in the Junk Belt was destroyed as well, joining the ever-expanding Junk Belt.

He closed his eyes. He reopened them as heavy footsteps were heard. Bela le Foe stood there. She looked very dishevelled and unhappy.

"Finally, the captain shows her face. The chair is yours."

Bounty got up and she took her place, "Helmsman, take us slowly into docking bay fifty."

The massive Qwn that was the Helmsman nodded. As they docked, Bounty saw the armed guards and sighed. Axel looked concerned. Bela Le Foe walked off the ship first. Bounty followed next with Axel and Feldspar. Feldspar looked around and smiled. A very large muscular man walked towards them. He had large spikes on his shoulders and two thick spiked horns protruding from his forehead. The others also had spiky horns as well. Theirs were not as pronounced as his.

Bela hugged the man. "Big brother, thank you for greeting us."

The man smiled and patted her on the head. "We have much to catch up on, Bela. Accommodations have been provided for your crew. We will begin the loading process soon."

Bounty raised his eyebrow, then looked through his database and smiled. He looked out the viewport and saw a large planet below them.

Feldspar looked at him. "What's got you so happy?"

"We are above Planet Silver 3. This is where the Pure Silverans moved to after the war. Never thought I'd get here."

The large man smiled, "You are familiar with us?"

"Yes, I am. I have researched the Silveran species since I was young. Why are we the way we are? What does the environment change in us? As I can see by your horns and spikes, they are much larger than before and also have small spikes on the horns as well. Truly fascinating."

"Ha ha, well, you're welcome to the library. I'll have Rebecca escort you. She is our top historian."

Bounty walked off with an imposing female with curly amber hair. Bela watched him go. She breathed a sigh of relief.

Admiral Thorn looked down at his sister. "Something up between you and that man?"

"He is bad luck. I don't know how long I can keep him. I should never have taken him on in the first place."

"I'm sure he's not that bad."

Bounty rolled to a stop beside them and got up and dusted himself off. "Well, that could have gone better."

A voice yelled, "You rat bastard! I'll end you like I ended your brother!"

Admiral Thorn looked down at Bounty. "What has got elder Grave so worked up?"

"History."

"That bastard is the reason our people came to this planet."

"I did not banish you. You all decided you couldn't live with the other castes," Thorn chuckled.

"Well, I should thank you then."

Graves walked in, snarling, "What are you talking about, fool boy?"

"Ancient one, look at us. Look at what we accomplished. Meanwhile, look at what has become of Silver. Wrecked by war. Just now deciding to explore the Galaxy. Meanwhile, we have been at peace for thousands of years."

"Hmm, I see. You got off lucky this time, boy!"

"Now, can I please see the Library?"

"Oh, very well. I suppose I'll let you have a look if your intellect can handle it."

The two walked off. Bela smiled lightly but quickly walked off, forcing Thorn to catch up with her. The rest of the crew was escorted to their hotel rooms. The woman that was to escort Axel looked at him and gulped.

Gilda walked over. "Cool your jets, old man. Your body is smoking." The intensity went down as Axel sighed. Gilda walked with him.

"Gilda, I don't like the way things are going. The demon is planning something. I know not what."

"Isn't he always planning something? I have yet to see him as anything but a schemer."

"I promised Bela he would not revolt against her. But something happened a few nights ago in her room. The demon looked angry afterwards."

"There is nothing we can do. Even if we protect Bela, we die."

"I know the demon is very strong. None of us would last long against him."

The three weeks at Omega station passed by. Soon it was time for them to continue. Bela looked much better and her tension was gone as well. They arrived at the ship to see Bounty with his battle garb on. His blade hanging loosely by his side and his gun holstered. On his back was a pack.

Bela spoke, "Why are you not in uniform, commander?"

Bounty smiled sadly, "Because you are not my captain. Here are my papers for my dishonourable discharge for desertion. And my badge, may I suggest Axel as my replacement."

"What are you blathering about?"

"Captain, don't play dumb. It doesn't suit you. You made it very clear to me that you don't want me on your ship. This just puts it legally. I am a deserter by law."

Axel spoke, "Don't do this, Bounty. How are you going to get home? Have you thought this through?"

"I have and you do remember who I am. A teleport across the galaxy is nothing for me."

Feldspar looked over the papers. She shook her head and then handed them to Bela. "Captain, it's all legal. It's up to you to decide."

"I did tell him I regret ever bringing him aboard the ship. I also told him I never wanted to see him again. I accept his desertion. Please get on board, we still have a mission to complete."

The crew obeyed. Bounty stood with his back turned to them, looking at Silverthree.

Graves walked behind him. "You are a fool. Do you even realize what you have done?"

"I fulfilled my captain's desire."

"No, you fool, you doomed them. Do you even realize what inhabits the Junk Belt?"

"I did not realize the Junk Belt was inhabited."

"Then you are a fool. Nu-zed Void and Shyft inhabit the Junk Belt. One species uses biomass and the metal from the belt to craft ships and weapons. Sturdy stuff resistant to everything but a plasma blade. The others are serpentine barbarians who can breathe in the void and fuck up the minds of their prey. They feed on despair."

"I see, well, the crew has fought worse."

"I disagree, the Nu-zed and the Shyft are beyond what you may have faced on Silver. They are forged by the Void."

"Hmm. Well, I guess my exploration will have to wait. I'll be back for a tour of the planet sometime. I am eager to see what you have done with the place."

Thorn smiled, "Well, as long as you keep my beloved sister safe, you are welcome back. If not, forget about coming back."

"Very well, Grand Admiral. I will most definitely keep her safe."

Bounty made sure his body and clothing were runes protected, then vanished and reappeared out in space. He began walking towards The Doomshroud. He reached the Junk Belt as the Doomshroud got stuck between floating debris. He saw the crew looking at him, sitting on the junk with a cigar in his mouth. He waved as his com crackled.

"Bounty Hunter 13 speaking, how may I help direct your call?"

Bela Le Foe's voice crackled over the speaker, "What the fucking hell are you doing here?"

"Your brother hired me to be your bodyguard. Apparently, the Junk Belt is home to many denizens that see us air breathers as prey. The Admiral is concerned for your safety."

"Damnit, fine. Teleport him aboard. Keep him confined in prison. I don't want to see his face."

Bounty appeared in a large spacious cell and began meditating. He could feel the presence of something. It was trying to gain entrance to his mind. He smiled. The creature suddenly appeared, clutching her head. Her slit eyes were watering and her non-mouth was crying in pain. Bounty entered her mindscape and spoke directly to her head.

"So you like what you see?" Images swirled of pain and torture.

"Yes, it hurts. You should watch your prey more closely. Images swirled of freedom."

"Of course, I'll free you from this pain, but first, you will submit to me." The words stop echoed throughout her brain space.

"Submit to me and I will."

The words stop echoed through her brain space.

Bounty opened his eye and saw the pathetic Shyft writhing on the ground. He sighed and released his hold on her mind. The writhing stopped. She breathed laboriously. He noticed Gilda watching him.

"Hello, Gilda. How may I help you?'

"Just came down here when I felt a large spike of psy energy. Thought you may be trying to escape. Who's your friend?"

"One of the denizens I mentioned. This is Gabrixisalshalksea the Shyft."

"I'll call her Gabby. How did she get in there with you?"

"They're all over the ship. If you notice any of the crew acting strangely, these things are the cause of it."

"I'll mention it to Axel and Vinyl. I'm guessing these things would feel threatened and attacked if they know we are onto them?"

"Not just that. They could also force those under their sway to commit suicide. You are already down many crew. Any more and you may not be able to complete your mission."

***

Bounty Hunter 13 sat in his cell, petting the female Shyft in his lap as she wrapped her four arms around him. She had been evicted from the Shyft hive mind and was lonely. Bounty smirked and wrapped her in his coat. It had been a month since anyone had bothered to check on him. Thanks to his nanomachines, though, he did not need food or drink. He heard someone coming and saw Ashka. She was being followed by a very large Shyft. He saw the images of the war chief and nodded. He also noticed a gun in her hands.

He heard QiKong's stern yet soft voice, "Ashka, wait!"

He also saw Gilda, Vinyl, Feldspar, Kim, and Bela Le Foe following Axel. Bounty lit his cigar and blew out a red smoke. *It begins.* He saw the crew surround Ashka. They were concerned and none of their voices seemed to get through to her. She looked even more stressed. He stood and walked towards the cell door. He got a closer look. Ashka was crying. She had a laser pistol pointing at her head.

Bounty spoke, "Ashka, please put down the gun. I did not sacrifice a lung to see you waste yourself."

Ashka jumped but responded, "You don't get it, old man. No one believes me. They all think I'm crazy."

"Why do they think you're crazy?"

"I tell them I see blue four-armed serpentine-faced bipeds. They laugh at me."

Bounty looked around at the concerned faces. "How long have you seen these creatures?'

"Since we entered the Junk Belt."

"I see. I believe you. You are not crazy, Ashka. What you see is real. They are the Shyft. Please give me the gun."

"Stop laughing at me!"

"No one is laughing. Oh, right, hang on." He fired his pistol and a blue snake-faced, bald-headed four-armed creature dropped with a large hole in its chest. "Can you understand me now?"

She dropped her gun and looked around at the worried faces in fear. "Wha? How'd I get here?"

"You were being controlled by a creature known as the Shyft. They are a very real threat and live in the Junk Belt. We are near their primary hive. Therefore their strength has been multiplied. He was making you hear laughing and mocking voices. These creatures feed off negative emotions."

Bela glared at him. "Why are you still here?"

"I don't know, Bela. Maybe someone put me here or should I call you Queen Xraxis of the Shyft?"

Her image disguise dropped, revealing a sinewy serpentine woman with four arms and a large shell on her back. "You saw through my morph. You are dangerous. No wonder the one known as Bela Le Foe fears you."

"Speaking of where is she or will I have to rip it from your mind?"

She saw the other members pointing guns at her. "Bup, bup, bup. I hold your captain and fifty per cent of the crew hostage. You kill me, I kill them."

"Kill her."

"Wait, don't you care about your crew?"

"Yes, and I've taken care of it."

"Wait! How?"

"I'm Bounty Hunter 13."

"Shit! I'm sorry, I'll run away and make my people leave you alone. Just don't kill me!"

"Then run back to your hive. This ship will be coming back through the Junk Belt. Leave it alone. I care little about any other ship that enters the Belt. They are yours."

"Got it, bye."

She vanished, leaving the crew stunned. "Your captain and crew are in the other cells."

The lights became brighter, revealing the rest of the crew covered in wire-like vines. All were alive and just waking up. Bounty sat back down.

"Oh and I'm out of provisions. Can you please send someone to bring something? It's been over a month of confinement. I can only survive so long without nutrients."

Bela spoke, "I'm sorry, why are you here."

"Oh, then I guess I was in communication with the Shyft Queen. Your brother sent me to keep you safe. Seems she also confined me here."

"I'll send someone down with food. You can stay in there for all I care."

"Fine with me. When you do go back through the Junk Belt and pass Oblivion Station, could you be so kind as to eject me into space?"

"What?"

Gilda spoke, "Yeah, he space-walked here. Your doppelganger told us to teleport him to the prison. He's been down here a month and two weeks now."

"Space walked without a suit?"

Gunnar chuckled, "Oh yeah, it's entirely possible for a Grey Silveran to survive in space. They have six lungs. Two for air, two for water, and two for other atmospheres or even non-atmospheres. They are also incredibly resilient to subzero temperatures. They used to have a very fierce space army. At one point, it was theorized they conquered half the known galaxy. Then the Magus came along and pushed them all the way back to Silver One."

Bounty was resting his head against the wall listening to the conversation. He inhaled through the cigar. He sighed and exhaled red smoke. He felt Gabby prodding his mind. He smiled and allowed her to feed on his emotions. She snuggled deeper into his jacket. She needed the hivemind to survive. He had become her queen.

***

The Doomshroud had soon escaped the Junk Belt. Bela Le Foe stared in shock at the massive station in front of her. It was shaped like a cube. It was also facing off against another space station. The com chimed.

"This is Omega Supreme Grand Admiral Jason Halberd of the Intergalactic transport station Asteroid Cube. Please evacuate to a safe distance. We have been battling Plasma Station for the last three Void Days. It is being controlled by a monster known as The Master of all Soul Killers. I cannot guarantee your safety if you insist on passing through."

Axel spoke, "Very well, we will back off for now. But we are on a schedule."

Bela watched the battle with interest. She then frowned. The pattern of attack had changed.

Ashka spoke, "Captain, I am picking up a disturbance on levels six through eight. I think we have been boarded."

A voice crackled over the com, "Hahaha, pathetic mortals. You think you can kill a god. I am Master of all Soul Killers. I have your ship under control. Once my thralls enter your upper deck and kill you, I will use your ship as a kamikaze ship."

"Oh, do be quiet, MaSK. I will not stand by and let my allies succumb."

Axel watched as a small figure appeared in space. It shot forward and was soon at Plasma Station. Bela stared in horror as a blinding explosion ripped through space. When the energy died down Plasma Station was in ruins. A massive floating head appeared. It began firing lasers from its eyes. It suddenly took on a grotesque scream and vaporized.

Ashka spoke, "Captain, the intruders have ceased to exist."

The view screen turned on and Bounty stood there floating, his body smouldering. He was also nude. "Requesting permission to be teleported back to my cell, please."

Bela gasped, "You need medical attention. I'll teleport you to the med bay."

"I'm fine."

Jason Halberd spoke over the comm, "No, you are not. You killed a soul killer. You need cleansing. I'm teleporting you over to our med bay. Captain, please dock at bay nine, so we can purify your crew members and ship."

"I... very well. You theoretically outrank me. Axel and Solan bring us to bay nine." The massive Qwn spoke, "Very good, Captain. Bringing her in now."

Bela was led into the purifying chamber as Bounty was being purified by a female who looked unimpressed with his physique.

He spoke, "Please ignore the burned section. Nothing you do will remove the burn."

"Impossible I can heal anything. What caused this burn?"

"Nuclear psionic detonation. Absorbed the energy into my being will be forever burned because of it, which is why I'm unconcerned about toxins from MaSK."

"You're always tainted! How do you live like this?"

"It's simple. One day at a time and step by step."

"Well, I've done all I can. He's all yours, Carl. Make him some new clothes."

A large pitch-black panther-like feline with white scars across his face stalked into the room, his tail swishing in agitation.

The cat spoke, "Of course, m'lady. Please follow me, Beast of Silver."

"You know me?"

"No, I do not. But our resident Priest Paul Prophetsword recognized the power from your detonation."

"Ah, I thought I felt a follower of God Silver here. Lead the way, mister cat."

The two walked off, leaving Bela and the rest of the crew behind. Axel looked nervous and pale.

Bela spoke, "What's got you so tense?"

Axel spoke, "My kind don't get along well with purifying techniques."

"You're a Brown Silveran. I've seen plenty of your kind get purified with no reaction."

"Boss, now don't be dense. You saw my true being on Acid/Green."

The woman spoke, "You're a true being? As in this form I see in front of me is only an illusion?"

"Not quite. I am all flesh and blood until I am mortally wounded. Then this body goes into hibernation to heal. My true form takes shape then and controls my actions until I am removed from the situation that mortally injured me."

"I see. Be you holy or infernal?"

"Depends on who you ask. My kind worships the Fire Djinn Efreet. Now whether Efreet is holy or infernal is all up for debate. We see him as holy."

"I see. Is there anyone else here who hides behind a mask?"

Judas and William both stepped forward. William's body changed into a massive bipedal and muscular wolf while Judas allowed his Vampire features to reveal. The woman sighed and motioned those two aside along with Axel. She cleansed the rest. That was until she arrived at Feldspar.

"My powers don't work on you. Why?"

"A girl's entitled to her secrets. Just know that MaSK's taint cannot affect me."

"I see. Jason, can you send a contingent down with Paul? These people need to be escorted to the chambers while I cleanse their ship. I also need Paul to cleanse some that may have an aversion to my technique."

"Very well, Tiara, they are on their way."

A monk wearing all green walked in, followed by several heavily armed guards.

"I do apologize for the appearance of the guards. You are not under arrest. We've just been at war with MaSK for so long that they haven't gotten the chance to remove their power armour. General Matilda Gaston will be your escort."

Matilda stepped forward and motioned the crew to follow her. Bela spoke, "Priest of Silver, I want your word that you will not harm my three crew members with your purifying energy."

"Believe me, my dear, God Silver will not harm them and cannot harm them from what I see. The Last King of the Stone Vampires, a Wolf god of planet Hollow Moon, and an Efreet. Your crew will be fine."

Bela gulped and walked away with the guard that stayed behind to wait for her. She arrived just as a feast was being brought out. She saw a massive bear sitting next to the cat, Carl. She blinked but shrugged it off. The priest walked in with her three crew members and she visibly relaxed. She looked around in curiosity.

"Gilda, where is Bounty Hunter 13?"

"He refused to join us in our feast. He said he had some issues to bring up to God Silver. Also said you'd be calmer without him around."

"He's right. I'm just shocked he's not here."

"You need to let up on your hatred of him. The man is innocent for the most part."

"I don't hate him. He's bad luck. Everything has gone to hell since I took him on. The attack at Casualty Station should have tipped me off. I would prefer not to have him, but my brother hired him to be my Bodyguard."

"I see. Well, regardless, let's enjoy this feast."

Bounty sat stroking the slender Shyft female. "I cannot keep her alive for much longer, Silver. She needs a large Hivemind to survive."

"Don't worry, boyo. I may have something in mind for her, but she would need to be sent to the future sometime after your death. The new beings I am shaping need to have an originator."

"She's all yours. Be careful with her. I care deeply for her like I would my own child."

"Yes, I see that. But do not worry yourself. She will be well taken care of." The Shyft vanished and in her place was a little girl swaddled tightly.

"Not what I was expecting, but very well. Bounty Hunter 13, meet your new daughter Omega."

"Well, shit. She has massive organ failure from the time shift." Bounty quickly rummaged through his bag and pulled out a child-sized stasis chamber. He quickly placed the girl inside it and injected her with nanomachines to stabilize her. He then put the stasis chamber away and sighed, "Well, I still have Bounty Hunter 26."

"Speaking of, how has he taken your new look?"

"Eh, he's not a fan, but he's barely around. He's taken on the mantle of Protector of City Silver. I fear it'll be the death of him."

"Remember, Bounty, time always is shifting. What you may have seen may or may not come to pass."

"I am aware of that old man. But some things are etched on the prophecy stone of fate. They are destined to happen regardless of what we do to prevent them."

"I disagree. I fought my fate all my life."

"And look what happened. You became God Silver. How'd that go for you?"

"Fair, but what you see, if it does come to pass, would be catastrophic for the population."

"And the Pale Elves will sweep in and take over. Yes, I know."

"You must prevent that at all costs. The Pale Elves will wipe out all Silveran species."

"I can only do so much, Silver. You would need an army of me to accomplish something like that."

"Hmm, now that is an intriguing concept. Goodbye, for now, Demon of Silver. Plans need to be made."

Bounty shook his head and went back to meditating. *It would take a few days for the ship to be fully cleansed. Then ten days for them to reach the end of known space. Then thirty days to reach the locked sector.* He shook his head. Standing near the doorway to the temple was the large grey Taur, Gunnar Rhapsody. He shook his head and then left the temple as a coughing fit overtook him. *Soon my time will come. It has certainly been interesting to see the galaxy. I will miss this.*

The next day Bela sat in a chair in the Public Park and recreation area. She was watching what was left of her crew and marvelling at the exotic fauna. She saw the large bear talking with the massive black panther—Carl. She smiled quietly, then went back to reading her book on the history of Planet Silver. Hunter clan was always mentioned all the way back to the founding days. Bounty Hunter jr. had been the first King of the Silver Throne. When he died, he gave the throne to his constant companion Artur Arul. Artur had ruled for many years before he and his clan were slain by one Zmatek. That was the start of the Chaos War. The Chaos War lasted until Bounty Hunter 11 joined up with the armies of Zorlin Ankara and made a final push. Zorlin was given the throne of Silver for their victory. The Silveran's had spread throughout the galaxy by now and then disaster struck. A cult known as the Rasputin cult had a revival and called themselves the Magus. They had come from planet Vatica and pushed the Silveran species back to Silver and devastated them to the point where it was just now that they had recovered enough to explore the galaxy, not as conquerors but as travellers and explorers. She closed her eyes. The Silverans have been through much. *Those that refused to acknowledge the rule of Blu Silver had left Silver and moved to a new planet. They called this one New Silver. My family was at the forefront of this exodus. My brother was the only one begging me to come with them. My family cared little for me since I was not a Pure Silveran.*

"Captain, you seem lost in thought. Care to join us for a picnic?"

"No thanks, Feldspar. I have some introspection to do."

"Suit yourself. Just remember, everybody needs a friend. You shouldn't withdraw like Bounty Hunter 13. It's not healthy."

"Thank you for your concern Feldspar, but I'll be fine."

***

Bounty was once again sitting in a cell. He willingly offered to be here since he knew Bela Le Foe was very uncomfortable with him being around her. He shuffled his deck of cards and pulled out a joker. He smiled.

"What are you doing, Demon?"

He looked up to see Gilda and Vinyl. He smirked, "Amusing myself. This deck of cards was given to me by Jason Halberd, my cousin."

"Why amuse yourself with a deck of cards?"

"Because Vinyl, this deck is special. The cards are all blank and reveal the truth when looked at."

"What do you see, Bounty?"

"The Fool, The Joker, and Mad Harlequin."

"All calling you out saying you're foolish."

Gilda whispered, "Or the wildcard. Why would you see those three, though?"

"Does it matter, Gilda? It's not like you care for me anyway."

"Don't say things like that, Bounty."

"I suppose if I had any friends, it would be the ones I've fought battles alongside, but enough of that. Why are you here?"

Vinyl spoke in her scratchy voice, "We came to check on you. Axel is worried you are denying yourself contact with others."

"What if I am? Why does it matter? I am the Demon of Silver. That's not just a title, it's a fact. Nobody cares for demons. It was given to me as a way to appease God Silver while at the same time banishing me from ever setting foot in City Silver as long as clan Silver rules."

"Bounty..."

"What's wrong, Gilda? Worry doesn't suit you."

"You can't just be alone."

"And why not? My children are grown and long gone. Four of them despise me, like everyone else on Eastern Silver."

"Bounty, please!"

Bounty sighed, "Gilda, I know you care slightly for me. You wouldn't have had sex with me if you didn't."

"That's why I'm so worried. I'm pregnant with your child. I'll need your help raising him. I can't go back to my people until he is grown. While the Oni god allowed my pregnancy, my people are ashamed of me. So please get help with your issues."

"Gilda... fine, I'll try to be more accommodating. By the by, did either of you happen to bring down any Fire Whisky?"

"No, did you want some?"

"I am mildly thirsty. I'll give you a pack of smokes if you bring me some," Gilda grinned. "Now we're talking."

***

Bela le Foe stared at the station before her. It was shaped like a Gothic Cathedral. It was currently locked onto them with over ten thousand autocannons. The crew was on edge.

Bounty walked onto the main deck. He stared at the space station and growled. He walked over to the communication station and typed in a specific code.

A face appeared on screen nine. "Who the fucking hell are you? And how did you get that code?"

"I am Bounty Hunter 13 of the Silveran Space Walkers. And I am Bounty Hunter 13."

"Oh great. You. Why are you Walkers invading our sector?"

"Not invading, exploring. King Silver of the continent Silver has joined up with Queen Scorpi Ankara, the third of Noamaiza and King Kulld of Norvcryog to explore Galaxy Silver."

"And why come this far?"

"My captain Bela le Foe was given orders to gain access to the locked sector. There are many things in the locked sector that the kings and queens of Planet Silver want. And while I would prefer keeping them there, my captain was denied the ability to come back to Silver if she did not collect them."

"I see, very well, Bounty Hunter 13. Tell your pilot to dock with bay ten. We will give you supplies and also have some of our people assist you in gaining access to the locked sector. Welcome to Planet White."

"Thank you, Supreme Grand Wizard."

"Feh."

The com station went dark and Solan slowly piloted the ship towards bay ten. As they docked, ninety heavily armed pale white soldiers stood, guns drawn. They all had neon pink hair and were led by a female with two large antlers on her head, neon pink hair styled in a mohawk, and a pink eyepatch on her right eye. The eyepatch covered a long jagged scar that went from her forehead to her chin, giving her a cocky lopsided grin. Her crimson eye glittered with sinister intent.

Bounty walked out and up to the woman. "Hello, Rebecca. How are you doing?"

"Like I'd tell you."

"Yes, yes, please have your men lower their weapons. I would like this to go as smoothly as possible."

She decked him and tackled him smashing his face into the ship. She continued to do this while her men boarded the ship and dragged the crew out.

Bela cried out, "What is the meaning of this?"

Bounty spoke between getting his face smashed into the floor, "This is the welcoming committee. The only way we're going to get supplies is if we beat them. Their guns are loaded with non-lethal shots, so do your best."

"Why are you letting her beat you? I saw you get stabbed through the chest and destroy your assassin."

"Heh, well, I kind of deserve this beating."

Rebecca spoke, "Damn bastard was given my hand in marriage, but he died on our wedding day. I was left at the altar."

Bounty spit out some blood and spoke, "Yes, it was supposed to be a wedding between Clan Hunter and Clan Hawthorne. She's my cousin."

Bela spoke as she blocked the attack from one of the soldiers before striking him with her tail. "Wait. Isn't that incestual?"

"And the problem here is? Regardless, Hawthorne is distantly related to clan Hunter. Her father promised my father that she would be my bride when we came of age. Unfortunately, my father died before this happened. When we finally joined, I was slain by my clone Leon von Psycheo."

Gilda stood on top of ten soldiers. "Grey Silveran family ties have always been incestual. It's a common occurrence to see brothers marry sisters, sisters marry sisters, brothers marry brothers, fathers taking on their daughters as concubines, some even taking their sons as sexual partners, and mothers to maintain status marrying their sons."

"That's abhorrent!"

Axel finished five with a flourish. "To you maybe, but to a Grey Silveran, normalcy."

By now, the eighty-nine soldiers that Rebecca brought were out cold. Rebecca looked up as a green fist connected with her face. She rolled back and groaned. Bounty got up out of the hole she had made while bashing his face in.

He walked over and helped Rebecca up. "I think this is a win, Rebecca. Start having the supplies loaded."

"Ugh, fine. But I still beat you."

Bounty cracked his neck and held his face. "Yes, yes, you did. Good job."

Bela stared at them, blinking in confusion. Gilda brought her out of the way of the loaders. When the loaders had finished, six people in black and gold heavy power armour walked onto the ship, followed by Rebecca. Bounty saw the insignia of the Gatemasters on the power armour and frowned. He sighed and shook his head and went on board, following the rest of the crew. He walked down to the cell area and sat in one of the cells.

Rebecca had followed him down and was now staring at his cell. "Why are you in there?"

"Captain Le Foe is uncomfortable with me being in the same area as her. She believes I am... bad luck. She's not wrong."

"So you sit down here alone?"

"Every now and then, Gilda, Vinyl, Feldspar, or Axel come to visit, but that is getting to be few and far between. I suspect once we hit the locked sector, I may be visited more often."

"Why are you helping those that don't want you? Why are you?"

"Because they, deep down, care for me. I may be marked outcast because you left me at the altar, but they look past that and see me as a cog in the great wheel."

"I don't know why I am. I am going to claim it's because Thorn paid me to keep his sister safe. But the reality is much more murky than that. I was well respected until Bela Le Foe found out my true identity. To her, I was first mate Dutch Hunter, but now I am that accursed Bounty Hunter 13, he who will usurp me because he thinks he knows better."

"You wouldn't actually usurp her, would you?"

"No, even though I am not thrilled with the mission, I will follow."

"You keep saying that. What is so dangerous that you would prefer to stay away?"

"I'll just say there is a reason that it's called the Locked Sector." Gilda walked in. "Boss, uh, we have a slight problem."

"Yes, what is it, Gilda?"

"The head of the uh... Gatekeepers is doing his best to piss us off. He's making racial slurs and treating all of us as sub-sapient. The captain is doing her best to keep things smooth, but she's reaching a breaking point."

"Very well, Gilda, I'll be up shortly."

Rebecca looked at Bounty. "You are only going to prove his point if you say anything. I've ignored him for my entire career."

"I'm not going to do anything that will hurt his ego. People have a way of shutting up when I'm around."

"That's true."

Bounty walked down the hallway to the bridge and saw two Gatekeepers in front of the door. He approached them and they blocked his access. He spoke in a dark, more violent voice than his normal one. "Move or be moved."

The two quickly obliged him and he entered the bridge to see Gilda on the floor, bleeding. He also saw Axel smouldering as he tried to rein in his anger; he was held against the wall by two Gatekeepers. Judas lay against a console, holding his side where blood was seeping from. The rest of the bridge crew were also injured and bleeding out. Captain Bela had a sword against her neck. He saw Gunnar leaning against a console with his head caved in.

Bounty roared, "What is the meaning of this?"

The Gatekeepers turned and opened fire on him. When the smoke cleared, Bounty still stood. His mask had been knocked off, thus exposing his burn. "I'll ask again. What is the meaning of this? Why have you attacked my crew?"

The commander of the Gatekeepers snarled, "You sub-sapients should know your place. You don't belong in space. You barbarians should have stayed on your dingy homeworld."

"Oh, commander, you wound me. I believe you have forgotten that the Silverans used to own the galaxy. Our genes are what helped create your kind. We helped jumpstart evolution on all the planets. So by calling us sub-sapient. You are calling yourself sub-sapient."

"That's it. I'm slicing your head off."

"Ooo, that's right, commander, prove my point."

Bounty waved his hand and the crew vanished. He sent them down to the med bay. "Now then, if you wish to kill me, bring it on. If not, then I suggest you pilot us towards the locked sector and open a path for us."

"You don't give orders, you beast."

Bounty blocked the attack and threw the commander off him. He struck one of the consols, which exploded from the impact. The commander got up and made a pass again. This time Bounty struck him hard, shattering his chest armour. He shoved the commander again. This time the commander hit the nav console, which burst into flames and exploded.

"You're beginning to bore me, commander. If you're not going to make an effort, stay down."

The commander snarled and impaled Bounty with his javelin. Bounty looked down at the shaft sticking through him and yawned. The Gatekeepers stood there dumbfounded.

"Try again, Commander."

The commander stared at the javelin and at the bored Bounty. "Who are you?"

"Learn the name well, Commander. I am Bounty Hunter 13, Demon of Silver, Destroyer of the Magus, slayer of Lord Slayerhammer, slaughterer of the Psycheo Guild, Scourge of Slavers, yada, yada... You get the point?"

He snarled, "Then Demon, you know my name well. I am Commander Shogun Yu of the Planet White Gatekeepers. I will be your death. Just wait and see."

The Gatekeepers vanished, leaving Rebecca behind. She sat at one of the destroyed consoles and sighed. "Well, that could have gone better. Sorry Bounty. Looks like you will have to turn back. There's no way you can gain access to the locked sector without the Gatekeepers."

"I disagree, my dear. I have my own way of bypassing security."

"Of course you do. Ugh, fine I guess I have to do this."

She took off her armor and began undressing. Bounty raised his eyebrow. "You really think having sex with me will distract me from my goal."

"No, I think cockblocking you will."

"Oh, you are evil. I like evil. Come see what you can do."

***

Rebecca lay on the ground panting in post-coital bliss. She groaned and closed her eyes in exhaustion. By now, Bounty had gained access to the locked sector. He sighed, "Where do I begin?"

"I suggest you begin by telling me why one of God Silver's useless abominations is near my planet."

"Ah, you must be Alexander. Well, I have come looking for the blade of Bloodhawk, the destroyer. Also, my overseers wish to find something called the Armor of Chaos."

"Oh, then you are in the right place. Though there is a price for my information."

"Sure, let me take a guess first. You wish to be free of the Locked sector. Sure, I can arrange that."

"You can? Hmm, you may not be so useless after all. Very well, come down to the planet before you. I will show you where the sword is. I know not where the armour might be, but I can point you in the right direction."

Bounty looked around at the destroyed equipment. "Uh, If anybody still is able to, I need repairs done to the main deck."

"Axel to Bounty. I'll send Leslie and Solan up. Then I'll take over while the rest of the crew recovers. The captain has withdrawn to her quarters. I fear she may try something. Kim and Feldspar are heading there now."

"Just what I need, a suicidal captain. Hmph, well, if you can get her to move, send her down to my location. I may just be the thing to encourage her to live."

"You think too highly of yourself."

"No, her hatred of me can be her guiding light."

"Ah, very well, Demon. Good luck."

Bounty lifted Gunnar up and sighed. You lived a long and wealthy life, my friend. Let's get you some peace. He then burned the body. "Thayme Sidrodc uigde het suel. Thyme Havens Sunocm het seul." He drank the amber liquid and then tossed the glass on the fire, which erupted and then vanished. He turned around to go to the teleporter and saw Leslie and Solan standing there. He turned back around and hefted Rebecca up and walked out.

Solan looked at Leslie. "Uh, what did we intrude upon?"

Leslie shook his head. "We just saw the sacred fire of Silver, the chaotic one. Silverans pray to him when they burn their dead. That is the ultimate compliment a Silveran can give you. If they honour you as they would their dead."

Bounty arrived on the planet and heard a hum as Bela Le Foe materialised along with a massive muscular man with deep bronzed skin, dusky black hair, and teal eyes that glittered with bloodlust."

"Bela, who's your friend?"

"I'm surprised you are just noticing him. He's the new chief of security, Belias, son of Gorm."

"I have been in the cell blocks to give you space, so you'll have to pardon me if I don't recognise your main deck crew."

Belias spoke in a deep earthy voice, "So Demon, why are we here?"

"I am picking up a weapon that was forged in the Haven Prison by a vicious beast known as Bloodhawk the Destroyer. He proceeded to slaughter many Angelus and Daemus in his quest to kill the Judge of Souls and Judge of Flesh. I severed his arm, which fell down here. So for my penance, I am retrieving the blade to be locked up in the heavens. If the arm has regenerated into a being, I aim to kill the being."

A feminine voice spoke, "Oh, you aim to kill me? Ooo this oughta be fun. You do realise my blade kills people permanently and their soul ceases to exist. So If you think you can kill me, bring it on. I will relish your death, for I am Bloodscythe, the Annihilator."

"Oh, big name for such a small girl. You are already dead."

Her blade dropped from her hand as she saw her chest explode outwards. "Huh, how?"

Bounty wiped off his sword. "Next time, talk less."

Her eyes rolled back as she fell. Bounty vaporised her remains and picked up the glowing purple sword. It vanished as he felt it bind to his soul. *Oh, that's not good. Sorry WARDEN looks like the blade chose me as its new owner.*

Bela spoke, "Okay, how'd you do that?"

"I can move very fast if I want to. Also, she talked too much. The warrior who strikes first is often the one who will win, but the opposite could be true as well. Now I have a promise to keep." His voice changed to that of thunder and earthquakes. "I summon you ancient cathedral of Holy Energies, Alexander. Reveal yourself to these mortals and submit for judgment!"

The sky darkened and a massive cathedral-shaped machine descended. "What is the meaning of this? How do you know the ancient spells?"

"Old friend, we were once on different sides of the War Between the Gods. My predecessor, the first Silver was your close friend, some say sworn siblings. But he turned his back on you. I am the Twentieth Silver. I hold no animosity towards you."

"I hold animosity towards you, Silver. I was banished and imprisoned within this lost sector. But regardless, I am weak. What is my fate?"

"I unbind your chains. I was the one who bound you therefore, I unbind you. You are a free old friend. Use it well."

"I thank you, Silver, but I cannot forgive you yet. This is a proper step. Goodbye, little mortals, I have faith to spread."

The cathedral vanished and Bounty collapsed to the ground and coughed up some blood and spat it out. He stood and staggered slightly. "Oh, I wish he hadn't done that. Woa! Why is everything so blurry? Oh hey Bela, why are there three of you?"

He dropped to the ground with a thunderous thud, kicking up dust in the process. Bela pinged her com and the three were teleported to the main deck. Axel stood there with concern on his face.

"Let me guess, that massive spike in sanctified energy I felt was Alexander the holy being released? I hope Silver knows what he's doing."

Bela looked worriedly at Bounty. "He summoned a massive cathedral, yes. What was that?"

Belias growled, "That, captain, was not something we should have been able to witness. Our powerful friend here just got possessed by a God. God Silver, to be exact."

Axel groaned, "Of course, why else would he still try to access the locked sector? You damn fool. That is a lot of energy you don't have that you wasted."

Bounty groaned and held his head, "I needed to expunge excess energy anyway. Gah! What did I drink to make my head so blorp."

Axel shook his head. "Don't worry, Captain, he'll be back to his normal self in a few days. He just needs to eat a big meal, drink some water, and possibly sleep and he'll be good as new. Speaking of new. Boss, you better put this mask back on. Your skin is really disgusting."

Bounty replaced his half-mask and stood up. He walked out, but as he started to exit the door, he dropped again. Belias and Axel walked over and hoisted him up. They dragged him off to his room and set him down at his desk. Axel typed in an order on the computer and a two-foot wide slab of meat materialised in front of Bounty. He stirred and began to eat it. Several drinks appeared and were consumed.

Axel spoke, "Belias, you best get up to command. I'll keep an eye on the Demon." Belias nodded and walked out. Axel sat and picked up his glass. "You idiot, not right now. I'm eating"

***

Bela paced the deck Ashka was sitting behind the com playing a game on her computer. Next to Ashka was Vinyl garbed in a fishnet bodystocking and nothing else. Vinyl had an ethereal disk jockey table in front of her. She was furiously playing electro-trance music. Belias, son of Gorm, stood slouched over the tactical station as he was bored. They had been travelling through the locked sector, encountering nothing but uninhabited planets. The coordinates Bounty had gotten from Alexander was at the far reaches of the locked sector. Axel sat in the pilot's chair, smoking a cigar. The rest of the crew was still in traction. Especially Gilda, who had given birth prematurely.

Bela Le Foe snarled, "I need to get off the ship. This is infuriating."

Bounty arrived on deck holding a bundle. "We need to stop anyway. Gilda's taken a turn for the worse and her child is barely alive. I need to recharge my reserves, so does Vinyl."

The ship dropped out of the black hole and travelled near a large teal planet. Bounty climbed aboard a jump ship with Bela, Vinyl, and Axel. The ship shot towards the planet. As they exited the ship, a mysterious portal opened before them. A large leonid man walked out with eight people in long red dusters.

Bounty looked at them. "Scuse us, folks, but your portal is in our way."

The lion man looked over to the woman in a red duster with a red hat and golden brown hair.

"You said this planet was uninhabited?"

"It is Lord Scion. These are intruders."

Bounty spoke, "Yeah, not intruders. I am here to recharge my reserves and perform a ritual. These are my fellow crew members. I really need to be going. I have to reach a certain area by nightfall."

"Carmen, close the portal. They're inconsequential." Bounty walked past.

Bela whispered to Axel, "What ritual?"

"I don't know and honestly, I don't need to know. I suspect it has something to do with the bundle."

"You don't think it's necromancy, do you?"

"If it is, then there's nothing we can do about it. Just let it go. It's easier that way."

The Lion man motioned his men to their goal, but he stayed back. He spoke, "Argon, I am curious about that man. Make sure it's hidden well. I will catch up to you."

The one with greying hair and sunglasses nodded and walked off. Scion slid into the trees and followed the four unknowns. He arrived as they set up camp. He watched from the trees as the weird one in a duster with shoulder spikes sat down in a meditative posture.

"Stranger, you may join us instead of watching from the trees. Soup will be ready in ten minutes."

Scion walked out and sat down in front of the fire. "How did you see me?"

"My psychic sight. I am Bounty Hunter 13. Who might you be?"

"That is a name that holds ancient power. I, on the other hand, am Scion of the Crimson Guard."

"I am familiar with all types of organisations but have never heard of The Crimson Guard."

"Nor should you. We are not exactly from around these parts. In our home galaxy, we are the most feared fighting force."

"Ah, I see. Like Jason Halberd of Asteroid Cube, you come from another galaxy. I love it. Let me guess, you are the strongest of your galaxy?"

"I am, but how'd you know."

"Notice how my lips are not moving. I am inside your head."

"Hmp, of course, you are, which explains why the others are not on edge with me. They know you have everything under control."

Bounty finally spoke with his voice, "Oh Scion, they are on edge. You just can't see it. Captain Le Foe's tail is lashing in anxiety. Axel here has his hand on his gun in the event you try something. Vinyl is the only one unconcerned with you since she is asleep. So care to explain why you are here?"

"I am curious about you."

"Not here-here, on this planet here."

"Ah, that changes things. I am disposing of a dangerous artefact," Bela spoke roughly. "So our galaxy is a dumping ground?"

Scion smiled. "You are not technically in your galaxy. The locked sector is in between. At least six other galaxies have access to it. So yes, this is a dumping ground, which is why very few of these planets are uninhabited."

Bounty snorted, "Of course, it is, which is why God Silver imprisoned Alexander here. Also, why the Chaos' armour was hidden here."

Scion spoke, "Chaos' armour? You mean the armour that the descendants of Lord Badger presumably took to keep The Ancient Lord Chaos from ever resurfacing? Only to have it taken from them four different times."

"Yes, that is the armour. Consisting of a helm, gorget, cuirass, bracers, pauldrons, chauses, greaves, sabatons, a necklace, and four rings."

"You really think they'd be stupid enough to place them all on the same planet?"

"I do believe so, yes. After all, I am a Hunter clan member and we descended from Lord Badger."

"Well, good luck, but why would you be trying to resurrect Chaos?"

"I am not personally looking to retrieve them. However, the captain here cannot return home without them. So until she finds them, she is effectively banished from Silver one. While it's no loss for me to be banished, the others in the crew would like to go home."

"Again, good luck. I will probably be seeing more of you. After all, you seem to be a powerful individual like myself and others who you may meet on your journey. Well, I best be going. Goodbye, Bounty Hunter 13, until we meet again."

"Goodbye, Scion of the Crimson Guard. May the Gray Guide and Protect you."

Scion walked off, shaking his head and muttering something about fools. Bounty smiled and stirred the soup. When Bela fell asleep, Bounty put up protection runes. Vinyl stirred and looked around, only to doze off again. Axel was snoring against a tree, his Bal'heth blade resting in his lap.

Bounty walked off, soon arriving at a circle of stones. He laid the bundle that held his son down. The boy was unresponsive and dead. Bounty started chanting in a dark and ancient tongue. As he chanted, he started to do a dance. Dark energies swirled around him and black lightning shattered the sky. A wailing cry was heard and Bounty smiled. He picked up the bundle. He stroked the boy and allowed the boy access to his milk spike.

"Goroth ye wee shit welcome to the land of the living. You are Grongar Hunter now. It comes with a price. The Hunter clan is not well-liked. But you are strong."

A grey-green-skinned man with a copper scrap duster was leaning against his executioner's axe, watching Bounty.

Bounty spoke, "Andros, the Executioner for the Gods, if you are here, that can't bode well."

"Maybe... I am curious. You are using necro energies, yet you do not feel like the average Necromancer that I destroy on behalf of the Gods. Who are you?"

"I am Bounty Hunter 13 of Silver. Dubbed the Demon of Silver, his wrath made flesh."

"Lofty title for what is essentially a banished one."

"Yes, the Czar of City Silver gave me that title to appease God Silver. While at the same time making sure I knew I was never welcome in Silver's City as long as his line ruled."

"So why do you fight for those that desire you to disappear?"

"I am a warrior. Any fight is worth it, no matter the cost. I represent many bad aspects of the Silverans."

"Yet you yourself have some sort of softness. And I am not talking about you being fat."

"Is it that noticeable... ah well. And you are right. I care deeply for my family even if they do not care for me."

"You are a very interesting man, Bounty Hunter 13. I look forward to seeing what becomes of you."

"Sure, perhaps we'll meet again, Andros. I hope not. That axe of yours concerns me."

Andros vanished with an earthy chuckle. Bounty went back to the camp. Day broke and Bela Le Foe woke up and stretched. She saw Bounty was packing things up. She said, "Are we done here?"

Bounty nodded. "We are done, Captain. I am fully recharged, as is Vinyl. Do you understand the gravitas of your situation?"

"I think I do. This armour I am looking for has the essence of a powerful and ancient deity known as Chaos. Why would the lords of Silver want something like this?"

"It's not just Chaos. The one known as Zmatek was the First God Silver. He was banished because of his crimes. He forged the armour of Chaos so that there was always a way for him to be reborn. He killed many Gods in the War of the Gods to create this armour. But that is something in the past."

"Will you allow us to reclaim the armour?"

"That was the mission, was it not? As I told Mr Scion, I have no plans to interfere. You all wish to go home. I could care less about my predicament."

"Don't you have a family?"

"Yes, but they don't care for me. Four of my children despise me. I have no mate to be with. And my other children are all grown up and out of the house making names for themselves. So shall we continue on? The further I get from Planet Silver, the more energy I lose, so we will likely need to make another stop so I may recharge again."

"Yes, let's go."

Bounty nodded and motioned them to go ahead of him. He looked around, nodded and followed. Scion watched them go. He opened a slot on his gauntlet, "Scion to Bon Bon. I found the disturbance. It's a man with great power roiling through him. Pass the information on to Pike, Broan, Henry, and Buxxom."

***

Bounty lay on his bed. Gilda had recovered but was still under observation. He had placed Grongar in stasis and teleported both Omega and him back to his home. It would be many years before he could de-stasis them. He sighed and sat up. He ordered Fire Whisky and sat at the desk drinking in thought.

On the main deck, Bela Le Foe was sitting watching the warp go by. She shook her head and dozed off. In the simulator, Belias and Axel were sparring. Belias used his Bal'heth blade, while Axel used a fiery halberd he conjured. They were being watched by Solan and Rebecca.

Belias rumbled, "This feels wrong, Axel. You seem distracted. I asked you to give me a challenge."

"I'm sorry, Belias. I cannot shake the feeling that we were effectively banished from Silver under the guise of entering the Locked Sector to retrieve an artefact."

"It is what it is, Axel. We cannot change this fact. Fight like the warrior you claim to be. Or do I have to injure you to get the fight I want?"

"Alright, but you asked for this."

Fire erupted everywhere. It began to swirl around Axel as he danced through the flames. Smoke spilt off of him, giving him a ghostly look. The two clashed, their weapons striking hard and fast.

Rebecca smiled and shot forward. "You both just died. I win."

Solan chuckled, "That you do, girl. Very good."

Bounty looked out his window at the warp. He turned his head and then bolted out the door, only stopping as he barreled through the main deck door. "Captain, stop the ship! Stop the ship now!"

The warp vanished, only to be replaced by a massive planet. "What the hell is that?"

Bounty spoke, "I don't know, but I sense danger. Pull the ship back to a safe distance."

Ashka spoke, "Uhm, too late something has locked onto us and is dragging us towards the planet."

A serpentine voice hissed over the com. "Welcome one and all to the greatessst ssshow on earth. You will witnesss warriorsss of great renown battling each other for amussment. You have no chance to esscape."

Bounty, Axel, Rebecca, Solan, QiKong, Gilda, Vinyl, and Belias appeared in a fort. A snake woman flicked her tongue out and slithered around them. She fully healed Gilda and smiled as Bounty spoke, "Where did you put our ship?"

The woman smiled and caressed his cheek with her tail. "You have nothing to worry about except to sssurvive. You are part of the Naga Army. You will be facing against the Tiger Army,

The Eagle Army, The Triad, and the Bear Army. We only ssselected the best of your crew to fight."

Bounty grabbed the Naga by the neck and yanked her towards him. "What is the goal of this? Why should I help you?"

She struggled. "Please release me. I know not what the masster wantss."

Bounty snorted and released her. She fell to the ground gulping for air. Gilda knelt down and held her upright so she could get the most air in.

Bounty snarled, "I don't have time for games."

A man in teal and aquamarine walked into the camp. His serpentine eyes glowed with ancient power. "If you wish to see your crew alive, I suggest you play my game."

"Ophiuchus, Gods damn it! Why does this not surprise me? So your goal is to distract. Great. Fine, do we get the pleasure of knowing who we're up against?"

"No, that is part of the game."

"What do I get if I win?"

"Whatever you want. I can bring anything to me that you desire."

"I'm guessing the Naga is our leader?"

"No, she is the healer. I am the leader."

"Ah, we're on the bad guy's side."

"It's a narrow point of view but yet so true. Now meet your fellow allies. Liun Ba of Meteor, Koji Mada of Discordius, Deathseeker, Naga Shaft jr., Uji Honda of Silver, and Bob."

A large man wearing black and gold walked in. His eyes had a bestial quality to them and his face looked almost lionesque, especially since he had a mane of hair. On his head were two long feathers attached to a crown. This was Liun Ba of Meteor. Bounty could already tell Liun Ba would not be satisfied with the fight.

The next warrior to walk in wore a tiger pelt over his crimson armour. He had blond and red hair shaped like fire. He also had war paint on his face. His eyes were jovial and grey. This was Koji Mada. Bounty disliked him immediately for being too jolly.

Deathseeker walked out, his grey chest was uncovered and he bore a pike emblazoned with the crest of the Hunter clan. He looked very much like Bounty but older and more menacing. He smelled of rot, but that seemed to stem from his rage. The rage he barely held in. Every time Bounty saw him glance his way, he could feel cold anger directed at him.

The next was a very tall and thin fellow with dusty brown hair and stubble of the same colour on his face. He could barely be called a warrior. He looked weak, but Bounty could tell there was a deep fire burning under his visage. A fire that seemed familiar.

Uji Honda was a massive, bronzed skin male with a youthful face, but his hair was white and mane-like. He was clearly an Oni of Komodo. Bounty snorted. But Gilda was awed by him.

The final one, Bob, wore a grey and white business suit. He was bald but with a black goatee. Over one eye was an eyepatch and his grey skin glittered as if he was infused with some strange magic.

"Demon of Silver, while I enjoy the idea of seeing you fight. I need you to be in the role of strategist. Before you lie a map on this map, you will see the other armies you are up against. They are already making their moves, as you can see."

"What happens to those who die?"

"There is no death here. They will respawn at their camp."

"So, to get the prize, I must prove my strategic brilliance. Bah! Fine, let's play this game of yours."

Bounty conjured several screens over the map so he could see the battlefield.

He turned towards Liun Ba. "Liun Ba of Meteor, I would like for you to take the slasher division of Naga, Axel, and Solan to confront the Wolf Tiger Army. Koji Mada takes the crusher division of Naga along with Deathseeker, Belias and Vinyl to sunder the Bear Army. Uji Honda takes the Venomari division of Naga along with Gilda to mess with the Eagle Army."

Ophiuchus looked curiously at Bounty. "What of the Triad?"

"They are inconsequential right now since they are infighting. Let them sweep in and gather the dregs of the other armies after we rout them. That way, we only have one army to worry about, but if you are that concerned... Bob, Naga, and Rebecca break the Triad."

"Ah, but you seem to have forgotten the Scarab Army."

"Have I? Hmm... I am unconcerned with them that there are only four in the army. It would be a waste of resources to crush them."

"You may regret that decision."

"We'll see Ophiuchus, we'll see."

QiKong spoke, "I will go block the advance of the Scarab Army. It will be a good test of my strength."

Liun Ba marched with the army he was given. By his side were his allies Gau Shun, the camp crusher and Xu Rong, the wall breaker. He also had to deal with the orange-haired man, Axel, and the weird multi-horned being, Solan. He snorted in derision at the army in front of him. Axel let out a yell and charged into the Tiger Army. He was followed closely by Solan and the Naga. Liun Ba watched impassively.

"Xu Rong circles around with Gau Shun and stabs them in the back. Break their will to fight."

Gau Shun saluted, "Got it boss."

The Wolf Tiger Army broke before the attack. All fled or were routed except for a female who took a pose and, in a flurry of strikes, took down ten per cent of the Naga. She snarled and lunged at Axel, who ducked under her strike and grabbed her arm, snapping it like a twig. She mewled in pain.

"Axel, don't kill that one. She is to be our prisoner."

"Why? Oh, never mind, Solan, I don't want to know." He kicked her to the ground and forced her face into the dirt. "Good girl, submitting like this."

She whispered, "When you turn your back, I'll kill you."

Axel stomped on her back and chained her up using aether chains. He placed a collar around her neck and yanked on her chains, causing her to stand and stumble. The Naga Army was teleported out and Bounty placed the cat on display, much to the dismay of one of the Naga.

"So it is true, Shahirani, you are attracted to this cat. Well, so be it. You may join her." He chained the young Naga up as well.

Ophiuchus spoke, "Careful Demon. You don't want to piss off your army."

"I am well aware of that, Ophiuchus. As you will see shortly, the chains don't last long."

Koji Mada sat on a very large and muscular horse. Belias was smashing bear soldiers left and right. The pale woman, Vinyl, was using her conjured DJ table to take down many others. Her electro-trance music was catchy and Koji could see his pal Kane Nao moving to the beat.

Koji sighed, "We are to sunder them, not downright destroy them."

Belias' thundering voice rang out, "That's hard to do when these stubborn thick headed tankers don't retreat."

A massive rotund black and white Ursa jiggled out, "Hey! You punks think you can get away with taking down my clan. Think again. Shabang!"

Energy erupted out from him, sending Belias stumbling and knocking Vinyl out of her trance, causing her turntables to de-summon. Koji smiled and jumped off his horse. He charged the bear but was intercepted by a large man in power armour and another in furs and chainmail. Belias went to assist but was intercepted by a small obscenely pastel pink and blue cat-girl and a woman in a blue and pink flame embossed hoodie. She had pink and blue stripes in her hair as well. Half of which covered her right eye. Several shards formed around her and a blade came into existence.

Back at camp Bounty looked at the screen. He spoke, "Ophiuchus, is that my sister Eris?"

"No, that is your sister Eris from an alternating universe. One where her soul was nearly bound to you. You of that universe severed her soul from him and had the Soul Protector erase her memories of ever being a Hunter. She styles herself as Wyldfang now. The cat is her wife."

"I see, so the man with the horned badger mask sitting behind bars at the Wolf Tiger base is my brother Myst from that same alternate universe."

"Yes, you are awfully perceptive."

"Lucky guess, since I'm positive my actual brother would not be so willing to sit behind bars."

Back on the field of battle, Belias dodged a strike from the woman's blade. He jumped back and grabbed the unconscious Vinyl before leaping over the two women. Deathseeker kicked the armoured man into the other one, then grabbed both and smashed them together, the two fell in a daze. This allowed Koji to jump on his horse and the Naga Army teleported out, leaving a dumbstruck Bear Army behind.

Bounty stood smoking his medicinal cigar. He smiled. Axel spoke, "What's got you so chipper, Demon?"

"My siblings stand against me. This is the first time I'll actually be at a disadvantage. They're smarter and more intelligent than me. I am good at solving things the brute way. Would rather be at the front fighting. They were always more strategic than me. This will be fun."

Uji Honda leaned on his trident; he had been wounded in the leg by a flying kick from one of the Eagle warriors. His friend Giong had rescued him from a flock of the Hawk Army. He had ridden him back to the small camp on his iron horse. Rebecca was now tending to the wound. On the field of battle, the Naga Army was getting decimated. Gilda was facing a man with a feathered cloak.

"Young girl, why do you fight for these creatures?"

"I was asked to. Why do you fight with the Eagle Army?"

"My brother leads them. He and I are the only ones left on our timeline. We gotta stick together."

"I understand that so why have you not routed us yet? You clearly are the superior army."

"Aquila would not like that."

"Damn right, I wouldn't." Gilda turned to see a small horned eight-foot-tall man with teal and copper clothing. He looked like Bounty Hunter 13 if Bounty was a fourth pure Silveran.

The man continued, "My goal is to see what the hell Ophiuchus is thinking. Also, where the hell is your Bounty Hunter 13."

"At the main camp. Ophiuchus wanted him as the strategist."

"Of course he did. Pointless test. Begone!"

Gilda vanished along with the Naga Army, Uji Honda, Giong, and Rebecca. She appeared in the Naga Camp. Ophiuchus did not look pleased.

Admiral Yi of Meteor stood on his mighty ship. He had been given control of the Naga Air Force. Next to him stood Deng Zilong and Chen Lin, two of his allies. The Air Force was currently over the Eagle Army Aerie. Admiral Yi's Turtle ships were wreaking havoc with the Eagle Army. The Aerie was almost crushed, but his army had sustained numerous injuries and had lost a fourth of their fleet. The leader was due back any minute, according to his spy.

"Signal a retreat. We cannot risk losing more of our fleet. Especially if we are up against a god."

Aquila appeared. He stood on top of the highest point of the Aerie. He waved his hand and a rain of stones bombarded the fleet. Then a feather-made cloak-covered man appeared and waved his hand. Jagged spears shot from the ground. Yi's ship was impaled and he suffered a grievous injury to his armpit. The ships vanished and the Naga Army appeared at the main camp, with Yi immediately being tended to by the healers.

The Three leaders of the Triad stood looking across the great plains. One wore a mask, the other a turban, and the final a helmet. All three had large metal wings attached to their armour.

Bob cracked his knuckles and grinned darkly. Naga was sitting on a rock, just vibing and eating a Gargant Steak sandwich. Rebecca lit her cigar and combed back her pink hair. The large Triad Army marched onto the field from four different directions. Rebecca blew out a crimson smoke from her mouth that quickly engulfed the battlefield. A huge energy beam lanced out and exploded, sending many soldiers flying. As their bodies hit the ground, they vanished.

She picked up some interference coming from Naga's ear. He must have had some kind of ear bud in his ear. She vaguely heard, "Shagu, what are you doing, you cowardly Kiku bird? Our lives are at stake and you are running again."

She heard a dark chuckle and saw a blur. The aura from this blur was turquoise. She could see through her own smoke and what she saw scared her. Naga or as she heard him called, Shagu, was obliterating the army with his fists. She also saw the bald man, Bob, take off his eye patch and send out a beam of energy that exploded more of the troops. Both these men terrified her. They reminded her of her husband, Bounty Hunter 13.

She cried out, "We are supposed to break them, not outright destroy them. Cut back your attack!"

That was when the ground caved in and the Naga Army charged from the hole. It was a massacre. Eventually, the Triad called for a retreat. Rebecca stood staring in awe and terror at her small army. She shook herself off and ordered them to return to camp.

***

QiKong Djinnai stood staring at the four black armoured and scarab-encrusted filigree warriors. He smirked as they hammered away at his psionic wall. He was floating there. They were getting tired and soon gave up and walked away. QiKong nodded and vanished.

After the disastrous defeat by the Eagle Army, the Naga Army found themselves beset with woe. The Triad had swept in and taken over the Bear Army and the Scarab Army had taken over the Wolf Tiger Army. Those two armies then turned towards each other only to have the Eagle Army defeat the Triad and ally themselves with the Scarab Army. The two armies now had their sights set on the Naga.

Bounty stood facing a massive army. The Naga troops were routed. The female Naga Bounty had chained up had turned on them. She had joined up with the rotund Ursa that had given Koji trouble. In turn, the two of them freed the tiger woman and joined up with the Triad. They were now using their unique hand-to-hand combat styles to rip through Bounty's allies. However, there was some good news. The strangers that he was ordered to work with were devastated by the opposing army. Deathseeker was using his pike to send waves of fire through the enemy. Bob fired some kind of laser from his now uncovered eye that exploded on impact. Uji Honda was slicing through the enemy with his trident. The skinny man, Naga, was using his fists and the bodies of the enemy to fight. QiKong appeared and snapped his fingers, causing Gilda, Solan, Axel, Vinyl, Rebecca, himself, and Belias to vanish back to the Doomshroud. Soon, though, the four men could not keep up with the constantly respawning enemy and the unique fighting styles of the furious four. They pulled back to the camp. Ophiuchus was steaming.

"I thought you were the best! Clearly, I was wrong."

"No shit, your snakeness. I told you I am up against my siblings. They are better than I am when it comes to strategic brilliance. I am a warrior. I fight with my blade, not with my head."

Bounty blocked a strike coming at Ophiuchus from a woman in a brown duster with a giant sword. "Elena? Is that you?"

"Who the heck is Elena? I am Bon Bon Huntari, Queen of Rivles. Heir to Goddess Rivles and Avatar of War."

Another woman who looked almost like the first but with no shirt on under her duster attacked from the other side. "I am Elena Mack. Hello brother, been a while."

"Hello, Elena." Bounty rolled away from them and put up a barrier between Ophiuchus and the warriors that had appeared. "So, Ophiuchus, do I have permission to fight?"

"Oh, fine I guess you can fight since you are the last one standing from my army."

Bounty took off his half mask and put it in his bag. He removed his glasses and also put them away. Liun Ba impacted the side of the butte. They were near as a large and hairy man wearing a patchwork trench coat walked into view. The man tossed Gau Shun and Xu Rong to the ground. His eyes gleamed jovially as he balled up his hands and punched the ground. Jagged spikes of stone ripped through the ground, nearly impaling Bounty. Had he not dodged the spikes, it would have.

Scion walked up the steps. "Do not let him go full power. Buxxom, Broan, Pike, take him down now!"

A bimbo-like woman dressed in only fishnets and belts and a man wearing furs over his chainmail armour attacked. She with her whip and him with a spear. Then the power armour-wearing man charged at Bounty and, with bone-crushing force, struck him with his power hammer. The burnt side of Bounty cracked open the cracks leaking out Psionic energy and giving him a ghoulish appearance. He heard retching from the sides and saw Bob and Naga throw up. Deathseeker scoffed at his display and went back to picking his nails. Uju Honda shook himself off but was unable to attack because Bounty's Aura was too strong.

Buxxom struggled to follow through with her strike. Her whip dissolved from the energy. Bounty cried out in mock pain and his energy erupted. A storm whipped up and flames erupted everywhere. Elena cried out and was tossed into Bon Bon, who was then struck by Buxxom and Wyldfang. Aquila stood strong along with Lord Badger and the feather-cloaked man.

Aquila spoke as his allies were being buffeted by the strong wind and rain. Also, being scorched by the fire. "Ophiuchus! Enough of this silly test. Do you want your planet destroyed again?"

"The better question is, Aquila, do you and Scarabaeus want to see these mortals destroyed? The planet itself is connected to me and I to it. It cannot be destroyed unless I am erased from existence. These mortals are struggling against this unmatchable power. Make up your mind quickly."

Aquila growled and sighed. He tossed down his pike. Lord Badger tossed down Scarabaeus' axe. Bounty calmly replaced his mask and glasses, the storm died down and he stood victorious. He snorted.

"We done wasting my time? I hope so. Ophiuchus, I win. Give me the armour of Chaos so that the crew of the Doomshroud can go back home."

Aquila yelled, "Are you insane? Why would you want that?"

Bounty sighed, "Captain Bela Le Foe's mission was to retrieve the armour of Chaos. She is not to return home to her family unless she has the armour. I am sorry, but that is what I wish for."

Ophiuchus nodded. "It is so and it is done. I give you the armour of Chaos."

Bounty looked it over and smiled, several runes appeared and a duplicate of the armour was made. Bounty replaced the real armour with the duplicate armour.

"I give you the armour of Chaos, put it back. I have what I need." Aquila looked at Bounty. "Okay, not as stupid as I thought you'd be."

"Come now, Aquila, you know yourself better than this. I am Bounty Hunter 13."

"That's why I was concerned. Regardless I believe it's time to send you mortals home.

Bounty smiled and turned towards the horned badger-masked man. "I am glad to see there is a Myst Hunter that is not a complete ass. I am glad to have met you."

"You can see through my mask?"

"No, but I recognise my brother anywhere, just as I do my sister. But I have a feeling she should not know her past."

"You are better adjusted than my Bounty Hunter 13. I am glad to see there is hope for him yet. Goodbye, Demon of Silver, may the Gray be with you."

"Same to you, Lord Badger of the Inbetween."

**

Many space weeks later, Bounty sat on his bed. He was unable to meditate. Many things kept stirring in his head. Blood-stained bodies and looks of fury etched into his mind. He slumped in defeat and had the computer make him a glass of Moon Scorched Fire Wine. He sipped at it while watching the warp go by. They arrived at Omega Station to restock. Bounty thought about leaving but decided against it. He could visit Silver 3 another time. Eventually, they arrived at Planet Brown and Station 12. Bela had made sure there were enough provisions for the extra week it took. They docked with Station 12. Bounty stood with his hand on his sword. He was watching the dark brown ridged forehead Brownians work. The workers almost had a reverence as they passed both Axel and Belias, who were also keeping an eye on things. When loading was done, The workers insisted they take Axel and Belias for drinks.

Bounty smiled, "Go on, you two, I'll keep the ship here."

"Is that a good idea? You know how the captain feels about you."

"It'll be fine. Go have a drink with your new friends."

The workers basically dragged Belias and Axel off. Bounty sat down on a nearby crate. He looked out across the expanse of space. He heard a noise behind him. He turned to see Ashka. She looked scared.

"What's wrong, kid? You look like you are in pain."

"I am! Everything hurts. Why do I feel like I'm on fire?"

"How old were you when I gave you my lung?"

"Three hundred ninety-seven."

"And it's been three years in space since then, oh boy. Alright, I know what's going on. You are hitting your second cycle. And since you have nanomachines that are from my blood, you will be experiencing a different change. You will be gaining some Grey Silveran aspects. Alright, I can ease you through this."

He enveloped her in his duster; her screams of pain were muffled. Then turned into soft whimpers. He fed some of his energy into her, easing her pain. When he felt her shoulder spikes penetrate his skin, he knew the change had happened. He unwrapped her and saw blood dribbling down from her new shoulder and forearm spikes. He soothed her burning skin with a cooling gel. She sighed in relief.

"You did good, kid. Much better than my children when this happened to them."

"Is it always this painful?"

"No, the first time is the most painful. Now that the spikes have grown in, there won't be any pain during your next cycle."

***

Many moons later, The Doomshroud stalled above Planet Red. Bounty looked out across the stars and nodded.

"Captain, may I request leave? I have a mission to take care of below us."

"What kind of mission?"

"That is between me and God Red. I am sorry, that is all I can give you."

"Another God requests your aid. First, it was Planet Lizard where you used the chaos storm to infuse that weird armour with energy, followed by Metallic, where you did something you refuse to talk about. Then Planet Gold, where you, according to the priest, cleansed a Goldian from an ancient corruption."

"Correct!"

"Am I to guess the ship won't start until you complete this mysterious mission."

"Also Correct."

"Ugh, fine, dirty your hands. I care not."

Bounty vanished. Axel stood quietly until Gilda spoke, "What's on your mind?"

"Don't you hear it? The cries of the dead."

"I hear nothing, but that doesn't surprise me. I am not as attuned to the PsyQi as you."

Down on the planet, Bounty stood staring at a green-armoured knight with a red helmet. Next to him was a boy that had once been Argentorado 100. "Hello, Bluud. It's been a while. I see why you chose this place. It's the solstice and the sky is clear. Are you ready?"

"I am ready donor. Strike me down. I yearn for peace."

"You died three minutes ago. Your body lies on the ground. The boy killed you. I am here for your souls. You were never able to unify, were you?"

"No, I was not very much like Lord Psycheo. You killed him as well. You also ended the boy, Deathskull. You got your revenge."

"Not about revenge, Bluud. It's about redemption. The Gods of Red have deemed you worthy. They sought me out to aid you on your path to the havens. I will lead you there now. But first..."

Bounty incinerated the corpse. Before picking up the two soul crystals left behind. One murky grey, the other a shadowy black. He chanted with a dark tongue and a pillar of light struck him, causing him to cry in pain as his skin cracked. When the light vanished, only the boy stood there. He looked up at the sky and smiled.

"Be at peace Bludd de Gulch. Your soul will return as my son someday."

Bounty reappeared on deck, leaning on an onyx cane as his body smouldered. He wheezed out, "You are free to move the ship, Captain."

***

The Doomshroud docked with the spacewalker station over Silver. It had been a long and arduous nine years. Captain Le Foe sat on her chair, her scales polished and gleaming. All the uniforms were pristine and Bounty stood near her in chains and his battle duster. On the view screen was Galifon.

He spoke, "Welcome back, abominations. I hope your mission was successful."

Bela Le Foe sighed, "It most certainly was. We retrieved the Chaos armour as requested."

"Please beam the armour to my location so that we may authenticate it."

"It's been beamed over. We also managed to capture the fugitive Bounty Hunter 13 but at the cost of all our redshirts and the Dutch Hunter's life. We also sustained many injuries and had to restock many times, so if you give permission, my crew would like to disembark and return to their homes."

"Oh, I give permission. Permission for you all to die!"

A large laser beam struck the Doomshroud, causing it to explode. Meanwhile, at Hunter Corporation, Bounty stood in his battle duster unchained and smoking his cigar. Bela stared at the explosion.

"Seriously, that bastard was going to kill us?"

Bounty nodded. "He got what he wanted. The armour of Chaos. He sought to use its power for himself. Unfortunately, he will soon find out it's useless. To an explosive result."

"Wait, you're going to kill the leaders of the Union?"

"Can't kill what's already dead. Galifon assassinated them last week, which is why I asked you to dock with my company's station. As far as Lord Galifon is concerned, you all are dead. My freighter ships can get you all home under cover."

"Did you plan this?"

"Hardly that intelligent, ma'am. I am just sneaky and had spies keeping me up to date."

"You are by far the most terrifying man I've met. I see why everyone calls you a demon. Thank you for bringing my crew to their homes. I will take the Doomshroud to Silver Three to be with my brother."

"May the Grey be with you, Captain."

"What does that mean? What is the Grey?"

"The grey is a force of nature. There are four distinct realms, each has its own colour. White is pure, Black is shadows, brown is Inbetween, and grey is Grey. Grey absorbs both Pure and Shadow. It is unity. When I say may the Grey be with you, I am unifying myself with you, but it can also be a dissociation. Grey being the unity between Shadow and Purity. The more white you add, the lighter it gets, the more black you add, the darker it gets. There is a trifecta of patron deities. Most Gods, including Silver, are grey, the Shadow Lord is black, and the Fountainhead is white. Brown is an outlier because all colours go into brown it cannot be classified. Many Maverictype people are brown. Look at me through the Psychic sight that all species have."

"Oh, Gods! It's so grey I feel like I'm being consumed. How?"

"I am the embodiment of Silver. Thus am also the embodiment of the grey."

"Are you saying you're a God?"

"Not yet, no, but there have been many alternate universes where I have become God Silver or a God. I am trying to avoid Godhood, but things are in motion that I am having a hard time stopping."

"You see things?"

"Yes, being the Avatar of God Silver or the Wrath of God Silver made flesh, I do get premonitions and foresight. It's not something I enjoy."

"I feel sorry for you, Demon, but I do not regret how I've treated you."

"Nor should you. I know how despised I am. I wish you the best, Captain Le Foe. This will be our last meeting. However, there will be someone getting in contact with you at a later date. She is close to me."

Bela Le Foe walked back onto her ship and flew off into black hole travel. Bounty sighed and sat on a bench. A blond girl walked over to him.

"Hello, Father. Is that the one you told me about?"

"Yes, she is, Leda, yes, she is."

Silver Destiny: The Invasions

The world has experienced a golden age. A new power has been discovered and used. New lands have been born. With such a melting pot, war is inevitable. Silver is strong and such strength will be cowed. Beware the man with the pale face. His mind holds treachery. He will seek to instigate the destruction of the stars so that his land may be reborn. We Silverans have always been a warring species. Even as we advance technologically, we seek to conquer. It is in our blood—War—War never changes.

- Elder Pearl Roman of the Silveran Royal guard

The Invasion of Silver by Noamaiza

Raven Triogonal was watching the stars. The constellation of the Hunter was now overtaken by the constellation of the warrior. She sighed.

Bounty Hunter 26, her mate, spoke, "What has got you worried, Raven?"

"War is upon this land. Twelve days til Apocalypso." She then cried out and collapsed.

Bounty carried her prone form to the bed and checked her over. He looked outside to see the middle moon darken.

"Twelve days from now is Noční lov. And I thought our honeymoon couldn't get any more interesting. Sleep, my love. Tomorrow is a new day."

The next day Raven was still asleep. Bounty walked outside to see a young woman in street thug clothes trying to hack his hover truck. He walked up behind her. She looked malnourished and was clearly desperate. He cleared his throat. She gasped and turned, looking up at his imposing thirteen-foot height with fear.

He held out a peeled apple. "Here you go. Why are you trying to hijack my truck?"

She grabbed the apple from his hand and crouched down, eating it hungrily. "I saw a target. A vehicle like this fetches thousands of credits."

"So you have no home?"

"How did you know?"

"Only someone desperate would hijack a Hunter Corporations mobile assault vehicle."

She looked at the truck and then back at Bounty. "What will you do to me?"

"I see a hungry child needing a safe place to be. Welcome to the family. Come inside, my wife will be eager to meet you."

Succession

Beatrix Badger-Oda stood staring at the encroaching army. The South Noamaizans had decided to invade the north for resources. They were led by the vicious Amazonian War Queen Rosalyn Dark. She was doing her best to hold off the army with elemental walls while the Northern Army debated. She saw motion out of the corner of her eye and saw the Avatar of Kali charge the enemy. She went to assist. The

Northern Noamaizans suddenly charged forth from their camp. They made headway, but a large mech walked into view. It raised its palm and thousands of rockets were launched. The Northern Noamaizans were instantly destroyed. Beatrix charged towards Rosalyn.

"Ah, if it isn't that weakling Silver's pet mortal. I am a true follower of Artemis. Your weakness will be purged and the true power of my great goddess will be revealed."

"You're all talk bitch. Face me like a warrior."

She waved her hand and the Avatar of Kali vanished. She would save at least one Northern Noamaizan. The blade came for her. She dodged only to be pierced through the back. As she fell, her head severed from her shoulders and her arms and legs were amputated.

Rosalyn grinned and turned Beatrix's corpse into parts for a motorcycle. She lifted Beatrix's head to her face, "I will make you suffer your blasphemous ways. You will never be able to go to the heavens as long as I have your body." She then kissed the severed head on the lips.

Under the Apple Tree

In an old forest glade surrounded by trees with a small pond in the centre, Bounty sat with his companions, Avol and Vicky. Both were devoted to him. Avol lay his head on Bounty's chest.

"I surrender to you."

Bounty went rigid. "Boy, do not continue down that path."

"But, master, I love you. I want to be with you. I want unity with my father and master."

Bounty sighed and stroked Avol, "So be it, son."

"I surrender to you. I give my body, mind, and soul to you."

"I care little for your mind, but I accept your devotion." Bounty slit Avol's arm open and did the same to his. Placing his bloody arm on Avol's, he continued, "With the mingling of our blood, you are now bound to me. I own you. Your body mine to use, your soul mine to keep. This is your desire?"

"Yes, please, master!"

"Then so be it. You are my slave turned child turned lover turned mate. From this day forth, as long as you live, you belong to me. When you die, your soul will be mine. I grant you reprieve in the Havens, but once you reincarnate, you will be mine again."

Vicky slit her arm open as well and immediately mingled her blood with Bounty's. He looked at her and sighed, "You as well, my dear. I own your body and soul. When you reincarnate, you will find me and submit again to me."

She smiled and snuggled into her father's master's chest. She ground her naked vagina against his leg and let out a coo of happiness. Avol coughed and vomited blood. He drank from his canteen and spat out more blood. Bounty watched him.

"Your body fails you, Avol. You will be dead by morning."

"I know, Father. I wanted to spend one last night in ecstasy with you. I will take your full shaft and have the best orgasm."

"I am too big for you, Avol. You know that."

"That is why I will take it all. I am dead anyway. The least I can do is die in the throes of passion. That is why I desire to bind. I can't live without you. I need you. I don't want to be alone."

Bounty sighed and brought Avol onto his lap. Avol lay on his back as Vicky moved her hand up and down his shaft getting him hard. She did the same to Bounty and positioned Bounty's member so it could enter Avol. Avol used what strength he had left from his disease and slammed his butt down, allowing Bounty's member to impale him and it did. He felt it penetrate his organs. Blood flowed out his butt, allowing him to use it as a lubricant. He cried out in exuberance. His semen splashed against Vicky, who was eagerly awaiting it. As he orgasmed again, his body went limp and he ceased to breathe. Vicky lay her head against Avol and cried. She soon fell asleep. Bounty burnt Avol and carried Vicky home. He entered his home to see Bounty Hunter 26 and Devon waiting for him.

Bounty Hunter 26 shook his head. "Sorry, Father, we were too late. An assassin killed the others. Llonna is beside herself. I took the liberty of sedating her while Raven, my wife, performed last rites."

"Do you have the assassin?"

Devon spoke, "She escaped, but when going through the recordings, I saw when she entered. She spoke to a woman named Rosalyn Dark. She also somehow got ahold of a way to disable security. Don't worry, the AI is fine. She's a little frazzled that she was somehow disabled and is trying to upgrade herself, so it never happens again."

"Pity, however, we now know who we are up against. Rosalyn Dark is a powerful sorceress who, in the days of myth during the war of the gods, accidentally killed her husband Hercules due to the machinations of Hera, the goddess of jealousy. She was given immortality and he became a god."

"So she is like a god. She also has many millennia of power behind her, so that means we can expect a fierce rival."

Scars That Remain

Eris Hunter struggled valiantly against the strange-looking cat creature. She was in the Noamaizan Arena as a test for the warriors. She had been resuscitated four times before this one. Her battered body was barely holding together and this strange four-foot-tall cat with insect wings and a horn was proving a tough opponent. A beam of strange rainbow-like energy struck Eris in the chest. She cried out and fell with a gaping hole where her heart used to be. The crowd roared in approval. The cat licked the paw that she had fired the beam from and then the paw became a hand.

Rosalyn Dark walked out and looked at the corpse of Eris. She scoffed and flung the corpse into the air, where she fired a beam of red energy, which exploded when it touched Eris destroying her body. Eris was dragged out of the back in a new body, sobbing. Rosalyn Dark then walked away with the cat, who looked back worried.

As the two entered a room, the cat saw four other warriors. One was a woman in white and blue armour that exposed her muscled arms and fabulous set of thighs. This woman seemed almost like a goddess. The woman next to her, however, was far darker and menacing. This woman wore a skin-tight rubber catsuit and her pitch-black hair was darker than night. On the wall behind them were an amber-skinned woman leaning against the wall and a prismatic-haired female smoking what looked like a wonder reed. Sitting in front of them all was a very pale woman with ice-blue eyes and icy hair. She was dressed very elegantly and looked to be a lady of high class and wealth. She went and sat down near the corner so she could keep an eye on the five strangers.

Rosalyn smiled and spoke, "You five have proven yourselves capable. You have been chosen to pilot massive war machines capable of entire devastating lands. You will be led by my wife, Umbral. I expect you to follow without question."

The four nodded in agreement. The cat stood up along with the other four, and followed Rosalyn to a large chamber where a woman stood. This woman seemed to be made of shadow and fear. The shadows seemed to swarm around her in a hazy fog. She had glowing green eyes that caused the cat to shiver.

The rainbow-haired woman spoke in a scratchy, almost masculin voice, "Sweet rides, which one is mine?"

Rosalyn smiled, "That would be the one with wings. It can turn into a jet fighter as well. You are our eyes in the sky. Don't worry, you will see plenty of action."

"Bring it on."

As the small group got to examine their mechs, the small bipedal cat creature looked at the arena where Eris Hunter struggled against several Amazon warriors.

That night she slipped into the prison where Eris was held. She saw the bloody bodies that Eris had originally inhabited and soon found the current one strapped to a spiked chair. Her head was low and her body was broken. She barely stirred as the cat touched her.

The cat purred, "Oh, you poor thing. My name is Unicaterfly. You are the former bodyguard of Queen Scorpion Ankara. I read about you but look at you now."

Eris looked up weakly. "Here to gawk at me, kitten? Mock me for your own amusement? I failed and this is my punishment. Leave me alone! Go play with your war toys, they won't help you against my brother."

"I am more concerned with you. You have been through many deaths, it seems. I am sorry that I was one."

"You are a strange one. The others only torture me. Please leave before they find you. I don't want your death on my conscience as well."

"Oh, don't worry, cutie. I am invulnerable. No mortal-made weapon can hurt me. See, I have a secret. I come from the clouds."

"Then you should know this was inevitable. As soon as Athena and Artemis joined up, Goddess Silver was doomed along with all her followers."

The March through Harsh Terrain

The Noamaizan Army arrived at the shore of Continent Silver. They were attacked by a turret which disabled one of their ships, stranding it. The Rainbow haired woman destroyed the turret with her jet mech.

Rosalyn Dark smiled, "Great job Rainbow Fistcrush. See if you can do a flyover of the forest to chart us a path."

"Got it, boss. I'm splitting off now."

The army set up camp in a nearby ruined fort. The mechs were tended to make sure the current rainstorm wouldn't rust their parts. Rosalyn sat in her all-terrain mobile task force headquarters. Her beloved partner, Umbral, was with her.

Umbral was alerted to something. She went to the door to see a very tall and thin Bunny Elf. "What the hell do you want?"

"I apologise. I was told this is where I could find the general. I have a way through the forest. I can lead you through if you so desire."

"Let her in Umbral. If she has information to get us to City Silver faster, we should take it."

Umbral glared at the rabbit elf. Then escorted her into the command centre. Rosalyn Dark looked at her.

"Well, don't keep me waiting. Tell me how you will get us through the forest?"

"My lady, I am a druid priestess of the Entrencher. He is the firstborn of the woods. Thus I can use his power to lead your army safely through the Spiked Forest. I will order the trees to give you a path."

"Do so and you will be greatly rewarded."

"All I request is that you send an assassin after my rival Druid Priest Corvus Hunter. His grove is near the mountains. Nevermore is a roadblock to The Entrencher's grip. If you get us through. He will die."

"Then Lady Dark behold The Firstborn of the Woods' power."

The trees suddenly recoiled as if in fear. A large path opened up and Rosalyn ordered her army forward. A small unit split off and headed to the Grove of Nevermore.

When the small unit arrived, they saw a large Grey Silveran male with curly horns and a green beard. He scratched his chest lazily. In the pale light, they could barely make out a glowing purple symbol on his torso. He snorted and then vanished in a shower of feathers. He reappeared behind them in a shower of feathers and half their unit was cut down. He vanished again and another half fell. The final fourth became terrified. One of the priestesses prayed for safety from the man. Her body glowed and the armour of Athena appeared on her. She succeeded in stabbing the man. He pulled himself off the blade. He walked over to the massive tree and slumped over. The unit watched as their fallen allies became small pyres. They were then forcibly ejected from the grove.

***

The Bunny Elf grinned maniacally, "It is done. My master has total control now. I thank you, Mistress Dark. May you succeed in your goal." She smiled at him and vanished in a whirlwind of thorny vines.

Rosalyn looked across the field and ordered her army forward. She hopped on her motorcycle and caressed the severed head of Beatrix Badger. She grinned and licked her lips. Before them stood a small army of Silverans and Tuar. The Taur were well-armed and she ordered her strikers to deal with them. She whispered something to Umbraland UmbraIvanished. Bounty Hunter 26 stood on the wall of city Silver. He hefted his Telepeircer and fired. All but six of the mechs were destroyed. He then jumped down and waded into the battle. His massive thirteen-foot height dwarfed the eight-foot-tall Silverans. He even dwarfed the ten-foot-tall Taur.

His blade cut large swaths of the Noamaizan Army down. His white and black duster swirled through the Noamaizan Army, knocking many back with the strike of it. He jumped and landed shattering the earth with his halberd and causing the stone to impale many of the warriors. Many tried to jump on his back and stab him from behind.

He paid no attention to them and continued to cut down their battle sisters.

He squared off against a pastel pink and white mech with a large feline head. He sliced through the mech before it could even fire. The other five opened fire on him. He absorbed their nuclear flames into himself. He saw his target he turned the fire on the cycles vaporising all of them and their riders. Rosalyn Dark had jumped off her's before it was destroyed. She saw the smirking soul of Beatrix Badger vanish and roared in anger.

Her army was invigorated by her dark magic and soon had the upper hand. Bounty Hunter 26 looked at his readout and nodded. He saw the mechs turn to Silver; he snarled and put up a barrier around Silver; his allies were decimated. The mechs began bombarding City Silver with their rockets. He teleported into the city. Only sixty per cent of the population had been transported safely to the shelters. He saw his wife holding open the tele-tubes with her power.

"Raven, hold strong! I will try to gather who I can."

"Do not strain yourself, my love. We must survive."

Bounty Hunter 26 found his daughter and teleported her to his hover truck and sent the truck as far away as he could from city Silver. His twin sister, Devon, was zipping through the city with her transporter. She was gathering as many as she could and then driving them to the extraction point. The city was crumbling from the vibrations of the bombardment. As she reached the extraction point, the ground erupted in a fiery nuclear inferno. Her truck was vaporised. Raven closed the portal as the flames reached her, incinerating her instantly. Bounty Hunter 26 looked up at the night sky as the moons turned red. He tried to absorb the fire like his father before him, but he could not contain it.

As the inferno roared, Rosalyn Dark saw the massive form of her enemy become stone. She grinned and helped her troops destroy the remaining enemy. They fell back as the radiation became severe. She saw her soldiers fall one by one as they were poisoned by the rads. She cried out and ordered the remaining mechs to retreat to Noamaiza. She got aboard her headquarters and reversed it. Within minutes her troops were dead. A massive radiation storm whipped up, sending the poison into the sky. Soon all of Eastern Silver was covered in radioactive clouds.

Escape to the Wasteland

Lord Moth stood on top of his castle. He saw the radiation coming and pressed a button. The Psy wells activated, sending up a neutralising wall. They crackled as the radiation hit. His wife was with a child, but she sent out some of her psy energy as well, reinforcing the barrier. Deep underground in the wastes of Western Silver, an old man nearly crumbled from the deaths of three powerful Psyonics. He steadied himself, dusted himself off and continued deeper underground. He arrived at a large cavern with many faces carved into the walls. In front of an altar was a grotesque tentacled monstrosity that had once been an elf. It was lying on its back, taking labouring breaths all overlay bones and corpses.

The old man spoke in a deep baritone, "Entrencher, it seems you have overstepped your bounds. Behold the last of your false druids."

The old man pulled out a severed head of an elf with rabbit ears. He tossed it towards the behemoth. He struck the bloated tentacled monstrosity with a glowing purple sword. There was a silent yet deafening scream that emitted from the creature. As the old man removed his blade, the creature ceased to exist. He shook his head and tossed an infernal bomb behind him as he exited the caverns. The flames cleansed the caverns.

As the old man exited the caverns, he came face to face with a masked man wearing a brown and teal robe. The man spoke, "Bounty Hunter 13, you killed a god. What the hell are you thinking?"

"That was no god. Besides, I only sought vengeance since that so-called god killed my brother, Corvus."

"Hold up. Corvus lies dead?"

"Yes, he died protecting his grove from assassins from Noamaiza sent by one of the Entrencher's false druids, Firstborn of the Woods, my cybernetic behind. Now I am aiming to take out Rosalyn Dark."

"You sent the meteor to wipe out the City Amazonia."

"So what if I did? The balance is gone. Lord Shadow lies dead. The lady of the Pure lands has been usurped. All that is left is you. Lord badger of the Inbetween."

"You fool man. The balance cannot be disturbed. Do you even realise what untold catastrophe could happen? Only what is fated, dear brother. Lord Shadow had reverted to its original owner before Bounty Hunter 26 took the staff of shadows. But the lady of the pure lands still has been removed. I guess they did not appreciate Trinity Dragon."

"You scared me there for a second, Bounty. I thought you literally meant that the balance had been disrupted."

"Mhahaha! I suppose my wording did have ambiguity. Fear not, Mystic Hunter the fourth. I am still Lord Shadow. My son, daughter, and daughter-in-law lie dead, however, things will begin to progress further. Be prepared for the worst. Goodbye, brother. I wish you luck."

"Don't say that, Demon. You know how fickle Lady Luck is. She may take it as a challenge."

"I cannot take back what I said, brother. Go find Baron Samedi to help bury the dead. I will be joining them soon."

"Don't say things like that, Bounty."

"You have much to learn about being a guardian of the Inbetween. You will learn things in time. Things that you wish you never learnt. May the brown be with you, dear Myst."

"I... ugh. Very well, Bounty Hunter 13, may the Grey be with you," he said and vanished. Bounty laughed darkly and then vanished. He found the Mobile Headquarters of Rosalyn Dark. He batted aside Umbral as she tried to stop him. This gave Rosalyn enough time to prepare. She lunged at Bounty as he sidestepped her and felt his body get diced into pieces. He grinned as his soul was freed from his body.

Rosalyn cried out in fear as the soul in front of her overpowered her with how grey it was. Umbral charged and tried to cut through the soul only to have the mists surrounding her rip apart, sending her to the beyond. Rosalyn used all the powers at her disposal. Nothing seemed to affect the Demon of Silver. He grabbed her and pulled her into a neon orange portal. He tossed her in front of a strange purple and black being that seemed to shift between the masculin form and the feminine form. He walked through the portal, closing it behind him.

The creature spoke in both masculine and feminine voices, "Hello, lovely, I have been wanting to grab you for my collection for quite some time now. You killed Heracles, my plaything. Freeing him from my grasp. Now you will become my plaything. I am your new master Slaahn-hla-ge."

"No! Ah! I can't escape what trickery is this?"

"The Demon of Silver blocked your powers. Ready or not, here it is."

Slaahn-hla-ge then grabbed Rosalyn and warped her mind with extreme pleasure. Rosalyn was soon a willing thrall to her new owner.

Wandering Under the Moonlight

Bounty Hunter 13 sat in his private grove. The Nuclear fallout had not affected many species of plants, but it was slowly affecting the animals. He knew the elves were trying to purify the forest. *Did I do the right thing?*

The statue chuckled, "It is hard to say, boy. Was it right of you to destroy an entire civilisation because they attacked you? Was it right to drop a meteor on their home, killing countless innocents?"

"Yes, that is my question."

"Even I can't answer that. We are one and the same boy. What do you think?"

"I regret my rash decision. Their army was already killed by their own nuclear fallout. Wish I could turn back time, but I do not want to deal with the Time Police, especially if they send Shaguthor the Indomitable. Ugh, that guy."

"Ha, you are planning something. I highly recommend that you stop scheming. No good can come of it."

"God Silver, you know me too well. Do not worry about your pointy head. I will not change my actions."

A small voice spoke up, "Who are you talking to, big guy?"

Bounty looked down to see a three-foot tall cat with a single horn, big green eyes, pale pink fur, and two tattered moth wings curled up near a tree. She was wrapped tightly around herself.

He sighed, "I am already dead, Felicity Unicaterfly. You cannot kill what is dead."

"Not here for you, big guy. I came searching for Eris the Hunter. She vanished from her prison in Noamaiza. I came to volunteer myself to her."

"Why? Were you not part of the attack force?"

"Yes, but I deeply regret what she went through. See, I am from the clouds. I wanted fun but only saw death."

"You are a goddess?"

"No, I feel Eris thought the same thing. No, I am from the clouds."

"Oh, a Cloud Cuckoo Lander. I see. I have not seen Eris. Though knowing her, she will find me. I know of a place where you can stay. It's currently inhabited by some Maurarders that took up residence, but there is a secret room that I can hide you in. You have to have a strong stomach, though. The room is my personal prison for those souls that I have claimed over the years. Perpetually trapped in erotic art."

"Take me there."

"Then hold on tight, girl."

The two vanished and reappeared in a large spacious room with many statues in erotic poses. Some rubber, some stone, and some metal. She stared at them and then jumped when a teal rubber statue moved.

"Llona, what are you doing here? I thought Umbral had killed you."

"Sorry, Daddy. I was trying to hide from those Marauders. I tried to blend in, but this is stuffy. How are they alive?"

"Not exactly alive, trapped in deep pleasure until I free them from their contract. Deep in stasis, so all functions are shut down except the pleasure receptor in the brain."

"I see. Why?"

"These girls all agreed to give me their souls in exchange for my Mercenary skills or their souls were given to me by someone else. But how are you alive?"

"When I saw Lunatyc get stabbed, I hid. Then the marauders took over. Sorry, Daddy. I'm a coward."

"On the contrary, my dear girl. You saw you were out manoeuvred and retreated to safety. I am proud of you, but now I need you to use your Succubus skills and find when and where your sisters will get reincarnated. Do not interfere with their progress as new people only interfere when it seems they have remembered their past life."

"Okay, Papa. But can I get fed first?"

"Felicity, pleasure, my daughter. I wish to see if you will be right for my sister."

"Uh, right. Weird, but okay, I hope you enjoy."

Bounty disappeared and looked at the nuclear snowfall. He sighed and began to purify the air. As he was tainted in his youth by a nuclear detonation, he now could clean fallout from the land.

It would take him years, but he had time. He looked down as he idly scratched his stomach. *Damn, I am getting fat. Ugh, no surprise though. I have long lived beyond the thousand-year mark.*

After feeding the weird succubus, Felicity disappeared and reappeared in the grove to see if she could find the Demon of Silver. The night was cold and unforgiving. *I suppose I deserve this for what I helped the Noamaizans do. So cold. Oh, wait, what is this warmth?* Her eyes bolted open. She saw a curly-horned male with a fur cloak. His armour was grey and brown like the woods. She felt like feathers were touching her brain when she looked too closely at his face.

"H... hello. Who are you?"

The man smiled, "I should be asking the same. What is a Cloud Cuckoo Lander doing on the ground?"

"Being stupid. My name is Felicity Unicaterfly."

"Ah, the runaway queen. Seems you couldn't handle the ground."

"I have been through the land of Wonder. When you play chess with a Jabberwocky and talk to a smoking giant millipede, then you can tell me what I can and cannot handle."

"My apologies. Why are you out here?"

"After City Silver was destroyed, I wandered, hoping to heal my wounds, but my body can't keep up. I'm so cold."

"Ah, do not fret, wee one. I know of a place where you can rest and heal. Now lay your world-weary head upon my shoulder. I will take you there."

He lifted her up. She was heavier than he expected. He arrived at a large fortress. He slid into the fortress and arrived in a trophy room. He looked around and saw a small bed. He placed Felicity on the bed and a healing energy engulfed her. A buxom hologram appeared and nodded in approval. She turned to the man.

"So it is true. The old Gods are back. Has it gotten to that point already?"

The man smiled, "Not truly back yet. Lady of the Data realm. You chose to ascend by becoming one with this home. Back when you were still Bounty Hunter 3's daughter. Why?"

"My father needed a computer that could keep up with him. I was dying anyway. It was only in my self-interest of survival that I did it."

"Do you regret it?"

"No, many of my father's descendants were amazing people. I especially like this one. He is very intense. Almost reminds me of my father."

"You may be closer to the truth than you think."

***

The wasteland was unforgiving. A woman in powered armour was walking through the apocalypse. She was sluggish and weakening by the minute. *I have to keep going. My family depends on me to get provisions. I have to keep moving.*

She stumbled and collapsed, sobbing against the unforgiving dirt. The icy nuclear wind blew fiercely above her as her eyes started to fade. The last thing she saw was an old haggard face with two thick horns and a fu manchu. *So I finally die and get to go to hell. Figures.*

She awoke in a clean room with only a sheet covering her. She looked around frantically until a hologram of a busty woman appeared. "Do not fret, child. You are safe, as are your sisters. You were suffering from severe dehydration and nuclear corruption. My master retrieved you and cleaned you up. He is elsewhere at the moment but has told me to provide you with clothing and a place to recover along with your two sisters."

"What about the others? I had nine siblings."

"I am sorry, only three survived. According to your sister, the others got munched by the twins."

"What, no! No, no, no, I don't believe you!"

"It's true, sis. Lala and Lulu went mad, along with several others and killed everyone except five of us. They then ate their flesh."

"Why wasn't I faster?"

"It's not your fault, sis. There was a man who had been secretly raping them. It broke their minds and the Nuclear fallout seeping in through the vents didn't help."

Llona Cacophony watched the girls from the shadows. She wore a bright pink vest over her teal dress. *There they are. I hope they will soon remember their past. I need my sisters.*

Lord Badger of the Inbetween

In this timeline, Bounty Hunter 12 was a monster obsessed with creating a child that could rival the Eternals. He forced his children to worship his son Bounty Hunter 13 and be his sexual partners. After his death, his children managed to break his mental manipulations. The only one unable to break the indoctrination was Eris. Her family managed to erase her mind and she now goes by the name Wyldfang. Myst Hunter found himself attracted to the Inbetween realm. As he schemed from the Inbetween realm, his brother Bounty schemed from the shadow realm. Both schemed to get rid of their father's friend Zenthon Ankara. During this time period, their father's experiment began anew in a small household with ten children. One boy and nine girls. But this was no concern for Myst. He had larger issues on his hand.

"Where th' hell am I? I was following a cry for help."

"Oh my goodness! What are you?"

He looked down to see a small doll-like being. It was an adorable little mouse-like doll. "Have I gone insane?"

"Hardly, mister. My name is Chirripi. You are the only other full-bodied being I have seen since I arrived here. My only companion is that soul over there. He was lost when his world was written out of existence by The Writer. He rescued the other soul trapped here, but he is now stuck."

"I see. Maybe I can help him. So why are you here?"

"I arrived here after my partner was consumed by darkness. I lost my way and wound up here. I cannot leave until my partner is freed or until I find a new partner. Are you okay? You don't look so good."

"My body is so used to the Inbetween realm that any extended period away from it causes my body to become stressed."

"Oh, dear! Hang on! I think I can help you."

The little doll scurried around, creating many runes and stepped back. The runes encircled Myst and when they cleared, he found himself looking at a readout on a screen which went to static. He blinked as the screen then showed his surroundings.

"What is this?"

"It is the robes of the X. I am surprised at your mask. Both bull and badger features. Why is that?"

"One ancestor was a Taur-Anubi, while my family's genetic ancestor was a man called Lord Badger."

"Interesting. Well, this garb should allow you to travel without stress on your body."

"Thank you, little Chirripi. I would like for you to be my travelling companion. At least until we can find and free your partner."

"I'm not sure that is allowed. Hang on. Well, there's nothing in the rules preventing me. Okay. Let's help the young man over there find his way."

Myst walked over to the boy. "Son, why are you here? Are you alive?"

"I am alive, but I have lost my way. I do not recall who I am or why this place accepted me."

"Don't you worry, boy! I'll help you find your way."

He lifted the soul and hid it in his robes. He followed the faint memories the boy had of a girl with bright neon red hair. They arrived on an island with a vast ocean surrounding it. In the far distance, he could barely make out the skyline of a large city. There was a strange assortment of people on the beach, including what looked to be a Platypod of the Junk Heap of Silver. He could also see a strange Canis with a dopy but intelligent look on his smooshed face. Both were actively messing around with a boy that had steel grey hair while two girls who looked almost the same giggled. He saw the neon red-haired girl sitting alone on an outcropping staring at the sea. He nodded and the boy appeared to her before finally being returned to the havens. She wept tears of joy and sadness. Myst smiled and went back to the Inbetween realm along with the strange doll. They appeared in a wasteland surrounded on all sides by graves marked with axes, swords, and clubs.

"This is not the Inbetween. Where in the thirteen hells am I?"

Chirripi spoke, "Oh, not good. I'm going to hide in your robe. This is the Graveyard. The seekers of light and darkness clashed here. Sextillions died. It was the first war and it wiped us all out. The founders survived but were cast out of time. Sixteen survived and they rebuilt the universe. You wear the robes of the founders, the X robes. I suspect you arrived here thanks to a call. The others will be here shortly."

Myst looked around and saw the air shimmer. Six beings emerged, three female and three male, all wearing different masks. The three females wore the masks of an owl, a liger, and a crocodile. The males wore the masks of a bear, a fox, and a mask that was completely featureless.

The featureless mask spoke with a resonating baritone, "So Janna and Auroch are still missing. But who is this? A new body wears the mask of the Badger."

Owl spoke, "What is your name, stranger?"

Myst looked at them and smirked, "Names hold power. You may refer to me as Transient Spark."

Fox spoke in a light and flamboyant tenor, "Well then, Spark. Why did you summon us to the waking world?"

"I did no such thing. I was trying to return to my home but arrived here."

Liger spoke in a thick Irescotwel accent, "Ach, I don't believe you."

"What's not there to believe? I am new here. How could I summon you?"

Bear spoke in a deep earthy bass, "I believe you, for I feel the strings of the summoning call. They come from this grey box."

A new voice spoke, "Ah, there it is. Oh, hello, fellas. Nice to see you."

They all turned and Crocodile spoke, "Oh shit. You returned to us Auroch."

The gold-eyed man with black, brown, white, and grey hair looked contemplative. He smoothed out his black and brown robe before speaking, "Auroch, now there is a name I have not heard in ages. Hmm, anyhoo, I suspect you wonder what this box is."

Bear spoke, "Where is Janna?"

"She's not here, Arctos. I suspect she's still working on her plans."

Crocodile spoke, "Then tell us what is in the box?"

"Easy, my dear Korach. Fate's little book. Swiped from him when he erased many planets."

Owl whispered, "You seek us to help you rewrite fate?"

"No, Heather, I do not. I seek to start another cleanse. This is what we all sought when our guilds clashed. It worked. The universe was reborn."

Liger snarled, "It be a fool's idea. No one follows the old way anymore. The barbarian planets can't even fathom nature, much less light and darkness."

"Ah, that is where you are wrong, Tigon. The barbarian planets have evolved to be some of the fiercest beings in the entire galaxy of Silver. They would surprise you."

The featureless mask spoke, "Auroch, you are the fool. No one would willingly follow us."

"Malphense, my man. You are correct, which is why I have been searching for this box."

Fox mask sneered, "You seek us to help you open it and help you rewrite it, so we have our guilds back. Is this correct?"

"Brava, you hit the nail on the head, Urocyon. Once we have our guilds back, we can reignite the war between the dark and the Light. This time rewrite the universe in our own way."

Myst snorted. "This plan of yours sounds winged. You would need all of us to crack the lock on that thing. Twenty more of us to maybe possibly open it."

Malphense nodded. "I agree with Spark here. We do not have that kind of energy."

"Haha, that is right, but there is a way for even the most stubborn lock to open. We once fought with the ancient auto key axes. We may have lost the ability to wield them now, but there is one powerful warrior of light still out there. He is a boy by the name Sorven. He fought against the Nightmare Fifteen. He is currently doing battle with the Un Twelve. He has survived everything they throw at him. He is the key, haha, to open it."

Myst spoke, "Seems to be a foolish plan. Relying on things that may not even happen. What makes you so sure this Sorven will help us?"

"We capture his girl. Hold her hostage and when he unlocks her chains, he unlocks the box. Simple as that."

Myst growled slightly, then allowed an unsettling grin to touch his lips. "Then, old man, allow me to capture this girl. I am new and this will allow me to prove myself."

"Oh, ho! I love it. Not the old man part but the eagerness. Do this and you may join our ranks completely."

The others scoffed at the idea. Tigon spoke, "If you truly seek to help us. Then do so out of the willingness of your heart. Not for some reward."

Myst looked at Tigon, then smiled again, "Of course, of course, but I expect no reward. In fact, I don't even expect you to trust me. I am nothing, especially compared to the likes of you."

Myst walked off following a faint trail. He wandered for who knows how long since time has no meaning in the Inbetween. He soon arrived at a large city. Skyscrapers split the sky and there was constant humid rain. He waved his hand and a small barrier appeared, protecting him from getting wet. He arrived at a large park filled with trees. He found her. She was exiting the school, Angel's Grove Learning Center for the Mystically Advanced. He looked around and saw smoke on the horizon. Then he saw five dangerous-looking NorvCryogans leading an army to attack the school. He grabbed the girl and pulled her into the Inbetween right as the army attacked.

He reappeared with her in chains and set her on the box connecting the chains with the lock on the box. The others stared at him in shock.

Heather spoke, "How were you so fast? One second, you were gone, then the next, you appeared with your prey."

Myst spoke gruffly, "I am Lord Badger. I have many powers. Finding my goal quickly is one."

Auroch nodded. "It is just as I thought. Very good. The boy will come soon. Let us set up the welcoming committee."

Myst watched them all wander off. He heard in his head, "You can not allow the war to begin. In the old days, back before the War of the Gods, the war between Shadow and Light was devastating. I told you Sextillions died. For some pointless reason."

"Do not worry yourself, Chirripi shadows cannot exist without light, just as light can't exist without shadows. Darkness and light are two of the building blocks of the universe. As the Master of the Inbetween, I keep the balance intact. These fools will soon open the box. I will face them. They will kill me, but they will never upset the balance."

"Die! No, you can't die. I need you."

"Oh, don't worry, Chirripi. The Myst Hunter that will replace me is exactly the same. We will become one. My time is up."

He stood by the box, leaning on his staff. The boy that arrived was furious. "You bastard stole her. I will take her back."

The girl cried out, "Rico!"

"You are not Sorven. Ah, I see. I was off in my calculations. You desire the girl. Then you face me."

Myst vanished and reappeared behind Rico. He struck him hard, breaking his arm. Rico cried out but caught his blade with his other hand. It fell and sliced through Myst, who staggered back only to be enveloped in a brown light that faded, revealing a grey-skinned face. The new man smiled. He scoffed and waved his cybernetic hand, sending Rico flying. The new man looked at the girl and sighed. He picked up his fallen staff and waited. This time a battle-worn boy arrived. His clothes were tattered and he had blood dripping from many lacerations. Some parts of his skin had shadow burn on it. He looked at Myst and raised his blade.

"Don't be a fool, child! You can barely stand. Your pal Rico didn't even stand a chance against me. You are near death as it is."

The boy struggled to stand, only to stumble. He was caught by a very large Canis man with large muscles. This Canis had heavy armour on and a tower shield covered in blades and scales. A Syrieen flapped down and pulled out a nasty-looking thorny Rose Onyx staff.

The boy grinned. "Gof! Doka! You made it!"

The Canis smiled in his wolf-like way and spoke in a deep earthy voice, "You move way too fast, Sorven. We could barely keep up. Doka had to fly to find you."

Doka spoke in a lilting airy voice, "Had you not gone ahead, you would not be in such a condition. Void Heal!"

Sorven was repaired right before Myst's eyes. Myst grinned and walked off. Sorven spoke, "Hey, wait, what are you doing?"

"Not dealing with you. She's all yours."

"Uh, okay?"

He unlocked the chains holding the girl and the box popped open. In it was a book. Sorven picked it up and was instantly stabbed in the back by Auroch. He quickly took out both Gof and Doka. As he stood to deliver the killing blow to the girl, the book vanished. Myst walked over and waved his hand, allowing the image constructs he had created to vanish. He stood holding the book.

Auroch spoke, "Come now, Badger. Give me the book. We can rewrite history."

The others appeared wearing cracked masks and torn robes. Myst looked at them and scoffed. A large hole opened in the sky. A massive being beyond description wearing a blood-red robe descended from the sky. In his hand, he held a massive scythe.

The being spoke but, at the same time, did not speak. It was a whisper but also a roar. "There the thief is. You stole something from my brother, The Writer."

Myst raised the book up. "Oh, ancient Azrael, the Alpha Reaper. I give you the Book of Fate.

These morons tried to rewrite the world by their own means. As Lord of the Inbetween, the balance must be kept."

"You have done well, Lord Badger. Now step back so that I may do my duty."

Myst walked off as the scythe split the universe. The seekers ceased to exist. They had been sent to the Havens of the Dead Planets. Myst waited until the universe had righted itself before opening his robe.

Sorven stumbled out in a daze along with the girl, Rico, Gof, and Doka. Chirripi walked out as well. Myst waved his hand and the kids vanished along with Gof and Doka. He patted Chirripi on the head.

"Come along, my little friend. I felt a worrisome shift. Hold tight."

He picked Chirripi up and vanished. As he exited his portal, in front of him stood a green Troll. He looked at the Troll and then down at his gauntlet. "Damn, wrong time period. Oh hey, Jaina, so this is what you were doing in the past. Well, come on. May as well get you someplace safe. Oh and Gorphazon, you may as well come too. I will get you back to Kilgoth Prime."

The Troll spoke, "Lord Badger of the Inbetween, what are you looking for?"

Myst replied, "That is hard to say. I am just getting used to this role."

"I see. Well, you two had best get going. Lord Badger will not wait long."

Jaina and Gorphazon walked into the portal and it closed behind them. Myst led the two to a safe zone of the Inbetween. He then re-did his calculations and vanished again. He and Chirripi reappeared outside a cave as an old man walked out. He spoke, "Bounty Hunter 13, you killed a god. What the hell are you thinking?"

"That was no god. Besides, I only sought vengeance since that so-called god killed my brother, Corvus."

"Hold up. Corvus lies dead?"

"Yes, he died protecting his grove from assassins from Noamaiza sent by one of the Entrencher's false druids. Firstborn of the Woods my cybernetic behind. Now I am aiming to take out Rosalyn Dark."

"You sent the meteor to wipe out the City Amazonia."

"So what if I did? The balance is gone. Lord Shadow lies dead. The lady of the Pure lands has been usurped. All that is left is you. Lord Badger of the Inbetween"

"You fool man. The balance cannot be disturbed. Do you even realise what untold catastrophe could happen?"

"Only what is fated, dear brother. Lord Shadow had reverted to its original owner before Bounty Hunter 26 took the staff of shadows. But the lady of the pure lands still has been removed. I guess they did not appreciate Trinity Dragon."

"You scared me there for a second, Bounty. I thought you literally meant that the balance had been disrupted."

"Mhahaha! I suppose my wording did have ambiguity. Fear not, Mystic Hunter the fourth. I am still Lord Shadow. My son, daughter, and daughter-in-law lie dead, however, things will begin to progress further. Be prepared for the worst. Goodbye, brother. I wish you luck."

"Don't say that, Demon. You know how fickle Lady Luck is. She may take it as a challenge."

"I cannot take back what I said, brother. Go find Baron Samedi to help bury the dead. I will be joining them soon."

"Don't say things like that, Bounty."

"You have much to learn about being a guardian of the Inbetween. You will learn things in time. Things that you wish you never learnt. May the Brown be with you, dear Myst."

"I... ugh. Very well, Bounty Hunter 13, may the Grey be with you."

Chirripi eyed the old man and then looked up at her new friend. He patted her on the head. The two left the desert waste.

She finally spoke, "What is with that man and why is he so terrifying?"

"Bounty Hunter 13 knows many things. He has dabbled in dark mysticism. He took the mantle of Lord Shadow when he slew the previous Lord Shadow. He sees things. Things that scare even me. I have much to learn. I suppose I shall go and visit my master."

The two arrived in a snowy fortress. A massive Ursar stood along with other Ursars. They seemed to be debating. Finally, a large grey and white one spoke. "We have no choice, the boy is to be cared for."

Myst got closer to see a bloody and ragged Nu Silveran. The man was barely breathing and looked to be half frozen. Myst gasped, "Moonstalker!"

The Ursar looked at him with dangerous intent. The white and grey Ursar spoke, "Who might you be, stranger?"

"Lord Icefang, I come seeking knowledge. You once found me very much like my nephew here."

"Oh? Hmm. Ah, yes, very well. Can you heal him? As a master of ice, I can't do that."

"Yes."

Myst knelt down and allowed some healing psy to envelop his hand. He moved his hand over Moonstalker. The boy gasped for air and looked around wildly.

Lord Icefang smiled, "It is you. Young Moonstalker Hunter, you trespass on the lands of the Midwinter Dragon. You are lucky you still live. She is very ornery."

"I lost my way and got seduced by the lights. Ugh, I don't feel so good."

"Well, that is to be expected. Gale, get him to the healing temple."

A female Ursar nodded and hefted Moonstalker up. The rest followed her leaving the white and grey Ursar behind. He looked at Myst and grinned.

"Well, boyo seems like you ran into some issues. Come and have some food and drink. It seems you still have much to learn."

"Thank you, master."

"I am no one's master, boy. Come rest. Replenish your reserves."

***

Many moons later, Myst stared at the island in front of him with trepidation. This was the castle lands of the first Lord Badger. This Lord Badger had forced unification. His many enemies were buried beneath the island. He entered the dig site to see a crimson and purple Equus. He watched her dust off some stone before writing something down.

"Who are you that disturbs these forsaken lands?"

She yelped and stared around wildly. She saw a doll-like being waddle hop over to her. She looked at it curiously.

"Hullo, I am Chirripi. The big guy behind you is Lord Badger. You are messing with his land."

"Sorry, I was sent here to begin the excavation process. My queen detected strong magical interference from this land."

One of the walls opened and a large brutish Lizard man walked out. He saw Myst and grinned, "Aboot damn time you got here, boyo. I sent for yeh ten days ago."

Myst looked down at the Lizardman. "Don Demarco. What is one of my brother's thugs doing here."

"Thugs! Laddie no! I am merely an entrepreneur. I actually sent it for your brother, but it seems he is busy. Come follow me. You too, girlie."

The two followed him into a huge mausoleum antechamber. There were five doors. One was already open. The open one had the symbol of the Lizard God. The other four had symbols of the Bull God, The Elf God, the Silveran God, and the Equus God.

"Each door needs at least three representatives of the species. We found that out the hard way when we tried to open the Lizard door. Poor Gaston lost his scales in the backlash. Luckily he will regrow them. I found the best combination is one representative from each subspecies of the door."

The girl spoke, "How tedious! Can you tell me what you found behind your door?"

"Sorry, nothing of value if that is what you mean. Just a bunch of worn-out armour and weapons. Not even valuable."

"Still, I suppose curiosity must be quenched. So Lord Badger, do you have a ship we can use?"

"Do not worry, my purple friend. The others will arrive shortly. Let us go outside to meet them."

As they exited, they saw a large Silveran Spacewalker ship land on the beach. A girl in a jumpsuit walked out. Behind her was a woman in Amazon warrior garb, a deep grey-skinned man who looked almost like a demon, and a Black Silveran with fiery orange hair and crimson eyes.

The dark grey-skinned man spoke, "Why did you call us here?"

The Black Silveran smiled, "I presume we are needed, Dakon. Before us stands Lord Badger of the Inbetween lands. I presume he is a descendant of the First Lord Badger. Very much like Beatrix."

"But why?"

Myst spoke, "All will be revealed in time, just wait."

A small hover ship, cargo class, floated into view. It stopped at the beach as well. Three Taur walked out. One was a Taur Anubi, one was a Taur Bos, and the other was a Taur Bisonum. The

Taur Anubi snorted and lit a cigar.

An imposing Equus woman with a blank stare on her face walked out of a star hopper. She was holding a leash with a vibrantly and obscenely pink mare on the end of it. Another Winged Equus landed. She was toned with a rainbow mane and teal fur. She was also naked, showing off her piercings, penis, and tattoos.

The air behind Myst shimmered and three different elves appeared. One was red with the solar throne emblem on his armour. The other was deep underground grey with green hair and red eyes. She wore the armour of Arachne. The final one had a woody look about her. She was one of the Sylvani elves that lived deep in the forest with them and also was one of Jeane d'Arc's followers.

The follower of Jeane d'Arc spoke, "What is this shithole?"

Myst chuckled, "Ah, the brashness of youth. Welcome to the Mausoleum of Lord Badger. Back when Silver was still a young planet, Lord Badger tried to conquer the first continent. He succeeded. Come follow me."

The small group followed Myst to the mausoleum. He waved his hand and many small scones lit up. "The first species opposed Lord Badger. They were Silveran, Taur, Elf, Equus, and Scale Folk. Each army numbered in the thousands. But they had no chance against Lord Badger, the first of the Mystics. His Psi constructs destroyed them. Now as it nears the new Millennium, I allow you to reclaim your predecessor's bodies to return them to the havens."

Axel spoke, "And what if we do not claim the fallen?"

"They will be Reaped, regardless of each species has its own way of honouring the forgotten dead. Please stand on the corresponding sigil that matches your species."

The imperious grey Equus handed the pink one's leash to the teal one. "I cannot enter the tomb. Prismatic Crush, you, along with Kim, will escort Professor Starfall."

The teal mare nodded. "Come on, Egghead, get over here."

The purple Equus shuddered and stood next to Prismatic. The door under the Equus symbol glowed malevolently before a sound that sounded like glass breaking echoed through the chamber. The three walked through and the door crumbled, revealing a wall. They had no choice but to move forward.

Axel stood on the sigil of the Silverans. Dakon and Beatrix stood next to him. The ground opened up beneath them and they dropped down. The air shimmered near Myst as a large

Hyaenidae stood next to him. She lit a cigar and blew out crimson smoke. He waved it away from his face and looked at the four elves. They stood on their sigil and teleported away. The taur had already walked through their door.

Myst stepped on a stone. "So Feldspar and Shenzi, shall we go and meet up with the others?" The ground rumbled and three-fourths of the floor began lowering deep into the earth. They arrived just as Axel entered the mausoleum. Dakon was slightly singed.

Beatrix walked in. "That was a pointless endeavour. Especially since the Mass grave is here."

Myst chuckled, "Hardly pointless when it was a test. A test of willpower."

The Taur entered and the Taur-Anubi opened a flask and poured out a drink for his companions. They downed the drink.

"Ah, Doctor Rhapsody, you brought the booze."

The Taur-Anubi smiled, "That I did, you old goat. That I did."

Myst waited and looked down at his chrono readout. He scratched his chin. The Elves finally arrived. The follower of Jeane d'Arc was unconscious and the Sylvani Elf was bleeding.

Myst sighed and walked over. He healed the Sylvani Elf. "What happened?"

The Sun Elf spoke, "Damn bitch attacked us."

"Can't say I am surprised. Those not originally descended from the first ones may experience madness. The Arclands only arrived on this planet a thousand years ago. Same as Strawlia. She must have fallen victim to the Tzarbomba, a psychological drug that pervades this place. Only effective on beings not originally from Silver. Another reason why the first army lost so badly was; many were mercenaries from other planets, however, all were buried here and imprisoned. Your task is to bring them home, and honor their deaths properly."

Axel spoke, "What of the mercenaries?"

"I told you they will be Reaped regardless."

The dead were honoured and a fog rolled in. If one were to look closely at the fog, they would see the Wraiths doing their duty. Toreno, their king, stood by his flamberge, ready. Myst smiled and sent the groups home. He, too, returned to the Inbetween. The ancient castle of the Badger appeared ominously and sent out a beam of energy. The sands swirled and hid it again.

Winter

Bounty Hunter 13 trudged through the radioactive snow. *Curse those Noamaizan bitches. They took my son from me. They took my daughter from me. They took my people from me. Now, look what this place has been reduced to. City Silver is no more and a junk city has risen around the petrified form of my son. The only other fortified places are The Onyx Tower of God Silver and the semi-destroyed spaceship in the harbour. Not to mention my home, which has been taken over by the Raiders. How the fuck they infiltrated my home, I'll never know. All I know is my children, wives, and servants lie dead, but I got the last laugh. I hope you enjoy your new home Rosalyn Dark.*

He saw movement in the distance prepping his gun. *I hope it's not a mutate. I can handle a Mutate easily though if it is an Ultramutate, I may have to expend some psychic energy to destroy it. Power Armour smart whoever is in there knows that the armour reduces radiation. They're moving rather slowly. Hope it's not radiation poisoning.* Bounty neared the person in Power Armor. They were moving really slowly and looked to be stumbling. As he neared, the person fell into the snow.

Bounty helped them up. The person struggled, "Leave me be, just let me die."

"I think not. Please remove your helmet."

"No, I cannot leave my bunker without food. They depend on me. I'd rather die than see them starve."

"Please remove your helmet, so I can help you."

He finally helped the person remove their helmet, revealing a blond female with yellow retinas; however, her corneas were black with corruption. He sighed and pulled out a small vial of liquid. He poured it down her throat while she struggled to stay awake. He immediately saw the corruption retreat and her naturally green eyes return. She finally succumbed to sleep as her body began to shut down. Bounty quickly revitalised her organs by imbuing them with pure psychic energy. The psionic nuclear corruption was finally purged from her body.

He looked at her readout and found she was from Bunker 9, which was nearby. A good place to hunker down and wait out the oncoming radiation storm. *I just have to get us there before it hits.* He hefted the girl onto his shoulder like a sack of junk, which weighed about the same. He began jogging as fast as he could with his arthritic joints acting up. He got to the bunker and used the master code to open it up. One good thing about being the CEO of Hunter Corporation is I have the master code for all the bunkers we built to help The Silveran people survive Psionic Nuclear Fallout.

As the door spasmed and screeched while opening, Bounty holstered his gun so as not to seem threatening to the occupants of Bunker 9. He immediately grimaced as he smelled cooking flesh. He peered into the atrium and saw bloody bones and five cooking corpses. All female, by the looks of it. There were twelve kids feasting on the bodies like feral savages. He almost pulled out his gun when something grabbed him by the shoulder.

"Whoa, dude! Chill, I'm friendly."

"You must be Lena. I found your sister out in the waste, nearly dead from radiation poisoning."

"No, Lena got munched. I am Luna. Dude, you better follow me before those cannibals smell you."

"So what happened? Your sister left you only a day ago with enough provisions to last three days."

"My little sister clubbed Lena to death with her wrench. And when my other sisters tried to restrain her. Her twin attacked them. Lucy and I got out of the bloodbath. We pulled the ones who had not gone feral into the kitchen with us to wait out the attack. They just snapped, man. I don't get it."

"I suspect radiation seeped in through the filtered air. Messed their young minds up and drove them to cannibalism even though they had plenty of food. Regardless of what happened, I am going to have to put them down."

"Can you make it painless?"

"I can."

He could see the psychic radiation corruption in her aura. She wanted to violently enact vengeance on them. He could also see she was fighting with herself not to go feral. He vanished and appeared in the atrium. The leader of the cannibals was a young girl missing three front teeth. She was currently chewing on a penis. He saw several scars on her. And realised why it took so fast. She had been raped; therefore, her mind was already weakened by the rape. The Nuclear Psychic Corruption broke what remained of her mental defences. This had started to turn her into a spirit eater. Those of unnaturally vile behaviour and thought become these corrupted yeti-like beasts. They are always hungry. Permanently emaciated, often found in cannibal dens. They made a huge leap in sightings after the war between Noamaiza and Silver that caused vast amounts of Psy-Rads to flood eastern silver.

"You look tasty. Wonder if you'd be better fried or roasted."

"Unfortunately, you will be unable to find out."

Flames erupted everywhere, vaporising the corpses. Then it was followed by a whirling sandstorm which petrified and shrank the twins but reduced the others to dust. He proceeded to collect all the soul crystals and place them in a small box. He picked up the twins' statues and put them in his satchel. He snapped his fingers and the rest of the kids in Bunker 9 vanished. They reappeared in his junk haulier. They were all in stasis tubes as the corruption was cleaned from their system. He walked over to a wall and typed in a code. The wall opened, revealing a cave passage. He continued down the passage after closing the hidden door. He walked for miles under the mountains. He remembered his life before this one.

Two young people lay next to me in my bed. The boy, Avol, was one hundred, as was the girl. I had received them as a reward along with their gang from King Moth of the Rising Falls. They were my payment for helping settle a border dispute between the Canis and the Silverans. These two were the only ones who had taken a liking to me.

Jump forward two hundred years and the two had professed their desire to be permanently bound to me.

"Why are you so enamoured with me, boy?"

"I feel safe and comfortable with you. I thought you would have raped us the moment we arrived at your home, but you helped us. You became Father instead of Daddy."

"That's what makes this so strange, Avol. I am essentially your father. Why do you want to become my mate?"

Avol placed his lips on mine. "Because I love you so deeply. Not the love between a father and son but between a husband and his wife."

"I want you to think very hard on this, Avol. Clear your head and have sex with a few of the servant girls. This is a massive step." I looked up as the girl walked in, her red hair shimmering in the light. "Hello, Vicky. You're just in time to try and talk sense into your brother."

"I'm sorry, Papa, but I agree with him. I, too, would like to become your permanent mate."

"I see. Can you both think really hard about this decision? Talk to Corvus and Eris about your desire. Then if you still want this, we'll go through with it." The two left the room.

"Hi, brother!"

"Gah! Eris, don't do that! You nearly gave this old man a heart attack."

"You know it won't work. They are set strongly for this. You may as well get the rings ready. I don't get why you're so opposed to this idea."

"They went from being my slaves to being my children. Now they want to become my mate. What's next? I worry they will desire the final step. Binding their souls to me for eternity."

"So a full circle. I wouldn't worry about it. With the way the war is going, they may not live long."

"I will protect them to the best of my ability, Eris."

"I know, that's why you should marry them."

I ended up giving in to them, but war happened. Gunfire in the distance woke him from his memories. He quickly arrived at the disturbance to see a bunch of Shadow Elves facing off against Ultramutates. They were losing many trying to take down a corrupted Behemoth. He pulled out his sword and sliced the throats of numerous Ultramutates. Their heads flopped back as they hit the ground. He arrived at the Behemoth and chucked a grenade in its mouth. The bomb vaporised its head, causing it to hit the ground with a heavy thud, causing some of the stalagmites to drop.

A tall, slender female wearing a mask walked up to him. "Thank you for your assistance. Queen Mab of the Unseelie requests that you hunt down the rest of those things. Their camp is nearby in the ruins of Quarry Alpha."

"Tell Queen Mab I don't come cheap. One thousand gold, twenty rubies, and ten sapphires to clear out Ultramutates."

"That's doable. You clear them out and we will pay you well."

Bounty pulled out a contract. "Alright, sign here, initial here, sign here and finally, sign here. Thank you for your business. I will take care of your problem or my name isn't Bounty Hunter 13."

The woman gulped and looked around at the carnage. She sighed and began to order her remaining troops to gather the dead. Separating the elves from the Ultramutates. Bounty arrived at the quarry. He grimaced as he saw the infestation of Ultramutates and their gore bags. He tossed in an infernum bomb that exploded, setting everything on fire. The heat was so intense that all organic material was instantly vaporised. He stayed up above the inferno before descending deeper into the quarry. He dragged the fire with him due to his affinity with fire. Within hours he had cleared the entire quarry. He then waved his hand and all the fire vanished. He was at the prison facility. The Ultramutate guard was eviscerated by Bounty's chain blade. He opened the cages and led the prisoners out. He could see the nuclear corruption affecting them and gave them some soup to drink. In their hunger, they did. He sighed and teleported them to his truck and into stasis for healing.

He walked out of the quarry to see many Shadow elf soldiers with their weapons pointed at him. He spoke, "Did you come to help or to stab me in the back?"

Their general was a grey-skinned female riding a chair with spider legs. She spoke, "Why do you stand on our holy ground?"

"Queen Mab asked me to deal with these Ultramutates. As you can see, they are no more."

"We have been waging Holy War against those things for months now. Why would Queen Mab allow an outsider to touch our sacred land?"

The tall elf from before jogged into the cavern, her bounteous breasts bouncing with every step. She saw the weapons drawn. "Stay your hand, General Arachne. He is an ally."

"He touched our sacred land."

"While true, we would have needed to purify the land from those beasts anyway."

"He should not be allowed to live."

"Arachne, listen, do you want to go against a man who can clear thousands of monsters within three hours?"

"I would rather die than allow him to live."

A loud voice echoed throughout the chambers, "General Arachne. I am Queen Mab. Stay your hand and pull back towards the temple to escort the cleaners to the quarry. I paid good money to clear these blasphemous creatures out and will not stand to have my top General disrespect my wishes."

Arachne snarled but obeyed. She and her troops walked away from the quarry. Bounty watched them go and shook his head. He was handed a large box. He opened it and saw his payment.

He looked at the general. "Keep it. It was my pleasure to wipe out those things. Consider this payment for my company's mistake. Tell Queen Mab I thank her for not stabbing me in the back. Like several other employers did hence the contract."

He walked over to a wall and pushed a hidden stone that opened a portal which he walked through. It closed behind him, leaving the general dumbfounded.

Bounty looked at his map and shook his head. He walked down a tunnel and into another cavern. He could smell the sea. He grinned and leapt up, locking himself to the ceiling. He bypassed the Hunter Clan Gauntlet. He phased through the ceiling arriving in his family's ship bay. That was when the world went dark. When the light returned, he saw a dark-skinned man with a white skull with war paint on his face. The man wore a top hat and wore a purple suit with coattails.

He was chomping on a cigar. "You again? Ha... have you made your peace yet?"

"I have not, Baron. Why do we keep running into each other?"

"One day, I will dig your grave."

"I'm sure you will, but that day is not today."

The crossroads vanished and Bounty began his hunt. He typed a code into the computer that sent knockout gas all over his home. He then activated the turrets, which began firing knockout darts. He walked through the gas and began swiftly killing the bandits. Within thirteen hours, he had slain all the bandits. He stood over the last one and gave a dismissive snort. She vanished into the cell block below. All of the prisoners the bandits had collected were teleported to his living area.

He looked them over and saw multiple scars on several of them. He also noticed half were mutated from the radiation. They were female, but they had male genitalia. Those were the ones that had the most scars. He eyed a female with blond hair and tattoos of skulls on her shoulders. She was being held by a woman with fire for hair with two horns on her head and forearm spikes. His eyes narrowed in suspicion.

"Back off, man. If you are planning on raping her, use me instead."

The girl grabbed the one who spoke, "Markus! No! I can't keep letting you do this."

"It's alright, Star. I am your faithful guard and will gladly protect your body from these raiders."

Bounty snorted. "Bah, as you can see, you are no longer prisoners and can leave as you, please. Though I would suggest, you stay until the radiation storm passes. So as not to have massive organ failure just by stepping outside. However, Star, was it? May I speak with you in private?"

She got up and walked with Bounty to a side room.

He spoke, "How in the thirteen hells did you get reincarnated as a female, Aerick-Starr?"

"How do you know my past life?"

"It's me, Bounty Hunter 13."

"Fuck! I mean, hi, brother!"

"Yeah, don't play coy. Answer my question, please."

"Okay, okay, I got greedy. This body was meant for a different soul, but I jumped into the well before she could, so this is my punishment for doing that."

"I see. Well, in any event, welcome to the land of the living. I hope you aren't leading that poor kid on."

"I would never lead Markus on. The thing is, I have yet to get the courage to get penetrated. I was the one doing the penetration on Vera. What will she think of me now?"

"Star, if you truly love Marcus, you should speak with him. I'm sure he will return the affection."

"I should probably get back to Markus and my friends. It's unfortunate we had to meet like this."

"Remember my words Star. And don't try anything foolish."

"Yeah Yeah."

***

Bounty looked out across the wasteland that had once been Eastern Silver. He frowned. The radiation storm was intense, but he continued to meditate in it. He was at his hidden grove. He heard a noise and looked around to see a red-haired woman with milky white skin and two small horn nubs on her head, denoting she was partially Silveran. He raised his eyebrow at her. She looked malnourished. She was also struggling to breathe the radiation.

He sighed and pulled out a gas mask, "Child, put this on. It will help keep your lungs from getting damaged further."

She yelped and scuttled backwards until she hit the statue of God Silver. She looked up into the statue's face and cried bloody murder before succumbing to the enchanted sleep that Bounty had put her in. He looked at the statue.

"So, Silver, what do we have here?"

The statue's head moved and looked down at the girl. "We have an Irescotwelan. I am surprised to see one this far north. Their land was sunk by Athena and Artemis when they usurped power from my sister Goddess Silver. Many died, but my sister was able to get plenty to safety by either sending them to Sucryog, Diavonbre, or even the southern lands of Silver. It's unfortunate, but they have eked out a living." Bounty took a syringe out and withdrew blood from his body. He injected it into the girl, ordering the fresh nanite prepared to fix her body. She shuddered and Bounty wrapped her in a blanket. She was teleported to his home in a warm room. She stopped shuddering and relaxed visibly. The computer started an intensive scan to guarantee the girl would not reject the nanite.

Bounty Hunter 13 felt a shift in the PsyQi as the forest began moving away from a certain area. He sighed and got up. He walked through the frantically moving forest. He heard a whistle as a Camazotz class ship fell from the sky. He stepped out of the way as it impacted. He lit his cigar and inhaled the pain medication and exhaled a black cloud of smoke. He raised his eyebrow in curiosity. *Never done that before. Must be something dark in there. Oh goody.*

He pried open the destroyed vessel. He saw two teen girls, both with thick forehead horns that wound up and then flattened into an arrowhead at the tip. He looked them over, both had crimson and black hair. Also, both had green and silver eyes. The only difference between them was one seemed to have orange and grey skin while the other had red and grey skin. He looked at the data from the ship's computers and shook his head. As night fell, the girls began to stir. The orange and grey-skinned one was the first to awaken. Her aura flared to life as the constellation of the warrior lit up. Her aura was a menacing and dangerous gold.

Bounty winced, "Well, that's why. What is your name, girl?"

The girl looked up at him with her mismatched eyes. "I don't remember."

"Hmm... Alright, I think I will call you Reiga."

The other girl stirred and groaned, holding her head. "Who are you people? Why does one of you look like me?"

Bounty saw the Constellation of the Hunter. "Hello, Arctos, my name is Bounty Hunter 13. This girl next to me is your sister Reiga. I see you got a nasty bump on your head. Do you mind if I place you on a medical table and examine you?"

"No... no examinations. No needles, no knives."

"Woah! Okay, okay! I won't hurt you. Will you let me look at it? I won't place you on a table or do anything else except maybe touch it."

"That is fine. It really hurts."

Bounty moved her onyx hair back from her silver and green eye and looked at the cut that went deep. He sighed and gently touched it and healed her wound.

"Girls, if you trust me, I can find you a safe place to rest."

Reiga looked dangerously at Bounty, "You have a home nearby? I'm sure there's nothing left for us. I saw you examining those screens. If that is the case, stop beating around the bush."

"Very well. For someone who seems to have no memory, you sure are well-versed in technology. If you agree, I will escort you to my home, where I will provide for you until such a time as you think you can safely leave."

Reiga growled, "Fine, but don't do anything to us."

"Deal!"

He led the two to his home and got them settled in. He returned to the ship and looked it over. He rubbed his forehead. *Damn, of all the things to come back and bite me, it had to be my sexcapades with the Master of the Dimensional Knife. Great, two more daughters who I cannot raise right.*

***

Several days later, Bounty Hunter 13 looked at the megalopolis before him. At one time, this had been a glorious city, the City Silver. Now, this was a city of scavengers and traders. When the bombs dropped on Continent Silver, many starships had crashed into the planet. The survivors of this catastrophe had banded together to create a city. They chose to build the city around the petrified form of my son Bounty Hunter 26. The boy had tried to protect the city. Unfortunately, the Noamaizans had planted a megaton bomb right under the city. When Bounty had put up his psionic shield to protect the citizens from the falling bombs, he had played into the hands of the enemy. The bomb had registered his psionic use and went off. His body had been petrified when he had tried to pull the detonation into himself. Now his corpse stood there as a testament to the old world. The former city stood in ruins, now spotted with shattered starships.

"Welcome to Junkalopolis. Anywhere you are looking for specifically?"

Bounty looked down at the young man in a form-fitting void jumper. "Yeah, kid, point me to the closest bar."

"Syd's tavern down on the main street. Hard to miss!"

Bounty tossed the kid a few common currencies. Then he began his trek down the main street. Many of these ships were Roc class destroyers. There were Griffin class triple-person fighters. He noticed several Anzu class drop ships and a few Ziz class Ultraships. The Ziz class Ultraships had broken up upon entry and were in several pieces. He saw several Wolpertinger drop pods being used as walkways for the guards. Interspersed among the drop pods were several unknown drone pods. The markings on the drone pods called them Al-Mi'raj. The only thing that stood out from the rest of these ships was an Ouroboros class science ship. This was also the only one with a makeshift sign that proclaimed Welcome to Syd's Tavern. Our speciality today is the Obsidian Tornado.

Bounty entered the tavern. His eyes immediately adjusted to the dim light inside. There was a woman wearing a lab coat behind the makeshift counter. He saw many waiters and waitresses in the same form-fitting void jumpers he had been seeing on all the denizens of this Megalopolis. *So many different groups all banded together to survive. Fascinating!*

"Yo, dude, you gonna order something or just stare?"

Bounty looked at the woman. He saw out of the corner of his eye that he presumed it was Syd behind the counter, prepping a Hunter Corporation shotgun.

"Yeah, in a second, let these old eyes adjust to the darkness. Okay, I will have a Silveran Fire Whisky, please. Shaken hard before pouring. Put it on the rocks with a shot of Umber Rage."

"Trying to forget something?"

"Sure, we'll go with that."

"Any food?"

"Yeah, the sticks with the works."

The waitress left and a man wearing patchwork scrap armour walked up to him with his hand on his holstered gun. Bounty grimaced.

"Hello, Geezer, I'm 'ere to claim the Bounty on yer head. Your mug is well known."

"You don't want to do this, boy. Trust me."

The scrap-armoured thug fired his gun. Bounty sat there unimpressed and placed the bullet on the table. The thug snarled and fired repeatedly. Again Bounty placed the bullets on the table.

"Are you quite finished? I am hungry and thirsty and my drink has arrived."

The thug smashed the drink out of the waitress's hand. Bounty turned towards him, sighed and exhaled. The thug's arm lit aflame. The thug screamed and tried to put it out. It spread to his hand that he was using to put out his arm.

"Cease or it will spread. It's alcoholic based."

The thug continued to panic. Bounty winced and blood splattered his face. Syd had fired her shotgun. The waitress had the decent sense to flee behind the counter when the thug smashed the glass. Bounty shook his head as a few others got up. One pulled a knife and held it against one of the waitresses.

Bounty got up. "You kids really don't want to mess with me."

"Stay back, freak or the girl gets it."

"Relax, son. I am far away from you. See, I am unarmed. Now, why don't you let the girl go."

The thug fell backwards with a hole in his head. A small woman with a sombrero walked out of the shadows, her sniper rifle smoking. "Didn't you hear the man? The girl is not your target."

She up-turned a table as several of the thugs began firing at her. Bounty waded into the hail of bullets. He then crushed his fist into one of the thug's faces. He then proceeded to give the others a beatdown. Several snapped necks and broken bones. Later all twenty thugs were dead.

Bounty looked at the mess and sighed, "Another bar I can't go to anymore. Here, kid, this should pay for the damages."

"Actually, old dude. You did me a favour. That gang has been harassing my employees and me for a couple of months now. S'why I hired Tamita there and her friend, Gilda. They are the guards of this establishment."

A green-skinned Oni woman with several war braids and horns on her forehead walked out. She stared at Bounty with curiosity. The door hissed open as a man wearing a grey duster with tactical armour with a helmet, visor, and gas mask walked in. The Emblem on his duster showed him as a general of the Federation of Allied Planets.

Syd smiled as sweetly as she was hauling the dead to her incinerator. "Hello, General Plata."

"What in the thirteen hells is going on here? I had numerous reports of gunshots and screams."

"Nothing but a little wasteland justice. Greeble and his fellow thugs picked the wrong person to threaten. Well, you can see what happened to them."

"What did they pick a fight with, a Hell Claw?"

Gilda spoke, "No, something far more dangerous. A demon forged from the very land itself."

"What could take on what looks to be fifty thugs and kill them all?"

Tamit spoke, "That would be the Demon of God Silver, Bounty Hunter 13. He's wanted on numerous counts of murder. Mind you, this was from the war. "

"Is he still around? I may have a job for him?"

Bounty stood and walked over to the general. "He is. Mind you, I don't come cheap. Here is my price list and the contract you need to sign to hire me."

The general whistled in awe, "I see you clean out Ultramutates. I see you also do assassinations. Alright, here's your contract back. I need you to join up with a group I have hired to clear out a massive complex of raiders and Ultramutates. Their infighting has been wreaking havoc on our supply lines. I want no survivors."

Bounty looked over the contract and nodded. "Gotcha, no survivors. I noticed you marked payment when complete. Did you read where it says if you stab me in the back, I have a right to kill you?"

"I did read that. Don't worry! I don't plan on betraying someone like you. Meet me at sunset near the gate. The team I have assembled will be there."

"See you soon then, officer."

General Plata left and Bounty helped move the corpses to the incinerator. Gilda had called the medical brigade to pick up the ones still alive. Bounty would have preferred them dead. After he finished his meal, he went and visited the statue of his son.

A woman looked at him with curiosity. She was in a form-fitting jumper with a holstered gun on her side and a jetpack on her back. Hanging from the jetpack was her helmet.

She spoke, "Hiya, gramps. Funny meeting you here. Didn't you two have a falling out?"

"Yes, only because I pushed all of my children away."

"Well, he never did stop saying how worried he was about you. He died a hero, you know."

"Did he? He died a fool's death. This city did not deserve him."

"He died protecting people. How can that be foolish?"

"The Noamaizans planned for this. That's why they fired smaller, less damaging missiles at the city. When their psionic nuclear bomb sensed the psychic shield went up, it detonated. Sure, he saved those outside the city, but the radiation was so intense you all would have died anyway. He only prevented the inevitable."

"He gave us enough time to get to the shelters. That's pretty heroic if you ask me."

"The city still did not deserve his sacrifice. They destroyed the temple to God Silver and executed all who opposed them, so many died for a small amount of peace."

"Can't you say anything nice about him? He cared for you. He died protecting a city that hated him. More than you could say for yourself."

"Yeah yeah, I've heard it all before. He was a hero, but that doesn't exempt him from being an idiot."

"The least you could have done was die in his place. Then I would still have a Father, but no! Why are you even here?"

"Your head of security offered me a job. I took it."

"What job?"

"Ultramutates and Raiders are screwing with supply lines. I've been given the task to eradicate them."

"I hope you die, old man."

"Your sentiment is noted. Your father would be proud of you, Tran. You went from a street punk to a respected member of the law. Well, I best be going; it's almost sunset."

Bounty turned and walked off. Not noticing the small tear running down her scarred face. She sniffled and touched her father's statue before walking off to continue her rounds.

As the sun set towards the north, Bounty sat on a bench by the gate. He was currently halfway through his menthol, herbs, and opium cigar. He breathed out a stream of blue smoke that caused a nearby guard to flinch.

"Bounty, you're still sucking on that trash, I see."

"Ah, Axel, what are you doing this far from Diavonbre?"

"Investigating. Jinxi is here as well."

"Hey, boss. Woah, you got fat! Been a while. Heard you died."

"I did, Jinxi, but as you can see, I live again."

A large druid walked over to them and he used sign language to speak, "Hello, Bounty."

"Corvus. I'm surprised you are joining us. Did Nevermore send you?"

"Yes, brother. I am here to assist in a cleanse. Our family made these monsters. Now we must get rid of them."

"But must you get your hands dirty? I thought you swore off violence as a druid priest of Nevermore?"

"You and I both know that my hands are already dirty. I have saved many from what lurks in that forest. Now with the nuclear corruption infecting the beasts, many have gone feral and I must save my followers from them. Not to mention what happened during the Civil War."

The green-skinned woman, Gilda, walked up with a man in assault armour wearing a turban on his head.

"Salim, this is Bounty Hunter 13. He is an interesting person to deal with."

Bounty looked at Salim and saw that the man was somehow from the past. His aura showed time stress. Bounty smirked. *Things just got interesting!*

"Hello, Salim, I look forward to working with you. Gilda, I see you are back from Komodo with your memories intact."

"The Oni god made an exception. I think he has something planned."

"Don't they always?"

General Plata walked up with Tran and a woman wearing a duster that was open, exposing her skin to the world. She wore an armoured skirt with platform boots that had spikes. Bounty knew her well. Behind this woman was a grey-skinned Taur with grey fur.

"Beatrix Badger, what an interesting surprise. You are far from Noamaiza."

"General Plata grimaced, "Please play nice. I don't need you in fighting. I hired her to assist because she wants to earn forgiveness."

"No guarantees, General. The Noamaizan forces took much from me."

"They took from all of us. She is trying to earn forgiveness."

Bounty smiled a dark smile, "Do you still have what it takes, girl? Do you still have the will to back up your words?"

Beatrix snarled, "I have more than that old man."

"Prove it."

Corvus quickly got between them, signing, "Save the pissing contest for the battle ahead."

She spoke, "He started it."

"Yes, he did. That is due to him being a petty asshole. Don't stoop to his level. That's what he wants."

General Plata looked between the two and sighed. "If you two are done, we had best get moving."

Bounty felt feathers against his brain and looked up. "Hold, General. We have one more coming. He or she should be coming round that corner about now."

A man with antlers ran around the corner. He was panting. "Sorry, I'm late. I heard you were looking for mercenaries and went to the station. They said you were gone already."

Bounty smiled, "Well, then, you are here now. Let us head out."

Plata glared at Bounty but shook his head. The small group left the confines and safety of the city. Plata led them to the first post. Bounty looked at the destruction around him and shook his head. His ears twitched and he looked over the rubble. He walked over to a pile of stone and wood. The others were surveying the destruction with awe.

Bounty moved some of the larger stones away. He looked at the man lying there before him. "Ultra Magnus. Shit, if they managed to bring you this close to death, they must have become stronger."

The man coughed and spat blood on the ground. "They took her. I could not protect her. They took Wondra."

Bounty began tracing several runes in the air. The runes glowed as he pulled the Nuclear Corruption from Ultra Magnus' body. He waved his hand and a mushroom cloud exploded into existence many miles away. Ultra Magnus' body glowed blue as Bounty healed him.

Plata looked off to where the mushroom cloud had appeared. "That takes care of the Raiders. How?"

Bounty looked off in the distance. "No time for explanations. Post Two is under heavy attack."

Plata grimaced, "We'll never be able to get there in time on foot."

Bounty snorted and then typed something into his gauntlet. A hover truck with the logo of Hunter Corporation on it roared up to them and stopped. The back end opened, revealing a living area. Bounty beckoned them aboard and climbed into the driver's seat. He floated Ultra Magnus to the medical bay. They saw several tubes with children floating inside them. Another opened and Ultra Magnus was placed into it.

The truck closed up and Bounty drove off. Within ten minutes, they arrived at Post Two. The battle was still raging and Bounty opened the side of the truck halfway, allowing the warriors to fire his Gatling Gun array.

Plata looked at Bounty, "Not to look a gift horse in the mouth or anything, but what in the thirteen hells is going on?"

"Welcome to my command centre. Also, my scrap haulier. It used to be that I always had a team with me. But my own personality drove them away. Gilda and Beatrix know first-hand I am difficult to get along with."

"That's an understatement, Boss."

"Jinxi, where did you appear from?"

"I scouted out ahead. It doesn't look good. All the trading posts were destroyed and I followed the Ultramutates back to their main hub. I could not get into the door due to some powerful rune craft."

The gunfire ceased and Bounty walked out of the truck. He examined the Ultramutates before him. He frowned.

Tran spoke, "Gramps, what's wrong? You look concerned?"

Corvus was studying them as well. He also did not look happy. He signed, "What have you been doing, Bonty?"

Bounty looked at him. "I have not been doing anything, Corvus. These are not Hunter

Corporation. These have been made differently."

Axel spoke, "What do you mean differently? They look like Hunter Corporation Super Soldiers."

"They are based on the Super Soldier design that became the Ultramutates, but they have been changed. We used genetic engineering and Prevolution Biosludge to create the Super Soldiers. This is Forced Evolution."

The antlered man spoke, "You say forced. That would explain things. When I heard we were hunting Ultramutates, I got eager. They raided my family farm and took my sisters and mother. They killed my brothers and father. They said something about needing women for the grey one."

Plata spoke, "That would explain why only male corpses are left."

"Jinxi, can you show me on the map where the main base is?"

"Sure thing, Boss."

Gilda gulped. "We have incoming. There is a second wave."

Bounty looked up to see a fifteen-foot tall, nearly naked, grey-green-skinned barely female charging him. She was speaking with grunts and growls. The smaller Ultramutates charged the position. Everyone pulled back towards the truck.

"Jinxi get them to the hub of these things. I will meet you there."

"But boss, there is no way I'll be able to get in without your help."

"Beatrix can help you."

The truck roared off. Bounty stood with his sword drawn. He beheaded one of the smaller Ultramutates. The female growled and the smaller ones backed off. She then let out a roar that sounded like, "ME WANT SNU SNU!"

Bounty raised his eyebrow as the smaller ones bolted as if their lives depended on it. The big female charged in a violent way. She tackled Bounty and pinned him to the ground. She was doing her best to strip him of his clothes while grinding in a feral manner against his crotch. Bounty was surprised he could actually feel his bones beginning to break under her assault. Only one way out of this. He penetrated the large Ultramutate. She was startled. She suddenly went docile and began thrusting methodically instead of savagely. She cooed, then let out a savage howl before passing out. Bounty released his seed into her four wombs. He pushed her off him and scanned his body for broken bones. Nothing showed up broken, so he transported the beast to his truck. The medical bay was almost full now. He would need to teleport those in the med bay to his home's medical wing, but first, he would need to find his truck.

Bounty Hunter 13 arrived at the main hub of Ultramutate activity. He saw the door had been caved in and there were many Hellclaw and Ultramutate corpses on the ground. He noticed several other corpses that had been severely mutated as well. He entered the facility and heard over the intercom.

"Well, well, well, the dashing hero comes. He better hurry. I've been waiting to break him."

Bounty growled, "Bounty Hunter X-10. Why does that not surprise me?"

"Aw, is the old man grumpy? Maybe I should put you down for a nap."

Several turrets opened fire and Bounty destroyed them, causing a door to open. He walked through a hallway filled with gas and laser beams. He growled and threw a fireball blowing a massive hole in the central area from the explosion.

"Enough games X-10. What have you been up to?"

Bounty looked at the central area where a pit had been dug out and filled with some kind of glowing purple sludge. He saw several women dangling over the sludge. He saw Gilda, Tran, and Beatrix among the women. Plata and Salim were struggling to fight several Hellclaws. He could see the antlered one was already near death. The antlered one was being treated by the Taur. He faced the robot.

"So X-10, it looks like you have been busy."

Bounty Hunter X-10 tossed Corvus' body at Bounty. He caught it and shook his head. "Oh, X-10. Killing my brother. Tsk Tsk."

"Behold my ooze. You get to choose which bitch I drop. There's a button in front of you. Push it."

"You think I care? I'm a cruel man."

"You don't think I know that already? You are a freak who doesn't deserve life. Push the goddamn button."

Bounty fired a shot at Bounty Hunter X-10 with his 44 twelve shot. It deflected off an invisible wall and sliced through one of the woman's ropes. Her eyes widened in despair and she dropped.

"Muahahah, you think I didn't plan for that? You're too predictable. Behold the power of my ooze."

As the woman hit the purple sludge, she began to mutate rapidly. Her skin became deep grey and her eyes became yellow. She had no pupils. She grew two more sets of eyes and her body became taller and more muscular. Her slender form became bulky. She let out a roar of anguish as the metal bindings snapped and slashed her skin. Her muscles grew rapidly, pushing her skin to the limit it could hold and then her skin snapped in a gruesome way. The tattered skin soon became a part of the new skin that was taking its place. She roared in agony again and again. Thrashing in the sludge. She then was let loose and Bounty was now up against a fifteen-foot-tall Ultramutate.

Bounty snarled and waved his hand. The others vanished along with the injured. It was just Bounty, Bounty Hunter X-10, and the now enraged female Ultramutate Titan. Bounty Hunter X-10 snarled and tried to escape, but Bounty teleported behind him.

"Hello, robot."

He slit Bounty Hunter X-10's throat and immolated him. He made sure that X-10 could not transfer his soul to a machine by using a spare soul crystal he had on hand. Now all that was left was dealing with the Ultramutate Titan. She seemed unsure of herself, almost as if she was waging war inside her head. Bounty raised his eyebrow. She looked down at him and then knelt on one knee. Her head bowed to him. He heard her thoughts.

"You wish for me to kill you?" She nodded yes.

"I have a better Idea. I can bring you to a haven for beings like you. There is another I must drop off there as well."

She shook her head no.

"You are too unique to be slaughtered like an animal. How about this? I bring you to this sanctuary and if you still desire your death upon seeing it, I will grant it to you."

She shook her head yes.

"Very good." He typed an order into his gauntlet and a large ship landed outside. His armoured truck decloaked and trundled onto the ship. Corvus walked out, shaking his head.

Bounty smiled and led the Ultramutate Titan into the docking bay, where she sat down. He began to treat her as the bay door closed. The ship lifted off and soared over the lands and sea until it came upon a large island. The ship landed in the water near a beach. A very strange being stood there sipping on a coconut. He was incredibly mismatched.

"Sidrodc, you old goat! Great to see you."

"Boy."

"Mind if I drop some more chimaera off?"

"You are going to anyway."

"True, but you can ease them into their new life."

"What's in it for me?"

"Here, maybe this will change your tune."

Bounty pulled out a bag. He opened it, revealing a really old-looking book made of leather. Even the pages were leathery. Sidrodc eyed it, then shrugged. He tossed the half-drunk coconut over his shoulder and it exploded into confetti which came alive and did a jig before bursting into flames and dissipating.

"Very well, I agree. Now, where are they?"

"That's the help I need."

Bounty led Sidrodc into the docking bay and Sidrodc whistled in awe.

"They are going to need to be changed, but first, can you shrink the big one?"

"How did these beautiful beings come to be?"

"Purple sludge my robotic doppelganger created."

"Lovely."

He snapped his clawed hand and the Ultramutate Titan shrank. She was soon nine feet tall. She looked around the island with wonder in her eyes.

"Do you still wish death?"

"No! What is this place?"

"Welcome to the Island Sin Maag."

Sidrodc smiled and opened a portal so a very large man with crystal wings front facing horns and deep umber skin could walk out. He looked at the small being in front of him.

"Bounty Hunter 13. Why do you request my presence?"

"Great Admiral of the Twenty-Four Gods, S'hin. I humbly request you give aid to these Ultramutates that I captured. They are smart, but they cannot fit into public life. You took their predecessors, the Kimera and gave them sanctuary. I beseech you to take them as well."

"Oh, cut the bull crap Bonty. You know I hate that mashugana."

"First impressions count."

"Oi very well. They are welcome to my paradise. I will have Vela escort them."

A tiny, almost bug-like woman flitted towards them. She was followed by a Kimera with lizard-like features, eye stalks, big bug eyes, and a trenchcoat. The two looked at the Ultramutates and grinned. The portal closed and the giant being vanished.

The insect-like girl spoke, "Howdy! Welcome home, you beautiful monsters. I am Vela and this is the Private Inspector Mutant. We will be the ones to lead and introduce you to your fellow Kimera. See ya around B."

She led them off as Bounty stood there watching. He smirked and returned to the ship. Corvus stood there holding a bundle. He opened it and showed Bounty, the child.

Bounty took the child. "Corvus, I'm glad you're alive, but what is this?"

"He is the only offspring of you and that Ultramutate Titan who wanted snu snu, as she called it," Corvos signed.

"I see then he was born prematurely. No wonder his legs look like mine did after that disease."

"But that's not all. Thanks to whatever was in that sludge, he is almost an exact replica of you."

"So, like Bounty Hunter 26 or what?"

"Much different. While Bounty Hunter 26 was a clone of you and your male clone Leon von Psycheo, this one is by all accounts exactly like you down to the very genetics. He is a true clone of you."

"Well, that is fascinating. Would you like me to drop you off near the forest or will you be coming home?"

"Close to home but still the forest, please," Corvus explained while using sign language.

"Very well, brother."

***

Bounty was training his son. The boy was now one hundred ninety-nine. He watched in worry as the boy struggled to stand after a particularly nasty assault.

"Remember, Thirteen, your legs are your weakness. They hold you back. You are focusing on the pain too much."

"Father, it hurts too much. Can we please call it a night?" Bounty sighed

"Yeah, let's get you something to eat."

Bounty helped his son to his hover chair and walked with him towards the kitchen. Tomorrow Thirteen would be two hundred. He would need to do something special for the boy. That night as Thirteen slept, Bounty began working on cybernetic legs. By dawn, he felt a shift in the melody. He put the legs on a loader and hovered it over to Thirteen's room. The boy lay there sweating and crying in agony as his body changed. While Bounty's was explosive, and Bounty Hunter 26's was bloody, Thirteen's was slow and painful. As the change took place, Bounty paid close attention to Thirteen's legs. They were still fragile looking. Bounty sighed and wet a rag and began doing his best to comfort his son.

***

Several years passed and Thirteen had gotten used to the cybernetic leg armour that would help him move. He had been tasked with clearing out a raider den that had been assaulting Outpost Twelve. He had investigated this den and found that the raider leader was called Scrapper. Scrapper was a vicious sort because anyone who got in his way found themselves dismembered and killed and put on display. Thirteen looked at the gory cages and the various hooks and pikes that were adorned with body parts. He had been caught and was currently fighting for his life within the arena. He wished he had some backup.

In one of the cages was a woman wearing a hood that concealed her face. Her clothes were ripped and she had some blood on her. The blood was not hers. She was watching the arena with interest. She saw the man dodge a robot only to misstep and get hit by a buzzsaw trap. He cried out in agony as his legs were severed from his torso. She smirked and conjured a guitar. She played a power chord that obliterated her cell. She then began playing even more, sending numerous blasts of energy all over. Her guitar became an axe and she charged into the arena blasting apart traps and killing the meat bags which got in her way. She typed in a code on her gauntlet and a portal opened up beneath the man and his legs and he vanished. She jumped in and vanished soon after.

There was a dark-clothed woman holding a book of spells and another with blond hair and goggles. She was currently welding an android together.

The woman with torn clothes spoke as she came through the portal. "Yo, Lucy, did a beefy man in two pieces come through yet?"

The dark-clothed girl pointed in the direction of a cryotube where the man lay. That was when laughter echoed through the chamber they were in. A chaos portal opened up and a woman with scales on her bare chest, a Taur leg, a Syrien leg, a Banebear arm, a Felis arm ending in a demon claw, and small spikes and horns on her shoulders and head, respectively, walked in. She picked up the cryotube and disappeared back through the portal. The dark-clothed girl tried to keep it open, but the energy backlash sent her stumbling.

The blond looked up as she finished the android. "Alright, Stephani, you're good to go. Remember, we can always transfer your spirit into another body if this one cannot keep up. Woah, what happened to the hunk?"

Lucy held her bloodied face. "He was taken by a strange woman with scales."

"That would be our aunt Eris. Lunatic call pops. He needs to know."

"Already did, Leda."

Thirteen woke up on a table of sorts. He saw a female Kimera standing over him with many runes surrounding her. She was looking him over and giggling.

"Where am I? Who are you? What's going on?"

"You are on the derelict space station Cyteck. I am Eris, mistress of Chaos. I am giving you cybernetic legs that will grow with you."

"Why am I awake? Shouldn't this be done while asleep"

"Unfortunately, no, because I need to connect the legs to your body so that your own nervous system, muscular system, and blood can fuse with the Techorganic legs. Therefore you need to be awake so that I know when you're in pain."

A new voice spoke from the shadows, "That's awfully nasty of you, sis."

"Shut it, Demon! I don't want to hear it from you. Leave me to my work."

"Oh, I wasn't going to stop you, Eris. I do not have the chaos necessary for this to work, but at least let me be here to comfort my son while he's in pain."

"Don't interfere and you can stay."

Bounty nodded and sat down. He studied the runecraft and saw a damaged rune.

"Eris, before you continue, the rune that is meant to weld the metal to his flesh is broken."

She looked at it and frowned. "Still can't get the hang of that rune."

Bounty waved his hand and the rune reformed properly. Thirteen cried out in agony as his flesh became part of the metal and the metal became part of his flesh. Bounty soothed his son.

"The process will be over in three, two, one. How do you feel, boy?"

"I feel like shit, Dad."

"That's to be expected. Now move your legs, boy. I want to make sure all connections work."

Thirteen got up and began to walk. It felt natural to him. "Why does it feel like these are my real legs, Dad?"

"The Cyteck facility creates biometal that, when combined with flesh, can essentially replace anything lost. They were a rival of Hunter Corporations until they made the mistake of kidnapping several of our employees. When I went to retrieve the employees, I was met with mindless cyborgs that obeyed the will of James Cyteck. I mercy killed them. Then wiped out Cyteck industries. So Eris, how in the thirteen hells did you reactivate the station?"

Eris slumped. "It was the only way I could think of to contact you. Make you angry since I want to die."

"We'll talk later about you dying. But right now, I need to shut down this station again."

It took Bounty several minutes to fully deactivate the Cyteck station. He smiled a dark smile as he downloaded all the data the station had to offer. Cyteck would live on in Hunter Corporations. He teleported Thirteen home and turned to Eris.

"So death, huh? Why?"

"Look at me, brother. I am an abomination. Goddess Silver refuses to speak with me and I feel so worthless."

"Eris, come here." He wrapped her in a hug. "Look at you. You're beautiful the way you are."

"No, I'm not! Don't lie to me, Bonty."

"Even if I wanted to kill you, I couldn't. You are immortal. One of three chaos users in the whole galaxy. Sidrodc of the island of Sin-Maag and Shegor, the Duke of Madness of the planet Clockwork, are your other ones."

"Please, can't you do anything? My soul is normal, but my body is this. Please dismember me! Do something!"

Bounty let out a sigh and entered his sister's vagina. She cried out in ecstasy and began rhythmically thrusting against him. As she climaxed, he placed her head in a stasis jar. He followed that up by placing her arms and legs in four other jars. He finally placed her torso in another after releasing his seed into her womb. He sent the pieces to his trophy room. A three-foot-tall pink cat with moth wings and a horn saw them and snuggled up against one of the jars. How she got in was a mystery.

Eris' spirit appeared to him. "Thank you, brother. But why the sex?"

"It will allow your mind to be in bliss during your stasis. No more gloomy thoughts, just pure ecstasy. Rest easy, sister. When you finally come to terms with your condition, I will release you, but until that time comes, your body is a decoration in my trophy room."

"That will be a long time, brother. I hate my condition. I should never have dabbled with that book."

"Dear sister, it will be sooner than you think. You will be begging me to free you. But for now, rest. The black book is dangerous even to the most skilled Chaos user. Which is why I gave it back to its owner Sidrodc."

Eris closed her eyes and vanished. She saw the cat and gasped. She began stroking her head. The cat began purring a deep throaty purr.

Bounty teleported home but instead reappeared in the moors of Silver. He lit a cigar and placed it to his lips. He inhaled then exhaled a green smoke. He saw several warriors before him. All had red curly hair. They were clothed in kilts except for the women, who were clothed in animal furs.

A woman with black and red hair walked forward. "Demon of Silver, I am Lady Enigma. I beseech you to help us."

"And pray to tell me why I should help you?"

"Please, in a past life, we were married. I'm begging you. The Noamaizan forces stand at our door and you are the only one capable of defeating them."

Bounty closed his non-eye patch eye and sighed in defeat. "Very well, Vicky. I will assist. Lead the way."

Vicky smiled in relief and her soldiers formed up around her as Bounty followed. They arrived at a war-torn field. Bounty saw why Vicky was concerned. Before him stood five Noamaizan war mechs. Each was a different design. He saw their five pilots resting around a campfire. He saw one was standing guard while the others slept.

"So Vicky, why do you need my help? There's five of them and they're asleep."

"My warriors and I cannot get close to them. Every time we try, an invisible wall stops us. We even tried shooting, but the bullets vaporised on impact with the wall. We're also concerned about the mechs."

"The mechs are broken. The only thing they're good for right now is to hide behind in a gunfight."

"I saw one of the five girls repairing one of the mechs."

"Okay, now that is concerning. Very well, I'll take care of it."

"Thank you."

Bounty sat on the ground and extended his energy. He felt the invisible wall. He began searching for a weak point. He saw one of the women stir. She wore a form-fitting black catsuit. She then vanished. He pulled out his knife and blocked her strike. He saw six of the soldiers fall with their necks slit.

"So it is you. Hello Umbral. I thought I killed you and your team when you tried to assassinate me?"

The woman snarled, "You killed them, but I survived to seek my revenge."

"You deserved what you got. You killed my children and my wives. Not to mention the several servants I had."

"I will see your head on a pike on my mech for what you did to my team."

A cocky and scratchy voice cried out, "Alright, finally, some action! I'm gonna wreck them!"

Another voice said, "Woah there, Rainbow best refrain from an outright assault. There's more of them than us and we don't have our mechs."

"Like hell, I'm gonna let Umbral outdo me, Equinox!"

A rainbow fist smashed into the shield formation that the Irescotwel Silverans were using. The shields at the forefront were vaporised, leaving nine severely injured soldiers in their place. Bounty grimaced. He snapped his fingers and the Irescotwelans vanished except Vicky.

The woman with a white void jumper on spoke, "You think you can save them? Ha! Crap, I was too late in blocking the teleport. Oh well. Diamond Dust!"

Bounty stepped in front of Vicky as a wave of shards hit him. He quickly pulled Vicky into his hammerspace after knocking her out. The wave crystalised around him and he saw the woman wave her hand. What followed next could only be described as torturous as the crystal exploded. He felt his body shatter. He staggered from the hit. His armour was destroyed and he was bleeding from many wounds, his blood was being pulled back into his body as the nanites desperately tried to repair him. He had a massive hole where his stomach used to be. He transferred Vicky to his home.

He smirked, "You just pissed me off."

The four stared in horror at Bounty's gruesome visage. He placed his hand on his face and took off his half-mask. Two of the girls vomited as they saw his cracked and charred skin from the nuclear detonation he absorbed from his youth. He looked even more monstrous now. His aura flared dangerously. Umbra backed off. She suddenly went very stiff and bolted to behind her mech, where she curled up in a fetal position pleading with her goddesses to protect her.

The only one unfazed by Bounty's visage was the one in a blue and gold jumpsuit. She pulled out her sword and smiled a dark smile that would have sent a chill down a lesser man's spine.

"Demon of Silver, I have heard of your exploits. I was brought up to be your equal. I even slew that bitch Beatrix Badger. I will now send you to the grave."

Bounty huffed, "All talk. Let's see you in action."

He instinctively knew this would be his death, so he ordered his nanites to pull to a specific area. He then extracted them and sent them into storage. He immediately felt his life force giving out. He smiled and sent multiple energy bursts towards the mechs. The invisible wall shattered and five of the mechs were destroyed. Umbra yelped and teleported away from the falling wreckage. Diana snarled and swung her sword while she had an opening. Bounty blocked it. He grinned and kicked her off of him.

"Equinox! Rene! Stop gagging and attack him. There's only one of him and he's almost dead!"

Equinox slammed her foot on the ground sending a path of stone spikes at Bounty. He rolled out of the way, but a rainbow fist connected with his body. He saw the diamond wave coming at him, so he used his psionic energy to block it. He smiled a deadly smile as his psionic energy lanced through the final mech.

He then used his remaining strength to wrap the girls in his aura. Diana broke free, but that was inconsequential. She drove her sword into his eye to try and disrupt what he was doing. His life force finally burned through his body, causing it to disintegrate, but he was done. All the girls except Diana were silvery statues, all in erotic poses. They vanished to his trophy room and his soul manifested. Diana stood there in shock.

Bounty spoke, "So Diana, how does it feel to be the last one standing? You succeeded in killing me, but I had the last laugh."

"You monster! Is it not enough to wipe out my city and kill my warriors? But to take my friends from me as well!"

"Your people started this war. This is the consequence of facing the Demon of Silver."

Her voice changed. "I will not stop hunting you, Demon! I will see your soul broken and destroyed by my hand."

"Good luck with that, Artemis. Enjoy the rest of your mortality friendless and alone."

Diana collapsed as Artemis released her from her control. "Don't walk away from me, Demon! You coward! Face me!"

He saw Diana looking around the devastated battlefield with tears in her eyes. He sighed and snapped his fingers. Her friends appeared and became flesh and blood instead of statues. He felt a blade connect with his chest. He looked down at the void-forged blade and sighed.

Artemis grinned maniacally as she withdrew it. She swung for his head. He phased through the blade and caught her hand. He twisted her hand, breaking it and took the blade. He forced it through her armour and then her chest. She choked on her blood.

"Artemis. I gave your favoured child back her friends. You can never hope to beat me. Just give up and leave me alone. I am an old man in a world that doesn't want him."

"I'll kill you, then I'll kill that wretched God Silver. You bastards took my people from me. I will see you burn for your transgression."

"Begone!"

Artemis screamed in fury as she was banished back to the Havens. Bounty watched impassively as Diana and her friends reunited. He used the wreckage of the four mechs to create a fortified fort for them. He waved his hand and they all fell asleep. He placed them in the fort and moved it as far away from the Irescotwel Silveran territory as he could without it going anywhere near the other territories.

"So, boy, are you ready?"

"I am Baron. You may bury me or what is left of me." He then allowed himself to be brought to the havens for judgement.

Reiga stood nearby. She had also come to this place to help the Iresotwel people. She followed the teleport and arrived in Noamaiza near a large home. She looked around and saw in the distance what she was looking for. She entered the scrap bunker and stood over the sleeping form of Umbral. She growled and stabbed Umbral with a silvery purple sword. Umbral's soul was absorbed into the sword. She picked it up. "That is for nearly killing my mother. While my father may have failed in killing you, I will see you pay."

She turned to see Equinox standing there with a shotgun aimed at her. She smirked and opened a portal to the Infernum. She stepped through and closed the portal. Equinox turned and walked back down the hall. She marked Umbral's name off the list.

Rainbow spoke, "This only leaves Rene and us. Diana refuses to stay. What will we do?"

"Nothing for now. The only thing we can do is help Beatrix Badger with rebuilding Amazonia. Maybe that will save us in the end."

"How many died because of us?"

"By all accounts, the entire city of Silver had one million people living there; only a handful made it out before Rosalyn's bomb went off. That doesn't even count the five thousand our mechs wiped out. We won, but so many died on both sides. Was it worth it?"

"Rosalyn Dark would say yes, but Rosalyn was unhinged. Wish I could have seen that before the war. Should have figured it out because of what she did to that girl, Eris Hunter."

"And how she turned Beatrix's corpse into her personal motorcycle, but we were blinded by power."

***

Deep in the wasteland of Western Silver, a man with combat armour stood on the outskirts of Marauder territory. This was the violent Forged Marauders land. He lit his cigar and snorted. He entered the land and was immediately beset by the smell of rot. He continued on. He came across many bodies. All led to a large skyscraper that was partially destroyed. His target was there. He entered the skyscraper and fired upon the ferals that inhabited the building. As he cleared them out, he kept hearing a dark and ghostly echo. He grimaced and entered the sub-basement.

The geiger counter on his arm spiked to crimson. He placed his gas mask on. He beheld in front of him a massive monolith with a naked woman reaching out from it. All over the monolith were elaborately drawn skulls. And the base of the monolith lay an altar that held a virulent purple and green knife. He killed the unholy abomination that was the priest. He heard in his head *Uuuhgg-Qualthoth, Uuuhgg-Quathoth. Dark and ancient. Beast from beyond. My skin is screaming. I am becoming one of them.*

Uuuhgg-Qualtoth, Uuuhgg-Qualthoth, burn the impure of blood. Book of Kriv'be'knih, Knife of Kremvh, I have found your temple. She of the monolith beacons me.

Uuhgg-Quathoth! Uuuhg-Qualthoth!

He fired his gun again and a glowing creature fell lifeless. He placed a blue book on the altar. It glowed green and then incinerated. He placed a red book on the altar. It glowed green and then incinerated. He looked at the remaining purple book. He snarled and placed it on the altar. The monolith seemed to scream and the naked woman became a skeleton. His geiger counter fell back to normal.

A menacing voice spoke, "You may have foiled my plan this time, Deathseeker, but in the end, I will be victorious."

The man snorted and turned. His body glowed white and the building became fire. "We will see, Lord Dragon. We will see."

He walked out to see a woman wearing atomic green robes. She looked at him. He snorted. "Best leave back to your pool of radiation Lady of Nuklea. The dark god is banished for now."

"What of the Lepidoptera?"

"Inconsequential! They are busy dealing with the Entrencher and the Harvester. They will be unable to bother you."

"Then I must thank you on behalf of Nuklea. I wish you to find your peace Deathseeker, but deep in my heart, I know you will never find it."

"Hmph... I will be off then. Unless there is anything else you need."

"Goodbye, Deathseeker. May the wastes guide you."

***

Bounty Hunter 13 awoke in his home in a new body. He sighed and checked on the Irescotwelans. Vicky was lying next to him. She was moving her hand up and down his member. She smiled up at him.

"Master, you're awake!"

"Uh, what? I thought you were Lady Enigma now?"

"I couldn't stand it. I gave my name and title to my sister. I also made sure they got transport back to our home. Thank you for assisting us."

"You're welcome, sweetie. If only Avol were here."

She smiled, "I guess I'll just have to do the work for him." She wrapped her lips around his member and let out a content moan.

Bounty sighed and placed his head back down on his pillow. *Well, things seem to have worked out. Let's hope nothing else happens to Silver.*

***

One day after the bombs destroyed City Silver. A woman sat with a knife in her hands. She had just watched her army get decimated by their own fallout. She was depressed. Her hand shook as she dragged the knife down her arm. She sobbed as no blood came out. An old man was watching her. He was sitting at a tea table sipping his tea.

The demonic man sighed. He finally spoke up, "Child, what are you doing to yourself?" His sonorous yet surprisingly gentle voice seemed to alert her without terrifying her.

She looked up, startled, saying, "Who are you?"

The demonic man smiled a sharp smile and said, "You're too far down the metaphorical rabbit hole, Alice."

Her eye twitched as she spoke, "Name's Dusk. Not Alice."

He chuckled, then smiled and spoke in a soothing tone, "Since when? You seem like an Alice to me. Curiosity got the better of you. Now I am here to keep you from going mad. Come, sit, and have some tea."

"Well, I suppose some tea would be nice. Do you have any eel grass herbal tea?"

"I do. Why have you been trying to kill yourself?

"I watched my army get decimated by a Hunter. Then the rest die from the psionic nuclear fallout from the destruction of City Silver. I fled like a coward. Now I can't bleed."

"You seem to bleed fine to me. I see the madness in your eyes."

"But the knife."

"Is very real. And very sharp. I see bone and muscle. How long have you been doing this?"

"Twenty-six hours."

"Hmm... Regardless girl, you are very close to death, but the choice is yours. I have a knife that will work and finish you off. Or you can find a new path and recover."

"I will find a new path."

"Smart choice. We are here."

She looked around the junk city. A black armoured man wearing a duster over his combat armour strode into view. He wore a gas mask that covered his face. He saw her and knelt down to feel for a pulse. Satisfied, he typed a code into his gauntlet and a truck trundled down the street. It bore the symbol of a medical serpent. He helped the med bot lifted her into the truck and it trundled off.

***

A pale white-skinned man with no discernable nose stood smoking a pipe. He was waiting. A large and imposing shadow landed near him and became a skeleton dressed in a tuxedo and top hat.

"Hello, Joe. Been waiting for you. The Inbetween has suffered a shift. It is time we check it out."

The two walked off and came upon a man dressed in brown and white robes with a horned badger mask. Next to him was a living stuffed doll. He was sitting on a black stone. As they arrived, he looked up. "Who are you two strangers?"

"I am Jason Inferno. This dapper bone man is Joe. Who are you?"

"I am Lord Badger."

"I can see that, Badger. Who are you in real life?"

"That is my own personal name. I will not give that out to strangers."

"We are part of the Council of Dreams. We outrank you."

"Don't you have something better to worry about, Jason Inferno? Your Space Islands were annihilated in the great rewrite. Your sister ascended to godhood and is a part of the Organos Pantheon, but she is missing. Presumed captured."

"Look here you.."

Joe spoke, "Calm down, Holy. We are in the lands of the Inbetween. This is his realm. What we were in the past is no longer. I was the hero of All Hallows Eve. I was the Master of Screams with my wife by my side. I was King Joe Boneskeleton. Tell me, don't you miss your island?"

Holy sighed and spoke, "Keep your head on, Joe. The islands were all turned into continents and then erased; we just have to live with them. All I did was hunt demons down. I was the slayer Jason Inferno. Demons feared me."

Joe's hands leapt off and ran forward. Joe spoke, "Well, Mr Inferno, I'd shake your hand if I had mine. Follow the hands. Whoopsie, there goes my body. Catch my head, Whee!"

Jason grabbed Joe's Skull and ran after the wayfaring body parts. Badger smiled and followed them. They came upon a cave and saw the body parts inside. Joe's head rolled into the cave and the parts attached to him. He rose slowly from the ground.

"How's it going, folks? Have any of you seen my hand?"

He looked down to see his hand on the back of the girl. The hand saw him and bolted. He raced around the cave, attempting to catch his hand. The six lizardmen looked at the strange bone man and began laughing. The hand attached itself to Joe.

"Ah, I see Lizard Gods have swiped you, Lady Jaina. Now don't be shy. Scream for me!"

Shadows enveloped the cave and the Lizard Gods screeched in terror as they were devoured by unknown shadow beasts. Badger watched impassively from outside. He was holding Jason back. When the screams died down, Jaina emerged from the cave holding the small girl. Joe Boneskeleton patted the other girl on the head.

"There we go, Lucy. Why are you here?"

Badger looked at the spooky girl. "Lucy Cacophony-Hunter? How did you get here?"

"You know me?"

"Uh, yes. I am familiar with your father's work. Bounty Hunter 13, the Lord of Shadows one of the pains in my behind I have to keep track of."

"Can you take me to him? All I remember is having a knife coming at me, then I was here."

"Yes, if I can locate him. You lot come along. It will be interesting to see what happens to you."

He opened a portal to the Gray. They arrived in the Havens. A large reaper stood before them.

He was dressed in grey and black. He looked down at the two. "Ah, I was wondering what happened to you two. Don't worry! I am not here to erase you. For some reason, The Writer decided to drop the two of you into the Inbetween world. He placed the others up here. So welcome to The Havens. Allow me to escort you to your designated area."

Jason and Joe followed him. Badger looked down at Lucy and the girl. He looked around. Finally, he saw what he was looking for.

"Daemus Xotl, can you escort these girls to the line of Judgement?"

The red and gray-skinned being with a crown of horns and two large wings looked at the girls. She led them to the line and left.

"Someone will be with you shortly."

A man with deep ebony skin and gold eyes, wearing business casual and silver glasses, walked over to Lucy.

"Hello, little Lucy and Lica. Your father has been concerned about your disappearance. I am here to make things go smoothly."

Lucy spoke, "Who are you?"

"I am Nox Tarot, your father's business associate."

"Oh, you're that nice man who attempted to rebuild our home."

"Yes, I am. I can't believe the Lizard Gods tried to steal your soul."

"Well, even Father says that I have a strong connection with the PsyQi. That may have been why they were trying to harvest me. Don't know why they would be harvesting Lica."

Lica looked down and shuffled her feet uncomfortably. "They may have wanted information on my experiments with bio mecha and psycraft."

Nox looked at Lica, concerned, "You were trying to play god? That is going to be a tough sell. Well, I never turn down a challenge."

Hunters Journey

Amari Hunter stood kneeling over the body of her dead sister, Trinity. She stood and looked around. The armoured woman who had killed her grinned savagely.

"You are a Hunter. I will enjoy rending you apart like I did to your pathetic excuse for a sister. She could not see The Pure World for what it was. A cleansing wash to rid the galaxy of your filth. And start anew. I will be that reckoning. And you will be dead."

"You done talking, Jeanne d'Arc?"

"I will cut you up and feed you to the carrion birds. I will gut you and strangle you with your entrails. I will… hurk."

Amari got up and the Psy blade she had conjured vanished. Jeanne d'Arc fell in two. "You talk too much."

Amari lit both bodies aflame and drank the amber liquid that had been summoned from the flames. She tossed the glass on the pyre. She sighed and left the pyre to burn. She vanished and reappeared on Diavonbre. She entered her bunker and opened her book, then closed it. She walked out of her bunker to see Axel Wulf and his mate Shenzi Fang.

She spoke, "I hate to interrupt, but I have a question."

He turned back to her. "You are not interrupting anything, Amari. What's the question?"

"Do you have any books on the realms?"

"Realms? What realms?"

"Shadow, Inbetween, Pure, Wood, Infernum, or anything that even mentions those realms."

"Now, how would you know about them… doesn't matter. I have no books like that. However, if you go to the lands of Bahamut and speak with Bahamut himself, you may gain some insight."

"Thank you, brother."

"Uh, sure, no problem. Stay safe little one."

"I am the daughter of Bounty Hunter 12."

"Yeah, that's why I said stay safe. Your clan has a habit of finding trouble where it is not."

"I know, which is why I stayed out of the story till now."

"You know what? I am not even going to ask. So my sanity stays intact. Have fun but not too much fun. You are always welcome back here."

"Thank you, Master Wulf."

"I am no one's master, girl. Now get moving. You don't want to be caught without shelter during the midday."

***

Nine moon rises later, Amari entered into the Dragonstorm valley. She was met by a platinum pink Lizard Girl with chrome pink metal wings. She bowed to the girl.

The girl spoke, "Hey, now, no bowing. I hate that. So what is the mysterious seventh sibling of Bounty Hunter 13 doing here?"

"I need to speak with Bahamut. Axel sent me in regards to a question I had."

"Oh well then. Belias, you can lower the gun. She is harmless for the most part."

A massive man bulging with muscles landed behind Amari. His wild orange hair made it look like he had an inferno for a mane. His six horns glinted as the sun rose. Amari gulped.

Belias spoke in a deep rumble that Amari could feel in her bones. "I have never heard Bounty Hunter 13 speak of you. Nor has Axel. Who are you?"

Amari spoke, "I have been busy researching. I also requested Axel to keep my presence a secret since, well, you know how well anyone with the last name of Hunter is treated."

"Ah, yes. Your brother had the same issue. Very well, but I have my eyes on you. I protect Dragonknife pass."

"I would have it no other way. Jinxi, may I speak with Bahamut?"

Jinxi shuffled her clawed feet. "Uh, a slight problem there. Bahamut has entered into a deep meditation. He cannot be disturbed during the process. But I am quite knowledgeable. I may be able to help you."

"Is there a private place we can speak? I don't trust the sky."

"I understand. The gods do like to fuck with you, mortals. Follow, but you must not use any power of yours as we enter Dragonfire citadel."

Amari nodded and entered into the large stone gate. Jinkie led her to a smaller temple and sat her down.

"So what is the question?"

Amari looked up at the suddenly imposing Jinxi. "I was looking for information on the realms."

Jinxi grinned, baring her sharp teeth. "Oh? Why would you want that information?"

"I have been seeing troubling images in my head. I have seen a man cloaked in shadows with a large silver splotch on his right side. I have also seen a dark man with feathers that make me sleepy. I have seen a twilight-robed man who strikes fear in my soul. And finally, I have seen a mysterious man wearing white and brown armour and a horned badger helmet. I know they represent the realms from my readings, but there is not enough information."

"Well, that is a tricky subject. Hmm. It is a good thing we are in the Temple of Thunder. Ramuh! Can I pass along the secret teachings of the Druids?"

A deep thunderous voice echoed through the chamber as bolts of lightning split the air and a smell of ozone permeated the sanctum. "Nevermore and I are not thrilled with the idea of an outsider knowing Druidic Secrets. However, as she is the sister of Nevermore's faithful, we will allow it."

Jinxi smiled again. "Thank you very much, old man. I owe you a tasty cupcake."

"Well, now that is more like it."

As the lightning calmed down, Jinxi spoke, "Okay, now that that is taken care of. How much do you know about the rules of our galaxy?"

"From what I have read. Throughout the galaxy is a melody that only certain people can hear. During the ancient days, there was a huge conflict between Darkness and Light. The galaxy was nearly wiped out. Then beings known as the Fountainhead spread throughout the galaxy. They forged the first species and became the first gods. That is all I know."

"Okay then. You seem to know more than most people. That is good. It makes it easier. Okay, so The Fountainhead were considered beings from the Pure Realm, the Realm of Holy. One of the major leaders of Holy was Alexander. He created a sect of monks Dubbed Guardians of the Pure Realm. That was before he was betrayed by his sworn brother, Zmatek, the first God Silver and the first God of Chaos."

"Chaos? Never heard of it."

"Chaos is easy to explain. Every being is chaotic. Chaos has no order or logic. By all accounts, you shouldn't work. Your biology is strange. Also, by all accounts, this world should not work, but that is the beauty of Chaos. It is the first building block of the entire universe."

"Okay, but what does that have to do with the men I see?"

"Well, that is the tricky part. As it stands, I can only tell you about the feathered man. He is the embodiment of the woods. But he is also an embodiment of the sky. He is Nevermore's faithful. Nevermore was a god from Planet Gothico and Gothica. He found a following here among the Syrien of the Aerys. He is now considered one of the major Death Gods of Silver."

"The Woods. Yes, I remember. Most of the Woods of Silver are its own Realm that exists between past, present, and future. The trees are their own species and are highly intelligent."

"Not just Silver. Silver is its own network, but almost a third of the forests in the galaxy are sentient life. The Druids worship in the woods and the woods protect them. There are many Druid Groves, but only a few are well known. To the irradiated West Silver, in the radioactive lake, is the Druid sanctum of Nuklea. To the East of Komodo and Diavonbre are the Thunderous sanctums of Ramuh. Of course, we are considered Druids for the seekers, but Bahamut is not a Druidic God. North is Nevermore and his champion on Eastern Silver. That is the only one available to Seekers. The Aerys refuse outsiders. Then the most curious of Druidic gods, created from legends and stories, is Lepidoptera. He is known, but not by much. Seekers refuse to go near his sanctuary. The gore turns them away."

"So the feathered man is a Druid and Champion of Nevermore. He lives on Eastern Silver. Okay, that is where Bounty Hunter 13 lives. In our father's old house. Thank you, Jinxie. I think I will go visit my brother."

"Ooo, boy. May the Grey guide and protect you."

"The same to you, Jinxi. Now how do I get out of here without being jolted?"

"You don't. The lightning is to cleanse you. It's not painful, just tingly."

Amari walked through the curtain of lightning and shuddered as the numbness went away. A flame-haired woman stood leaning against the door.

She smirked, "So you are Amari Hunter. I felt you are trying to get knowledge about the Infernum. Come along. I will escort you to Continent Silver through the Infernum. Prepare yourself."

"Uh, who are you?"

The woman smiled a fanged smile. "I am Hannah, the master of the Dimensional Knife. You are a curious child who seeks knowledge."

The two walked through the fiery portal only to appear in a suburban neighbourhood with a fiery lake and a river of magma flowing through it. A man wearing many robes appeared.

He spoke, "You are not the ones I am expecting. Hmm, portals got crossed. Hannah, be a dear and find these mortals for me."

Hannah looked at the picture and opened a portal. Eight girls walked from that portal and looked around.

The eldest spoke, "Hey, I thought our... ugh, brother-in-law was supposed to meet us here."

The robed man spoke, "He is busy making the dinner you all will enjoy. Your sister asked me to pick you up."

The tomboy spoke in a rough voice, "Fuck this! Open the fuckin portal back up. I'm outta here."

The elder slapped her. "Laura! Play nice. I don't want to be here anymore than you do. Nor do any of us. But we promised we'd come to dinner once a year."

"Ugh, fine, but I'll complain the entire way."

They boarded the ship along with Hannah and Amari. The robed man turned on the boat's motor and it sped off. He arrived at a large home. The small group stepped off.

Hannah spoke, "Charon, this is the home King of Demons chose to make residence in?"

Charon chuckled, "Yes, he did. It makes him feel at home. You do remember what happened to him, right?"

"Oh yeah. Oh, here is your payment for guiding us across the river Styx."

"Domo Arigato."

Charon sped off down the river as the elder sister rang the doorbell. A woman dressed in a black dress with thigh-high socks and leather knee-high boots opened the door. Her eyes were covered by her hair which was dyed black. Her roots were showing blond, however, she spoke, "Oh, you are early. Please come in."

"Let's get this over with. Hello Luci, it's been some time. Nice to see you."

"Cut the sarcasm, dear sister. I know none of you wants to be here."

The tomboy snarled, "Yeah and this is the last fucking year since the contract ends this year. Then you can go fuck off."

Luci let them in. "Have a seat, siblings. I am sure you know my daughter. Vulpes, say hi to you aunts, then you can go away if you so desire."

The white-haired girl in torn jeans and distressed jacket scoffed, "Hello, aunt Loren, hello, aunt Luny, and hello, aunt Logan. The rest of you can go suck a dick."

The tomboy snarled, "If only Luci sucked a dick, you wouldn't be here."

"Leave my daughter out of your feud with me, Linda."

Vulpes spoke, "We done here? Good, I'm going online." She walked upstairs and slammed her door shut.

A deep earthy voice spoke, "Hello, Hannah, you seem to have come at the wrong time. I do apologize that you had to see this. By the way, why are you here?"

"Well, I was going to show Amari Hunter the Infernum. However, my portal got mixed with their portal. So now I need permission from you, cousin, to leave. I also need permission to show her the other Hells."

"Ah, well, in that case, I request you stay for dinner. It will be much easier for Luci and I to have someone else take reign of the conversation; otherwise, it gets awkward."

"I didn't even realize you were married?"

"Well, not in the traditional sense. She sold her soul to me. I gave her what she desired. Her daughter did the same. Plus, she reminds me of my Luci."

"Your Luci was a psychopath bent on destroying you."

"Okay, so not exactly like my Luci. If you all would like to, dinner is ready. Have a seat at the table since this does mark the last year you will be required, per contract, to be here. I have cooked up something very special for you to commemorate the occasion. Enjoy."

They entered the dining room to see a cooked body on the table that looked like Luci. The King of Demons spoke, "Since y'all want to be so vindictive towards Luci. I have taken the liberty of designing this meat based on her naked body. Oh, don't worry. It's not actually cannibalism. It just looks that way. Dig in."

Luci shook her head and then sliced off her meaty doppelganger's breast. She set it on her plate. "Husband, you said you would save this for our wedding night."

"Ah, but that is tonight. As per the contract, the last day of the requirement for your family to be here is on your wedding night."

"Oh, you sneaky zomnagile."

"I thought you'd like it. Welcome to the family."

Luny, the sister in purple, spoke, "Mmm, let me have your cunt, Luci. It looks so juicy."

"Here you go, Luny. I hope you enjoy it."

"I do like eating cunts, love."

Laura scoffed, "You're as bad as she is. Ugh, this is so wrong on so many levels. I think I'll just have the potato salad."

Lauren, the sister in teal, who looked like a blond bimbo, said, "Luci, I'd like your other breast unless you want to save that for your husband."

Luci smiled, "Here you go, sis. It's almost as plump and juicy as your tits are."

"I'd say so. Logan, pass the honey, please."

The sister, with a mechanic uniform on, handed Lauren the jar of honey. "Here, sis. Hey Luci, I'd like a chunk of your meaty ass."

"Here you go, Logan. Anyone else wants a bite of my ass?"

The eldest sister shook her head. "I guess since we are doing this. I'll take a piece as well, but have it on the record that I am appalled by this feast."

Hannah spoke, "Cousin, I am not very hungry and Amari looks like she's going to be sick. Can I get the amulet of your permission to visit the other Hells?"

"Hah, of course, Hannah. Here you go. Now I am going to enjoy the situational Schadenfreude."

She led Amari to a large door. A massive three-headed hound started barking at them.

Hannah smiled, "Here is the amulet, Kerberus. See, we are friends."

The dog borfed the allowed Hannah and Amari to pet it before stepping aside, allowing them to enter the Under Realm.

As they entered, the pathway changed suddenly. Amari cried out as she fell. She landed on the void and floated back to the path. She looked around. Hannah chuckled as she led her further into the Under Realm. The walkway was made of a dark rainbow, while ethereal purple flames sparkled in the inky blackness that surrounded the path. The flames burned brightly and then began to form a large city. Amari watched the city form. It looked like the old marble cities of Groemece. Back when Noamaiza was devoted to the worship of Zeus and Jupiter before Goddess Silver took over. They soon arrived at a massive temple complex. They were met by a handsome man holding a top with a ♆ topped with a ♆.

The man smiled, "Hello, Amari Hunter. I welcome you to my lands."

"You are Hades. Oh wow. You were like my favourite god growing up."

"Oh? Well, a fan is a fan. Why do you come this way?"

Hannah spoke, "We are going to the planet Hell Two and the pathway split, forcing us to come here."

"Ah, well, welcome. Persephone will take you to your destination."

***

"Sorry about that, Amari. We really should not have started with hell the first then moved from there."

"It's okay, Hannah. Ugh, how is Lust so damn powerful? She nearly ripped apart my brain."

"That was not Lust. Lust was the planet's name. That was Slaahn-hla-ge. She is the Prince of Lust. Lucifer usually keeps a tight leash on her, but Lucifer's been distracted."

"Is there a way we can skip the last ones?"

"Hmm, yes, but you still must suffer through clockwork."

"Why?"

"Hello there, Shegor, the Duke of Madness. I have brought you, Amari Hunter."

The man dressed in a black and gold coat with his white hair slicked back and his horns polished turned towards them. He smiled. To Amari, his deep voice almost sounded like her brother's.

"Hello there, Hannah. It has been a while since you visited. How are our daughters?"

"They are with Bounty Hunter 13. He is their father now. I know this makes little difference. I leave her in your care, old man. She seeks to know about the Infernum. I figured the best one to teach her would be her brother from a different timeline."

"Ah, very well, H-poo, I will teach her forbidden knowledge. But you got to come to visit more often."

"Don't call me that, but I will think about it. I really must be going. Her next stop is Planet Silver."

The old man smiled and motioned for Amari to sit. She did as he poured himself a cup of tea that looked amber but smelled like coffee. He lay a bunch of tea packets before her. She looked at them and then picked out the one that said Organos Tea with Juniper and Black Hemlock. Since poison did not affect Silverans due to their genetics, Black Hemlock was a favourite among tea drinkers. She especially loved it due to its bold flavour.

"So Alice, what brings you to the rabbit hole."

"Uh, what?"

"Hmm, okay, let's try this again. You are Alice falling down the rabbit hole seeking knowledge that you don't know you are seeking."

Another voice spoke, "Dear brother, don't mess with her. She may very well burn the cheese. We can't have it raining cats and dogs now."

"That is why I am doing this, Lord of Madness. Things must be dealt with a certain way or else the croutons explode. Now Alice, you have leapt headfirst down the rabbit hole. What can old Cheshire deliver to you?"

Amari blinked in confusion and shook her head. "I think I am going mad."

Shegor cackled, "Well, as they say, madness is relative. Isn't that right, my lord?"

"Haha! That never ceases to bring joy to the gelatin, but we must be serious here for once. She is not here to be driven mad by us. She is here to learn about the Infernum. You wrote the book on the Infernum."

"Ah, fair enough. Well, Amari, you lucked out. The Alice in you has gone and the White Rabbit has lost his time."

Amari blinked again. "Oh, I get it now. You must treat everyone like they have gone mad because I seek the knowledge you were testing me. I failed."

"The flowrat squeaks."

"I am sorry. I need a moment. I have never failed at gaining knowledge in the past."

A grey woman in a gold bikini armour ran up. "My lords! Generals Dretk and Jalal are at Tangerine; the walls just fell."

"Ah, so it begins. Very well. Amari Hunter, this is the book I wrote as a mortal. It will give you what you seek. I have a business to attend to. My rival has made her move. Jump through the moths and you will arrive at the second stop of your journey."

Amari finished her tea and entered the circle of moths; they glowed neon red and flew off. She found herself in a vast city made from scrap and junk. Standing in the middle of the city was a large black Ouroboros class science ship. A large sign declared Welcome to the Scrap Heap traders and scavvers welcome. Marauders, keep out! A man wearing black combat armour covered by a white-tan duster walked over.

Through his black combat helmet and gas mask, he spoke, "Hmm, I am not sure I like people randomly appearing. I am Captain Plata of the Junk City Police. You are an unfamiliar face, so I am afraid I must put you under quarantine until you are registered. Please come with me."

Amari nodded and followed. She soon arrived at a medium building with the Logo of the Silveran Marine and a Tactical emblem on it. Okay, so at least I know I am on Planet Silver or, more specifically, Continent Silver, but where on Continent Silver, am I? As she entered, she saw one of the one-foot-tall bipedal lagomorphs standing on the large desk, having an active conversation with a giant green-skinned behemoth of a man in scrap armour with a chain gun on his back.

The green man spoke in a rough, earthy voice, "Hey, boss. Rufio's been trying to get a hold of you. But there seems to be some kind of interference."

The bunny girl spoke, "Hello, master. Who is the new girl?"

Plata sighed, "I am not your master, Jackie. And would you take that collar off?"

"Nuh uh, reminds me of my failure, so I don't fail again."

"Ugh, always with this. Grath, I need you to interrogate this woman. She appeared from thin air. Jackie can join you to see how it's done. Looks like I need to investigate our dish. Before the interrogation, please tell Rufio if I am not back from investigating the dish within the hour to come to find me."

A watery voice spoke, "There is no need for that old friend."

A tall and thin man walked in wearing a green t-shirt with brown cargo pants. His hair was perpetually long and unkempt.

Plata shook his head, then shook the man's hand. "Shaggy, you son of a bitch. Why are you here?"

The man spoke, "Please, as a lieutenant in the Time Police, this woman intrigues me. She is an unknown. Almost as if she was a last-minute addition. By the way, her name is Amari Hunter. I am sure you are familiar with the Hunter clan?"

"Oh yes, very familiar. Had to deal with two of them over on Eastern Silver."

Amari spoke, "Who in my family did you work alongside?"

"Not so much work as tried to keep him under control. The Demon of Silver and his brother."

"I have not heard of the Demon of Silver. This journey keeps getting curiouser and curiouser."

Shaggy spoke, "Regardless, I am here. As soon as I leave, the interference with your radio will go away."

Amari spoke, "The Time Police, what is that?"

A man in high-performance combat armour walked out. His bare arm was covered in scars. He spoke, "The Time Police keep the balance of time. They arrest anyone who fucks with the timeline. Before you stand Shaguthor, the indomitable, the only Time Police that makes The Demon of Silver cringe with worry."

"Whoa, something I don't know. Unheard of. Awesome, I get to learn something new."

Shaguthor chuckled, "There is not much else you need to know about us that is not in our name. We are not exactly common knowledge. The only reason these officers know about us is that I have been actively trying to recruit them for our organization. It also keeps me sane. I am used to being around mortals. However, the mortals I hung out with passed away many centuries ago."

Amari smiled, "Well, I am not much, but I would gladly hang with you."

"Haha, little mortal but also strangely not mortal. Hmm. I will think about it. You are a curious one. Almost as if you shouldn't exist. Who messed up the timeline? I do apologize, Plata, but I must research this disturbance."

Shaguthor vanished in a wave of tentacles. Captain Plata shook his head and then sighed in relief. "Glad to see he has taken an interest in someone else."

"Is that a good or bad thing?"

"Ah, I wouldn't worry about it too much. You are an anomaly. Frankly, you seem normal to me. Or as normal as any Silveran. Any reports, Rufio?"

"None only thing is some wasteland justice in the marketplace, but it has been handled by Curry."

Amari spoke, "So if you guys don't do anything, what is the reason for this building?"

Jackie hopped down from the desk and scurried up to Amari and climbed up to her shoulder. She chittered, "That's a very bad observation. We do things. The wasteland holds many Raider and Marauder gangs. Our job is to keep them from the city when they get too close. We are elite. The other fellows handle the disputes."

Plata chuckled, "Jackie, down! Come up on my shoulder."

The bunny jumped down and landed, then scurried up Plata's leg and coat, then onto his shoulder. He scratched her chin and her foot began thumping in excitement.

Rufio spoke, "Well if all we are dealing with today is a visit by Shagutor, I think it's time for a drink."

Plata nodded. "We could all use a drink. Keep your radios on in the event the automated alert system warns of a Marauder attack."

The four left the building, followed by Amari. She spoke, "So, am I still quarantined or not?"

Plata spoke, "I don't think so. Shaguthor says you're fine, so you are good to go."

She followed them to the big black ouroboros class science ship, which had a sign out front that said *Welcome to Sid's Tavern. Our special today is Blackfire Rum.* As she entered the brightly lit sterile bar, she had to let her eyes adjust. She saw a massive creature with giant claws and spines that could rend steel. She gulped as it sniffed her, then snorted and moved away from the door.

Plata spoke, "That was Jakx the Hellclaw. He is smarter than other Hellclaws and also smaller. He is the bouncer for this establishment. He doesn't like to speak much."

The four sat down at a larger table while Amari sat down at the bar. She looked around until she was taken out of her awe by a country voice, "Hey there, suga. First bar you been to? Name's Sid, you seem awfully familiar."

Amari looked at the busty Amber Elf with her hair tied up in a ponytail. She wore a jumpsuit that bore the insignia of the Silveran Spacewalkers. Over the jumpsuit, she wore a science coat with a Hunter Corporations shotgun strapped to her back.

Amari spoke, "Yes, in fact, this is the first time I have truly left my home for an extended period of time. My name is Amari Hunter and you must be the owner of this establishment."

"That's right, sug. What'll it be?"

"Oh, right. Uh, I don't really drink Alcoholic beverages. I do like some Black Hemlock tea."

"Ah, then here you go, sweetie. I already had some brewed up. Not everyone drinks booze here. Hunter, ah, that is why you seem familiar. I had dealings with your brother in the past or I assume he's your brother. The Demon of Silver, Bounty Hunter… well, we won't finish that his name is bad luck."

The radio next to her crackled to life. "Automated Alert number seventy-five. We have an unidentified anomaly coming fast from the east. All guards, please recall to the Eastern wall."

She saw Plata and his team get up and hurry out the door. She looked over to see Sid checking her shotgun and cleaning it up. The radio crackled again. This time it was Commander Plata's voice, "Hey, Sid… uh, we need you to have someone escort Amari to the east gate. There is, and I can't believe I am saying this, a pink dragon here that requests her presence. Yes, I know what I am seeing, Rufio. No, the beer was not spiked. Ugh, just calm down."

The radio cut off and Sid raised her eyebrow. "Hey, Gilda, be a dear and bring Miss Hunter to the east gate."

A green-skinned Oni of Komodo walked out and looked down at Amari then rolled her non-covered eye.

"Sure thing. Not like I have anything else to do while recovering. Come along, kid."

Amari paid for the tea and had it put in a to-go cup. Syd smiled and waved as she left. She followed Gilda.

"Uh, Gilda, was it? What is an Oni doing here?"

"Hah! Not a day goes by without that same question in my head. But I am here because I have been banished from my tribe and The Oni Gods have abandoned me, so I have moved to Silver, where I am more welcomed than I am on Komodo. We are here."

Amari looked at the large Platinum Pink Dragon before her. She blinked, then grinned, "Hello, sister-in-law. Why are you here?"

"I could ask you the same love. You were supposed to be at Nevermore's Druid Grove three days ago."

"Yeah, I know, but then I had to sit through a cannibal dinner, a mad god, and a portal that dropped me here instead of Eastern Silver."

"Woof, sorry about that, kiddo."

"Hey, I'm older than you."

"Haha, yes, that is true. Hop on. It'll be easier flying there instead of trusting a teleport. Thanks a bundle, Captain Plata. Axel, The Fury of The Dancing Flames says hello."

Plata was quiet for a second, then, "Jinxi! What the hell!"

Jinxi flapped her metal wings hard, sending a cloud of dust up. Then she spoke, "Bye! She was over the horizon before they could even register her voice."

Jinxi touched down outside the forest of Eastern Silver. She shuddered as her body went back to its Silveran size.

"Here, Amari, you may want to put this radiation damper on. Eastern Silver is far more radioactive than western Silver. It will be some time before it can be considered habitable again. The clearest part is by the mountains where City Silver was rebuilt. Well, there and here in the forest because Bounty has been absorbing the radiation into himself to clean the land quicker. It's his penance for what he has done."

"What has he done?"

A heavy and deep voice layered with weariness from life spoke, "Aside from the millions I have killed. Oh, not much. Hello, Amari."

"Big Brother!" She hugged Bounty Hunter 13 tightly.

He smiled a world-weary smile. "It's been some time since we talked. What brings you to Silver?"

"I seek information."

"Oh? Well, my guess is that you are seeking a druid."

"Yes and the shadow man who has been watching me, the white-haired twilit man who scares me, oh and also the strange badger-faced man."

"Well, I can definitely tell you that the shadow man who has been keeping an eye on you is not me. Even though I am the Shadow Lord."

"Who is it then?"

"I can't tell you, for he likes to remain secretive, but he does care for you. Regardless, Druidism is not my domain. Let us go see Corvus. He will be quite pleased to see you."

Jinxi said, "I'll let you take it from here, Bounty. I must get back to Diavonbre. I can't risk being too far away since Bahamut is sleeping."

"Very good. Oh and have a merry Lucy's Day."

"Oh goody, it's that day of the year. Winter Solstice. Ugh, I am sure you love the darkness."

"Ugh, the shadows are hard to control this time of year. Stay safe and I hope General Winter brings you what you desire."

She flew off and Bounty led Amari to the Druid Grove of Nevermore. He spoke, "This is where I leave you temporarily, dear sister. I must attend to my duties. Also, the crow doesn't like me in his sacred space."

"Don't stray too far, brother. My next stop is the land of shadows."

"Hah, well, if you can't find me, I will be in my Forest Glade, keeping the storm at bay."

As Bounty sat meditating, the thunderous storm crashed through the skies. *You want me to what? No, I heard you, but are you insane Silver. Have you finally cracked and gone mad? Ugh, fine, but mark it down as this plan is stupid and risky. Way too risky. We do not know what the Taur built Coldharbour to contain. And also, you are fucking nuts if you think old Coldharbour will surrender to me. Ugh, fine but I will complain the entire time.* Bounty got up and as he walked towards Nevermore's Druid Grove, he bumped into Amari. She seemed out of it.

"Hey, sis, what's with the empty look?"

Some semblance of normality came back to her as her eyes lit back up. "Ugh, are all the Druid gods like that?"

"Ah, you got to commune with the Daeva. No, not all the Druid gods have a Daeva associated with their name. Merwyn and Hannah, the bearer of the Dimensional Knife, along with Ramuh the Lightning Druid and Lepidoptera, do not have Daeva. Also, most Druids do not worship a god they worship nature, damn hippies."

"I am ready to see the Shadow Lands Bounty. I am eager to know about the Lord of Shadows."

"We will go there as soon as I take care of some business in the dark part of the forest."

"Wait, we are going to the Dark Crater."

"Oh, hell no. The dark part of the forest is where the secretive Guild has their headquarters. It is also where the Taur built Coldharbour's temple during the war between us and them. The darkness comes from the crater, but it is harmless where we are going. The closer we get to the crater, the more dangerous it is. We are coming up on the Ruins of the Onyx Tower. Keep close. This is Silver's domain."

Amari looked around at the massive chunks of Onyx. At one point in history, the large tower she saw before her was ten times larger.

"Is it true that the tower was built by a wizard to contain death?"

"Yes and no. Yes, to the wizard part. He did manage to capture Azrael, the Alpha Reaper. However, the tower was not built to contain Azrael. He wanted to capture Damsel Death. Thanks to the unity of The Scorpion Queen, Silas Huntari, Argentorado Red 10, and Goldar, the demon of the skies, Azrael was freed. This is one of many Onyx Towers. Each tower is associated with an element required to build a Silveran. Or at least that is what the stories say. The Dark wizard built over this tower with his own. His was destroyed while this one still stands."

"So four aliens came together to help a god?"

"I would not say the Eternals are Gods. They are aspects of the universe. Far more important than gods. Unlike gods, they can't die until the heat death of the universe. And four aliens, as you call them, were actually the beginnings of a long and prosperous alliance between planets Silver, Red, Gold, and Grey. We are here."

Amari looked up from her writing and saw a large black wall. Bounty handed her a tag. "Put this on before we enter the darkness. The Guild won't shoot at you as long as you wear this. It marks you as me."

"And what of you?"

"Haha, well, I am the Shadow Lord." He enveloped himself in darkness, nearly blending in with the wall of shadows.

The two entered the dark part of the forest. It was perpetual twilight here. Not much sun could get through the darkness. However, the trees looked healthy, if not a little scared.

A woman walked out from behind a gate and she spoke with a very deep voice, "Halt! Who is it that tries to pass through Guild territory?"

Bounty spoke through her, "I am Dutch Hunter. You have me on file. I also helped your husband with his problem."

"It's you... ugh... fine. We are having some issues with intruders, so don't interfere."

"Sure thing Contessa."

Bounty quickly hurried Amari past the gate. She spoke in her normal voice, "Warn me next time you decide to use me as a puppet. That was extremely weird and uncomfortable."

"Sorry, Amari. Contessa is a good girl, but she is very strict with Guild rules. Especially since she is number two, we must quickly get through this area before we are noticed by the Midnight Druids."

"Who are the Midnight Druids?"

"Notice how the trees look unnaturally healthy. The Midnight Druids care for the trees in the dark part of the forest. The shadows here are clean. However, the closer we get to the crater, the more the shadows become tainted. You will also notice the trees do not exist in the tainted lands. They moved away from the Dark Crater and nothing grows there. I am going to insist you wear my duster. It will protect you from the tainted darkness. It doesn't affect me since I am the Shadow Lord."

She took off her coat and placed his coat on. Her breasts flopped out. She looked for buttons and then shyly held them together.

"I feel really exposed, Bounty."

"Hmm, don't worry about it. We are the only ones here."

"Okay, now that kind of makes me mad. Are you not attracted to my massive breasts."

"Oh boy, calm down, Amari. I don't get aroused anymore or did you forget about my experimental nanomachines."

"Sorry, it's just that sometimes I get the urge to be stared at. I don't get much attention."

Bounty wrapped his arm around her. "Amari, you are a wonderful girl and any male or female or hermaphrodite would be lucky to have you as a lover."

He felt her go limp and lifted her up. Sleep well, sister. You are not meant to see what is coming. He walked into a large courtyard with ruined buildings and stalls all over. He entered the massive temple and looked at the statue before him. It was a Taur, but his horns were fiery. His shoulder spikes were jagged and his bull face was scarred all over. He was sitting in a meditative posture.

Bounty spoke, "Awaken Coldharbour. By orders of God Silver."

The statue moved. "God Silver, now that is a name I have not heard in centuries. Why is there a Silveran in my temple? Especially since your kind killed my people."

"Not all of your kind are dead. Many have moved to The Upper Depths, but I am here to give you a chance at not disappearing."

"Oh? How? My kind no longer worships the old gods. They worship Anubis and the gods of science."

"Not all. The other Pyramid gods are also worshipped. Only a select few are scientists. The old ways are still going strong. I am here to give you some power. I am a worshipper of many dead gods. Tribal Silver, Dread Goddess, Many of the First ones, and now you. Silver is my Patron God, but I have the power to spare."

"How then will you worship me?"

"As we speak, an Island is being made. I will move your temple there. I will also take an icon of you to my home, where my private temple is."

"You are willing to move my temple even though you do not know what it was built for."

"I know it was built to hold the last vestiges of the Blood Clan. Their taint has already been released from the mountains. They do not scare me."

"If what you say is true, then you are a fool. The Blood clan is more powerful than you can imagine. Their leader was called the destroyer for a reason."

"Bloodhawk the Destroyer does not scare me. I have already injured him in the Havens. He will fall in the end. They all do."

"Hmm, so be it, Pawn of God Silver. Free me."

Deep underwater, Thull Thanos awoke temporarily. He looked around curiously. The water seemed calm, but then an unknown island popped into existence over by The Upper Depths. His facial tentacles shifted into a thinking position. He slowly turned and his watery wings caused a small whirlpool to form. He then felt a shift in the Melody. He let out a watery chuckle and then fell back asleep.

On the newly formed island, a large temple complex appeared. It was cleansed from its broken appearance. Coldharbour was alive. He felt rejuvenated, then shuddered. "Is this the power God Silver has? He is more dangerous than I thought, but I now owe him. Ugh!"

Bounty let the wind whip around him. The howls of the damned threatened to blow him over. When it finally calmed, an imposing man stood there.

"You have released me from my prison. Who are you so I may honour you with death."

"I am Bounty Hunter 13. You will be the one to suffer death if you face me."

"Hmm, I can see you are quite strong. Very well, but when next we meet, my hand will not hesitate to kill you."

"Goodbye, Bloodfang Invictus. I am afraid all that will happen is your son, the destroyer, will perish along with your clan."

The man seemed to sag slightly then he vanished. Bounty opened a portal to the Shadow Lands and awoke Amari. Amari looked around at the glowing crystals and the many pathways that snaked through the darkness. Some on her level, some high above her and some upside down. It was an Escheresque nightmare inducing dizziness trying to comprehend what she was seeing.

As she started to lose consciousness a snapping brought her to focus. "Let's not focus on the scenery, child. Focus on me. I am real."

She blinked and looked intensely at her brother. "What happened?"

"The illusions of the Shadow Lands nearly consumed you."

"Ugh, my head…"

"Yes, it took me a while to get used to the place as well. It is strongest during the Winter Solstice. General Winter will bring his army of Lesser Eternals to the planes of Nightmares. He will fight to hold the darkness at bay. He will succeed but will also injure me in the process."

"So what is the Shadow Lands?"

"As you are aware, in the beginning, there was darkness. From that darkness came the great cow, Bessie. As her udders overflowed, the Space Platypus came into existence. It laid the egg that became the universe. But where did the Space Platypus come from, you may ask. It came from darkness. This darkness. Do not let the stories fool you! Darkness is not entirely evil! And light is not entirely good. One cannot exist without the other. Unfortunately, there are those who wholeheartedly believe that darkness is evil."

"Who is that?"

Bounty looked to see where she was pointing on a black sandy beach overlooking an inky ocean and a large moon-like crystal in the sky. A woman was sitting there. Her body was covered in cerulean armour and by her side was an axe.

"That is new. I have never before seen her. Let's find out, hmm."

As they neared her, she stirred and turned, revealing a shapely woman with platinum blue hair. Around her neck was a necklace of a nine-pointed star.

"Ah, a Lightbringer. More specifically, a Lightbringer who seems lost. Who are you to intrude upon the Land of Shadows?"

She got up and raised her axe, but a tall man in red, black, and brown robes held her back.

He spoke in a deep voice, "Do not attack him, Amber. He is the Lord of Shadows and the master of these lands. Hello Shadow Lord, I am Darkness in Twilight in Light."

"Hello, DiTiL. Why are there Lightbringers in my Realm?"

"I am not a lightbringer. I was a fool who tried too hard to control what could not be controlled and paid for it with my essence. I am but a shadow of my former self. Amber is here because she became lost in the darkness after trying to rescue her friend. He is now safeish in the Castle of Cards."

"Ah, I see. Well, Amber, if you are willing, I can send you back to the Grey," she spoke. "The Grey?"

"Sorry, the land of the Mortals. You do not belong here. The longer you stay, the more the darkness will eat at you until you become like the darkness. I can already see the shadow burns on your soul."

"If you can, that would be amazing."

"Hmm, something is wrong. I can't open a portal for you. Oh, I see. You and DiTiL are from before the great rewrite. Your land was erased from existence by the Writer. That is no problem. The portal I am opening will bring you somewhere safe."

Sorry, Brother. I know you hate intruders. A portal opened and Bounty led the three through to a large open space with sand. Many Lightbringer axes littered the ground. Walls upon walls of black stone cascaded down like waterfalls. A man stood there dressed in white and brown. His badger mask was horned.

He spoke like an earthquake, "Why are you intruders here in the Inbetween?"

Bounty spoke as the shadows vanished from him, revealing the large burn on his right side. He opened his bag and pulled out a half mask that he put on the right side of his face. "Hello, Lord Badger. I am sorry to intrude. Especially here. But I have a Lightbringer who was from before the great rewrite. She was lost in my Lands."

"Ah, I see. Very well. Follow close and do not stray from the path."

Amari stared at her brother and then spoke, "I had heard stories of your looks but never believed them. How are you still alive?"

Bounty looked down at her and then smiled. "Who says I am? I kid, I kid. As I am naturally attuned to fire when the Psionic Nuclear bomb dropped at the Pyramids of Chombra, I was able to absorb the nuclear fire."

"We are here, puny mortals."

Bounty spoke, "Cut the crap, Badger. You and I both know there are no mortals here."

Lord Badger looked behind him and Amari could have sworn she saw the mask's lips turn up in a smirk. She blinked and the mask was back to normal.

"Words must be spoken, Demon of Silver or our mystique will fade. You should know that more than anyone."

"Ugh, fair is fair, Lord Badger. The mortal here needs a safe spot where she can recover from being in the Lands of Shadow for an unknown amount of time and Master Darkness in Twilight in Light also needs to recover."

"DiTiL? What the hell is he doing alive? He tried to digitalize the Compendium of Space Islands. Ooof, must have been some explosion to send you to Darkness."

DiTiL spoke, "It was big enough that it shredded a Lightbringer's Armour revealing who he was to his friends. Like I said, I was a fool in my youth."

"Regardless of what or when we are here. You will be safe here until a Reaper can come to claim your soul for judgement."

A stone monolith rose from the ground. Badger escorted the two inside. He then walked out by himself.

"So, Bounty Hunter 13, why are you actually here?"

"Amari wishes to learn about the strange man with a badger mask who has been keeping an eye on her."

"Ah, I see you saw me. Must work on that."

"No, you likely were very careful not to be seen. However, she is as strong as me if she ever decided to use that strength."

"Ah, yes, she was born right after you and before the conjoined ones."

"Yes, and she was already intelligent and able to understand the words that were spoken."

"Amari, what you are about to see is not to be mentioned. Do you understand?"

"Corvus said the same thing and I will say to you what I said to him. I live by myself on the lands owned by Axel Wulf. I speak to nobody but him and his wife, Shenzi. And as you should know, he is an Efreet, so he knows forbidden things."

"Then behold my face, sister."

The mask retracted into the man's armour and he lowered his hood. Amari saw her face, Corvus' face, and Bounty's face. She then saw the cybernetic arm that he had. "Myst!?"

"Yes, little sister, it is me."

"Okay, what the shmutz is going on?"

Bounty spoke, "I took on the Mantle of Lord Shadow when I slew Czar Zenthin Ankara the Shadow. Myst became Lord Badger when the previous Lord Badger was slain by a Lightbringer. Corvus chose to devote himself to the Raven, Nevermore. Nevermore needed a new follower to be able to equal God Silver. Because while Nevermore is a Druid god, he was the primary God of Planets Grey, Gothico, Gothica, and Punkx. Silver only allowed him to be a God of Silver as long as he had followers equal to or greater than Silver had."

Myst spoke, "The newest Silver cares little about what his predecessors did. He is far too lenient and has been letting the Gods of Silver walk all over him."

Bounty spoke, "It will end in war. Yes, I know you have had this rant before, dear brother, but for now, I think it is time to return to your duties. We have a Lightbringer coming up the road."

Bounty enveloped himself in shadows. Myst's mask covered his face again as a man with spiked hair and a large chain axe arrived at the crossroads where they were standing. Next to this man was a large Canis with a tower shield that looked like it could also be used as a hammer. Also near them was a slender Syrien with a rose-shaped staff. Behind them stood an imposing woman with yellow armour and a helmet in the shape of a Saberfang Tiger Felis.

Amari spoke, "Wait, I thought you were killed by Jeanne d'Arc."

The woman looked down at them and then sagged slightly. "I was. My soul is trapped in this armour until the Lady of the Pure World can find a replacement."

Bounty scoffed, "The Fountainhead cursed you in other words."

"Silence, Beast of Shadows! Ugh anyway... Lord Badger, I bring unto you these three Lightbringers. They were slain in battle with a mighty foe. I need you to allow them to recover to try to fight this foe again."

Lord Badger spoke, "If they are dead, they belong to the Reaper."

"This foe is looking to start the Lightbringer war up again."

Lord Shadow and Lord Badger spoke in unison, "What!"

Bounty cleared his throat. "My guess is that is not a good thing. Boy! I bestow upon you the chain axe of Darkness wield it with the chain axe of Light and the chain axe of Twilight. That should give you an edge in the battle."

The boy looked at the black onyx chain axe and then at the crystalline chain axe he already held. He looked up at Bounty with fear.

Lord Badger spoke as he opened a portal, "Do not be afraid. The darkness is as much needed as the light. The door is not yet open, you have time. This time you will succeed. Go now and stop the fool who desires to bring the war to the realms."

He patted the boy's but to encourage him through the portal and it closed as soon as the three entered. Bounty pulled the shadows back into the Cane of Shadows, which he put his weight on to maintain standing. Lord Badger's mask retracted back into his armour and he shook his head.

"You can't keep doing that, Bounty. Your body can only take so much of a beating before it gives up."

"My body is already giving up. I will need to retire for a bit."

Amari spoke, "Is that a good idea? I have heard rumours from Norvcryog that they seek to invade Silver."

"Like Myst said, my body is no longer able to keep up with me. So Trinity, why have you not attacked me like you tried to do with Corvus?"

The yellow armored woman spoke "I am no longer the Lady of the Pure World. But like you said The Fountainhead cursed me when I accidentally discovered them. I blame my adopted father. He tried to push me too far."

"As well you should. Lord Dragon is not someone who is trustworthy. He seeks something. I can only suspect what he seeks is not a good thing."

"Are you angry with me Bounty?"

"Why would I be angry with you, Trinity?"

"Because of my past actions."

"Your past actions caused you to be forced to be on a life support unit. You have already suffered enough. Also, I am old and tired. Why waste time on being angry about something so insignificant?"

"You have changed, Demon of Silver."

"I had the best return Amari to her home. She has learned enough to make the right assumptions. Come along, Amari. That is enough knowledge for today."

"Yes, I think you are right, brother. I need time to process what you, Corvus, and Myst have taught me."

A portal opened and the four walked through. Myst placed his mask back on. They looked at her large bunker. There was a cackle and a very large Hyenidae emerged from the underbrush. She lunged at Amari and then hugged her tightly.

Amari patted her on the back. "Hello, Shenzi. I am glad to see you too." Bounty smiled, then vanished along with Lord Badger and Trinity.

Invasion of Continent Silver by Continent Norvcryog

Age of the Hunt

King Nachtkrap of the NorvCryogans stood in front of his Generals Rubezahl, Changeling, Faust, Fossegrim, and The Dread Wolf. They were looking down on a map of the Continent Silver.

Faust spoke, "Damn him, damn that man called Demon of Silver. He slaughtered us all without a care."

Changeling hissed, "Yess, you fool, we know. Our firsst invasion wass a failure thankss to him, but rumours state that he has laid down hiss sword and refuses to raise it."

Rubezahl spoke in a deep baritone, "Those are only rumours. Until our God Odin One-Eye gives us the word, we must refrain from invading."

Fossegrim smirked, "I have already taken the liberty to conquer Northern Silver. That old man called demon did nothing to stop us. We must march on City Silver while he lays dormant."

The Dread Wolf smiled a sinister smile. "I agree with you, Grimm. Now, how about the others? My Lord, you have been awfully silent."

Nachtkrap shook his head. "Sorry, I was lost in thought. I am worried about attacking my older brother. Will it curse me as a traitor?"

Dread Wolf snarled, "That imbecile betrayed your clan. He is nothing. Your great-father gave you the throne on his deathbed. You are the rightful heir and your brother will die for his betrayal. If necessary, I will kill him for you so you do not have to get his blood on your hands."

Changling spoke, "All of uss would gladly sspill hiss blood. We await your orders."

Fossgrimm nodded. "We already have a foothold let us go all out. Blitzkrieg them before they can do anything."

"I trust all of your judgements on this. Very well raise the banners of war. Crush all who oppose us."

The generals, in unison, spoke, "For the empire, for Old One-eye, for glory in death or victory! For Valhalla!"

Dread Wolf stood at the entrance of the tunnel they had forced the denizens of North Silver to create. He entered along with the rest of the army, with Rubezahl behind all of them, forcing the conscripts on. As the army exited the tunnel, it collapsed, crushing Rubezahl.

Fossegrim snorted. "What an ignoble death. Pity. Who gets his army?"

Dread Wolf smiled, "Have Faust take half and you take the other half. I also want both of you to split up and flank City Silver on two sides. I want our army to surround the city. No one should escape the city with their lives intact."

The army did as ordered. Within hours City Silver was surrounded. They bombarded the junk walls of City Silver with heavy siege engines. The walls crumbled before them. They swarmed the city. The guards were overwhelmed and decimated. Dread Wolf made sure all the guards were beheaded and their bodies strung up on banners to reduce the moral of the populace.

The king walked out. In his hands were two blades forged with a blood-red metal. He was alone.

"Fool, you think to challenge us!" the king smiled

***

Three days prior, king sat on his throne. He was staring at a grizzled old man with white streaks in his coarse black hair. His eyepatch covered the unnaturally smooth side of his face. His other side was weathered and tired looking. He was wearing glasses and smoking a cigar that burned with green energy.

"Bounty Hunter 13, I heard you were in my city last night. What did I tell you?"

The man laughed, "Never to set foot in your lands. I was just checking on the progress you made. Why did you rebuild?"

"Broken ships are not stable, so I moved those willing and rebuilt, but we are off-topic. I warned you I would execute you if you entered my city."

"Ha! Many a king has said that. I still stand."

"I know you are never to set foot in my city. I banish you. We do not need your help."

"Good, I was calling to tell you I was retired anyway. And also to give you a warning. The north is going to be occupied. They will come for you. You turned your back on them. They will kill you if they get ahold of you."

"Then I will defend myself. I am of Norvcryog. I will die with a blade in my hand and despite my treachery, I will be welcomed to Valhalla."

"What of your family?"

"If I die, they will die. It matters little."

***

The king charged the line of soldiers. He tossed them aside; his zerker nature took over. His blood-red blades kill indiscriminately. As he killed a general, Faust stabbed him in the chest. He swung, beheading Faust, only to have the Dread Wolf walk over and rip out his throat. The last thing he saw before darkness was his headless body being cut up by the Norvcryog army.

Dread Wolf howled in glee, then spoke, "Remaining commanders round up all the pretty women in the city and put them out to be used by the army. Capture the children and they will make good conscripts. Kill everyone else. This bloodshed will bring glory to our cause."

The commanders passed on the orders and the army went forth. Dread Wolf entered the castle. He sent troops to secure the former king's family for execution.

One of the soldiers came back shaking. "I am sorry, my lord, but the only thing we found was this."

The soldier held up a playing card with a horned symbol on the back of it. On the front was a jester. "So they escaped. Pity."

He beheaded the poor sap who gave him the bad news and sat on the throne of the city. He grinned. The sounds of carnage invigorated him. A greasy man in a blue embroidered robe walked in. When the guard tried to stop him, he clenched his fist. The guard crumpled in on himself with a disgusting squelch and a spray of blood. Dread Wolf looked at the man curiously.

"So you are the one known as The Dread Wolf of the North."

"That is me. Who are you?"

"I am Lord Dragon. I see great things for you. I look forward to assisting you in your task."

"I do not need help. Especially from a Pale Elf."

"Pity, very well, your reign of terror will be swift. You will conquer the east of Continent Silver all the way down to Angela's Grove. But your fate will end in your defeat at the end of the year. Have fun!"

Lord Dragon vanished, leaving behind an amused Dread Wolf. "We'll see Lord Dragon. We'll see."

Day broke in the devastated city. Blood and gore coated the streets and walls. The army was currently enjoying their gift. The many young and pretty girls trapped in stocks and being violently used. All the currency is being rounded up to send to Norvcryog City. Any icons of the gods, other than the Norvecryog pantheon, burned or melted down. Everything else burned or melted down. Only the ruins remained.

Bounty stood on a hillside watching impassively. In his arms lay two children and a woman. He turned and walked off. He went back to his home and placed them in stasis chambers. It would be a bloody year.

During week six of the occupation, the army was getting restless. All the women had either starved to death or had been killed while in coitus. Dread Wolf looked at his map. He stared at it. Finally getting up, he summoned the generals and commanders.

"Men, we must conquer the rest of this Odin-forsaken land. Cleanse it of these heathens. In these chips are your orders. Follow them. I don't want any mistakes."

The commanders and generals saluted and walked out to regain control of their armies.

The Forest's Revenge

General Jottun stood in front of his army. "Commanders, I want you to split up and reconnaissance the forest. We must find a way to get to The Ship, a medium city built

on the wreck of a spaceship that crashed here when the bombs fell."

The commanders dispersed as General Jottun entered the forest with the first team. The Sylvan Elves took offence towards Jottun for entering their sacred lands. His unit was slaughtered instantly.

Commander Lori Nacht stood waiting for her siblings to get their tools. As soon as they did, she led them into the forest. The first night went smoothly and they made great progress, but night fell and they camped out in a strange glade with an onyx boulder in the middle of a small pond. The pond had smooth pebbles covering the bottom. It was surrounded by coniferous Spike Trees. In one corner of the glade was a large statue depicting a demon-like entity. Next to the statue was an altar with a strange horned symbol on it.

Lori stayed vigil. She was especially concerned with the statue on the boulder. It was another demon-like being in a meditative pose. Soon her vigil was up and her sister Lenni took vigil. It was now the midnight hour. Lenni did not notice her dark sister Lusi walk to the meditating statue.

Lusi sat next to the meditating statue and it spoke, "So, little girl, why do you and your family intrude upon my sanctuary?"

"So you are real. Figured. We just needed a rest. We have a long walk ahead of us."

"Yes, I hear. Going to The Ship. Even though I am retired, I must warn you tomorrow begins Noční lov. Beware when the three moons turn red. For three days, the forest will be more alive. In the old days, we Silverans would sacrifice prisoners of war in the forest. It was to prevent the forest from overrunning our land. Now that there are so few cities left, the forest is reclaiming the land. Tomorrow if you are in the forest, it will begin its hunt. Your blood will give it sustenance."

"Is there anything we can do to avoid death?"

"Yes, look for the old ruined forts from the wars. There you will be safe from both the forest and the Sylvani Elves."

"Can you give me more help? How can we find these forts?"

"I would prefer not to help my enemy, but you and your family are young. Very well. Here is a map marking all the old forts leading to the ocean. Now all your family has to do is trust you to lead them to safety."

The horizon broke into a fairy purple and fiery orange. The sun shattered the dark pushing it away. The meditating statue was gone leaving only Lusi resting on the onyx boulder. Luk, the only boy, waded through the water and climbed the boulder he picked up Lusi.

She murmured, "Beware the red moons."

She jolted awake as the water touched her and began to look around wildly. She saw the blue eyes of her brother and sighed in relief, snuggling into his chest. As soon as the two got to shore, Lusi grabbed the scouter. She quickly and feverishly put in numerous locations.

Her elder sister Lunatick spoke, "What's got you scared?"

"I just had a nightmare that gave me all these locations. It also reminded me of a myth I read about when getting ready for this war, Noční lov."

"Hunters Blood Night? What does that old fable have to do with anything?"

"The forest will come alive and eat us. Please trust me."

"Alright, if it's got you so freaked out. We trust you. Isn't that right, Commander?" Lori nodded. "Even if I have a hard time believing in a fairytale, I will trust you."

"Alright girls, we move out in ten. That should give us time."

Luk spoke, "Commander should we warn the others?"

"Yes, we should. Lana notifies the rest of the army."

"On it, sis. Oh, sorry, Commander."

"It's alright. You girls can be informal with me."

"Commander, they're laughing at us."

"Then eat something and let's get moving."

They followed the trail of ruined forts, only stopping near a circle of mushrooms to eat lunch. As night fell, they came upon a large fort with a demonic statue standing with what looked to be a cigar in his mouth. Blue smoke billowed from the mouth of the statue.

"You who dares to step foot on the sacred grounds of Silver? Beware the sirens song. Do not mistake my words for generosity. Your kind invaded my lands. Keep your radio on. I wish to see you suffer."

The statue vanished, allowing them access to the fort. Lana kept the radio off. As the three full moons rose into the night sky, they burned blood red. The radio turned on. Throughout the night, all they heard were the screams of the dying. As dawn broke the sky, Lana lay holding her twin tightly. Her twin sister's mascara was running down her face from her crying all night long. Lua, the joker of the group, sat in the fetal position with a bit of vomit next to her.

The statue walked in, smoking a cigar. He looked at them and then smiled a fanged smile, "You survived the first night. Good for you. Now let's make this more difficult for you."

He pulled out a gun that vaporized their rations. "Let's see you survive night two." He vanished, allowing them to leave. There were only enough rations for lunch.

Lori spoke, "You girls eat. I can stand to not eat food. You too, Luk."

Luk shook his head. "No thanks, my stomach is still knotted from last night."

They finished lunch and continued on. As the shadows of dusk began encroaching, they still had not found a safe fort.

That was when a large man with a bushy beard and a cloak made of feathers walked into view. He sighed and motioned them to follow him. He struck a vine out of the way. They followed him to a small, mostly ruined fort. He motioned to the top, where it was mostly intact and signalled them to stay there.

Lori collapsed against the wall as soon as they entered the top floor. Lenni hurried over there and helped her sister into a sitting position.

"Sis, I will take the first vigil. Here are my rations. Eat something, please."

Lenni watched as her siblings slept. The radio was still on and more dying and terrified cries were heard over it. She walked over to Lynne, who was manning the radio while Lana slept tightly, holding her twin Löla. She brushed Lynne's shoulder, causing Lynne to slump into slumber. Her eyes became draconic and her hair went straight, revealing two horn nubs. She made sure her sisters and Luk slept throughout the night. She rummaged inside her hammerspace and laid out a meal of dried salted meat, nuts and apples. She began peeling the apples from their hard outer shell and finished as the sun rose. Her draconic eyes went back to normal and her horns vanished beneath her wavy hair.

She smiled, "Good morning, girls. Did you sleep well?"

They looked at the feast before them. Without questioning it, they began eating. The only one who looked mildly put off was Lusi. They began their trek. No one noticed two glowing green eyes watching them. The forest was mildly pissed off that there were still survivors. As night fell, the forest began actively attacking Lori's family. Lunatik was the first to fall; her cries of terror drove her siblings on. Lynne fell next; she couldn't even cry out before her head was severed. Lua started to jump at any movement, finally running in terror. By the time they found safety, only Lori, Lusi, Luk, and Lenni remained. Lori was shaking and she clutched her siblings close that night.

Dawn finally came. Lori lifted Lusi up and began walking while Lenni grabbed Luk. They soon arrived in a beach area with a large cave. Across the way, they could see Dragon's Den Island.

Lori spoke, "Lenni, I am going to investigate that cave. If I don't come out within the hour, expect my demise. Take care of them, please."

"I will set up a safe place for them at that fort with the horned emblem. But if you don't come back, I will need to get provisions and find The Ship."

"I understand, but please if I don't come back, stay with them until they awake."

"I will."

Lori walked into the cave. As her eyes adjusted to the light in the cave, she immediately saw two turrets pointing in her direction. She closed her eyes, letting a tear fall before they opened fire. Her eyes opened and she was in a cell with her dead siblings.

"What?"

Lunatik rushed her and hugged her tightly. "We made it, sis."

"But I saw you die. How?"

The large statue that they had encountered throughout their mission walked in, smoking a cigar. He exhaled blue smoke and then spoke, "I tricked you. Your siblings were teleported here as soon as they died. I have been taking care of them. Just waiting on the last three."

"Leave them alone!"

"Nope!"

Meanwhile, at the fort, Lusi was kissing Luk. Her overzealous passion was preventing him from thinking straight. The two were soon naked. He was deep inside her when he burst. His seed spilt into her womb. Their passion drained they passed out. Two glowing blue eyes were watching them. Lenni smiled and inhaled the lust in the air absorbing it. Her hunger sated, she teleported to

The Ship. She ordered her provisions and then entered a nightclub. She waved at a woman in fishnets and tattered black clothing.

The woman walked over and smiled, "Lloda, you came back. How was it?"

"Well, I met the reincarnation of Lunatic. She didn't recognize me, which is good. It's better she doesn't remember anything. How are you, Lucy?"

"Enjoying myself for once. I suppose that father is still being a bitch."

"He refuses to enter this war. I fear he will have to."

"I feel sorry for the enemy when he does. Gotta go. My dance is up next. See you around."

The large man with a feathered cloak walked into the fort. He saw his prey. He shook his head. He placed their clothes on them, then picked them up and vanished. He reappeared in prison in a vortex of feathers.

He signed, "Here you go, brother, the final one is at The Ship and I suspect she will be here shortly."

The man with the cigar spoke, "Thank you, Corvus. I'll clean them up and place them with their siblings. How are the others?"

"Getting used to being prisoners of my Druid grove. They are well cared for and I'll release them in a month."

"Alright. Good luck, brother."

"How are you?"

"More traumatized than I thought from all the battles I've been in. Shegor says that he is surprised I'm not completely mad yet. Zarkanus agreed with him."

"So you are serious. You are not going to enter this war?"

"No, I suspect I'll have no choice soon. The Dread Wolf encroaches upon The Rising Falls. Quazar Moth can only hold out for at most three years before the walls are breached. I fear for her safety. Meanwhile, I have heard rumours of double dealings by the Supervillains of Angela's Grove, while no surprise there. I feel that the Heroes will fall then there goes Angela's Grove. I also sense my death on the horizon. Especially since it sounds like The Dread Wolf is pressuring The Magus, Mystics, Psykiks, and Bards to submit, if they do, nowhere is safe. The Gods are getting worried. They are urging Silver to do something. He wants me to get involved."

"Bounty, if you get involved, you die!"

Bounty dried off Luk and Lusi, then placed them in with their siblings. "What happens, happens, Corvus. I am prepared either way."

Corvus shook his head and then vanished in a burst of feathers. Bounty snuffed out his cigar and walked out of prison.

"Hello, Lloda or should I call you Lenni now?"

"Father. You have my siblings held captive. Release them."

"Or what?"

"I don't know. Usually, that works."

"I am not in a generous mood today. You may join them." He handed her a card and walked off. She looked at him, smiled then entered the prison. She joined her sisters in the cell. They were all asleep when she did this. She lay her head against Lori and fell asleep herself.

In the middle of the night, she awoke to a gentle nudge. Her eyes became draconic as she opened them. Lunatick was sitting there.

"Lunatick, shouldn't you be asleep?"

"No, especially since I needed to confirm something."

"What?"

"Ou are Lloda Hunter."

"Shh. Not so loud, love."

"Why did you choose this family?"

"I had no choice. Little Lusi made the same mistake as my Lucy. She tried to summon a spirit, but hers would have destroyed the whole block. I couldn't let that happen, so I took its place. I thought you didn't recognize me."

"I didn't, sis, but it took me until seeing my life flash before my eyes when that vine grabbed me to do so. Why is the former father acting so bitchy?"

"He has PTSD. The many wars he's been through have affected him deeply. He swore he would not enter this war."

"He won't have a choice. I just wish there was a way we could save Sam and her unit of our lovers."

Bounty had overheard the request and sighed. He knew where this Sam was.

She was stationed at The Rising Falls. He sighed. Shook his head, then vanished.

The Horned Crowned King

Carolyn Pine stood with the army outside a massive holo-shielded and walled city. The army was in the hundreds of thousands. Her unit was filled with all the conscripts. She shuddered as Grand General Goval Volt signalled the bombardment. The holo shield stayed strong, but a mechanical man walked over to it. He pulled out a long black blade and plunged it into the holo shield shattering the first layer of defences. He smirked and pointed his sword towards the wall. The army charged.

Many turrets opened fire. The bombers fired at the turrets causing them to crumble. The wall fell soon after. A large horned man stood in their way. He was ten feet tall, with a large burn on half of his body. He wore an eyepatch over the frighteningly smooth right side of his face. Where the burn on his body was, he was smoking a cigar that glowed orange. He exhaled silver smoke and vanished. He appeared next to Carolyn. She barely had time to cry out as flames engulfed her. Her unit was soon vaporized. The rest of the army had entered the city.

The burned man vanished and entered the castle. He watched from inside as Quazar Moth walked out with her staff raised.

"Bloody Rainbow Explosion!"

The invaders were ripped apart by a rainbow explosion. Quazar was overextending her power as her rainbow explosions ripped through the enemy army. She gasped in shock as a bullet entered her throat. She fell to the ground below. She staggered up, clutching her throat. She kept firing Rainbows. Her elite guard had soon formed up around her. They were fierce looking. One was a fiery woman with grey skin and forearm spikes. Another was a slender Olayazcan with a red hooded sweater on. Next to him stood a three-eyed man with glowing amber eyes. This man quickly healed Quazar. There was also a well-toned girl with teal hair that could be used as a shield if necessary. There was a woman with a spell book and another holding a shotgun. Finally, a girl with heavy power armour wielding a flaming blade. It did not take long for the elite guard to be overwhelmed.

"I surrender, leave my people be."

Volt walked over to her, smiled and ripped her shirt off. He took her staff and snapped it in half. He ordered her guard to be chained up to totem poles that signified Volt conquering this land.

He then motioned for the cyborg to come over.

"As the one who breached these walls, you get to fuck her first. Then she will be passed around. In the meantime, rape and pillage as you see fit."

The army dispersed in fervour. As they were raped and pillaged to their heart's content, they were being stalked and killed. The burned man was swift and merciless. He walked into the square to see Quazar bloody and filthy. She lay there almost lifeless, her rear end pointed up while her upper body was low to the ground. Her elite guard fared no better. All were in some form of the post-sex pose. The fiery grey woman with forearm spikes was barely breathing as her neck was tied up with a noose. The burned man snarled and ripped the head off the cyborg and vaporized his body. He then swung his blade, bisecting Grand General Volt. He picked up Quazar.

"Sorry, I'm so late little sis. I would have been here sooner had I known there were this many."

Her empty eyes watered and she lay her head against him. "I'm sorry I was so weak."

"Oh, Star. You did well. You aren't Bounty Hunter 13. I am the only one in our family able to handle such overwhelming odds. I'm proud of you. Now rest. I'll make sure The Rising Falls is well protected."

He unhooked the guard and carried them all inside the castle. He placed them into healing tubes and sighed. He began to collect her most trusted allies. He placed them all into tubes. He shook his head in disappointment. He snapped his fingers and a young man appeared.

"Hello, Bounty. It's been a while since we talked. Here's your throne back. If you want it."

"You know my stance, Father."

"Fine, I'll get Thirteen to take it. Can you stay and help him?"

"I will. But don't expect us to help you with anything else."

"I don't."

Thirteen Hunter appeared and looked at his father. He sighed in defeat and sat on the throne. It glowed, accepting him as the new ruler. The burned man vanished, leaving his sons to rule. They left the Totems of Volt up to make it look like The Rising Falls was under Norvcryogan's control. They then called their families to their sides and began the long process of rebuilding The Rising Falls.

***

Dread Wolf stood, his yellow eyes glaring. He had successfully brought the Mystics to his side. Then forcibly subjugated the Magus and Psykicks of Silver. They were arrayed before him.

"You know the fate of those who deny me. Now carve us a path through this impassable river. I wish to strike hard and fast. Generals execute those that fail."

They obeyed and within minutes, the younger ones lay on the ground, their powers exhausted. They were immediately executed. Soon a passable bridge had been made. Three-fourths of the Mystics, magus, and Psykicks lay dead. Their bodies were left for the carrion animals.

General Gorgon said, "Take the rest of these prisoners and find where the Demon of Silver is. When he is found, take them and kill him. In the meantime, force the Bards to submit."

Gorgon bowed and his troops hauled away the remaining Psykicks, Mystics, and Magus.

Dread Wolf drove his army on. They marched through the night. He sent twelve units under General Changeling to begin the siege of The City Under the Mountains. They arrived at the massive Dwarv Silveran city that was partially under the mountain and partially outside the mountain. The city outside was filled with Jottun, Oruk, and Trolglin Silverans. The inside was reserved for the Dwarv and their slaves, the Gnomish Silverans. Changeling ordered the bolt throwers to open fire. The city walls glowed with ancient power and then reflected the bolts wiping out Changeling's entire army. He stared at the city in fear and shock. He gulped and fled.

Meanwhile, Dread Wolf walked into the city of Angela's grove. He was instantly set upon by the one known as Ultra Magnus. He flicked his wrist, slicing through Ultra Magnus' throat. Ultra Magnus starred in wide-eyed horror. That was when the Supervillains, led by Ultra Magnus' mortal rival Lot Lethlor came into view.

Lot spoke, "Hello, oh great overlords. We come bearing gifts for your advancement."

He motioned towards a large cell filled with many prisoners. Dread Wolf snarled, "What of it?"

"Well, these people are the ones that the heroes hold dear. The heroes will not face you if their loved ones are in danger. The moment one or more hero revolts, the cell will release a toxic nerve agent that will kill the prisoners instantly."

"I like your style, but how do I know you won't betray me."

"You are wise to question a villain like me. All we ask is that we can go wild. Robberies, extortions, all the stuff the heroes try to prevent. Without interference."

"I will give you that as long as you remain loyal."

"Don't worry, my great overlord. We are loyal to you."

"Then prove your worth by escorting my generals to key points in the city. Assist them in controlling the populace and you will have all your greedy hands desire."

Changeling ran into Dread Wolf, his fear was unabated and he fell to the ground. Dread Wolf looked down at him. "I see you failed Changeling. Pity I had high hopes for you."

He flicked his wrist and Changeling's legs detached from his body, allowing his blood to spill out. Dread Wolf flicked his wrist again and Changeling screamed as his stumps sealed. "Be glad for that much. I could have executed you. Put him in the worst part of the city."

General Fin Nacht stood staring at Little Komodo in Angela's Grove. He had already conquered it. By his side was Jenny Oda, the Schizhuan, protector of the middle lands. She was the one who kept mortals safe from gods and vice versa. She had willingly submitted to him to protect her people. There was a commotion in the market and he saw a medium red drake slam into his guards, sending two flyings and impacting the wall below him. One flew through his window. He looked at Jenny and she sighed and jumped down.

She cried out, "Do not do this, Jason. Your family was well respected. Retreat and I can make sure the Yinglongs are safe from the wrath of our overlords."

"You are the only traitor Jenny. I will not submit."

Fin kicked the drake in the head. "Then you will suffer."

His guards formed up and pulled out Iron spears and chains. They swung the chains and caught Jason around the wrists and foot claws. He cried out in pain. They quickly submerged his hands in molten iron and pinned them to the ground. They tightened the chains and stabbed his wings, pinning them to his back so he couldn't use them. Two iron shackles were produced and placed around his ankles before the chain was pulled, taught and embedded into the nearby buildings. He would not be able to thrash around now without killing civilians.

He whined in pain. Jenny turned away and quickly bowed as a large man with wolf-like features walked into the market. He only had one eye. The other had a scar going through it and an eyepatch covering it. He looked at the drake and brushed his hand along the scales.

"What a magnificent beast that you caught, General."

"Thank you, my lord, but he is not a beast. He was the protector of Little Komodo, Jason

Yinglong."

"Ah, that changes things. I see you used iron on him."

"Yes, my lord. The Schizhuan taught me the weakness of all mystic-like creatures."

"His scales are sturdy. I have always wanted a dragon scale cuirass. Cut off his claws and use them to cut the scales off. I would like a new cuirass in a month's time. I do want him to stay alive and suffer for his impudence."

He walked over to Jason's face and tilted his head. He grinned evilly before plunging his claw into Jason's right eye and ripping it out. "Fin, be a good man and give this to the Yinglong family. Tell them I am keeping an eye on them. Oh and also film him fucking his mother. I wish to be entertained. Afterwards, kill her."

"I must apologize, my lord. I can film them having sex, but it would not be a good idea to execute the mother. If she is alive, she can be used as a bartering chip. If she dies, he has nothing left to live for and will rampage."

"Hmm, good point. Very well, Fin, I will not have her executed. But cut out the boy's teeth while they have sex. I wish to see how dragon blood affects copulation."

"I can do that for you, my lord."

"You, Schizhuan, pour molten iron in the drake's eye socket to cauterize and stop the bleeding. Do it now or suffer."

Jenny swallowed and took a forge pourer and dunked it in the molten iron and poured the cup of iron into Jason's eye socket. He cried out in pain and smashed his tail, hitting the Dread Wolf.

The Dread Wolf climbed out of the small crater and snarled, "Slice his tail off, grill it and serve it for dinner."

The guards did as ordered. By now, Jason was too weak to scream. He just lay there.

***

Over in Little Olayazca, General Changeling sat in his hover chair. Dread Wolf had severed his legs for failing to capture The City Under the Mountain and had sent him here. His guards were struggling to deal with the many criminals and vigilantes here. Especially one Miguel Tiger. The Tiger family was the thorn on his side. He did not have enough guards to deal with them and the thieves led by Black Grackle. A knife hit the side of the building he was near and exploded, sending him flying. He watched as Black Grackle entered into his vault and stole his wealth. He lay wheezing on the side of the road, unable to fight. A woman wearing Amazon armour walked over to him. She helped him into his chair and blocked a claw strike from Blanco Pantero.

"Wondra, you treacherous minx, why are you here?"

"Ronaldo, cease this fruitless endeavour. The Norvcryogans have won. Cease and lenience will be given to you and your family."

"I, Blanco Pantero, will never submit to a traitor to her own people." Wondra snarled, then pulled out her sword.

"Then die."

The sword was kicked out of her hand and a platinum burst shredded her armour. She staggered back as Platina Danger smashed into the ground in front of her.

"You stay away from my husband, bitch!"

Fear crossed Wondra's face. She grabbed General Changeling and ran. There was an enraged roar behind her. She kept running until she got him to a safe building. She collapsed against the wall panting.

"Bout damn time you sshowed up. Remember we hold your girlfriend hosstage. You obey uss."

She snarled but held her tongue

"Now ssince you are naked kneel and pleassure me bitch."

She obeyed unwillingly when he had released all over her, he fell asleep. She curled up in the corner, crying. Blanco Pantero and Platina Danger walked into the building. She picked Wondra up after cutting open her arm, leaving behind a blood puddle. She then cauterized the wound and walked off with Blanco Pantero still holding the abused form of Wondra.

***

In the centre of Angela's grove was a large multi-tiered building. This building was surrounded by a massive park that served as a forest getaway for the city. This building was Angela's Grove Schooling Center. It was currently under siege by General Rosso Crymsin and the Undertakers.

A young teen was waiting in ambush, he was transparent so only his friends and allies could see him, but the enemy could not. He took possession of one of the soldiers and smashed him into a wall. On the roof of the building, a woman in black and green with black eye shadow and lipstick stood holding a large chain gun. She was strong for her deceptively slender frame. She opened fire. She wiped out a unit causing one of the Undertakers, a man in cerulean, to jump up the building to confront her personally. That was just what she wanted.

"Truck, he's halfway up the building, blow the wall."

The wall exploded, sending the cerulean-clad man plummeting. He hit the ground with a sickening crunch and lay unmoving. A white energy field grabbed Truck and yanked him to the ground. It did the same to the goth woman. It engulfed the building pulling out all the defenders. Breaking bones as it yanked them through the wall. They were forced into kneeling positions as the army primed their guns.

Crymsin spoke, "I will be merciful and give you each a chance to surrender. Now witness the fate of all who deny a surrender."

She pulled out a gun and pointed it at Truck. She fired and his head ceased to exist. His corpse dropped to the ground as the blood spilled from his neck.

"That is for the death of Azul."

That display quickly caused the defenders to surrender. Collars were slapped on each of them. "If you try to challenge us again, these collars will electrocute you. If you still challenge us, they explode. Do not try anything funny. We own you now. You will obey."

As the army dispersed, leaving the Undertakers in charge, Crymsin spoke into her gauntlet. "Dread Wolf, the school has finally been taken."

"Good job General Crymsin. With that, Angela's Grove is ours. All that is left is to hear from Grand General Trollhammer. Make sure the students are available for the army to use and enjoy."

"Very well, sir. Anything else?"

"No, General Crymsin, that is all for now."

***

Rip Trollhammer stood looking at the formidable city Under the Mountain. He lowered his binoculars. He had a small infiltration unit of zerkers set up. His commanders were Tor of the Ulfhednar Wolfzerkers, Grag of the Svinfylking Boarzerkers, and Gaston of the Bearzerkers.

He spoke, "The only obstacle is the wall which can destroy any army. There is a gate that we would need to open to avoid the wall. The problem I see is will the wall try to eradicate us if we climb it?"

His second in command, one of the Ulfhednar, Commander Tor Odinheart, spoke, "Only one way to find out. I will try to scale the wall."

Odinheart bounded off on all fours. He arrived at the wall and pulled out his grappling hook. He swung it and it hooked the wall. He began climbing. When he reached the top, he slunk across the battlements, killing any guard he saw. He then opened the gate. Trollhammer led the zerkers into the city.

"Gaston, light the fires."

Gaston and his unit of Berserkers slaughtered anything that was in their way. They lit fires to smoke the civilians out to round them up. The city outside was burning. Trollhammer lifted his warhammer and smashed the inner gate down with a mighty blow. Grag, you and the Svinfylking wipe out the defenders, no survivors."

The defenders of the inner city were slaughtered like animals. His mighty warhammer flashing with chaotic power, Trollhammer singlehandedly routed the defenders. His zerkers soon had finished their missions.

Trollhammer's small army marched into the under the castle. They slew everyone inside. The floor was slick with blood. And the walls were covered in gore. Trollhammer stood over the young king and smashed his head into the throne. He kicked the boy's body aside and sat on the throne.

"Grag, I want a report of all the captured goods. Then send word to Dread Wolf that The City under the Mountains is ours."

The large boar man grunted in acknowledgement. Trollhammer smiled and put his hands behind his head and leaned back. He put his feet up on the corpse of the king and exhaled a sigh of relief.

Death of the Waster and the Warriors Grave

Bounty Hunter 13 finished piling the corpses of the fallen Magus, Psykicks, and Mystics. He lit them aflame. "Thayme Sidrodc uigde het seul, thamy havens sunocm het seoul." He downed the amber liquid summoned during the prayer and tossed the glass onto the flame, causing it to burn intensely. He walked towards his home and saw several people standing in his way. He then heard ghostly Polka music and grimaced. Polka Knights is just what I need on the eve of my death. He sighed and lit his cigar.

Gorgon stood there holding a barbed sword that he pointed at Bounty. "Demon of Silver. Tonight I rid this worthless continent of you. You, Bards, know what to do. You refuse, you die."

Numerous other Bards walked into view, including one that was on a hovering pipe organ. He grimaced and pulled out his blade. "I just wanted to relax, but it seems my fate has been chosen. Come tonight, my blade will taste flesh once again!"

The cacophony of instruments started. Bounty dodged a burst of fire. He leapt back from several ice bursts. He knew he would be unable to stand against this many Bards. He just needed to wear their numbers down. Gunfire cut down several of the Bards. Bounty saw his rescuers. It was his daughter's new family, the ones from the forest. He raised his eyebrow and flipped back from a wind strike.

"You fool kids! Get off the battlefield. My destiny lies in death. You still have many years to go. Don't waste them on an old man."

Gorgon snarled, "Commander Lori Nacht, what is the meaning of this betrayal?"

"Sorry, General. We were paid handsomely to help him."

"Then I will end your worthless lives."

Bounty rolled out of the way from the ghostly dancers wearing lederhosen. The dancers struck the Nacht family, causing them to fall instantly to the ground in agony. Bounty snapped his fingers and the Nacht family vanished. Several invisible blades sliced into him, causing him to stagger right into an eruption of stone that embedded into him. He gasped and threw his sword severing Gorgon's head. That was when The Dread Wolf appeared. He looked over Bounty's blade and then smiled. He swung it a few times, then walked over to Bounty. He sliced down, cutting Bounty's head off. He then raised it up towards his face and sneered.

"Pathetic. I expected more from you." He ripped the horns off of the head and tossed it aside. "Leave the corpse for the carrion animals. He deserves no honour."

Dark laughter echoed across the field. "And with that, you have proven worthless. Behold your folly. You have denied the Gods and have executed all the people who don't worship your pantheon. You may have conquered Eastern Silver, but your days are numbered."

Two large meteors dropped from the sky. One fell on the capital of Norvcryog, wiping it out. The other fell on the tenth city Silver. Dread Wolf watched as the body of Bounty Hunter 13 burst into flames and vanished. He became enraged. He howled and slew many of the Bards before leaving. His rage was unabated, he roared, "You gods are weak and pathetic. You want me? Come face me! I will end your pathetic existence like those of your worthless followers."

***

General Fin Nacht watched as the Sichuan was ripped apart by the red drake, Jason Yinglong. Jason turned back into his mortal form, revealing the many scars on his body where the iron pierced his skin. He had jagged dragon teeth and his one blue eye glowed with hatred. The allies that broke him free finished off the guards and turned towards him.

General Nacht saw his life flash before his eyes and kneeled in terror. Madam Yinglong walked out and stroked her son's hair. "Do not taint your claws with his blood. Remember, he saved me from the wrath of his leader. You have exacted vengeance on the one who harmed and betrayed you. That is enough."

Jason lay his head against his mother, tears dripping from his one good eye. She held him and looked at General Nacht. "You had the best leave. I may have been able to reign in my son's impulses, but his friends are still here."

Fin Nacht nodded and bolted. He soon grew tired and collapsed on the ground outside Angela's Grove. He awoke in a prison cell with Lori Nacht, his niece, standing over him.

"Welcome to Hunter prison, uncle. My master brought you here until such a time as he deems you worthy of being released back on Norvcryog."

"So you are a traitor?"

"I am. I owe the Hunters greatly. They rescued my sisters and brother from being devoured by the forest. They care more about us than any of the Nacht family did. You lot didn't even bother to attend father and mother's funeral."

"Get out of my sight. You are no longer worthy of calling yourself a Nacht."

"So be it. Enjoy your stay." She walked off, leaving her former uncle alone in prison.

Back at Angela's Grove, Changeling lay choking in a pool of his own blood. Wondra stood over him, her blade bloody.

"Any last words before I end you?"

"Suck my dick, you worthless whore. That's all you're good for."

She struck, severing his head, then she collapsed to the ground crying. Platina Danger held her close as she wept. Blanco Pantero took Wondra in his arms as Platina Danger vaporized the body of Changeling. They walked off with Blanco Pantero still holding Wondra.

"For the Daughter of Bounty Hunter 12, you surpassed my expectations." Platina Danger and Blanco Pantera stopped, then turned to see The Dragon. Wondra coughed, "What do you mean by that?"

"You are Bounty Hunter 13's twin sister, so to speak. Born from one of Bounty Hunter 12's wife's duplicates. She had the ability to duplicate herself. Each of her four duplicates managed to get pregnant with his spawn. You show great promise and I am offering you a chance to join the elite."

"Oh fuck off! I know your plans well, Lord Dragon. I don't want any part of it."

"Then you will die like the rest of these worthless heroes."

He vanished in a gout of poisonous green fire leaving Blanco Pantera to shake his head and walk off with Platina Danger beside him.

A spirit stalked through the ruins of Angela's Grove school. He was outraged at the display of power. The children of this school lay in pools of semen, blood and urine. All were beaten and broken down. All had been thoroughly used to the point of death for some of them. As the spirit beheaded the last of the grunts, he noticed movement in the corner of his eye. Another spirit lay in the corner whimpering and holding a goth girlnear his chest.

The spirit walked over. "Relax, David, she'll be fine. You did well in protecting her."

"She's so cold and weak. Why couldn't I be stronger to help them."

"You're only a teenager."

"Where were you?"

"I was retired."

"Had you been here, none of this would have happened."

"Maybe or maybe I would have died and this still would have happened. Who's tosay?"

"Why are you here?"

"Killing some Undertakers."

"Never show your face here again."

"Understood! Your girlfriend is healed. Now turn visible and let her warm up."

The spirit walked off, coming upon three girls chained together and being used by the Undertakers. Crymsin was sitting back, masturbating to their pained cries. She slashed the breast of the girl next to her and filled her cup with the girl's blood, then drank it. She sneered and struck the girl to the ground and put her feet up on the girl's back. She leaned back in the chair she had made of a girl and lit a cigarette with the candle near her left side. The candelabra was another girl bound and chained tightly so as to be unable to move.

Her head rolled to the ground and the men using the girls were slaughtered. The Undertakers fell dead as well. Bounty unchained the girls and undid the girls used as the chair and candelabras. He walked away after healing the physical wounds. His spirit continued on. He smiled and appeared near The City Under the Mountains. He entered the ruins and shook his head sadly. He quickly killed the zerkers as they slept off their drug-induced frenzy. He released the Goblinoids, Trolglin, Oruk, and Jottun. He moved on to the Underkeep. He saw Trollhammer smashing down a Dwarv statue andkicking one of the Gnomish Silverans. She whimpered. He then picked her up and was about to rape her when he fell, a stream of blood exploding from his chest. The Gnomish Silveran saw a flash of a purple blade but nothing else. She looked around.

Bounty smiled and healed her body, putting her to sleep. He continued on and saw that only a few Dwarv remained. The rest had been slaughtered. Their corpses were all over the place. Bounty began the task at hand. He carried all the bodies to the main hall. He layed them out and made sure all their pieces were together. He saw he had an audience. They couldn't see him, all they saw were their families' corpses being moved. A barrier formed, preventing them from accessing further. Fire erupted everywhere. Followed by a deluge and when the steam and smoke had cleared, all the bodies were gone in their place headstones. Some had caught a glimpse of a tall spiked man. Bounty walked out of the destroyed city.

At The Ruins a Wolf's Shattered Dream

Throughout the night, Dread Wolf paced the ruins of City Silver. All his hard work now lay in rubble. He heard many things through messengers. Trollhammer and his zerkers lay dead The City Under the Mountain had been reclaimed. Angela's grove was reclaimed and all but a few generals and commanders were slaughtered. The heroes reclaimed their city after their families and loved ones were rescued. Even the Rising Falls had been reclaimed. He kicked a stone, shattering it.

He howled at the three full moons in anger. The sky spilt down rain and a massive storm picked up. The Gods descended from the Havens. Their rage at Dread Wolf spurred them on. He smiled as they landed and attacked. He ripped into them using his teeth and claws. None survived his fury. As three Gods remained, he beheaded two and grabbed the female, Artemis. He pinned her to the ground andviolently raped her. He bit into her marking her as his. The next three days, he broke her. Reducing her to a sex toy, Bounty walked into the ruins.

"About time I caught up to you, Dread Wolf."

"What the fuck! How are you still here?"

"You killed me and left my body for the animals. Souls exist, you know. But regardless, I am not welcome in the Havens anyway."

"Ha! You are worthless. What makes you think you can beat me, if the Gods themselves can not!"

"I am the Demon of God Silver. His wrath made flesh. Now that my soul is unleashed from the body, I have no limiters. Feel my power and despair."

Energy erupted, sending Dread Wolf reeling. He clutched his head in agony as the PsyQi energy tore through his body. He gasped as a purple blade jettisoned from his sternum. He stared in wide-eyed horror.

"The funny thing about this blade is that it kills the soul. Goodbye for eternity."

The body of Dread Wolf fell empty. His body became dust and then vanished as if he had never existed. Bounty looked down at Artemis. He sighed. He lifted her up and cleansed her mind and body. She would still have the stain of dishonour, but she was whole. He set her back down.

"There you go, Artemis. Rest, I'll get you back home so you can ascend back to the Havens."

"Please kill me!"

"I can not. At least as a soul. This is the only blade I have and you don't want to cease existing."

"Please, I would rather cease to exist than live with what he did to me!"

"Artemis, there is another reason I say no. I despise you. I despise what you did to my land, what your people did to my homeland. I would gladly wipe you from existence, but if I do, what's to stop me from slaughtering the next God or Goddess who tries to conquer Silver."

"Please, I'm begging you!"

"Artemis! Sleep."

She went limp and Bounty picked her up and carried her to the location of Beatrix. He set her down near Beatrix's hut and vanished as Beatrix opened the door. Bounty saw that she had given herself war tattoos. She looked much fiercer now than when he worked alongside her. She looked directly at him and smirked. He smiled back and vanished. He arrived at his home and saw his little wives resting next to each other. The boy was at full mast while the girl giggled and stroked his member.

He gasped out when he saw Bounty and released his seed. He rushed to Bounty and hugged him tightly. "Master, you're home. I was so scared."

"I am still dead, Avol. But I am glad to see you alive. Once I get my body back, I'll entertain your desires."

"Yes! Thank you so much, master husband."

Bounty smiled a sad smile and went to his grove. He sat on his meditation stone. He turned towards the statue of God Silver. "Do I deserve them, Silver?"

"I can say with certainty that you do. Even the most reviled man deserves some happiness. You deserve them as much as you deserved, Feldspar. It could be argued that you don't, but I have no desire to start that argument. You are a living being."

"Then why do I feel I don't deserve their love and desire? Why can I not return their affection? They love me, it's true. They love me as much as Feldspar did. Why do I feel so apathetic? Why do I still struggle through existence? I have witnessed and caused so much death. I don't deserve anything."

"That is why. You don't deserve anything for your violent ways. But that is what makes this so special. They can look past your cruel past. They see you as theirhusband. They love you even after their death. Understand this you need to heal. This will allow you to heal. Your mind is filled with treachery and death. I know we tried to keep you from this war. You ended up being dragged into it anyway. Now as the continent rebuilds yet again, you must pull yourself from helping. You need to heal. Enjoy your family, Bounty. The horizon is dark."

Gods and Their Politics Part 1

God Silver sat surrounded by many of the other Silvers. Each of them played an important role. His was to watch. He sat in his wheelchair as his Angelus nurse extracted some poison from his body. The God Silver who gardens sat across from him. The God Silver who fights stood near the door smoking what looked to be a cigar. The God Silver who determines sat reclining and reading his grimoire next to Lizard Silver, as he called himself. The final ones, The God Silver who listens and the God Silver who speaks walked in. All of them looked tired.

God Silver looked at his group. "Is everyone here? Good, we have some pressing matters to attend to. As you all know, the New Millennium is upon us. As is custom, the other Gods have a chance to challenge me to become the New primary God of Silver. This is more difficult ever since my incident last millenia with the first Oni God. And then Bloodmare just a few decades ago. I have accrued many enemies and very few Allies. Now, more than ever, I need to rely on you a lot."

The God Silver who fights blew out red smoke from his mouth. "Worry not, old timer, I can fight on your behalf since I am you. I will relish the challenge."

"Yes, I figured you would like that. I also need someone to tell all the gods about the assembly. Whether they listen or not is entirely up to them."

The God Silver who speaks replied, "I will be your messenger." He then vanished.

It came to pass on the eve of the new millennium several hundred gods arranged themselves according to where they stood in regards to God Silver. In the neutral area behind the Seat of Nevermore sat many of the gods from different planets that had gained a following on Silver. Nevermore would be the voice of the neutral party. He stood facing the podium where The Great Silver Dragon stood. Along with him were Noctua, his daughter, the Sand Trio and their disciple, The Great Khan, Ophiuchus, Samedi, Nuka, Uncle Moon, Gaia of Silver and her son Titan, Lucky Seven, Ramah the Lightning Druid, Shogun III, and Slaan-ha-Ie. There were ninety more in the neutral party. They either came from various planets in Galaxy Silver or were from continents on Silver who did not care what happened to God SIlver

Only a few of the Allies of God Silver sat behind the God Silver who gardens. These included God Silver who speaks, God Silver who listens, and God Silver who determines. The others were

Eefreet of the Holy Flames and Bahamut from Diavonbre, Electranikka, Lucifer the Morning Star, and Mitra White Lotus from Misogoke. The Godof Si'n Mag, Feldspar, Nemesio the Feathered Serpent, and Ares Invictus sat to the left along with Demon King Oda, Lord Badger of Organos, and Zarkanus from Komodo. These were God Silver's staunchest allies. Or, at the very least, were allied with Continent Silver and thus God Silver. There were fifty more who didn't bother to show up since they had no desire to watch and or have fun fighting Silver.

Those that heavily opposed or outright hated God Silver were led by Athena of Noamaiza. They would have been led by The God of the Oni, but he no longer existed. They were numerous. She had earned the right since, in an alternate timeline, the Noamaizans had conquered Continent Silver. Then they got wiped out. She had just recently regained Godhood. Alongside her were Prisma of the Tuar, Alexander the Holy Cathedral, The God of The Oni formerly called Sol Invictus, and Old Odin One-eye. These were gods who hated Silver with a Passion.

In front of the assembled Gods Stood a massive Silver Dragon with ancient energy behind his eyes. Many Gods revered The Great Silver Dragon as the Creator. Next to him sat God Silver, who watched being tended to by his Angelus nurse. Also near him were Razorfang in his humanoid form, Zaratan the Island Maker in his Humanoid form, Thull Thanos of the Thulhuid, WARDEN, and The Burned Walker.

The Great Silver Dragon spoke, "You know the rules. Every God gets a chance to duel God Silver. If you win, you become the new main God of Silver. The planet's name stays the same, but you get all the power until the next Millennium fight. Begin."

One after another, the Gods, who wanted, challenged Silver. They were all beaten. Finally, Athena walked into the ring.

She smiled, "I challenge the real God Silver. Not this one. The real true God Silver. The one sitting in his chair. The old freak."

God Silver smirked, "You think just because I'm old and weak, you can beat me? Very well, girl. But if I win, you go back to being a mortal."

"Put your money where your mouth is, old timer."

God Silver stood with his flared energy, knocking everyone off their seats. The ground cracked with each step he took. He stood at full height, towering over Athena. She looked up at him. Seeing fire in his eyes, she gulped. He waved his hand. She was vaporized instantly.

"Anyone else wants to challenge me? I didn't think so." He walked back over to his seat and sat down.

God Silver who fights, smiled as the next one walked forward. She was young and unknown to him. Her skin was like onyx; she had six arms and four eyes. Her horns were jagged and curved back. She smiled and pulled out a flaming sword from her chest. He grinned and the two clashed. She blocked a killing blow with her shield.

This was when the unexpected and unforeseen happened. As she knocked him off his feet, a boy appeared. He looked like a miniature God Silver. Her blade connected with the boy. All six God Silvers were shocked.

The Great Silver Dragon looked at the boy. "It seems that we have a winner. The boy is a God Silver. So congratulations, girl. You win by technicality. Who are you?"

"I am Goddess Velris."

"I see, like the Goddess Rivles of Galaxy X. Very well. Congratulations, Velris, you are the new primary God of Silver. See God Silver for your followers."

"That's a problem, Silver Dragon. I have no followers except The Hunter clan. They will not want to worship a usurper."

"Then your duty is to find her followers."

"So be it. Come along, boy, we have much to discuss."

The Old Man Silver had the boy wheel his chair out with him in it. The God Silver who determines looked at speaks and listens. The three grabbed Velris and walked out leaving a dumbstruck fights to be consoled by gardens. The God Silver who watches finished scribbling in his notebook. The Gods dispersed. Eefreet and Bahamut gave dirty looks at the door the boy left through. Aquila the void walker, smiled and vanished to spread the word to the allies of God Silver of what happened. Their choice was to remain as allies to Silver or to become allies of Velris.

The first void walker encountered was Brinn, also known as the Skin Changer. She had been instrumental in the first War of the Gods. She looked at him with worry in her eyes.

"I felt a major disturbance. Almost as if the Balance had been shifted. What is going on?"

"God Silver is no longer the primarch of the planet. He has been replaced by Goddess Velris. You have a choice to make, young one. Will you maintain your allegiance to Silver or transfer it to Velris?"

"I am one of the four blades of Silver; therefore, my allegiance stands."

"Very good. This means you are to assist Velris if she needs it. God Silver is being forced to assist her as well."

"I have no plans of rebelling. I know what happened back in the day of the War of The Gods. I don't want to experience that again."

Aquila the void walker, vanished and reappeared near a large serpent temple. He raised his eyebrow and entered to see Victoria the third blade of Silver, being drained of her energy. He sighed. And looked at the giant serpent god.

"So Uncle Sandhands shows his true desire."

"Who are you?"

"I am the void walker. An associate of God Silver, now God of the Hunter clan. You have one of his allies trapped in what looks to be a machine designed to drain her immortality. I am sorry I can not allow you to go through with this."

"Hahahah, you think you can kill me?"

A purple blade jettisoned from Uncle Sandhands chest. He looked down at it in shock as he ceased to exist. "I know I can. Are you alright, Victoria?"

"Now I am, thank you. What was that feeling I felt earlier?"

"God Silver is no longer the primarch of the planet. He has been replaced by Goddess Velris. You have a choice to make, young one. Will you maintain your allegiance to Silver or transfer it to Velris?"

"I have always been loyal to Silver. I see no reason to deny my loyalty."

"Very good. Let's make sure there's no lasting damage from what Sandhandsdid."

He checked her over, nodding. He snapped his fingers and she vanished. Heblocked the blade of Grandfather Thundermouth. He then caught the second and third blade. Thundermouth snarled and stabbed at him with a short dagger. It connected. The Void Walker smirked, severing Thundermouth's four arms and then impaling him with the purple blade.

He saw the remaining Reptoids and spoke, "Don't try anything stupid. You don't want another War of the Gods. Consider their deaths my warning."

He vanished before they could do anything. He sighed and mentally warned every God on

Silver about the Reptoid's intentions. He also reminded them of The War of The Gods and how destructive it was.

Deep below the Veltan Scar, eight giant creatures awoke. In the Onyx Tower God Silver opened his eyes from his rest. He had finished talking to the boy who had lost his position. He smiled.

"So it begins."

"What was that old man?"

"The Gods grow restless. They are still furious over their loss to Dread Wolf. I will need your help, boy."

"Help with what?"

"My dear mortal Bounty Hunter 13 is jaded and tired from life. He needs his rest. Your job is to create some powerful children for him. Six of them. At least two must be twins."

"Why does this need to happen?"

"He cannot be everywhere at once. Even though he wishes he could. Two for continent Komodo, one for Sucryog, one for Misogoke, one for Diavonbre, and finally, one you can place on Silver. The one on Silver's goal, in the end, is to help Velris gain followers."

"Your favoured mortal has powerful children already. Bounty Hunter 26, Thirteen Hunter, Omega Hunter, Orion Hunter, and Grongar Hunter, to name a few."

"Ah, but they are trapped in the Haven of Dead Planets. Thanks to the machinations of the Shogun Clan. How those bastards descend from God Shogun is a question I have yet to find an answer to."

"Very well, old man, I will do so. What of the rumours of war?"

"If the gods wish to fight, so be it. I will summon my blades when the time comes. I feel, though, that none would be so foolish as to attack another god. Especially since I demonstrated what I was capable of. But if they choose to be idiots, I will entrust my cousin Ophiuchus to create a planet where they can fight to their heart's content."

"I can assure you that the war will happen here. I already felt the Chthonic Titans awake. Whether you like it or not. This planet will be ravaged."

"Will it, though? We've had four major meteors strike the planet. Our people have survived

Nuclear winter. Our people have survived the First War of the Gods. They will survive this."

"I hope you are right."

The younger Silver walked over to a crafting table. He studied the plans for a new race of Silveran's, their defining features would represent Velris. Two thick horns curved up from their foreheads, two to six arms depending on genus, and soft hair on their heads. While he was doing this, he began designing the children the oldtimer wanted. He smiled as the pieces came together.

"Old man, I have what you desired. Meet Sin Seeker and Midnight Seeker. They are a unity of all the Komodo races except Ganeshians, Rakshasa, Canis, and Gatorillo."

"I like them already. They do not stand out much; therefore, they can stay hidden much longer."

"Next, I have Nightmare. He will end up on Sucryog. He is meant to be very similar to his father. I designed him to stand out and be a fierce warrior."

"Very good, child."

"I have two designs based on the Neon Punks of Misogoke. This one here is Bridgette and this one is Margogonin, Margo for short."

"I like Margo. Fuse aspects of Bridgette with her. Give her a chimeric aspect."

"So something like this?"

Young Silver pushed the two forms together, creating a being split right down the middle.

"Yes, but make the combination less pronounced, then you got it."

"Alright. Next is Roanquake for Diavonbre. I made her plant-like in appearance to unify her with the continent's jungles and forests. Of which she will protect."

"Good, good. Give her a few aspects of both Efreet and Bahamut and we have ago."

"Very well. Lastly is Brandi. As you can see, I made her an exact replica of Velris. Minus the extra set of eyes. Her birth will mark Velris coming to power. So people will worship Velris."

"Good, that should appease the Great Silver Dragon. You did well, boy. Which makes me wonder how you were defeated so easily."

"When you just come into being as a blade connects with your skull, you cannot really defend yourself. I can prove my fighting prowess if you desire."

"No thanks, my body is old. My joints hurt and poison from Oni Sol and all those who despise me has made me tired. If you wish to spar, speak with God Silver who fights. I'm sure he would love to fight you for breaking his winning streak."

***

Ares Invictus broke through a crumbling wall as Aphrodite Areia slammed into him. He got up from the rubble and dusted himself off.

"That all you got, girl? I have been a war god longer than you, try harder."

"That may be so old man, but God Silver is no more. I can do as I please. I will kill you and take your power for myself."

"Ha ha! Very good. Then come Aphrodite of War! Kill me if you can." Aphrodite stabbed with her spear only to have it go through the wall. AresInvictus struck her hard from behind, sending her to the ground. He followed that up by kicking her so hard that she launched through the air and into a volcano. She walked out of the volcano and saw she was on Noamaiza. She snarled and lobbed a molten rock at Continent Silver. She returned to her havens in a fury.

She motioned one of her winged messengers over. "Bring this message to Old One-Eye, Oni Invictus, and Prisma. I desire to speak with them. Also, on your way out, get someone to bring me Athena's mortal form. I need my companion back."

The winged messenger saluted and flapped out. A Pale man watched impassively as a molten rock flew past him. He shook his head in disappointment.

"So it is true. Doctor Fluorescent stands at my doorstep."

"Hello, old friend, it's been a while. What do you call yourself now?"

"I am Sidrodc. Always have been. So why does the phoenix armlet stand beforeme?"

"The Gods will be going to war."

"Again? What set them off this time, a slice of bologna?"

"Rage and fury at their loss to the Demigod Dread Wolf. General fury at GodSilver. Some desire to conquer the land. A new head god was appointed and that lit the dry brush."

"Wait, Silver is no longer the head of Planet Silver?"

"Correct, he is just the God of the Hunter clan now. The new head god is the Goddess Velris, who is forged from onyx."

"I see. Well, how unfortunate. Just when I was getting used to God Silver the Fiftieth, he had to go and burn the cheese."

"Yes, well, I fear this is all playing into the hands of The Leader of the Pale Elves."

"Lord Dragon is nothing to worry about. Believe me, that he was a fool when I knew him and he's a fool now. A scheming fool. But a fool nonetheless. But why tell me this?"

"The fountainhead were the progenitors of all the gods and mortals beyond the Star Vale. We came through the veil to teach these mortals and help them evolve from their pseudo-beings. We became gods. Many fell into the trap of Godhood. That has only progressed. The Pale Elves came from planet Organos before it was erased in the big retcon. They were on par with us fountainheads. And while I trained you and you trained Thyne Gregor who was slain by Lord Dragon. Lord Dragon has been advancing since the time of Bounty Hunter."

"Yes, I am aware of the amount of time Lord Dragon has been alive. I suspect Velris will be good for Silver. The old man has constantly been ascending his other self and it has grown as stale as month-old crackers. We needed a good shakeup. First, the Gods found what it was like to be overpowered, then they took a nosedive when Dread Wolf slaughtered them all. Now we have a second war. I wonder which gods will survive and which ones won't."

"I wish I wouldn't survive."

"Ha! Suck it up, old man. I've been living in this mismatched form for millenia. Never will I see myself as a Fountainhead again. But it's fun to mess with people. I can't sit idly. No, I can't move at all because Chaos is a wonderful, wonderful thing!"

"You make less and less sense every time I meet with you, brother."

"Cheese for everybody! Tata Phoenix."

Doctor Fluorescent shook his head and walked away. He came upon the magma rock, now cooled. He saw young Velris sitting on it.

"What are you doing, girl?"

"Hello. Which one are you?"

"I am Doctor Flourescent."

"Ah, hi there. To answer your question, I am thinking. Also, am I going mad or did a massive mausoleum appear?"

"You are not going mad. Looks like Bounty Hunter 13 is going to sleep after his severe defeat at the hands of Lord Shogun."

"He's the one that Silver favours, right?"

"Yes, he is and if you were smart, you'd find a favoured as well."

"Hmm, is there anything else I should know?"

"If you wish to be as skilled as Silver, you would be wise to gather four blades for your cult. Silver has Ares Invictus, Brinn the Skin Changer, Nemesio the Featheredserpent, Lucifer of the Morning Star, and Victoria, rider of victory. These four fought by his side during the first War of the Gods and recently, Nemesio allied with him."

"I see, do you have any recommendations?"

"That is your decision. I will, however, point you in the direction that young Artemis is in her mortal form."

Velris arrived at a large druid grove. She was about to enter when a large grey man with fur and feathers on his cloak appeared in a swirl of feathers. He began to make motions with his hands. Velris tried to understand. That was when a blond woman in a turquoise uniform appeared. Velris could feel hellish energies from this new woman.

The woman spoke, "Uncle Corvus says that you should not be here, immortal usurper."

"I am not an usurper. I won legally. Regardless I am here for the mortal husk that was once Artemis."

Corvus began moving his hands again and the demon girl spoke, "Uncle Corvus says that the one known as Artemis needs to heal mentally."

"Tell your uncle I need her as my blade."

"Tell him yourself. He's mute, not deaf."

"What is a demon from the Hell Sector doing here anyway? Do you have sway over him? For if you do..."

Corvus growled then a booming voice, not his own, came from his mouth. "You do not speak to my niece that way. She is the daughter of Bounty Hunter 13. I am growing tired of you, Velris. Seek out Sekhmet. You may be surprised by what comes of it. Now begone from my sacred grove!"

As Velris fled, Corvus collapsed against the gate. His niece hefted him up to standing and placed his arm around her shoulders. She half carried him to the tree in the centre of the grove.

She lay him down against it. Then drew a protection rune around her as the tree pulled him inside. She placed a feather in her hair and then went into the large temple to Nevermore. She would watch over the temple while her uncle recovered. Her family was in the Havens and she was the only one alive right now. She felt alone.

A scratchy voice spoke, "Ah, little Lodi. I was wondering who was here in the temple."

"Lady Strigidae, I see you still live."

"Yes, my curse keeps me from dying. Oh, by any chance, have you seen Lucky?"

"Yeah, she was in my room last night. She should still be there. We had a goodromp."

"Ha Ha! Good on her. Good on you as well. Maybe you'll finally settle down."

"And what of you, Ava Ursa? Lucky cares deeply for you."

"I am old. I am not right for her. Duke is all I need."

"So you say, but I see and feel the way you look at her and my uncle."

"Ha! I suppose that I do desire someone else besides Duke to fuck my brains out, but I hold that desire in."

"I could help you as well."

Lodi smiled; she may not be feeling so alone anymore. Now that she had two willing playthings. She frowned and quickly went back into the grove. A portal opened and a red-haired Silveran with horns that curved behind her ears fell out. She was panting. Lodi hurried over to her and spoke, "You are trespassing in my uncle's sacred Grove to Nevermore. Who do you think you are?"

The woman looked up at her and whispered, "Rani, is that you? No, that can't be right. Please help them. They have been captured. I tried to save them." The woman passed out. Lodi looked at her and then around.

She went to the Tree of Nevermore and touched it. The Crow Daeva appeared. He looked at her and then at the woman on the ground. "Why do you summon me, Lodi Cacaphony?"

"Sorry, uncle is unconscious and Nevermore won't speak to me since I am not a follower. Who is she? And who is them?"

The Crow Daeva nodded his head. "I see... no... okay, I can help you."

"Uh, what?"

"Corvus is unhappy that I am sharing this with you, but time is of the essence. Corvus has five sisters that he has kept hidden from your father. Therefore, you do not know of them. They are in trouble. Congratulations, you get to help them. Please go through the portal. I will send you some backup. Destroy all who oppose you."

War, War Never changes

Lodi Cacophony-Hunter stood on a large plateau. She looked around her at the strange flora and fauna. One thing was for certain she was not on Silver anymore.

A tall man dressed in a black feathered headdress stood smoking a pipe. His reddish-tan skin glittered eerily in the moonlight. He looked up as a blond woman with horns appeared from a portal. He chuckled, "Ah, Lodi Hunter. Welcome to Gunmetal. I am Chief Swift-fang Coyote. I knew your father. The Crow of Death sent me an omen that you would be here. I am to help you find the ones taken from you."

Lodi was startled out of her awe. She looked over the man who had spooked her. His horns went straight up in a spiral. She shuddered at his presence. "I still don't understand. You are the one Nevermore sent to help me?"

"Indeed I am. We are to hunt down the fool who took your aunts and kill him and all who helped him. The first of your aunts is on this planet. I know where she is. She was purchased by a man who looked to use her to further his ambitions. She is bound in chains and unable to fend for herself. Shall we run as swiftly as Lord Roadrunner?"

"Lead the way Master Coyote."

"I am nobody's master. Regardless, I will try to run slow."

"I can keep up. Don't worry about me." Her hair became longer and more spikey and her horns became more jagged. She grew a tail from her waist and wings from her back. She grinned.

"Ah, a succubus bound to the soul of a mortal. How intriguing. Then follow demon. We must make haste."

***

By nightfall, the two had arrived at a large fortress. Heavily defended from all sides and angles. Swift-Fang Coyote spoke, "I will create a diversion. None must live. Can you handle this?"

"I have seen my fair share of death. I do not want blood on my hands."

"Then I will be the one to slaughter, just try not to get hurt in the explosion."

"You need not worry about me. I will kill if necessary."

"Let us hope it does not come to that. Here I go. Your aunt is in the back of the compound, near the mountain. She is being heavily sedated. He may also be trying to brainwash her. To snap her out of her trance, flash the symbol of the Hunter. Or hit her over the head with this stuff."

"You seem awfully familiar with what is going on."

"Don't worry about it. I have been spying on this place for a long time. Looking for a reason to attack and destroy it. The capture of your aunt has given me this reason."

"Am I just a pawn for you to use?"

"My dear girl, we are all pawns. Go save your aunt. Oh, and watch out for shrapnel."

He started to chuck grenades and fire missiles from a missile launcher she had not seen on him before. The compound lit up with explosions and she slipped inside during the confusion. Through the fire and the flames, she could hear mad cackling. She shook herself off from the creeping cold she felt. She soon arrived at a steel door. She saw the flames warp into a being that ripped the door off the wall. The flames followed her as she entered the chamber. She saw the man standing there with a woman wearing teal with turquoise horns that had small flames on them.

The man said, "You are too late to save Kori Hunter. She is my puppet now. Slave, slaughter the little bitch."

Kori shot forward only to be slammed into a wall. Lodi stood there holding the staff emblazoned with the Hunter clan crest at the top. Kori cried out as her mind was restored.

The flames engulfed the man. He cried out, "No! Not you! Lucifer, I killed you. No, you will not take me. No!"

The flames vanished, leaving behind no evidence of any of the people this compound once held. Kori shook her head and groaned. She looked at Lodi, then blinked in confusion. She looked down at herself and touched her body to make sure she was still in existence

Kori spoke, "I am here, but I am also there. What the hell is going on?"

An androgynous being appeared wearing a fishnet body stocking and their body seemed to be altering between both masculin and feminine forms. Their hair was an onyx inferno that cloaked them.

It spoke, "The Hell indeed... Lodi Cacophony-Hunter, this is Kori Hunter-Huntari. She is Bounty Hunter 13's twin sister... sorta. Kori Hunter, this is Lodi Cacophony. She is Bounty Hunter 13's daughter... ish."

Lodi crossed her arms. "Lucifer, I should have figured it was you with the deranged cackling.

The hell was that? Was I just a tool for you to get to somebody who owed you a soul?"

"Yes and no. My dear girl, I claimed many souls tonight. My main goal with this was to reunite you with your darling aunt."

"Yeah, I call bullshit, but whatever. I am used to being a pawn. Comeon Kori, let's get you someplace safe."

As the two left, Lucifer shook their head and vanished. Kori looked around at the devastation and the one who caused it.

She spoke, "Oh! I know you. Chief Coyote, you found somebody to help spring me. I also thank you for giving her the tools to break me free from hypnosis."

Swift-Fang Coyote smiled, "I am glad to see you in one piece. Bounty would kill me if some harm came to you. I am glad you did not have to kill anybody, Lodi. I saw your guardian demon following you."

"Weird way to say nuisance, but okay, Guardian Demon, it is."

"Are you not a Guardian Demon to your sisters after they reincarnate? Lucifer is no different. You were once one of his children before you were summoned."

"Yeah, well, not anymore. I was fused with the soul of Lodi Cacophony. It still hurts me to see my family pass. When will that leave?"

"It won't ever leave you. You are immortal. Your family always returns to you. Also, soon you will have your father since he is an idiot who keeps fighting his fate."

"I guess you are right. Thanks… so how do we get off-planet so we can save the others?"

Swift-Fang struck a bell and a fiery portal opened, revealing a shapely grey-skinned woman with spikes on her forearms and two impressive orange horns.

He spoke, "Hanna, I'm surprised you came in person."

The woman spoke, "I was curious who had an Infernal Bell. It has been a long time since one of those has chimed. But it also figures one of Bounty Hunter 13's minions would have one."

"I am not a minion, ma'am. Do not treat me as such. Bounty and I have not spoken in thousands of years. He couldn't even be bothered to help me when the Magus attacked my planet."

Hanna sighed. "Yea, that sounds like him. I apologize on behalf of my mate. He can be a stubborn and forgetful man. Though I feel this is more a supernatural forgetfulness than actual forgetfulness. Almost as if you should not exist."

"Are you insinuating what I think you are?"

"Maybe, but we can discuss this later. Not in front of non-initiates."

Lodi scoffed, "I studied under Corvus Hunter. He takes care of me. You'd be surprised at all the things I know."

Hanna smirked, "Probably not as surprised as you think. Corvus knows things we do not and I am sure he taught you all of them. I think he is training you to replace him if necessary. As Bounty has Bounty Hunter 26, Corvus has you. So do you think you know what we are talking about?"

"Yes, The Book of the Forgotten, a book that has many names written down inside of it to keep them safe. But because of its name, the person exists physically but also does not exist in the memory of people."

Hanna blinked in confusion. "That sounds horrid. But that would explain why some remember the Chief here and some don't. I concede you know more about this than I do. Regardless, let's get you to the next sibling. Oh and Kori, you heard none of this, got it?"

Kori rolled her eyes. "Yeah, I know how it goes."

Hannah brought Kori and Llodi through the portal. Lodi looked around and frowned. "What planet is this?"

Hannah spoke, "Planet Bronze. Now I must be on my way. Look for Azolas Dul, he can help you."

A silky smooth voice spoke, "I am here already, Hannah. You know I don't like random Infernum Portals opening up. Who knows what could come through? My people are tired of all these damn Infernals trying to invade our land."

Hannah closed the portal after sliding through it. Lodi looked at the man in front of her. He had metallic bronze skin and wore a black tusked gas mask over his mouth. His eyes were crimson slits and he had no nose. He also wore a coat over Copper chest armour. On his back was a nasty-looking double-bladed voulge. He had a purple topknot and the rest of his head was bald. To her, he almost looked like one of the Djinn from Diavonbrey back home.

Kori spoke, "You must be Azolas Dul? You know where my sister is?"

Azolas spoke, "I do indeed know where she is. The Cult of The Black Oblivia Lord has her to use as a sacrifice to summon the Lord of Destruction and Rebellion, Mahzune Dazun. He is one of the few Infernal Lords of Order. He represents HOPE but the Cult of the Black Oblivia Lord desires to summon him to take Bronze in his name. They have seriously misunderstood his domain.

Regardless, he is a very dangerous Godling."

Kori sighed, "Well, can you bring us there or not?"

"Ha, you are the impatient one. Yes, I can. We are here. I do not know where the altar is specifically, but you should be able to find it."

Lodi was searching with her mind's eye. She found the location. "Mr. Dul, can you plant a bomb right about here?"

"Yes, what kind of bomb do you need?"

"Strong enough to break through stone and metal."

"Here we go... why here?"

Lodi formed a psy bubble around the bomb. It exploded, creating a large hole. She dropped down, followed by Azolas and Kori. They landed on the altar and Lodi immediately grabbed the woman on the altar and leapt back up. Azolas looked at the dazed Cultists and smiled under his mask. He withdrew his voulge and ripped into them.

He tossed some guns to Kori, who shrugged and opened fire. He tossed a bomb towards the machine that was going to be used to tear a portal to the Sideways, which is where the Obliva Gods resided. He grabbed Kori and jet packed through the hole as the bomb exploded.

Kori looked at the dazed woman and said, "Hello, Rani. Glad to see you in one piece."

Rani blinked, then shook her head to clear it. "What hit me and where am I?"

Azolas spoke, "You are on Planet Bronze and you were imprisoned by some cultists that no longer exist, thanks to yours truly."

"Ugh, you are way too cocky for my taste. I need coffee before I deal with you."

Lodi spoke, "Uh, I don't quite know where my next target is. Do you mind getting these two back to Planet Silver? Or even the Factory Moon of White Gold?"

"I can certainly do that. Thank you for getting me to these cultists. Your ride is here."

She saw a Stingray-shaped ship land. Its ramp opened and a balding man walked out. He had black and grey camo on and two guns at his hips. He smirked as she walked over to him.

"You are Deathknight. My father says you are the best gunslinger he has ever seen."

"Name's Luke Darkfaith, kiddo. Deathknight is my title and I am retired now. So please call me Luke."

"Thank you, Luke, for bringing me to my next location. Speaking of where are we going?"

As they walked onto the ship, Luke said, "Planet Grey. Lord Slayerhammer has kidnapped your aunt. He's hoping to ransom her. However, the ransom will not happen. I understand you would like to avoid killing, which is why I'm coming with you."

"I can kill if I have to."

"Oh, don't concern yourself. The Coyote told me you have witnessed quite a bit of death already. I would like you not to get your hands dirty."

Lodi sighed, "Thank you for your concern. I appreciate the thought."

"I do apologize. Do you want to fight? It seems you feel conflicted."

"The Crow sent me to rescue them myself since Uncle Corvus was unable to due to illness. I feel like I am not holding up my end of the bargain by letting others do the fighting."

"Ah, but you have rescued your Aunts. So to me, that seems like you are holding your end of the bargain."

"I... suppose if I look at it that way, I don't feel so useless."

"Here's a gun. Do you know how to shoot one of these?"

"My father trained me on a rail six-shooter. I think I can handle firing a .45 triple shot."

"Show me. We have quite a bit of planet-hopping to go. We are going a long way so we can get behind him, so to speak."

She looked at the targets and opened fire in rapid succession. All were direct hits to vital areas. "Satisfied?"

"Oh yes, indeed, you are good. You would make a great Deathknight. Thank you for humouring an old man."

"Thanks for letting me blow off some steam."

"Ha ha, we are here. Get ready."

She exited the ship to see a man dressed in spikey copper-coloured armour. He had a mighty hammer on his back that looked like it could smash up a person to indistinguishable mush.

"You have the ransom?"

"Are you Lord Slayerhammer? If so, yes, I do."

"Strip to prove you are unarmed."

"Do you want me to use the pole to dance as well?"

"Bitch do it or this goth bitch gets it."

Lodi removed her clothing, allowing her ample breasts to jiggle a bit as she dropped her skirt. She was keeping a close eye on Lord Slayerhammer and could see he was getting an erection easily since his tight pants left nothing to the imagination.

"Kick the skirt over here so I can grab the Credit chip inside."

Lodi pouted and then seductively stretched her leg in a way that allowed a bit of her vagina to show. He was sweating now. She grinned and lightly kicked the skirt over in a playful manner. He lowered his guard and his head became a fine red mist. Her aunt wiped a bit of the blood off her face and stepped aside as he dropped. She picked up the bloody skirt and looked in the pockets of it.

"You little minx, there's no credit chip inside. Nice job."

Lodi started to dress herself. "You act surprised even though you know what I am."

"Here, I have a spare skirt you can use. I don't want you to get this filth's blood on you. How do you know I know what you are?"

"You are Lucifer Ankara. The only surviving Ankara left. You are well known. As are your psionic feats. I also read your book "ThePhysiologyofIncubiandSuccubi.""

"Yes, I was taken in by the Ankara clan. But my real name is Lucinda Hunter. Call me Lucy. You know me, but who are you?"

"I am your niece Lodi Cacophony. Though I suppose it's Lodi Hunter now. Your brother, Bounty, took my siblings and I in after our house was destroyed. He helped raise us alongside our parents and became like a second father to us."

"Oh, you are the one I spoke to when making my book. You had knowledge as a Succubus that was quite useful. But I always found it curious that you knew so much about Succubi even though you, by all accounts, are a mortal who has not dabbled in Infernalmancy."

"Wrong on all accounts. My little sister, also called Lucy, tried to summon me to give her the power to seduce her brother into impregnating her. Her older sister, Lodi, was watching over her and when she came to check on her, she tripped and fell right into my half-corporeal form, thus fuzing the two of our souls together permanently. The backlash caused the house to explode as her family was coming up the driveway."

"And she was unharmed?"

"Yes. I do believe it was Lodi who saved her. Lodi tripped in such a way that as our souls fuzed, causing the backlash, her body fell on top of Lucy as the house collapsed around them. And since she was now part Succubus thanks to the fusion, she was protected thus, Lucy was protected."

Luke spoke, "If the two of you are done talkin', you ready to lift off? I am going to take you to your final Aunt, who is imprisoned in Amber stasis on Planet Sanguine. My spy does not know what imprisoned her, just that she fears it might be for using her body as an incubator for something."

"Is there a reason she thinks this?"

"Get on and I'll explain on the way." The two boarded the ship and Luke continued, "About fifty-odd years ago, some Magus remnants split back off from the Mystics. They took the inhospitable Sanguine and terraformed it, making it their new base of operations. They then teamed up with a strange species from beyond the known space. These things are insect-like with black carapaces that are immune to most damage. The only thing able to damage this carapace is their scorpion-like tails and their acidic blood."

Lucinda spoke, "So you think they are using Mayari as an experiment in hybridizing these creatures?"

"While I can't say if that's the case, I fear it may be the case."

They arrived on Sanguine. Stinger one opened fire on the Magus stronghold.

While Luke was distracting the Magus, Lucinda and Lodi snuck into the facility. They were stopped by a man wearing red. He shook his head, holding them back. On his back was a trident emblazoned with a stylized Thulhuid head. They felt like they were drowning by just looking at the thing. They peeked around the corner to see a half naked teenager garbed in a black spiked carapace. She was currently raping a woman with purple hair, two curved horns on her forehead, and one cycloptic eye.

She grunted. "You will make many babies. You are strong."

An amber-skinned woman with black hair wearing pink spoke, "Marcia Wong, release my wife right now!"

Marcia spoke, "Sorry slut, but I am making my babies strong. Your sister is no longer here. I am the queen of the Zenos."

"Please, Marcia, I'm begging you to snap out of it."

"Shh… you will be next in line for fertilization. This meat sack must be filled first."

There was a large explosion and the wall caved in. A woman wearing bio armour walked in her frail form, barely able to stand. She vanished and appeared next to Marcia. She pulled Marcia off the woman allowing the aedeagus to be seen. She scoffed and grabbed the Insectoid-like helmet that Marcia wore. She ripped it off and swiftly finished Marcia off so she would not suffer from the wounds.

The man sighed and walked out. "Omega, what did I tell you?"

The woman in bio armour spoke, "Sorry, Uncle Cardinalis, I was getting bored. Who are your friends?"

"They were about to intrude on a discrete mission."

Lucinda spoke, "Meaning, we were about to blow the cover. What a mess! Oh hey, Amy."

The woman in pink blinked in confusion. "Lucinda Hunter? Ugh, what are you doing here?"

"Came to rescue my sister."

The purple-haired woman spoke, "I didn't need rescuing, but thanks."

"Oh, not you, Lee. No, my other sister. You there, Omega, where are the Amber Stasis chambers?"

Lodi spoke, "Wait, Omega! I thought you were still in recovery?"

The woman in Bio armour spoke as she lowered her hood. "Lodi? What in the Thirteen Hells are you doing here?"

"I came to rescue our aunt, Mayari. Uncle Corvus sent me in his place since he is recovering."

"Okay, this is getting super confusing. The Amber Stasis chamber is through here. Queen Zeno stores her prey in the Amber until she is ready to impregnate them."

The group walked into the storage chamber and saw that Queen Zeno had infested many of the Magus into her drones. Cardinalis finished each of them off since they were dying anyway. He then placed a mark on each of the Amber Pods that had somebody inside the pods were then teleported away. They finally reached Mayari's pod and Cardinalis placed a different mark on it that caused the Amber to melt, allowing Mayari to be free.

She spoke groggily, "Old man, what took you so long?"

"Sorry, sis had to play the role of babysitter." Mayari shook herself off and Cardinalis helped her up. "Can you walk?"

"Don't have land legs yet. Ugh, my head. I feel like I just got done partying after a show. Only, the only naked chick is me."

"Not quite. Captain Lee Tangara is also naked."

The purple-haired woman spoke, "Yeah, thanks for the reminder. Now can we get out of here? My nips can cut glass right now."

They walked outside to see Stinger One waiting as they boarded. Both Mayari and Lee were placed in quarantine in the event they had been impregnated with the alien creatures. The Magus facility was in ruins and all the zombie Magus were dead. Stinger One fired a missile as it lifted off that vaporized the facility.

Luke finished his scans and nodded. Cardinalis spoke, "So what is the prognosis?"

"They show no signs of being pregnant nor are either playing host to a queen hybrid, unlike Marcia."

The two looked at the dead body of Marcia and Cardinalis shook his head. "We had still best get them to Hunter Corporations HQ on the Factory Moon White Gold."

"Not a good idea. I suggest Hunter Station. It's smaller and far easier to contain a creature than a whole planet."

"Hmm, you are right. Set the course. I also have samples from these Zenos; they seem oddly familiar to me."

After the group was dropped off, Omega stayed on Stinger One. Her image disguise dropped, revealing a red and blue-haired woman with Pure Silveran features. Luke looked at her and then smirked.

"Quit staring, Luke. I had to disguise myself as Omega. She was the last one I was in contact with before the battle between the Hunter clan and Shogun clan."

"I said nothing, Cherry. I don't know why you even bothered to hide yourself."

"Shogun Yu is still looking for any surviving Hunter clan members. If he is not slain soon, his corruption by the Dragon will be complete. Then the Dragon will have another puppet to play with."

Rhapsody in Grey

Gunnar Rhapsody stood on the outskirts of The Upper Depths. He was awaiting a man Coldharbour had ordered him to accompany. Gunnar could feel the eyes of the Taur Bisonom guards on him. As he was a grey-furred and blue-skinned Taur Anubi, he was considered dangerous. He was, after all, a spitting image of the Taur traitor, Bounty Hunter 12.

A large Hydra Class ship came into view. Its jets hummed as it skimmed the water. It then stopped at the dock and a woman wearing a white duster walked out.

She spoke, "Grand Commander Gunnar Rhapsody?"

"I am."

"Not much for talk huh? Names Beatrix. Come aboard and we can set off."

Gunnar followed and looked around. He raised his eyebrow at the eclectic group before him. At the head of the group was a massive Primata bulging with muscles. He also saw the Silveran woman, an Oni of Komodo, an Elf, and a Dwarf. He snorted.

The Primata lumbered over to him. "You are the final piece of the puzzle. I am Predator Apex of the Primata. Welcome to the Eclipse. Now all of you listen up. Our mission is to hunt down a dangerous man. His name is Shogun Yu. He slaughtered my stepdaughter's family. She has asked me to hire the best mercenaries money can buy. But since I didn't have much, you lot will have to do. That is only the cover mission. Now in actuality, we are collecting a dangerous artefact for my friend Amari Hunter. It is a book that has been hidden away in a complex devoted to Lord Badger. As I understand to unlock this complex, I need Taur, Silveran, Oni, Elf, and Dwarf blood."

Gunnar snorted, "I have been to the Island of Lord Badger. You are correct in the assumption that blood is needed. However, the blood does not have to be spilled. As long as we are of pure descent, you should be able to unlock whatever the complex needs."

"Well, that is good to know. We will be arriving at our destination shortly."

They flew over the Island of Lord Badger. They could see many excavations going on. The ship landed at a large-scale excavation. A strange-looking woman walked out of a tent. She was pale blue-skinned with a purple mane of hair and strange tendrils dangling from her cheekbones. Her eyes gleamed amethyst and her sharp teeth reminded Gunnar of a Bladefin. Is she one of the taur experiments in genetics? I wonder. Hmm. This may bode ill.

She spoke in a harsh voice that reminded Gunnar of two swords smashing together. "You are

Predator Apex. I am Aurora of the Drani. You are the one who is looking for something significant, no?"

Apex smiled, "I am the one looking. But my friends and I must see The Labyrinth first. I have an idea of how to get through it."

"Of course, Predator. Right this way, please."

Gunnar followed the small group to a massive ziggurat. He frowned. The energy radiating from it was nearly blinding him.

Beatrix spoke, "Hey, are you alright? You don't look so good."

Gunnar looked down at her and then snorted. "I'll be fine. I am still standing. What of you? Can you not feel what lies behind these doors?"

"Oh yeah, but when you are stuck working for Bounty Hunter 13, you get used to overwhelming psy energy very fast."

"Yes, I suppose that is equally true for you as well. And possibly that Oni girl."

"She is mysterious, no? But you are equally mysterious. You seem to know quite a bit more than you are letting on."

"I am from the loins of Coldharbour. So I may or may not know what is about to happen."

"Gross but useful."

They were soon at the door of the labyrinth. The massive symbol on the door glowed ominously before the door rumbled open.

Apex Predator spoke, "Welcome to Lord Badgers Labyrinth. As you can see, there are two doors before us. One requires the blood of the first ones and the other requires Silveran blood. I do not know why more do I particularly care why."

The Elf spoke, "Should we not be concerned why? After all we are walking into paths unknown."

"Thing is, like I said, I do not know why."

Gunnar rumbled, "The first ones were the Lizards. Followed closely by the Elves, Dwarves, and Thulhuid. As the symbol is of Elven origins, you can see why Elf's blood is needed. The second symbol is of Silveran origins. But it is ancient Silveran, meaning those with Silveran blood can open it. The first Silverans looked like the Taur. Then the ones commonly associated with Silver and finally, the Oni. Each one replaced the one prior. So they say."

Apex scoffed, "Whoever they are, they certainly created an annoyance."

"You are not wrong, Predator."

The Oni spoke, "But will it open? I am not full Oni. I am Green Silveran with Oni heritage."

Gunnar chuckled, "Yes, Gilda, it will work. I am full-blooded Taur, and Beatrix is full-blooded Silveran. The door will open. What we find behind it, I do not know."

"How do you know me because I do not know you."

"The Doomshroud before you had your child and before that bastard Shogun III killed me."

"Oh wow. You were the stranger that seemed to be Bounty's shadow."

"Yes."

The doors cracked open and then fully opened, allowing the small team to split up. Predator Apex went with the Elf and Dwarf, while Aurora went with Gunnar, Beatrix, and Gilda. Gunnar looked around at the walls and then snorted. He stepped down on a pressure plate and the walls shattered as the traps crumbled.

"This place is ancient. I highly doubt any of the traps work anymore." Gilda smirked, "Oh, so it's going to be boring."

Aurora shook her head. "Just because some spikes and darts don't work at first does not mean we should let down our guard. Lord Badger was crafty. Craftier than some others. Who knows what else he may have in store for us here."

Beatrix just continued to walk forward. She kicked open a wall and continued through other walls, not even trying to figure out traps or puzzles. They soon arrived in a long corridor with many murals on it.

Book of the Forgotten

Aurora examined the murals intently. She was taking pictures and etchings and examining them through an aura lens.

"This is incredibly fascinating. This details the Forgotten. There are names here that are not in any history book. It also seems that there is a lost continent of Silver."

A voice spoke with a strange, almost rocky accent, "Not lost, my child. Hidden away and forgotten by even The Writer himself."

Beatrix spoke, "Hello, old man. I thought I felt your presence."

"Ah, Beatrix Badger-Oda. Goddess Silver's little mortal. And direct descendent of the Conqueror himself."

Gunnar looked at the man before them. He looked like a pure-blooded Silveran, except he had scales all over his body instead of smooth skin like a regular Pure Silveran. He also had rough hair instead of the smooth hair. The fact of the matter was he looked like a lizard.

"What are you?"

"I am a Silveran or what would have been the Silveran species had the Dragons been allowed to finish their creation. Had not the Fountainhead come to our planet, this is what the primary species would be. I am God Silver. Or Lizard Silver if you feel uncomfortable. I was the firstborn of The Great Silver Dragon. He was my father, with Gaia Silver being my mother."

"I see. Hmm, very interesting. You seem to hold no animosity towards the Silverans. Nor the Silver Gods."

"Old man Silver and Goddess Silver do not bother me. Therefore I have no animosity towards them. I am also quite happy with how they have organized Silver. The Old Man is a broken man. He stays hidden. I think that is where the other Gods' animosity lies. They have been left to their own devices. As I am Silver, so to speak, my devices are his devices."

Gilda snorted, "Of course, that makes perfect sense. So why are you here?"

"I am one of the Forgotten. Did not Apex Predator tell you? He is searching for the Book of the Forgotten. This book has written in it everything The Writer forgot in his great rewrite. And he forgot many things. As such, since we Lizard Silverans were forgotten, here we are."

Gunnar smirked. "Before you open your mouth Gilda be aware. Just because something is forgotten by the many, it can be remembered by the few. The Scale folk believe in the Great Silver

Dragon. Thus he exists, but he is the one who remembers what his children could have been. Therefore Lizard Silver also exists. As he exists, so do his people."

"I see, but how do you know this?"

"Because Coldharbour, the God of the Taur, was forgotten. The Taur forgot him. But he exists because he was originally God Silver. As God Silver exists, so too does he only at a weakened state. We Taur were the Original Silverans. Then the spiky guys came along and we have been at each other's throats since then. As I am the only follower of Coldharbour left, I know many things that should not be known."

Aurora finished with her examinations and turned around. She walked over to a door and touched six glyphs that glowed. The door vanished. And they walked through only to bump into Apex.

Apex was panting. "Aboot damn time you got here. The Dwarf and the Elf are both fighting strange-looking Silverans."

Lizard Silver walked past them and the sounds of fighting ceased. Gunnar caught the Dwarf as he was tossed aside while Gilda got barreled over by the Elf. He set the Dwarf down and helped Gilda and the Elf up. They entered the chambers to see the Lizard Silverans bowed before Lizard Silver.

He turned to them and spoke, "Apex Predator, you seek the Book of the Forgotten. I can give it to you, but first, you must offer me something in return."

Apex dusted himself off. "What do you seek?"

"Zakar, stand and step forward." A female did so. "You there, Bull, impregnate my daughter."

Gunnar chuckled, "And why should I? What is in it for me?"

"Do not the Taur experiment in genetic manipulations?"

"Ah, I see. You wish to see what two original Silverans would produce. Very well, I will do as you ask. In private."

"Go to the altar and do so."

The two walked to the altar. She whimpered and lifted her tail ever so slightly so her musk could be smelled. Gunnar put up a shield that made them invisible and he entered her. Her spike tail wrapped around him, cutting into his skin as she convulsed in ecstasy. When he was done with her, he was bloody and the altar was rubble. She lay on the rubble twitching and Lizard Silver chuckled.

"Well done, she is filled with eggs. You have earned the book. And earned my trust."

"Thank you, Silver. I hope they are what you seek."

The small group was teleported from the temple. They appeared in a space station. It was empty except for a few flickering lights. Many runes lit up and the station was bathed in a haunting blue glow. The book glowed as well and a woman who looked like Bounty Hunter 13 appeared.

"Ah, Predator Apex, I see you found the book I have been searching for. Now to undo what was done. Gunnar, please stand on the glyph that has the crest of the Rhapsody, Gilda, please stand on the glyph that has the crest of the storm of Susano'o, and Beatrix, please stand on the glyph that has the crest of Lord Badger. Elf girl, please stand on the crest of Silver, Dwarf, please stand on the crest that looks like boulders falling onto an anvil, and Apex, please stand on the glyph of the forest. I do hope I have enough power."

The shadows formed up into a demonic shape behind her, along with what looked to be a man wearing a badger mask. Also barely visible was a man cloaked in feathers that made one sleepy to look at. The three channelled their power into her and she let out a cry as the book opened. The station shook angrily. A grey wave washed throughout the galaxy of Silver. As it struck Planet Silver, a new continent appeared.

Deep underwater on Silver, old Thul Thanos awoke and grumbled as the tides changed. He searched for the source of the change. And saw a continent that should not have been there. He curled his face tendrils into a frown but felt a presence. He nodded and closed his bulbous eyes, the tides continued as normal.

The gods shuddered as the wave washed over them. Even Silver, who was unaffected by these things, couldn't help but shiver as the Forgotten became known. He looked down at Lizard Silver.

"So you come back. Ha! I love it. Help wheel me into the common area. I am sure the others have questions."

Lizard Silver nodded and pushed the wheelchair with Old Man Silver into the planning room. He stopped him at the head of the map. The other Silvers walked in.

They looked at the newcomer and God Silver, who Speaks spoke, "So what am I looking at here?"

Old Man Silver smiled. "Well, boyo, you are looking at what the Dragons wanted our kind to look like. However, Zmatek fucked that plan with a rusty machete. Zmatek wanted control of Silver; he tore that from the hands of Gaia Silver. He usurped her and was soon embroiled in a war he could not win. You know the rest. Meet Lizard Silver, God of the Lizard Silverans. Also, examine the map. You can see the Continent of Fantasy has reappeared. The continent was where the beings from Terra-Aert landed after their planet was destroyed. It is the land where the Serpenti and Gargoyles originate from. It is also home to The Crater, a large city made from the remains of a meteor that old Zmatek smashed into Silver to wipe out all species. So he could make Planet Silver in his image and become all-powerful. You know, classic villain stuff."

"I see there are also new landmarks. Should we be concerned that this weakens the barrier? I fear The Dragon will make his move."

"It does, but we want the Dragon to begin his plot. In the end, it will allow us to win against him. This shows that a new continent can become existent."

"What are you planning, Old Man?"

"Our time is coming to an end."

"What are you talking about?"

"You will see soon enough."

Eden Tower

Gunnar reappeared outside the Ziggurat, which had vanished as if it had never existed. He shrugged and waited. The others had soon appeared. However, the Elf and Dwarf looked worse for wear. Gunnar snapped his fingers and the two vanished. Apex was holding up Aurora, who looked really sick. Beatrix looked dazed and in a trance.

Apex spoke in his rumbling voice, "She is having an adverse effect to whatever that was. I think she was staring too hard at those fellows who appeared behind Amari Hunter."

Gilda threw up and then spat, "Okay! What in the Thirteen Hells happened?"

Gunnar spoke, "We just helped the Galaxy remember many things lost to them when The Writer rewrote the Universe."

"Okay, who is this Writer?"

"He is. Ugh, how do I put this? He is the one who lives beyond. He is the Eternal who wears a flowery shirt. He is the Creator. I am sure you have heard the theory that we are in a book. But who is the one who made our book? He is."

"I see. So when our story, so to speak, ends, so do we."

"Yes, but also no. A story is meant to be read over and over and The Writer likes his stories."

"Great, just another pawn in someone else's game. Ugh, mortality sucks."

"I have to agree with you but look on the bright side. We are about to have a fight on our hands."

The small group was surrounded by a platoon of soldiers. These soldiers had the emblem of chaos on their armour. Gunar brandished his axe and grinned a dark grin. Gilda unholstered her gun, Apex beat his chest in a display of dominance, and Beatrix shot forward. The soldiers fell and exploded into confetti which then also exploded. Beatrix was thrown by the explosion.

Gunnar leapt up and caught her. "You alright, girl?"

Beatrix shook her head. "What a nasty surprise! But yeah, I am fine."

Gunnar smiled, "Of course, I would not expect anything else from something the Lord of Chaos conjured."

"So we need to find the head and cut it off."

"Easier said than done, I'm afraid."

Aurora spoke, "Those were only scouts. Come I know where he is heading."

They followed her and arrived soon at a massive Onyx tower. Gunnar stared at it and spoke, "This is not one of the originals."

A voice spoke, "Oh, but it is. Zmatek tried to use this tower to remake Silver in his image. This was during the War of the Gods. He hid a copy of himself and the spiked Silveran species inside it. And now you have unearthed it. Not bad. But unfortunate for you."

They looked at the man wearing the Chaos Armor. Gunnar growled, "Lord Chaos, I presume?"

"Right on the money. Now I will kill you and claim what is my birthright."

"Come then, if you desire death, I will grant it to you."

A beam struck Chaos and a man covered in scars appeared. "Sorry, Mr. Rhapsody, but I will take care of this."

"You are?"

"I am Odin Hunter, son of Bounty Hunter 13. I must thank you for helping the world remember me."

"He's all yours. Just let me grab some popcorn first."

Gunnar conjured some popcorn and a chair and sat down. He then conjured some more chairs. Gilda looked at the battle between Odin Hunter and Chaos. Then back to the chair. She shuddered, remembering the dark fire burns and sat down. Gunnar handed her a bucket of popcorn.

"Come, Beatrix, there is no point in joining this fight. This is a battle between gods."

"Sorry, I have to do something behind the tower. Be right back."

Beatrix hid behind the tower. She saw nine figures advancing towards her. As they neared her, she spoke, "About damn time you kids got here. Look, I can only keep the guise of Beatrix up for so long. We must perform the ritual while chaos is distracted."

One of the men spoke, "Of course, Elder Sister. Ifrit, Anubis, and Hades take up your position. Now Fire! Shiva and I will help Carrah. Let us banish this wretched tower from Silver."

Odin smiled and continued to assault Chaos. He then positioned himself just right. As Chaos sent a beam of pure chaos at Odin, he dodged. It struck the tower and the tower vanished from existence. It had been teleported to a desolate planet right before the Locked sector.

A serpentine humanoid stared at the tower. "I hope you know what you are doing, Silver."

The man next to him spoke, "Ophiuchus, Silver, thank you for creating this planet. He did not want to destroy his predecessor's greatest work. But he also knows that it would only spell disaster for Planet Silver should it remain."

"Well, Void Walker, I can't say I blame him, but holy shit, man. A fourth Silveran Species."

"Soon to be only three. If Lord Dragon has his way, the Silverans will be wiped out, as if they haven't already."

"That's tough, pal. But we should leave before God Silver awakes."

"First though, let us make sure that this Silver does not become Zmatek. I will need to forge new memories for him. You may leave if you desire. But it would be helpful if you hid this planet temporarily."

"Way ahead of you. Good luck, Void Walker. You will need it."

"Ugh, now she has her eyes on me. Thanks for that." Ophiuchus chuckled and vanished.

Back on Planet Silver, Chaos was broken. He sat before Gunnar. Behind Gunnar stood Odin Hunter and his siblings.

Odin spoke, "Kill him before he regains his power."

Gunnar replied, "He is a mere pawn in the real Chaos scheme. Remove his armour and he becomes powerless. I cannot help you with that. The backlash would probably kill me since I am of advanced age. You lot are younger, sturdier, more malleable than these old bones."

Apex walked over to the man and snapped his neck while twisting off his helmet. Odin and his siblings removed the rest. A brown portal opened and a man in a horned badger mask walked out.

He spoke, "I will take those. Plans must be made. Oh, hey there, Odin. Your father sends his regards."

"Tell the old man I've played my part. He better pay up."

Bounty Hunter 13 walked through the portal. "Tell me yourself, kid. Here's your payment. I hope it suits you better than it did me. Come along, Lord Badger, we have some armour to dispose of."

"Sure, Sure, but how long will it remain disposed of?"

They watched as the portal closed. Gunnar spoke, "Well, that was anticlimactic. Eh, oh well.

Apex, what is next on the agenda?"

"Nothing, I will return you to your homes. We are done here."

"Yeah, drop me off on Silver. I'd rather stay away from the prying eyes of the Upper Depths right now."

Death of Shogun Yu

Gunnar stood on Silveran soil. He was thinking about something. He then heard a commotion. He saw his old ally Bounty Hunter 13, get beheaded and vanishes. He also saw a girl with gold skin in a wheelchair about to get slain. He intercepted the attacker.

"If it isn't Bounty Hunter 13's apprentice Mayhem de la Sol, so you did finally turn traitor."

"Gah! Why is everyone in the know except me? Forget it. Kill Zion. I'm outta here."

Gunnar sliced through the soldier and wiped off his blade. He looked down at the girl in the wheelchair. "Zion, huh? How are you doing, kiddo?"

"Not a kid, but terrible. We failed. All but ten of us died. We couldn't even protect Queen Cashmere. That was our one goal. Why?"

Gunnar sighed, "I suspect Bounty knew it was a losing battle. How many did you say survived?"

"Ten, myself, Lava, Amodu Wenceslas, Belladonna Psycheo, and some weird aliens that Lord Hunter had gathered for our forces."

"I see. So, did you get injured during the fight?"

"I did not. Bounty kept me safe or as safe as possible. I have fragile leg bones. If I try to stand, they will shatter. He should have left me for dead. I am unsure why he tried to keep me alive."

A large golem made of magma rose from the earth. He spoke in a voice that sounded like a raging inferno. "You are alive. I thought I felt your presence. That is good. Who's your new friend?"

Gunnar looked at the massive creature. "I am Gunnar Rhapsody. I also once worked with The Demon of Silver. And from what I have experienced with him, he likes to try to do his best to keep as many people alive as he can. Even if it alienates him."

Lava chuckled, "Yes, I have witnessed that as well, but he is also a schemer. If he thinks you still have a part to play, he will keep you alive to play your part. Hence why even though Mayhem left herself open for attack many times, he did not take advantage. For all logical reasons, she should be dead by now, but she still has a part to play hence her living status."

"So he could have prevented the betrayal but chose not to?"

Gunnar spoke, "Yes and no. See, had he prevented the betrayal, it would have altered the timeline. Something he is forbidden from doing."

"Stupid is what it is. He should have done something."

"And that is why he is hated by many. They see things the same way you do, but as he is also one of the four, he is forced to play by certain rules."

Zion spoke, "The four. Never heard of it."

"Nor should you have. It is a Druidic secret. Only a Druid can explain them to you, but you are in luck, as I am a Druid. The four. They are ascended. They hold sway over the four dimensions connected to the Grey. The Grey is our realm. Connected to Grey is the realm of chaos, the realm of the Inbetween, The Shadow Lands, and the Pure World. Also, the Infernum, but there is nobody in command of the Infernum. The realms keep balance. It can neither go one way or the other or else untold catastrophe will happen. Lord Shadow is the Master of the Shadowlands. Lord Shadow is Bounty Hunter 13."

"Oh, I see. I think I get it. Even if he wants to help, he has to obey the laws set for him as The Shadow Lord."

"Unfortunately, yes. Therefore even if he sees an event, he can't interfere."

"Ugh, anyway, thanks for the help. If you could, can you wheel me to the port so I may get a ship to get back home?"

"Yeah, but I would request you tag along with me for a bit, both you and Lava. I am needing to examine something, then find someone and kill them."

Lava chuckled, "I am all for revenge. I will join you. Hold on while I solidify and cool my body a bit."

Zion spoke, "I suppose I have no choice in the matter. I need somebody to push my chair. It has wheels instead of a hover unit. Too poor to afford a hover unit hence why I joined up with the Hundred so I could get paid."

"Gunnar raised his eyebrow. "And how were you going to get paid?" He then seemed to be lost in thought. "Ah, I see. Bounty says to check your account. He has wired payment to you."

"Uh, what? Whoa, okay, that is a nice payment, but how?"

"I can communicate with his soul. He is dead, but his soul is stuck in this realm since he's not accepted in the Havens. His body will piece itself back together over the course of a few decades.

In the meantime, he can still do things as normal."

"Well, I can finally afford the surgery I need to strengthen my legs. Maybe it won't be so bad now."

Gunnar pushed the chair over to one of the small ships that survived the battle with minimum damage. He looked at the dead bodies and sighed. He set Zion in the shade of the ship and began collecting the dead. When he was done, he saw a black stone that he enchanted. As he placed the stone atop the bodies, they lit up with gray fire.

"Thayme Sidrodc uigde het seul, thayme Havens sunocum het seul."

He downed the amber liquid and tossed the empty glass on the fire. It vanished, leaving behind the stone glowing with many names. The stone then vanished as well.

Lava spoke, "What was that?"

"That, my fiery friend, was something only a follower of Coldharbour can do. I allowed their names to be forever immortalized in stone. The Hundred will go down in legend. And when any remaining Hundred passes from this world, the stone will appear at the time of death and immortalize their name. Their souls may be in the heavens, but they will be forever remembered for the cause they fought. Even if it was a losing one."

"What of the traitors?"

"They, too, will be honoured. After all, they too fought for what they believed in."

"Awfully generous, considering that Silverans don't like treachery."

"Ah, but I am not a Silveran. I am Taur. We honour warriors, scientists, and bards. We also honor traitors well, most traitors, the only one profoundly despised by the Taur is Bounty Hunter 12. He not only was a traitor to the Taur but also a traitor to the Silverans. He would have been honoured had he chosen one path or the other, but instead, he chose neither. Some would say he broke certain taboos of the realm. And they would not be wrong."

"I see. Interesting... I have only lived on Mt Silver. This is my first foray into the lands of your meat bags. My wife, Fire Ruby, insisted I leave for a bit. She is going through the form change that all Silliconites go through at the turn of the millennium. She needs space because she will lash out. I also need space. We have been together for a millennium."

"Ha! Well, I am sure you are getting quite the experience."

"Speaking of... who is it you desire to slay?"

"He is called Shogun Yu. He was a Gatekeeper of planet White. He and his men severely injured many crewmembers of the Starship Doomshroud. His hammer split my skull. He also came to Silver. He was encouraged by Lord Dragon to attack Bounty Hunter 13 and his family. They slaughtered them and those they did not flay, gut, behead, or dismember, they tricked Bounty into sending them to the Haven of Dead Planets, where they will be trapped for eternity."

"Oof, that is nasty. So you seek his head?"

"Yes, but not because of revenge. But because of fate. I was fated to kill him the moment he bashed my skull in. He and I were linked at that moment. It shall be my blade that removes him from this land."

"Fates change. How do you know it will be you? I digress. Do you know where he is at?"

"No, but I know somebody who does. She lives in Junk City. Which is where we are going."

"I know the place well. I will meet you there."

Lava vanished. Gunnar boarded the ship and pushed Zion to the helm. He buckled her down and lifted off. A few sputters and dips later, the ship thudded outside a large gated city made of scrap metal and junked ships.

A man in combat armour stood on the upper walkway with a gun pointed at Gunnar. He spoke, "Who are you and why do you seek access to Junk City?"

"I am Gunnar Rhapsody. The girl next to me is my travelling companion Zion Glass. We seek shelter and to speak with General Plata."

"Alright, but no funny business."

The gate opened and Gunnar pushed Zion into the city. As they entered, they saw a woman in an orange sweater and skirt fucking a girl in a purple jumpsuit against the wall.

Gunnar chuckled, "Hello, Welma. I am guessing Shaguthor is in the city."

She turned her head to him and then hissed angrily, "I'm busy! But yeah, he is. How'd you know?"

"Simple, you are one of his constructs. Based on the girl he was fascinated with as a mortal. However, she didn't see him as a good mate and desired Daphne the Executioner. When the mortals he worked with passed away, he created constructs of them to pass the time with. Even though they are mere shadows of his friends."

"You're good. He's in Syd's tavern. Hard to miss. Now get out of here while I enjoy myself."

Gunnar pushed Zion past the two girls and onto the main thoroughfare of Junk City. She looked around in wonder. She was awed when they came upon a large Ouroboros class science ship nose down in the dirt with a sign outside that proclaimed Welcome to Syd's tavern. Today's special is Micro Brewed Black Spine Whisky.

Gunnar opened the door to the ship and pushed a button allowing a ramp to settle into the dirt. He pushed her up the ramp and stopped as a large Hellclaw sniffed them.

"You no smell familiar. You look dangerous. Bad smell means a bad man."

"I can assure you I mean no harm."

"Hold on for a bit. Must talk with Syd. Syd knows what to do."

"Go on and get your boss then. I can wait."

The Hellclaw walked off and Gunnar lit a cigar. He leaned against the bulkhead. Zion spoke, "Uh, what was that?"

"That my girl was a Hellclaw. Bioengineered before the war with Noamaiza along with the Super Soldiers. However, before they were released from production to fight on the front lines of the war, Noamaiza attacked and destroyed City Silver. They used a powerful nuclear psy bomb to blow up City Siver. Western Silver was irreparably irradiated by the explosion. The radiation mutated both the Hellclaws and the Super Soldiers. The Super Soldiers became the Ultramutates like that fellow over by the bar. While the Hellclaws became twelve-foot-tall savage pack hunters. This one is far more intelligent than the others. The others can't speak, nor do they operate alone."

"Kinda cool, so do you think they have Umbral Dissonance here?"

"That some kind of booze?"

"Some very strong whisky. The only thing that keeps the pain at bay."

The woman at the bar finished talking with the Hellclaw. She walked out from behind the bar and looked Gunnar over.

"He's alright, Jakx. Seems harmless enough," the Hellclaw spoke. "Boss says fine. Eye on you."

Gunnar smirked, "I wouldn't have it any other way."

He wheeled Zion over to the bar and Syd handed her a black liquid that smelled like cherry.

Zion smiled and started to sip at it. Gunnar walked over to Shaguthor.

"Hey, Shaggy! Trying to forget something?"

"I am not in the mood for chit-chat Gunnar Rhapsody."

"Heh, well, it's not you. I'm after."

"You seek Shogun Yu. I know. He's on Komodo. Allied with the Xin clan of Oni Hunters."

"Why, thank you. Now I know where to go."

"Ugh, leave me be, please."

Gunnar walked back over to Zion. He sat down and was handed a silvery liquid that smelled of stone and wood. He grinned, "Coldharbour's elixir. How did you come by this?"

Syd spoke, "I can replicate any alcoholic beverage. One of the popular ones is Blood Whisky. The replication removes the harmful effects of the drink but keeps the alcohol. So with Blood Whisky, a being beside the Vampires who drink it will no longer experience a blood rage or Moon form. For Coldharbours Elixir, one will not experience the bone chill."

"Ah, but the bone chill is the part that allows one to fully experience the terror that is Coldharbour."

"Ah, but that part doesn't affect you now, does it."

"Alright, I'll bite. How do you know I follow Coldharbour?"

"Aside from the fact you are a Taur on Silver. I can tell you don't follow the Pyramid gods because you don't have the amulet of Anubis dangling around your neck. You also dress more than they do. I can tell from the smell of blood on you that you are not one of the scientists of The Upper Depths. And the main reason... that is a Hunter Corporation tri-barrel .44 magnaburst. The Taur hates Hunter Corporation. Something about Bounty Hunter 12 and his treachery. Only an outsider Taur would wield something like that. And most outsider Taur worship Coldharbour."

"Bravo, I'm kinda impressed, especially since Coldharbour has been mostly forgotten."

"No, he hasn't or haven't you heard about his new temple."

"Last I remember, his temple was lost."

"Well, a few decades ago, an island appeared off the coast of The Upper Depths. When a team investigated the island, they found a massive pristine temple dedicated to Coldharbour. It's said Coldharbour spoke to them. He's back."

"Hmm, I must be getting old. I have not been paying attention. But lately, I have been on various adventures. So risking my life has been keeping me busy."

"Seriously, you should check it out. By the way, who's the rock monster behind you?"

"He calls himself Lava. He is one of the last remaining hundred Guardians of Princess Cashmere."

"Wait, what? Princess Cashmere lies dead?"

"Yes, she was betrayed by her bodyguard and maid, Meyhem De La Sol."

"How recent?"

"Very Recent. Three days ago."

A green Oni walked over. "What of Bounty Hunter 13?"

"He lies dead. He died shielding the Princess from a hail of bullets. But one of the bullets pierced through him and hit her. She died instantly."

"That's bullshit. Bounty has nanomachines in his body. He can get riddled with bullets without pain or death."

"Ah, but that is the way it played out. He was quickly beheaded afterwards by Mayhem herself."

"But the nanomachines should have healed him."

"Not if he took them out."

"He can do that?"

"Maybe, I am unfamiliar with his skill. But he does have the tech know-how to be able to do something like that."

Zion spoke, "Every word he says is true. Bounty Hunter 13 shielded the princess from armour-piercing rounds. A stray hit her in the head, killing her. He sent what few still lived away. Only ten. He then tried to get me to safety, only to have his head removed from his shoulders. My assailants were slain by Gunnar. I still live. I don't know why?"

The Oni sighed, "Name's Gilda, by the way. I am one of Bounty's wives. I know he likes to scheme. He probably kept you alive to tell the story. Or he somehow knew Gunnar would arrive at your location and protect you. He works in weird and mysterious ways."

"So I have heard. I don't see why a lame-legged person like me should have lived instead of a healthy warrior."

"Who knows? Anyway, If you guys are going to Komodo to take on Shogun Yu, I want in."

Gunnar chuckled, "I am glad to have you."

"I'll show the Oni God I am not too old to fight."

Gunnar paid for the drinks. He then gave a bit extra for the hassle. Lava, Zion, Gunnar, and Gilda left the tavern. He then focused on where he needed to go and a bell appeared. He struck the bell, causing a deep reverberation that caused a portal of grey to open. He walked through and Gilda pushed Zion through with Lava following.

They arrived at a large temple complex with a large Spotted Ursar waiting for them, along with a Striped Felis. A Serpenti lunged at them with a hiss while a Syrein struck from the sky. Gilda let out a roar and caught the Serpenti mid lunge and threw her into the Syrien. Both struck the ground unmoving.

Gunnar looked at the other two. He then smirked, "I'm not sure I like the welcoming committee, Master Oswin."

An old-looking Wukong walked out. "They are simply zealous. No such thing for the old ways. Nor patience of time. How is the old bull?"

"I could be better. Seems I'm out of the loop."

"Ah, yes, the Temple Island of Coldharbour. Yes, I felt that change in my bones. I see you have students as well."

"Not quite. They are travelling companions. We are hunting Shogun Yu."

"Then your bell brought you to the right place."

Gilda spoke, "Uh, hate to interrupt you old geezers, but what the hell!"

Gunnar spoke, "We of Coldharbour can call upon the Bells of Coldharbour to transport ourselves to any of Coldharbour's temples. The Bell should have announced our coming. Master Oswin is an old Priest of Coldharbour. The only one remaining. He keeps his temple safe by turning it into a dojo. He has trained many a student in hand-to-hand combat and blade dancing."

"Are they going to be okay?"

Oswin walked over to the two on the ground. "Get up. You did well, but I am slightly disappointed you attacked first. I thought I taught you better."

The Syrien spoke, "You were right, Master. I apologize for my overzealousness."

"Ah, don't worry about it. Students meet Master Gunnar Rhapsody. He is the one who trained me."

The Striped Felis walked over. "He looks unimpressive. I always thought that you said he was a giant."

"I was a child. So, of course, he was a giant."

Gunnar chuckled as his body changed. He became more muscular and also much taller. "What about now, little cat?"

"Okay, much more impressive. But how can you shift size like that?"

"By not actually shifting size. This is my normal height. I was trained by Bounty Hunter 13 to disguise my looks using the PsyQi. It is something the Hunter clan is very good at."

"So why do you seek Shogun Yu's head?"

"He slew me. He was the one who brought about my first death. Therefore he and I are linked. Like Lord Psycheo to Bounty Hunter 13, I must be the one to kill him."

"Then you should know he has his children. They are all violent. Now they work with Xin Fang and his clan. They call themselves the Holy order of Oni Hunters."

"That is good to know, but they are inconsequential. When Shogun Yu finds he is in a losing battle, he will send them away."

"But if he doesn't?"

"Then they will die."

Oswin spoke, "Then I wish you the best. They are at the temple of the Holy order. You can see it from here."

"Yes, I see a burning temple. Wait, why is it on fire?"

"Another seeks their death as well. He was sent by the Oni God to purge them. He is called Zallerion Skulldancer."

Gilda growled, "That whelp. Come on, get us there. I can't have him showing me up."

Gunnar chuckled and they vanished and reappeared at the foot of the hill. He sliced through an Oni hunter that they had appeared next to. Gilda let out a roar and charged into the others, her chain blade slicing through them like butter.

The blue-bone armoured boy backflipped and landed next to Gunnar. "What's got her in such a frenzy?"

"You. She wants to prove to the Oni God that she is still worthwhile."

"Ah, his whole if they reach a certain age, they are no longer useful to me deal. Only young Oni can fight and hold places of esteem."

"Yes, that."

"I am not even an Oni."

"Oh, I know that, Arcanus Hunter. The only survivor of the Hunter clan Massacre by the Shogun clan."

"Jeez, you know me?"

"Sure I do. You have the same scent as your father. With a hint of mint instead of cinnamon."

"Ha! You must be Gunnar Rhapsody. I have heard of you from my father. He seemed to think you were more deserving of accolades than he. Also, I am not the only survivor. There was one more."

"Oh yes, I am aware of him. Oops, hang on."

Gunar sliced through an Oni Hunter that had been trying to sneak up on Zion. He wheeled Zion over to a large stone that he conjured.

"Where was I? Oh yes."

He waved his hand and a large bell descended from the sky. He rang it three times and vanished through a grey portal. He exited it as the chimes were causing Shogun and his family to reel from the soundwaves. He threw the children out of the way and stood imposingly over Shogun Yu.

"Hello, old man. Remember me?

"I do. You are that sub sapient who I smashed your worthless head in."

"I'm returning the favour, you worthless sub-sapient."

Gunnar split through Shogun Yu's head and tossed his body off the cliff. Gunnar stood waiting to see if the Shogun Clan would attack him. None dared, in fact, they fled as soon as they saw their patriarch die.

Gunnar vanished and reappeared by Shogun Yu's body. He lit a flame. "Thayme Sidrodc uigde het seul, thyme Havens sunocme het seul."

Gilda spoke, "Why do you honour him as a Silveran?"

"Because he will hate it. And he will be stained by the fact one of the Subsapients he despises has honoured him as one of their own."

Gilda chuckled, then turned towards Arcanus. "So Zalleron Skulldancer, you seem to think you can replace me. I can't argue the fact that you are a skilled fighter. I am not fond of the animosity Oni God has shown towards me. But I will leave you to your duties. Let's get out of here, Gunnar. I am tired of this."

"Calm yourself, Gilda. We still need to return to Oswin, then get Zion here to a good doctor to help her with her ailment."

Arcanus looked down at Zion and then smiled, "Oh, I know somebody who can help you. Go to the Upper Depths and ask for Doctor Amagi Tanuk. She is a skilled healer and Mechanic."

Gunnar snorted in disdain. "Well, since that is on the way to my home, I can get you there."

Gunnar, Gilda, and Zion vanished and reappeared on the steps of the great temple. Oswin was smoking a thin reed that almost looked like a Wonder Weed.

Gunnar spoke, "Master Oswin, I did not know you smoked."

Oswin smiled, "It's something I have taken up in my old age. And yes, this is a Wonder Reed. It certainly helps calm my mind."

"That is the point of them. Where is Lava?"

"He decided to spar with my students. He is skilled for a Magmatite, but why is he out and about instead of with the Silliconites of Mt. Silver?"

"Something about his wife, Fire Ruby, needing space while she shifts form."

"Ah, so the millennium is finally upon us, is it? I had best get my students ready then. Old Scar will be by to challenge me for his right to be the Dragon Monk."

"But he is not destined for that role, is he? No, I see great things for that Spotted Ursar."

"You see too much at times, old friend. Far too much."

"That is just the way I am Master. Hey! Lava! You done yet? It's time to hit the road."

"Why yes, I am. How was your workout?"

"Good but also bad. I fear The Shogun Clan is still too powerful."

"I wouldn't worry about it. I saw a weird cat talking to Yuenu, the forest maiden. Kept talking in the third person. Called himself Seethrassa. However, he seemed to be a disguise of some sort."

Gunnar watched as Oswin coughed out some smoke. "Oh yes, Seethrassa. I know him well. You are correct on many of your observations, Lava."

Lava chuckled, then spoke, "I am needed back home. I guess Fire Ruby messed up and I need to fix it. Can you drop me off at the nearest volcano?"

"Sure, let's go."

After dropping Lava into Mt Chakra of Komodo, Gunnar drove his ship to the Upper Depths. He arrived and saw a blond woman in a mechanics jumper waiting for him.

She spoke, "Hello, Gunnar. Is this Zion The Glass?"

"Yes, I am Zion. Who are you?"

"I am Leda Cacophony, also known as Doctor Amagi Tanuk. You are going to be my patient. I will allow you to walk again."

"I am unsure of this procedure."

"It's free. My father has paid for it entirely. It will not be invasive. In fact, we won't be cutting you at all."

"I see. I am interested now. I think I am ready."

Gunnar chuckled, "Then I will give you to the care of Ms. Cacophony here. May the Gray be with you, Zion. We will meet again."

"Of course, we will. I desire solace and the new temple island may be just what I seek. I will see you there."

"Goodbye for now, then."

Leda wheeled Zion into the gates and they shut behind her. Gunnar boarded his ship and flew to the Island Temple of Coldharbour. As he entered the temple, the statue woke and smiled.

Silver Destiny: Hunter Clan

Legendary Hero: Sin Seeker Hunter

Deep within the forest, Yuenu, the Blade of the forest, screamed fruitlessly at the sky. She struck the ground causing a small tremor to happen, which in turn broke a strange seal very far away.

An earthy monotone voice spoke, "What has you in such a mood?"

"Leave me alone, Dread Goddess. I don't need you to fuck up my life as well."

"Hmm, well, I suppose I can't help you then."

"What?"

"You were deceived by Bounty Hunter 13 in one of his many disguises, Seethrasa, I believe. I know your desire was to have sex with one male from every species on Komodo. But Bounty Hunter 13 ruined that for you. I can relieve you of the children in your womb. Erase what has been done so that you may continue with your goal."

"I accept. I do not care what that means. Do this and I am yours."

"Haha... do not worry about it. I have no need for your soul. It is done. It will be like I had sex with him and not you. That is what history will remember."

***

A hooded man with two thick horns protruding from his temples stalked through the night. He was looking for something specific. He came upon a large farm with a mansion at the top of the hill overlooking the farm to the east and a jungle to the north. He banged on the door and then placed a bundle on the step.

The owner of the mansion walked out. He was a massive man made of muscle. He had a short sword drawn as if afraid of something. He heard a gurgle and looked down to see an amber baby with grey eyes looking up at him. He saw a note on the baby that said, "Take care of my children. I am entrusting them to you to watch over and train. I am being pursued. Name them how you wish. I call him Sin. She is Midnight. I wish you luck, Lord Xiang."

"My lord, what has you in a fright?"

"Nothing but wind, Miaoyi. I found this by the door. The heavens have answered your pleas for a child."

A fox woman stood by a phantom. She smiled and spoke, "Lord Dragon, I have found the one you crave to kill. Xiang Yu hides out in a mighty fortress near the southern jungles. It should not be hard to find. He has it on a large hill overlooking the jungle."

"You have done very well, Daji. Send Zhou of Shang my regards."

He then stabbed Daji in the stomach and kicked her off the ledge that led to his prison. He looked over the ledge as her body fell and smiled darkly.

Miaoyi was in the garden teaching a young Midnight Sin to farm. Sin Seeker sat in his father's lap, listening as he recounted the pre-age. Where demons and monsters came from.

***

In the beginning, the void was dark. Then the Eternals were born, the Eternals consisted of The Writer, a man in a green floral button-up shirt, a grey tank top under the shirt, and blue cargo pants. He has Emerald and Black hair with an amulet. He also has a book that is wrapped in buckles and leather. He is the oldest of the Eternals. Whatever he writes comes true. He was the creator of all, including Damsel Death.

His little brother is Morpheus, the Dream Master, who is an enigmatic being who seems to warp in reality around him. Morpheus has an older brother, the creator of the planets Azrael, the Alpha Reaper, who is a black armoured man with a white energy scythe. He and Damsel Death are twins. Damsel Death is a pale woman with black hair and black eyes. She wears a long flowing dress that is etched with black runes. Her aura is pitch black and she is Azrael's twin. She was created by Writer for Azrael.

The youngest siblings are Devastation, who is a rough-looking man. He wears a black duster with a cowboy hat. He is always seen with smoke trailing from his mouth. He is also known as war and annihilation. He is an expert brawler and favours fists over weapons.

Then came Lust, a girl with pink hair. She is nude all the time. Fear, who is Lust's twin and is a girl who wears all purple and has pink and purple hair. She's always happy and joyful. The third girl of the triplets is Euphoria, who is a tall woman with long black hair and golden eyes with black clothing all over. She is always gloomy and depressed. She speaks in a monotone.

The Eternals worked the galaxy in their hands. The Writer had control over everything, but Devastation yearned for control. He tried to steal the Writer's book with the help of Lust and in doing so, he was cast out. Lust was punished severely, for she was once known as Love; her clothes were destroyed and any cloth or metal she put on would burn her. Thus Love became the darker Lust. When Devastation was cast out, Azrael begged the Writer to place a pure being to counteract Devastation. A man with white hair, eyes and clothes was created and his name was Xeltar Purified.

Darkness washed over the universe and the beings were made. On one planet, beings with pointy ears and slender figures were born. These were the original design. One was a man and the other a woman. They were placed in a lush garden by Azrael to protect them from Devastation. In the Garden were three special trees: the tree of life, the tree of death and the tree of truth. Many animals were created, one was a minotaur who was given visions of an outside world. The other creatures were canines, felines, rodents, and other mammals and fish. In the darker parts of this garden planet were wolfmen, blood drinkers, moving shadows, and other dark monsters too horrible to be named. The two lived oblivious to the dangers around them and the life outside the planet. They had many children who travelled the world. Some joined the dark and some developed strange powers.

The Minotaur, one day, decided he wished to see the outside world. He travelled to the woman and spoke, "My queen if we eat of the tree of truth, we will learn the ways of the outsiders. We will become one like them. They are powerful and incredibly strong, almost perfect. Unlike us, we are imperfect."

The queen looked lovingly at the minotaur, she had been deceived by his words. She sought perfection in herself so she would be the perfect woman. The second act of evil was done that day deception was used. The queen went to the tree of truth and looked at the delectable fruit. Her lust for pure beauty took over and she grabbed a fruit and devoured it hungrily. Her teeth ripped it apart in her mouth. Her husband saw this and went to Azrael's temple.

He spoke, "My lord protector, my wife has disobeyed you. I fear I will be overcome to disobey you as well. She has eaten from the forbidden tree of truth. What shall I do?"

Azrael spoke through the statue, "I will send a being of my realm to help you. Your wife, I fear, may be lost depending on how much fruit she ate. Who was with her?"

"A minotaur. I know not which one."

"Hmm, I see. Very well."

As the beings were created, Devastation began his meddling. He created a being known as

Omega Chaos and he placed the monster in the dark parts of a galaxy known as Silver. This galaxy had already advanced far beyond what the Eternals had expected. To keep the species in line, Morpheus placed the cursed planet, which he called Hell, in the middle of a sector known as Silver. Devastation then advanced the Hellions and made twelve planets making the first Hell the thirteenth Hell. Devastation then created natural disasters and other terrible things. One of the most cruel things he did was help create the grand magus empire. He then taught the overlords to build Nuclear weapons. He became the patron god of the Grand Magus Empire. This strengthened him. He attempted to kill Morpheus and his other siblings in the Nightmare catastrophe. He was only stopped when Morpheus created the Fountainhead. Devastation countered this with the creation of the Tributary. A large war took place and Devastation was defeated. He was then sent to The Haven of Dead planets, where the dead gods and all the people who died after the planet that they were born on was destroyed and written out of existence. Thus the first age ended.

***

"Father, how do you know this?"

"I was taught this by my master, Sidrodc. As he taught me so, I teach you. One day you will teach someone and this knowledge will be passed on."

"When do I get to train with a blade, father?"

"Soon, my son. Soon."

As night fell, the three full moons glowed. Up in the sky, the Warrior constellation glowed ominously. Sin Seeker sat eating while his father meditated. His mother was finishing up the second portion of the meal. His sister Midnight looked scared. He looked outside as the moons turned red. The jungle began to move. Down beneath the hill that Xiang Yu's farm stood. Dark runes appeared and an army emerged. They were led by the Great Emperor of Evil Qin Shi. His army charged forward and soon had gotten up the hill. He teleported into the home. He stabbed Miaoyi in the chest and went for Xiang Yu's head. As his blow landed, he fell with his gut leaking out of him. Sin Seeker stood with a short blade drawn, blinking in surprise. His father and mother's corpses both vanished, leaving him alone with the army and his sister. He was quickly set upon by the enemy and struggled to defend himself. Midnight Seeker watched wide eyed. Finally snapping out of her shock, she grabbed a double-ended voulge off the wall and dove into the enemy. Her circular attacks decimate them. She finished it off with a slam sending the corpses flying.

***

Death of The Demon King Oda

It was nightfall and the three moons of Silver shined their pale light down on a massive mountain shaped like the head of a hound. Their ghostly glow made the white mountain glow in the night. Below the mountain, in a secret entrance, a man stood. This was Mitsuhide Akechi. He was waiting for something. Suddenly he opened the secret door and an army marched in. The Shrine city of Honnōji was located within White Wolf Mountain. The army quickly attacked.

***

Emperor Oda sat on his throne. Near him was his wife Noh-Wu, and his loyal retainer, a young boy or maybe a girl by the name of Ranmaru. It was known that he and Ranmaru had a sexual relationship. His other retainer, a frail-looking two-hundred-year-old by the name of Sin Seeker, stood on his other side holding two bundles. He looked at the twins and grimaced. The door burst open and a guard rushed in. He was quickly shot full of holes before he could even speak.

Emperor Oda pulled out a blade shooting purple energy off of it. The frail man, Sin Seeker, quickly slipped into the shadows as Mitsuhide attacked Emperor Oda. That was when the flames began. The clash between the Emperor and Mitsuhide led them into the flames while Ranmaru held off the army. Ranmaru did not last long as he was overwhelmed. The empress and her ninja attacked the remaining army. A burning door collapsed, blocking them from Sin Seekers' view. He quickly leapt up a sakura tree and slipped onto a ledge that led outside. He exited White Wolf Mountain and slid down the mountainside. He began walking until he came upon a small temple to the Moon Goddess Platinum. He entered the shrine and a priestess barred his way.

She spoke, "Get away, demon!"

Sin smiled, saying, "May I speak to the Sword Saint?"

She balked and bowed, leading him into the inner sanctuary. In front of them sat a monk dressed in loose robes. The monk opened his eyes and looked Sin Seeker over.

"Ah, the Hunter's spawn enters my sanctum."

"Master Lu Zhi, I am calling in a favour you owe me."

"Very well, Sin Seeker. What is it you ask of me?"

Sin Seeker handed one of the bundles to him, saying, "This is Rei Oda. Take care of her for me."

"The Emperor's daughter? So today was the day, then?"

"Yes"

"Very well, child! I will care for the girl."

Sin seeker still held one bundle, so he continued to walk until he came upon a caravan heading towards Lo-Yang, the home city of The Hero of Chaos. He paid the leader for a ride. The caravan entered the city about dawn and Sin Seeker stealthily leapt from building to building until he reached the palace. He entered a portcullis by bending the metal out of his way. He saw concubine Ts'ao and followed her into her room.

He spoke, "Lady Soso, I am calling in a favour you owe Emperor Oda. Take care of his daughter Liz and raise her well."

Soso turned at the whisper and only saw a bundle on the floor. She removed the wrapping to reveal a tiny girl looking at her with bright blue eyes. The girl giggled and cooed. Soso began nursing the child.

As he began walking back to his farm, he heard a low squeal and the sounds of something scrabbling against metal. He turned to see a tailless fox. It looked up at him and squeaked in fear as he knelt down and allowed it to snuffle his hand. He rummaged in his satchel and pulled out some jerky. The little creature devoured the jerky.

It spoke to him, "You is very kind, mister. I am Shimasake. My clan banishes me. Can I come with you?"

"Sure. I have plenty of room at my farm."

"Thank you. Thank you! Thank you! Could I have some more jerky?"

Sin Seeker handed another slice to Shimasake. She devoured it and leapt onto his shoulder.

***

Death of The Assassin

One year later, Sin Seeker stood on the edge of his farm. He was awaiting something. He saw a young woman jogging up his pathway. She stopped at him and bowed.

She spoke, "Master Sin Seeker, Lord Hideyoshi would like to have your assistance in finding the traitor Mitsuhide."

Sin Seeker smiled, "I have been waiting for you. My spy knew ahead of time about this message. It's only out of consideration that I await you."

The young woman gulped, "I am Tara Li. I suppose I will be working with you."

Sin Seeker smiled, "Did Hideyoshi tell you why you needed my help?"

"No, he didn't."

"Good, he keeps secrets well. Come along then."

"How do you plan on getting to the castle?"

Sin Seeker pushed a button and a hover cycle rose out of the ground. He got on and patted the seat behind him. Tara Li climbed nervously on. He kicked a bar and the cycle started. She clung to him as he sped off. In an hour, a massive pagoda rose before them. Sin Seeker parked his cycle in the yard and chuckled as Tara fell off the cycle. He helped her up and the two walked towards the entrance. Hideyoshi was standing in the lobby awaiting the allies. He clapped his hands joyfully as Sin Seeker walked in.

He spoke joyfully, "Master Sin Seeker, it is good to see you again. We had feared the worst when we couldn't find you. When the sword saint said you could be found, our hope was rekindled."

Sin Seeker grimaced, "Yes, well, I had to keep a low profile. Gracia was looking for me."

The shiver that the name Gracia sent down Hideyoshi's spine was noticeable. He nodded in agreement. Soon the generals had all arrived. The armies were going to march on Mt Tenno at Yamazaki. They would create a diversion while Sin Seeker and his ninjas would sneak into Mitsuhide's main camp and execute him. Tara Li would be reinforcing the Honda-Tokugawa forces. She seemed quite excited about that. Sin Seeker walked outside and went over to a rice paddy. Five youths stood tending the paddy.

He spoke, "We have our orders. Once the distraction starts, we are to slip into the enemy camp and kill Mitsuhide."

The one with a red streak in his hair spoke, "Sir, do you really plan on killing Mitsuhide? We all know Oda wanted to die."

The one with yellow in her hair. "Of course, he wouldn't," she then looked at Sin Seeker,

"Would you?"

Sin Seeker walked away and they rushed to catch up. They all got on their hoverbikes and rode off. When they arrived at the castle, they hid their cycles in the forest. Sin Seeker waited until the army marched into view. He and his team scaled the back wall using magnetic shoes. Sin Seeker saw a warlord that looked familiar. She had flowing black hair and eyes that could freeze the hearts of men. Her lips were a deep red that looked almost black. *So she has survived. Lady Nō, you devious minx. Now if she's here, where is her ninja Ninada?*

He saw a shadowy form leap over the parapets. He spoke, "Time to move faster. We cannot let the Kunoichi get to Mitsuhide."

The girl with pink in her hair. "But sir, Trini and I are Kunoichi."

"Just hurry up."

The seven of them got to the top of the wall and all vanished in a burst of steam. They appeared in the main room, where they saw Mitsuhide and his daughter Gracia fighting a very swift ninja. Sin Seeker threw his voulge and the hilt of it struck the ninja pinning her to the ground. She struggled as Gracia loomed over her charging up an energy orb.

"Stand down, Gracia!"

Gracia stopped and turned to Sin Seeker, her eyes widened and she lowered her arms, bowing slightly to Sin Seeker.

Sin Seeker turned to Mitsuhide. "I know why you killed Emperor Oda. He asked you to kill him if he became too cruel and corrupt. Now we must fake your and Gracia's deaths. However, you should just let the youth handle things from now on."

Sin Seeker pushed a button on his gauntlet and the two of them were teleported to his farm. He picked up his double voulge off the Kunoichi and knocked her unconscious. He hoisted her over his shoulder and then pushed a blue button as he and his ninja jumped out of the building. The room that Mitsuhide had been in blew up. Sin Seeker flipped and landed near Nō. He placed her Kunoichi near her and walked away. His ninja had vanished as soon as they had touched down.

***

Sin Seeker's Rage
Sin Seeker Xiang stood on the outskirts of Shizugatake. He was tall, muscular and eager to join the fight. However, he had been ordered to maintain the defense of Hideyoshi's main camp. He was fuming.

The elegant woman next to him spoke, "Calm yourself, Lord Xiang. You must maintain a steady composure."

"Lady Nene, please have your husband reconsider. My sister is out there fighting against our army. I am the only one who can beat her."

A man wearing tiger skin over his green armour walked in with a young woman bound up. He tossed her before Sin Seeker and Nene.

Nene spoke, "Kiyomasa Kato, good job. Thank you for defeating such a powerful warrior."

Sin Seeker stared down at his sister as Hideyoshi walked out of his tent to see her.

Hideyoshi spoke, "Midnight Sin Xiang, you fought to defend my rival. Here is my sword. If you have any honour at all, you will commit Seppuku for your treachery."

She looked up at him and then nodded. Kiyomasa Kato undid her bindings. She looked over to Sin Seeker, who sighed and primed his axe. As she stabbed herself, Sin Seeker beheaded her. He glared daggers at Hideyoshi and vanished after incinerating his sister. That was when Shizugatake castle suddenly went up in flames. Hideyoshi rushed to the castle and entered. He saw Sin Seeker standing over the dying forms of Shibata Katsuie and Oichi Oda. He saw Oichi's daughters from her first marriage and tried to herd them out. Sin Seeker advanced, causing the girls to flee.

"Goodbye, Hideyoshi. I hope you find success. But I can never forgive you for what you did. I understand why, but my loyalty is now my own. Do not call for my aid again. I will not answer."

The flames became intense, forcing Hideyoshi to flee the burning castle. His last look of Sin Seeker was a demon that became obscured when a pillar crashed down, blocking his view.

***

Assault On Orkea

It was the middle of winter many years later when Sin Seeker, now a hermit, received a knock at his door. He opened it to see Kiyomasa Kato. He looked at the green armoured man and sighed.

"Pray tell why you are here?"

"Hideyoshi requests your aid. As do many of us generals."

"I thought I made it clear you lot should not expect my aid for what you did."

"I understand that, Lord Xiang. However, all of Napja is unified under Hideyoshi. He is seeking to expand his rule to the Orkea region. Then onto Central Komodo. We would like your help to realize this goal."

Sin Seeker looked thoughtful for a moment. "Very well, Kiyomasa, I will assist, but only because Hideyoshi is dying. This is a fool's errand, but I will do my best to assist you."

***

Sin Seeker stood on the castle ship Vol as it hovered over the water. He was waiting for the attack to commence. It had been many long and tiresome years with Orkea and Napja fighting and then retreating. But this was the final battle. Money had run out, as had troops. He had witnessed so many atrocities by the Napja army. Rivers had run red with blood as the Napja forces slaughtered civilians and soldiers alike. He was waiting. Next to him sat a man wearing tattered jeans and a spike-studded shirt. On his wrists were spike-studded gauntlets and he had dyed his white hair blue and black to match his clothing. He was playing the sitar.

"Do calm down, Lord Xiang. Nothing is going to happen today."

"We are up against Yi Sun-sin. He is one of the best admirals of Orkea. No one has been able to counter his Adamantine ships. Watch out!"

Sin Seeker blocked an attack from a man wearing armour plus a bunch of Oni skin. Sin Seeker snarled.

The man spoke menacingly, "All Oni must die. I am the retribution of The Holy Order. Xin Fang!"

"Well, Xin Fang, you picked the wrong person to attack."

He threw Xin Fang overboard and sent an arrow through Xin Fang's shoulder. Xin Fang continued to swim away with one arm. Sin Seeker snorted and continued to pace. The Castle ship Vol was in the strait of Norang. It was a small strait. Not much manoeuvrability. Sin Seeker heard the orders to retreat over his com. He watched as the ships tried to but were blocked by the Orkea navy. He saw Yi Sun-sin on his ship, now blocked the only way out of the strait. A ship opened fire on the castle ship and was disabled. As it floated near, Sin Seeker landed on it along with many troops. He saw Deng Zilong, the commander of the Central Komodo legion and Sun-sin's ally. The troops massacred the ship's crew. Including Deng Zilong. Sin Seeker snarled.

He teleported back onto the Castle Ship Vol. "Motochika, I can find no honor here. All I have witnessed during this useless invasion are numerous massacres of the innocents. Goodbye, I suspect you will win this battle. Or, at the very least, be able to retreat."

Sin Seeker vanished and reappeared on his small Roc class fighter. He watched as Admiral Yi pursued the fleet and watched as Yi's ship was struck by a repeater. He sent one of his bug drones down to see how things were.

Yi Sun-sin leaned heavily against the wall. His son Yi Hoe and his nephew Yi Wan were staring in shock. Sun-sin whispered, "The war is at its height. Wear my armour and beat the drums. Do not announce my death." Yi Wan was the first to regain composure and quickly brought the corpse of Yi Sun-sin into his office. He came out wearing his uncle's armour.

As the Navy of Napja finally retreated, Sin Seeker saw one ship finally arrive at Yi Sun-sin's. He turned into his drone's frequency and saw Chen Lin, the ally from the Central Komodo board and thanked Sun-sin for his many rescue attempts only to see Chen Lin fall to the ground three times, wailing. He smiled a sad smile. Then recalled his drone and left for his home, where he received word of Lord Hideyoshi's death from cancer.

***

Battle of Succession

Five years later, he had heard rumors of two of Hideyoshi's retainers squaring off for power. Both sides had marched their forces to Sekigahara. Some big names were involved in this battle. Not only was one army led by Jacen Tokugawa and his bodyguard Uji Honda but the other side had the intelligent strategists Sakon Shima and Otani Yoshitsugu. Yoshitsugu also had a retainer named Gosuke.

However, Jacen had the support of the Oni clan Aku led by Akuseru the Black. He decided to join up with the West led by one Mitsunari the Profound. He knew that was the side his ninja would have favoured since they belonged to the Templar Masons, a group of Oni Hunters.

He jumped on his hovercycle and rode off. He arrived at the battlefield just as it was going downhill for the west. Over half of Mitsunari's forces had turned traitors. He only had the support of clan Mori, clan Chosokabe, clan Ankokuji, Clan Konishi, and clan Shimazu.

Sin saw his ninja square off against Ujiyasu Honda and get slaughtered. He watched as Shimazu's son charged Akuseru and got kicked off his mount by Tara Li.

Tara Li got shot by Shimazu's son, only for the son to get stabbed by Akuseru. He sighed and hefted his blade, seeing clan Mori struggling against some of the traitors they were up on a mountain. He vanished in a puff of steam and reappeared near the traitors. He carved through them, allowing the Mori-Chosokabe forces to advance. He then vanished again, only to reappear near Shima Sakon. He looked at the shotgun hole in Sakon's chest and sighed, causing the body to burst into flames. He then waved his hand, sending the flames across the field of gunners. The screams of the dying filled the air as he vanished again and reappeared near Otani. Otani sat there, too sick to move his loyal retainer Gosuke stood near him. He was about to plunge his kataa into his chest.

Sin Seeker held his hand and said, "I have assisted Lord Mitsunari's cause. The battle turns in your favour. Please stay your hand."

Otani looked up at Sin and gave a brief smile before plunging his kataa into his chest. Gosuke kneeled and sobbed before raising his axe. However, Otani burst into flames before Gosuke could behead him. Sin walked away from the spot and saw Jacen facing Mitsunari. The two fought, but Jacen's flame cannon spear soon fired, immolating Mitsunari. Sin Seeker walked over to the wounded form of Tara Li and blocked the spear of Uji Honda, the leader of the Oni. He noticed the Black Blade of the Oda hanging loosely around Uji's waist. He smiled and the two clashed, his double voulge sending waves of air while Honda's spear Tonbo-Giri sent energy crackling through the air.

"Ah, nephew, you fight with strong vigour. Truly a sight to behold. But I am called Uji Honda, the unbeatable for a reason."

The other Oni began chanting and an ethereal sound formed around the two warriors. The Monkey King appeared behind Sin Seeker and mimicked his movements, becoming ethereal. Sin Seeker and Uji's blades clashed as a psychic storm formed overhead, causing thick bolts of lightning to strike the ground. Sin Seeker smiled viciously as his body changed. He was going into his second cycle. His body grew small spikes on his shoulders and his muscles became more defined. He finally let out a roar as his psychic energy exploded outwards, completing the transformation. Akuseru, the other Oni, and Uji were thrown back and when the smoke cleared, Sin Seeker and Tara Li vanished along with the blade of the Oda. Jacen hurried over to his bodyguard to make sure he was well. He then sent his loyal generals away so he could have some peace to mourn the fallen.

***

War In Central Komodo

Sin Seeker arrived at his home and set Tara Li in a bed. He saw Shimasake walk out with some ointment. She began tending to Tara as Sin Seeker went for a walk. He arrived at a secluded glade and meditated. He vanished in a puff of steam and appeared at Lo-Yang he entered Lady Soso's room while she slept and placed The Devil Blade next to her robes, with a note bequeathing it to the young Liz.

Two hundred years passed. During this time, he followed numerous reports out of Najpa about the various goings on of Emperor Tokugawa. He also was paying attention specifically to the dissent among Central Komodo about one Tung Po. He arrived in his glade, where he saw an amber elf who was sitting under a tree in the glade of ferns and trees. His armour was gold and red. Around his waist was wrapped a flail. On his back, he had a naginata, Yari, and Odachi. On one hip, he had a gun and the other was a dagger. He had sinewy black hair that was tied in a bob and held a mask that looked like an Oni's face.

He was speaking to a very tall wild man. "Three years have passed since Tung Po's death. The imperial throne is vacant. I do not know how the rest of the year will fare. But I do know that it will be interesting. I foresee us meeting your kin soon, Keiji."

The tall man with wild hair spoke, "I await my mother, Yuenu's offspring. If he's anything like your step-uncle, I will be very disappointed."

"Trust me, Keiji. He is nothing like me. You two will get along fine."

"When do you foresee us meeting him then."

"Three, two, one, enter stage right, Sin Seeker."

From the right of where the two were sitting, entered Sin Seeker. He looked at the two men, raised his eyebrow and sat on a stone.

He spoke, "I would question why you two are in my glade, but I have been dealing with some troubling issues lately and am too tired to question things."

Shimasake had appeared and was sniffing around Keiji. He was eyeing her warily. Her ears perked up as she spoke, "Sin, he smells like you!"

Sin Seeker looked at Keiji and spoke, "Who are you two?"

The amber elf spoke, "I am Toshiie Maeda. This is my nephew Keiji Uesugi. We have been waiting for you. My sister-in-law asked me to help you."

Sin Seeker nodded, saying, "I sure could use it. Who is your sister-in-law? So that I may thank her."

"She is the Forge maiden Feldspar, your mother."

"I see... so she still lives, that is good. So Keiji, this means we are brothers. Excellent, I look forward to your skills in battle. Come back to my farm and we can have a feast.

***

After the feast, Sin Seeker walked through the woods he called home. He arrived in a clearing where a stone-skinned woman lay holding a small, winged Equus girl. He saw the stone-like woman struggle up and get into a fighting stance.

"I mean no harm. I was just walking when I came upon you two. You're injured. Come, let me take a look."

***

Introducing the Bear of Hizen

Three years later, Sin Seeker was visiting the bar that Keiji, his half-brother, had introduced him to. The bar's name was Monkey. He was sitting next to Keiji. He ordered a burning red drink that smelled of grapes and apples. His adopted daughter, Bubbles, had joined him and was sitting drinking a fizzy beverage with a chunk of whipped ice in it. Shimasake leapt up and landed on Keiji's massive hair. She snuggled up and fell asleep, dreaming about chasing small animals. Keiji was feeling a soft, gentle kick every now and then. Shimasake was yipping in her sleep. He downed his drink in one gulp.

A voice rang out, "Keiji, you son of a bitch!"

Keiji turned only to get punched in the face by an enraged bear with red and amber fur. The bear was ten feet tall and both his hands were covered in a metal gauntlet with spikes on them. He had an eyepatch and a two-pronged scar across his face. Keiji moved with the strike and struck the bear in the solar plexus twice. This caused the bear to stumble, allowing Keiji to put him in a headlock.

Keiji chuckled, "Dancing Bear in Sky, you still can't beat me."

Dancing Bear chuckled, rumbling the floor below him with it. The two got up and bowed to each other.

"Why don't you join us for a drink, Sky?"

"I would love to."

Sin Seeker spoke, "You two know each other?"

Dancing Bear growled, "I know this wily snake we have been hunting together since we were young. Name's Dancing Bear in Sky. Yours?"

"Sin Seeker and this little equus is Bubbles. And my sister is around here somewhere."

Keiji pointed to his hair where a small one-tailed kitsune slept, periodically twitching her paws.

***

The Folly of the Way of Peace

The air was thick and humid. It was always thick and humid during the summer years on the Continent Komodo. A small village sat quietly in the middle of a massive forest. The villagers knew the outside world but had no care for it. They prefer the forest. They are protected. The sun rose over the forest as one of the tall elephantine-like Ganeshans walked into the village. He was passing through along with a man who led the Way of Peace. This man had been given a tome by The Immortal of the Southern Mountains. The Ganeshan looked around, twitched his trunk and smiled as the people flocked to the Great Teacher.

The Ganeshian spoke, "Master Zhang Jue, I have led you to this village. However, I have urgent business to attend to, so I will have to leave now."

Zhang Jue responded, "Very well, Gor Gor'e, my brothers and I thank you for your help. I hope you will consider giving us aid. The firmament has perished, the Yellow Sky will soon rise; in this year of hunter, let there be prosperity in the world!"

Gor Gor'e shook his head sadly, "No, I am afraid you must walk this path alone. Peace, brother!" Gor Gor'e turned his back and walked away, vanishing in a cloud of vines.

A girl of nearly two hundred ran up to Zhang Jue and cried, "Master, master! You must help me, my brother is very ill. If he dies, I have no place to go. Please, I know you can heal him."

"Very well, my child. Bring me to him and his ailment will be purged."

The two walked towards a farm on the outskirts of the small village. As they entered, Zhang Jue fell, overwhelmed by a psychic disturbance. He hit the floor and the young girl helped him up. She led him towards a closed door. As they entered the room, Zhang Jue noticed a man of about six hundred. The man was very pale, even for an Amber Silveran. There was a sheen of sweat covering the man and his clothing. Around him, a psychic squall played havoc with the air. Zhang Jue placed his hands over the man's body and began pulling the psychic energy chanting in an ethereal language. As his chanting increased, the psychic energy squall began to stabilize. The man woke to see Zhang Jue kneeling beside him.

He spoke, "I Thank you, elderly one. How can I repay you for waking me from that horrible dream?"

"Just remember this in the event we meet again."

It was the hottest day of the hottest month in the hottest year on record. Sin Seeker was standing on a bluff overlooking a large-scale battlefield. Off to the west, he saw Huangfu Song's unit suddenly get drenched and could barely make out large rain golems decimating the garrison. He was going to aid them when he saw a flash of green. He zoomed in as best he could and saw the young Drakon Liu Suen and her two bodyguards. He then turned his attention east and saw Lady Soso advancing slowly behind her bodyguard due to the huge tornado-strength winds. He sighed and looked south. He could see the Yellow Cloak leader Zhang Jue. His Way of Peace rebels had done a number on the army of the Emperor of Central Komodo.

He watched as the battle eventually led to the altar garrison of Zhang Jue. He vanished in a puff of steam and reappeared as Ts'ao Liz's cousin fell to the fire-breathing drake that guarded Zhang Jue. The boy roared, "You imperial villains. I am the flame of the Way of Peace. You can not get through my righteous fury. Brother Zhang Jue will remain safe from your blades."

He appeared and dropped down with Bubbles and her mother. Her mother was severely suffering from the poison in her system. Shimasake clung to his hair as he spoke, "Don't worry. I got this."

He shot forward and the dragonling dropped to the ground. He arrived at the door and slid into Zhang Jue's chamber. He pretended to remove a helmet as Ts'ao Liz entered the chambers. Behind her stood the Green Drakon in rags, A large Panther-like woman, and a red-skinned golden-eyed woman with long hair tied up in many war braids. He grimaced since he knew her well. That was Shogun Pei, the granddaughter of the self-proclaimed God of War, Shogun Yu. He snorted.

Zhang Jue spoke, "Thank you, Lord Xiang for saving my brothers and I. We are vastly indebted to you."

"No, master Zhang Jue, it is I who should thank you. You healed me of my ailment. I just ask you to stay out of trouble for me. Lady Liu Suen, I ask you to keep Zhang Jue safe from harm. The people need a preacher."

**

The Usurper Falls

Sin Seeker walked into Yuan Shao's main camp as he was giving a rousing speech befitting his pompous attitude. He was accompanied by Bubbles and his sister Shimasake who was using her powers to make herself look like a beautiful woman. He walked over to Gongsun Zinnia, her bodyguard, and Liu Suen.

He spoke, "I will be assisting you in your attack. I suspect that you will need the help. Hulao Gate is defended by Liun Ba and his student Fang Ryofu. Shall we head out?"

The small army began trekking west. Liu Suen, due to her dragon heritage, was slow in advance because of the deep snow. She was following Sin Seeker and Zhang Jue, who was burning through the snow. She was also behind Chang Vicki and Shogun Pei to stay warm. The wind was blowing at their front, so she was protected from the cold because of their two massive bodies. She was having a pleasant conversation with a green-skinned elf who wore silver armour. This was the Little Dragon.

Bubbles, as she learned was Equus' name, seemed to enjoy the cold. She was gliding across the sky as a scout.

She spoke to the two-hundred-year-old woman, "What is your name? I heard your brother talk to your equine friend, but I never got yours."

The girl smiled. "My name is Shimasake. Big brother took me in when I was cast out from my clan. He is very generous like that. He made me his sister since I refuse to be his daughter."

"That is very interesting. Why did you refuse to be his daughter? If you don't mind me asking."

"Well, I was just suffering from the fact my elder sister Diao Kyna disowned me and also that my mother, Zhang Chunhua, refused to even acknowledge my existence. All my tails were cut off as well. So I was angry and betrayed until Sin came along. He nursed me back to sanity and offered me adoption. I asked if I could be a sister instead because my clan cannot stand to be controlled by a man."

"Ah, I see. Does your Kitsune blood grant you reprieve from this cold?"

She seemed startled that Liu Suen saw through her disguise but smiled. "It does not, but we Kitsune can handle extreme temperatures. I once knew a Kitsune who was frozen in ice for six hundred years."

As the two continued to walk, Liu Suen heard something. It sounded like a woman fighting. She turned her head and saw a flash of red. The woman wore red leather skin-tight armour. She saw she was a Felis of the Tiger army. She was wielding a bow and periodically would blast the enemy with fire. Behind her, she saw a red-bearded Rakshasa whose sword was on fire and slashing at the enemy. Along with them were two Rakshasa females doing a blade dance cutting up the apparent ambush. The bow wielder attracted her. Her cat-like features were not as pronounced as the male and two females behind her.

"Sin Seeker, Shogun Pei, Chang Vicki! We must help them."

Sin Seeker turned his head and saw the three Rakshasa and one Felis fighting an ambush of one hundred. He yelled, "Bubbles! Give them hell!"

The leathery-winged Equus with cat-like eyes descended. She opened fire with a mini-chain gun strafing the enemies. They scattered, sustaining numerous casualties.

Liu Suen rushed to the side of the girl in red. "Are you alright, my lady?"

The girl smiled and swished her tail against her in a flirtatious manner. Her voice was like a purr, "Ooo, thank you, my lady, for your concern. I have withstood twice as many grunts in other battles. My siblings and I could use your help getting the supply captains escorted."

Sin Seeker looked around at the Tiger army. They were staring at his forehead. He brushed his skin and smiled. His two horns were visible. "You know it's impolite to stare. I may think of it as a challenge."

He noticed immediately that all the troops looked anywhere but at him. He turned towards the generals. "I apologize. I am Sin Seeker and who are you?"

The twin Rakshasa girls stepped forward. The one with darker colouring spoke first, "I am Diao Fukyu my quieter sibling is Xiao Fukmii. You're a cutie; looking for a concubine?"

Sin Seeker patted her on the head. "I am far too old for you. I'm sure you'll find somebody. Speaking of... where are the supply captains?"

The red-bearded Rakshasa nodded off to the east. "They were supposed to be coming from the supply base near here. I suggest we go check it out."

As Sin Seeker escorted Liu Suen and the Tiger army towards the supply base, they saw smoke. They rushed the base only to see it on fire. The black smoke rises from the cold earth.

The bearded Rakshasa roared, "No! Gods damn it. Those were the only supplies we had. Now we will have to retreat. Who did this blow to our honour?"

One of the lesser troop captains yelled, "Lord Sol Quan, it was Ding Yuan and his clan. He will pay for defiling our honour."

The other troops roared in approval.

After Clan Sol had left to avenge their honour, Sin Seeker, Liu Suen, and her sisters continued to march through the pass. As they reached Hulao Gate, a massive amber elf dropped down on them, riding a fiery red Cyberhorse. His hair was pulled back and worn in a golden headdress. He has donned a flowery-patterned battle coat that looked heavy and was lined with kevlar. Aside from the coat that reached his ankles, he was also encased in black body armour decorated with images of a lion. He wore a gold belt depicting a demon's maw and had sharp spikes.

A dark pink-haired woman landed next to him. She wore a black and grey duster that fluttered in the cold wind; she looked more dangerous than Liun Ba.

"I am the mighty Liun Ba. Face me if you dare. I have killed millions of worthless peons. So send your strongest that I may cut them down."

Several Generals arrayed themselves in battle formation Draco. Liun Ba was a fierce fighter and soon slain all the generals but one. This was the bodyguard of Kong Rong, Wu Anguo. Wu Anguo managed to use his heavy axe as a shield and weapon. Their fight lasted six rounds before Fang Ryofu slashed Wu Anguo's back, causing him to falter and get his arm cut off by Liun Ba.

Liu Suen faltered at this display, but when she saw Chang Vicki charge Liun Ba, she resolved to fight. She and Shogun Pei quickly caught up to Liun Ba and engaged him in battle. This allowed Sin Seeker to help Wu Anguo. Almost immediately, Liun Ba was knocked from his hovercycle. He rose from the ground and swung his halberd. Chang Vicki blocked the blow but faltered until Shogun Pei assisted with her hammer, but still, the halberd inched closer. Liu Suen joined in with her daggers. The three united and were able to force his blade back. The three fought with a fervour only reserved for those that are cornered. Liun Ba, inexhaustible, threw them back. He raised his halberd for a killing blow. Sin Seeker blocked the deadly blade with his double voulge. Liun Ba saw Sin Seekers' grey eyes and leapt back.

He jumped onto his cycle, growling, "So Hunter's spawn fights against me. Very well, you may pass. I care not what happens to that swine. But mark my words, we will meet again."

Liun Ba then galloped off, leaving a baffled Sin Seeker in his dust. The girl snarled, "Come at me if you want to die!"

Fang Ryofu sliced through a foolish general who had dared to charge her. She then cleaved an arm off another general.

This caused numerous generals to flee, screaming, "I... I... It's Fang Ryofu! Run for your lives!"

Liu Suen, Chang Vicki, and Shogun Pei squared off against Fang Ryofu. Shogun Pei wielded a great hammer shaped like a dragon. Chang Vicki held a two-pronged purple metal spear shaped like serpents. Liu Suen held two small double-pronged daggers that she swung with quick accuracy. It took thirty rounds before Fang Ryofu

was able to break free. That was when Sin Seeker charged her with his double voulge extended.

She snarled at Sin Seeker as he rammed her away from the gate allowing the three sisters to get a reprieve. His monkey-style bladed strikes kept her occupied. The two were whipping up a whirlwind with their combat.

Liu Suen yelled, "Man, the siege tank we are blasting down this gate."

Shimasake stepped out of the way of the large tank as it lumbered into her path. She motioned Bubbles to land next to her. Bubbles did so and the tank opened fire. With six bursts, the gate disintegrated and the coalition entered Baoyang castle.

As they entered Baoyang, a lingerie-clad girl spoke, "Alright, Ding Yuan. Get your forces out here and kill these traitors."

A red elf leapt from the rafters and slammed his great sword into the ground. He spun it around, causing several of Yuan Shao's forces to get cleaved in twain. Zhang Jue and Chang Vicki attacked him first with fire, then Chang Vicki punched him through a wall taking the battle into the next room.

There was a screech of a bird as a small Syrien appeared from a vortex of feathers. She wore white Taoist robes to contrast her inky black skin. On her head was a huge conical straw hat. It hid her face from observation. She vanished in a vortex of feathers and appeared behind Liu Suen, who blocked her attack while Bubbles lifted off to deal with her in the air. Shimasake jumped onto Liu Suen's shoulder, saying, "Let me be your eyes." She then felt an electrical jolt hit her brain. She blinked only to see purple, then saw the path that the Syrien took and began her assault.

The wall was blasted in as a tall female Red Silveran walked in. Her small horns were exposed due to her elegant headdress. Sin Seeker was thrown into the wall near her; he got up and dusted himself off. She smiled a toothy smile as one of the grunts yelled, "It's... it's... it's Ding Cui. Run!"

All the grunt troops dropped their weapons and trampled each other to get out of the vicinity.

Sin Seeker grinned as he pulled out his double voulge. She lowered her pike at him. The two clashed blades. Sin Seeker was spinning his voulge while using his monkey-style strikes. He was deftly blocking each of her strikes. He threw her back with a well-aimed kick. She stumbled and glared daggers at him. She threw her pike and it impaled both Tung Ming and Tung Bai. She grinned and left.

There was a burst of feathers as the Syrien appeared. She spoke in a melodious tone, "I am Chinkyuu. My lady Fang Ryofu was charged with treason by her highness Tung Bai. She refused Lady Tung's advances. Our forces will withdraw for now, but we will meet again."

Sin Seeker watched her vanish in a vortex of black feathers. He grimaced and held his side.

Bubbles saw this movement and said, "You're injured!"

Sin Seeker grunted as he moved to face her. "It's nothing. I had worse injuries than this."

Bubbles looked unconvinced but shrugged it off, saying, "Well, at least let the healers look at it."

***

The Hunters Blood

It was the height of the hunter's blood moon when all three of planet Silver's moons were shown red. Sin Seeker sat under a cherry blossom tree, sipping at some wine. He was alone, having sent his sister to bed. He had hidden his clan so that they would be safe. He knew what tonight was. It was half past midnight when the moons were at their peak when the three sisters walked into his garden.

Shogun Pei spoke first, raising her hammer. "I have come for you, Sin Seeker Hunter. You thought you could hide your heritage from a Shogun."

Liu Suen sighed as she unsheathed her knives. "I am sorry, Sin Seeker. She overheard Zhang Jue's deathbed confession. I am afraid I must help her kill you. Sisterhood comes before friendship."

Sin took off his shades. "No, you will do no such thing, girl. This is between Shogun Pei and I know, however, the treachery you have committed will be repaid."

Shogun Pei roared, "Enough talk! You die tonight, Hunter!"

She swung her hammer, crashing it into Sin Seeker. He was flung into the nearby cliff. He grunted as he felt his back crack. He didn't have time to defend himself as she mercilessly smashed her hammer into him. His armour shattered as he got up. He saw the dragoon hammer open its jaw. It closed over his chest, puncturing his heart and lungs. He also felt his jugular tear as he blacked out. She unhooked the jaw and polished the fangs. The blood had been absorbed by the hammer.

Chang Vicki spoke, "Shouldn't we bury the body?"

Shogun Pei snarled, "The birds can have him. His family is a scourge in this world. They deserve no honour."

As they left the orchard, a man with bronzed skin and inky hair descended from the heavens. His rugged features and many battle scars marked him as the great Khan. He muttered a blessing under his breath that was merely a whisper on the wind. He then lifted Sin Seeker up in his lower two arms and vanished. Liu Suen had heard the blessing and paled noticeably. She collapsed on the ground in panic. Her two sisters rushed to her aid. She was led to her bed, where she took ill.

***

Swordsmen in the Plains

Many years had passed and Sin Seeker was six hundred. He sat in his field, meditating as Tara Li practised her kicks. Next to her stood Dancing Bear in Sky and his brother Keiji Uesugi. He could also see his two-hundred fifty-year-old Equus daughter practising her sharpshooting. On his head sat his little adoptive sister Shimasake. He also saw a worried Tung Bai shaking near him. He went over and sat next to her. He placed his arm around her and she snuggled into his cloak. He knew she had yet to recover from the trauma she received at Chang'alextraza. Her mind was broken, but her body had been healed nicely. He closed his eyes and thought back.

He remembered when he saw an army of yellow-turbaned warriors marching through town. He saw their great teacher and felt a voice in his head Go north towards the city of XiaPi. On your way, make sure to stop and save the Equus girl.

Sin Seeker turned to Tara Li. "Kid, we get to go help the allied forces at XiaPi."

The two walked off since XiaPi was only six miles away and Sin Seeker's cycle was in the shop. He saw a group of bandits led by The White Wolf of Baihu. They were struggling against a small Equine-headed girl with golden eyes. He joined the fray and routed the Baihu army. He helped the foal to her feet and she grabbed his hand, dragging him inside her home. He saw a gargoyle woman sleeping in a hammock with her veins bulging. He recognized the poison in her body and quickly rummaged through his satchel. He stuck a needle into her veins and administered the antidote.

She stirred. "Take care of my little girl."

Her body vanished along with their home. He looked down at the terrified expression on the foal's face.

He squatted so he was almost face-to-face with her. "Hello there, small one. I am Sin Seeker. And although I know it's terrifying to be left alone with a strange man in a strange place. I hope we can get along."

The foal looked into his eyes and grinned. "Okay, mistah. Momma calls me Bubbles. She was always sayin' she could not hold her form because of the poison. But she forced herself to so she could find me a good home. Youse is that man."

Little Bubbles wrapped her small arms around Sin Seeker and he picked her up. The three continued to walk as the fog rolled in.

He arrived at XiaPi with his small troop. He could see the army of Ts'ao and the army of Liu struggling against three pink-haired women in black armour. The three were joined by two girls with orange hair.

Keiji spoke, "Those are Khwarezmian. What they are doing here is beyond me. Be careful when attacking them because their kind is collectively known as beasts. One can even prove hard for ten men. Those pink-haired girls look to me like they are from clan Ryofu. I am not sure about the orange-haired ones."

Shimasake spoke, "What about the ones on the walls? I see a black and red armoured male with two horns, a blue-haired girl, a red-haired man, and another red-haired girl. There also looks to be one of the legendary Aces with them."

Dancing Bear in Sky spoke in a low growl, "You guys concern yourselves with the army of Khwarezmia. I see little Ts'ao Liz running towards the floodgates. I worry about an ambush."

Sin Seeker smiled, patted Tung Bai, and stood stretching his muscled form as he picked up his voulge. She looked pleadingly at him, but that was when he heard a commotion in the village. He used his enhanced sight and saw a golden army attacking the villagers. He saw the standard of Yuan Millia. He then saw a blue armoured man leading the army.

The man was suddenly attacked by a Ganeshian monk. The blue armoured man was Chunyu

Qiong, one of Yuan Millia's top generals. He smiled and handed some Knives to Tung Bai and motioned her to follow him. Tara Li followed closely behind as Keiji jumped on his dragon horse and shot off. If one were to look closely, one would see a small fox clinging for dear life as she clung to his hair. Dancing Bear in Sky vanished in a splash of water.

Dancing Bear appeared next to a group of soldiers and tossed them into the rest of the army; he grabbed one by the head and slammed him into the ground before tossing him and barreling over a legion of troops. Keiji swung his fork and sliced through Qiong's face. Ripping apart his nose and leaving a permanent gash. Qiong called for a retreat. The soldiers scrambled and fled. His advisor GuoTu threw a blast of burning wind, which Sin Seeker deflected by spinning his voulge. He then shot forward and bisected GuoTu.

The Ganeshian spoke, "Warmaster Sin Seeker, I am the Duke of Heaven Gor Gor'e Eliphan. When the yellow cloaks were routed, I hid. I am here to lend my knowledge to your army."

Next to him stood a girl who looked almost exactly like Ts'ao Liz. This caused Sin to blink in confusion.

She smiled, "Hoi unca Sin."

Sin Seeker frowned, "You must be Tarot Hunter, Arcanus' daughter."

"Thas right unca. You remember me."

"How is the old geezer."

"Paw is doin' great. Mistah Ts'ao Ang is using him as a body double while he consolidates his forces against Emperor Tokugawa."

"Good."

It was night by the time Sin Seeker and his allies arrived at Gundu's plains. He looked at the array of forces both on Ts'ao Liz's side and Yuan Millia's side. He saw the supply depot was guarded by Chunyu Qiong and a very effeminate man wearing butterfly wings and booty shorts with nine streamers flowing off it. He saw the units led by Wen Alice and Yan Ling march towards the front lines. Off in the distance, looking down on the entire battlefield, were Fang Ryofu and her allies. Much more concerning, however, was a red standard that portrayed a bestial face.

Sin muttered, "What the hell are Orkeans doing here?'

Gore Gor'e spoke, "It would seem they are allied with the Yuan."

Dancing Bear spoke, "Then it would seem little Liz will need our help. Especially since I see old friends of ours." He pointed towards a group of hunters clad in Oni scalps and armour.

Sin Seeker snarled, "Is that the Xin clan? Well, I know who dies tonight." They arrived at the camp of Ts'ao Liz to see her nearly panicking.

Dancing Bear walked over to her "Baccē cintā mata karō. Maiṁ surakṣita rakhēṅgē."

She turned to them, her eyes lighting up with joy. "Wǒmen zhōngyú yǒu jīhuì niǔzhuǎn júmiàn!"

She noticed the rest of them and squeaked, "Who are all of you?"

"I am Sin Seeker. The wild man is my brother Keiji. Next to him are Tara Li, Gor Goré, and Bubbles, and I see you have already met Dancing Bear in Sky. We are here to help you since the Xin clan under Yuan Millia nearly wiped out my village."

"I appreciate the aid. But why me?"

"You show promise. I also heard what happened at Wancheng Castle. Having your army nearly destroyed means this battle, you are outnumbered. I have turned many battles in favour of the ones that I assist."

There was a shout, "Open the gates."

They turned to see a beleaguered army led by Liz's five phoenix generals. Her eyes widened in fear.

Her general, Shin Rip, came up to her and bowed low. "We have lost our footing in the Orkea region."

"How?"

"Yuan Millia's allies Impyrado Red and Ashphar Blue attacked with their army. Their general was the legendary conqueror Konishi Yukinaga. Yes, the same one that killed him."

Konishi threatened us with the line, "Fight if you want to die or let us pass."

However, Lord Song Sanghyeon responded, "It will be easy for me to die but difficult for you to pass." He then Personally led the troops in our final charge. After his death, we ordered a retreat. This is what is left of our army. And it looks like Impyrado Red followed us here.

Sin Seeker nodded, "Alright, Liz have your five generals and Shin Rip advance on Baima and Yanjin. Master Wolf, you will go with them since I know you are well adept at fighting overwhelming numbers. Lady Rei, you will take Keiji and Dancing Bear to the supply depot of

Wucho and destroy it to demoralize the enemy. General Zhu Chu, your strength will be needed with that. I will take care of Fang Ryofu and the Orkeans. The strange man behind you will stay here with the rest of my group to guard the main camp."

Gor Gor'e spoke, "I disagree. I will take Tarot and Lady Xu to cause a distraction to lead Liu Suen, Shogun Pei, Chang Viki, and The Little Dragon away from the front lines."

Sin nodded in agreement, but before he could raise his voulge, two heads were thrown at his feet. A muscular woman wielding a spear shaped like a dragon's head walked into view. On her hip was a handgun and on her other was a scabbard that held a blue-handled sword.

"I have slain the Generals Wen Alice and Yan Fa-Ping."

Liz looked astonished, "Thank you, Shogun Feng Yinping. I am very fortunate that you are here, but I wish for you to stay longer and assist in distracting some of Yuan Millia's forces."

"Very well, Lady Ts'ao. But know that when I succeed, I am no longer a part of your army. Let us go, Xu Hana. I wish to see your prowess in battle."

The white-cloaked bandit smiled, "I wish to see yours as well."

Sin nodded and leapt up the stone banks towards Fang Ryofu. Not noticing the Xin clan sneaking towards Ts'ao Liz's camp. The army dispersed to enact Sin Seeker's plans.

***

The three moons glowed intensely through the clouds. It was the time of year when two were red. Two red moons signified it was the sacrificial season. In the old days, clans would send their prisoners into the forests, never to return. Sin Seeker arrived just as Fang Ryofu began her charge. He slammed into her Mecha Horse, Red Hair, sending her flying off of it. Her small cadre of generals surrounded him. He waved his hand, sending them in all directions before charging Fang Ryofu. That was when the Orkean army leapt from hiding.

Impyrado Red spoke hauntingly, "We were going to ambush clan Fang, however, it seems a demon is alive and in front of me. By the decree of Empress Ecti and the rules placed down by the inquisition, I declare your death."

Sin Seeker avoided the pike thrown by Fang Ryofu. "You done yammering? If so, show me what you're made of!"

***

Dancing Bear rolled out of the way of laser claws. The effeminate man floated into the air only to divebomb Dancing Bear.

Dancing Bear snorted and adjusted his gauntlets. "You are a little late to the party. Your depot is in flames and your ally is down. Join us and your talent will not be wasted."

"Ahh! Your efforts are dazzling! You shall see me shine as well… Yes, even brighter than now."

Keiji looked down upon Chunyu Qiong. "What have you to say?"

Chunyu Qiong sighed, "The sky decides the victor. What need of you to ask?"

Zhu Chu slammed Chunyu Qiong's head in. Rei gasped, "He surrendered. Why did you kill him?"

Zhu Chu spoke roughly, "He would have betrayed us since he views Lady Ts'ao Liz as a traitor. Turning on her old friend Yuan Millia to conquer this land. He was also too easily swayed in our favour. So who's to say he would not turn on us like he did the Yuans."

Rei turned towards the effeminate man. "And what of you? Will you turn on us so easily?"

"I Chang He will do no such thing. Yuan Millia could not match the beauty of battle like you. I would be honoured to fight alongside one whose battle beauty is as magnifique as yours."

Dancing Bear looked at the sky. He felt a chill in his bones. Ts'ao Liz is in trouble. How did we overlook the Xin clan? He vanished and reappeared in Liz's main camp.

***

Gor Gor'e snarled out a challenge to Yuan Xi, Yuan Shang, and Yuan Tan, the three older brothers of Millia. Their self-righteous honour immediately drew them out. Along with them came Liu Suen, Shogun Pei, Chang Viki, and The Little Dragon. He pulled back, causing the small legion to advance. That was when Shogun Feng Yinping arrived with Xu Hana.

Gor Gor'e sighed, "What unfortunate timing."

Tarot gasped and immediately pulled out her firearms. She managed one shot off, killing Yuan Xi. That was when she was stabbed through the abdomen by The Little Dragon. She tumbled and lay there clutching her stomach.

Yuan Shang yelled at Liu Suen, "Your sister fights for the enemy! You were a spy all along."

He then charged at Suen, nearly decapitating her before he fell in half from a swift strike from Chang Viki. Shogun Feng Yinping finished off Yuan Tan. She held her blade out to stop her daughter's siblings from attacking Gor Gor'e. The three immediately retreated along with the Little Dragon. Gor Gor'e knelt down and began mending Tarot Hunter. He summoned paper warriors to guard them. Xu Hana just smiled.

***

Sin Seeker had managed to maim the generals sent by Empress Ecti, causing them to call in their ship and retreat. He was now facing the combined might of the Khwarezmian army and Fang Ryofu's siblings and cousins Fang Ling, Lu Li'ing, Fang Ling Ling, Lu Lingli, and Lu DaliaZil. He had lost sight of Fang Ryofu and Lu Fang. He managed to push the girls back. But he was too close to the edge of the cliff he climbed. Ling Ling used her nine li staff and tripped him. Sending him tumbling down the cliff. Fang Ryofu slowly climbed the hill leading to the cliff. She was supporting Lu Fang, who was missing his arm. A tall brown silveran stood puffing on a reed. He looked down the cliff with disinterest.

Fang Ryofu spoke, "Yuan Millia is a lost cause. Let us retreat to fight another day."

***

Dancing Bear appeared in Ts'ao Liz's main camp. He looked around, seeing Bubbles hovering over Tara Li protectively and saw Shimasake hiding under some rubble. He then noticed Ts'ao Liz had her void blade drawn and was about to kill her girlfriend. He adjusted his gauntlets and blocked the blow. He fought valiantly but ultimately was unsuccessful. He collapsed as Liz's blade pierced his body.

***

Smoke On the Water and Fire Burns the Horizon

Sin Seeker sat on his porch strumming his Nadrian-made sitar. It was calming to him. After nearly losing Dancing Bear ten years ago, he had taken it up. Keiji was in the training yard along with Bubbles, Tara Li, and Tung Bai. The four of them had started with yoga and then had gone into tai chi. Tarot Hunter lay on a cot listening to the sitar. Her eyes closed as she recovered from her recent fever. Gor Gor'e was in the shrine meditating. A thin female with a yellow streak in her hair limped onto his land. She saw him and reached out before falling over from dehydration. He saw her and snapped his fingers, causing her to teleport right to him. He felt for a pulse, satisfied he brought her into his home and placed her on a medical table. He hooked her up and she began the process of rehydrating.

He examined her and muttered to himself. "Trini, so you somehow survived Sekigahara. It's been hundreds of years since that battle."

There was a small commotion outside and Sin Seeker went to investigate. He saw a crowd of people surrounding what could only be described as a wrestling ring. He saw a grey-green-skinned humanoid wearing a jester's hat. The creature grabbed his opponent, lifted him up by the legs and flipped him onto the ground. He then leapt high into the air and landed full bodily on the poor sap. He finally lifted him up.

The announcer yelled, "I can't believe it. No! Yes, it's his Atomic catapult knee strike. And Tian Shin is out. There you have it, folks. Our Legendary Drunken Duke Jester "The Shadow" Grave has done it again. Is there anyone who can stop him?"

Sin Seeker smiled and leapt into the ring. He saw the drunken duke lunge. He rolled away and popped up behind Jester. He grabbed Jester and suplexed him. He then followed this up by lifting the Jester onto his shoulders, leaping up and proceeding to drop while bending Jester's back painfully. The crowd roared their approval. That was when things got messy several Rakshasa attacked the crowd. Their incendiary attacks immolate those unlucky enough to be hit.

The ring caught fire as Sin Seeker helped Jester Grave up. The two then were back to back as Ebony General Han Guy attacked them. His second Hun Han the red fell with his head twisted off. The Shadow stood with Hun Han's head before tossing it into the fire. Han Guy ordered the Rakshasa troops to retreat.

Han Guy spoke, "You are Flying General Sin Seeker Hunter, are you not?" Sin nodded as Guy continued, "Well, you don't look nearly as terrifying as all the stories say. Ha ha, Sol Qu'an has nothing to fear from you."

A large rakshasa near him spoke, "Come, General Han, the fleet is ready to depart. We will crush Ts'ao Liz at the cliffs of Ganesh. Then this land will be ours."

The two left, leaving The Shadow and Sin Seeker to ponder. "Finally, Sin spoke, "Well, Shadow, do you want to join my merry little band of outcasts?"

The hulking man smiled a yellow-fanged smile. "I would be glad to join you. It seems I will be entertained more with you anyway."

***

Sin looked across the river, Yang. He saw the massive statue of the god Ganesh along with the many pillars that identified Ganeshian temples and homes. He looked over west to see Wukong pass, which led to the land of the Monkey King. He saw a large hover truck loaded with cannons and ballistae parking at the end of the pass. To the south, he saw the swamp that Yang empties into and the rugged huts of the Gatorilaians, monstrous alligator-headed gorilla men. He sighed as he saw Ts'ao Liz's ships chaining together. To the northeast, he saw a small shrine being erected and a small ship landing. He zoomed in to see Liu Suen and the Little Dragon disembark. He also noticed Shogun Pei and Chang Viki head towards the pass, most likely reaching it by nightfall. With them were an armoured Draconian and a Gatorillo in bestial garb. Ts'ao Liz's ships were arrayed southeast of the shrine.

Gor Gor'e spoke, "It looks to me like Sol Maria and her family are planning a fire attack. If my senses tell me right, they have the strategists Zhou Yu, Lusu, Lumeng, and Luxun summoning fire spirits."

Tallon Li spoke, "If my guess is correct, the ships will catch fire and Ts'ao Liz will have to escape through Wukong pass. I will go there with Trini, Tung Bai, and Shimasake to help her out."

Keiji stood and, with one swift motion, launched the four onto his dragon horse, following close behind as they went to Wukong Pass. Sin Seeker tapped his glasses again, viewing the battlefield. He saw a small rowboat near his position.

"Come, Shadow! We will launch an attack on Han Guy as soon as he makes his fire attack. I'll show him how terrifying I can be. Gor Gor'e, watch the battle unfold and keep me updated."

The two slid down the cliff they were on. It was about midday. Various skirmishes were being fought between Ts'ao and Sol. As the sun set, Agent Gracia Akechi and Bubbles appeared near Gor Gor'e. With them was Dancing Bear in Sky and a small army of Oni.

The Oni leader was an obese muscular man. He spoke, "I am Menghuo, King of the Nanmen. We have come to support Grand General Sin Seeker. Where would you like us?"

Gor Gor'e spoke, "King Menghuo, I would like you and your wife to destroy The Sleeping Dragon's altar. The rest of your soldiers need to head towards Wukong Pass with Dancing Bear, Bubbles and Gracia."

"May I take my brother-in-law and brother with me along with Wutu-gu? I will need them for backup."

Gor Gor'e nodded in acknowledgement and the four headed towards the altar. Bubbles and the others began trekking towards Wukong Pass.

Gor Gor'e smiled a dark smile and began conjuring runes. As dusk fell, he felt the wind blow towards Ts'ao Liz's fleet. He saw Sin Seeker standing in the path of several burning boats. He waved his four-fingered hands and the runes shattered. The purple dust flew across the battlefield. Many Rakshasa collapsed.

He was only partially paying attention to the battle. He heard a leaf crack and blocked the spear thrust from Miao Fang and then rolled to avoid the attack from Miao Miao. He let out a bellow as a sword went through his shoulder. It was from Sol Yi. He wrapped his trunk around Yi and tossed him over the cliff, only to see him jump off orange runes and land next to him. He snorted and used his spade to slash at Miao Miao, who avoided his attack leading him right into the blade of White Tiger. He looked down at the triple-edged blade and quickly reversed time by two seconds.

He lunged at Miao Miao, who dodged. This time, however, Gor Gor'e angled his body in such a way that caused his tusk to be struck by the blade. His tusk broke in half and he kicked that tusk, causing it to imbed itself into White Tiger's stomach. White Tiger spit up blood and fell off the cliff.

Miao Miao purred, "You done fucked up, old geezer."

Her energy claws sliced through his back. He stumbled forward and felt a boot to his back. Then there was a burst of energy and he was flung far. He did a somersault and landed hard on his feet. He saw Zilong, the little dragon charge Liz and he intercepted them.

***

Dancing Bear sat on his rowboat, waiting for the fire. He was smoking a wonder reed. He heard a commotion and looked up to see several Rakshasa sneak on board Ts'ao Liz's dragon ship. He smiled and kicked off the boat causing it to float to shore. He saw Ts'ao Liz standing surrounded by fire resisting Hsün Yü's pull. The Rakshasa attacked and he let out a loud roar that sent them scurrying.

Dancing Bear spoke, "Get moving, girl. I will not allow you to die while Sin Seeker wants you to live."

He sighed as she stood paralyzed before gently grabbing her with his teeth and setting her on his back as he went down on all fours. Hsün Yü clambered up as well, holding onto Liz as he shot off. Within minutes they had arrived at Wukong Pass. He saw a yellow-haired Oni with yellow tattoos all over wielding a rod with a bestial skull on top. She was with several Oni dressed only in furs and bones. They all pulled out exotic-looking bone weaponry. Dancing Bear eyed them warily.

She spoke, "Go, we will hold off the enemy along with Lord Bear. I yearn to rend Sol Maria asunder."

As Ts'ao Liz fled, many Rakshasa and Felis arrived. They were led by Sol Kuang and Sol Lang, Sol Maria's older brothers.

Dancing Bear let out a roar, "Come at me if you wish to die. The Bear of Hizen stands strong. I will rip you up and chew on your entrails."

Two foolhardy Felis warriors bedecked in heavy metal attacked. Their axes shattered against Dancing Bear's fur. He then sliced them in half with his claws. The Oni attacked. Sol Lang quickly turned tail and ran. Sol Kuang struggled to break free of the encirclement. Eventually, he fled along with six striped felis warrior women. The rest lay bloody on the ground.

Dancing Bear turned towards the Oni leader. "Who in the thirteen hells are you?"

The woman smiled, "I am Jasmine Deval. I was trained by King Menghuo and Queen Zhu Rong. My husband is Wutu-gu, master of the titanium skin technique. I see you are also a skin master."

Dancing Bear nodded. "Yes, I am master of the Orochichalum skin. Come, let us meet up with your husband and the other Nanmen."

***

Sin Seeker stood on the mast of the central Dragon Ship. He watched as the seven boats of fire smashed through the hull. He saw Han Guy jump off the ship and strike the ship with his anchor rod. From the flames, several Rakshasa warriors began throwing fireballs. He watched Ts'ao Ang dive into the water along with The Giant Archer and The One-Eyed Wolf. He saw a young woman with a very cold aura about her dive and swim towards Wukong Pass.

Han Guy laughed only to see his troops petrified with fear. He saw in the fires a huge demonic man wielding a double voulge. The fires became neon blue as the man attacked. His troops screamed in terror and dove into the water. Only one man stood strong, Hanzo Dang. Han Guy lifted his club and swung it at the demon. Watching in horror as the club passed through the demon. He was struck from behind by Sin Seeker, who threw him off the ship, shorting out his electronics and causing him to slowly sink into the water.

Hanzo Dang dove into the water and hauled Han Guy to safety. Sin Seeker spoke, "Now do you see why I am feared, Han Guy? Next time I will not be so merciful."

The Shadow spoke, "I can see I chose the right person to follow. Your mastery of fire is as incredible as it is effective."

The two left and met up with Dancing Bear on his way from meeting up with the Nanmen. Sin Seeker watched the fleet burn, remembering the past.

It was evening when young Ranmaru entered his meditation chamber. The boy was naked and covered in Lord Oda's semen. He lay in front of Sin Seeker, who saw whip marks on the boy's back, most likely from Nohime getting rough.

"I take it that the task Nobunaga and Nohime had for you was entertainment?"

Ranmaru nodded with tears in his eyes. He whispered, "Why can they not see me for my mastery of the sword? Why is it every night they fuck me?'

"The same reason I did. You are young and excitable, but do you remember what I taught you? You can use that to your advantage."

***

Sin Seeker watched as the Sakura tree burned. He was on a ledge overlooking the flames. Two assassins came at him. They were bisected. Ranmaru stood there holding his sword and bleeding. His clothes were tattered by the fire.

"Please, master Seeker. I am dying. Will you fuck me one last time so I may embrace death willingly? In the arms of the only one I cared about?"

Sin placed the two bundles down. He brought Ranmaru close to him. He dropped his image disguise revealing a ten-foot-tall elf. He lifted up Ranmaru's five-foot form and penetrated him. Ranmaru screamed in ecstasy and pain. He orgasmed almost instantly before his spirit left him. Sin Seeker placed him at the foot of the Sakura tree and left with the bundles as the flames consumed him.

Sin Seeker conjured a glass of amber liquid. "Thayme Sidrodc uigde het seul, thame havens sunocme het seul."

He downed the glass before walking towards Wukong Pass with The Shadow and Dancing Bear.

A violent feminine voice rang out, "Sin Seeker, I challenge you!"

Sin Seeker turned towards the voice and saw Fang Ryofu and her army. She stood there with her sisters and brother. She was also leaning cockilly on Kao Shun, the camp crusher. He smiled and waved his allies on. He lunged, sending her limited troops scurrying. He had not realized he was still in his true form. His thick three foot long and three-foot-tall horns glinted in flames. His razor-sharp shoulder and upper spikes cut through the air with a whistling sound. Fang Ryofu was tackled in full force. He heard something break as he crashed into her. He smiled his fanged smile causing her sisters to bolt. Her brother looked around, seeing no one. He grabbed the unconscious Fang Ryofu and carried her away. Sin turned around and as the flames obscured him, he put his image disguise back on. The flames turned the sky orange with their intensity.

***

Keiji surveyed Wukong pass and then placed Bubbles and Shimasake near the third junction before galloping on to the fourth junction. He saw a purple sphere fly past him. He then saw Tung Bai exit the sphere along with a dangerous-looking kunoichi dressed in a Gothican dress. He raised his eyebrow and then shrugged before spotting his target slinking into range. His target being Chang Vicki. She was a muscular woman with wild pitch-black hair. The way she moved reminded him of a Moon Saber Cat with hints of a Pantheris. She wielded a spear shaped like a serpent. He grimaced, recognizing that spear as an ancient Serpenti Ankh-orochi spear.

***

Bubbles stopped Ts'ao Liz with her gatling bow. "Hold on a bit. There is an ambush in the clearing. Let my aunt take care of it." She then saw Liz zone out as she continued, "Liu Suen's general Weiyan is nearby." She rolled her eyes, seeing drool coming from Ts'ao Liz's mouth as she stared at Shimasake's Kunlun form.

As Shimasake finished, Bubbles waved her on, "Okay, you're good to go."

***

Keiji watched as Chang Vicki threw her spear towards Ts'ao Liz, narrowly missing her. He whooped and charged down the incline. He slashed at Vicki, who dove for her spear. He smiled as he saw Ts'ao Liz slip by. He leapt off his horse and smashed the explosive end of his spear into the ground, causing a bevy of stones to fly up and trip up Chang Vicki. She caught herself by bouncing off the palms of her hands and flipping onto his shoulders. He felt her muscular thighs flex, trying to crush his windpipe.

"Ya know, I usually take the girl on a date before getting freaky. How's next Wodensday sound."

"Why you…"

"Gotcha!"

He then flicked his mane and struck her in the vagina. She let out a yelp and released him. He took this opportunity to strike her off. She lay there twitching before roaring in pure rage.

She charged Keiji, who caught her with the shaft of his spear, flinging her into the cliff and causing a small rockslide. She was effectively buried and trapped. He leapt over the stones, pulled out her unconscious body and walked towards the end of the pass.

***

Tara Li and Trini Trung stood waiting. Trini had insisted on fighting. Tara was basically holding her up at this point. She saw a flash of red and heard bells.

A blade narrowly missed her as she turned. She used her cloak to tie Trini to her back before blocking another dagger strike.

The man in front of her was an Amber elf. He had long spiky wild hair. His chest was bare except for a bandolier going from his shoulder to his waist. All across his waist were bells.

A deep voice spoke, "Gun Jing, stand down. Can you not see one is unable to give a good fight? It would be dishonourable to kill one who can not fight back."

She turned to see a red-robed man with shoulder-length hair tied up in twelve war braids. His black skin glittered with a golden sheen under the moonlight. His eyes were wolfish and orange. Another black and gold-skinned silveran walked into view. He had a green robe and leaned heavily on a battle rake. He stumbled and was caught by a pigtailed four-foot girl with an amazing rack. She helped him sit.

She looked worriedly at The other man, "Lumeng, if we fight here, we are routed. Lord Lusu's health is at risk."

"Do not worry, Luxun, as long as Gun Jing holds his hand. We will survive the night."

Gun Jing spoke, "'Bout time you got here, old man. Why should I not kill these two?"

Keiji walked into the clearin.g "Because of me!"

Gun Jing immediately sheathed his knives. "Woah! I give. I give. Don't want to mess with The Wild Kabukimono."

Keiji handed a flask to the green-robed man. "How are you holding up, Lusu?"

"I am just winded. Thanks for the whisky."

***

Sin Seeker arrived just as Ts'ao Liz exited Wukong Pass, along with Zhu Chu and Xu Hana guarding her. She slumped hard against Hsün Yü. That was when Shogun Feng Yinping came into view. The troops looked horrified. Sin Seeker pulled out his voulge to attack.

Feng Yinping spoke, "I can find no honor here. Lady Ts'ao Liz, my debt to you is repaid. Get going before I change my mind."

Liz nodded and hurried on. Feng Yinping vanished into the night, leaving the wind to blow against Sin Seeker's back.

***

Dragon vs Wolf

Sin Seeker stood outside the Supply Depot at Mount Chaqi in the province of Huangzhong. The young and ambitious Liu Suen had marched her troops here. She wanted to gain Huangzhong so she could declare herself queen. He looked out across the battlefield and grimaced. He overlooked the battle, ground he saw the standards of Ts'ao Ang on mount Dingjun. Near the base of Dingjun stood the standard of Guo Huai, a rather sickly fellow, and The Giant Archer, Ts'ao Ang's cousin. He saw the standards of Chang Ho, an effeminate man with a dark and brooding side, near the two others. He grimaced. This battle will be the death of me. I don't like our odds.

Gor Gor'e stood on a lookout tower. "I don't like the looks of this battle Sin Seeker. Coming in from the north, we have Zilong, the little Dragon and Ma Chao, the Dragon of Xiliang. From the east, Liu Suen leads along with Chang Vicki and that bestial gatorillo Wei Yan. She also has the Sleeping Dragon and a devious-looking man."

Jester Grave snorted as he stretched. "That would be The Marquis who Schemes, Fa Zheng. I will take care of him."

Gor Gor'e spoke, "It looks like an old man is moving to the front lines. He seems to be coming towards us. And he is being supported in his march by Wei Yan."

Sin Seeker turned towards a purple and teal-cloaked man. "Well, Master Suma E, what say you to this turn of events?"

"Have Shadow attack, Fa Zheng. I will need you to stay here guarding the depot, but the rest of your men will head to the centre and support Zhu Chu and Ts'ao Zhen. If we can hold the centre, this battle will be ours."

Gor Gor'e spoke in alarm, "Boss, the Fledgling Phoenix has come up on our rear. Through Phoenix Gorge."

Suma E smiled and sent up a blue spark. Twenty-seven gunners opened fire on The Fledgling Phoenix and its forces. Many were slaughtered, but The Phoenix refused to die. He waved his fan, causing a gale to whip up, obscuring the gunners. That was when boulders started rolling down the gorge. The rest were killed, but The Phoenix still continued his march. The boulders shattered before him. Sin Seeker readied his voulge as the Phoenix got into range. Ice erupted from the ground, becoming black crystals that impaled the Fledgling Phoenix.

Suma E humphed, "Well, that takes care of that nuisance." He then vanished in a gout of purple smoke.

Sin Seeker heard a voice in his head. "That will be one to watch. He is dangerous."

Another more feminine whispered, "But his son Zhao seems nice enough. I would support him."

Sin Seeker grimaced before a shout alerted him. The depot was in flames. The Gatorillo Wei Yan was hooting in joy. Gor Gor'e jumped off his watch tower. "Where the hell did he come from?"

Wei Yan slashed Gor Gor'e across the chest before throwing him off the mountain. Sin Seeker charged only to be riddled with arrows. As The Elderly Archer fired upon him, he slumped forward. One of the voices spoke, "Don't die on us now, boy. Let me take over."

Two ethereal battle axes appeared on Sin Seeker's arms and his body took the form of The Oni Katsuie Shibata. As the spirit took over, visions of the past flooded Sin Seeker.

He was on the battlefield at Shizugatake. Katsuie Shibata was holed up in his castle with Lady Oichi. Sin Seeker had been begged to come back by Hideyoshi. He walked into the castle easily enough. The flames that Katsuie had set revealed his true form. He saw Katsuie sitting in front of his tea set. Oichi was near him, both were slowly bleeding out. They had committed suicide together instead of fleeing. He looked around before swinging his blade ending their suffering. He also noticed Ranmaru's sister, Jinsu. It looked to him as if she had been forced to commit suicide. He saw Hideyoshi struggling to grab three female toddlers. As he advanced, the three girls whimpered. Hideyoshi then was easily able to herd them out of the burning building. He sighed and knelt in front of the bodies. He whispered as the flames crawled up the bodies, "Srobab heset seuls iltun hety anc nifd epaec. Thame Sidrodc slebs heset iebdos"

As Sin Seeker regained his body, he found himself at the foot of the mountain fending off several soldiers while protecting The Giant Archer's body. He let out a wild bellow spinning around and he bisected the soldiers. He caused The Giant Archers' body to burst into flames. He then weakly advanced on the centre garrison, which had not fared much better.

***

Jester Grave stood near Liu Suen's main camp. He walked in, bashing the soldier's heads together as they charged him. He grabbed a commander by the helmet before swinging him into a group of others. Fa Zheng and Chang Vicki advanced. He saw Chuko Liang, the sleeping dragon near who he presumed was Huang Yueying, the white serpent. Both were eyeing him suspiciously. As Chang Vicki lunged at him, he grabbed her in a chokehold before body-slamming her to the ground. She lay dazed in the crater he created.

Fa Zheng spun a razor-tipped cloth at him. He dodged before jumping onto the spinning cloth and kicking hard. Not realizing his own strength. Fa Zheng fell without a head. The head rolled into the crater he had created and onto Chang Vicki, who yelped and scurried as far from it as she could. Liu Suen brought out a young Oruk girl and held a gun to her temple.

She spoke, "If you try to stop us, your daughter will die. Got it?"

Jester growled, "Leave my baby out of this."

The girl squirmed free but was shot in the back. Liu Suen stared dumbly at her smoking gun. Her eyes were wide in shock. Jester rushed his falling daughter and caught her. He growled and hurried out of the camp.

***

The Tarot Hunter lay in the middle of a dozen bodies with knives sticking out of them. She panted weakly, clutching at a spear that had penetrated her vagina. It was currently sticking out of her stomach. Her eyes were fading as she trembled. Sin Seeker knelt and vaporized the spear. He then petrified her and shrunk her. He placed the small statuette in his bag before jogging off. He found the broken body of Gor Gor'e among some stones by the river. He was barely breathing and his intestines were hanging out. Sin grimaced and also petrified and shrunk Gor Gor'e. He continued on towards Liu Suen's main camp. He saw the body of Chang Ho and went over. He heard, "Chunyu Qiong, why must you mock me? You and I will meet soon. Please forgive… me…"

He waved his hand, causing Chang Ho to burst into flames. He looked around the narrow pass and saw a hidden mark. He growled, "Suma E planned this to happen. He wanted both Chang Ho and The Giant Archer to die in this battle. But why did he spare Zhu Chu and Ts'ao Zhen?"

Suma E appeared and fired an ice spear at Sin Seeker, impaling him against the mark. "Too many strong warriors dying would cause suspicion. You have outlived your usefulness Sin Seeker. I will be the one to rule these lands." He then vanished as Jester Grave walked into the pass. Jester Grave lay a green-skinned female oruk near Sin Seeker. Sin Seeker pulled himself off the icy spear and waved his hand, causing the girl to shrink and petrify. He grunted and pushed a button on his gauntlet, causing a small ship to materialize above them. A small lift lowered, allowing Jester to help Sin Seeker onto it. It was raised and locked. The ship sped away towards Sin Seeker's farm.

It landed and several automated bots rushed out of a hole in the ground. They brought the stasis tubes out and began bringing them to the hidden med centre. It was so technologically advanced it could even bring the dead back to life.

Jester watched with curiosity as the med centre worked. It slowly repaired the damage done to Gor Gor'e and Tarot. Sin Seeker sat on one of the beds. The robot nurse carefully extracted the arrows and burned the wounds shut. He could see many scars on Sin Seeker's torso.

Jester Graves spoke, "Care to explain those scars."

"They were from my first death. Also, the reason I helped out Ts'ao Liz and her brother. I first assisted Liu Suen. It was my fault. I should have known they'd get curious about who I was. When the yellow cloak leader Zhang Jue died in Liu Suen's care, he revealed my lineage. He asked Liu Suen to support me, but she was devoted to Shogun Pei. They are sisters, after all. Shogun Pei convinced her that the remnant of the Hunter clan should be purged. My father was the only survivor of the clash between the Hunter clan and the Shogun clan. He bedded one of the amber elves named Yuenu, the lady of the forest. I was the result, along with a twin sister."

"What happened to your sister?"

"Dead. She died during the battle of Shizugatake. Hideyoshi was against the Oni Shibata Katsuie. She was on Katsuie's side. I was on Hideyoshi's side. She killed many of his troops. So when the master of the dagger axe, Kato Kiyomasa, captured her, she was forced to kill herself."

"So what of the scars?"

"Shogun Pei used her hammer and embedded me into a cliff. Pretty sure I died that night. The three moons were red. It was the time of year when, in the old days, sacrifices would be made to the forest. I woke up here in this bed. My body fully renewed into what you see now."

***

The Battle of the Big Bridge

Keiji had heard troubling news. Over in Cheng province, Shogun Pei had marched on Ts'ao Ren, the turtle tank warrior's castle at the fan. He only had the support of Dancing Bear in Sky, Tara Li, Bubbles, and Shimasake. The rest were helping Sin Seeker at Mount Chaqi. He snorted and kicked a pole causing a small hover sledge to rise from the ground.

Dear Keiji,

I have created this sledge to attach to your dragon-horse. It is reinforced titanium, along with numerous of my own runes. It should be able to withstand the speed at which you will be riding. I foresaw Fan Castle falling. Do not be rash and don't expect to be able to turn the tide of battle so easily. I am entrusting my daughter in your hands. Keep her safe along with the others. By the time you reach Fan Castle, it will be flooded. Take great care in your advance. Shogun Pei and her siblings are not to be trifled with. The goal of the coalition is to kill Shogun Pei and as many of her siblings as we can. Try not to let the Turtle fall. If you can turn the tide of battle, do so but do not put yourself and others at undue risk.

Your half-brother,

Sin Seeker

Keiji watched as the sled attached to Matsukaze the girls boarded and he got on Matsukaze's back. She shot off. They soon arrived at Fan Castle. He saw the Maeda banner on a hill north. So that was where he parked. He walked into the camp to hear arguing.

"Don't be a fool, Pang De! If you reinforce the floodgates, Shogun Suo will kill you."

A blue armoured dragon man spoke, "I am already dead. I pierced Shogun Pei's arm with a poisoned arrow. My coffin will come into good use."

Pang De left carrying a steel coffin on his back. Dancing Bear followed quietly. Keiji saw Dancing Bear sneak off but pretended to ignore it. He walked up to the yellow and gold-clothed ninja.

"Hello, Matsu! It's surprising to see you here."

She turned towards him in disbelief. "Keiji! You... you are alive!"

"What'd you think? I was dead?"

"Yes! You never contacted us after you went off with Sin Seeker. Your uncle was beside himself. Thinking he sent you to your doom."

"How is the old geezer?"

A grey-skinned silveran walked into view. He was wearing a loincloth and nothing else. He picked up his bane bear cloak and put it on. A blue metal sword hung from a loose belt. He turned his burning red eyes towards Keiji and spoke, "Last I saw, Toshi was duelling Shogun Ping and winning."

"Brovone Bjorn, why are you here? I thought you had a beef with the Maeda clan."

"The enemy of my enemy is my friend. So why are you here?"

"I have come in support of Ts'ao Ren the Turtle Tank. Sin Seeker sent me via note. What has happened so far."

Toshie limped into camp, holding his bleeding arm. "Ping is dead. He got me good, though. I nearly lost my arm. Ah, Keiji, I was wondering what happened to you. We could use your unique flair. I am sorry about your father. He died a noble death."

"Eh, death happens. Where do you need me to smash."

"We could use you at the floodgates. We heard disturbing news that Shogun Suo was planning on demolishing them."

"I already have a man aiding Pang De."

"Then how about Fan Bridge? We could use your spear to protect our supply line."

Keiji nodded, "Brovone Bjorn protect little Bubbles here. She is my niece. Tara Li aid Ma'a Maeda in striking the centre and making a path for our support from Lumeng."

Matsu spoke, "What makes you think The Tigers will help the Wolves."

A red-cloaked boy walked into camp. His midriff was showing and his red tiger eyes glimmered with intelligence. He was leading a female by a chain attached to her collar. She looked subdued.

He handed the chain to Keiji, saying, "This is Ka'ai, daughter of the bear of the Hojo. She betrayed us, leading to her mother disowning her. I hand her off to you as a show of good faith that the Tigers will aid the Wolves."

Keiji growled, "I don't condone slavery, but I will accept your show of good faith by taking this slave."

The two bowed to each other and the boy's breasts flopped out of her chest wrap. She blushed and tried to run. Keiji stopped her. "You will want to stay. We are currently surrounded by water. It looks as though the floodgates burst anyway."

***

Pang De was struggling against the mighty kicks of Shogun Suo. He blocked with his coffin before slamming it into Suo's head. Suo went down but took advantage of his falling and stabbed into Pang De's crotch before slicing up as Pang De fell. Dancing Bear took this opportunity to strike Shogun Suo from behind after finishing off Zhao Cang the Black. Shogun Suo lunged at Dancing Bear. He dodged and tried to strike back, only to be thrown toward Pang De's fallen form. He righted himself with a flip and used his paw to gesture rudely at Shogun Suo.

***

Tara Li had gotten to the centre castle along with Ma'a Maeda right as the floodgates broke. They were both on the ramparts along with Ts'ao Ren and his brother Ts'ao Chung. She could see Shogun Pei and her army setting up catapults. One of the catapults exploded, sending the troops near it flying. Their corpses splattered into the water with sloshy thuds. She saw Ma'a put away her bazooka. She blinked since she did not see where it came from.

Ma'a reached her arm into some blue sparkles near her medical satchel and pulled out a very large gun with a miniature nuke missile. She fired it off, destroying the cliff on which more catapults were being built. She smirked before replacing it back into the sparkles.

***

Dancing Bear snarled as he dodged another kick from Shogun Suo. He was trying to protect the injured Pang De. Another strike came from behind. He was now facing Shogun Xing and Shogun Suo. He slashed into Suo's armour, rending it and nearly eviscerating Suo. Suo stumbled back and fell into the rushing water, getting swept away. While Xing was distracted by his brother being drowned, he was kicked into the water as well. Xu Hana appeared on the horizon, rushing as fast as she could. She collapsed near Pang De and tried unsuccessfully to stop the bleeding.

Dancing Bear grunted, "He's gone, girl. Nothing we can do."

Dancing Bear's ears flattened against his head as a miniature nuclear explosion reduced a cliff nearby to rubble. He lay Pang De in his coffin and closed the lid before climbing on top of it and grabbing Xu Hana. "Hang on, girl, it's about to get radical."

Several rocks tumbled down, smashing into the coffin and sending it flying into the rushing water. He grabbed a piece of wood and began moving the coffin towards the bridge leading into Fancheng castle.

"O sole mio sta nfronte a te"

"Aren't you making light of the situation?'

"Of course, girl. What point is there in being gloomy? He knew his time was up the moment he shot Shogun Pei with that arrow. He also knew going to the floodgates was suicide. Also, we're winning. Shogun Pei's forces have been reduced by half. No, wait by three-fourths. Several dozen have just surrendered to Lumeng and Luxun. She will be making one last charge against the castle. She is surrounded."

***

Keiji stood on the bridge to the Maeda fortifications; he swung his fork, killing several grunts and throwing their bodies into the river. A fearsome beast of a drake lunged at Keiji with his club. Keiji blocked easily and vaulted over him. Several gunners opened fire, cutting into the bestial man.

Keiji smirked, "Did I just blow your mind or what? So long, Zhao Lei, I wasn't the better man. You just got led feet." He then whistled and rode off towards Fan Castle as Zhao Lei dropped into the water. His body floated there with green ribbons flowing out of twenty-seven craters in his flesh.

***

Shogun Pei struggled through the small pass toward Fan Castle. She smashed through several of the traitorous tigers. She finally made it to the bridge in front of fan. She saw Lumeng standing there. He slashed his pike at her. She let the blade glance off her shoulder before letting out a poisonous mist from her mouth. He began coughing and keeled over. She kicked him aside and sent an explosive wave toward the gates. It impacted, causing the gates to shatter. She rushed the gate tossing aside Tara Li, who had tried to jump-kick her from the walls. She dodged a grenade flung by Ma'a Maeda. She crashed into Dancing Bear, who managed to sever her injured arm. One of the Tigers picked up the hammer and walked away.

She dropped her hammer. "Guess it's unarmed combat with you."

Dancing Bear raised his eyebrow at her before being grabbed by a tall winged humanoid and dragged into the air.

"Liu Feng thought you would be too cowardly to assist. Guess I got to wing it." He then severed Liu Feng's left-wing, sending the drake crashing into the ground.

He saw Shogun Pei charge Ts'ao Ren only to fall with a spear in her chest. Keiji stood there and pulled out his spear and incinerated the dead Drakons and Shogun Pei. He sighed and got off his horse.

"We had best be going. Sin Seeker and the others returned from Mount Qi. They were decimated. Tarot Hunter, Gor Gor'e, and apparently Jester Grave's daughter are all in critical condition. We will go back to the Maeda camp. But first, Liu Feng, I know you are still alive. Go tell your sister that the shogun clan is routed. Reveal to her that Shogun Pei is dead. Tell her this is what happens to those that betray the trust of Sin Seeker."

The winged Drakon got up and bolted. Keiji handed Ka'ai to Tara Li. Ma'a Maeda climbed into the sled as well as Brovone Bjorn, who was currently serving as Bubbles' perch.

Dancing Bear chuckled, "I'll catch up. I have some unfinished business to attend to."

Keiji shot off, leaving Dancing Bear in the dust. Dancing Bear turned to see Chang Vicki charging onto the scene.

"You are too late to save your sister. She is dead, but do not worry. You will be joining her soon."

"That is what you think. I am Chang Vicki, the indomitable. You are nothing but a lowly bandit."

"How drunk are you?"

"I have been sober for four years."

"Well, then come kill me if you can."

The two clashed on the bridge leading towards Malachite Forest. They were evenly matched. Dancing Bear jumped over her and sent her tumbling into the mud. She got up and sliced her hand with her spear. She stabbed at him several times, her blood powering up her spear with each thrust. In her wild fury, she did not even realize her body was weakening. The Serpenti spear was consuming her life force. Her eyes began to get blurry as she felt her hand get severed. The spear dropped along with her hand. Her hand shrivelled up as it was absorbed into the spear.

Dancing Bear sat down next to her sobbing body. He cauterized the wound and stroked her fur.

"Why did you kill her?"

"Liu Suen betrayed Sin Seeker. He still has the wounds from that day as jagged scars across his body. Shogun Pei killed him, but he was revitalized. Now he claims his due. I was only the sword. Now I can kill you or you can leave and try to sway Liu Suen from her destructive path. She may listen to you. Sin Seeker does not want to kill her. He has already claimed his due. But if she insists on continuing this path, he will stop her."

"Kill me. I do not want to live without my sister."

"No, you are redeemable."

Both looked up to see a four-armed bronze-skinned man with inky black hair and two horns jutting up from his forehead. He held a staff in one hand, an axe in another, and a fan in the third. His fourth was empty.

"I have seen your warrior's spirit, Chang Vicki. It is pure, unlike Shogun Pei's, which was dark. You are being given a chance. You can join Liu Suen and work to change her mind or I can take you now. Your choice will either save Liu Suen or kill her."

She stared into the man's Realgar eyes before bowing her head. "I will try to save my sister."

The man smirked knowingly. He lifted the Serpenti spear out of the muck and it became orpiment instead of blackish green. There were azurite bands circling it and a jewel that was the colour sanguine. He handed the spear to her after restoring her hand.

"Chang Vicki, you are to be my voice. I am the great Khan. My mark is now on you."

He vanished along with Chang Vicki, leaving Dancing Bear alone.

***

The Battle Without Justice

Sin Seeker growled and cursed his luck. He was near a robed being with grey Serpent eyes, the being looked like death.

"Seethrassa believes we are outnumbered. Surrounded on all sides by Drakon. Seethrassa thinks we should… run."

Sin Seeker snarled, "I would have to agree with you. I hate running from a fight. My father would never run."

"Seethrassa knows Bounty Hunter 13. Lately, all he does is run. His body fails him at times."

"Does it now? Well, Seethrassa or should I say Bounty Hunter 13, what is your plan now that we are surrounded?"

As his body changed into that of a thirteen-foot tall man with four-foot horns and sharp spikes on his shoulders and arms, "Uh oh, you see things. Of course, I would not doubt Sin Seeker would see things, but do you see what the Tigers are planning?"

Sin seeker looked around and sighed. "Fire, of course."

The two saw their opening and burst through, with the sons of Shogun rushing after them. The portcullis closed and Shogun Xing managed to get through another before it closed. Sin Seeker smiled devilishly as flames erupted all across the battlefield. Xing could only watch in horror as his younger brother Suo was incinerated.

The demonic form of Sin Seeker turned towards Xing and spoke, "One more Shogun dead. My clan will be avenged. You are next, child."

Xing passed out in fear, nearly peeing himself. Sin Smirked and the gates opened. He hoisted the boy up and walked towards the centre pass of Xiaoting. He tossed Xing at Shogun Feng Yinping's feet. She gulped and lifted her brother up. She backed away and fled.

The tall man had vanished, only to be replaced by the cat. "Seethrassa will see you around Hunter's spawn."

"Yes, you will, Father. Yes, you will."

The Little Dragon fled towards Liu Suen. As Sin Seeker neared Liu Suen's main camp, he came across one of Liu Suen's generals demolishing the tiger forces.

Pan Zhang, one of the tigers, spoke, "Fu Rong, friend, why not surrender? Your army is routed?"

"Dogs! Do you think a mountain will yield?"

Fu Rong charged Pan Zhang only to be decapitated by his voulge. Sin Seeker eventually came upon the ship of Cheng Ji; he was easily sinking many Tiger Ships with his cannon fork. But he could not last long.

Sin Seeker spoke, "I suggest you abandon ship. Liu Suen has already begun to evacuate."

"I have never fled from battle throughout my military career. Besides, the Empress is currently in a dangerous situation."

Sin Seeker sighed and continued on, hearing a very large explosion behind him as Cheng Ji was obliterated. He came across The Little Dragon fending off an attack along with one of the Southern Oni.

The Oni spoke, "My lord go protect Liu Suen. I got this."

"Very well Shamo'ke. Stay safe, my friend."

Shamo'ke dodged an attack by Gun Jing. Gun Jing started to cough violently, even spitting up some blood. He was helped up by Pan Zhang. Gun Jing charged again, this time using his machine gun arm to fire at Shamo'ke. A bullet struck Shamo'ke's arm but was only a glancing blow. He swung his short pike, slashing Gun Jing. Gun Jing fell lifeless. Pan Zhang pulled Shogun Pei's hammer out of the aether and smashed it into Shamo'ke, crushing his chest and killing him.

Shogun Feng Yinping arrived behind him as Shamo'ke fell. Her eyes were full of fury. She pulled out a short black blade and stabbed Pan Zhang in the heart. She took her sister's hammer and then saw Sin Seeker standing there. Her fury is unabated. She charged him. Sin Seeker dodged her furious attack. He kept dodging until she collapsed on the ground sobbing.

Through her sobs, she spoke, "You murdered my daughter. You murdered my brothers. Why won't you kill me? I have nothing to live for."

"I disagree unless you only act like you are receptive towards my advances."

Sin Seeker saw the black-armoured Lu Lingli, daughter of the famed Lu Bu, walk into the clearing. She sat and snuggled up against Shogun Feng Yinping Sin Seeker, leaving the two there, making sure flames wouldn't touch them. He finally caught up to Liu Suen. She was being carried by Chang Vicki. He saw the tiger army catching up. He tapped a ledge causing a small landslide blocking Chang Vicki and Liu Suen from view. The Sleeping Dragon arrived as reinforcements. Only to end up being an escort to the last remaining ship. As Sin Seeker watched it sail away, he sighed.

He spoke to the shadowy form next to him. "How long does she have Brovone?'

"I give her a little over a year before she finally falls. Pity she could have been the one to lead this war-torn land."

Sin Seeker nodded, "I suspect the new Central Komodo emperor will be Suma Zhao. His father is ambitious but will not survive long and his brother will make too many enemies and get assassinated. I hope to the gods I am wrong, though. Since it will mean young Ts'ao Liz will not survive long either."

***

Sanctuary of the Two Geniuses

It was four hundred war-torn years as each of the three primary kingdoms fought to claim Central Komodo as their own. Eventually, it had fallen to the wolves and dragons. Ts'ao Liz had vanished along with her sister Rei and her strategist. Ts'ao Ang had begun to grey and was now in charge of the Wolves. The tigers had allied themselves fully with the wolves. Sin Seeker figured it was to build their power. The beginning of the end would be at the Wukong plains.

Sin Seeker stood inside the small fortified village of Wukong. The small monkey people were eager for his protection. Jester Grave scratched the head of one of the females on his shoulder. She chittered happily.

Sin Seeker chuckled before looking out upon the Wukong Plains. "I see why your family needed us. Both the Dragons and the Wolves have captured many Wukong as slaves. Gor Gor'e, what do you think our plan of action should be?"

Gor Gor'e Eliphan snorted, "I recommend you and Brovone Bjorn stay here with Jester Grave. I see the Khwarezmian army on the horizon. Dancing Bear and Keiji will begin clearing out the front-line villages while leading me through them to place protection runes. Tara Li, Bubbles, Ma'a Maeda, and Trini will snipe from the cliffs south of here. Tara Li is to be the lookout while the other three snipe with tranq darts. I want to reduce the number of deaths in this battle. Shimasake, you and Tung Bai sneak into the Dragon camp and convince Shogun Feng Yinping to charge the enemy. If my plan is correct, she will meet up with Lu Lingli and take her out of the fight."

Sin Seeker nodded, "Well then, let's go. We should also keep an eye out for any other Wukong that may have been captured or imprisoned."

Dancing Bear began clearing the front. He looked up at the three moons and saw they were blood red. His pulse quickened and he began moving faster. They finally reached the last village. Keiji swung his spear, severing a general's arm. The general's second in command called for a retreat.

Keiji looked around and saw numerous explosive barrels. "God dammit, it's a trap."

Gunfire erupted, causing explosives to ignite. The fire quickly spread across the dry ground brush. Keiji looked around. Dancing Bear was smouldering but unharmed and his innate fire resistance had saved him from the blast. He was still dazed and had shrapnel in his skin but otherwise unharmed. They rushed over to the mangled form of Gor Gor'e.

Dancing Bear was furious. "Those bastards, I'll kill 'em all."

The fire wrapped around Gor Gor'e, causing him to vanish. It then took the form of him saying, "Do not get enraged, friend. I knew today was my last day. Protect Sin Seeker. He will need your aid. The Wukong are safe. That is what those protection runes were for. May you remember The Way of Peace."

He vanished, leaving behind an awestruck Keiji and Dancing Bear. The two then watched as Fang Ryofu entered the battlefield. She looked terrible. Lu Lingli and Shogun Feng Yingping met up and duelled. The two then fought each other towards the forest and disappeared into the trees. The fire began to become intense as it raced along the dry brush. Both sides of the battlefield were burning. Sin Seeker charged Fang Ryofu. She struggled under his blows. Finally collapsing, the flames blocked them from view.

Sin Seeker stood with his voulge raised. "Why do you still fight?"

"My army may have abandoned me, but I will not stop until Ding Cui and Ding Yuan are avenged."

A blue-armoured man walked into the middle of the flames. The flames became a deep red revealing his true form.

"That is enough, you two. Sin Seeker, this is the new body of Midnight Sin. You two need to stop this useless argument. Sun Maria and Ts'ao Liz have both passed."

Before he could continue, he fell with an icy crystal jutting out of his stomach. Suma Shi stood there. He fired off two more bolts of ice, causing Sin Seeker to take them.

Sin snarled, "I will not fall to the same tricks twice. Flee now! Tell your father Ts'ao Ang lies dead."

Suma Shi fled as Sin Seeker lifted Arcanus up on his shoulder. He brought his ship down and placed Arcanus in the medical sector. He then vanished and reappeared outside the Dragon base. The Sleeping Dragon walked out along with his wife, the White Serpent. She was holding her dagger axe at the ready.

Sin Seeker looked down at The Sleeping Dragon as he sipped his tea. The Sleeping Dragon looked tired. The White Serpent also looked tired, but hers was more from supporting her husband than illness.

"I appreciate all the trouble you are going through to try and kill me, Chuko Liang. However, I am a Silveran and hemlock does not affect me, nor does arsenic, but the tea is nice."

The sleeping dragon sighed. "Yes. I figured It would not work for you. You have been a curious thorn in my tactics. A wild card I did not account for. It is time for me to pass on. A pity this will be the last we meet. I enjoyed matching wits with you."

The Sleeping Dragon closed his eyes and raised his head to the stars. There was a meteor shower as three moons glowed red…

***

The Monkey King stood overlooking the Wukong plains. Next to him was a serpentine woman with an icy aura and a muscular male with a fiery aura.

"I win. Pay up."

The man spoke, "How did you know this would come to pass, Sun Wukong?"

"Simple, Fu Xi, I was there when Sin Seeker was re-born. I saw his destiny."

"So you cheated?"

"In inelegant terms, yes, Nuwa, I cheated. But regardless of how it happened, I win."

"Ugh, fine, here's your payment."

"Pleasure doing business with you."

Fu Xi laughed and raised a beer stein to the Monkey King before drinking it.

***

Sin Seeker stood staring up at the three full moons overlooking Wukong Plains.

His ship was waiting for him. He was soon joined by Keiji, Dancing Bear, Fang Ryofu, and Bubbles. Shimasaki jumped up on his horns and nestled into his hair. The others were just arriving. For him, the war was over. His small family boarded his ship and left for his farm. He arrived at his farm to see Ts'ao Liz and she knelt at his feet.

He patted her head. "Welcome home, Lady Ts'ao. May you prosper under my banner."

Invasion of Silver by the Equus

A tall Kimeran stood staring down at a purple Equus girl. Her hair is platinum purple.

He spoke, "Circles within Circles within circles. It's always about Circles. God, I hate Circles. They are too orderly."

The white mare behind the purple one spoke, "What are you talking about, Sidrodc?"

"What am I talking about? Oh yes, you seek to invade Continent Silver no?"

"How do you know that?"

"I am Chaos, you know. But that is not why I am here. No, I am actually here to stop you from this path of foolishness."

"My mind is set, you old goat. Nothing you can do will change my mind."

"I see that. However, be warned you are only going to be slaughtering your people if you do this. Continent Silver is home to one of the Great Onix Towers. Part of the Prime Circle."

The purple one spoke, "You keep mentioning circles. What does that mean?"

"Solaria, you have not explained the PsyQi to your student. What is wrong with you?"

"It's never come up. There is no reason for it. We are not Silverans."

"Gravy and Biscuits, girl! You risk detonating a bomb. Oops, the cheese is burning. I must be off. Taa taa…" He vanished in a shower of confetti that then detonated, covering the entire castle in painted polka dots.

"Ignore him, Dusk. He is mad as a hatter. We must focus on our invasion of Continent Silver. The last dregs of the Silverans must be eliminated before they can rebuild. They are abominations. I have spent many moons talking and making alliances. Our allies have already whittled them down."

"I must take a stand and say that we do not have the manpower at this time to make such a plan. We can't even keep those Lunar Rebels at bay. What makes you think that we can invade Silver?"

"We can. Trust me."

"Ugh, you are my teacher. Very well. When you need me to lead the attack, I will, but until then, I'll be in my library on Island Thatchvill."

As she left the castle and got on her airship, a moist pink pillow slapped into her muzzle. She looked at the naked plump pink bottom of her friend, Kim, floating in midair.

"Dammit, Kim. This is not a good time."

Kim's face popped out of a portal behind her. "Oh, but every time is a good time for face tushi. So why are you so distracted, no boobs?"

"Circles. I am distracted by circles."

"Ooo, I like circles. They are round and bouncy like boobs. They form everything from the lowly Atom to the biggest tower. Why circles, though? Oh that is a conundrum. What a fun word to say con... undrum. Oops, gotta go. Somebody forgot a foal's birthday. Gotta go make them happy."

Dusk shook her head and wiped off her muzzle as Kim disappeared.

"What a curious creature. I like her. So little Alice has dove into the rabbit hole."

"Yes, I have. What is so important about circles?"

"Like your friend said, they are the basis for everything. They are also pure. A circle is ever a circle. But one wrong twitch and a circle can become an oval. They are orderly. A circle has no end. It just continues to loop."

"You sound sane, Sidrodc."

"Ah, that is because I am not Sidrodc. The old goat has been alive for aeons. It has started to affect his mind. Hello Alice, I am Doctor Fluorescent, but you may refer to me as Master Phoenix."

Dusk turned around to see a well-dressed man wearing a lab coat. However, the thing that stood out to her was that his forearm was replaced by a void metal vambrace. This vambrace had the emblem of a burning phoenix on it. It also seemed to glow ominously.

"What are you?"

"I am me. That is all you need to know."

"I seek knowledge."

"I know. And I will help you. But not here. Not while the sun is up. I will see you later, Alice."

Dusk flew her airship to her home on Island Thatchville. She landed on her tower and exited the ship. A slender lizard boy walked out, holding a robe for her. She put it on since she kept her library relatively cold and dry so as not to damage her precious books.

"Razor, Can you try to keep the others occupied? I have some intensive research and would like to not be disturbed by my friend's antics."

The boy nodded and jumped off the tower and extended his wings to glide to the ground. Dusk watched him go, then sighed. Now where is the book on Pre-Silver History? She walked through her library until she bumped into a solid body.

"Ah, Alice, your journey through the Rabbit Hole begins. I do believe this is the book you are looking for, but it is a load of Taur shit. Literally. Like the Taur who wrote it was just seeing what shit he wrote down, people would believe. I can tell you the truth, but first, a game."

"What kind of game are we talking about Phoenix?"

"Muahaha! Just a game of war. Let us begin, shall we?"

***

Dusk found herself on Continent Silver. She was next to her friends and all of them were dressed in Solar Empire armor, except Kim, who was nowhere to be seen. Prism Rush, her rainbow-haired friend, was sporting two mechanical wings and her right eye was missing. She had an eyepatch over her eye. Behind them were three Imposing mares, one in pink crystal-like armour, one in platinum polished armour, and one in fiery gold armour. Before them lay the ruins of City Silver.

Prisma spoke in her scratchy butch voice, "Hey, egghead, get your head out of the clouds. We await your orders. Her lordship wants us to go circle around through the forest and strike from the back while the guardian of the ruins is distracted. We are just waiting on your command to move out."

"Right! Uh, let's go then."

She walked towards the forest. Her troops followed her. "You have made your first move, young Dusk. Now it's my turn!"

The three full moons became crimson. The forest became violent. As she and her troops rushed through the forest, it consumed them one by one. She arrived at a small glade with a big black stone in the middle of a pond. The forest did not come near this place. They would be safe for now.

"Set up a small camp, we move at dawn."

She counted the number of troops left. Only a fourth remained. She shuddered and spoke, "Jackie, what in the thirteen hells was that?"

An amber mare, well-toned except for her thighs which were pure muscle, walked over. "Sorry suga ah don't quite know. Ah, have never seen plant life act like that."

A mare that looked like somebody threw up a bunch of pastel colours spoke quietly, "That was, is still, Nocni Iov. As a forest dweller, I know the history well. Back in the old days, when Silverans were a bunch of warring tribes, they would sacrifice their prisoners to the forest so it would not encroach upon their farms and villages. The first of every month is Nocni Iov. And it is said that the Demon of Silver was born on the thirteenth Nocni Iov of the year. It's also when he is at his strongest."

"And dare I ask what month this is."

"Thirteenth. We are going to be massacred."

Jackie spoke harshly, "Can that line of thought, Butterfly? We will survive this."

Prisma nodded. "Right! We faced down the horrors before. A little forest isn't going to stop us."

Dusk nodded and lay down. Then saw on the black stone a statue of a pure Silveran. She swore she could see smoke coming from its nose as it lit a cigar. She then saw two silvery fiery voids open where his eyes should have been. He stared directly at her and she bolted upright. She looked around and it was just about dawn. She saw Jackie fixing up some stew. She walked over.

"Why are you cooking? Where is Kim?"

"Uh, suga, are you okay? Kim was executed for being part Silveran along with many others. You were the one to sign the order on behalf of Solaria."

"I… what? But… oh goddess."

"It's alright, suga. None of us knew that she and Rene were part Silveran. It was a shock to all of us. I did hate you for it. Rene was my girlfriend and we had plans to get married, but as of now, we can't afford to hate you. You lead us."

"So I also must have missed the part where Prisma became a cyborg?"

"Uh, maybe. That was at the first stages of the war when we all fought against the Lunar Rebels. She was the guard of Lady Selene. You cleaved her wings off as she tried to dive at you from the sky. When she still tried to defend her lady, your blade sliced through her face giving her that scar. She was saved from the block when Selene surrendered to Solaria. However, she was forced to be a slave in the quarry for a year as punishment."

Prisma spoke, "It was better than the alternative, which was becoming a breeder for this army. Getting constantly raped and constantly giving birth. Fuck that! A bit of hard labour under rocks that could crush you was preferable. We had best get the men fed and on the road. The attack has begun."

After a meal, the troops moved out. The forest was still very alive and by the time she got out of the forest, only herself, Jackie, and Butterfly remained. Prisma had been snagged by a vine and pulled under the foliage. The sound of her terrified screams still echoed in Dusk's head.

She was behind the guardian of the ruins now. It had taken them six hours to get there. She saw Solaria still fighting against the Demon of Silver, but the others were dead. Selene lay against a wall with some rebar sticking through her sternum. The crystal armoured mare was headless and spilling blood from her neck. All the soldiers were destroyed. Some burned up, while others were missing parts. She saw one of the female soldiers trying to hold her intestines in, to no avail.

Butterfly cried out and collapsed. Seeing all the death had put her in a catatonic state. Jackie was currently clearing her stomach of breakfast. She rushed the Demon of Silver and as his halberd came at her face, she blacked out.

***

She awoke in her library panting. She looked around only to see Doctor Fluorescent clapping his hands.

"Very good but not up to standards. But you played my game. So I am obligated to answer any and all questions you may have."

"Okay, so what are you?"

"Hmm, a tricky question. Once, I was Doctor Johnny Fluorescent of the Fountainhead. I was one of the first Fountainheads to reach the Star Vale. The planet I was resting on had a cult dedicated to the worship of Firebirds. They found me. They went to sacrifice me to their Firebird, but I escaped and found a void metal vambrace in a cavern. The cultists found me and came to attack me, but the vambrace incinerated them. In the confusion, I had accidentally touched the vambrace and it fused with me. My soul is now permanently bound to this vambrace. And since Void Metal only will be destroyed at the end of the universe, I am immortal. This is my nine-hundredth body. I have been both male and female. I have even been a gelatinous humanoid."

"Okay, more questions raised but unimportant. My main question is, what are the Towers?"

"Hmm, better to show you than tell you. Prepare yourself, Alice. We are going back in time."

***

"Welcome to the first continent. Do not worry about changing anything. We can't interact with the past like this. Since this is not actual time travel."

"The first continent?"

"Yes, just watch."

She saw three large dragons. One was Silver, one was copper, and one was white. Near the Silver dragon, she saw a large turtle. And finally, a tentacled man with wing stubs on his back. His squid-like face scrunched up in annoyance.

"Great Silver Dragon, why must we take orders from these interlopers?"

"Ha ha, the same could be said of you, Thul Thanos. We are not taking orders. We are merely helping them with their plan. They wish to forge the beings of this land into something better."

"But we already have the Thulhuid and Scalefolk. You yourself forged the Scalefolk and the Thulhuid are my children. Of course, there are also the Elves and the Dwarves that came with my children."

"The beings on this planet came before you. But not before my Scalefolk. The Scalefolk are not meant to inhabit this land. They were forged for warmer temperatures."

The Turtle spoke, "They are here. Welcome esteemed visitors from beyond the stars. Why have you called us here?"

The leader of the strange beings spoke, "I am Zmatek of the Fountainhead. We were sent here to help bring intelligence to the beings beyond the Star Vale. You have a magnificent planet. So intriguing."

Silver Dragon spoke, "Why thank you, but it is not our planet. Gaia Silver is our mother. She is asleep now. What do you need to help create people for this land?"

The woman next to Zmatek spoke, "I need a great forge built on the crossed leylines. At the start of each leyline, I need a great tower made of black stone built."

"Oh well, I suppose we can assist you. I am well versed in the leylines of Silver. My dragons and I will build these towers. Come Razorfang, we have work to do."

The Turtle spoke, "I will begin the making of the forge you need. Thul Thanos, you have a large forge mountain, do you not?"

"I do, old man. The first of my ships to land here was a great forge. All our ships came from that one, but Midwinter will need to help. It is covered in Ice and snow right now and has cooled considerably."

"That I can do, Thul Thanos."

Dusk watched time fly by as the towers were built. When they were done, Seven Onyx towers with seven different symbols were fully built. There seemed to be no doors or windows, just a massive pillar holding up the sky.

"Impressive, aren't they? Null for lord Phantos of what will be Komodo, Fire For the Forge mistress Sylar Silver, Stone for the Holy Alexander, Wind for Webspinner on what will become Diavonbre, Music for Lucifer of what will become Misogoke, Water for the great bear on what will be NorvCryog, and finally Lord Zmatek soon to become the dark lord Chaos he gets the tower of thorny vines on what will soon become Silver. The great forge is also on Silver. The tallest mountain of the great crystalline pass. Mount Silver. A large volcano where the Fire Nymphs live among the Firebirds of Silver."

"What do these elements represent?"

"Let's watch further."

She saw the Dragons and the Fountainhead gather around a huge forge. The great Silver Dragon blew a stream of silver flame out his mouth lighting the forge.

Sylar spoke, "First, from the Tower Null, bring forth the blades for the bones."

Phantos layed out many blades that were hooked and dangerous looking. He lay them out in a vaguely humanoid form, including two at the top.

"Next, Lucifer, send your voice to cover the bones."

The one called Lucifer began to sing a dark and mournful song that then became a vigorous number about exploration and war.

"Next, Husband, please wrap your black vines around the blades to connect them together."

Zmatek wrapped thorny black vines around the music and the blades. Soon the forge was covered in his blood from the thorns.

"Now Alexander, the stone that will become the skin. Place it down on top of everything."

A stone body was placed on top of it all. The forge glowed and all the elements came together. A Bull like head with two horns took form first. Followed by a furry body with spikes on the shoulders, knees and elbows.

"Hmm, not what I was expecting. Regardless we will forge another place it aside."

They set the statue-like body up and did the process again. This time a body with no bull-like head formed. This one was non-furry.

"That is better. Alright, let's get the others formed."

Dusk watched as a large Ape was forged. Followed by a large bear. Then to her horror, a bipedal chitinous creature that she knew all too well. She watched as Zmatek hid the non-furry spiked being. Their bodies burned. To give them life, Webspinner gave them intelligence and folktales. The Great Bear gave them life's essence, blood. Their bodies cooled and life was given.

***

They were back in the library and Dusk spoke, "That was wrong, where are the Equus?"

"The Equus were not born until later. You are a byproduct of Taur genetic engineering."

"I don't believe you."

"If you don't believe me, then why are we even bothering with these questions?"

"Say you are right. Where would I find that information?"

"The Great Library of Lord Badger, but only a select few can get there. And those that do refuse to ever leave and they become twisted. There is another way. There are rumours that the Hunter clan has access to ancient information. Their clan is always in pursuit of knowledge. But if you do not believe me, why would you believe them?"

"If we were not among the first races, where are we? And which were the first races?"

"You are among the fourth generation of races. The first races were The Trees, Dragons, Fluffy Puffies, Dwarves, Elves, and Thulhuid. The second generations were the Scalefolk, Kytan, Taur, Ursar, Primata, Rodentia, and Ganeshian. The third generations were the Silverans and Centaurs. The fourth generations were the Oni, Equus, Doebuck, Satyrians, Felis, and Canis. The fifth generations were the Syrien, Goblins, Oruk, Troll, and Hyenidae."

"If you are right and I am not agreeing with you, this means that the Equus are science experiments."

"Aren't all races science experiments? The stories say you were created by the gods. I find it amusing. There are no gods. We Fountainhead created the first beings on every planet. Aside from the Dragons, obviously. And even then, we didn't hit all the planets. The R continuum fucked about for amusement and created the Rainbow Sector. The Xeran created life on all the planets leading from the locked sector to the junk belt aside from the Rainbow Sector. The three progenitors then got into a fight and the junk belt was made from the destroyed planets. Hell, it could even be said we Fountainhead are science experiments."

"What do you mean by that?"

"That is none of your concern. Ignore what I said. There are some things better left unknown."

"Well, you said any question. Nothing is off-limits. What do you mean by the Fountainhead being science experiments?"

"Ugh, I did say that. Hmm, how best to explain to a mortal how the galaxy was born? Hmm. Alright, so Silveran mythology states that the universe was created from the great cow Bessie's udders. As her milk flowed, a platypus came from it and birthed an egg. That egg hatched, becoming the galaxy of Silver. But if that is the case, how did Bessie come to exist?"

"I don't know?"

"It is theorized that the Universe was written."

"Like this is some story and we are all a part of it."

"Yes."

"But what happens when the story is over?"

"Some would say we cease to exist. Others would say the story begins again. Cycle after cycle. Some would argue that the universe has been rewritten many times. This iteration of the universe is just one of many renewals."

"How can I learn this?"

"Hmm, speak with the Druid Butterfly and get her permission to learn druidic secrets. That would be the next step."

"So what is the true importance of the Onyx Towers?"

"They each lay on a powerful leyline of Silver. They help spread the PsyQi all over Silver so as not to let it overload one place."

"There's that word again PsyQi. Sidrodc said it as well. But Solaria says that is a Silveran thing."

"Solaria's deranged and has become corrupt with power. But that is how I see it. The PsyQi surrounds us. It inhabits us. What you call magic is actually the PsyQi. All elements come from the PsyQi. It is one of the primary building blocks of the universe. Every species can use the PsyQi. It goes by many names Shadow, Light, The Grey, Brown, and Infernum. Some would call it Chaos. But it is more than that. It is basically lifeforce. Those who can connect to the PsyQi can see through it. That is another reason why the Demon of Silver is so strong. He was born blind. He uses the PsyQi to see. So he can see what somebody is planning before they do."

"That is all I want to know. Now I know what my next step is. Thank you for teaching me."

"That is one of my reasons for existing. Knowledge must be shared. Goodbye, Dusk. Do try not to get your fire extinguished too quickly."

He vanished in a shower of red feathers, which dissipated. She was alone. She shook her head and then opened the book she was looking for. As night fell, she slipped out after putting a blanket on Razor as he slept. She slid through the forest. And arrived at a small cottage. She would not bring Butterfly into her schemes. She tapped at the cottage door and an imposing grey Equus opened the door. She had stripes all over her well-toned and naked body. She looked at Dusk and then smiled a dangerous smile.

"Ah, young Dusk of Solaria's loins, how may Zora assist you?"

"Zora, I seek knowledge that is taboo. I seek to know a Druidic secret."

"Oh, tell Zora why you seek her and not your friend, the shy one?"

"I do not want to risk hurting her."

"But you are willing to hurt Zora? Hmm. Oh, Zora supposes she can help young Dusk. But Dusk must be willing to do whatever Zora asks of her. Zora's methods are extreme."

"I am willing."

"We will see."

Zora blindfolded her and bound her arms and legs after stripping her. She then bound her arms and legs to her waist and placed her on a hook so she hung off the ground.

"Uh, this seems kind of sexual. Is it necessary?"

"Zora did not say Dusk could speak. You seek taboo knowledge. Zora is a very horny mare."

She wrapped Dusk's muzzle shut and began to pleasure her. She also pleasured herself. She combined their two fluids together and dumped them in a cauldron. The smell of Musk filled the cabin. Then it was replaced by the smell of burning wood.

"Inhale the fumes, young Dusk. And I will give you the knowledge you seek."

Dusk took a deep breath in. Her mind began to spin. The blindfold was removed and she saw Zora standing there dressed in bone armour.

Zora removed the wrap around her muzzle. "What do you seek from Madam Webspinner?"

"I was told the next step in my desire to learn about the Towers of Silver and the PsyQi would be to talk to a Druid and learn Druidic secrets."

"Oh, that is a dangerous line of knowledge. Zora can certainly help you with your problem. Zora can see now why you came to Zora and not Lady Butterfly. What do you know of creation?"

"Nothing."

"Then we shall start there. In the beginning, The Writer wrote into existence the great Space cow Bessie. Along with Bessie, he wrote into existence his siblings. Morpheus the Dream Weaver, Damsel Death, Azrael the Alpha Reaper, Devastation, Lust, Euphoria, and Lady Luck. The Eternals then helped the galaxy form. Azrael created the Judge of Soul, the Judge of Flesh and the Guardian of the Well of Souls. Bessie began spilling milk from her udders and from that milk came the platypus. The platypus laid an egg which hatched and the galaxy was born. The devastation was not thrilled with his brother's creation. He sent the Mouse that smashes and all manners of plague, diseases, and mortality to the galaxy. Morpheus took pity on the people and sent The Psycho Fish to help them imagine and tell stories with their imagination so they would feel better about themselves."

"Zora that is enough!"

"Ah, Lady Butterfly, you are supposed to be asleep."

"I was woken by what sounded like someone giving away secrets. She was sent to see me, but she came to see you instead. Cowardice, most likely. Do not give away any more knowledge. She must earn it the hard way."

"Ah, but she has already inhaled the fumes. She must learn now."

"Damn it, Zora. You know the rules. I am the Head of the Equus Druidic Order. This must go through me."

"She is your friend. She was concerned that she might hurt you."

"Ugh! Dusk! Fine! Continue but don't do it again."

"You are here now. Why not tell her yourself."

"How far is she?"

"She sees the bone armour of Gaia."

"Oh, dear, okay, so as Zora was saying, Morpheus gave the denizens of the universe Imagination. But imagination can lead to dangerous things. Four Beings decided that there had to be something working behind the scenes. The first was the Xeran Azmodai, the second was the R Continuum R, the third was the Fountainhead Sidrodc and the final was unnamed. I do mean that literally, his name was Unnamed. Unnamed was a powerful wizard and Schemer. He desired ultimate knowledge. How to create life, it destroyed him."

"I know about the Fountainhead. I actually met a Doctor Fluorescent."

"I know. He's the one that woke me up. But to continue. Azmodai sent out many Xeran to go to the planets beyond the junk belt. R sent his Continuum to two sectors that amused him. And Sidrodc sent The Fountainhead to the planets beyond the Star Vale. They were so skilled that eventually they breached the Star Vale and entered into the galaxy proper."

"Gaia Silver welcomed them. They returned that welcome by destroying everything she had built. They warped her powers to create life. They did not appreciate her or how she was forming life."

"It sounds as though Gaia Silver is bitter."

"I am. I mean, she is."

"Zora thinks things must get back on the rails. There are five things you must know. One, the dichotomy between Light and Dark is not as black and white as you may think. Lord Shadow commands darkness, but it is not evil. Lady of the Pure Lands commands light, but it is not so good. One can't exist without the other. Two Balance is always shifting. Just because you think you have the upper hand, you don't. Three Grey and Brown are the Inbetween lands. Lord Badger is an asshole, he commands the Brown."

"Who commands the Grey?"

"The Grey is our land. The land of Mortals and Gods alike. Badger, Shadow, and Lady are the three higher beings. There are others, though. Recently Technology and Woodsman have become like Badger. Rumours swirl that there is actually somebody in charge of The Grey, but they have not made themselves known."

Butterfly whispered, "The great Lich is the one rumoured to be. Who the great Lich is, nobody knows. Then you have Chaos. Sidrodc is the master of Chaos and all Chaos Spawn come from him. He has many children and grandchildren."

Dusk spoke, "People like that don't deserve to exist."

Butterfly glared angrily at Dusk, then regained composure. "I think that is enough for you to get a grasp on it. Just be aware that there are things that are more dangerous than what I told you. There are things out there that can instantly corrupt a person."

Dusk passed out and awoke in her bed. Jackie was standing over her.

"Shoot, suga thought you were dead for a bit there. Flora and I found ya on the ground outside the farm. You were not breathing."

"I feel funny."

"You have been out for six days. Oh, and this order came in the mail for you to sign. Solaria seemed quite pissed off that you were unconscious."

"Oh, then I had best sign it. This is an order to execute all Equus that may be part Silveran. Oh man, this is huge."

Dusk signed the order. Jackie looked at her and then shook her head. "Razor, would you be a darlin and send this back to Solaria."

"Sure thing Jackie. I just hope Dusk knows what she's doing."

"I'm sure she does."

***

Many months later, Dusk stood next to Solaria as the prisoners were brought forward. These were all who had been found to share some Silveran blood. Dusk recognized many of them from Thatchville. She saw among the prisoners were Rene and Kim. Kim had uncharacteristically straight hair. While Rene looked like she had been put through the wringer.

As the executions began, Dusk saw a maniacal gleam in her mentor's eyes. She forced herself to watch. So she would not appear weak in front of Solaria. Then came the part where Rene was brought forward. They placed her face down on the chopping block. That was when a Black-armoured Equus male walked out of a portal. What skin Dusk could see was pink. He opened fire and killed the Executioner and several guardsmen. He grabbed Rene and Kim and entered the portal again as a fireball smashed into the ground where he had been standing. Solaria was on fire with rage. She personally incinerated all in the courtyard. Guard and prisoner alike.

"Come Dusk, we have a war to plan. That was clearly one of Selene's people."

"I follow my liege. We will make sure those Lunar Rebels get what's coming to them."

Razor sighed and looked up at the sky.

***

Razor sat meditating with his mentor Zhang Jue and his mentor's brothers, Zhang Bao, Zhang Mancheng, and Zhang Liang. This was the Way of Peace. Their rebellion was moving smoothly. Their slogan, *the blue sky has fallen, the yellow sky rises*, had successfully recruited many to their cause, but that had been many moons ago. This was the hottest day in the hottest month of the hottest year. Their army was currently being eliminated. The emperor had sent out a decree calling all supporters to put down their rebellion. The supporters showed up Ts'ao Liz of the Wolves, Tung Cho of the Susuine, Liu Suen of the Drakkon (like himself), Sol Jia of the Tigers, and Yuan Shao of the Elves, to name a few.

He watched as each of the brothers left to go deal with the Empire in their section of the battlefield. None came back. He stood and walked towards the door. He opened it and then closed it behind him. He watched as the Empire came up the hill. He exhaled fire. But one was pushing through the fire while protecting Ts'ao Liz.

"You imperial villains will never get past my righteous flames! I will protect Zhang Jue with my life!"

He gasped as a blur struck him. Dragging him through the door and setting the shrine aflame. He stared up at the amber-skinned demon with awe. The man smiled at him.

***

Razor shook his head as he entered the forest. The demon of Komodo had saved him and Zhang Jue. But he had been forced to place Zhang Jue under the care of Liu Suen. He was destined for another path. The Demon of Komodo had taken in a Gargoyle and her Equus daughter, but the

Gargoyle was becoming weaker the longer she stayed away from her ancestral home. He brought her here. She was now sleeping. Until such a time, she felt revived. He sighed. Dusk had strayed. There was still hope for her. If only the influence of Solaria could be purged.

He looked at the small hut he had been building for himself. He had placed a goodbye note to Dusk on her bed. He donned his yellow robe and placed the yellow head wrap on his head. As he meditated, he could see Zhang Jue, Zhang Bao, Zhang Mancheng, and Zhang Liang smiling at him from the Havens. He also saw a giant Ganeshian stroking his trunk, standing behind Zhang Jue. The way of peace was still alive as long as he drew breath.

The Lunar Rebellion leader, Selene, was watching the stars. She felt a fiery presence next to her and turned to see an orange-haired elf.

"What is my Sister's abomination doing here?"

"Aunty Selene. It's always a pleasure. How goes the science experiment? Oh wait, she turned against you. I see the Pit of the Dead is working well for you. What is this the fourth time you failed?"

"Silence, elf. Why are you here anyway?"

"I am here to warn you. Solaria is on her way with an army made of elite units. A man in black Equus armour interfered with her execution of all those Equus with a sliver of Silveran blood in them. She thinks it was one of your knights."

"Firstly, my knights don't wear black. They wear white like the moonlight. Secondly, how would I interfere when this is the first I am hearing of it."

"Regardless, dear aunty, they are on their way."

"Ugh, thank you for the warning Sunspot. My troops will be ready for her."

Sunspot vanished and found herself in the forest of Island Thatchville. She looked around and saw a small hut with a yellow flag flapping in the breeze. She saw an Amber-skinned Mare knocking at the door.

"Come on, Razor. You know Dusk needs you. Why do you hide from us?"

A voice came from the hut, "Jackie, I told you Dusk has become tainted. I am retired. I can't keep up with her ambitions. She is blindly following Solaris. It's been proven true. She allowed her two supposed friends to be executed along with a fourth of the Thatchvill citizens. Including children."

"I guess you are right. But it is our duty as her friends to help her. Even if it's just you, Butterfly, and myself."

"No Jackie I am done. Leave me to my meditations."

"Razor, we can't just give up."

The one called Razor exited from the hut garbed in a yellow cloak. He was holding onto a staff with the top carved into the shape of a lion's head. He seemed to tower over Jackie.

"Oh shit, you are not Razor. Who are you?"

"I am Razor. Master Razor of the Way of Peace. The Razor you knew was my disguise. As a Drakkon of Komodo, I can shift my size. So I became smaller and almost boy-like to understand the Equus. But I have seen I understand nothing. Leave me be, Jackie. Allow me this peace. I must honour my brothers who have passed on before me."

Sunspot raised her pierced eyebrow. "Sorry to interrupt this unique squabble, but where am I?"

Razor looked over to her. "Ah, young Sunspot, biological daughter to Solaris. Welcome to the outskirts of the Island Thatchville."

"You know me?"

"I know of you, yes. I read some of Solaris' history. It seems that you are the reason she hates Silveran's so much."

"Yes, my father was a Silveran. He abandoned Solaris to raise me. She couldn't even do that right. The moment she got a whiff of what Selene was doing, she stole Selene's plans and made her own. She promptly tore the poor thing's soul in two, creating two different girls. She then dumped them in a river to drown. I suppose it's better than Selene's corpse pit. At least they survived."

Jackie blinked, "Uh, what?"

Razor shook his head, "Don't concern yourself with it, Jackie. Go back to your farm."

"Why are you so stubborn?"

"Why are you?"

"Ugh!"

Jackie walked off. Leaving Sunspot and Razor alone. Sunspot spoke, "So why the yellow?"

"I am a follower of the Way of Peace. A Tao sect from continent Komodo. My elder brother, Zhang Jue, was our leader. Obviously, not biological but by faith. I was the youngest. They were masters of sorcery. I was a Drakkon. Unfortunately, our sect was destroyed by the Allies of the Emperor. Many of my friends were slaughtered in the battle. I survived along with Zhang Jue. But eventually, I came here. I have tried to keep Dusk Moonbeam on a path of righteousness. I failed. She is too enamoured with Solaris, so I quit."

"Can you teach me?"

"Hmm, I think if you are willing, I am able. Come meditate with me."

The two walked into the hut as a large Equus man in black armour watched from the woods. She took off her helmet, revealing a magenta face with bright pink hair. She also had a scar across her right eye. Suddenly she vanished to be replaced by a bouncy pink mare. Kim vanished again, only to have the black armored mare appear again. She walked through a portal to see who else she could save.

***

Dusk oversaw the battle. She was on the front lines using her magic to help boost the Solar Empire soldier's energy and power. She jumped back as a cyan blur tried to tackle her from above. She swung and sliced through the mare's wings. The mare turned her rainbow hair dirty with dust.

"By Prisma, you will fall to me, solar witch."

"Don't push your luck, Dash! We were friends. Please surrender."

"Fuck you, Dusk. You blindly follow a dictator."

Dash cried out as Dusk's sword split her face open. "Then perish."

The guard quickly stopped Dusk. "The Moon Tyrant has surrendered. All her followers that still live have been given the choice to be breeders or quarry workers. Stay your blade, my lady."

The guard then turned towards Dash. "So rebel scum, what will it be, give your body to the breeding hall or work in the quarry?"

Dash held her hand to her face. "I would rather work in the quarry. At least the Stoen family takes care of their workers."

Dash was led off to the prison ship. Dusk stood sweaty as Solaris descended from the sky.

"My student, you did admirably. You may pick from any of the mares that were sent to the breeder pens. She will serve you unquestionably. I understand you lost your help recently."

"I did. Razor abandoned me. When I find him, I will kill him."

"Oh. I can certainly see the fire in your eyes. But unfortunately, he has diplomatic immunity. He is a representative of Komodo and also a Dragon. We would risk angering the Dragons if we slew one of their own. I can't have them join the fight when we attack Silver."

"Fine, may I see the breeder mares? I need to relieve some tension."

"Of course, my dear student. Follow through the portal."

As they exited the portal the smell of sweat and sex filled Dusk's nostrils. She looked around at all the bodies chained up. She was led to a room where the prison ship was being unloaded. She looked each of the new breeders over. Finally, seeing a well-endowed filly. She grinned predatorily, "I want her."

The girl was brought over. They forced her into a subservient position. A collar was slapped around her neck and then she screamed. They removed the slave brand from her rear end and forced her to look her new master in the eyes. As the enslavement took hold, she whimpered. Dusk grinned and took hold of the girl.

***

Rene looked around her. She was in some kind of forest. She was startled when she saw an electric blue-haired woman walk out of the woods. The woman had male genitalia and wore only a fishnet body stocking with her nipples covered by tape.

"Ah, lady Techna I am Vinyl Darkspeed. I welcome you to Continent Silver."

"I have not gone by Techna for years. After the temples to our lady of Electronica were shut down by the Solar Empress, I gave up that name."

"Oh? Well, regardless, welcome to Continent Silver Rene of the Equus. It seems you were spared the chopping block."

"Yes, by a strangely familiar stallion. He brought me here. Why?"

"To keep you safe from the tyrant sun. I am here to welcome you because I am a follower of Electranikka like yourself. Also here to visit my girlfriend and hopeful mate."

Vinyl led Techna out of the forest. They arrived at a large castle with many turrets scanning the forest. A large pink stallion in black armour awaited them.

He spoke in a scratchy feminine voice, "Hi Rene, glad to see you made it in one piece. Welcome to my father's home."

"Darling, do I know you?"

The stallion vanished only to be replaced by the bouncy boisterous nudist Kim who then vanished again to be replaced by the stallion. "The name is Pie. I am one of Kim's personalities. I take her trauma and exist to prevent any more trauma."

"Oh darling, that sounds absolutely dreadful. How do you do it?"

"How do you breathe? My existence is the same. A normal function. Come inside before the Elves get confident."

***

Dusk stood staring at the massive army before her. Solaria stood dressed for war. Jackie and Prism Dash were by her side. Prism still wore her slave collar to keep her in line. Dusk felt invigorated. Next to Solaria was her brother, Steel Storm. Behind them were Selene and her brother's Elven wife, Candy Aphrodite. All were dressed for war. She was in her wizard robes and eagerly awaiting orders from her leader.

Solaria spoke, "Today, we take over continent Silver. Today we will gain victory over the wretched Silverans. Today we have become top of the food chain. To war, to victory, to death and glory! Board the ships to our destiny!"

The army marched aboard the ships and the ships lifted off and quickly arrived at Continent Silver. They landed on a vastly open plain with a huge ruined city in the distance.

Butterfly was shuddering. "The forest has fled to avoid destruction. The ground calls for our blood."

Jackie spoke, "Get ahold of yourself, suga. Solaria's burning fury is upon us."

Solaria spoke, "Dusk, I would like for you to circle around and strike from the rear. If we catch the guardian of the ruins in a pincer attack, we will win."

Dusk saluted, "Yes, my Empress. I will not fail you."

"I should hope not. I put quite a bit of faith in you, my dear student. If you fail, your head will join the others on my trophy wall."

Dusk led her forces toward the tree line. All of a sudden, they were engulfed by the trees.

Forest was all around her. It soon became night. The three moons were full and glowed red. The forest came to life. Her army fled through the forest. By the time they reached a small glade, she was down by about half. They were all shaken. They rested a few hours, then braved the forest again. By the time they exited the forest, only herself, Prism, Jackie, and Butterfly remained.

Jackie spoke, "By the Infernum, what was that? I ain't never seen forests act like that."

Butterfly spoke as her body changed, "That my dear mortal was my beloved forest claiming its due. It is Nocni Iov, the first of the thirteenth month. Every month on the first day, my forest awakens to its primal nature. In the old days, sacrifices of blood were made to the forest to grant the cities and villages safety from being encroached upon, but now, only a handful of Silverans remain. Soon my beloved Elves will claim their rightful land. And then they will claim all other lands that belong to them. Those wretched fountainheads usurped control of my planet. Zmatek made sure I was bound and locked away, but then I found a good host. Someone with a soft heart who loved nature. She gave me her body and I was free."

Jackie looked her over. "Are you saying that Butterfly is actually Gaia Silver? Shit. I knew something was up when I first met her... you."

"You know of the old ways?"

"I do. My family was originally Druids. We still use some Druid techniques in our farming. Why else do you think our land is so fertile."

Dusk shook her head and rushed to aid her Empress. She was behind the guardian of the ruins now. It had taken them six hours to get there. She saw Solaria still fighting against the Demon of Silver, but the others were dead. Selene lay against a wall with some rebar sticking through her sternum. The crystal-armoured Elf, Candy Aphrodite, was headless and spilling blood from her neck. She was still holding onto Steel Wind, who was cleaved in twain. All the soldiers were destroyed. Some burned up, while others were missing parts. She saw one of the female soldiers trying to hold her intestines in, to no avail. Solaria was struggling against the Demon of Silver. His body glowing grey, he was a terrible sight to behold

She rushed him only to find herself thrown by his glaive. "Stay down if you know what is good for you. This is between my ex-mate and I."

She struggled up but found herself engulfed by vines that seemed to put her to sleep. Solaria screamed in a rage but soon fell. She was smouldering from the flames.

"You let Lord Dragon corrupt you with his gems. You blasphemed against the natural order. You played god and lost. I was right about you. You were too ambitious. Goodbye, Solaria. Goodbye, my daughter. May the Havens heal you."

Solaria screamed in rage and charged the Demon of Silver, only to find her head missing from her shoulders. As she fell, she vowed revenge. Her soul split in two. One-half went to the Havens. The other, vowing revenge, vanished in a malstrom. Gaia Silver watched as he piled the dead. He then lit them aflame. He said a prayer and the pyre vanished. Gaia Silver watched as he knelt down and placed the mare, trying to hold her guts in stasis healing.

She then made herself known, "Bounty Hunter 13! Demon of God Silver. You are the only one to stand in my way from total control. I have watched your kind defile my lands and attack my children."

"Damn Elves, sorry, your children attacked my people first. So Gaia Silver, how do you propose to end me?"

A massive bipedal dragon rose from the ocean and charged toward Bounty. "Ah, one of your regulators. But there is one problem here. I know that if I damage him enough, he will go back to sleep."

The regulator exhaled atomic fire. The fire engulfed Bounty, who warped it into a towering dragon made of fire and darkness. "You think to use fire against me. I am affiliated with fire. It anointed me at my rebirth."

The fire dragon slashed through the flesh dragon. "Go back to the depths from where you came, Gogrial. Your fire can't harm me."

Bounty slashed Gogrial again and again, forcing the lizard to flee. He would heal in the ocean under the care of Thull Thanos. He stood with the inferno raging around him. He stared down Gaia Silver. She let out a whimper and vanished. He turned towards Jackie and Prism. Prism cried out and grabbed Jackie and the vines that held Dusk and bolted to the ships. She quickly lifted one off and fled. Bounty screamed in agony and the flames vanished. He lay in the still-burning crater. He put out the fires before they reached him, but he could not move. He had used all of his energy and the reserves he had built up. He looked up at the stars and then a pink face staring down at him.

Kim spoke, "Hi, Dad. Glad to see you still breathe. Need some help?"

"Hello, Kimberlite. Ugh. I guess you can help me."

"Oki doki, up you go. Let's get you home to rest."

"I can't rest, Kim. I fear the Shogun clan has made their move."

"Can't be helped. You can't fight like this. Come on. Time to put you down for a nap, old timer."

***

Dusk woke in a hospital room. Jackie stood over her. Looked like she had just gotten off work. She was sweaty and Dusk could see the rivulets of sweat dripping down Jackie's muscular body. Her heart leapt to her throat.

"Good to see you awake, sugar cube. How do you feel now that the toxins are removed from your system?"

"I feel awake. Oh gods, what did I do in my blind devotion to Solaria?"

"Quite a bit. But that is over now. All that is left is to face the judge and the consequences of your actions. I will be here every step of the way and should you face execution, I will be there to support you in the end. Rene is dead, so I have to move on."

"I'm sorry."

"Hmm, feels hollow. You must work on that if you wish to avoid the guillotine." Dusk looked at Jackie and then saw Prism Dash behind her.

Prism Dash spoke, "Hey egghead, uh, we have a small, very big, very pink issue."

Pie walked in holding a shotgun. "Hello, Dusk. I see you are well. My name is Pie. You and I met already when I saved Rene and Kim from the chopping block that you sentenced them to."

Dusk nodded, "I suppose you are here to kill me, then?"

"Not quite. Kim has moved back in with her father. But Rene says she can't trust you anymore. She is severing your friendship and she apologizes to Jackie that she can't break up in person."

Jackie smiled. "Well, tell her no hard feelings. I wish her the best."

Pie nodded, then glared at Dusk. "My father says you had best stay away from Continent Silver for now. He will slay you if you step foot on Silver. He also says that there is a great cataclysm coming to the Equus Islands. He suggests you prepare for it."

"Tell the Demon of Silver I don't take orders from him."

"Your sentiment is noted. Goodbye, Dusk."

Pie vanished and reappeared on Continent Silver outside Bounty Hunter 13's home. She looked around at the Elf corpses and then sighed. She piled them up and burned them. It begins again.

Reiga and The Dream Factory

If a giant space Platypus exists in the milk of the space cow Bessy who lays an egg that hatches the universe. There are openings for madness. However, there is one universally known rule. Don't let the mouse that smashes on your shoulder, for he will only spout hate. And don't let the Psycho Fish cut through your thoughts too fast or you become like the mad monk Salim- Al-Jafar who thought the earth was trying to consume him because his feet would sink in the sand. Well, after all, the earth was trying to consume him.

-Attributed to Pliny the Mad BH 1320-1510

Reiga Hunter lay feverish. Her red hair was matted against her scalp. Her father was keeping a cool wind blowing against her. He muttered under his breath an Ancient Silveran prayer. Roughly translated as The Hunter scouts ahead of the Warrior. The Warrior will guide you with his blade from the Prisoner with his chains.

Reiga had been poisoned from an assassination attempt on her father's life. The Assassin had been none other than her elder sister, Cherry. Cherry was currently fretting.

"I'm sorry, old man. I messed up. I didn't mean for her to get hurt. Poison usually doesn't affect you."

"It's all right, Cherry. I didn't expect her to jump in front of your blade. Our game must be put on hold. Go get Corvus. He is well-versed in poison extraction. Her non-Silveran DNA is being affected by the poison. The Silveran part of her DNA is fighting the poison. That is why she is so feverish."

"Is she going to be alright?"

"Possibly, but she has a better chance if you rush to go get Corvus."

"Right," Cherry said and rushed out.

***

Reiga looked around her. The land she was somehow in was chaotic. There was constant rain soaking the jungle. "Ugh, where am I?"

A large drake swooped down and landed. He adjusted his tie. "Ah, young madam Reiga Hunter, daughter of Hanna, the master of the Dimensional Knife."

"You know me?"

"Why yes, I do. I am the Grumphing. My brother Jabberwocky is friends with your mother."

"Why am I here, Mr Grumphing?"

"Poor Lica is having a psychotic break. You are here to discover why. Follow the Flowrat and it will take you to Madness."

"Squeak?"

"Yes, little one, she is the one. Now go."

As Reiga followed the flowery rat, she heard through the air.

>Two pranced down the twisted road singing
>
>To sing, to dine, to die on this bleak black road
>
>a Grumphing

***

>In the golden rice field, two sat singing
>
>to dine to sing, to die on this graining field, a Grumphing

***

>Upon the field, they saw a flowrat
>
>(a rat of flower and fur) it sang
>
>Why sing to die in this merry field
>
>a Grumphing

***

>In reply, two sang
>
>We sing to dine and dine to sing

***

>The flowrat sighed and left the two alone, singing
>
>The Grumphing doth appear to dine a rhyme

***

>The Grumphing is said to be of serpent and bat large and mighty
>
>the Grumphing sat in the thrones of highest kaep

the Grumphing

It flies like the dniw and sings like a drib

(it colour is black as death and breaths chillingly)

It welf over the grainy field and landed

singing

why live to dine to sing

until the deathbells they do ring

***

They in response, we sing to sing and dine to dine for our deathbells they do chime

For we die to sing to dine in the faerie vine

of the other line

***

As the Grumphing looked on, they faded and were gone into eternity

the great banquet in the sky

She was startled when she came face to face with a skull wearing a top hat and ruffled neck poof. He was holding a purple and pink cat that seemed to be made of smoke.

The cat spoke, "Ah, the young warrior made of stars. I have been eagerly awaiting you. Please follow Madness. He will bring you to her."

The cat left behind his sinister smile as he faded away. The skeletal man nodded and beckoned Reiga to follow him. She did.

As she arrived, she heard it in her head.

She first went to see Lica, the addict who was most knowledgeable in dreaming since she was a dreamer trapped in the dreams of dreams. She was sitting on her throne, stroking the giant pink and purple tiger that was her pet. This was Chess and he was a strange one. His body was always smoking, which gave the throne room a spooky pink and purple glow.

Reiga was startled. "Curious and curiouser. How did I arrive here? I was in the Jungle just a second ago."

Lica purred as Chess' smoke filled her body. Her eyes opened to reveal one pink and one purple, Chess spoke, "Dreams have ways of moving you. Now for why you are here. My mistress is sick. I fear we may need to call upon the chronicler and most ancient Z. He will know. Yes, this yummy situation can be resolved with his help."

An old man in blue walked in. Upon his shoulder sat a red and black Cheshire. This Cheshire cackled and bounded to the throne. It, too, sat in Lica's lap. Its smoke filled the room and a dark voice echoed through the chamber. "Her mind is boring. She feels normal. Madness takes our guest to the obstruction."

The skeleton nodded and walked off, with Reiga following him. They arrived at a swirling tornado over a large hole. She looked at it in trepidation, then peered over the edge. Madness tapped her, sending her into the hole. Only for her to rise in the wind as she vanished, she heard.

The bright blue sky looks down on a brown and grey barren wasteland running around a lush and green tropical valley with crystalline golden beaches

A gently flowing river cuts through it

people swim in designated spots on these crystalline beaches while others put up bright and colourful tents

A raven-haired girl jogs along the beach she perches on a blue boulder

Her pale skin has a light sheen of sweat a drop falls down into the waters where fish play tag and catch while tossing a golden pebble

with hints of silver specks.

As she appeared in a strange looking town with smoke from smokestacks in the distance. She found she was wearing a long coat with a bird mask that covered her face. She felt for her horns and instead felt a large hat. She looked down in a puddle and saw a plague doctor staring back at her.

A voice spoke, "Ello govna welcome to jolly London towne. You must be one of those doctors that seek out the plague to destroy it. I myself am a doctor. A doctor of the mind."

She spoke in her best masculin voice, "I am looking for someone. Here is her picture. She may be in serious danger."

"Ah that is young Alice. Her family's home burned down recently and she was sent to the sanitarium since it broke her mind. I am her doctor. Cornelius Vonderape at your service."

"Cornelius, huh! Hmm. My, my, we are in trouble now. I see your mind before my eyes. Your secrets laid bare. You raped and murdered Alice's sister Dorothy. Then to cover your tracks, you set her home on fire. She saw what you did. Now I see what you do to her. Goodbye, wonder rape the world will not mourn your death."

His body was combusted as she walked away. His black soul vanished. She arrived at Arkham Sanitarium. She slid through the hallways like a shadow. She soon arrived at Alice's room. The girl was chained to the bed with heavy bindings that stopped her struggling. Her eyes had deep dark circles under them. She was gagged, likely to prevent her screaming. Reiga touched her and she looked up pleading. Reiga removed the gag and hushed her whimpers. Her front teeth had been ripped out so that

Cornelius could use her. The room became ominous as Reiga undid the bindings. A red, black, purple, and pink portal opened. Reiga brought Alice through. The portal closed and she heard a lock. Before her was a huge factory floor, she felt her body transform. She looked down to see she was a crow. She muttered angrily under her breath.

Alice looked around her in awe. "What happened to the Land of Wonder? And who are you?"

Reiga sighed, "I am Nevermore. You are trapped in the dark recesses of your mind. Like Frankenstein's Monster, you must journey to find yourself. This is a dark blasphemy of the Land of Wonder. Your abused mind will heal as you travel. I will assist you to the best of my ability. I believe this knife is yours."

Alice looked at the purple steel butcher's knife. "Ah, the Vorpal blade. It is lighter than I remember."

***

The two were soon in a large glass cage. A large being that spewed grease and oil sat, making dolls. He looked at the two of them with hatred in his eyes. Her blade went snickity snackerty and he died as his skull split open and the oil poured out of him. It engulfed the two and they passed out.

Alice stirred and saw in front of her a cowboy riding a Tyrannosaurus Rex. He held out his hand, saying, "Well, howdy pardner looks like you took a tumble."

"Uh, where am I?"

"You are at the station of dreams."

Reiga hopped angrily in her bird form, then flapped her wings and landed on Alice's shoulder. She shook herself and then began preening her feathers. The cowboy eyed her warily, then shrugged.

"Well, lil' lady, why don't you board the train? Seems you need to be somewhere. But don't quite know where. The Train is Names Jones. This big fella is Rexy. What is yours?"

"I am Alice."

"Well, Alice, welcome to the Rabbit Hole."

The train opened, allowing them access to a white room with a bench. She could see the entire train. On one side, she saw a nun wearing lingerie next to a large red demon in a suit reading his newspaper. She could also see a woman that looked to be made of plastic with massive balloons on her chest. She was taken aback.

"This train takes us dream actors to our jobs. Rexy and I are going to old west steam town. Those three are being dropped off at the labia. The big guy that looks bloated is going to the child's dream area."

"He seems out of place for that kind of dream."

"Hardly, he is not a dream actor. He is the guardian of the children. He makes sure their dreams are happy and playful. Unless they need a nightmare to help them, that is his task, for he died to protect them."

"Oh, I think I remember him. In my dreams. After I was abused by my therapist."

"Ah, you are that Alice. Well, this changes things. No wonder that bird seems uncomfortable. She is not a bird."

Rexy spoke, "Yo Jones stop with the chatting. Our stop is coming up."

"So sorry. I hope you find where you belong, Alice."

The train stopped and the door opened, allowing Jones and Rexy to get off and several amorphous blobs to get on.

The bloated man hovered over her and examined her. He then looked at Reiga and shook his head. He floated aside to reveal a woman with her hair covering her eyes wearing white. The woman was drenched and dripping water as she stood there.

The woman spoke, "Hello, Alice. I am Sadaki, you seem nice."

"Uh, hello, how do you know me?"

"A guess. It's usually an Alice who looks so baffled by the dreams. I am heading to the haunted house where dreams of ghosts and ghouls happen. Near the Nightmare factory."

"I think I was there already."

"Oh no, not the place you were. No, that was a portion of your mind. A portion that is no longer there."

"How do you know?"

"I am a Psy ghost. Your mind is laid bare before my eyes." Reiga cawed at Sadako, who backed off. "My apologies. I didn't mean to intrude upon it. Your guardian is very protective."

"She has helped me. Wait, how do I know it's a she?"

Sadako shrugged and then spoke, "Ah, we are coming up on the labia. Soon our friends over there will be leaving.

"Huh, I would have thought there would be more overtly sexual dreams. That is one of the most common."

"And you think a large train entering a vagina is not sexual?"

"Okay, that is true. Hmm. What is after the labia?"

"By mere coincidence, The Haunted House. Since spooky dreams are usually the most common, those include falling, fighting, and nightmares."

"Why that way?"

"We are nearing the end of the line. After the haunted house is a realm of madness, we call it Wonder. Up is down, left is right, jumping is falling, flying is walking. And don't even get me started on the creepy Guardian of Wonder. Chess, the pink and purple Cheshire cat and his pet, Lica, the addict."

Reiga ruffled her feathers and then hopped over to Alice's other shoulder. As they neared the station, she saw the demon, nun, and plastic woman get up. The train stopped and ejaculated steam. The three got off along with many of the amorphous blobs. The train continued. Creepy carnival music began blaring over the speakers as the train pulled into a massive mansion castle hybrid, where Sadaki got off along with the rest of the amorphous blobs.

The train suddenly lurched forward with alarming speed. Reiga caught herself by flapping her wings. Alice was not so lucky. The train suddenly vanished and Alice fell into a black, red, purple, and pink portal. As the two exited, Reiga became her normal self and Alice disappeared.

Lica, the addict, woke up. "Uh, my head, it was absolutely horrible. So normal. Oh, hello, little bird. Thank you for reuniting me with my mind, but now you must leave."

Rega yelped as another portal opened up under her, sending her through. She woke with a start gasping in terror. A large grey hand was on her shoulder and she looked up into the swirling grey eyes of her father.

"Ugh, what a weird dream."

A red and black Cheshire appeared on her father's shoulder. He disappeared, leaving behind his smile and in her head, she heard. Or was it a dream? Thank you, little bird.

Her father brushed his shoulder, erasing the smile. "She is looking much better, Corvus. Thank you for your help."

Reiga looked over to see her uncle in his black feathered cloak. She reached out to him and he took her hand and smiled a knowing smile. She sighed in relief. Then closed her eyes.

Corvus signed (She just needs to rest and recover, Bounty, as do you. That wound is looking worse by the day.)

"What my burn. Yes, I know. My time is coming again. But this time, I don't think I'll be the same."

A voice came from Corvus' throat. "We can only hope. Ascension is nigh, Demon of Silver. My priest will also be ascending. For he is the last protector of the Daeva."

"Nevermore. Why did you turn my girl into a bird?"

"She is as much a part of me as she is of you. Hanna was working under my influence when she decided to sleep with you. Therefore it is only logical that in the lands of dreams, she would be a bird. She also seeks to fly free."

"Am I holding her back?"

"No, her sister is. The poor thing still cannot remember what or who she is."

"Rest well, Reiga, my girl. Tomorrow is another day."

Legend of Nightmare Hunter

It was dusk when a grey-skinned boy entered the village. Only one moon shone in the night sky. The other two were dark. The boy was leaning tiredly on an anchor-like weapon. There was a striped equus next to him.

"Sorry, Shaman, thanks for the assist. I am glad you found me instead of something more vicious."

"You were foreseen by the spirits, oh Nightmare of Hunter's loins. Thank you for your seed that I so desperately need."

She led him to the inn where a bard was playing on his lute while teaching a small girl to play the drum. She walked with him to the counter and he pulled out a ring.

"A room for two, please. I will be paying by chip."

The innkeeper, a striped sabre fang felis, smiled a fanged smile. "Big spender, huh? Shall I have silencing wards placed in the room as well?"

"Yes, please."

"And shall I have one of the dancers in your room for entertainment, sir?"

The shaman purred, "Oh, I would like that very much," as the boy heard ringing in his ears from the recent explosion. "The younger, the better."

The innkeeper nodded excitedly. "I have the perfect girl for you. She is well-used because of her age. But she is very good with what she does."

The boy scanned the ring before placing it back into his shirt. The two were escorted up to the room as several Felis finished placing the wards on the room. A small red-skinned elf was unceremoniously tossed into the room. She wore nothing except her chain collar. Her tiny breasts were pierced with tags, as was her abused jewel. She kept her head down as the shaman walked over to her.

"Do you see the plight of this land, oh Nightmare of Hunter's loins? Many a child is enslaved to entertain. The Crystalline Empire does nothing. In fact, they promote the enslavement of the lesser species. This land needs someone to fight for it. Will you be that or will you be another tyrant?"

The boy examined the child and a guttural feral growl escaped his lips. The girl slumped over unconscious and the boy walked over to the shaman. The shaman was startled until she felt him enter her flower. Her eyes widened in shock, quickly turning to lust. Soon she was bent over the bed, getting a pounding. Her screams of ecstasy being absorbed by the wards. She felt his climax into her womb and she climaxed again, for the sixth time. She blacked out. As the sun shone in the next morning, she was greeted to the dawn by a hearty breakfast of mushrooms and eggs.

She saw the child curled up next to her with a silvery brand on her rear. The grey-skinned boy was sitting out on the deck smoking a long thin reed. It emitted a pale green smoke that seemed otherworldly. She gasped as she saw his eyes. She prostrated herself.

"Get up. I despise people doing that." Replacing his shades after cleaning them, he continued, "You seem to know my name, yet I don't know yours."

"I am Zinnia, my lord."

"Well, Zinnia, you are pregnant with a daughter. Be careful foaling her, she's going to be big."

"Please let me accompany you. I wish to be your slutty cum dumpster."

"This is why I had reservations about sexual relations with you. You have been broken. But I suppose it's mostly my fault for being so energetic."

He waved his hand in a small pattern that caused her eyes to glaze over; he then blew the smoke in her face causing her to awaken.

"Ugh, what happened last night? I remember seeing you on the beach, but then nothing."

"You were drugged by my pheromones. You will have a daughter after last night's excursion."

"That is to be expected since I feel sick. I will raise her well. Be safe should you need me. I am Zinnia. I shall be on my way."

"Stay safe, Zinnia. I suspect this is only the first time we meet."

Zinnia left, leaving the child alone with her new master. She looked up fearfully at him.

"I am Nightmare. Who are you?"

"I am a fucking Slut."

"Okay. How about this? You are Astrid. As Astrid, you are expected to be my companion only. Your body is mine. Okay, Astrid, let's remove all of these chains and piercings."

An hour later, he had fully removed all the chains and piercings from her young, abused body. He also healed her. He cleaned off some of the dirt on her body. Her mental wounds would not heal for a while.

***

It was midday when General Wenceslas of the Cerulean Stalwarts heard a commotion. He had no backup, but he did have his blade. He removed the blue blade from its sheath. He entered the forest to see a young man with an anchor weapon and an eyepatch defending a teen red elf from one of Sucryog's most dangerous predators, the Trihelm Scorpio. He went to aid the young man only to see him explode, vaporizing the Trihelm Scorpio while remaining unscathed.

He then saw the youngster collapse and saw the man's back with a purple burn. The Trihelm had bit him. He called for a drop-ship on his communicator. The small craft appeared on the horizon with two smaller bikes as guards. The bikes transformed into heavily armed feminine robots.

A well-armoured knight walked out, his servos hissing against the cold wind. The helmet retracted, revealing a golden-eyed demon with red skin and midnight-black hair.

"Nurse Raven, good to see you. He fended off a Trihelm by himself and got poisoned. This girl seems to be his daughter. Or something."

"I will see what I can do, General Wenceslas, but Trihelm poisons kill immediately."

Nightmare struggled to his feet. "I am no ordinary man. Give me a suit like you and I will heal up in a couple of hundred years."

"You are a Grey Silveran?"

"I see my image disguise failed. Unsurprising since my body is going into Overdrive trying to purge the poison from my body."

Wenceslas groaned. "Can you at least get examined back at Bastion Three while we fit you with Orochicalum armour?"

The three boarded the small ship and sped off to a small fortress near the phantom Woodlands. Wenceslas was immediately set upon by numerous white-coated soldiers as he exited the ship.

"Gods dammit! Fragin Wights. We gotta get moving."

He pulled out two pistols and began firing into the soldiers. Nightmare grunted and exited the ship. He saw Wenceslas being besieged. Growling under his breath, he chokeslammed one of the grunts causing a purple burn to appear on his neck, which caused him to foam at the mouth as he died from the Trihelm poison. As Nightmare finished several off, they fled.

"That is why I need the armour. Not for my protection but for those that come into contact with me."

"Fukin idiots. Why would you charge into an army? Y'all should've escaped."

"Not my style, Captain. Plus, I need to go into the armoury. I have a Silveran here who is sweating out Trihelm poison."

"Shi' really. Alrigh' put him in a sterile chamber that we can purge after his fitting. I'll get the armoury bots up and running."

"Thank you, Captain Psycheo. We are coming into the sterile chamber now."

Captain Psycheo stood outside the chamber. She was wearing black bikini armour that had spikes all over it. She was smoking a thin reed that burned purple. Her midnight purple hair seemed to glow in the lights of the hallway. Her purple lips and eyes seemed to beckon Nightmare.

"Bewitching sight, isn't she, boy?"

"Wha..."

"Well, snap out of it. She prefers the fairer sex."

Lady Psycheo smirked. "Alright, old man. That's enough yammering. Get out and sterilize your suit. The bots need all the room they can get."

***

Twelve years passed while the Cerulean Stalwarts fortified their positions around the forest. It was around this time King Syvarin Kold of the Crystal Empire fell in battle against the rebel Draugr army. His son Silt Kold took the throne by force from his older brother Sven.

Bards from then on would sing, "Old King Kold was a violent old soul. He took the throne and broke his bones. Now he lies in barrow land."

Under Silt, the empire expanded exponentially. Any city opposed to them was ransacked and forced under the iron boot of progress. The Rebel Draugr and the heretic Weights also experienced growth. During this time, with enemies on all sides, General Wenceslas went out on a mission to assist one of the bastions. With him were Nightmare and Astrid. Astrid was in a blue duster that was covered in personalized runes that Nightmare had imbued into it.

Nightmare was letting his suit air out against the cold frost. There was whistling as several arrows sliced into his flesh and detonated. He staggered back, bleeding from a foot-wide hole in his chest. He grunted and fired a burst of energy, killing the archers. Wenceslas growled and pulled out his blue blade.

That was when the stealth fighters uncloaked and slit Nightmare's throat. He beheaded the agent. But due to the blood loss, he fell. He grabbed his ring weakly and impaled his chest with the small pointed end. Wenceslas found himself surrounded but grabbed Nightmare and Astrid before running. Several explosive arrows later, he got to a clearing. He, too, sagged to the ground. He could feel shrapnel in his back from his suit. He started laughing when he saw an onyx wall nearby with golden words on it.

Astrid looked at him. "What's so funny?"

"I am the last of the Hundred Guardians[3] to fall. My friend Belladonna passed before me during childbirth. I have been taking care of her daughter since. Many of us perished in the battle against the Pale Elf army. Only twelve survived to live long lives. But the stone only appears at the end of our life. Some sort of spell Lord Bounty Hunter 13 put on it to remember us by. Here take this core to Bastion Twelve. I suspect it's the only one besides Bastion Three to survive. This was a premeditated attack. The Spriggan warriors usually attack us en masse. And Nightmare, I know you are listening. Wait to burn me until Lady Psycheo gets here. Tell her she grew up to be just like her mother. And I am proud of her."

The stone wall glowed and the name Amodu Wenceslas: Anti-Paladin, appeared before the stone vanished. Nightmare pushed a button on Wenceslas' gauntlet before struggling to his feet. A protective layer formed over his skin as he lifted Astrid up and closed his armour. Several hundred Spriggan rangers entered the clearing.

Nightmare rasped, "You picked the wrong prey to hunt on Noční lov. No one leaves this clearing alive."

The leader laughed before exploding in a shower of gore. Nightmare surrounded the clearing in neon purple fire. Seconds passed, but that was all it took. Several hundred Spriggan rangers ceased to exist. The night sky glowed red from the Hunters Blood Moon. Nightmare replaced his shades over his glowing purple eye. He then sat down and began meditating.

Lady Psycheo walked into the clearing after passing through the strange neon purple flames. The fire vanished and formed a small campfire in front of Nightmare. She nearly peed in fear since

---

[3] See index of names for a list of the hundred.

the flames made Nightmare seem sinister.

Nightmare rasped, "Hello, Alena Psycheo. It took you long enough. Your father says he's proud of you and that you grew to be so much like your mother. But I have a question. When did you decide these bastions needed to fall?"

She sat teary-eyed next to Wenceslas. "Around the same time, Silt Kold took my daughters and wife as leverage. He sent me my wife's hand, saying if I did not convince the Spriggan Rangers to destroy the Cerulean Stalwarts, her head would be next."

"I see. Well, I hope he will not harm them. Go ahead and report the destruction of the Cerulean Stalwarts."

"I cannot. Bastion Twelve still exists."

Rav-en walked up behind Alena with her blade drawn. "The old man raised you as his own. You helped him find the Cerulean Stalwarts. Now you betray us. You will not leave this clearing alive."

Nightmare rasped, "Sheath your blade Rav-en. She will be punished by the dead, not the living. That is the Cerulean Stalwarts way. You can already see the mark of betrayal on her back and it will only expand the more that pass. And when she dies, should they deem her unloyal, her soul will be torn up and destroyed."

"Why would you do this?"

"My children and wife are held prisoner by King Silt Kold. I have no choice in the matter!"

"You bore me." Nightmare waved his hand, causing Alena to slump. He then manipulated her like a puppet.

King Kold appeared on a small holo screen. "Is it done?" she spoke. "Yes, now release my daughters and wife."

"Heh, you still remain. Are you, not Cerulean Stalwart? Since you failed your mission, they die."

Nightmare snarled, causing a poisonous rift to open he walked through and beheaded the two guards. He opened the cell that held her daughters and wife. He then released the other prisoners as well. He sent them all through the rift and tossed a Stalwart bomb. It detonated as he walked through the rift and closed it behind him. He noticed that Alena was awake.

Alena stared slack-jawed at him. "How the hell are you fully healed?"

Nightmare sat down in front of the purple fire. "I am Nightmare Hunter. Like my father, Bounty Hunter 13, I have nanites in my blood. Thanks to your little betrayal, I had to inject them early."

Nightmare set Wenceslas and the dead rangers alight. Causing the purple flames to dissipate.

"What are you planning on doing with all these people."

"Well, those that belong to the Spriggan Rangers can leave back to their hidden village. Those that belong to the Wight Knights can go back to their lands. And those in the Rebel Draugr army may leave as well. The more enemies King Kold has, the more I can operate under the radar."

"Why?"

"I am the reckoning of the twenty. Kold has pissed them off and they wish to see him and his allies sundered."

***

Five years passed as Nightmare watched over Astrid. He had turned Alena into Bastion Twelve and she was being kept prisoner there. Rav-en had allowed a small leniency and let Alena's wife and daughter stay with her. King Kold was having many problems with the various rebellions. He was soon assassinated by his son, who took over. The cruelty of the Crystal Throne became worse. Nightmare sighed as another voice begged him to do something. The twenty gods of Sucryog were being persistent.

"Come, Astrid. We have a pilgrimage to the twenty Sucryog god's statues."

"Really, Father, you know what they want."

"As much fun as it would be to wipe out the Crystal Empire right now, I do not have enough resources to do so. After all, it is just going to be me right now. But with the gods lending me their blessings, I will be able to do more damage."

A jovial yet sinister voice cut through the air. "That is total bullcrap and you know it."

"What is it now, Agnuines?"

"Oh, you hurt me, Nightmare. Can't a guy just talk with his pal?"

"Now, who's bullcraping?"

"Ahh, haha! My rivals and I already gave you a blessing, as you call it. Go destroy the Empire of Kold. There is something far more sinister coming and it will be better for you to clean one mess up before another adds to it."

"I am unsure if you are serious or not."

"I am very serious, boy. Kold is of little consequence. Kill him and end his tyranny."

"Why do I feel something terrible will happen if I do so?"

"We Gods are fickle. Who's to say our blessing will stick if you don't? But you have nothing to fear from me, Malca, and the Huntsman. The others... are very meshuggah."

"I'm sure they'd say the same of you."

"Please, stop with the flattery. It gets you everywhere with me. Now go, my devilish fiend. Go and take down the Kold empire."

Nightmare scoffed and walked off. Astrid quickly followed him. He waited for her, then placed her in a stasis sleep. He slipped into the Crystal City, leaping from building to building. He soon arrived at the Crystal Castle, where the Crystal throne sat. He filled the castle with noxious clouds. He quickly killed King Kold and his allies. He looked down at the baby snoozing in his mother's arms. He grimaced and saw the bodyguard of the Boy. She was wearing a gas mask and had a gun pointed at him.

"The Twenty have their vengeance. Take the boy and flee. I may very well regret this decision."

The bodyguard nodded and easily lifted the woman and her son. She teleported out. She exited the city as a wave of energy washed over the city. She saw a silver aurora in the sky and gulped. The throne had chosen its true master.

Nightmare sat on the Crystal Throne and heard Anguines' dark jovial laughter. He spoke, "I know you're there, Anguines. Now why did the throne choose me?"

"Ah, now, where is the fun in that? May I suggest finding the book 'The Gems of The Dragon'? Written by someone close to you."

Several years later, Nightmare stood on the docks awaiting something. A small craft pulled up. A man in dragon armour with short black hair and green eyes exited the craft. He bowed slightly to Nightmare.

"I am surprised a Shogun clan would seek a Hunter clan's help."

"My ancestors were foolish. They were poisoned by Lord Dragon and their minds were clouded by his lies. My allies and I have come to give our aid in restoring the Crystal Throne and Crystal Fortress. My lord, may I present to you Lu Fang, the flowery monk, Hu Sanniang, the ten feet of blue, and Wang Ying, the stumpy tiger."

"I received word of you coming. I welcome you four to Sucryog. I am glad to have you. For I also received a premonition of the Ash Elves invading my land. So I would like the defences to be fortified."

***

One Thousand Years Ago

Thull Thanos of the Thullhuid slept peacefully underwater. His large eye opened and his mouth tentacles twitched. His other eye opened and he rose from the water. He saw a small boat bearing the mark of the Hunter clan. It was currently being sucked down a whirlpool. He lifted the boat from the water. Looking closely at it, he noticed it was more of a raft. On the raft unconscious was a boy of barely three hundred. He looked like he had been well used. Thull Thanos grumbled and probed the boy's mind. Fenix Ankara huh... well that needs to change.

Thull Thanos smiled a tentacled smile and placed the boy on Sucryog. He then went back to his sleep. The tides came and went as the three moons went through several cycles. Thull Thanos awoke again. This time he felt the boy, Fenix, was now a man. He was being buried the way the Sucryogans bury their dead by placing them on a boat and burning them. As Fenix's spirit left its body, Thull Thanos collected it. He then dozed off again while moving the tides like he had been doing for an eternity. He awoke again, this time feeling a deep despair from above him. He looked up but could not see anything. He tilted his head in annoyance and rose from the water.

He could see the source of the despair. It was a young woman whose soul seemed as ancient as his. "What is the Dread Goddess doing on my doorstep?"

She looked up at him, surprised, "I am lamenting that I cannot get a man out of my mind. I try not to have the same mate every time I revitalize myself. But he is once again in my life."

"Ah, Bounty Hunter 13 does seem to have that effect."

"You know him then?"

"Hardly, he is an oddity that I always have to ignore while I sleep."

"You know me, but I do not know you. Who are you?"

"Hmm, how do I explain my existence to a Goddess? I am the sleeper of the tides. I rule the oceans and waterways of Silver. Once I was but a Terah Aert Thullhuid, but as Terah Aert fell into chaos and destruction, I led my people to a new world on our mountain ships. We landed here and I evolved into a different being. My many children took to praying to me. I have since become more. I am Thull Thanos of the Thullhuid."

"You were one of the first ones! Alongside the likes of The Silver Dragon and Zaratan, the sea turtle."

"Yes, I suspect I am. For not only did my kind travel the stars to arrive here, but we also somehow went back in time. The Writer sure pulled a fast one with that. But that is not why I am awake. Why do you despair? Do you not care for the one you pine over?"

"I do. It's just I have already given him two children. A third is just overkill."

"Ah, so you are pregnant?"

"Yes, but I am scared of this one. This one is different. I do not detect a soul in it."

"Hmm, has The Writer pulled another fast one on me?"

"What do you mean?"

"I have a soul in need of a body. The boy was badly abused and left afloat on the sea. I sent him to Sucryog, where he became a famous king. But he passed away a century ago. I have his soul in my keeping."

"You think the soul of Fenix Ankara is to be reborn as my son?"

"Yes, I do believe so."

***

"Anguines you bastard! Show yourself."

"What have you in such a fit, Nightmare?"

"You said this book will give me answers. It has nothing. None of the books in the Library explains why the throne chose me. All they talked about was some Silveran legend by the name of Fenix. He was the first to unify all of Sucryog. The Crystallans built this city to honour him."

"And that doesn't seem suspicious to you? Are you purposefully playing stupid or are you this dumb?"

"Are you saying I am somehow related to this Fenix fellow?"

"Yes, I am. But maybe you need to speak more with the Wretched Abyss than the god of debauchery and wine."

A sinister and inky voice spoke, "I have heard my name and I come. Ah, Anguines of the Revelry Realms, you summon me?"

"I do no such thing, but our mutual mortal does." "Ah, Nightmare Hunter."

Nightmare looked at the inky void in front of him. "Ugh, hello, Ink. Do you have anything on The first ruler of the Crystal Throne, Fenix?"

"Ooo tasty subject that. Yes, I do. What can you give in return? Hold up, wait, is that book The Gems of the Dragon?"

"Yes, it is. Written by Bounty Hunter 13, my father."

"Then a mutual trade. I take that book and you get the history of the Crystal Empire."

"Why would you need… ah, never mind, I don't want to know. Here you go."

"And here you go, favoured mortal."

***

Bounty Hunter 13 stood atop the Crystal Tower. Ah, so the Wretched Abyss gets ahold of my book. I hope he chokes on it. Now where is Othas Li?

Bouty looked to the distance, where he saw a massive ashy storm approaching.

Not Dathgo… wait, what the hell?

Bounty teleported to where the ash storm was. He saw before him a twisted man with a skeletal frame and a large tiki mask covering half of his body. The man saw him and grinned before tossing a cybernetic ash elf before he ripped it apart.

"Ah, so it is you, Dathgo, the Ash demon. I see you slew Othas Li, the steampunk cyborg. Good for you. A pity you have only hastened your downfall."

"Ha, that is what you think. I have the Heart of Magnus Invictus. As long as it still beats, I am immortal."

"That old waste of space is still here. Ugh, figures you four would meddle with it." As Dathgo swung his sabre at Bounty, Bounty dodged and grabbed the body of Othas Li and vanished.

***

Nightmare paced restlessly under a statue of a horned god. The statue was watching him. It finally spoke, "Boyo, what have you so troubled."

Nightmare was startled. "Who said that?"

The statue spoke, "Look up."

"Okay, I must be going mad. I hear a statue speak."

"I am merely using this statue as a conduit to speak with you. I am God Silver who Speaks. You are Nightmare Hunter, son of The Demon of Silver."

"Sorry, this is a new experience. Usually, the gods who speak with me show up in a physical form."

"Ah, sorry, how's this?" The air shimmered, and an imposing man appeared with two thick horns coming from his temples, shoulder spikes, white hair on both his head and chin, wrinkles, swirling void grey eyes, and a long grey and gold duster.

"Father?"

"Yes, but no. Like I said, I am the God Silver who Speaks. So what have you troubled so?"

"The Crystal Throne chose me as its ruler. And I am somehow a descendant of Fenix Ankara. I can't be a part of the clan that hastened the downfall of our people. It seems wrong."

"Oh well, I suppose a lesson is in order. The Hunter clan and Ankara clan have been well connected since Bounty Hunter 12 was sworn brothers with Zenthin Ankara, The Shadow Lord. He was given The Shadow Lord's daughter, Mar-la Ankara's hand in marriage. It unified the two clans. And from that union was born The Demon of Silver and, to a lesser extent, his siblings."

"So even Father was an Ankara?"

"Yes, but at the same time, no. You see, the soul is what gives your body its form and shape. As Bounty Hunter 13's soul was also Hunter clan, he is more akin to Hunter than Ankara. You, however, are more akin to Ankara than Hunter which baffles me, but I also detect some kind of watery interference. So for some time, your soul was in the care of Thul Thanos of the Thullhuid. Hmmm, anyway, how is your daughter?"

"She is currently in Crystal stasis. She got severely hurt and was near death. It drove her mad. Though I suspect one of the Sucryog gods is more involved with that than the near-death experience."

***

Lord Badger wandered the Inbetween. He was searching for something. He had felt a strange interference and was investigating where it came from. He grimaced as a sharp pain jolted through his head. *Dammit, Bounty, what did you do?* I gotta find this interference or these headaches will continue. He soon came upon a temple and entered it. On a pedestal, he saw a miniature city. It was made from some unknown metal. He touched the city only to have it pull him into it.

***

Eris Hunter followed the Chaos wail to a large volcano spitting out ash. She looked at it and then grimaced when she saw Malaxia, the Ash Elf queen. Malaxia was grinning madly. She cut down a construct and then continued up the path. Eris followed and as she entered the volcano, she saw the still beating heart of Magnus Invictus. She snorted. She saw Malaxia try to touch the heart only to be incinerated by a forcefield. She studied the forcefield for a second, then grinned. It suddenly went critical and dissolved, leaving the heart unprotected.

She vanished as Dathgo appeared and swung his spiked blade at her. He tried to reinstate the shield, but a sharp scream echoed in his head, causing him to explode. The heart shattered into a gory mess as Bounty Hunter 13 stabbed a purple blade into the heart. He scoffed and vanished as the mountain erupted.

***

Nightmare was resting as he rested, terrors gripped his brain. He was facing down Lizardmen and Dragons and they were decimating his ships. Then as his ship landed on a Jungle Island, his troops turned on him. He woke in a panic only to have a firm handhold him down. He looked at the strange creature before him. It had a squid-like torso and walked on tentacles. It had a weird bulbous head that had a tentacled beard that covered its mouth. Its eyes all six of them blinked and one of the tentacles curled up almost like it was shushing him.

It seemed to say, "You are Nightmare Hunter? I need you to stay calm. You are surrounded by Ash Elves. They have not noticed you yet. And Mountains willing, they won't. Follow, please. The forest is unsafe for a king."

Nightmare nodded and the creature's facial tentacles curled up in a smile. He followed the creature to a large cave entrance. A Striped Equus was waiting for him.

She smiled, "Ah, good, Thul Anarch found you. I was concerned when I saw the raiding party of Ashen ones."

Nightmare spoke through his rebreather, "Thank you for your concern Zinnia. But how did you know where I was?"

"Nevermore sees all. And he wishes to keep you safe."

"Oh goody, another God I have never heard of with his eye on me. First was God Silver."

"Nevermore is allied with Silver and you are Hunter clan. So, of course, Silver has his eye on you. There are others as well. But they have stayed away. The Sucryogan Oblivia Gods are the masters of this continent. You will meet another soon. One that is not allied with Silver or those opposed to Silver."

A soft feminine yet at the same time masculin voice cut through the air, "I am already here."

Zinnia pulled out a shaman staff while Thul Anarch summoned a watery blade. Nightmare sighed.

Nightmare spoke, "Hello Volvek, I have been waiting for you."

"Have you now? Hmm. Why?"

"Ever since I saw your kind attacking my city in my dreams I have been awaiting the day we will meet. But since you are not actually here right now. That day will be on the battlefield. Good luck with your mortality Volvek."

"How do you know?"

"I felt the heart get destroyed. You are mortal now. Well, for the most part. As long as the people believe you are a god, you are a god."

"I must say I am impressed with the research you put into this. Were we not on different sides of this conflict I may have enjoyed conversing with you."

"This conflict can still end peacefully."

"No, I don't think it can. Too many of my people resent the Crystal Empire. They are in a battle-hungry mood. They desire to avenge the many years of enslavement by your predecessors."

"Then I hope your blades are sharp and your guns well-oiled."

"See you in battle, Nightmare of Hunter's loins."

"Hmph, see you in battle dual one."

Zinnia stared at Nightmare with concern. Then gently hugged him. He patted her back and stood up.

"I best be getting back to the Crystal City."

Thul Anarch smiled as a watery portal opened. "Hold your breath and step on through. You will arrive in your throne room."

"Here goes nothing."

Nightmare dove through the portal and rolled to a stop by the foot of his throne. He scoffed and sat down. He summoned his generals and began debating with them how to defend the city.

***

Seven Hundred Years Ago

"Father! The Shogun clan is here. They are prepared for our battle."

"Thank you, Nightmare. Now get aboard the ship."

"Father, I can fight with you."

"Nightmare! Do not make me knock you out. Please just get on the ship."

"Ugh, why is it so important I not fight?"

"What is coming next will be too traumatizing for you. I can't, no, I won't put you through that."

Nightmare went to leave as his siblings and father went to go to battle. He shook his head. Then secretly followed. As he walked on the battlefield, something felt off. Arcanus saw him and shook his head. That was when the Shogun clan turned off a stealth cloak. Nightmare looked at the horror. Many of his siblings lay flayed and chopped up. Their organs spilt everywhere. Fire erupted from his father as his father became enraged. That was when he was grabbed by Arcanus and pulled away from the battlefield. Arcanus dragged him onto the ship and sped off. He watched as a strange explosion happened. The shockwave came for the ship. Arcanus vanished and the ship was struck, sending it out of control. That was the last thing he remembered until waking up next to a Striped Equus covered in his sperm. He cleaned her up and incinerated the sheets. He cooked breakfast as she awoke.

***

Current Day

Nightmare stared at the encroaching horde of Ash Elves. There were thousands of them. His small force could not hold them back.

"Men, the walls are strong. I want you to begin going throughout the city and tell all denizens to retreat to the safe zone. Then I want you to guard the safe zone. Do not worry about me. I have faced down the denizens of Oblivia. A bunch of snooty soot Elves are nothing to me."

The soldiers did as they were told. Many felt relieved they did not have to fight the Ash Elf army. Nightmare sighed and typed an order into his gauntlet. Many turrets popped out of the wall and opened fire on the encroaching Ash Elf army. The screams of the dying filled the air. However, he suddenly felt his connection to Oblivia weaken and saw many Elf sorcerers summoning an army from the Oblivia realms. He grimaced as he heard Anguines' dark laughter in his head. He shook his head. Then smiled a dark smile. The Oblivia gods may have forsaken him aside from Anguines, the Horned Hunter, and Malca, the vengeful demon. But he had a trick up his sleeve. He pulled out a red flower that seemed to be the blood drop of a god in flower form. He heard in his head where did you get that, boy? He responded I received it from the Duke of Madness. He warned me not to trust the gods of Oblivia. Just because you and The Huntsman have not abandoned me does not mean I won't use the black warrior. Anguine responded if you summon the Black warrior, you can forget about my boon. Nightmare chuckled and then lit the rose aflame. A red-haired and red-bearded man appeared dressed in pure black power armour with small motifs of roses. His left arm below the elbow was a void forged sword. He had a tower shield on his right arm. His black horns glistened in the moonlight. Two ethereal ravens appeared and a large horse made of stars came into existence. The Black Warrior mounted his steed and charged into battle.

"I hereby revoke my blessing. You are no longer the one chosen to wield my weapon as if I needed your weapon Anguines. Do you know what I did with all of the artefacts I received from the Oblivia gods? I put them in a safe, never to be seen by mortal eyes. So go ahead and take your blessing back. Go find a different mortal to fuck with."

"I will, you abhorrent brat. I will. And they will come for you. They will kill you. I look forward to your screams as you die."

"Good luck with that. Chrome curse you. Chrome curse all of you. Except you Malca and you as well, Hunt I like you."

As the Black Warrior slaughtered the Ash Elves, Volvek appeared on the field of battle. He banished the Black Warrior and ordered his men to open fire on Nightmare. The hail of arrows, bullets, and lasers came at Nightmare, he pulled out his sword, gifted to him by his father. He swung it and an energy wave sliced through the hail causing most of it to ignite and disintegrate. Without warning, several of the Ash Elves became hulking bestial creatures and turned on their fellow warriors. The moons became blood red. The Black Knight reappeared and continued his onslaught.

"I see you pissed off the Oblivia Gods. Good, boyo."

"Hello, Father it's been a while. I see Devon is with you."

The woman in a black duster and green battle-kini spoke, "I am not here with Father. Once I learned you were alive, I had to come see you."

"Well, then, that certainly is serendipitous. I welcome the help you are offering."

"Come, little brother, let us show these ashen ones what the Hunter clan can do."

The two jumped down and charged into the remaining warriors, cutting many down on their path to Volvek. Bounty leaned against one of the towers and lit his cigar and inhaled the pain medicine. He breathed out a teal mist that caused him to raise an eyebrow.

He spoke, "Malca the vengeful and Hunt. Well, well, well, I am surprised. I thought Ebonvoid was your enemy?"

The blue-skinned man with six horns and tusks spoke, "An enemy of an enemy is a friend. We are all brothers in arms. As I am indebted to Silver for allowing me to exist, I am not planning on forsaking one of his chosen."

The man with a Horned Doebuck skull for a head and a large spear spoke, "As I am the Master of the Hunt, the prey is anything. Your son gloriously turned the predator into the prey. He is still worthy of being my champion."

"Of course, I would not expect it either way."

"Will you not join in the hunt?"

"Only when I am needed, which should be soon. Volvek is coming."

Both Malca and Hunt vanished. Bounty Hunter 13 stood on the battlements waiting. Soon almost all of the Ash Elves had been routed. That was when Volvek appeared. He was androgynous with both ash-white skin and deep red skin. He spoke with both a male and female voice that dispelled the enchantment on the Elves who Hunt had turned. He then spoke again, causing The Black Warrior to vanish. Bounty had recalled him to his plane of existence. He was no longer needed. Bounty placed the black thorny rose back in his hammerspace. As Devon was thrown into the wall by Volvek's voice, Bounty jumped down from the battlements. He landed with a thunderous thud and kicked up a lot of dust which he then sent forward, obscuring Volvek's vision. He caught the wounded form of Devon and teleported her back to his ship.

Volvek smiled and sang. His voice let loose numerous ancient spells. Bounty struggled to stay standing. The wall was beginning to crack. A wave of incandescent blue struck Volvek, causing him to fall. His mouth was sealed by a rune.

Nightmare spoke, "You are the last of the triumvirate to be standing. I applaud your stubbornness. However, it only gets you death."

Bounty spoke, "Hold your blade, Nightmare. Do not strike him down. He must still suffer. You strike him down. Now he will get what he wants."

"Then what will you have me do, Father? His kind is trying to destroy my city and the people I protect."

"Mark him as a traitor. You may not know the mark, but you can create it."

"How?"

"Place your hands on his shoulders. Now focus your anger and despair into your palms. Perfect, he has been marked a traitor. The first king has been avenged."

A black mark appeared on Volvek's torso. It spread until his entire chest was covered in it. His eyes widened in despair as Bounty stood over him.

Bounty spoke, "You and the triumvirate betrayed and murdered the first king of Sucryog. You then found the heart of Magnus Invictus. You stole his power to become like gods. Well, now it has been destroyed. Your power will wane. Make amends before the end and maybe you will receive peace. Now be gone and never come back."

Bounty snapped his fingers and Volvek and his entire army vanished. He, too, teleported away.

"You did it, Father. You won!"

"Did I, Astrid? It feels hollow."

"A hollow victory is still a victory."

"I do suppose you are right. Let's go home. Maybe one day your grandfather will come back. He seemed tired."

The two walked back into the city of crystals. Nightmare made sure all knew the war was over. That night he dreamed of fire. He dreamed his city would come under attack by pale-skinned elves with slime dripping off of them.

The Hunter's Prize

Bounty Hunter 13 stood next to Gilda Taka-doji, Axel Wulf, the Fury of the Dancing Flames, and Vinyl Darkspeed. They were awaiting their three new companions. Behind them stood a Gigas Silveran by the name of Belias. Next to him was a fierce-looking Hyenidae.

The Hyenidae spoke, "You better keep my mate safe or I will rip your throat out."

Bounty smiled, "I promise you, Shenzi, I will keep him safe."

Belias rumbled, "You better hold true to your word Demon of Silver. I will not stand by as my sworn brother goes into combat in a weakened state."

Axel sighed, "Do not worry about me, you two. Worry about defending the Bahamut, Shenzi, and Efreet alliance. I can hold my own against whatever this mission has to offer."

Bounty spoke, "It should, in theory, be very easy. Escort three warriors to their destination. And escort the winner home. We shouldn't even have to raise our hands in battle. But we are there as observers. Well, I am there as a judge and these three are there to make sure my judgement is not tainted. One of the warriors is a Silveran. So they are to keep me from automatically declaring the Silveran a winner."

Belias rumbled, "That may be what was told to you. But things have a habit of going sideways while you are around."

"Fair enough. But do not fret. Even if hell opens and the army of demons attacks, he will remain safe."

Axel spoke, "I worry that you account for that."

"Don't"

A scratchy feminine voice cut through the air like a spear. "So you are the goons who are guarding us to our destination."

Bounty shook his head. "That we are. We have been paid good money to keep you safe and well-rested on your journey to the Trial Grounds. Thank you for meeting us in a timely manner. I am…"

"Bounty Hunter 13, we know. You are the Demon of Silver and a general pain in the ass."

"You know me well then. Since you know me, how about you introduce yourselves to my companions here."

The woman who spoke was a garish-looking grey silveran. Her skin was almost pink and her hair was a muddied blue. She was naked except for some war paint and tribal tattoos. She had a scabbard on her back and in her hand, she held a bloody steel blade.

The woman spoke again, "We already know them. Axel Wulf, follower of Efreet, Vinyl Darkspeed follower of Techna, and Gilda of the Oni, a traitor to her kind."

"Well, if you know us, why not tell us your names?"

"Fuck that. Get us to the proving grounds."

"Oh, I can tell I am going to love this journey. Get on the truck."

A hover truck materialized behind them, blocking any escape or second thoughts they may have had. It opened up, revealing an array of auto-cannons and chain guns. Bounty motioned them to get on. The Taur snorted and got on first while the other two went timid, seeing all the guns. Gilda and Axel grabbed the Oni man and dragged him on, while Vinyl and Bounty grabbed the Silveran woman. The truck closed and sped off. Bounty sat in the driver's seat while Gilda sat next to him. Vinyl was in another room playing electro-trance music and worshipping her goddess, which left Axel watching the three warriors.

Gilda spoke, "So what's the story with them? Ever since the Oni God deemed me unworthy, I have been out of the loop."

Bounty shook his head and then pulled up three profiles. "The Taur is The Eighth Explorer of Perfection, with Eyes of Electrum and the Raiment of Blood, Howl of Tortuga. She was a pirate queen. She led the Seven Pirate Lords of the Maw of Kraken. She plundered many ships and small coastal villages. She is wanted by the Anubi for murdering Lord Gazron of the Bisonum. Howl of Tortuga was captured not too long ago and sent to this duel to be removed. Her barbaric ways make her a social outcast of the heavily scientific Tuar."

"She seems capable. Why get rid of someone so skilled?"

"Not my place to ask. I have been paid to get them there and once a winner has been decided to finish them off."

"Eesh... okay, so who is the Oni?"

"That is The Dreaming Plunderer of the West, Zahomnodziel Devilblood. He was sent by the Oni god because he is old. He is still fighting, but you know how the Oni god is. He likes to have the youth in charge and shuns the old since he thinks the youth are more suited for his purpose."

"Yeah, that is why I am no longer in his favour. He found your son to be more suited to his desires."

"Yeah, I heard Arcanus proved himself worthy of being an Oni even though he is not an Oni. He is called Zalleron Skulldancer now. I have my misgivings, but Arcanus seems to feel good about it."

"Whatever… okay, so who is the last one, that weird-looking Silveran girl."

"Yeah, she is an interesting one. There is a reason she is called The Dishonor of the Serpent. Ashanes Drakewatcher was once a fervent follower of Silver. She obeyed his law, even the parts that seemed to contradict the other parts. However, she has recently become increasingly disrespectful of him and the other Battle monks of Silver. The clincher was when she defaced his statue. I tried to tell him it was his own damn fault. She is a teenager and is trying to find her way in a world that is increasingly opposed to God Silver. But the disrespect was too much and he sent her to duel the other two."

"You opposed your God?"

"Haha! Yes, I can talk back at him since he was once a Bounty Hunter 13. I am the only one, though. I do my best to keep him on the level. And I am not thrilled about this duel. Especially the part where I sacrifice the winner."

"Can't you save them somehow?"

"Yes, but it would dishonor them. They truly believe that this is an Honorable thing to fight each other to see which is the stronger species."

"Is it not?"

"I feel it just creates more division. Silverans, Taur, and Oni, do not get along even though they are, by all accounts, the same species, just with different looks. It has always been this way. It did not help that the Silverans slew many Taur during the Chaos War and then banished the rest to the Upper Depths. Then, of course, the Oni God and God Silver have always butted heads. Especially since Elder Silver slew the first Oni god in a fit of rage after he was poisoned by the Gods who wanted him destroyed."

"Yeah, but this Oni god seems to at least dream Silverans are okay as long as they prove themselves to him. I mean, he did allow you and I to have a child together. Even if that child is now banished to who knows where, thanks to the Shogun clan."

"Haven of Dead Planets. The planets that were wiped out in the great rewrite went to their own dimension and were placed in stasis. Thus the Haven of Dead Planets was created. There is no way to retrieve my children who got sent there. They are lost to me."

"I would say don't give up hope. But from my understanding of the Havens, no one can escape the Haven of Dead Planets. It is a pity my only child, with you, is permanently gone."

"Ah, but do you still desire me? Because I still desire you. Especially now that my little wives, Avol and Vicky, are no longer willing to be reborn. They desire peace in the Havens and I do not blame them one bit."

"I have always desired you, Bounty. Your intense fire at the Pyramids of Chombra kindled something in me. I can't get you outta my head. Now I know what Feldspar feels like."

"Yes, her desire was so strong she had to move to the other end of the galaxy to get away from me. I have had five children with her. Cherry is a skilled mercenary and assassin, Sin Seeker and Midnight are warriors in their own right, Nightmare is the King of the Crystal Empire, and Kim is still being raised by her adoptive family on the Equus Islands. But as long as your desire is strong for me and my desire is strong for you, there is a slim chance you may have another child. Afterall, you are still part Green Silveran. Your Oni blood was muddied because your father was a Green Oni who desired a Silveran woman. His desire was so strong he overcame the limit that The Oni God had on all Oni. You came from that union."

She blushed, "I never told anyone that. How did you know."

"When you were in my medical bay recovering from your Darkfire Burns, my computer ran a few tests on your blood to make sure there was no chance of a bad reaction to the treatment. I also know your relationship with She-who-devours-the-cock-of- her enemy-and-crushes-heads-with-her-thighs."

"Alexandra is my little psychopath of a sister and I wouldn't 'ave it any other way. I am also guessing you know about my relation to Maungirtha?"

"Yes. Just as you know about my siblings and our father and also our grandfather."

"You are related to the Ankara clan through a union between your father, Bounty Hunter 12, and Zenthin Ankara's daughter, Marlana Ankara."

"Yes. By all accounts, I could have taken the throne when I slew Zen Aka, but I chose not to. So I let his last son take it. Do I regret allowing Blu Silver on the throne? No, not really, even if it effectively banished me from City Silver."

"So why do we need to be observers?"

"The Gods claim it's to keep me partial. However, I suspect there is a deeper plan involved. These three are essentially sacrifices for what I do not know."

"Easier to not know. I suspect if we knew, the sacrifice would not work."

"You are probably right."

The truck soon arrived at a large open expanse. There was nothing around for miles. Bounty looked at his map and nodded. He began carving a glyph on the ground. When the glyph was created, he brought the three out. He placed a statue of The Oni God at the west point of the glyph. A statue to Silver on the eastern point of the glyph, the statue to The Dread Goddess on the southern point of the glyph, and the Statue to Coldharbour, the God of the Warrior Taur, on the northern point of the glyph.

"Stand by your respective God. Vinyl and Axel, you will need to stand by the Dread Goddess. Gilda, please stand next to The Dreaming Plunderer of the West. Howl of Tortuga, while the Taur-Bos do not worship any gods, the Bisonum do, please stand next to the statue of Coldharbour."

"Fuck that. Since the Anubi are the ones who want me dead, put up the statue to Anubis."

"Very well." Bounty removed the statue of Coldharbour and replaced it with the statue of Anubis. "Finally, we come to you, Ashanes. Please stand next to the statue of God Silver."

"So it is true we are to die here."

"I would try to comfort you and say no, but unfortunately, that is a lie. Each of your respective Gods wishes to be rid of you for… reasons."

"Was I so terrible?"

Bounty sighed and lit his cigar. "Begin the fight. Each of you is a skilled warrior. I am an impartial judge from this point on."

Ashanes pulled out a glaive but was immediately put down when Howl of Tortuga shot her. She crawled over to Silver's statue and lay against it as she began to fade.

Her purple blood travelled down the glyph and several parts lit up as it hit the large bowl in the centre. Bounty watched curiously as her body healed, but she was chained up to the statue of Silver.

Howl of Tortuga tried to shoot Devilblood, but he rolled out of the way of her attack. He summoned fire in his hands and began to throw fire at her. She deftly dodged the fire bolts, but as she dodged, his stream of fire struck her. As she burned, he stabbed her with his naginata. He pinned her to Anubis with the naginata and her blood flowed into the glyph and even more lit up. He pulled out a spiked club and challenged Bounty to fight him. Bounty shook his head and exhaled a black stream of smoke. As the smoke hit Devilblood, Bounty shot forward and severed his arm. It dropped to the ground with a heavy and wet thud.

Bounty looked at the kneeling Oni and sighed, "I am sorry, God Silver, I can't go through with this."

The statue to Silver spoke, "Hmm... oh, I accounted for your meshuggah. Vinyl, please play Electrione hymn seventeen, Axel, please light the braziers, and Gilda stab Bounty Hunter 13."

Gilda cried out, "What?"

"For the ritual to work, his blood is needed. It's not like you can kill him. These three have given their blood. Now he must give his. Do you understand?"

Gilda sighed and stabbed Bounty through the chest. A massive grey and black-cloaked being emerged from the glyph on the ground.

It spoke in a haunting basso profundo, "You summoned me, The Reaper of Nothing?"

"Yes, you have a duty to perform. There are still souls trapped in the Haven of Dead Planets. Retrieve them so they may be Judged by the Judge of Soul."

"I have my orders." The Reaper vanished.

Bounty pulled Gilda's sword out of his chest. "One millimetre to the left and my heart would have been penetrated. Close call. Never in my entire career have my heart been that close to being eliminated. Good job, Gilda."

"Did I hear God Silver right? That Reaper is going to the Haven of Dead planets?"

Silver spoke, "He is, yes. The Writer has written it, so it shall be. Now I do believe you have a wedding to get to."

Bounty spoke, "Oh yes, thank you for the reminder. Corvus is finally settling down, but first,

I had best collect the fallen. So why did you spare them and how did you get that past Anubis and The Oni God?"

"What the jackal and the sun do not know will not hurt them. Plus, Old Anubis and I have an understanding. He is a god of judgment and he certainly adores Howl of Tortuga's work."

Bounty began placing the statues back into his hammerspace. He then lit the glyph on fire, causing the collected blood to be sacrificed by fire. He then erased the glyph so no one else could use it. He shifted his attention to a blue-skinned teenager with a black mohawk and goatee. He was wearing a black vest with blue jeans. His shoulders were exposed, allowing his two sharp shoulder spikes to glisten under the sunlight. His muscles bulged as he set his trident on his shoulders. His swirling grey eyes put Bounty on edge.

He spoke, "This is not my Timeline. Where am I?"

Bounty spoke as he took off his black psy dampener glasses and handed them to the boy. "Kid, you are on Planet Silver. I believe this is Timeline Gamma. Put these on before you continue. Which Timeline were you looking for?"

"I do not know. You look like my father, but you smell less sulfury."

As Bounty spoke, he tied a black cloth to cover his eyes. "Hmm, I see. You are from Timeline Beta, where your father ascended to Shegor, the Duke of Madness. So why did you not go to him?"

A voice spoke, "I placed him here. I had forgotten about him. But have re-written him to become your son. Bounty Hunter 13 meets Bounty Hunter 1014. In his timeline, he was born from an excess of your energy. In this timeline, he is a byproduct of your ritual. He was dubbed the Demon Slayer by his family. That trident of his can destroy those from the Hell sector."

"Very well, Writer. I will do my best to adjust him to this reality."

Gilda called out, "Hey, old-timer. You coming or not? The Truck won't leave without you since you are the only one who knows how to operate these controls."

"Sorry, Gilda, I was just finishing up making sure there was no trace left of the glyph. Come along, son. The future is ahead of you."

The two walked into the truck and Bounty Hunter 1014 looked around. He saw Axel, Gilda, and Vinyl looking at him in curiosity.

Bounty Hunter 13 spoke, "Remember how I said even if the Jaws of Hell open and demons attack. Well, they can't. This young man destroyed them before they could escape to our world.

Meet my son Bounty Hunter 1014."

Gilda looked him over and then shuddered "he seems as strong if not stronger than you."

"As he should. He was a byproduct of the ritual. Now then, I am going to make a few stops, then we will go to Corvus' wedding."

They arrived at a large ship which the truck trundled aboard. Bounty escorted the three out. He then set a course for The Maw of Kraken. As he arrived, several turrets popped out of the water.

Bounty spoke into his com channel, "This is Captain Argon Slayer code seven nine nine twenty. I request permission to land."

A young male voice spoke over the com, "Dad? What the hell are you doing here? Uh, very well, land at port twenty."

"Thank you, Llude."

Bounty docked and exited the ship carrying Howl of Tortuga. Before them stood a tanned boy with white and blond hair, blue eyes, and a black gas mask over his lower face. He raised his eyebrow at Bounty. Next to him stood a woman in ratty purple jeans and a well-worn leather jacket. Also, there was a smaller woman in all black with a hood covering her eyes.

The boy, Llude, spoke, "Okay, Dad, what the hell is going on? That is not your ship."

"Old ship got destroyed. This is the new one and I am here to drop off a Taur who is hiding from her people. Meet Captain Howl of Tortuga. You may need to get her to the medical centre. She lost quite a bit of blood."

"Is that the only reason you are here, Father?"

"Yes and no. I do not know if you received an invite to your uncle's wedding."

"We did, but I don't think we can make it. Ever since we were put in charge here, we have been fortifying the Maw. Strange ships have been seen all over like they are scouting or something."

"Yes, those would be the Pale Elven ships and you are right. They are scouting. Planning and scheming on how to invade all the locations of Silver. They want to conquer Silver."

"Of course they do. Stay safe, Father."

"You too, son. You too."

A med boat floated over and they loaded up Howl of Tortuga. Bounty climbed aboard his ship and it vanished.

Llude looked at the empty space and shook his head. "Alright, girls, let's get back to work." He and his sisters walked off.

Bounty's ship reappeared above a mountain. He began to lower towards a large temple complex. He landed on one of the loading docks and supported Devilblood as he walked off. There was an Amber Elf monk with a shaved head waiting. The monk looked at the Oni and then nodded. He took Devilblood's weight and walked him into the monastery as Bounty lifted off and sped away. He arrived at a massive island floating on the clouds. He landed and looked around. He could see a rave off in the distance and smiled.

"Eris, oh Eris, where are you, my Kimeric sister?"

A Kimera poofed into view, drinking a black tar-like substance. "Ello broda!" She then coughed up a frog that shook its fist at her and hopped off. "Ooo, frog in my throat hate it when that happens. So what brings my sexy sibling here?"

"Hello, Eris. It's been a while. How is Felicity?"

"Much better now that we live up here. She seems much perkier and friskier up here than down there. So who is the weird girl?"

"Eris, this is Ashanes. She was once a follower of God Silver. I would like you to take care of her for a while. You should have plenty of knowledge raising a teenager since our daughter is still around up here, I think."

"Yes, Jazzica is up here still, but I think she may be going to train under Beatrix Badger-Oda soon. I think it will be good for her."

"No doubt about it. Beatrix is as strong as I am. She will train her right."

"I will gladly take care of the girl. Mmm, it is so good to see and feel and feel you again, brother."

"Keep it in your pants."

"No! I want no need to feel your monster cock inside me. My walls spasming in ecstasy as I ride you."

Bounty grimaced as she lunged for him. Her claws dug into his chest as she gripped him. He sighed as she dry-humped him, desperate for a reaction from him. He entered her, causing her to freeze up. She then let out a pitiful mewl and lay her head against his neck sobbing. He stroked her.

"What is wrong, sis? You don't want this, do you? But you can't help yourself. You hate the gnawing need for something to distract you from your trauma. I know the feeling. I was the same when my children were slain. Even more so when the Hundred Guardians of Princess Cashmere were torn apart. My PTSD caused me to seek out distractions. Just like yours is."

"How can I get help? I am an abomination."

As Bounty climaxed inside Eris, she let out a feral howl and slammed her face into his chest. She climbed off him and cleaned him off. Then curled up in a fetal position stroking her tail. Bounty placed a book near her.

"This is a way to summon Shegor, the Duke of Madness and Zarkanus, the healer. They are how I received help for my PTSD. They will help you as well. See you around, sis. Maybe next time won't be so bad."

He walked into his ship as she grabbed the book. Ashanes watched the ship disappear and shrugged. She knelt down and offered her hand to Eris. Eris looked up at her and then smiled a weak smile.

***

Bounty landed his ship at his home. As he exited the ship, Bounty Hunter 1014 spoke, "Is this your home?"

"Our home, dear boy. Our home. If you like, you can settle in or you can come with me to your uncle's wedding."

"I think I would like to stay here for now. It is taking me some time to get used to this timeline. I think I'd like to visit the archives of City Silver."

"City Silver is destroyed, but you are in luck; I do have a copy of the Silveran Archives here. Computer escort Bounty Hunter 1014 to the library, please."

A holographic female appeared. "Of course, my lord. So you are His Lordship's newest child. You have much to learn. Follow, please."

The two walked off as Bounty Hunter 13 vanished. He appeared outside the Sacred Grove of Nevermore. He grimaced as he felt weakened. Because he was considered undead by Nevermore, he was not entirely welcome to be here. He pulled on his red duster and slicked back his black and grey hair. He pulled out a second pair of black psy dampener glasses and placed them on his head.

Corvus walked out of the grove in his feathered cloak. He signed, "What the hell are you doing here, Argon the Slayer?" He looked as though he had just gone through an ordeal. He looked tired and worn out.

Axel spoke, "Bounty, stop pulling the man's leg."

"He's my brother. I have to have some fun."

Corvus blinked, then signed, "Wait a minute. You... ugh, fine, of course. Thank you for coming to Bounty. I also see that Myst is here as well. I don't know who the girl is with Hanna, but she didn't set off any alarms."

"Quasar Moth, former princess of the Rising Falls. However, her title was revoked when it was proven that she was not a direct descendant of Lord Moth. Also known as Star."

Corvus signed, "I am presuming Aerick-Starr?"

"Bingo."

Corvus signed, "I am surprised you showed up. You never got along with the Equus."

"Hate to break it to you, Corvus, but I also have an Equus daughter. Sunspot, daughter of Empress Solaria of the Solar Empire. Damn bitch!"

"Hey, my mom's not that big of a bitch. I mean, she did banish me, okay, okay, she is a super bitch."

"Hello, Sunny."

"You stop it. Sunspot, get it memorized."

"I am just poking fun at you. Why are you here?"

"Oh, Hinewai is my friend. She invited me."

"Cool cool. I see Nevermore went all out for this."

Corvus chuckled and signed, "He even got High Priest Poh to officiate the ceremony."

"I see an unfamiliar face. Who is the fellow with the dark skin and white hair?"

Corvus signed, "Ah, that guy. He is the Priest of Ramuh, the Lightning Druid. He may even be an aspect of Ramuh."

"So, is the Lepidoptera going to be here?"

Corvus signed, "No, thank the twenty."

"I take it. You are still sore with it."

Corvus signed, "Understatement of the year. Anyway, I am glad to see you, brother."

"Who's the Elf?"

Corvus signed, "That is Eva Ursa the Strigidae. Her apprentice is around here somewhere. Ah, the Shadow Elf is by Ramuh. Her name is Lucky."

"I see. Well, you certainly have a strange group in your grove."

The two walked towards a large Cathedral stylized in the way a temple from Planet Gothic would look. Inside this cathedral was a man making preparations. This was High Priest Poh. He was a tall man in a red trench coat, black pants, and a crow-shaped gasmask. He placed his red-gloved hands on his black obsidian staff and tapped the staff twice. Everyone quieted down.

He spoke in a booming tenor, "In her tomb, by the side of the sea, Astarte Ullallume sleeps nevermore. Souls cascade the sounding bell tolls for thee. Songs of Nevermore waft through the breeze. Bless the child of the conqueror worm. The bells ring out the golden bug as the souls waft through the breeze singing forever more."

He motioned for the metallic blue mare with a rainbow mane and two wing stumps forward. He then did the same to Corvus. He placed their hands together and tied them with a bead and feather cord. He then drew in the dirt surrounding them the mark of Nevermore.

He continued the ceremony. "Once upon the dawn so wary, there we ponder so weak and bleary, as the sun shines bleak and scary. Hold our hands to the coming night when we dance without abandon. Two souls, one flock. Mask of Prospero's red death breathes new life into the pendulum swinging, swinging Nevermore. Fall to Usher's house and bend the binding of these two souls. May they never break forever, evermore."

As the cord burned up, permanently binding the two in marriage, the mystically enhanced gothic cathedral's ceiling lit up with the night sky as purple, white and blue beams covered the fake sky. Nebulae were seen alongside constellations as midnight purple feathers flew all over the place. Bounty scoffed rather extravagant of you, Nevermore.

Corvus and his wife both bowed to a large statue of Nevermore that was at the centre of the cathedral. Bounty looked around and then teleported in front of Corvus as a thunderous shot rang out and a large hole appeared in Bounty's chest and he hit the ground on one knee. He summoned the Staff of Shadows and used it to pull himself up. Several of the attendees threw back their cloaks and opened fire. His son, Moonstalker, tore open one of the masked beings with his claws. But he had opened himself up and was filled with bullets. He slashed one more throat open before he succumbed. Bounty snapped his fingers and all the weddinggoers vanished. He struggled up and lunged at one of the beings. He struck hard, knocking the helmet loose to see a pale elf with cerulean black hair.

"Damn it, you Pale Elf bastards. Interrupting a joyous occasion. None leave alive."

A female stepped forward. "That is what you think, old man."

"Mayhem, you damn traitor. So these are your troops. Well, no matter, before I expire, I will take as many of you with me as I can."

A voice spoke, "Come now, old timer, you can't possibly take all of them by yourself. Allow me to lend my axe."

A man in black and silver scarab armour attacked the Pale Elves. Bounty had healed enough and teleported all the pale elves, himself, and the man out. He lit the cathedral aflame, cleansing it of blood and bodies. As he reappeared in the wastes of West Silver, he cracked his neck and rolled his arm. The Cane of Shadows vanished and a large black halberd appeared in his hand. He joined the man in combat.

"Thank you, Leon, for coming. Though, to be honest, I was not expecting you."

"I am not the only one here, though. I may be dead like you will be soon. But I can lend you a hand in glorious combat."

A man wearing a bear skin cloak and a loin cloth sliced through one of the Pale ones. His green steel sword glinted in the harsh sunlight.

"Good to see you, Lord Bear."

The man chuckled, "That is awfully formal of you, considering your son Sin Seeker calls me by my name."

"Sorry Brovone Bjorn. Formality is always recommended with demigods."

"Ha ha! I guess for some of us, like Achilies, that is true."

The three slew the elves until only Mayhem remained. Bounty spoke, "It is not yet her time to die. I thank you for your help, Lord Bear. Sorry, Brovone. Thank you as well, my clone, but it is time to return to your posts."

The two vanished as Bounty sat down; he had withdrawn his nanites and placed them in storage. "Go on, girl, do your duty."

Mayhem screamed at him, "You always say that. When I betrayed Cashmere, you said it. Now you say it as I aim to kill you, why?"

"Why? You are far too immature to know, but I will tell you that I foresaw both your betrayal and my death at your hands. So do your duty, pawn of fate."

Her blade sliced through him as he dissolved into dust. She vanished as a large forest cloaked perpetually in night appeared along with a stone coffin.

***

Corvus walked back into his grove with Ramuh and his wife. Sunspot had taken Hinewai to the Equus Islands, but the two soon returned.

"So Ramuh, it seems you were right to be concerned about security. Looks like I have some work to do."

Ramuh spoke in an earthy voice, "You will do no such thing. Let me fortify this grove you need to spend time with your family. Don't be like Bounty Hunter 13"

In the in-between, Lord Badger stared down Lord Bear. Lord Badger spoke, "Is it done?"

Brovone Bjorn smiled, "Yes, Lord Badger, it is done. Bounty lies dead or as dead as he can be. Everything is going as planned though I wish Moonstalker had not perished as well."

"Moonstalker wanted to prove himself and he did. He got his warrior's death and was burned in ceremonial flames as is honourable. He will still need to go through the Havens, but he will return tempered by his experience."

"Now, if my assistance is no longer needed, I will return to Komodo."

"May the grey guide you, Lord Bear."

Brovone Bjorn scoffed and then vanished through a portal.

***

Gods and Politics Part 2

An Onyx-skinned woman with firey orange runes all over her stone-like flesh walked through the water. She had been shaken by the fury of Nevermore and shuddered as the cold water invigorated her and washed off her terror. She journeyed east and soon arrived on Diavonbre. Before her, stood two brown-skinned men, one of them was larger and more muscular than the first. Also standing with them was a small pink-skinned girl with scales on her shoulders. She was clearly pregnant. Velris tried to see what was in her womb but cringed at the overpowering grey that she saw.

The brown-skinned man with orange and grey hair chuckled. "So you are Goddess Velris. I see you understand what is in my sister's womb."

"All I see is grey. Who are you, people?"

"I am Axel, the Fury of the Dancing Flames. The big guy is Belias the Gigas and This small one is Jinkxi, the daughter of Bahamut. She is pregnant with the next generation or what will be the next generation. The birth of her daughter will mark a new age of Diavonbre denizens. But as the new head goddess, you should already know this."

"I just became the head goddess."

Jinkxi spoke harshly, "Stop bull-crapping yourself. The gods know nothing, all you are are immortal beings worshipped. I am a goddess since I have worshippers. Axel is a god as well. You know nothing because you are not actual Gods. Just a higher being than us. You see grey because I bear Bounty Hunter 13's daughter. She will keep the Pale ones in check. Something the Gods cannot do."

"Calm yourself, Jinkxi. Velris here is the new head god whether we like it or not."

"She usurped power from God Silver, Axel. Why should I play nice?"

"She won by the laws set in place. Do not fall into the trap many of the Gods are falling into. Speaking of, we are being watched. Reveal yourself, Sekhmet!"

A massive feline woman walked out wearing scarab armour and was dressed for war. Her fur glowed in such a way that it made her look like she was on fire. She grinned, causing Velris to quiver with fear.

Sekhmet spoke in a voice that rumbled through Velris' bones, "I hear you are seeking allies, little onyx skin."

"I am or was told to by Doctor Fluorescent."

"I am willing if you are able to defeat me. Do so in front of the allies of God Silver and I will join you."

Velris withdrew her magma sword from her chest and charged Sekhmet. Sekhmet grinned and struck her as she charged past. Her large paw smashed into Velris' face sending her down. She held her hand to her face. She whimpered. She got up and sheathed her blade. She took a fighting stance and caught Sekhmet's paw as it came in for another blow. Sekhmet grinned again, this time her face was super close to Velris'.

"I like you already. Very good. You are stubborn, however. That could get you defeated. Hmm. Don't make me regret my choice, child. I will be your blade."

Velris gulped at the fiery eyes of Sekhmet and knelt down. "Teach me how to fight."

Axel laughed. "Oh, this should be entertaining, but I have places to be. Come Shenzi and Belias, we have plans to make." Velris watched as the brush moved and a massive Hyenidae walked out. The woman smiled and giggled darkly before disappearing again. Jinxi snarled and stormed off.

Velris gulped, "I don't think they like me."

Sekhmet smiled, "Of course, they don't. They have been allies with God Silver's Chosen mortal for a long time. Now you appear as the new head god of Silver. God Silver has been relegated to a minor God that sits wrong with them. You will find many who hold that grudge. But there are also many who despise Old Silver. Your allegiance is unknown. Those that oppose will try to get you to join them. I trust you to make your own way. But be warned, I was once a follower of Silver."

The two walked away. A brown elf with grey and orange hair watched them before smirking an evil smile. He walked into a cave and knelt before a statue of a woman in Amazonian armour.

"Lady Athena. I come with news. The new God, Velris, has no strong allies. She has joined up with Sekhmet, but the hatred that Bahamut's chosen and my brother, Efreet's Chosen, have for her can be tasted. She may find you to be her new friend."

"Hmm... I hope so. The more opposed to God Silver, the better we are at removing him permanently. Thank you, dear. Begin with the plan. Since Efreet forsook you, kill his followers. That will make him weak. Easily destroyed."

"Yes, oh, great Lady of War."

Efreet looked down upon his favoured. He nodded. "Axel, my boy. Your brother has begun to attack my followers. He and those who think I forsook them are aiming to destroy me. Can you handle this or do I need to give you help?"

"Fear not, Efreet. Ever since you chose me over him, we have not seen eye to eye. We may have been twins with a unique bond, but my blade will not hesitate. Especially since I know his will not."

"I knew I chose the right one to give power to. Your brother held darkness in his heart. He could not handle the cleansing fire."

Axel smiled and left the small shrine. He soon arrived at the location his brother was attacking. He was startled when he saw a Pride of Sphinx join the battle alongside a flock of Harpies. He spoke, "Vicki, Shenzi, no mercy."

The air shimmered and a vaguely serpentine shape shot off. There was deranged cackling and a pack of Hyaenidae appeared and began massacring the attackers.

Axel blocked the attack from his brother. "Hello, Alex. Been some time. I appreciate the attempt."

"You! I will kill you and when I do, I will claim your Efreet as my own."

"Sorry, bro. You just lost. In your rage, you got distracted. Good luck."

Alex looked down at his body to see a spear stabbed deep within his torso. He spits up blood and falls to the side. Axel incinerated the body. He then proceeded to assist his allies in the cleanse. When all of those that followed Alex were dead, Axel piled them up and incinerated their bodies as well. The fog rolled in and he saw the Wraiths led by their King, Toreno, clearing the souls from the field of battle. He bowed slightly as Toreno passed him. The Wraith nodded. Axel and his allies were left in the fog. Leaving the Wraiths to do their duty.

***

Velris shivered. She was staring at a massive cathedral made of Silver, stone, and Marble. The blizzard raged around her. This was the sacred temple to her next ally.

Sekhmet snorted. "Damn flashy for a bird."

A large shadowy woman appeared. "Oh, goody, a podunk sand dweller. Why do you disturb my mistress' rest?"

Velris spoke between shivers, "I seek The Silver Raven. I am a new goddess and was told by Lucifer that she might assist me."

"Oh? Hmm, what's his game? Regardless, follow! If you can pass the door, she will meet you and consider your request."

As Velris neared the temple, she noticed the door was flanked on either side by massive pillars. But even more alarming was that the pillars all seemed to be monstrous in nature, like they were alive.

Sekhmet sighed, "Come on, Velris. No need to fear this place."

Velris nodded and entered the door. The shadowy woman was sitting on a throne. Her body shifted and changed so that the shadows no longer surrounded her. The shadows flowed off of her like a cloak. She was a massive Hawk-headed woman wearing silver armour. The shadows formed into wings and she looked down at Velris.

"Why do you seek my aid, new Goddess?"

"My predecessor God Silver allied himself with Nevermore. You are on equal footing with Nevermore."

"Hmm, yes, I suppose I am. Nevermore has been preoccupied with The Entrencher, the so-called Firstborn of the Woods."

"Will you aid me?"

"Oh, very well. I am rather bored up here by myself. I may also know someone who may help you as well."

"May I ask your name?"

"Hmm. It has been a while. Call me Cuervo Plateado."

"Thank you Cuervo Plateado. I am honoured that you would assist me."

***

The black raven, Nevermore, sidestepped a tentacle. "I thought Bounty Hunter 13 killed you? Ugh, you stink!"

The creature waved its tentacle in an obscene way. "Do you speak to your mother that way?"

The two clashed again, but this time, the Entrencher got a hold of Nevermore. He struggled as the vines gripped him and began injecting him with a toxin he was unfamiliar with. A large axe struck the vines shattering them. It flew back into the hands of its master. A large Doebuck stood there with his horns gilded with silver and bronze. His sinewy muscles hefted the large war axe and swung it again right into the head of The Entrencher.

Another horned being but with horns that were ornamental, not true horns, walked over and pulled the vines off of Nevermore. This androgynous being nodded and rummaged in their satchel. They pulled out a vial with a toxic purple substance in it. They forced it down Nevermore's throat.

He coughed and shook his feathers. "Ugh, tastes as bad as it looked. Thanks for the asist Wilderking. Also, thank you, Horned God."

The Doebuck spoke in an earthy voice, "Good to see you too, old man. Shall we finish off this blasphemy for good?"

A being cloaked in leaves descended from the sky. He spoke, "You hold no power to kill this creature. Allow me."

The man stabbed down with a sword designed to look like wood. It emitted a purple glow before the creature disintegrated. The three stared at this newcomer.

Nevermore spoke, "You are a new face. Are you a new god?"

The man spoke with the wind through the trees. "No, far from it, actually. I am an old god. I was once known as the Woodsman."

"You were one of the first ones!"

"That is correct. I see you have insight. Who are you?"

"I am Nevermore of Gothic, though the Syrieen of Silver has also taken me as one of their Gods. So have some Druids."

"Ah, you and the so-called Firstborn of the Woods have been the ones fighting for control of the forest. I admire your tenacity. I am glad I could help. But I must go, many more Blasphemous creatures are coming. Be warned, Wood Gods. The Pale ones have allied themselves with Evil. Lord Dragon leads them. Begin your preparations to fortify my lands. If I am needed again, I will come."

"Thank you, Lord of the Woods."

"Ha! I'll be seeing you."

He vanished as quickly as he came. Leaving the two Wood Gods and one Sky God to contemplate their predicament.

Susano'o stood facing down the remaining five Serpent gods. The Lizard gods had already been subdued by The Silver Dragon. But these five were stubborn. They had managed to inject him with their venom. He could feel it draining him and empowering them. He staggered back.

Before charging forward, he bisected two of the Serpent gods as he passed. He staggered and fell. He was caught by two large grey hands.

"Hold up, old man. You can't continue to fight like this. Allow me."

Susano'o saw through his fading eyes a massive grey demon with thunder for hair and a large scar that bisected his face giving him an unsettling grin.

A horned Monkey man landed. "Oh, woah, hold up! Who the hell are you?"

"Hello, Sun Wukong. You owe me ten grand. However, I am not here for that."

"Braid the Deathseeker. Shit. Well, we welcome the help. These Raptorians have been pushing us back badly."

"Good. Well not good for you. Good for me. Means I can let lose a bit."

"Not too much, this is a nice planet, after all."

"Oh, don't worry."

Electricity crackled around Braid as his body became more muscular. He disappeared in a flash and reappeared. The Raptorians fell and disintegrated only to reform as a massive eight-headed dragon.

Sun Wukong stared up at the monstrosity. "Yamata Orochi, Fuck!"

The large dragon laughed and spewed a noxious poison from his mouth. Only for the poison to be replaced by blood as his heads dropped one by one. The ground erupted in Iron spears that lifted the corpse of Orochi from the earth. Suddenly and without any warning, Orochi ceased to exist. Braid engulfed the area in a holy fire that eradicated the blood from all surfaces, including the assembled Komodo Gods. He landed and rummaged through his satchel. He pulled out a small pill. He opened Susanoo's mouth and dropped the pill in. He massaged the pill down his throat and then let loose a massive bolt of lightning that crackled all over Susano'o, who coughed and rolled to the side. He looked around and saw Braid standing there. He curled up and let out an unmanly whimper.

"Oh, how the mighty have fallen. Regardless, consider your debt repaid, Sun Wukong. I must continue my search for a worthy opponent."

A man wearing red and gold armour spoke, "Who are you to cause such fear in Lord Susanoo's eyes? Even more so with Wukong, who has no fear."

"I am Braid the Deathseeker. Forsaken by my father because I didn't match what he wanted from a prophecy. My name and birthright have stolen by my little brother. All I have left is Death."

"I see. Well, Deathseeker, I am Fu Xi. I am honoured one with your lineage would assist us."

"Oh, can the pleasantries please? I am not one to be so honourable. Make preparations, Komodo gods. The Pale Elves have allied themselves with blasphemy. They will seek to destroy you just as I destroyed Yamata Orochi. War is upon this land whether you like it or not. Goodbye."

Braid vanished. A woman walked into view along with a large feline and an even larger bird. She looked at the gods in front of her. "Uh, hi there, I am looking for Shavi the Diamond Dust."

A frosty woman rose from the stone. "Who is asking?"

"I am Velris, the new head of Silver."

"Ah, the one who beat God Silver in combat. I am who you seek."

"Please join with me as my blade. If I can get a Komodo God on my side, I will prove that I am better than Silver since no Komodo god has openly allied with him."

"You are wrong. For he has five allies here. Oni Shibata, Oichi-hime, Oda Nobunaga, No, and Mithra of the White Lotus."

"Then I was given false information. I apologize if I angered you with my lie."

"Oh, hardly. I was correcting you. I am willing."

Susano'o had regained his composure and snorted in disdain. He walked off. Fu Xi watched him go and motioned a strange bipedal racoon creature with massive balls that it walked on over. The creature nodded and waddled off.

***

A Phantom passed over the land. It was a masculine form. It seemed to be searching for something. It descended and arrived on Diavonbre. It looked around and picked something up off the ground. It flew off. Soon it arrived on Misogoke. It found what it was looking for. It descended and passed one of the trains heading to the inner circle. It discreetly entered the train and the train overheated and lit a flame. Three beings died in the fire. The rest were spared. The Shadow placed what it was looking for on an altar in the Caverns of Fate. The Altar glowed and an image of an Ankh appeared. The cavern shook as three beings appeared.

The large man with six wings, three horns, and a jagged scar from his left shoulder to his right hip looked down at the shadow. He spoke in a voice not unlike thunder, "Why did you summon us, creature?"

"I am the Shadowman first mortal to ascend to godhood. I have come bearing a warning. God Silver is no longer the top God of Planet Silver. He was replaced by an unknown Goddess by the name of Velris. You will be forced either to side with him, her, or the Aphrodite of War in the coming conflict. Make your choice wisely, for after the conflict will arise an even more powerful threat by the name of Lord Dragon. He will lead his Pale Elf army to destroy all beings on this planet. For he seeks to become like God."

The female with flowing white hair, gold eyes, and skin like diamonds spoke, "Why tell us this?"

"You are from the Planet Myth. The only planet out there that can rival Planet Silver. Your kind beat back the Silverans when they conquered the galaxy. You also succeeded in obliterating the Magus Empire when they tried to do the same. Your planet survived the Great Rewrite. The rival Gods of this planet will seek to have that power on their side."

The man with two wings, four horns, fire for his eyes, and smoke for his skin spoke, "We side with Scarabaeus and whatever he chooses. He assisted us in our time of need."

"I am not sure that is a wise choice. But it is your choice. I will not make you choose. I just hope things work out. The Pale ones cannot be allowed to take this planet. They were meant to be written out of existence."

The massive one with the scars growled. "We have made our decision, Shadowy one. I am Ankh, the Anointed master of the arcane. You killed my mortal form to give me this warning. Therefore you are a dangerous threat."

The smoky one spoke, "Calm down, dear brother. He was right to do what he did. It would have been the only way we'd listen."

"But Argon. I had a family. I was happy. I enjoyed mortality."

"I know, brother. You were, after all, a mortal before my brother took over your body after his death. Morrigan, do you share Ankh's sentiment?"

"I was a sex slave as a mortal. I feel much better in my true form. I do, however, agree with his sentiment. Who are you shadowy one to decide such things."

"I am Shadowman first to ascend to Godhood. I am the First Lord of Shadows. I do apologize for my trickery. I can also assure you, Ankh the Anointed that your mortal family will be well cared for. My descendant, Bounty Hunter 13, will see to that."

"Now I am concerned. Bounty Hunter 13 is not exactly well-liked, even among the gods."

"Yet you chose to side with his patron, God Silver. Yes, that is right, Scarabaeus is close allies with Silver. He was once Lord Psycheo, Bounty Hunter 13's clone. And like his genetics, he ascended to godhood."

"Hmm... if you can promise my wife and daughter's safety. I will not strike you down."

"I assure you, Ankh. I may be synonymous with darkness in people, but I am trustworthy. Your family will be safe. The Demon of Silver stands unyielding."

An electric blue-haired Nephilim walked into the caverns. She had heard the magic melody of the universe change. This was a change that concerned her. Well, her goddess was concerned she was not. She stared at the three beings in front of her. Lit her cigarette and left the cave. Shaking her head in refusal.

Shadowman spoke, "Dj Darkspeed. Please pass a message on to Bounty Hunter 13. Lord Shadow commands him to take in the family of Nextar. Their head of household passed away in a train accident."

Darkspeed stopped moving and spoke in a scratchy voice, "Ugh! Nope did not drink enough booze to deal with this. If I can find him, I'll tell him. In the meantime, I will take the family under my protection. Is this satisfactory to you?"

Ankh spoke, "Better you than the Demon of Silver."

"I hear you, bro. Don't worry. They'll be safe with me and Tavi."

Shadowman nodded. "Now that that is settled, I bid you farewell." Shadowman disappeared into the aether. Leaving Ankh the anointed and his siblings alone in the cave."

Morrigan spoke, "Well. That happened. Hey, Darkspeed, wait up. I have some questions."

***

Far above the Continent Noamaiza on Mount Olympus, Zeus sat fuming. "Aphrodite, why should I allow that traitor One-Eye to set foot in my domain?"

"Please, nephew, this is neutral land. I can't let him on Noamaiza proper since he is a male."

"Ugh! Tell me again this fool idea of yours."

"It's not foolish to want change. Silver is weak. He doesn't have it in him to oppose all of us who hate him. If we ally with Old One-eye, Prisma, and Jeanne d'Arc, we can overthrow the wretched Silver for good. Both God Silver and Goddess Silver."

"Very well, girl, I will allow you to hold your meeting here. However, I will not risk my followers in this endeavour. Athena, I give you your Immortality back. That is all I will do to help. I have no desire to fight Silver. He has left me alone and has not bothered me. You seem to be the only one of our pantheon desiring his demise."

A sinister voice cut through the air. "You are so useless."

"Hello, One-eye."

"Why did you summon me, Aphrodite of War?"

Aphrodite smiled, "With your assistance, I can finally take down God Silver."

"Hmm... intriguing. I do suppose now is a good time to strike since he has been stripped of his title. What, though, of the new one?"

A young voice spoke, "Velris is inconsequential. She is weak. She will be easily disposed of once Silver lies dead."

Zeus looked at the newcomer. She wore bright silver armour. Her spear glistened as if made of the sun. Her young face hid her age. He snorted and took a sip of wine.

Athena spoke, "Jeanne d'Arc welcome. I am sure you heard the plan."

"I did. I have already made plans to eliminate Velris. You need not worry about her."

Athena snarled, "Silver must fall first. Do not screw this up."

"I will do no such thing. As soon as Silver lies dead, she will die."

The sky rumbled with ancient energy. A gout of flame blew a hole through the clouds they were sitting on. A woman made of pure light rose through the hole. She opened her eyes, revealing black holes. She was furious.

"You are the one who killed Trinity Dragon. You stole her power without my permission. I am Daybreak. I was the first one to ascend. The Pure Lands chose me. I chose those who can use my power. You killed the one I chose. I did not give you permission to use my power."

Jeanne smirked, "Like, I care what you think. I am from Neo Tarah-Aert. I don't follow your rules."

Jeanne was stabbed at Daybreak. Her spear disintegrated before it even touched Daybreak. Zeus rolled his eyes and got up. He walked out of the room and locked the door behind him. Athena stared at the door with trepidation. A sudden urge to flee overtook her and she bolted.

Aphrodite watched her close ally leave. She pulled out a bow and fired at Daybreak. The arrow pierced Daybreak's skin. Daybreak looked down at the void metal arrow. She grabbed Jeanne and threw her at Aphrodite. Aphrodite opened fire and all of her arrows struck Daybreak. But now she had no arrows. Daybreak shattered her defences and came close to her. Her touch burned Aphrodite. Aphrodite fell to the ground smouldering. Jeanne backed up only to hit the legs of Old One-eye. He looked down at her cowardice and stabbed her through the heart. She went rigid, then became ice and then shattered, leaving behind a soul crystal. He walked over to Aphrodite and ended her suffering. He stared down Daybreak only to see a void forged blade in his sternum. The Oni God, Shuten-Doji, stood behind him along with Alexander. Alexander tossed the body of Prisma on the ground as well. Prisma stared up at Daybreak.

"Oh goddess, please spare me my life. I swear I had nothing to do with these two."

Daybreak looked at her. "Did your kind not try to kill the Silverans?"

"Yes, but that was ages ago."

"Hmm. If you swear to uphold your purpose, I will spare you, but only if you work with Sylar. She was once God Silver's wife before he deemed her unworthy and tortured her. She is my new battery since Jeanne d'Arc killed Trinity Dragon, my first battery. Do not make me regret my decision."

Daybreak vanished, leaving the wounded Prisma, the mechanical Alexander, and the Oni God to ponder their circumstances. The Sky darkened and a red-cloaked man descended from the portal he landed and harvested the bodies. He then looked at the three living gods.

"I am Azrael, the Alpha Reaper. I am the one who claims your souls when you die. I am the one who judges your souls when you die. Be warned, those who oppose Silver, a test is coming. Will you work alongside Silver in the coming catastrophe or will you die along with the other gods of this planet?"

He vanished with the three souls. Shuten-doji scoffed but shook his head.

"I know what is coming. They have already tried to wipe out Orkea. They almost succeeded. Damnable Pale Elven Wizards have allied with creatures even I can't comprehend."

Velris stared at the feathered and bone-armoured man before her. He had olive tan skin and coarse black hair. He stared down at her.

She spoke, "You are Nemesio the Feathered Serpent, are you not?"

"I am. Why are you on Olayazca?"

A dark woody voice spoke, "She is here because I sent for her."

"Very well, Wolfthorne, but Olayazca stands with Silver."

"I know very well your allegiances. I am not here to cause any trouble."

"I hope you are right."

Nemesio walked off with a slight limp. Wolfthorne watched him go and shook her head. "Boy ascended too early. His body is failing him because of it. But you, you intrigue me. That is not a good thing."

Velris stared at the wolf-cat-bear-ape hybrid. "You wish to see me?"

"Yes, young one. I wish to join you, but what I see is a weakling."

"But I beat God Silver."

"Had not that young man appeared as your blade came down, you would have lost. You would have been up against a Bounty Hunter 13."

"What?"

"You didn't know? All the God Silvers in that room are ascended Bounty Hunter 13s from different timelines. Even the Bounty Hunter, 13 of this timeline, is on track to ascend to godhood."

"I can't allow that to happen. Bounty Hunter 13 is already too powerful as is. I have watched him for some time."

"Hahaha! Oh, you poor naive girl. The Writer has a way of making sure things come to pass. You cannot escape the drums of fate. We are all pawns in the long run. I see now why you are so weak. You have much to learn. I will teach you."

***

Nemesio stood near a woman with a noseless face. She had ritual scars all over her body. Her chitinous bio armour pulsed with blood. She had long brown hair and two grey eyes.

"Jaina Yu-Harle, the trickster goddess of Organos. Why do you seek me out?"

"I have heard the call, Nemesio the Feathered Serpent. Something reached out to me and called me here."

A young voice spoke, "That would be me."

The two turned to see a small girl with pale skin, black hair tied in a noose that she kept around her neck, wearing all black except for blood-purple stockings. She held a doll with no head in her hands.

Nemesio blinked in confusion. "Wendy Morte, I thought you were fictional."

"That's the thing about being forgotten. I can sneak around investigating things."

"Why then did you call Yu-Harle and I here?"

"To pass on a warning to the gods of Organos and Olayazca. The Pale elf known as Lord Dragon has made his move. He has allied himself with the Blasphemy from beyond time and space Athwntheziluxbthyvzsor. The Pale Elves will soon march to conquer Silver. Be prepared for a hard fight. We must hold them at bay. They can not be allowed to conquer."

Nemesio scoffed, "For if they do, then all of the Gods will die. Yes, I know. I was given that information by Bounty Hunter 13."

"Then you know what trouble we are in. Now is the time to stand strong, not split apart."

"Do not worry, Wendy Morte, Organos and Olayazca have no desire to go to war over politics. We will stand together for the sake of the planet."

An earthy voice that shook the ground spoke, "That is what I like to see."

The three turned to see a man wearing a robe with a badger hood. He held in his hand a claw that glistened black. Jaina fell to her knees in prayer.

"Ah, you are the one known as the Trickster. I have heard of your exploits. Yes, it is I, Lord Badger, the ascended."

Nemesio looked at this newcomer. He sighed and spoke, "You have been watching us. Why then did you send Wendy instead of saying the warning yourself?"

Badger looked at the feathered serpent. "How do you know I sent her?"

"Come now, Lord Badger. I am allied with Bounty Hunter 13, the Lord of Shadows. I know your signature very well."

"Ah, you know the old ways. Yes, I did send Wendy. She needed the power boost and I granted it to her. Many of the Organos gods have been forgotten. It is my duty to keep them remembered.

So I send them to give messages in my place."

"I appreciate the warning. The Pale Elves will regret ever stepping foot in the lands of Olayazca."

Velris stopped suddenly and looked around. Wolfthorne smiled. "You hear the Magic Melody of the universe. A shift has taken place. Time will tell if this is a good shift or a bad shift. You may want to up your pace."

Velris arrived at a small cave. Nuklea walked out, holding a bundle. She eyed Velris warily.

"Which god are you?"

Nuklea smirked, "I am the Goddess of the Atom. I am she who prevents radiation poisoning. You may refer to me as Nuklea."

Wolfthorne looked at the bundle. "Ah, where did you find her?"

Nuklea looked at Wolfthorne and frowned. "She was found by a radiation pool. I have healed her of rads, but for some reason, she is dying still."

Wolfthorne examined the bundle and then nodded. "Lady Velris, you have the opportunity to shape a living being. Come here, allow me to show you how."

Velris picked up the bundle in her lower two arms and unwrapped it. There was a blue-black frail, looking being emaciated with no mouth and four arms. Wolfthorn stroked the girl.

"Now, Lady Velris, I need you to focus on the wastes, absorb the radiation around you and imbue the girl with it. Then when that has happened, give her a mouth and hair."

The three moons turned aquamarine as Velris glowed a fiery orange. Her onyx skin suddenly cracked, revealing many runes that also glowed an ominous orange. The child glowed orange and suddenly started crying. Velris stroked the girl giving her a pronounced chest, black hair, and ruby eyes. She struggled and Wolfthorne stroked her hair.

"You are doing well. Allow me to reinforce you."

Cuervo smiled a beaky smile and stepped over and reinforced Velris and Wolfthorne. Sekhmet nodded and watched. Nuklea seemed intrigued. The girl now glowed with three different colours. Magma Orange from Velris, Black Silver from Cuervo, and Burnt Mahogany from Wolfthorne. A powerful scent filled the area. It almost smelled like Cinnamon. A haggard old man with wrinkles walked into view. Grey energy was flowing off of him. Half of him was burned and scarred, the other old and wrinkly.

The girl smiled, "You got fat, my queen."

The man smiled a fanged smile, "I am not your queen anymore, Gabby. You are now your own being. Goddess Velris, you have ushered in a new age of Planet Silver. By creating Brandi, you have started a chain reaction. Now many of those with Silveran blood will be changed into their new form. I also thank you for finding my daughter."

Velris looked at him. "Demon of God Silver, I can't allow you to ascend. You must be destroyed."

"Hmm, well, good luck with that, Lady Velris. My final battle approaches. Lord Dragon has made his move. The Pale Elves have allied with the Blasphemy from beyond Time and Space Athwntheziluxbthyvzsor. They will invade soon. It will be up to you and your blades to stop them. The Silverans are no more. You have killed them. Now you must revive them. Your work is not yet over."

She pulled her sword from her chest and charged the old man. He caught her blade and stabbed it back into her. He stared at her, his eyes glowed grey and void-like. He kicked her hard, sending her rolling. She gasped for air and struggled up. A wave of Ice encased him. Then it shattered several stone spears struck up from the ground and impaled the man.

He laughed, "You can't kill what's already dead. The Blood clan made sure of that. Heed my warning Velris. The pale Elves will try to take continent Silver. You will be destroyed if they do. Get your priorities straight. My destiny is set and no matter what you do, it will not change. I tried that already. If you fight me, you will be weak when fighting the Pale Elven Gods. They will destroy you and then Planet Silver will be theirs. Gather your allies. Come, Brandi! Your siblings await you."

The blue-black-skinned four-armed girl smiled and skipped over to him "Yes, Father Queen."

"Again, not your queen anymore. You are no longer a Shyft. You are a Silveran." Velris roared in anger and charged him, only to be intercepted by Sekhmet.

Sekhmet purred, "I warned you not to test my allegiance Lady Velris."

Velris slashed down with her sword and bisected Sekhmet. She stared at the dead goddess and gasped. She dropped her sword and tried to reverse time. A large man appeared. He was lanky with shaggy hair. The ground erupted in tentacles.

"I am Inspector Shaguthor of the Time Police. What is the meaning of this?" Velris whimpered.

"I didn't mean to. Please, I didn't mean to."

Shaguthor looked down at the bisected remains of Sekhmet. He shook his head. "I'll allow it. But don't mess with time or you will feel my wrath. It is alright, Chief Inspector Hunter."

A man who looked like the old man from earlier but without the burn walked over. His brown trench coat flapped in an unseen wind. He lit a cigar. "I would have allowed it as well, inspector, as much as I despise messing with time. Sekhmet cannot be allowed to become nonexistent. She is still needed."

Shaguthor rolled time back and Velris charged the old man. Sekhmet intervened. "I warned you not to test my allegiance Lady Velris."

Velris stopped mid-swing and looked around in shock. Sekhmet vanished in a swirl of sand.

Cuervo walked over. "What is wrong, Velris?"

"Major deja vu. Uh, where did Sekhmet go?"

Wolfthorne looked around. "She went back to Diavonbre. Congratulations, Velris. You have already made an enemy of Continent Diavonbre."

A voice spoke, "Oh, don't worry, they'll come around."

The three looked over to see a brown trench coat fluttering in the wind. Time froze and a man came into form.

Velris snarled, "Bounty Hunter 13, you are still here?"

"Wrong but also right. Inspector Bounty Hunter 13 of the Time Police. You messed with time by reversing it so you would not kill Sekhmet. I am here to warn you. We Time Police do not appreciate mortals or Gods messing with time. This is your only warning. If you do it again, I will send my most powerful officer against you to arrest you. Shaguthor will do so by any means necessary. Goodbye, new Goddess. Don't cross the Time Police."

Velris nodded. "I will uphold the law, Inspector. I swear."

"Hmph"

The inspector vanished, leaving the scorched wasteland to whip up dust in his place.

Velris gulped, then watched as the sky darkened. She saw before her a massive non being. It was covered in slime and tendrils. She cried out as it seemed to reach for her. A large wing whipped her in the face snapping her out of her trance. She shook her head and saw a man wearing a black biker jacket with a black fedora on his white hair. His eyes were deep crimson and glowed with strange energies. He folded his wing back and snorted as he looked down at her.

He spoke with a soothing yet sinister voice, "Hello, little goddess. You seem troubled. Hmm."

"What was that that I saw?"

"Ah, the horror from beyond time and space. It is Lord Dragon's ally. You saw the future. If my pale brethren take over."

"You are a Pale Elf?"

"Not anymore. Hmm. I am one of the ascended. You interest me. I am Genov's Witness. You may call me Seraphot, the One-Winged Daeva. My dread companions and I have seen you and have watched you."

"Why the one wing?"

"The other was ripped from my back by Nevermore during our climactic battle for planet Gothic. He used the fabled Climhazard and severed my godhood from me. That was a millenia ago. It took me this long to reconstitute my being. But you are a new Goddess. I wish to become your ally. You will need my companions and I as your allies. And we would be happy to help you out."

"Who are your companions? I need to know who wants to work with me."

"Ah, yes. Appear, my friends. Come greet the new goddess."

A clown-like man appeared painted white with crimson stripes all over his body. His blond hair was short and slicked back. On his back were two wings of bone, two wings of leather, and two wings of feathers. The world screamed in terror at his presence. A tall, androgynous man with purple hair and fur on his arms and legs appeared next; he held a book in his hand that he was reading from. He turned his head to look at her and she saw blue fire in his eyes. A creature appeared and whipped up a whirlwind. When the wind died down, a monk stood there covered in fleshy grey vines that connected him to the creature. He was menacing yet pleasant to look at. But she could feel evil intentions swimming off of him. Finally, a man in a tattered black duster with red and white hair appeared. He was by far the most normal looking of them, yet she could tell he was a powerful sorcerer.

The clown spoke in a voice of malice, "I am the Mad Jester of the Moon. I am the God of Magic."

The androgynous man spoke in a melodious voice with sinister undertones, "I am the White Lord of Destruction. It was a science experiment gone wrong. I was created to be the bringer of destruction, but I was deemed a failure. I am the God of Desire and War. I regret that I was a part of wiping out the Silverans. I was only fulfilling my purpose."

The monk scoffed. "We all fulfilled our purpose. Why should we help this little usurper?"

The man with red and white hair sighed. "Because, Seemoore Delta, we need her to bring us back to full power. We have all lost a piece of our godhood. She will help us be remembered."

"Oh, I suppose you are correct, Chancellor. New Goddess, what say you? We help you. You help us."

"I believe you can help me. But I fear your intentions."

An old crone riding a mortar and pestle flew into view. She spoke in her scratchy voice, "As well you should. Lady Velris, there is a reason these men make the world scream. I came to investigate. However, I can see you need their help as much as they need yours. God Silver is strong. Those that oppose him fear this strength. But you will be as feared as he is. They will turn on you as quickly as they turned on him. These men can be strong allies, but if you deny them, they may join your rivals and then you will be outmatched."

The Chancellor smiled, "You should listen to Baba Yaga. She is the wisest of the gods. And has been around since the first war of the gods back when Planet Silver was young."

Baba Yaga smiled a snaggle-toothed smile. She whistled and a hut sped into view. It was on the top of bird's legs. She hopped into the hut and it sped off. She disappeared over the horizon.

The Chancellor spoke, "What is your decision Lady Velris?"

A deep voice spoke, "Do not listen to the sweet words of a snake. He is a parasite upon the stars. If you give them power, they will destroy you."

She turned around to see the God Silver, who speaks standing there smoking a cigar. Next to him was the God Silver, who fought standing with his great sword resting on his shoulder. The Chancellor hissed and recoiled from their energy.

"Why should I listen to you?"

"I have been the god of this planet for aeons. You have been the god of this planet for mere days. With age comes wisdom. I have seen many timelines. No good will come from allowing these men power. Leave them powerless."

"You don't tell me what to do. I will allow them to join my cabal."

"Then you are a fool. I had hoped better of you. Goodbye, Lady Velris. I hope you can hold back the darkness before it consumes you."

The two vanished and reappeared in an onyx meeting room. God Silver, who Speaks, sat near God Silver, who Fights. Both were near God Silver, who listens and God Silver, who was just born. God Silver who Gardens wheeled God Silver who Watches in.

Watches smiled, "Is everyone here? Good. What is the consensus, my friends?"

Fights scoffed, "I see no merit in continuing to examine Velris. She has chosen her path. I say we take back our title by force."

Speaks shook his head. "That is not a wise Idea. We are already struggling with Alexander and Sylar's allies. The Arcland Gods are also being a thorn in our side. We do not need to fight Velris and her allies, no matter how seedy they are."

A voice spoke, "Then maybe it is time to bring in someone else."

A large man walked in with his black hair undone. It was windswept, like he had been riding at great speeds.

God Silver spoke, "Who are you? You seem familiar."

"I should, for I am a part of you. All Bounty Hunter 13's were born under the three constellations, even if one was unknown. The hunter, the warrior, and the prisoner. Parts of each constellation are shown during your birth. My soul is the prisoner. I hid my soul many eons ago to gain immortality. I hid it in the stars."

"You are Koschei, the one dubbed deathless."

"Yes, I am. Only the heat death of the universe will end me."

"Why do you seek us, Koschei?"

"I have witnessed Planet Silver split the first continent into many. I have seen two new continents appear from nothing. I feel pity on the Pale ones, for they have been deceived by a dark desire. Many do not speak up for fear of being devoured by the horror from beyond time and space. The Horror that one Lord Dragon has sided with."

"Yes, Lord Dragon desires to conquer Silver and wipe out all non-Pale Elves. Are you suggesting we let him?"

"No, I am suggesting nothing of the sort. I can not say what I am suggesting. For this is a game to me and I can not be forthright."

Listens nodded. "I believe I know of what you speak. You are saying we should allow Velris to join with those four dark men. But only because they will be relegated to a new continent. One that will house all the Pale Elves that survive the coming war. They will desire their old gods back. No horror god that was forced upon them."

Koschei grinned, "Very good. But can you achieve this alone?"

God Silver, who watches, spoke, "We are never alone. We have our blades. We have our allies. The war has yet to begin. Lord Dragon has yet to make his first move. We have time."

"Do you?"

Silver Destiny Finale

The Future of Bounty Hunter 13 Part 1

The vastness of space was cold and lonely. Bounty Hunter 13 stood in the cold darkness studying the strange planet in front of him. Before him stood a giant space dragon, a massive space phoenix, and a gargantuan space bull. They seemed to be guarding this planet. Is this the fabled Planet Fountainhead, progenitors of my people?

The bull turned towards him and then spoke, "This is not the Planet Fountainhead. You are trespassing here, godling. Leave before we crush you."

The Phoenix spoke in a feminine voice, "Now… now, Old Bull, he is here because we summoned him here."

The dragon spoke in a voice that surrounded Bounty in shadows, "You are required here, Argon Terrinos, The Slayer."

Bounty tilted his head. "I am not this Argon Terrinos. Who is Argon the Slayer?"

"He is you, yet you are not him. His soul is trapped in you, bound to your soul, but he is not part of your soul."

Bounty grimaced, "Fine, what is Argon the Slayer required to do?"

"Kill the False God King of this planet. Release his daughter from her prison and release her clone from the augments she was forced to gain. You may have help that we choose."

The Phoenix waved her wing and Gilda's soul appeared in the vast chill. Gilda looked terrified.

Bounty walked over to her. "This is a test, Gilda. Do not concern yourself with what is going on. For some unknown reason, we were chosen to help this Planet."

A wolf appeared and howled, causing Llodi to appear as well. She seemed unaffected by this strangeness. She walked over to her father.

"And why is Llodi here?"

"In her resides the soul of Argon's daughter. A promise was kept that must be fulfilled."

The four spoke in unison, "Free Planet City Vale from the False King."

***

Five Figures stood looking out across the midday forest. Before they rose a black, silver, red, and gold wall; behind this wall was a complex of traps and mazes.

"Okay, this place gives me the chills. I can feel untold powers and hear dark whispers. I strongly oppose the idea of us going in there."

"Do not worry your little head Kar-en."

"Shut it, Mayhem. The dark priestess is right. We are trespassing on holy ground." The red and pink-haired woman rolled her eyes. "I would hardly call the tomb of Bounty Hunter 13 holy. More like accursed."

The Dwarven Silveran in bronze and platinum armour growled: "Either way, lass, we are trespassing."

Mayhem snorted, "Regardless, we are going in. I am not afraid of ghosts."

The small group waited while Kar-en opened an invisible door. The dark priestess smiled as the group walked in. Few will survive. I just hope I am one of them.

Mayhem spoke, "Jar-ed, Wi'ili-am, Xen-a will go explore that way. Fer-ol, Sk-na, and I will go this way. Dwarf, you take the rest forward."

The red and pink-haired woman, Xen-a, was the first to trigger a trap. She had lit a lamp to see the murals on the wall. Wi'ili-am was eviscerated by numerous hooks and wires. His blood flowed into a hole in the ground deactivating the trap. She looked at the mural and recorded what she saw. On the mural were seven figures. One was a Banebear, one was a horned skull, one was a Rocziz, one was a Mooncatz, one was a Shadowolf, one was a Hsigo, and the last looked vaguely serpentine. She saw them arrayed with their backs to a wall.

"Jar-ed, what do you make of this?"

"If my lore is correct, each symbol represents one of the seven groups that defended Princess Jubilee Cashmere from the Pale Elf army. The skull represents Bounty Hunter 13 and his allies. The rest have no idea what they represent. All history remembers is that eighty-eight of them died and Princess Cashmere was executed."

The two continued on through the murals depicting the clash and defeat of the hundred. They saw the mark of a traitor on one. Followed by the execution of Princess Cashmere. As they exited into the atrium, they triggered another trap. Seven spears stabbed into Jar-ed. He dropped, triggering another flamethrower trap that incinerated his body.

Xen-a gulped as she entered the large circular path overlooking a large lake. In the middle of the lake, on a large butte, lay a single coffin. She stepped on a pressure plate and fell with numerous arrows in her body.

Fer-ol and Mayhem stood over the dissolving body of Sk-na. She had stepped in acid and in trying to extract herself, had triggered an acid waterfall. The acid vanished as quickly as it appeared. The two continued on until entering into a large area with a lake. Fer-ol looked across the lake to the Odpočívadlo na Hunter. He grimaced. The railing broke. He cried out in shock before falling into the water. As he tried to swim towards the butte in the middle of the lake, it began swirling. Huge waves slammed into him. He was tossed around like a ragdoll.

Mayhem watched this impassively. She then saw the walls on the other end bulge. Ten huge grinders appeared on the wall. And began rolling, pulling Fer-ol towards them. His limp body was unable to resist. There was a sound akin to two stones being smashed together as his body became mulch.

***

Bounty dodged the attack from the winged woman. She screamed in rage at him only to find herself on fire. Her eyes widened in terror as she tried to put them out. But she could not. A woman appeared and waved her hand, causing the flames to vanish.

Gilda's soul walked over and healed the woman with what little healing techniques she knew.

Bounty floated into the castle and saw the False God. He drew the Blade of Vorpal or, as it was formerly known, the Blade of Bloodhawk the Destroyer. He stabbed the king and he became nothing. The oppressiveness of the planet became less oppressive.

The Four space beasts pulled him up into space along with Llodi and Gilda. There was a blinding flash of grey and Bounty grunted in pain as it felt like his soul had been ripped in two.

He saw Gilda fall and then get up, holding her head as a woman walked out of her. This woman was brown-haired and blue-eyed. She looked around in curiosity, then down.

Gilda watched this woman warily, then happened to turn towards Bounty as a man walked out of him. This man looked almost exactly like Bounty, except his face was heavier than Bounty's.

The woman rushed him. "Argon, it's you. What is going on? Last I remember, I had a black axe coming at my head."

Argon spoke in a voice that sounded very much like Bounty's. "We were slain, but for some reason, instead of our souls going to the Havens, we were bound to two powerful souls that were just being born. I do not know why."

The bull spoke, "Because, my child, you were a Magus. Your sins were unforgivable. However, that schemer God Silver had plans for you. He redeemed your souls by binding you with his chosen warrior and young Gilda Taka-doji. He also desired your strength to help his chosen warrior. Be glad you were freed from your binding. For Bounty Hunter 13's fate is immortality. And as was promised to you as you died, God Silver releases you from his scheme alongside your second wife Harmony and your daughter Raleigh."

Bounty grimaced as Gilda vanished then he was pulled back to his tomb.

***

Mayhem watched this impassively. She then saw the walls on the other end bulge. Ten huge grinders appeared on the wall. And began rolling, pulling Fer-ol towards them. His limp body was unable to resist. There was a sound akin to two stones being smashed together as his body became mulch.

A dark grave voice spoke in her ear, "Ah, there you are, Mayhem. It's been a while. How is the traitor?"

Mayhem paled, "I did what I had to do. Leave me be."

"Blood for blood. You killed Princess Cashmere and the eighty guardians. Your life was forfeited the moment your sword sliced me open."

She cried out and jumped, gliding over to the black tomb, she raised her sword. And struck.

***

The air was crisp. The winter was nearly upon the land. There was a deafening explosion that rents the air asunder. The three moons were full, creating an almost daylight brightness to the midnight hour. It was a witching hour as Bounty opened his eyes. He blinked in confusion as a pale elf stared down at him. She had a purple sheen to her black hair and piercing pink eyes.

He murmured, "Raven?"

She spoke, "Oh good, he's alive."

She wrapped a purple cloth over her eyes and stood up. She reached her hand down to help him up. He took it and got up. Her strength surprised him. He looked around seeing three others. One was a dwarf and the other was a bald brown man with one arm. The third seemed almost equine. He noticed pink skin and saw two blue eyes staring through the helmet.

"So why are you here?'

The pale elf spoke, "My companions and I were on a quest when we came upon your terrifying tomb. We don't quite know how you got resurrected."

"I know how. Who are you folks anyway?"

The pale elf fidgeted before saying, "I am unable to tell you my name. Names hold power."

The dwarf nodded at this, but the dark-skinned man spoke, "I am Captain Oneida Blacksin, leader of these rogues. The equine is Pie. She lost her voice in an accident. Welcome to the future."

Bounty saw Mayhem lying in tatters. She was still alive. He walked over to her and looked her in the eyes. He snorted and snapped his fingers, causing her to petrify and shrink. He placed the statue in a bag that mystically appeared. He then walked over to the arrow-riddled body of Xen-a and she, too, became stone. He removed the arrows from her petrified body and placed her statue in his bag as well. The purple-clothed pale elf watched Bounty as he looked at his tomb. He shook his head and the entire structure and surrounding forest vanished, leaving them standing in a wasteland. It was midday.

Bounty spoke, "You kids might want to keep up with me. We are in the apocalyptic lands of Western Silver."

Oneida spoke, "You seem awfully unconcerned that hundreds of years have passed. You are the last Pure Silveran in existence. And the fact you don't know half of us."

"This is not my first resurrection, nor will it be my last. My soul is not welcome in the Havens. So I have experienced the world moving on while my soul meditated on my coffin. I also really don't particularly care about my travelling companions."

"So you have seen what the Pale Elves did to your people. What did they do to all the horned beings on this planet?"

"Of course. Mass genocide. They failed, though. The Taur, Doebuck, and Satyrian are still alive. So are the Silveran species. The Pale ones never did get a foothold on the other continents. So there are still Silverans in existence, just not here."

"That may be so, but you are the last on this continent."

"Oneida, was it? I have been the last for a long time."

Bounty looked at the ship before him. He smirked, "You didn't tell me you were captain of the Blackheart Pirates."

A massive rino man with numerous cybernetic augments walked out of the ship "No boy-o, that would be me."

"Rino von Rhino, what a surprise. Not really, but good to see you, old friend."

"Bounty Hunter 13, you conniving bastard. You're alive! Thought you died shielding Princess Cashmere from a hail of bullets?"

"Rumors of my death have been greatly exaggerated, I see."

"Let's get aboard Blackheart One before we get discovered out here. By the way, welcome back. Been a long time since someone did a good old-fashioned purge around here."

"Who says I came back to kill the Pale elves?"

The mystery woman, Kar-en, spoke, "That is why we resurrected you. There needs to be a culling. Many of the pale ones are using forbidden magicx and wreaking havoc all over the place. The common people are in a state of constant peril. Your expertise is needed."

"Well, then, I suppose that is why I am here. Very well. Then my blade will taste elven blood again."

***

Sucryog

Steam billowed out of the way as Blackheart One landed. A large man in blue armour watched from the battlements of The Crystal Castle. Next to him stood a woman in Black, Silver, and Red serpent armour. Her battleaxe had a serpent coiling around the hilt. Her black and purple hair billowed in the wind. On his other side was a Stripped Equus dressed in minimalistic Shaman clothes. The army of the Pale Elves were in a heavy defensive formation. It was as if they were trying to stall the Crystal Army. The sky became dark and a sharp wind whipped up. A purple and green miasma wrapped around the pale ones.

"Get your men away from the enemy. They are summoning an aspect."

Turning around, the man in blue spoke, "Who dares tell me what to do?"

"I dare boyo."

"Father? But you died!"

"Yes… well, as you can see, I am alive again. Now listen carefully, Nightmare. Pull your troops back now!"

"All troops pull back to the main wall. We must protect the walls."

The troops pulled back. Soon a creature beyond description emerged from a portal that the pale ones had guarded. It absorbed many of the Pale Elves before it turned its focus on the Crystal Castle. The perverse abomination smashed one of its thin, sinewy arms down. The arm splattered all over the upper wall causing smaller abominations to form out of the muck.

Nightmare snarled, "Flamers open fire. Do not worry about friendly fire, the armour will protect them. Burn the abominations!"

The shaman assisted the flamers with their task. Meanwhile, the creature was still trying to overwhelm the Crystal Empire forces. Bounty Hunter 13 jumped down.

"Captain Oneida, please concentrate fire on the creature. Rino, I need you to send the Pale Elves to their dread gods. Have the dwarf and the spooky lady help you."

"I got you covered, Demon. Rino will not move to attack as long as that thing exists in this realm."

"I'll take care of it. Watch your eyes."

Flames erupted all over the battleground. The flames coalesced into a towering dragon that was part fire and part shadow. There was deranged and maniacal laughter coming from within the fiery dragon. Within a minute, the unknowable and blasphemous creature was incinerated. Rino charged out of the ship along with the woman and the dwarf. They were joined by Nightmare and the woman with the serpentine axe. Only two elves remained after the onslaught. Bounty towered over them.

The female with a scar across her face spoke, "Please spare us."

Bounty snarled, "Why should I? Your kind didn't spare any when you tried to purge my kind from existence."

"Please! That was before my time. Please have mercy!"

"Argh! Fine! Tie them up and toss 'em in the holding cells. If they try anything, execute them."

Rino nodded and, with the assistance of Nightmare, escorted the two aboard the ship.

The Dwarf smiled, "Awfully generous of you, Demon of Silver. It's a good thing you didn't stoop to the level of the Pale ones. Gives you good marks."

"So this is a test, is it Ro-jath the Bronzed Titan?"

"How?"

"I am almost a god. Also, you stink of death. Specifically like a reaper."

"So the rumours are true."

"Yes, I am not welcome in the Havens. The gods fear me for some reason. My destiny is ascension. Though I abhor the idea."

"Father! I am glad to see you safe."

"Oh, Nightmare, I was always destined to come back from my exile. But I see time has not been kind to you. What happened?"

"It's a long story. Started when my ship crashed and a shaman found and healed me. I must introduce you to my family. You and your allies are welcome to stay the night. I know you must desire to push on."

"No, no, the Pale Elves can wait. I have not had a meal in almost a hundred years. I could use this time to catch up with you. Did you have any children?"

"Come on, Father. I'll introduce you."

Ro-jath watched them leave. He nearly collapsed from anxiety. "Rokos, my dear, I think we bit off far more than we could chew."

The woman smiled a mysterious smile. "Come, my nervous companion. I'm sure a good ale will ease your mind. He did pass our little exam. I just wish we had stopped that aberration from gaining a foothold in this land."

Rino snorted and walked off. "Come on, you two wimps. It was banished with the fires of hell. I think we all could use a stiff drink."

The three walked off, with Oneida quickly following behind them after locking up the ship. "Seriously, we are going to leave those two elves unsupervised? Ahg, come on!"

Pie watched them leave and vanish. She appeared in the containment facility. She made sure her weapon was visible. She stared down the two Pale Elves. "Try anything and my cupcake launcher will be so far down your throat you won't have time to defend yourself. Anyway here is some food. My companions seem to be joining a party celebrating your defeat, which begs the question. Why did you surrender so easily, Queen Schlaughter?"

The woman gulped. "I saw the fury of God Silver. Why wouldn't I surrender?"

"Sure, we'll go with that. My eyes are on you. You as well, mister assassin. Do not tempt my master's generosity."

The woman nodded. "I am locked in here. I wouldn't dare try anything. You and your dark master scare me."

Pie's eyes narrowed suspiciously, then she shrugged and walked off. She entered the main deck. Her body drastically changed into that of a vibrantly pink poofy-haired equine girl dressed in a baker's uniform. She opened her private communicator.

"Kimberly to Dusk Moonbeam. Do you copy?"

"It's two am here, Kim. I'm busy with Jackie. What's up?"

"The mysterious anomaly on Sucryog has been dealt with. It was Pale Elves trying to conquer by summoning an abomination from the beyond realm. My master took care of it."

"Who is this mysterious master of yours? Oooh, Jackie right there. Ah! Gottagobye!"

Kim smiled slily then her body changed into the armoured Pie.

"Kim, you must give me a warning when you take over. What if I was in the middle of a warzone."

"Sorry, Pie, you know Dusk freaks when she sees you or Screwy."

"Just give me a warning next time, even if it's a popper popping."

"Yessiree will do that. One party cannon explosion."

Pie rolled her eyes and looked at the aurora spewing forth from the towers in the Crystal Empire.

Bounty Hunter 13 had eaten his fill. He slipped out of the city as the three moons rose to prominence in the sky. He entered the forest to find a peaceful place to meditate. He saw a large hover altar sitting in an empty clearing. His curiosity got the better of him and he began to examine the altar.

"Try not to damage my temple, stranger."

Bounty looked around. "Ah, Nevermore, is that you?"

"Bounty Hunter 13, why are you on Sucryog?"

"Cleaning up a little infestation of Pale Elves. What about you?"

"My little priestess lives here, so I visit. My main home is still Silver even though your brother holds the forest at bay and does not have time to worship me."

"How is Corvus?"

"He could be better. But like you, he fights."

"Care if I meditate here or is this your sacred grove?"

"Ha! Go ahead. My little priestess is currently drunk and trying to bed your son, her father."

"Seems to be the case with my family. I see you over there, Karen of Rokos. Why have you followed me?"

"I am curious about you, Demon of Silver. You called me Raven. Who is she that I resemble?"

"Raven Triagonal was a powerful sorceress. She was the reason for what we on continent Silver call the Veltan Scar. She ascended to godhood when the Noamaizan Nukes detonated. Now she is called Lady Pegasus. Like my son Bounty Hunter 26, she was destroyed in the explosion. Unlike my son, however, she became a goddess. He became as reviled as me. He was recently banished by Shogun Yu to the Haven of Dead Planets."

"You mean The End of Worlds?"

"Yes, he, along with his siblings who fought alongside us in the battle between Clan Hunter and Clan Shogun. The rest were cruelly killed and displayed to demoralize me. It only enraged me. I fell into their trap. In my fury, I triggered the spell that banished my children to non-existence."

"I see. I am sorry that happened to you."

"What's done is done. I have had many years to think about what I did. It was inevitable. Had I not triggered it, one of them would have."

"I'll leave you alone then."

"It's alright if you wish to stay. I will not be conversing but am thrilled that some reapers desire to test me. See you in the morning either way."

"He scares me, Nevermore."

"As well he should, little one. He is the Wrath of God Silver made flesh."

A sinister voice cut through the air. "Made up title made up god. There is only one true god and it is beyond anything you can imagine."

Karen summoned an ethereal sword into her hand. She looked around and was promptly stabbed through the abdomen. She grunted and staggered back. She caught sight of a scaled being with blood-red scales and blood-red eyes. The creature went for Bounty but was incinerated before it could even get close. Karen saw two fiery silver voids in Bounty's eye sockets. His dark glasses were off, as well as his tattered duster. He seemed more than mortal. It sent shivers down her back. She cried out as her wound was ripped from her body and shown on Bounty's body. She looked down to see she was fully healed. She looked at him. Seeing an old man instead of the terror she saw before. His glasses were back on, along with his coat.

She fled the grove. He snorted and went back to meditation. She soon arrived at the Crystal Castle to see the Cerulean armoured Nightmare waiting for her. He spoke through his helmet.

"What was that immense power I felt from the grove where Shaman Zinna placed her altar?"

"A Bloodclan ripped open my chest and was vaporized by a horrific monster. The monster became your father."

"Did the monster have glowing silver voids for eyes?"

"Yes. It was terrifying and I have seen Azrael, the Alpha Reaper."

"Hmph! Sounds like father allowed a fraction of his power to be felt."

"He holds that much inside him. How is he alive?"

"Hah! You act as if he was ever alive, but I kid. He has always been powerful. He was born under three red moons with the constellations of the Hunter and Warrior glowing through the psionic storm he created at his birth. Don't fear what he is. That is why he is alone. Too many fear him. It's sad, really. His friends live on other planets and refuse to contact him. He is a stubborn old coot, so he doesn't speak with them. He has watched his family be killed multiple times. He has watched the world move on. He has become the villain of his own story. I don't blame you for your fear."

"I see. Why are you still awake?"

"Someone's got to guard the city."

The next day saw Oneida and Ro-Jath nursing hangovers. Rino von Rhino was waiting. Pie walked over with an unconscious Karen slung over her shoulder. Bounty walked out of the forest, smoking what looked like a cigar.

"I see you still inhale that crap, old man."

"That I do, Rino. It is the only thing to keep the pain at bay. What is the plan?"

"I was going to ask you that."

Nightmare walked over. "I just got word from my friend. The Equus Islands suffered a severe cataclysm. They were forced to become one Island. The death toll is immeasurable. The Pale bastards took this opportunity to try and wipe out the survivors. I would like you to assist them. Please! Father, I know you have had unfavourable dealings with the Equus before."

"I will do my best to assist them. Do not worry yourself, Nightmare."

Blackheart One lifted off and flew off. Nightmare looked on. He was worried. He typed in a code on his gauntlet and spoke "Nightmare Hunter to all in range. The Blood clan has begun its plan. Be prepared for anything. I will see you at home when this war is over."

***

Equus Islands

An amber-skinned Equine-headed girl stood on the outskirts of a large, partially destroyed city. Her gauntlet chirped as a message came through "Nightmare Hunter to all in range. The Blood clan has begun its plan. Be prepared for anything. I will see you at home when this war is over."

She had a cigarette in her mouth and was about to light it when a very attractive and buff Equine-headed woman bumped into her. The mare was blond and freckled. She licked her lips, knocking out her cigarette.

"Dammit, all that was my last one."

The Freckled woman turned her head to look at her. "Hello there, sugar cube. Didn't see you there. You must be Sunspot. Dusk has been in a tizzy since ya contacted her."

"You know Dusk?"

"Sure do suga, she's mah wife. Been married for six years now. Come on in. Mind the rubble. City's looked much better than this."

"Yeah, I know. Who are you?"

"Name's Jackie Apple-Moonbeam."

"Cute name for a cute girl."

"Shucks, suga. But I'm happily married. Heya Rainbow. Tell Dusk I've found her guest."

Sunspot looked up to see a punk woman with electric rainbow hair. Her jaw dropped. She blinked and the woman was gone.

"Keep your mouth open like that and you'd make a great bug catcher." Sunspot quickly closed her mouth. "Who was that?"

"New to these parts then. That was Rainbow Boom. She's captain of the unity guard. She's also married to a force of nature. So don't be getting any ideas."

"Why are all the hot ones taken?"

"Don't let it get ya down, sugar cube. I'm sure someone like you has gotten a lot of tail."

"No, not really."

"Well, keep an open mind, hun. You are about to enter into a cornucopia of lesbians. All of Dusk's cohorts are sexy. Most of us are taken. Regardless sug, we're here."

Sunspot looked at the large glowing tree. It dwarfed all of the skyscrapers nearby. She was led into the tree and saw a commotion of barely clothed women. They were getting ready for a sleepover or an orgy; either way, Sunspot was taken aback.

She gulped and fidgeted. A dusky purple mare rushed her. "Sunspot, you came back. It's great to see you."

"Hi, Dusk. It's been a while. I wish it were under better circumstances."

"Why, what happened?"

"A bunch of pale-skinned elves attacked and nearly wiped out Aqualan. Thankfully an elite unit of Centaurs and Taur are helping hold the line. I came to warn you because we saw a bunch of the pale ones head this way."

***

"Obliterate the pale bastards. Elementalist's open fire." A large muscular yet oddly feminine bull shouted.

A volley of elements splashed against the Pale Elf army. Several elves were slain, but the arcane armor of the others protected them.

The bull shouted again, "We must hold the enemy here. Sharpshooters fire now. We must prevent them from entering the ruins."

Several more elves fell, but the allied soldiers were exhausted and slowly being whittled down. The wall in front of the bull exploded as a large slimy horror burst into existence. Its appearance sent the allied forces into shock and the Pale Elves slaughtered many. The bull pulled out a serrated blade and charged the creature. He was flung back as fire erupted in the form of a bipedal winged and horned dragon partially made of shadows and fire.

Massive amounts of gunfire erupted from a leviathan class ship. The Elves were decimated. The dragon made of fire and shadows vaporized the slimy horror before vanishing. It was replaced by a Silveran with a grey sleeveless duster. He was smouldering. His face was burned on one side and the other was old, scarred, and wrinkly.

The bull smiled, "Bounty Hunter 13, you old devil. You show up here on my turf."

"And save your worthless hide, D…"

The two embraced passionately. D… whispered, "Thanks, little bro."

"Not a problem, sister, brother."

Bounty smiled and looked over to see Karen in awe. "Who's your friend and why does she look so stunned?"

"This is Karen and I'm pretty sure she's in awe that you are remembered by me. After all, you don't exist."

"That's what mortals are meant to think. Regardless little bro. We need to hightail it to the City of the Giant Tree. A portion of the Pale Elves split off along with a blood clan blasphemy. The kids can mop up here."

"Come on aboard, the Blackheart one."

The ship lifted off with one pale elf prisoner from this battle. The rest were being slaughtered by the combined forces of the Aqualan Equus, Centaur, and Taur army.

***

Dusk stood on the wall looking at the encroaching army. She was wearing crystalline body armour. Three of the others also wore the same crystal-like body armor. The rainbow maned woman wore a skin-tight bodysuit. She was standing near the very large-breasted model-like a mare that looked like someone threw up a bunch of pastel colours. This mare was in a trance and a large vine ripped open the ground and tore through several elves. Several of those elves threw fire at the vine igniting it.

The pastel mare cried in pain and collapsed. This sent Rainbow Boom into a rage. She shot up through the sky and dived at the Pale Elves. She leveled out, causing a rainbow-like mushroom cloud to expand and vaporise half of the Pale Elf army. A fearsome-looking red and purple

Arachnetaur smiled and sent out a web of blood-red energy. It engulfed Rainbow, causing her to turn on her friends. She shot into the air again.

Dusk cried out, "Everybody brace for Rainbow Nuclear detonation."

A white mare with electric purple hair spoke, "Not on my watch, dahling."

The white mare went into a trance as electro-trance music filled the air. She summoned two ethereal disk jockey tables and massive ethereal speakers. The music got louder and more intense. As Rainbow rocketed to the ground, a burst of sound sent her flying back up. She was unconscious. The white mare turned her speakers on the Pale Elf army.

She sang in a very scratchy voice, "Base bomb, bass bomb, blow them all to hell!"

The sound ripped into the pale elves several fell to the ground in tatters. Others had their chest imploded from the bass. Soon only fifty of the thousand Pale Elves remained. The Arachnetaur spun another red web and sent it toward the white mare. She saw it coming and evaded it. It struck two of the crystal armored mares and they turned on the others. That was when a Leviathan class ship descended from the clouds. There was a whump as a large effeminate bull landed on the battlements. He got up and shook off the dust from his landing in a very dog-like fashion. Right behind him landed a dwarf in copper armour wielding a coppery red headsman axe. Also, a one-armed mahogany brown gunslinger flipped and opened fire on one of the controlled mares.

A large inferno ignited the battleground, killing even more of the Pale Elves. In that inferno was an old man. This man faced off against the Arachnetaur. The Arachnetaur's legs became blades and she flung herself at the old man. He avoided the spin attack. Sunspot jumped into the inferno and joined the old man in battle.

"Hey, boss. Been a while."

"Sunspot, what are you doing here?"

"Unhappy to see me, Father?"

"No, just surprised. I got the impression that you didn't care for young Dusk."

"She grew on me. I see you have seen better days."

"Oh, not really. Just forgot to pick up my mask from home."

The Arachnetaur screamed, "Why can't I touch you? Who are you to be so quick?"

"I am the wrath of God Silver made flesh. I am the demon of the lands of Silver doom of the northern lands. Killer of the queen of Noamaiza. I am the Lord of Shadows Bounty Hunter 13."

"You died! You don't exist! How!"

Sunspot huffed, "He's the fucking demon of Silver. How do you think?" She then sucked in all the fire around her and exhaled a violent stream of magma that melted the Arachnetaur. "Was getting tired of that conversation anyway."

She staggered and Bounty caught her. She was sound asleep. He smiled and wrapped some of his dusters around her. He extended his hand and caught Rainbow Boom as her unconscious form descended from the sky where it had been thrown. He jumped and landed on the battlements. He handed Rainbow to the pastel mare.

"I believe this belongs to you, Gaia of Silver's loins."

"Don't call me that. I am Butterfly of the Equus."

"Sorry, Butterfly. You want her or not?"

Butterfly took Rainbow and began mending her broken bones. Bounty snapped his fingers and the two enthralled mares went limp and were freed from their enthrallment. He looked down at Dusk. She looked up at him and gulped. That was when Kim landed on his shoulder. She tilted her head at Dusk and grinned,"Heya, no boobs. This is my enigmatic master. Your father." "What!"

"Yes, silly. He is the man whose seed led to what the nasty queens used to create you, Pixie, and Glimmer Grimm. He also fucked her royal pain, Solaria, creating Moonsong and Sunspot."

"You lie! How can I be the offspring of that demon?"

"Duh, his sperm was used to fertilise an egg. That egg grew into a fetus, which became you."

Jackie walked over with her shotgun over her shoulder. "Relax sugar cube. I can sense your anxiety all the way across the courtyard."

"Kim says this beast is my father."

"I see it. You both smell very similar and you also have that purty horn on your head that seems very similar in structure to his."

Sunspot stirred, woke up and spoke in a burned voice, "Only one way to find out,Dusk."

"Fine, do it."

Sunspot unwrapped herself from Bounty's duster and landed with a wump. Shegot up and wove a strange pattern in the air. The energy web lanced out. It stuck to Glimmer Grimm,

Moonsong, Pixie, Dusk, and Bounty. It glowed a silvery light that wove its way between Bounty and the girls. It also wove a dark blue light that vanished. Signifying their mother was gone.

Dusk gasped, "No! No! I can't be half Silveran. Mistress Solaria said all Silverans were monsters and demons. They are below us. Your web is wrong."

Jackie sighed, "Don't fret any. She'll get over it. I suspect she'll be researching until dawn."

Bounty shook his head. "Oh, I am well aware of the hatred the Equus have for my kind. I think nothing of it. She would not be the first of my children to despise me. Nor will she be the last. Good luck to you, young Jackie. Sunspot, you are welcome to join my party to assist your siblings."

"No thanks, Pops. I will be here to help rebuild this land. After all, I am a Hunter."

"Yes, you are. Good luck, but I must be on my way. My blade has many souls to claim."

Bounty boarded the ship along with Ro-jath and Oneida. D.. whispered into his ear, "See you later, little brother." Then gave him a little peck on the cheek.

Bounty sighed, "I will definitely see you, D… I just hope I can help you."

***

Komodo

A medium cargo freighter met Blackheart one halfway to the continent Komodo. Rino von Rhino spoke, "This is Blackheart One, to an unknown cargo ship. You are in my airspace. Move or be crushed."

A scratchy female voice spoke, "Rino, you old bastard. I've been looking everywhere for you. I am here to pick up my father. We need him immediately over at the Junk Heap."

"Leda, what have I told you? Regardless, I have him. Dock in the cargo bay and he'll be waiting."

Bounty stood along with Ro-jath and Karen in the cargo bay as a grey and black boxy ship landed. A young woman wearing only mechanic overalls walked out. She rushed Bounty and embraced him.

"Daddy, we need help. Lude, Lucy, Stella, Jordyyn, and Rona Alexandra can't hold out much longer. Loddi has expanded her power and is near death. Lunatic was also critically injured. Please come with me."

"Alright, kid. I'm coming. Just relax. I taught Lude everything I knew. We have several days before he's in serious danger."

"We are outnumbered."

"Ah, I see. Get the ship moving then."

The smaller craft sped off. Rino sighed, "Alright, it looks like it's just you and me, Oneida."

"And Pie. She is still here."

"Hello, big guy!"

"Jeez, don't scare me like that, Pie. Nearly gave me a heart attack. Just hope the three of us can make a difference."

Oneida scoffed, "I think we'll be fine. After all, we are teaming up with Sin Seeker Hunter and his family."

"Fair enough. I just hope they leave some of those Pale Elves to us."

"Less work I have to do, the better I am. I'm not as spry as you are."

"Haha! Come, my ebony friend, we have much to do."

Blackheart One floated over the lands of Komodo. Pie spoke, "We have an issue, Captain!"

Oneida sighed, "I see it. This is the largest landmass. Nine regions, each being besieged. How do you want to proceed?"

A voice crackled over the com, "Yo, Blackheart One. Name's Keiji. Boss says he's got Napja and central Komodo Covered. We may even be able to hit the Oni Lands and Orkea."

"Tell Sin Seeker thanks. He just took a load off my shoulders. We have only three of us here. Bounty had an issue rise up elsewhere."

"He says you best get moving before you get targeted. See you at the rendezvous point."

"See you, kids, there. Good luck. Chrome, be with your blade."

"Hah!"

Rino's mechanically augmented voice cut through the air, "So from what I am hearing, we only have to deal with the regions of Nadria, Teimvan, Lapan, Naldihta, and Miaomongqiang."

"That's correct, Rino. How do you want to play this hand?"

"I will take Nadria since it is a larger region. I don't need sleep thanks to my augments. I would suggest Pie take Miaohmongqiang since they revere horses. She might have an easier time. She should then attempt to hit Lapan. Though since Lapan lies near the rendezvous point, we may all be there by the time she gets there. We will then take a boat to the Raginrepos region and assist there. That is if we have to. I don't think the Ts'ao would let it fall. Which leaves you with the smaller regions of Tiemvan and Naldihta."

"Great. I suspect I'll find help down there. I hope. Alright, dropping you two off, then I'm heading out to get my ass kicked."

"You'll do fine, my one-armed companion. You are the best gunslinger in the Blacksin mercenary force."

"If only that were true. Away I go."

***

Oneida appeared on the outskirts of a small village. A yellow-skinned Oni stood in front of the entrance to the village. She looked furious.

Oneida was cautious. "Greetings, yellow one. I am Captain Oneida Blacksin. I am here to assist in the repelling of the Pale Elves."

"You are too late brown skin. I have killed them all and disposed of their corpses. Now I await my next challenge."

"I do not wish to fight you. You are small. Almost like a child."

"Oh, that is it, you ecewbvbn."

"Eh, wha?"

She lunged at him, snarling, "I am Tallon Yellow Fang, conqueror of Naldihta. You are nothing but a bald one-armed loser."

Oneida reeled from her furious assault. He was blocking her attacks with his gun. That was when lightning struck in between them. A large muscular bronze-skinned male with tattoos of dragons all over his chest stopped her assault. He crackled with electricity. His eyes looked like black fire opals and his yellow hair was like a void.

He spoke with a voice that was deep like thunder. "Calm yourself, young one. This man is your next challenge. He is a gunslinger from another planet. You are to assist him in his cleanse of these lands. The blasphemous Pale Elves need to be cleaned. Do your duty."

She bowed. "Yes, Lord Susano'o."

Oneida sighed in relief. He looked at the God in front of him. "Impressive, but are you the real Susano'o?"

"You dare question the creator of the Oni?"

"See, there's something about you that seems off. Far too flashy for Susano'o. Yes, you look like him, but your aura is off. Your aura seems to be made of shadows and darkness."

"You are too perceptive. Truly you are the one-armed slayer."

The false Susano'o warped. A large muscular man with green hair and yellow eyes stood there. On one hand, he held a pike emblazoned with the Hunter clan crest.

Tallon gasped, "Lord Hunter!"

Oneida looked at the new man with a raised eyebrow. "Lord Hunter?"

"Yes, I am Braid the Deathseeker. Also known as Lord Dutch Hunter. My little brother not only stole my true name, he also took my false name as his own."

"Spare me the sob story, I care little about family squabbles. I only care about fighting the Pale Elves as I was hired to do. So Braid, will you be in my way or are you here to help?"

"Tallon!"

"Yes, my lord master."

"Come, we have much to do and little time to do it in."

"Where you go, I follow."

"Ugh. Come along."

Braid walked off, forcing Oneida to catch up with him. They arrived at a large ornate castle that was under siege by ninety units of Pale Elves. Each with their own fell beast from beyond space and time.

Oneida grimaced, "Seems my death has arrived."

Braid looked down at him and then snorted, "I disagree. It may look like we are outnumbered, but clearly, the Pale Ones are being held at bay. Shall we join the fray?"

"It will be a glorious battle." Oneida then charged into the army, opening fire with his gun.

Tallon pulled out her bone-like blade and sliced through several of the Pale Elves. Braid sighed and lit his cigar. He unholstered his Septa Barrel Rail Minigun and opened fire. The rapid sound of electricity-propelled spikes sounded through the air. He then brushed his hand against several runes on the gun and element attacks were added to the spikes. Fire, Ice, Wind, Lightning, and stone effects slammed into the enemy. When the dust and smoke finally cleared, only one slimy horror and a massive muscular blood clan member remained.

The horror advanced, forcing Tallon to flee. Oneida fared better, but still, the fear aura this creature sent out caused his morale to wilt. Suddenly and without warning, his body changed. His missing arm became a large bio canon. His bald head grew a mohawk and his eyes glowed with ancient energy. He braced himself against one of the statues by the gate and opened fire with a powerful beam of molten metal. He roared in rage, "This is the Spear that will pierce the heavens. Rage of my ancestors."

The horror was pierced with the molten metal and writhed as it ate through its body. Eventually, nothing remained. The Blood Clan member snorted and wiped off some blood and slime from his face.

He spoke, "That's all you got. So be it. I Blood Fury will be your death."

The man grew in size and two large cannons emerged from his armor. His arms became bladed and his hair became wires that connected to his armor. He went to swipe at the castle but was blocked.

He looked down at Braid, who was currently holding back his arm with a fiery sickle. Braid was smiling a dark smile. The sickle cut through Blood Fury's arm, disintegrating it. Blood Fury reeled back in shock, creating an opening that Braid exploited. He sliced through Blood Fury's waist, incinerating both halves of Blood Fury. His sickle vanished and he ignited his body with white fire. The white fire spread, cleansing the land of the Pale Elf bodies and their corruptive toxins. The flamesvanished and Oneida was back to normal. He shook his head, clearing it of whatever fog he had been in. Tallon slunk back, looking dejected. Braid dusted himself off and walked over to Tallon.

"Good job, kid. Let's keep going. I am sure Captain Oneida will be thankful for ourhelp."

Tallon looked up at Braid and shakily spoke, "You're not mad at my cowardice?"

"What cowardice. All I saw was a warrior making a tactical retreat when she wentup against something far beyond her abilities."

She fell to her knees in a bow. "Thank you, Master!"

He lifted her up. "Come, my dear, we have much to do and so very little time to do it in. Are you coming, Captain Oneida, if that is your real name?"

"Oh, it's my real name, alright."

"What was that cybernetic horror that shot molten metal at that eldritch horror?"

"That is me. When under great stress, my adrenaline kick-starts my nanoextension. I am sure you are familiar with the God Efreet?"

"I am. All Efreet worshipers, when near death, can transform into an aspect of their God. Is that what I witnessed?"

"Sort of. Many Blacksin mercenaries are experiments from Neo Tarrah-Aehrt. Like all of those from that Cyborg planet, I have a strain of Mecha DNA. The experiments I was subjected to enhanced that strain. Creating an Artificial being insideof me. He and I worked things out and he takes control of my body when I am subjected to great stress. I am the reason there are no longer any Areas of Neo Tarah-Aehrt. I destroyed Area 100, Area 300, Area 500, and Area 700. My second in command took out the others."

"We are here. Thank you for helping us pass the time."

"Hmm, no problem. What is your story?"

"Not the time for that. As long as we have the capital of Teimvan, I will say nothing about myself."

The three looked upon the partially destroyed city that was currently being besieged by a giant eight-headed serpent.

Oneida growled, "Oh fuck this."

Braid snorted, "You wanted to die. I suspect you were right. Today is that day. Come, let us find the Blood clan member in charge of that thing."

Tallon spoke weakly, "That is the Blood Clan member. That is Blood Orochi."

"Well, Fuck. Okay, new plan. Slaughter the pale elves and lead that thing towardsCentral Komodo. If we can get the help of the Legendary Hero Sin Seeker, we may just stand a chance."

The three began to slay any Pale Elf soldiers that tried to attack them. Soon only Blood Orochi remained. The massive eight-headed serpent shifted his focus to Braid. Braid smirked. He snapped his fingers and Oneida and Tallon vanished along with the serpent. He looked around and nodded in approval. He then walked off, white flames followed him.

***

Pie twitched in agitation. The small girl who she had just saved was poking and prodding her in awe. The small cat-like child suddenly recoiled and jumped. She mewled in fear. Pie gently scooped her up and scratched behind her ear. The kittenbegan purring. Pie then wrapped her up in a protective blanket and slid her into her hammerspace. The girl was out cold and unconscious. Pie turned towards a large muscular woman riding a large quadrupedal Equine-like beast. The creature had pale white fur on its face and two large antler-like protrusions on its head. It also had spikes on its massive, almost ape-like, front legs. The woman was as fearsome as her mount. She had bronze skin and serpentine eyes that glowed orange. Her hair was a deep umber and she wore ornate dynastic armor.

Pie growled, "So The Great Khan did have a daughter."

The woman spoke sternly, "Yes and I don't like your tone, horse."

"Hmph. I suppose you are hunting down Pale Elves?"

"I am. Will you be in my way?"

"No, since I am hunting them down as well."

"Dare I ask what a chaos spawn is doing killing Pale Elves."

"Nothing drastic. My master, Bounty Hunter 13, seeks to clean their taint from the land. Leading up to his final confrontation with The Dragon."

"Hmm... very well. I will lend you my aid."

"Good because we are here."

"What! How?"

"Adoy!!! I am chaos born."

"Ugh! Let's get this over with."

They surveyed the damage. Two slimy horrors wandered around, consuming anything in their way. Above it all was a pale woman with blood red eyes and blood pouring down her face, her hair was brackish green, and she had crystalline claws on her hands. She let out a powerful screech that levelled a guard tower. That was when a cupcake splatted into her face. She turned towards Pi, who grinned evilly.

Without warning, the cupcake on her face exploded, destroying her head and causing her lifeless body to drop onto one of the horrors. It turned towards Pie and advanced.

The daughter of The Great Khan charged the beast with a roar. She executed it, causing it to form into two horrors instead of one. She was taken aback, then six cupcakes splattered the two beasts and they were incinerated in the following explosion. A slide whistle sounded and confetti burst into existence, tangling up the other horror before also exploding and incinerating it. The Daughter of the Great Khan stared in shock.

Pie spoke, "Well, that takes care of that. Oh, hello, Mister Cat. I believe this little bundle belongs to you."

The massive bipedal panther man snarled, "Mister Cat! I am the great Miao Fang. Show some respect!"

"How about I show respect when you keep a better eye on your children."

"Very well, strange one. I can accept that. Miao Miao, Mishka's okay."

A tall buxom snow leopard woman walked out of one of the castle gates. "Oh, you found her, did you? I see she succeeded in finding someone to help us."

"Name's Pie. I am sure you are familiar with the buff hottie behind me. I leave you three to clean up. I gotta be somewhere." She vanished without a trace after leaving behind some dried meat for them.

Miao Miao smiled, "What a strange character. Hello Kutu. Been a while."

"Mistress, I see you found a mate."

"That I did candy lips. That I did."

**

An old man in combat armour and a turban stood on the ramparts of the junk cityof Mahabharata. He sliced through one of the Pale Elf warriors that had leapt at him. His twin scimitars flashed in the Dusk, slaughtering Pale Elves left and right. He leapt back as a massive claw smashed into the ground in front of him. He looked up at the blasphemy of mechanical and biological components dripping with obscene slime and emitting powerful fear pollen. He snorted in disdain. As the creature smashed its hand down again, the old man charged up the arm. He sliced through the creature's neck and began plummeting towards the ground. He was caught by a large rhino-headed man.

The Rhino man chuckled, "You trying to kill yourself, Salim Saladin?"

"You know me?"

"That I do, old man. However, now is not the time for that. Allow me to assist in your battle."

"I will take all the help I can get."

There was a below and three Ganeshans entered into the fray. They were quickly followed by an army of White Silveran's. The leader of these Silveran's had painted his antlers gold. The tide of battle shifted dramatically. As the Rhino man's jetpack turned off, he set Salim down. Salim joined in the battle.

"Rino von Rhino. What are you doing in my lands?"

"Hanuman? Well, this is awkward."

The large monkey man with several cybernetic augments stared down at his former comrade. "Well, answer me."

"I am here on mercenary business. The Demon of Silver has been resurrected. He is going to be taking his world back from the Pale Elf god. I have been hired to assist some reapers in testing the Demon of Silver. So here I am assisting in the purge of Pale Elves."

"Hmm, I see. Are you not playing into Lord Dragon's hands? Does he not want to bring his dark ally into our universe?"

"Yes. But I think you forget that Bounty Hunter 13 may as well be called a god at this point. He will be the one to destroy Lord Dragon. He will also ascend to godhood when he does."

"We will see. But for now, I will join you in your cleanse of our lands. This battle is going to be long and hard. I fear for the lives of our warriors."

"I don't. You have five insanely god-like heroes on the field of battle. Bhima the Terror, Arjuna the Goliath, Salim Saladin the Time traveller, Bhishma the one who can match Asura, and Rishyasringa the Antlered. There is no way in the thirteen hells that those men can be defeated."

"I hate to break it to you, old man. One has already fallen. Look."

Rino von Rhino looked across the field of battle to see Bhishma riddled with many black arrows. So filled was he with them that they held him above the ground. Rino shook his head and pulled out his cyber sword. He ignited the blade with its vibration and heat setting. He charged into the battle, cutting through the Elves like a plasma laser through an ice cube. With each strike, he not only cleaved them in half butalso incinerated them in a fiery explosion. He caught the wounded form of Salim Saladinand Bhima. Arjuna joined him, firing off numerous ethereal arrows from his vorpal bow. They soon arrived at the side of Rishyasringa. He looked to be on the verge of death. The three Ganeshians were dead. They died protecting Rishyasringa. The White Silveran was bleeding from many cuts that seeped a black ooze.

Suddenly his body began to glow. All the Silverans on the field of battle glowed with the same light. Rino quickly put Salim and Bhima down and retreated to a safe distance, just in time for a massive aura explosion that sent a cascade of psy energy out. When the light show cleared, the Silveran warriors stood changed.

They all had four to six arms, large horns protruding from their foreheads, and silky hair. The only thing unchanged was their various skin tones. The horns on their heads were also serrated like antlers but not actual antlers.

Only a dozen Pale Elves remained, along with two smouldering horrors and a large red bison man. The Pale Elves fled in terror. The Bison man stood firm and ordered his horrors forward. Salim slashed through the two horrors and went for the red Bison man. He was launched by a hit from the bison and hit the wall of the castle with a sickening crunch.

Rino walked forward and pulled out his two sixty-calibre twelve-shot pistols and opened fire. The Bison man remained standing but now had twenty-four new holes in his body. He snorted and charged. His head glowed with energy and he shattered the stones in his way. Rino dodged the attack.

The bison man roared, "I am Bloodbison the Juggernaut. You are an ant compared to me."

He charged again, but as he neared Rino. He was lifted into the air. He struggled and looked down to see Rino's snarling face.

"Ants can lift many times their own weight. You are insignificant. So long, Bloodbison."

There was a squelck as Rino dug his fingers into Bloodbison's skin. Then a sqlork as he ripped Bloodbison in half. Fire engulfed him and he was cleansed of the tainted blood. A large green-eyed Silveran with green hair and six muscular arms walked onto the field of battle. A fire followed him as he walked, purging the land of the tainted Pale Elf blood. The man spared a moment and bowed to Bhishma and the fallen Ganeshians. He then incinerated them.

"Thayme Sidrodc uigde het seul. Thayme Havens sunocme het seul." Hedowned the amber drink that was conjured during this prayer and threw the empty glass on the burning bodies incinerating them. He continued on his way. The flames followed obediently.

Rino looked at the mango and could almost swear he saw a hulking demon with a large triangular helmet. He blinked and the man was gone. The horrors conjured by Bloodbison had been incinerated by the holy flames. Sent back to their dimension. Rino went over to Salim's prone form. He was about to leave when Salim opened his eyes and stood up he stretched, popping his bones back into place.

Rino smirked, "Still alive, I see. Good. See you around and tell Hanuman he is welcome back anytime."

"Thank you for your assistance Rino von Rhino. We would have lost this land without your help."

Rino walked off after lighting the cigar he sorted. "You did most of the work, old man. Hasta la Vista."

Rino ignited his jetpack again and flew off, leaving a small crater which he launched from.

***

A ten-foot-tall amber-skinned man with two small horns on his head sliced through a hulking horror from beyond the known realms. He blocked an attack from a heavily armoured Pale Elf. He leapt over the elf and slit his throat as he landed. The elffell, gurgling. He jumped back in a flip and landed near another ten-foot-tall man with wild hair and a kimono on. A woman was near them, both panting. She was very voluptuous and designed to look as attractive as possible.

The amber man with horns spoke, "Keiji, I need you to grab Trini and get yourself and Shimasake to a safe distance. If you see Dancing Bear in Sky, grab him as well."

"Will you be alright, brother?"

"I will be fine. After all, I am Sin Seeker Hunter."

"Alright! Rip and Tear, brother, Rip and Tear!"

Sin Seeker smiled and spun his double voulge shredding many of the Pale elves that were near him and clearing a path for his family to escape. They did. He let out a terrible roar as his image disguise fell. A thirteen-foot-tall amber-skinned Silveran stood there. His horns weathered and cracked with age. Sharp jagged spikes on his shoulders that were painted gold. His deep cobalt eyes crackled with ancient energies. His aura flared, vaporising more Pale Elves. That was when many ships appeared. They began spitting out soldiers by the thousands. Many horrors were with them. Sin Seeker snarled and continued his relentless attack.

Keiji was watching from the plateau. He heard Dancing Bear say, "We have to go back and help him. Why is he doing this alone?"

A female voice spoke, "He has the energy to spare you all were on your last leg. If only I wasn't so weak, I'd be down there helping him."

Keiji scoffed, "Right, Ryofu? Right? You were nearly bisected by one of those horrors. Tara barely made it out alive. Also, chill. We have company."

A large multi-headed serpent dropped from the sky. It was followed by two figures who were launched towards the plateau. The figures were caught mid-air by a heavily armoured Equus. Who was, in turn, caught by a rhino man with mechanical enhancements? The small group landed, kicking up dust.

The rhino man spoke, "Captain Oneida, care to explain what in the thirteen hells that thing is?"

The dark-skinned man grunted as he got up. "Hate to break it to you, Rino, that is Blood Orochi. Bastard was destroying the capital of Teimvan. He had routed the entire army. Some man calling himself Braid sent him and us here."

Shimasake poked her head out of Keiji's hair. She yipped, "Holy crap, you assholes are alive?"

Oneida spoke, "Hello, Shimasake. Yes, Rino and I are still in one piece. No thanks to you."

"Hey, I was busy. Lousy portal."

Rino spoke, "Yeah, how did you wind up on Meteor?"

"When brother attacked XiaPi, which was under the control of Liun Ba, the Beast of Meteor, a giant tree man appeared and teleported him away. I was caught in the beam since I had been there trying to stop my little sister, the Kitsune known as Diao Kyna, from being a fool."

Keiji spoke, "Ah, so that is where you disappeared to. Sin Seeker seemed to think you had run away."

The small Kitsune crossed her arms. "I was very tempted to. But Meteor did not approve of my existence. He sent me back almost immediately."

A monkey man dropped into existence and spoke, "That does not surprise me. He was very leery of us being on his planet."

Rino spoke, "Hello, Hanuman care to help us out here?"

"Yeah, and I brought some friends."

A large muscular bronze-skinned male with tattoos of dragons all over his chest announced his appearance with thunder. He crackled with electricity. His eyes looked like black fire opals and his yellow hair was like a void. Next to him stood a fierce tigress dressed in a tight rubber catsuit that showed off her assets. Next to her stood a spotted Ursar that seemed to glow with draconic power. There was also a blue-skinned manwith void black hair. His numerous scars glowed slightly, making him look like a constellation.

"You brought them here! Hanuman, you asshole. I owe them money."

"Yes, I know and they promised to void your debt."

"You can't trust anything the Mistress of the Drunken Tiger style says. And you brought The Dragon Warrior as well. Are you trying to get overkill here?"

Dancing Bear in Sky spoke, "Look what's done is done. I am more concerned that Susanoo is here. He is not a fan of anyone who follows God Silver."

Hanuman scoffed, "What God is? Silver has created many an enemy. Even I disapprove of him. But that thing is far beyond the abilities of mortals. Susanoo sees this and has agreed to help. I do not know why Rama is here, but who cares? We need the help."

Sin Seeker slashed through many horrors. He saw to his left Susanoo, an Oni God, attack the many-headed serpent that had fallen from the sky. As Susanoo attacked, two of the heads circled around him and bit him. He was nearly bisected. Sin Seeker saw a golden beam strike the serpent heads, attacking Susanoo and destroying them. They immediately regrew. Their colouring was off, though. Instead of blood red, they were now black as shadows. They were also oozing like the horrors that Sin Seeker had just dispatched. The spotted ursar was thrown into the cliff that Keiji and the others were on. The feline woman yelped as two of the heads grabbed her and tried their best to rip her apart.

Sin Seeker snarled and sliced through those two heads and incinerated them and cauterised the stumps they came from. Blood Orochi focused its attention on Sin Seeker.

One of the many heads remaining spoke, "You have managed to injure me, mortal. Who are you so that I may know your name after you die."

Sin Seeker snorted, "I am Sin Seeker Hunter. Son of the Demon of Silver. Born of the Sword Maiden and raised by the Conqueror from Qin, Xiang Yu. You are a shadow of Orochi born from his fury."

"That may be so, but I have everything he had and now more. By becoming Blood Clan, I have gained powers from beyond space and time. I have the power to reduce you to atoms should I so desire."

"Sure you do. Why haven't you used those powers?"

"You question me?"

"Heh, the distraction worked."

Sin Seeker was in the air, ready to plunge down on Blood Orochi to slice off all heads at once when a large green-eyed Silveran with six muscular arms walked onto the field of battle. A fire followed him as he walked, purging the land of the tainted Pale Elf blood. He looked up at Blood Orochi and scoffed. Fire engulfed Blood Orochi, destroying him.

Sin Seeker looked at the man as he landed. "So you are Father's equal." A voice not Sin Seeker's own came from his mouth. "Braid the Deathseeker you have wandered the lands of Silver for many centuries. Ever since Bounty Hunter 12 disowned you. Even though by all accounts you matched the prophecy. I'll give you a choice. Remain a wanderer or join up with your little brother."

Braid snarled, "Screw you, God Silver. That kid stole my name, stole my fake name, and stole my inheritance. I will never become a Hunter. That was made clear to me. I am a wanderer and shall remain so until I die."

"Very well, Braid the Deathseeker. I look forward to seeing what becomes of you."

Sin Seeker gasped and fell unconscious since his body could not handle long exposure to god powers. Shimasake rushed over to him.

Rino spoke gruffly, "He'll be fine. He is Bounty Hunter 13's kid. Unfortunately, my friends and I must leave you. Bounty Hunter 13 needs us at the Junk Heap. I wish you the best of luck. Please make sure Drunken Tiger and Dragon Warrior are fine. Susanoo, good luck. Give my regards to Gilda Taka-doji."

Susanoo turned, but Rino von Rhino, Captain Oneida, and Pie were gone. He scoffed and vanished back to his domain.

***

The Junk Heap

A white and yellow-haired boy stood next to a female with a teal dress on. He was Llude Hunter and he stood bleeding from many wounds. He was stubbornly fighting. He had killed many

Pale Elves.

The girl murmured, "Llude, love, we cannot keep this up. I am sorry my power fails me and I don't know how much more you can take."

"We have to keep up, Llodi. The others are relying on us to keep them safe. Leda and Loda went to find help. We are children of Bounty Hunter 13. We can't give up!"

A Pale Elf general with light combat armour stood on his ship watching impassively as his troops were being killed by one boy. The boy was failing, however, it was only a matter of time. He sighed and walked over to the comm unit.

He spoke, "Child of the hunter, you have killed many of my troops. I applaud your stubbornness. But you cannot hold out. This is your last chance, surrender and your family will be spared. You will be the only one to die. If you continue to resist us, all of you will die."

Llude looked at the General. "Do you promise to spare my sisters?"

"I do. Does this mean you surrender?"

"I need a guarantee."

"My word as a warrior. I will not lay a finger on your family."

Llodi cried out as a commander of the Pale Elves stabbed her in the back. She fell. Llude snarled and beheaded the commander. "Fuck you! You Pale bastard!"

The general looked away as his troops converged on the pirate fortress. There was a commotion.

A large ship came into view and opened fire. All of his ships were destroyed as a second ship from the air opened fire. He was shocked and jumped off his ship as it came under fire. He walked out of the water and pushed the hair from his eyes. He blinked in confusion. He saw a large Cybernetically enhanced Rhino man, a black armoured man with a horse head helmet, a one-armed warrior holding a shotgun, and a bronze armoured dwarf.

"The hell! Attack you worthless maggots. We still outnumber them."

His troops opened fire with their ballistic magic. The remaining war machines on the battlefield also opened fire. Then the fire started. A man wearing classical pirate gear stood atop the great heap throwing flaming orbs down at his men. Terror gripped the general as he saw the mouth of the Infernum. A hulking demon with black horns cut down all of his soldiers in the blink of an eye. The war machines blew up and the demon advanced towards him.

Llude spoke, "Father, stop. It's over. Give the man a chance to surrender."

"Why should I! His kind never did the same for me."

"You need to calm down. I can feel your fury in my bones. You scare me rightnow."

The demon sighed and sagged; he seemed to age thousands of years. Within thespan of seconds, before him, stood an old and tired Pure Silveran.

"My son seems to think you deserve mercy. I am Bounty Hunter 13. You are General Galverion the Butcher. Do you surrender?"

"I have no choice in the matter. My army is obliterated. You may do with me what you will."

"Ugh, fine. You will join the others in the prison. Pie, please escort him to the cellblock."

The equine helmeted man nodded. He motioned Galverion to follow. He obeyed.

As he entered the cell block, the man spoke in a gruff female voice, "You are very lucky Master Llude was able to restrain Lord Hunter. You are also lucky in that you get to spend time with her royal pain, Balarna Schlaughter, and mister assassin. Get in and don't try anything."

Outside, Bounty was surveying the wounded. His children lay battered. Llodi was the only one near death, however. He sighed and began mending Llodi's stab wound.

He heard a rustle and looked up to see Luci and Llude kiss passionately. He also saw her kiss Rona Alexandra, Llude's girlfriend.

Again I witness my children's incestual desires. Why is my family like this? Hmm, I suppose I have no one to blame but myself. The way I treat Eris certainly rubbed off on them.

"You seem lost in thought, Demon of Silver."

Bounty snorted, "Just rethinking my example to my children. Why are you here, Karen? I thought you and Ro-jath were doing last rights outside?"

"We finished early. I came to check up on you. Who are all these kids?"

"My children. They are in their sixth reincarnation. I found them in a slavecompound. Along with a bunch of their schoolmates. Killed all the slavers and did what I could to return the kids to their rightful homes. A few were unlucky in that their parents had sold them to the slavers. My hand was not merciful."

"I believe your hand has never been merciful. You have trillions of deaths on your hands. I feel it. I do not know why Ro-Jath and I are here. I find you irredeemable. But I am only an observer."

"My dear reaper, you are correct. I will never be able to redeem myself. I don't particularly care about that. The gods fear me. People once feared me. The only thing I can do is make sure my children don't taint their hands with hundreds of thousands of deaths. I am the Demon of Silver. I don't expect redemption."

"Ugh! I'll leave you to your work. Know, however, that I have my eye on you."

"I expect nothing less."

He waited until Karen left before slumping his back. He looked down at Llodi. She was healed and looking up at him with watery teal eyes.

"Oh, don't be like that, Llodi."

"But daddy?"

"Llodi, I was a very cruel man to my enemies. I was a powerful warrior who killed without mercy. I am an evil entity in almost every culture and religion this world and other worlds have to offer. I am old and set in my ways."

The boy scoffed, "Are you saying I am irredeemable as well, Father?"

"No, Llude. You have not killed as many as I have. You are still young. The only child of mine that I fear went down the same path was Thirteen and possibly Bounty Hunter 26. They have styled themselves The High Vizier and the Left Hand of the Demon, respectively."

The eldest girl with platinum blond hair, who almost looked bimbofied spoke, "Father, why do you act like this? You were always kind to us. Why do you not expect redemption?"

"Lida. I am covered in the blood of my enemies. Their deaths have tainted my soul. A soul which was already tainted by nuclear fire. My soul gets closer and closer to black with every battle I am in. The more I kill, the more I am tainted. It's just how our souls work. You have very little taint even though you have killed hundreds of the Pale elves. But you are also on your sixth reincarnation. The soul heals from taint when it is reincarnated. As I am unable to reincarnate, the taint grows."

The black-haired girl with arcane symbols on her skin and in all-black spoke in a monotone, "Can't the gods allow you to be reborn?"

"No, Luci. And even if they allowed it, I would not accept their offer. It's not their choice to make. Only the Judge of Souls and The Judge of Flesh can decide that. Plus, I don't have a Holy

Lawyer. The one, the Havens, would have the same animosity towards me as the gods do."

A tall butch punk-looking girl with brown hair chimed in, "Then let us take some of your burdens. We are warriors as well. We can kill as well as you can."

"Remove yourself from that way of thinking, Lunatic. You have a wife and daughter to care for. You also have a fairly noble career as a Rock n Roll Bard. You are famous all over. You do not need to taint your soul. Especially on my behalf."

A brown-haired girl in a lab coat and eyeglasses spoke, "Father, you can't do this alone. We are your children, maybe not by blood, but certainly by nurture. You helped raise us. You took over when Mother and Father passed away. You took care of us even when we forgot who you were. And while I still don't believe in the pseudoscience of the soul, the scientific proof is that we love you and want to help."

"I understand that, Lica. I don't want you to be tainted like me. I don't want other faiths to see you as monsters. I definitely do not want you to turn out like me. Despised by many and liked by few."

The kids looked hurt. Bounty shook his head. "Enough of that. Don't you kids have a celebration to go to? I hear Tortuga will be filled to the brim today since you pirates beat back the invaders."

That seemed to raise their spirits. Bounty finished mending them and sent them on their way. He sat down as Ro-jath walked in.

"You look like hell warmed over, boyo. Hold up, you are bleeding! I'll get the nurse."

"Don't worry about it Ro-jath the Bronzed Titan. This is how I heal people. I take their wound and put it on me, healing them in the process."

"That seems a wee bit dangerous."

"I have nanomachines inside my corpse that keep repairing me."

"Eh, What?! You're undead!"

"Might as well be. I'm sure you overheard my conversation with Karen. I am not welcome in the havens. At one time, when I died, I could get a new body. But now, now, I am no longer welcome. So I have to piece together my broken body and inhabit it."

"Hmm... is your pride getting in the way of your health? No one is not allowed in the havens. That is a falsehood. Whoever told you that was lying through their teeth."

"That may be so. But I do know the gods themselves hate me. The only ones ambivalent to me are Silver, Bahamut, Coldharbour, Efreet, Anguines, and Nevermore. The rest fear me. Even those who claim to be allies of God Silver."

"So you stay alive to spite them or to ease their tensions."

"So I don't have to deal with it."

"I am unsure about you, Demon of Silver. You are nice to your children. However, you are not nice to others. You claim to be set in your ways. But deep down, I think you desire change. You just have yet to find it."

"It matters little. I have killed so many people. It is better this way." "I disagree. Everyone gets a chance."

"Ha! I admire your tenacity Ro-jath. I can see why the reaper is using you. But I can guarantee that I will be judged unworthy. She dislikes me ever since she saw me vaporise a blood clan member that stabbed her. Like the gods, she is scared of me."

"Hmm... that is worrisome. After the celebration, where will we be heading?"

"Misogoke, the continent of volcanoes and rings. My daughter seeks aid."

A snarling voice spat, "Ah, so the Demon does care... where was that when I needed it, Father?"

Bounty looked up to see a mohawked man wearing classical pirate garb. His bladed shotgun was holstered and his ice-blue eyes glared angrily.

"Ah, Bounty Hunter 39, this is where you fled."

"Hmph... fled more like was forced to."

"I offered you a place to stay."

"Yeah, under your watchful eye. No! I had enough of you and your ilk."

"Bounty... ugh, so stubborn. You are too much like me. How is the pillaginggoing?"

"Well, as you can see, I am the head of the Twelve Pirate Kings. So... I got that goin for me."

"I am glad to see you have made a name for yourself. Away from me. If only Bounty Hunter 52 had that drive. Ah well..."

"I am not here to make amends, Father. I am here to see your withered old husk. That perfection you had is no more; you are dry and shrivelled up."

"Pleasure seeing you too, boy."

***

Misogoke

A very pale woman with black and electric blue hair stood looking at the moonrise. Her body was covered in tattoos, some glowed strangely as the moons rose to prominence. She was waiting for something. Her mother stood near her naked with her penis hanging limply.

"Mother, can you at least put on some pants?"

"I cannot, Margogonin, my religion forbids it."

"Ugh, you are the worst mother. I don't know what Mom ever saw in you."

A grey-skinned woman with ash-black hair walked up the incline. She sighed, "Are you two at it again? Margo, love, your mother has always been there for you. Why can't you accept her quirks? And Vinyl, you forgot your nipple tape at home. I went back and got it for you."

"Aw, Tavi, you didn't have to do that. Bounty has seen everything."

"I know, love. But we have time. The Pale Elves are still trying to break through the inner ring. The brigands of the inner ring are putting up a heck of a fight. I almost envy them. Do you know how long it has been since I drew enemy blood?"

The pale woman with Electric blue hair grinned, "Oh, my sweet violent Tavi. You drew my blood last night."

The younger woman scoffed, "You two are way too horny. There is a tree over there. Go fuck yourself."

Vinyl cackled, "Can't he's almost here."

A large ship flowed over the waters. It was parked on a beach near their home. A large Pure Silveran male walked out, his grey and tattered duster flipping in the sudden gale that had whipped up. Behind him was a woman in a black and purple dress with a blindfold on. She seemed otherworldly. Vinyl scoffed and jumped down from the cliff. She landed in front of Bounty as he lit his cigar.

Vinyl spoke in her scratchy, mechanically enhanced voice, "Hey Boss, it has been a while. Glad to see you're still kicking."

"Hello, pale one. You seem unusually chipper from the last time we talked. Been having some fun?"

"You know it. Come, Tavi and Margo await us."

Bounty looked up the cliff to see a grey-skinned woman looking down at him. He smiled. He collected Karen and Vinyl and jumped. He landed near Tavi with a whump. He set the two down. Vinyl was erect from the rush.

Tavi Darkspeed smiled, "Hey, boss, glad to see you still know how to make an entrance."

"Hello, Tallon. I see you are dressed for battle. What is the situation?"

"Tavi and the situation is your daughter needs help. I would love to tear apart the Pale Elves, but my claws are not as sharp as they once were. Vinyl can only do so much in invigorating the brigands of the inner ring. They are currently fighting a losing battle. Will you assist us again?"

"As it stands, my dear apprentice, I have no choice in the matter. I am being judged on how I deal with the Pale Elves. So lead us to the Inner Ring. My blade will be swift."

"Stop, please. I do not wish to relive the pain of the past. And why can't your ship take us there."

The ship lifted off and flew off towards The Arclands. "That is why Tavi. They have business elsewhere."

Tavi looked up at Bounty. "When did you get so old?"

"I have always looked worn out. My half-mask kept it hidden. I do not have it, so my grotesque features stand out."

"I knew about the mask. That's not what I meant."

"Come, Tavi. We have much to do and little time to do it. Are you still alive, Vinyl?"

"Hah! Margo and I will catch up. Go, my little Tavi needs to wet her claws withblood."

Bounty looked back at Vinyl. He smirked then the five of them vanished. They reappeared on the outskirts of the Inner Ring. They were on the tracks that connected the Inner Ring to the Middle Ring.

"Well, we are here, I guess. Let us cleanse the Pale Elves from our lands."

Margogonin stepped forward as the ground erupted, causing the tracks to shatter and fall into the ocean. Margo cried out in anger and rushed the Pale Elf army. Electro-trance music filled the air as she tore into the front-line troops. Within minutes, she found herself at a disadvantage. As a blade came at her head, she saw her life flash before her eyes. She was taken out of her trance as a large black halberd blocked the strike. She blinked to see her father there, impassively blocking the blade.

"Keep an eye on your surroundings, girl. Never charge into a fight in anger. You are lucky I have been at your side since your attack. You left yourself open numerous times."

"You were blown up."

"I had a Psionic shield up. Your mothers are fine. In fact, they have been helping you."

"I'm sorry, old man. I messed up."

"Learn from your mistake. Now help us mop up. Now that you are sane."

"Yes, sir."

The Pale Elves were quickly routed. Viny smiled as Tavi licked some blood off of her face. She then kissed Tavi in passion. The two were soon making love in a pool of blood and corpses. Bounty groaned in annoyance. He felt something on his shoulder and looked back to see Margogongin supporting Karen.

"Where'd you find her?"

"She was right behind you, summoning a spectral sword. I feared you were under attack, so I knocked her out. She isn't breathing. Is she okay?"

Bounty looked Karen over and shook his head. "She's fine, aren't you?" Karen moved. "Damn, I thought I was playing dead nicely."

"Why were you trying to attack my father?"

"I don't trust him."

"Let her down, Margo. She is here to study me. She is a reaper or something like that. Sent to decide my fate, my death. Whether I'll be erased from existence or other things, she also is scared of me, so there is no need to make her fear you as well."

"Why is she scared?"

"She saw my true power. You know the fiery silver eyes that so fascinated you when you were young."

"Oh, well, I am sorry, Miss Reaper. I understand you perfectly now. Will you be joining us in our victory celebration?"

Bounty smiled, "Of course, I would not miss Tavi's cooking for anything. And that means

Karen will be joining us as well. But let's let Tavi and Vinyl finish what they are doing. Come, let's collect the dead. And Kar-en, thank you for disposing of that general who tried to attack me while my back was turned."

***

The Pale Elf Army landed on the continent known as Straulia. As they exited their ship, they were attacked by flying piranha jellyfish. Their horrors tried to advance but were set upon by small grey Ursa with knives for claws. Then the thirty-foot-tall scorpions and spiders arrived. It was a feeding frenzy. Only one elf survived since she fled to her ship. As she tried lifting off, a brown ten-foot tall kangaroo man with massive muscles, pointy ears, and a beady face squatted and then jumped. His foot hit the side of her ship, sending it careening into the ocean.

The kangaroo smirked and scratched his balls in superiority.

The Hunter Clan is Reborn

Orion Hunter stood next to his older sister Omega. She was with Li'l Boom, her wife. The three had been sent into a strange rift by an explosion. They were with four others. The first was a massive and muscular green Silveran, with horns that went straight back, named Grongar. The second was his older sister Jubilee. The third was the eldest among them, Bounty Hunter 26, his body a mass of scars and burns from a long-forgotten war. The fourth was unknown to him.

Omega was a thin woman with a large chest. Her black hair shined almost purple in the light of wherever they were. Her umber eyes looked worried. She was looking around this realm. Where they were standing looked like a Metropolis frozen in mid-collapse, she saw large crystal clumps and also people frozen in place, almost like statues.

Bounty Hunter 26 spoke, "Do not touch the crystals. They are predators. You touch them and you become like these statues. Also, don't touch the statues either."

The green-skinned male with his fangs jutting up from his jaw spoke, "Where th' hell are we?"

"You are not far off, Grongar. This is End of Worlds. It supposedly is where dead planets are stored."

"So a literal hell... good, maybe I can find a worthy opponent here."

Orion snorted. "I highly doubt that. We are in an inhospitable environment. Theoretically, we should already be dead. Those damnable Shogun sent us here."

Jubilee spoke, "And yet we still live, brother."

Orion snarled, "Yet we still live. What was the reason they sent us here?"

Omega replied, "To torture us, Orion. I suspect they sent us here to suffer. There is no escape from this realm."

One of the crystal golems turned towards them, followed by others. They advanced slowly and glitchy. Their bodies seem to phase in and out of existence.

A deep booming voice spoke, "I SEE THAT THE HUNTER FAMILY LIES IN DANGER… I CAN HELP YOU. JUST FOLLOW MY INSTRUCTIONS. ABOVE YOU. CLIMB THE BUILDINGS, THE GOLEMS CANNOT STICK TO THE STONE, BUT YOU CAN. CLIMB AND I WILL OPEN A PORTAL FOR YOU."

The group began climbing the crumbling skyscraper that was frozen in mid-fall.

The pale white glowing sky glinted off their armour. They finally reached the portal and jumped through. The vortex spits them out in a forest.

Grongar spoke, "Well, shit. I remember this place. A past life. The name Goroth comes to mind. What Trickery is this?"

"DO NOT FRET, YOUNG ONE. I HAVE SENT YOU HERE TO RESCUE YOUR FORMER CLAN. THIS WORLD WAS ERASED FROM EXISTENCE BY MY BROTHER, THE WRITER. HE FEELS SORRY FOR THE MORTALS THAT GOT TRAPPED HERE BECAUSE OF THEIR DEATH. I AM AZRAEL, THE ALPHA MASTER OF DEATH. YOU WILL BE MY TOOL. YOU HELP ME; I GET YOU OUT OF THE END OF THE WORLDS. DO WE HAVE A DEAL? SORRY, I FELT LIKE SAYING THAT. YOU HAVE NO CHOICE IN THE MATTER."

The mysterious man spoke, "Regardless of choice, ancient one, we will play yourgame. But how do you expect Grongar to free them?"

Grongar looked down to see a black scythe in his hands. It glowed purple in the eerie light of the forest. "The blackguard scythe. An ancient weapon of my former people. You wish for me to kill them?"

All that answered was jovial laughter. Grongar frowned but began walking. He was relying on his past life as Goroth to guide him. They soon arrived at a clearing where a man with a long white beard and a large hat sat resting. Next to him rested a sitar. His eyes were closed at the moment and he seemed almost dead.

Grongar spoke "Elder! Time to move!"

The older man opened his eyes. "Goroth, my boy. I thought I told you to go with therest."

"Oh right, forgot. I am no longer Goroth. My name is Grongar. I am here to freeyou from eternal damnation. Come, Elder, we must find the others."

"I would question your sanity, boy, but I see no familiar stars and the sky glows a pale white." He grunted as he stood, his joints popping and grabbed his Sitar. "Well, let's go then."

The small group continued through the forest. They soon arrived at a large battlefield with several people lying on the ground.

The elder spoke, "Grongar did I send my family to their death?"

"You died while playing your Sitar. Your last words were for us to continue without you. We did. We were ambushed by the Pale Elves. We moved to defend the priestess but, well, as you can see, we did not last long."

"What of the ranger, priestess and our little assassin."

"The ranger rode off to the west with the priestess on Narfi. The assassin and I went to attack the main fortress of the Pale Elves."

Grongar kicked the prone form of a man wearing legionnaire armour. The man got up as Grongar kicked the prone form of the others. Soon all were standing, staring in awe at the land.

The female with two scimitars spoke, "Goroth, what is the meaning of this?"

"You are dead dear sister. I am here to save your soul. I am no longer Goroth,though. My new name is Grongar. Come, we still have four more to save."

The large group walked into the forest following the trail of footprints left behind by Narfi. They found Narfi riddled with barbed arrows and the ranger leaning against a tree pinned to it by more arrows. Bounty Hunter 26 pulled out the arrows and Grongar woke the two up.

"Priestess, run! Wait, where am I? Where is the Priestess?"

The Elder grasped the man, "Relax, ranger. You are dead. We are in a hell of sorts. The priestess is still missing. We are looking for her, though."

"Father, I was too weak to lead the clan."

"Nonsense boy, you did excellent work. The Pale Elves outsmarted us with their tricky ways. Now let us find the priestess."

The ranger was helped onto Narfi since his legs did not work. He led the group through the forest. They arrived at a river where they saw a female in skimpy clothing with a serpent staff fighting off a bunch of crystal golems. Grongar snarled and waved his hand in a rune shape. The rune glowed and blasted the golems into the water. A shield appeared on his arm and he stepped in front of the priestess. Another golem charged and was shattered by the shield. Grongar looked at the giant shell on his arm and grinned.

The priestess spoke, "Do my eyes deceive me or am I haunted by the dead?"

"Neither priestess, I am here to free your soul from hell."

"Goroth, but you went with our assassin to kill the leader of the Elven assholes."

"Well, it was a trap and I was slain along with her. But I was the only one tosomehow get to the Havens. The rest of you were written out of existence. But that has changed and I am here to rescue you all from this realm."

"I'll believe it when I see it."

The group traversed back the way they came and after many miles, they arrived at a fortress in mid-explosion. Grongar looked around and saw a small body frozen in midair. He leapt up the rubble and scooped the form up before plummeting toward the ground. He landed on an air bubble that was summoned by Bounty Hunter 26.

"Girl, it's time to awaken."

The small girl blinked her eyes and gasped in joy, wrapping her arms around Grongar. He handed her over to the Elder and then spoke, "I will now free all of you."

The scythe appeared in his hand and he swung it. There was a sound of a bell clanging and a bus appeared. The door opened and a cloaked man walked out andmotioned them to enter. As the group walked forward, the man stopped Bounty Hunter 26 and his family. He motioned for Grongar to step forward.

"YOU HAVE DONE WELL, GRONGAR HUNTER. YOU HAVE PASSED YOUR TEST. COME, AND I WILL BRING YOU TO THE HAVENS ALONG WITH CLAN RAGOTH. UNFORTUNATELY, THE OTHERS STILL NEED TO PASS THEIR TESTS. GOODBYE, HUNTER CLAN MINUS GRONGAR. GOOD LUCK"

The bus vanished, leaving Orion, Omega, Li'l Boom, Jubilee, the mystery man, and Bounty Hunter 26. A portal opened and they walked through it. They arrived in a land made of a strange rainbow-like metal.

"I SEE THAT YOU HAVE ARRIVED AT YOUR NEXT DESTINATION. WELCOME TO BISMUTH. YOUR GOAL HERE IS TO RESCUE THE GEM KNIGHTS AND The BEINGS ONLY KNOWN AS PRISM RUSH, LAU REN, AND JACKIE. THIS IS A TEST FOR JUBILEE AND OMEGA'S WIFE"

They came upon a group of beings in the middle of being dismembered by abunch of humanoid crystals. There was a red-brown-skinned girl, a massive woman with garnet armour, a shorter woman with blue skin and purple armour, and a pale pinkarmoured dancer.

The girl with red skin spoke, "Redwood, there's too many of them. Where is Stefania?"

"I don't know, Parvati. We just have to hold out."

The swarm defeated the women. Their mangled bodies lay in pieces on the ground, then reformed as the swarm attacked again. Li'l Boom charged into the fray, her two spears slicing through the enemy army. She leapt back as a large granite foot in sandals smashed into the ground.

The giant granite statue spoke, "You took my little starlight and corrupted her. Your fate has been sealed, little organic."

Jubilee jumped up and sent a wave of pure energy into the granite statue, causing it to crumble. She stood there panting before collapsing unconscious. The bus arrived and the cloaked man walked out and retrieved Jubilee. He motioned Redwood and the others on the bus.

Parvati spoke, "Wait, what about Stefania?"

"SHE AWAITS YOU AT YOUR DESTINATION. NOW HURRY BEFORE THOSE THINGS REFORM AND ATTACK."

They hurried off until they came upon a large Rainbow Pyramid. It was guarded by a large rainbow-haired minotaur with pale skin and crimson eyes. Her lower legs were covered in coarse cobalt blue fur. They could barely make out a slender jackal-headed female with a bow armed and ready for attacks. She stared at them with angry green eyes. Several arrows impacted the ground and exploded. Her companion snarled in rage and shot forward with surprising speed.

"Boom, boom! You murderous bitch! I'll kill you!"

Li'l Boom jumped back from the onslaught. Omega tried to go help but found herself trapped in place. She struggled desperately, trying to free herself.

Bounty Hunter 26 spoke, "Don't bother, sweetie. This being a test for her, we cannot interfere. Just relax and everything will work out."

"They'll kill her. I have to help her."

A large explosion blocked their view and when it had dissipated, Li'l Boom had Prism Rush impaled on her spear. The other spear was embedded in Lau Ren, whodropped into the crater that Li'l Boom had created. She was standing atop Jackie, a Minotaur. The Bus appeared and the grey and black-cloaked reaper walked out.

"NOT HOW I WOULD HAVE DONE IT. BUT YOU PASS. I WILL GIVE YOU A MINUTE TO SAY GOODBYE TO OMEGA. SHE IS NEEDED ELSEWHERE."

"I am a ready reaper. If I say goodbye, it will hold her back. Better for her to be mad at me."

Li'l boom entered the bus and it vanished as another portal opened. The mystery man forcefully grabbed Omega and pulled her through, with the others following closely behind. They arrived in a jungle near a temple to a serpent deity.

They saw two brown-skinned men with a mohawk made of spikes on their heads. They were locked in a constant battle. Whenever they would die, they'd be returned to fighting. Both looked worn down by the constant resurrection. Both were tall with black hair. Only one was broad and thick, while the other was skinny and frail. Their choice of weapons was also different. The broader one used handguns and a shotgun, while the frail one used a trident. The broader one was bald with a goatee, while the thin one had his hair braided into a long war braid. The thin one had a bushy beard and moustache. He also wore a robe with a jetpack. The broader one wore a form-fitting nanotech armour and a cape.

The mystery man stepped forward and spoke, "Lenzo! Xerxes! Cease this meaningless fight. If you truly wish to end it, fight me!"

The broader one, Lenzo, spoke, "Fuck off, brother. This does not concern you."

The thin one, Xerxes, spoke, "Thirteen Hunter. How did you escape my wrath?"

"Skill and the fact you two were written out of existence."

Thirteen Hunter pulled out his flamberge and pointed it at the two of them in a display of dominance. They took the bait and attacked in a fit of wrath. Thirteen Hunter soon had cleaved Xerxes in half and stood over the wounded form of Lenzo.

"Surrender, please, brother. This has gone on long enough."

"You truly are our father's son, which is why I proudly say. Finish me. I will not submit to that weakling's blood."

"So be it."

Thirteen sliced down and Lenzo fell for the last time. The bus came and brought the two onboard.

The reaper spoke, "COME THIRTEEN, HUNTER. YOUR TASK IS COMPLETE."

"I cannot reaper. I must see my siblings through the coming trial."

"I AGREE. GO THEN WITH THE BLESSING OF AZRAEL, THE ALPHA REAPER. THE FINAL DESTINATION IS THROUGH THAT WORMHOLE."

The group were about to enter the wormhole when the Havens of Dead Planets shuddered.

Before them stood a man in a black sleeveless duster with a black cowboy hat and smoke coming from his mouth. Two men appeared wearing the same outfit. They were Silverans, but one had blue skin and the other had red. They were joined by Two women. The women looked alike, except one had frizzy orange hair and a deranged look in her eyes, while the other had olive skin and a look of calm danger in her eyes.

The red-skinned man spoke, "Ah, nephew, I see you are the one in this land. Behold the Eternal known as Devastation. I am Nemo. The man next to me is Cain. Beside us is Pandora and Izzy "Boom Boom" Hunter. We, too, were trapped in this realmbut not because of the Shogun Clan. We were trapped here by the Hellphayth clan. Damnable Gellians tricked us. We came here when we felt another strain of our clan Appear in the Havens of Dead Planets. Shall we help you release Devastation?"

Bounty spoke, "Why? Was he not imprisoned here as punishment?"

Cain, the blue-skinned man, spoke, "He was, but he is now needed. The Pale Ones have nearly conquered Planet Silver. They worshipped him in ancient times. He is to be released to blunt the one they follow now. Lord Dragon, once known as Fringe."

Devastation snarled, "That whelp is still alive? Come face me, judge me."

Bounty Hunter 26 pulled out his halberd. He was ready for battle. He attacked with a flurry of blows that were all easily deflected by Devastation. Cain and Nemo joined in their furious assault and knocked Devastation off his feet. He took off his duster and tossed it aside, where Thirteen picked it up. Devastation flexed every muscle in his body. He then charged Bounty, trying to suplex him. Bounty stood strong and a black blade jettisoned from Devastation's back. Bounty pushed him through the portal.

The rest followed Bounty through the portal and it sealed behind them. Bounty withdrew his blade from Devastation, who vanished. The small group looked around where they had exited and saw that they had arrived in a seemingly deserted space station. Omega stood garbed in some kind of black armour that looked organic, with a hood that hid her face in shadows so only her gold eyes were visible. There was a tall, thin-faced woman next to her, garbed in a crop top with spiked bangles and fingerless gloves. She also had on ripped jeans. Her short hair was a neon blue with pale neon blue highlights. She also had pierced eyebrows and a nose ring. Next to her stood a woman in a trenchcoat and sleek padded leather leggings. This woman had fiery orange hair and seemed younger than the other.

Thirteen looked her over, then looked worried. Orion spoke, "Thirteen, was it? Why do you look worried?"

"Because, boy, I have not seen armour like that since a past life. I remember this station well. It is Plasma Station, a derelict space fortress that watches over Zabara Irridon."

"Why does it worry you so?"

Omega looked at the armour then whispered, "Fuck I know this armour. My past life before the erasure of our timeline. Warlord Novanoir and the Nu-Zed Void. This is that final battle."

The tall woman with neon blue hair spoke, "I don't quite know what's going on here. Kate and I were in the middle of fighting while my boss escaped. Then you weirdos popped out of a wormhole."

The orange-haired girl pulled out a communicator from her trench coat pocket. "Wayne, have you detected any anomalies?"

There was a thick voice that answered, "Yeah, spacetime got vorped. Is everything okay in there!"

"Uh, Doc B got away. Ronaldo and the tweebs went after her. And three weirdos with horns just popped out of a portal."

Bounty Hunter 26 spoke, "Four of us. Count again."

Ember turned towards him and then gasped, "The Demon of Silver!"

"That's my father. I am Bounty Hunter 26, the Left Hand of the Demon. You must be Ember Hawthorn. So we are back on the right timeline. Very good."

He pointed his glaive at Ember and said, "Surrender."

She quickly put her assault rifle away and kneeled before Bounty. He walked into the light and Kate threw up.

A southern voice spoke, "Woah dude, what happened to your face?"

"Ah, you must be Ronaldo. I survived a psionic nuclear detonation that heavily burned the left side of my body."

Kate threw up again. That was when they heard skittering. Ember dragged Kate and Ronaldo to her ship. It lifted off soon after two girls wearing lab coats boarded.

Bounty Hunter 26 scoffed and looked around. Nine heavily armoured creatures with black bio-armour strolled into the docking bay they were in. One of the creatures pointed a serpentine whip at them, which became rigid and formed into a vicious spear. They spoke in guttural hisses and snarls.

"Yeah… no." Bounty Hunter 26 threw a fireball which impacted their armour and set them on fire. He looked around and saw a derelict drop ship. He motioned everyone to get aboard and went into a meditative stance. The ship came to life and he began to do some gentle movements that caused the ship to jerk and then move forward. He clenched his fist and the wall was blown apart. They were free. But he had used too much psychic energy and collapsed. Thirteen growled and shoved his hand forward, causing the ship to shoot straight towards Zabara Irridon.

Izzy "Boom Boom" Hunter typed in a code into her gauntlet. A large cargo ship appeared. Can slashed through one of the Nu-Zed Voids that charged them. The cargo ship landed and the four quickly got on board. The single-eyed woman with purple hair and an Oni horn spoke, "Hi guys, where too?"

Cain spoke, "Hello, Lee. Let's get back to Planet Silver. We have been trapped in that place for far too long. Well, we have, you have been free."

A woman wearing a crop top pink sweater and pink leggings spoke, "I told you it was a bad idea to face Lord Hellphayth by yourself, but no one listens to Amy Tangara."

"Well, dear sister-in-law, we thought we could destroy him, but no. That job fell to somebody else. By the way, do you know who defeated him?"

Lee spoke, "Yeah, our nephew Odin Hunter slew Hellphayth in an explosion from days of being crucified by the Hellphayth of planet Vatika. He wiped out the entire planet. All the souls were then captured by the Seven Great Demon Dukes of the inner Seven Hells."

"Except Lord Hellphayth himself, I am to assume."

Amy spoke, "Yeah, that's right, Cain. Not even the King of the Thirteen Hells could capture his soul. He joined up with a clan by the name of Blood. Lee felt your resurrection and rushed here as quickly as she could. It was just serendipity that we received your distress beacon."

"Cool... cool... now let's get out of here before the Nu-Zed Void get confident."

***

There was a deafening crash outside as a purple-skinned woman began torturing a dark pink girl. She looked up as a lizard man rushed in. "My lady. A massive drop ship just impacted outside. It destroyed the statue to your glorious image."

The woman snarled, "Deal with it, Shatter. I am in the middle of something."

"As you wish."

Shatter walked out of the castle that looked like it had been painted like the colours of dawn and dusk. With him were four girls on chains that he held. There was also a woman dressed as a cowgirl. She had her shotgun primed and ready for anything. The people were being escorted to their homes by various guards dressed in the same colours as the castle.

A porcelain doll woman wearing a see-through top and ripped jeans with a jacket over the top walked into the square. With her was a frail-looking model and a green-skinned druid.

Bounty Hunter 26 walked out, being supported by Thirteen. Omega followed with Orion next to her. Orion spoke, "Sorry for the destruction. We underestimated our velocity. Where are we?"

Shatter spoke, "You have landed in the lands of the Luminous court. You destroyed the statue of our beloved Luminous Princess Dawn Dusk. What do you have to say for yourselves."

Bounty Hunter 26 snorted. "Please bring your beloved dictator out here. I have a message for her."

"Princess Dusk is busy right now. Whatever you have to say to her can be said tome."

"What does the invader want, Shatter?"

"My lady! You should really stay inside."

"Ah, the violent destroyer of the sacred lands of God Silver. How many died foryour amusement. I wonder if you still hear the screams at night when you sleep."

"Jackie, please execute the follower of that wretched demon God Silver. He taintsmy vision."

The woman dressed as a cowgirl quickly pointed her gun at Bounty Hunter 26's head. Thirteen placed his hand on the gun and lowered it.

"I apologise for my brother. He is still doped up on pain medication. As you can see, he is severely burned on one side of his body. He has no idea what he says."

"We don't allow no worshiper of Silver here in our town. Ah, I'll give you a second chance. But keep yer mouth shut."

"We just need to charter a ship to Iridion."

Dusk snarled, "What is taking so long, Jackie?"

"I see no icon of Silver on him. He's drugged out of his mind. Ain't no point in killing a junkie. Especially a junkie with ties to Iridion."

"Well, do something. Sixty lashes should teach him."

Bounty Hunter 26 was forced to the ground and his shirt torn off. The sight of his cracked and charred skin caused several guards to throw up. Even Dusk Dawn was having trouble keeping her lunch down. She quickly turned around and rushed inside. Shatter was the only one unfazed. Jackie pulled out a bullwhip and struck. Blood immediately gushed out of his skin and as the whip recoiled, the blood splattered on her face. She spluttered and when she saw bone through the whip mark, she, too, threw up.

"Bunch of pansies can't even stand the sight of blood. Are we done here?"

Shatter spoke, "Yeah, I don't think any more is going to happen. Butterfly, please treat this man's wound, then find him a way off this continent."

The model nodded and, with the help of the porcelain doll woman and the green-skinned woman, got Bounty Hunter 26 onto a stretcher and into the back of an ambulance."

Thirteen spoke, "You would not happen to know of a place on the outskirts where we can stay. As you can see, our ship is unsalvageable."

"Yeah, you can stay with the Onyx clan. Bubbles, be a dear and escort these things to The quarry. Have Feldspar deal with them."

A grey-skinned woman with a golden eye, an eyepatch, and light blond hair jumped down from a building nearby. She landed with the grace of a flying sumo wrestler and shook her head to clear her vision.

She got up and wobbled slightly, causing Shatter to facepalm. "Alright," he saw an albino with neon blue hair, "DJ Techna, would you be so kind as to get these... peopleout of here before the princess has them executed?"

The woman saluted, then steadied Bubbles and motioned Orion and the others to follow her. Thirteen stayed behind after cloaking himself. He followed after the ambulance. He soon arrived at a massive animal sanctuary. But also a hospital was next to it. He frowned and slipped into the sanctuary. He was knocked unconscious as soon as he entered.

***

Orion looked around the massive quarry that they were being led through. He could see many crystals forming. He was amazed. Omega, on the other hand, was worried. A place like this was great for hiding bodies. They came upon a large wooden home that seemed to be growing out of the quarry wall. Techna banged on the door and then vanished. Bubbles shook her head.

A tall, voluptuous woman opened the door. She was shiny with sweat. She looked down at them. Orion's jaw nearly fell off as he looked her over.

Bubbles spoke, "Hello, missus Shale. Is Feldspar home?"

"Bubbles, what an unfortunate surprise. Yeah, Feldspar is getting out of the shower. Sandstone is in the kitchen if you want something to drink. I'll find a place for these people."

"Mistah Shatter said you guys could take care of them. He doesn't want the princess getting testy. She's already fuming."

A voice spoke in monotone, "Shale let the Hunter clan in. You're letting out thecold."

Shale escorted Orion and Omega in, then motioned them to sit. She helpedSandstone brought out the drinks as an imperious muscular woman walked downstairs in a sports bra and shorts. She was still slightly damp from her shower and her sports bra had absorbed some of the water, revealing some skin. Like her sister, she was grey-skinned with grey, dusky purple hair; even her eyes were grey. She had two small horns on her forehead.

Omega spoke, "You seem to know us. Why?"

"Your father was one of my many mates before I moved here. He and I had a daughter named Cherry. She killed me during the rebellion of Brovone Bjorn. From what I understand, your father was wrought with grief."

Omega shrugged, "That was way before our time. Now Father is just resigned to the fact his family always dies. He's slightly distant because of it."

"Oh sweetie, I'm sorry to hear that. Your father was sweet, but every good thing must come to an end."

Bubbles walked in with an icepack on her head, where it looked like she had rammed into a cabinet. "Missus Feldspar, I need to speak with you privately. It's regarding what you wanted me to look into."

"Come into my office."

***

Thirteen found himself dangling upside down by chains. He was currently looking at two shapely green legs with a small fuzz of orange on them. He saw two amber legs walk next to the green ones.

A soft voice spoke, "Treesie, who's your friend?"

The green legs turned towards the amber legs and he heard a kissing noise. The green legs spoke, "He's just a trespasser, I found while meditating in the garden. Let me deal with him, please."

"Oh, Treesie, he's just here to keep an eye on us so we don't hurt his elder brother."

Thirteen groaned, "Damn it, why did it have to be you. Butterfly of Gaia's order, I am the High Vizier of God Silver. You have a lot of explaining to do."

"I no longer report to any gods. Leave me alone. What's so hard about that."

"Honestly, this is annoying for me too. Can you let me down before I take myself down?"

He heard clinking as the green legs went to his side and he felt one leg come undone, then the other. He dropped to the ground. As he tried to get up, his mechanical legs screeched in protest. *Oh great, I get reincarnated with these things. Why could not Azrael give me back my organic legs?*

Treesie gulped as she stared down at Thirteen. He summoned a black staff with the crest of Hunter on the top. He used it to help himself up before he pulled out a wrench and began banging on his leg with it. The screeching stopped and he visibly relaxed. The three looked around as a large roar echoed throughout the chamber.

The wall caved in and a large blue and silver dragon burst in. "Where is she?"

Treesie quickly began vocalizing a deranged-sounding throat song. The dragon struggled to maintain form. It eventually collapsed into the porcelain doll-like woman that had left with them.

She shook her head, "I'm sorry, darling. I lost control."

"It's okay, Rene. I have plenty in my budget to repair whatever gets broken."

Thirteen raised his eyebrow. "What have you so distraught? I know my brother spoke of a complex devoted to God Silver that was destroyed."

Butterfly shook her head. "No much different than that atrocity. Our friend disappeared quite a while ago after talking to that tyrant about her destruction of the Silver complex. We have been trying to find her since."

They heard heavy footsteps "Hmph, sounds like a job for the Left Hand of the Demon."

Thirteen turned towards his brother. "That is probably the worst idea ever. We are alien invaders. Causing such devastation would certainly lead to us being marked as shoot-on sight. Then how will we get to Irridion?"

"Steal a boat after proving our might."

"You think too much like Father.

Bounty Hunter 26 pulled out his Fogpike. "Yes, brother, I know."

Butterfly spoke, "Woah, whoa, hold on. At least listen before you go psycho killer on Dawn Dusk."

Rene spoke, "I'm sorry, dahlin' we have an opportunity for revenge. I wish to helpthem."

Treesie hummed in thought, then smiled. "Well, since you don't want to back down.

I say you strike where it hurts. The four leaders have a meeting every month. This month happens to be at the Castle of Dawn and Dusk. They will have their elite guards there. So…"

Bounty Hunter 26 smiled darkly. "We kill all of them for their holy purge. I like the idea. When is the meeting?"

Butterfly shook her head in sadness. "Three days from now. Please reconsider. I can keep you two safe. Let the aliens die, you don't have to join them."

Rene stroked Butterfly sadly. "I am sorry, dahling. Our brothers and sisters in faith cry out for vengeance. It must be carried out."

Thirteen smiled sadly. He could not dull his brother's fury. It would be a massacre. He unholstered his Magnum Long-Range Negashooter and began checking the components. He pulled out his Telepiercer and also checked its components. When he was satisfied, he holstered them both and began to sharpen his flamberge.

***

"So the tyrant has her in her dungeon?"

"Little worse than that. She is torturing her and trying to drain her of her powers."

"I see. Thank you for your report, Bubbles. It is as I feared."

"The meeting of the royals will be in three days. If we can strike before, then we won't have any casualties."

"No, I am afraid we will have to strike the day of. With all the royals distracted, we can sneak in and out."

Omega was downstairs hearing all this. She shook her head disapprovingly. Orion looked at her and sighed.

"I suppose you have a better idea than what they are planning?"

"I don't. I am just sad that it will not work. Knowing brother, he has already planned to massacre them all."

"How do you know?"

"Bounty Hunter 26 is the left hand of the demon. Remember, our father is called the Wrath of God Silver."

Sandstone looked at them. "You can hear them?"

"Yes, our clan has really good hearing."

Shale grinned evilly, "Then you can tell us what they are saying."

"They are talking about breaking your sister Kim out of a high-security torture chamber."

"Finally, some action. I'll contact the gang."

Upstairs, Bubbles smiled. "I believe your sisters heard us."

"Good, that gives me more people to work with."

***

Jackie stood in the centre of town. She saw a woman who dyed her hair a neon rainbow run past.

"Prism Bolt! What is going on?"

"All of my guards have come down with a strange plague. I am trying to find the militia members to use them as guards. The high gathering is today at Princess Dawn Dusk's castle. I need guards."

"Well, shoot, hun. Let me grab McIntosh and I'll meet you at the castle."

"Thanks, Jackie. I knew I could count on your help. Grab anyone else from themilitia, you see."

"Will do sugar cube."

Several hours later, Jackie stood at the doors to the castle. She only had a massive red-skinned man next to her. He was wearing the armour of the Holy Order.

"Sorry for taking you out of retirement, McIntosh."

The red man held his hand against his throat and a mechanized voice came out of his mouth. "It's alright, sis. Wasn't doing much anyway."

Prism Bolt came into view looking dejected. As she walked up to Jackie, she sighed, "No one. Everyone seems to be sick. I don't know what happened."

McIntosh spoke, "Gaia's benevolence. I remember seeing her in my dreams last night. She said it would be a bloody day and if we feared our death, she would save us."

Jackie shook her head. "Yep, I can see her doing that. I can also see why no one wants to be around today."

"Hey losers, what's got you down?"

Prism Bolt looked up to see her rival, Lightning Runner. "I have no guards to protect Dawn Dusk with and there's a big meeting of the royals today."

"Sheeit, well, count me in. I'm the best there is."

"Yeah yeah, heard it all before. Put your money where your mouth is."

***

Bounty Hunter 26 looked at Thirteen, who had finished off reassembling his gun for the eleventh time. He looked towards Treesie and Rene. He saw sadness in Butterfly's eyes. He looked around the room and saw the four he had been introduced to. Techna, Lyra, Gilda of Gryphon, and Bonniebell. Both Gilda and Bonniebell were armed to the teeth. Lyra was playing her banjo to soothe Butterfly. Treesie and Rene were prepped for war. Both had the rune armor of God Silver on their clothing or, in the case of Treesie, her bare skin since she had no clothes on. Both also wore bandoliers filled with various bullets and grenades.

Thirteen spoke, "You don't have to do this. Bounty and I can do this without help."

Rene huffed, "You think I don't know this. You are the Voice of the Demon. Your brother is The Left Hand of the Demon. No! I know full well you two can handle this. I want revenge. Do you know what it's like to see all those you care about rounded up and slaughtered in front of the whole village?"

Thirteen was about to say something when Bounty Hunter 26 stopped him by shaking his head. Then he motioned the small group to follow him. The plan was to have Thirteen do most of the slaughter since he was the most armed. Bounty Hunter 26 would be using his Psychic energy to protect the group. But judging by how Rene was on the warpath, she likely would be the one to be doing a lot of the killing.

They arrived at the castle. Bounty Hunter 26 saw numerous guards of the Holy Order. He also noticed the woman in a cowboy outfit on the wall with two heavily armed men. There were two women with wings doing flybys, along with several other winged guards. He also saw the grand ship of the Crystalium Commonwealth. He saw the heavily armoured warship of Queen Solarium of Infernum and the Lunatic battle cruiser. The rulers are all here. Lucky me.

Deep down in the dungeon of Dawn Dusk, a pink-skinned elf lay chained up to a machine. Her hair was long and her eyes grey. In her mind, there were three other personalities. The bouncy jovial Kim, who was currently asleep, so the more vicious one could reign. The vicious one was (pi). Now Pi was the one who protected the more innocent Kim so she did not have to suffer through heartbreak or other traumatizing experiences. Unfortunately, this experience was testing her limits. Next to her was the chaotic one called Screwy. Screwy held untold chaos powers and the machine was tapping directly into Screwy. She was incredibly weak at this time.

Pi looked up at the massive pink-tinted dragon. Bahamut, I cannot keep this up. What should I do? I must preserve Kim's innocence. The Dragon fixed a critical eye on Pi in life, there are many dangers that all people must face. You have done your duty well, but it is time to let go. Kim needs to grow up. If you would wake her, she would tell you this herself. She appreciates you and would never ask you to leave, but she also doesn't want you to strain yourself.

Kim's eyes opened and instead of grey, they were deep crimson. Her hair became bouncy and her skin took on a more hot pink look. Pi's skin was regular pink and, Screwy's was Steel Pink, the Dragon's was magenta. Kim looked around and saw Shatter standing there.

"Hi, Shatter. You may want to get your girls to a safe area. Big things are about to go down. But first, could you be a sweetie and turn off this machine?"

"I can't, Kim. I'm sorry."

"Okidoki, but seriously you may want to hide your girls and yourself for a while. It's safer for them."

"What are you talking about?'

The machine started crackling with energy. The damping coils shattered and Shatter bolted. All the protections that Dawn Dusk had put in place overloaded and melted the machine.

Outside was chaos. Nineteen guards currently lay dead and the rest were fighting off the combined efforts of Rene and Thirteen. That was when the transport vehicles were obliterated by gigantic stone pillars that erupted from the ground. A furious Shale stood there, her eyes glowing with ancient energy. Behind her were Omega and Orion. Next to them stood Bubbles and Sandstone. Sandstone was hiding behind her hair, not wanting to watch the destruction.

Feldspar waved her hand and the Pillars shattered. The shards went flying. Many more guards now littered the ground.

"Sandstone, sweetie, I need you to tend to the wounded."

The girl with her hair over her face shook her head. "Something big is going to happen. I don't want to be at the epicentre."

Bounty Hunter 26 looked around. "Thirteen, Rene, Treesie pull back towards my sister Omega. You too Vinyl, Lyra, and Bonnibell."

The small group pulled back as the ground exploded. Bounty Hunter 26 shielded his eyes from the massive magenta dragon that rose from the ground. Its amber eyes looked around and saw Feldspar. It scrabbled out of the opening and pronked over to her. Feldspar smiled and scratched the Dragon's chin.

Dawn Dusk walked out, followed by Solaria, Selene, and Sin. On the wall of the castle, Jackie and McIntosh stood near a man wearing polished steel armour. He spoke, "Paladin McIntosh, I want you to take down that demon."

"Eeyup."

Jakie spoke, "Now hold on yer holiness. The rulers are out there. They can handle numerous demons. Or was that a lie made to make them look good?"

"Jackie, It's mah duty as a Paladin of the Holy Order to eradicate those of hellish origins."

McIntosh jumped down and calmly walked towards Feldspar. She saw him and shook her head. Orion walked towards McIntosh with his trident. The two warriors squared off and the rulers attacked. Bounty Hunter 26 was thrown to the ground by the maniacal Selene. She grew claws and tried to tear him open. He calmly gripped her claws with his hands and squeezed. She howled in agony as her hands were crushed. He tossed her aside and she rolled several times before hitting a fountain. She struggled to her feet and saw Solaria throwing fire at the other demonic man.

Bounty Hunter 26 stood and dusted himself off. "Empress Solaria of Infernum, Queen Selene of Lunatic, Concubine Sin of Crystalium, and Princess Dawn Dusk of Luminous, you have slain my followers and destroyed many other religions. The Gods have seen your tyranny and have allowed me to seek retribution on their behalf. God Silver has decreed you burn."

Nuclear green flames erupted around Bounty Hunter 26. He advanced towards Selene and she cried out in fear. A whip of fire wrapped around Sin, causing her body to wither to dust. Her husband jumped down and stabbed Bounty through the back in a rage. But the flames wrapped around him and he, too, became dust. When she could no longer feel the chaotic energy she had absorbed from Kim, Dawn Dusk panicked and began using every spell in her arsenal.

Solarium snarled in a fury, "You think fire can kill me? I am the Sun."

She erupted in fire and her bolts became beams and explosions. Thirteen sighed and jumped away from another explosion. He jumped up and grabbed Solaria before dragging her to the ground. His legs began melting under the fury of her fire. Suddenly she went limp. A sinewy spear was embedded in her neck. Omega stood panting, her armour cracked and smouldering. She tried to remain standing, but her frail body was not meant for this kind of activity and she collapsed. Thirteen caught her and lay her aside. He, however, was stuck. His legs had melted in such a way that he could not move them, but they were still in one piece.

Orion had McIntosh on the ropes. He calmly and mechanically took down every defence that McIntosh tried to defend with. He jumped out of the way of a woman covered in electricity. She rolled to a stop lying in a crater as if dead. Another woman, this one with rainbow hair, dove at him. She kicked him hard enough that it sent him off balance. This allowed McIntosh to stab Orion. The knife broke on his skin. McIntosh looked shocked, but that didn't last long as the rainbow-haired woman was caught in the air by Orion and slammed into him, sending them both to the ground. Orion stoodthere and snorted steam from his nose. He raised his trident for the kill but stabbed it into the ground near McIntosh's head.

"I win. Now you need to give it a break. You are the last of your order. I may have need of that in the future."

Dawn Dusk stood there in a fury. She was also terrified and fighting for her life. She had just watched Solaria and Sin get murdered. In Front of her stood Rene and Kim.

Kim spoke, "Dawn, it doesn't have to end like this. You still have a choice."

Rene snarled, "Yes, she can die for killing all my followers."

"Hasn't she suffered enough?"

"How can you say that? She had you locked up and was draining you of all your life force."

"That is true, but she is still our friend deep down."

Dawn Dusk screamed in a feral-like manner and charged the two of them. A shot rang out and she dropped to the ground with a hole in her back. Jackie stood there, her gun smoking. She wiped a tear from her eyes. Then grabbed Kim in a hug. Kim stroked her hair.

"Ahm, so sorry, Sugarcube. Ah, didn't know what she was doing."

Kim smiled, "Don't be sad, be glad. I'm alive and well. I'm just sorry you had to kill her. You shouldn't have her tainted blood on your hands."

Bounty Hunter 26 spoke, "As touching as this reunion is. You need to choose a new leader."

He examined the statue of Selene. Shaking his head in a sad manner, he shrank it down and placed it in his satchel. Shatter walked out with his hands raised in surrender.

Thirteen spoke, "Ah, just the man I was looking for. King Shatter of Infernum. Recall your troops and get a mechanic over here so I can move again."

"You call me King. Why?"

"You are the last royal alive. Therefore the thrones are yours. I suggest you find help. You will need it."

Bounty Hunter 26 looked at them and smirked, "Thirteen, stop messing with the boy. There needs to be a serious leader."

"I'm Prince Shatter of Infernum. I have helped reign in Dawn Dusk's more violent tendencies. I am the best you got."

Bounty smiled, "Well, maybe I underestimated you."

***

King Shatter had been appointed ruler. Orion stood on the dock looking across the ocean. He frowned. Thirteen stood next to him, holding a snoozing Omega. Bounty Hunter 26 was currently loading supplies onto a hover ship.

He turned Thirteen. "What happens if I don't want to do this?"

"I will not force you, Orion. You are the son of Bounty Hunter 13, regardless of what happens. I wish for you to see the state Iridion is in before you make any judgment."

"Very well, brother."

They boarded the ship and saw Feldspar with her three sisters. Feldspar was nude and holding Kim near her. Kim giggled and playfully sucked on her breast.

Sandstone was in the corner blushing at this but was currently masturbating. Orion saw Thirteen massage his forehead and walk over to the bar. Bounty walked over to Sandstone and sat next to her. She ignored him, focusing on her sisters. Omega was still sleeping in Thirteen's arms at the bar. Orion just stared.

Shale spoke, "Sorry about my sisters. They wish to be your entertainment while we travel to Iridion. Enjoy the show. Once the ship starts its path, I will give you a little something. Don't think I didn't notice how you looked at me when I opened the door."

The ship sped off; they would arrive at Iridion within the next five days. About mid-day, the ship stopped near an island. The group disembarked for lunch. Sandstone had grown attached to Bounty and was being held up by him as she ground against him. Her eyes glazed over and her tongue lolled out of her mouth as she thrusted. He sighed. They found a nice shady spot and set up a table. Soon a feast was ready.

Sandstone was still desperately riding Bounty Hunter 26. He sighed and placed his hand against her neck. She went limp and he peeled her off of him. "Food looks good, Feldspar."

"Of course, I am one of the best cooks."

"Yes, being the goddess of hearth and home has its benefits. But that is not who you were before, Dread Goddess."

"Oh, you are your father's son, alright."

"Omega, who was now up, spoke, "Wait, she's a goddess?"

"They're all goddesses. Little Kim is Bahamut's daughter, Shale is the goddess of miners, and Sandstone is the goddess of healing and architecture, which makes me surprised that she could not stop having sex with me. I know I'm not that similar to my father."

"She's been pent up."

"Ah, that would explain it. So Dread Goddess, I did not know there were any followers of you on Zabra."

"There are not. I am trying to stay away from Planet Silver. My desire for your father is too strong."

"Why not accept this? Maybe you two were meant for each other."

"I hope not, but I fear you are correct. Many of my alternate timelinedoppelgangers have stayed with him. I will see what happens, but for now, leave me to my quiet life."

The group ate and relaxed until the sun started its descent into the under realm. They boarded the ship and it set off. Shale stayed close to Orion throughout the night. Sandstone did the same for Bounty. Thirteen, however, stood on deck watching the stars go by. He was unsettled.

Omega walked out in her underwear. "Thirteen, was it? Why are you still awake?"

"Well, I have a feeling in the pit of my stomach that something will go wrong."

"We're the Hunter clan. Doesn't everything go wrong for us?"

"Yes, I suppose you are right. Still, this feeling of unease is troubling."

A voice spoke, "I wouldn't worry too much about it. You'll be dead soon." Numerous shadowy assassins jumped the two. Omega jumped back from one, only to get stabbed through the chest by another. She staggered back and tumbled down the stairs to the sleeping quarters.

Thirteen snarled as he was impaled with a spear. "You made the wrong move."

Thirteen sliced the head off the assassin, causing it to burst into a fine mist that flowed back to the man who spoke, "Kill one another takes its place even you cannot last long against hundreds of them."

Thirteen smirked and sent a beam of fire through the horde. It impacted the man who snarled and snuffed it out. Thirteen charged the man. The man blocked his attacks while his shadow puppets stabbed at and lacerated Thirteen. Thirteen could feel his life fading from him. He struck hard in one last desperate strike. The assassin that had come aboard exploded as Bounty Hunter 26 entered the fray.

As Thirteen passed out, he heard, "I got you, little bro. Rest easy."

Six more assassins appeared; one looked at the charred corpse of his companion and huffed. "Well, that was pointless. So you are Prince Orion's adopted family. Pathetic. I've seen Void Crabs more dangerous than you. However, you are the last one alive besides Orion. Now he can watch as we slay the rest of his family in front of his eyes before we drag him before the king for execution."

"Well, are you going to talk or are you going to kill me."

The assassins all summoned shadow puppets and Bounty Hunter 26 smiled a deadly smile. He shot forward at blinding speeds and bisected three of the assassins before teleporting and beheading two more. He then appeared in front of the one who spoke and stabbed him through the heart.

"How about now?"

"How?"

The assassin dropped dead along with the other five. Orion stood staring at his older brother with shock, terror and dread in his eyes.

"Come along, boy and let's see what we can do for our siblings. Also, for Feldspar and her siblings."

"My sisters and I are okay, but Omega lies on the brink of death and I can see that Thirteen looks close as well. Sandstone is doing what she can to bring back Omega."

Bounty looked at Feldspar and sighed, "She was stabbed by pure darkness, so she is tainted by shadow poison. She will need to be hit with a blast of purifying energy before she can be healed. The same goes for Thirteen."

"I see. Now I know what we're dealing with. Bring Thirteen down to us so we may cleanse and heal him as well."

"I will not need that, Lady Feldspar. Shadows and I get along well. Considering I am an Aberration, life and death are meaningless to me."

The two turned to see Thirteen standing with black smoke pouring from his wounds. His eyes were a deep copper and his hair had become grey in some areas. He tried to move forward but dropped to the deck on his face.

"Ow! Stupid legs."

Bounty shook off his awe and went to help his brother up. "You are too much like our father. At least let Feldspar and her sisters examine you."

"Oh, very well, brother. I will need help moving, though."

Bounty lifted his brother up easily and walked down the stairs leaving an awed Orion behind.

"You best come down as well, young one. In case there are other assassins."

Orion nodded and walked down with Feldspar. As soon as he left, the girl known as Bubbles popped her head out of a box. She climbed out and looked around, grimacing.

"Lady Bubbles, are you sure about this?"

"Of course, Techna or are you Rene now? These guys are our only chance of getting back to Planet Silver. Without wasting ten grand to charter a ship to Silver. Neither of us have that kind of money. So unless you want to continue to whore yourself out for meger cash, this is it."

"It's Rene in control. I have yet to listen to the Sacred Music of Elecktranikka. And what gives you the right to call me a whore?"

"Sorry, but you take cash for sex that is prostitution. Even if it's part of your worshipping of Electranikka."

"Come on, losers get me out of here!"

"Sorry, Gilda. Hang on."

The two pulled out a Gryphonum from the box and she shook herself off. The three shoved the corpses overboard and lay out under the stars. Dawn came and Omega had made a little recovery. The trauma from the battle and now her near-death experience made her already weak body even weaker.

"If only I had the same healing skills as my father, I could help Sandstone with her healing."

Thirteen shook his head and stroked Omega's hair. He moved his hand away to see it covered in black sweat. He spoke while wiping his hand off, "Sandstone, please cease what you are doing. Leave this to me. Her sweat is incredibly toxic right now. Shale, purify your sister and leave with her. I need all of you up on the main deck. I need space to work."

Bounty spoke, "Don't do anything foolish, brother."

"Trust me, Bounty."

Bounty shook his head and left the chamber. Thirteen formed many runes around Omega. He then meditated he mentally dove into her mindscape. He saw her chained up by darkness and walked into view. There was a screech as the shadows recoiled from him. They formed up around their prey and lifted her into the air, using her as acore for a giant shadow demon. Thirteen shook his head and smirked before the staff of shadows appeared in his hand. A beam of pure darkness shot out and struck the shadow demon, causing a portal to open and sucking it inside, leaving a tainted Omega behind. The inky blackness swirled around her. Thirteen touched her and the darkness vanished; he overpowered it and pulled it into his being. His grey spirit just became more grey. He exited her mindscape and saw a feathered serpent demon standing over her.

"Ah, aboot time you showed up, Nemisio."

"So you were expecting me, Thirteen Hunter. Why does this not surprise me?"

"You always did favour her over any of us. She also enjoyed your presence as achild. While you were still mortal."

"It looks as though you have everything under control."

"No, not really. She still needs your cleansing wash before she can awake."

"Very well, though, you must answer my question before I help you. What did thisto my favoured?"

"The answer is simple. We were assaulted by a shadowy assassin whocontrolled darkness puppets. He nearly killed me as well. But because of my affinity with darkness, I was able to survive. She has no affinity with darkness, fire, crystal, or stone-like her siblings."

"Very good I am allowed to help you now."

Thirteen began meditating to recover what he just used up. He raised his eyebrow and his soul split from his body.

Up on deck, Bounty stared at the three trespassers. They cringed under his scrutiny.

"So let me get this straight. You three are from Planet Silver and wish to get back there. And you think we can help with that?"

Bubbles spoke, "Yes, uncle, I know you can help with that."

"And who's daughter are you?"

"I am Bubbles Hunter, daughter of Sin Seeker Hunter."

"I do not know any Sin Seeker in our family."

"You have much to learn then. Once you and your siblings were killed and banished by the Shogun Clan, Grandpa was forced by the gods to help them create powerful followers. It didn't help that he wanted to get rid of the pain the Shogun caused him."

"So he fucked many women. Great. How many siblings do I have now?"

"Fifteen. That is on top of those that are older than you."

Bounty sighed and shook his head. "Well, get me up to date on all the happenings and I will do my best to get you home."

"Sure thing, uncle."

They walked down to see Thirteen sipping a cup of tea with Nemisio while Omega rested in his arms.

"Come, join us, Bounty. The tea is very revitalizing."

"This is by far the most normal I have seen you, Thirteen."

***

It was about midnight when they arrived at the continent of Irridon. It had been an arduous five days, but Feldspar and her sisters had done their best to entertain the Hunter clan. Bounty Hunter 26 and his siblings disembarked the ship along with Bubbles, Rene, and Gilda Gryphon. Feldspar waved them goodbye and the ship disembarked.

They walked through the city on the way to the castle avoiding the guards. When they arrived at the castle, they saw many corpses hanging from their necks. Some were in cages hanging over the fire. Others were impaled on poles. The sign above the courtyard had written on it. This is the fate of those who challenge my rule. Look upon them and despair.

Thirteen spoke, "Behold Orion what the usurpers family did to your people. He is a tyrant and despot. You are the only one fit to rule this land. What say you?"

"Fucking hell, man. I guess I have no choice in this matter. I thought I didn't want to be king, but seeing this display was horrifying. I will take the throne, but how?"

"How do you think? I chose not to go with the reaper for this very reason. I will kill the king on your behalf, and you will take the throne and execute me to appease your people."

"I don't like it, brother. Maybe I can just banish you and forbid you from coming back ever again."

Bounty shook his head. "Think on that later first, you must claim the throne."

Orion aimed his trident at the castle. "I am Orion of Iridion. I am the true king of this city. If you wish to dispute my claim, you may do so with your blade."

A voice from the castle tower spoke, "You have no proof. Guards kill this interloper."

The guards opened fire. Orion stood his ground then swung his trident in an arc, sending the bullets back. He then opened fire with his trident. Meanwhile, Thirteen had arrived in the tower, where he saw the gluttonous man who held the throne. He was currently raping a ten-year-old girl. There were several other ten-year-olds chained up in various erotic positions. All looked well used. The glutton's head fell off his shoulders and Thirteen tossed his corpse out of the tower. The corpse impacted the ground with a squelch. Thirteen undid the chains on the children.

Bounty Hunter 26 looked at the corpse and spoke, "Guards, your king lies dead. If you desire further proof of Orion's claim to the throne, allow him to sit on it. If it does not accept him as ruler, you may kill him."

The gunfire slowed and a large muscular woman with many scars and a missing eye walked out. "I am Queen Rebecca Dreadhand. I will allow this. Guards cease-fire."

She escorted Orion, Omega, and Bounty inside, where there were many guards armed with their guns drawn and ready to fire. She led Orion to the throne. As he sat down, it glowed brightly and a wave of energy washed throughout the kingdom. She stared in horror at Orion.

She fell on her knees in front of him prostrate and bore her breasts in a display of submission. "Your servant awaits her punishment, my king."

Orion shook his head. "No punishment. Your husband lies dead. That is all that is needed."

One of the guards spoke, "What of the slayer of our king? Will you just sit by and let them live?"

"Has there not been enough death? Look at the courtyard, look at the corpses of your people. Look at the children your king rapes every night. It was a mercy that he died."

"Still, my lord, we would feel better about your rule if justice for your predecessor's death was met."

"I feel there has been enough death in my kingdom. Bring him before me." The guards threw Thirteen in front of Orion. "Here is the assassin, my lord."

"You have been found guilty of regicide. I decree you shall hereby be banished across the galaxy to Planet Silver. You are to never return if you are seen here again, you will be executed."

The guards murmured in discontent and Orion sighed. He pulled out his gun and fired, striking

Thirteen in the head. Thirteen slumped to the ground and burst into flames before vanishing. The guards nodded in approval.

Orion spoke, "Now I will be investigating all of the nobles and guards. I want this to be a country of unity. I do not want to see any other tyrant like my predecessor."

Bounty Hunter 26 spoke, "Your Highness, my sibling and I would like to charter a ship off the planet. But we are low on funds…"

"Lady Dreadhand, please escort these aliens to the docking bay and give them the oldest scrap ship you have, but not so old as to be irreparable."

Rebecca nodded and ushered Bounty out. Omega, Bubbles, Gilda, and Rene followed. Orion sighed in defeat and slumped in his chair.

***

Bounty Hunter 26 looked over the controls of the scrap ship. He shook his head and lifted off. Omega was clinging to the chair in terror as the ship screeched and squawked as its junk engine stormed to life. They only made it as far as Plasma Station before the ship began showing signs of wear.

"Pain in my freaking ass. This ship sucks! Ugh."

He landed on Plasma Station and sent out a distress signal on a certain frequency. A massive Leviathan class destroyer dropped out of a black warp hole which disappeared behind it. A woman's face appeared on his junk screen. She was blonde and wore a mechanic's jumpsuit and wore goggles on her head.

"This is Admiral Leda Hunter of the starship Doomshroud. I have received your distress code. Who am I speaking to?"

Bounty Hunter 26 smirked, "Hello, sister. You are speaking with Supreme Grand General Bounty Hunter 26, the Left Hand of the Demon of Silver."

"Holy shit, bro, you're alive?"

"Barely. As you can see, we have had some difficulty."

"Well, I'll send Lude over with a hopper so we can get you back here."

"Unless the hoppers have gotten bigger, you'll need two. I can space walk overthere."

"Wait, who else is with you?"

"Omega, apparently the Daughter of a Sin Seeker Hunter, a Gryphonum, and a follower of the Rave goddess Elektranikka."

"Oh, that's where they disappeared to. Okay, I'll also send Loni and Lida as well. I don't want you to spacewalk here in this condition."

The wall in front of the junk ship exploded, allowing them to see space. Bounty Hunter 26 spoke, "We await your hoppers then."

"Always with the destruction, brother."

"Sorry, my hand slipped."

The three hoppers had soon arrived and Bounty stood guard while the others boarded. He was wary of the Nu-zhed Void. His non-burnt ear flicked in agitation. Finally, he relaxed and boarded the hopper piloted by Lude. The hopper landed inside the Doomshroud. He exited and looked around.

"Looks about the same as when Father was an officer for the Silveran Space Walkers."

Lude smirked, "It should. We purchased it from the fleet as our personal flagship once Bela le Foe passed away. To think they were going to scrap it."

Leda spoke as she entered the bay, "It still works but is starting to show signs of age. Hi big brother." She hugged Bounty and he gently patted her back. "Mm, you still smell so good."

"Get ahold of yourself, Leda. Well, anyway, you can still smell me if you want, but give me a tour first."

"Okay, big bro."

She grasped his hand and led him out the door. Lude just smirked. He followed soon after, along with Omega. Rene and Bubbles had already dragged Gilda off. Loni sighed.

She opened a communicator. "Hey, boss. I think we need to get the family together."

The voice over the speaker replied, "Loni, my boy, what's got you so glum?"

"Bounty Hunter 26 lives and the girls are already getting excited."

"Ah, I see. Well, keep an eye on things. Are there any others?"

"Only Omega. The rest, I think, are lost forever."

"Highly unlikely that Twenty-Six would leave them behind. I suspect they are in the havens. Did you all find Sin Seeker's daughter?"

"Yeah, we have her."

"I'll send out a call. Thanks for the notification."

"Yeah, boss, see you shortly."

On the command deck, Leda was inhaling Bounty Hunter 26's scent. He shook his head and looked at the controls. He managed to open a black warp to Silver and the Doomshroud went through. It reappeared near The Factory Moon White Gold. A large docking station came into view.

A dark-skinned man in a purple business suit with glasses over his red eyes appeared on the screen. "Ah, young Bounty Hunter 26, I see you are back from your foray into the land of dead planets. Welcome back. If you could just dock with Station Hunter, we will have a transport ship for you to get home."

"Thank you, Nox. I see Father has made some changes since my passing."

"Yes. Since he couldn't kill himself, he made many of what he calls improvements."

"Oof. Wait, couldn't you just release him?"

"No, because he is not allowed in the Havens. The gods are incredibly fearful and antagonistic towards him."

"That must have been rough."

"It worked out, though. He is much better now after a bit of therapy with Zarkanus and Shegor. Also, once Vicky and Avol returned to him, he recovered faster."

Leda snuggled deeply into Bounty's coat, her hand was down her pants as she buried her face into him. Her sisters were looking at her with envy. Bounty saw this and frowned. Omega looked dejected. The group boarded the transport ship and it flew down to their father's home in the forest. Bounty Hunter 26 looked at the devastation of the many wars that had taken place once he passed. He sighed. The forest had become much larger now. He could see the Hunter clan fortress as they approached.

The ship docked and he exited. The first thing he saw was a dusky purple-coloured horse-headed girl. He raised his eye, especially since she was stark naked and ploughing another amber horse-headed girl with a toned body and well-defined muscles.

Lude spoke, "Dusk, stop sucking face with Jackie and say hi to your older brother!"

The dusky girl jumped and turned. She looked at Bounty and immediately began measuring his body. "You look different from the others. Why?"

"Others?"

"It's because he is our father's clone."

Bounty turned to see a twelve-foot-tall four-armed well-muscled man with two thick horns that seemed familiar.

"Oh, look at her go. She did the same to me when she saw my legs."

Bounty looked down and smiled. "Thirteen Hunter, you glorious bastard you planned to be shot in the head."

"I shot myself in the head. Orion was showing weakness. I dominated him into killing me. And apparently, like father, I am not welcome in the Havens."

Lude had walked off with Lucy in tow by now. The others had departed as well. Omega was still there. She was sitting on several cargo crates. Her eyes welled up and she hid her face in her hood to prevent the tears from being seen.

A hand touched her shoulder. "Hey, sweetie, why so glum?"

She looked up to see a pale pink face with deep red eyes and orange hair. "Boomie, you came back!"

"Why wouldn't I honey?"

The two hugged and Li'l Boom stroked Omega's head. She rocked Omega until she fell asleep and smiled. Li'l Boom lifted her up easily and carried her to their room. Dusk dragged Bounty Hunter 26 to the main area, where he saw several other Equus, as his brother called them.

Dusk spoke, "Girls, you gotta see our brother. He is incredibly different from the others."

Bounty looked down as he was suddenly bombarded with eight girls, all asking various questions.

"Girls! Girls, one question at a time, please! Woa, be careful of what you touch. If you knock a certain thing loose, you'll be in for a nasty surprise."

A massive man in dark blue power armour walked in. He spoke in a mechanically augmented voice, "And pray, dear brother, what is that?"

"Hello, Nightmare. I'd rather not have a bunch of vomit to clean up."

"Ha ha! Girls, our brother is a near exact replica of our father. He was touched by radioactive fire when he was young and absorbed it into his being. Like Father, he is permanently disfigured because of it."

Dusk looked at the new person and raised her eyebrow. "You don't think we can handle it?"

Nightmare spoke, "Then a question is in order. Have you seen what charred a burned flesh looks like?"

"I only know that my mentor was the goddess of the sun. I have seen her kill people but not burn them. Burning would mean honourable death. All those who opposed her were dishonourable in her eyes."

"Then you had best be careful at what you examine on Bounty Hunter 26."

"So Nightmare, I am guessing Arcanus is around here somewhere."

"He is currently with his daughter as she burns off some energy in the training grounds."

"Why are you here?"

"We came because it's been too long since our family reunited. There are many new faces, as you can see."

"I do see. Let me catch up with my brothers, girls. Then I'll be happy to entertain your questions."

The amber-skinned Equus lit her cigarette with fire conjured from her finger. "Sure, we can wait. Right girls?"

They all nodded and went back to doing what they had been doing before. Bounty Hunter 26 walked off with Nightmare.

"So, care to explain why they seem to have dual souls?"

"Yes. I'm sure you remember our father's fling with Galaxia, the star cutter?"

"Who could forget? She was an interesting warrior goddess."

"Well, she gave birth to three daughters and hid the fact from him. Well, during his slump after you, Goroth, Omega, and Orion were sent to the haven for dead planets, one of those daughters, in her quest for power, slept with him. Her daughter is the amber firemancer. She was led down dark paths by The Dragon. She learned certain thingsthat she tried to implement. Her experiment backfired on her, however. Her sisters found out about it. They stole the data from her and did their own version. Those girls are what you see."

"How are the others, except the Amber one, our sisters then?"

"Solaris infused father's DNA with a fraction of her power."

"Ah, I see where this is going. That kind of energy burns through bodies quickly."

"It does. Four of those girls are undead, sorta."

"So the dual soul is what?"

"Where they get their power. Several chthonic beasts made the bad choice of encouraging Solaris, Selene, and their little sister Cadence de Aphrodite. In turn, their bodies were ripped apart and their souls taken and infused into the girls."

"Fuck how strong are they?"

"Well, Sunspot, the amber girl, destroyed a city with her power and, in turn, was disowned and banished by her mother."

"Well, not as strong as Father, myself, or Thirteen, who could vaporize the planet if we actually let loose. But pretty strong to be able to destroy a city."

They arrived at the training centre and saw Arcanus in the refreshment room. His daughter was still duelling hard light holograms. She seemed to be inexhaustible. Nightmare took this time to leave.

Bounty smirked and walked into the refreshment room. "So old age is finally getting to you, huh, Arcanus."

"You wish. No! Just waiting for Sin Seeker to show up. He said he'd be here with his family to train with Tarot and I. Ah, here he comes."

Bounty turned to see Bubbles coming down the hallway with a slender but imposing Amber Silveran. With this, Silveran was a woman who looked almost like him, but she had deep crimson hair while he had pitch black. Behind them was a large, wild, looking man with long spiky hair. Amidst the hair was a small six-tailed fox snoozing in her makeshift nest.

The amber-skinned Silveran spoke, "Arcanus, who is this?"

"Sin Seeker, this is our older brother Bounty Hunter 26."

"The Left Hand of the Demon? Is he going to be training with us?"

"If he so desires."

"Well, maybe I'll actually have a challenge then. If he decides to train with us."

***

Omega entered the sex dungeon. She was going to thoroughly punish Li'l Boom for not saying goodbye. As she entered, she saw Lude and Lucy having intercourse on the Spine Bed along with an Olayazcan girl who wore a strapon and held a whip. She smirked, but what really intrigued her was Lunatyc and a mystery girl enjoying the Vibro speakers. She also saw Jubilee using the tentacle pit and strangely enough, Lloda was in the corner fully clothed but had a glowing hot pink aura about her. She shrugged and shoved Li'l Boom onto the Destroyer Mach 13. She grinned devilishly as Li'l Boom looked deep into her eyes, eagerly awaiting what was to come.

***

Thirteen sat in the garden smoking his cigar. He saw Nightmare with his suit open, revealing a sickly pale man with a blighted purple gash across his chest.

"You know, Nightmare, I could heal that for you."

"I know your process of healing wounds like this. I would not wish this on anyone."

"Fair, however, let me at least extract the poison."

"If you can do that, I owe you a blowjob."

"Haha, no thanks. This is from the generosity of my cold dead heart."

Thirteen traced many runes around Nightmare. He then placed a large crystal on the ground in front of him. He placed several runes around the crystal as well. As he was doing this, three beings were watching him from the copse of trees. Thirteen sat down between the crystal and Nightmare but off to the side. He entered a meditative state. A blighted purple glow emanated from Nightmare, entered into Thirteen and then exited Thirteen into the crystal. It took two hours for Thirteen to fully extract the poison from Nightmare's system.

As Thirteen finished, a voice spoke, "How did you do that?"

Thirteen opened his eyes and saw a very large wolf-like Nu Silveran. "Who are you?"

"I am Moonstalker, the scourge of the north. Now answer my question."

"It's not something easily learned. Have you heard of transference healing?"

"Yes, where an idiot takes the wound of another to heal them."

"Well, this is almost like transference. I used runecraft to extract the poison and send it into a crystal. The crystal is now a class seventeen poison bomb. I learned the process from Corvus Hunter."

"So you are Hunter clan. Why does your scent seem unfamiliar then?"

"I am a little after your time. I was born after the Noamaizans destroyed City Silver with a psionic Nuclear Bomb."

"Ah, one of the tainted ones. What is your name?"

"I am Thirteen Hunter, The Voice of the Demon and High Vizier of God Silver."

"Hmm. Lofty titles for one such as you."

"I earned them."

A feminine voice spoke from the copse of trees, "Don't antagonize him, Moonstalker. I read about him. He's his father's exact duplicate. But unlike father, he has no qualms about killing his family members."

Moonstalker replied, "I disagree, Cherry. Father killed several of his siblings."

"While true, he did not kill his children. We were killed by his clone Lord Psycheo."

Thirteen spoke, "Cherry? As in the little bitch who tried to assassinate King Blu

Silver and kickstarted The Silver Knight's rebellion."

A heavily scarred and vine-covered woman walked out. Her eyes were blood red and she looked wilted. "Yes, that is me."

"What happened to you?"

"I was a fool and paid for it with my body."

"I see. Would you like to be healed?"

"No one has been able to heal me, but if you can. I will be indebted to you."

Thirteen smirked and waved his hand in a strange pattern. Cherry let out a pitiful whimper as her body changed. Vines shot from Thirteen's arm and wrapped around Cherry. She struggled but was soon silenced. When the vines withdrew back to Thirteen's arm, Cherry collapsed. She gasped as she looked at herself. She was cleansed of her affliction.

"You actually healed me! God, how strong are you?"

Nightmare chuckled, "You only saw a fraction of his power. Look at him through the PsyQi."

Moonstalker and Cherry both did as told. Cherry gasped, "So much grey. I feel like I'm being consumed."

Moonstalker grunted, "So you are truly father's duplicate. I see. Like Bounty Hunter 26, you share the father's curse. Pathetic."

A four-armed onyx-skinned woman with four orange serpentine eyes walked in. She spoke, "Watch your tongue Moonstalker. Many of us share Father's curse."

Moonstalker snarled, "Why are you here, Brandi? I thought I told you not to come near me."

"I came to meditate and overheard your little squabble."

Thirteen smirked, "As a pure blooded Nu Silveran I suspect you see us and our half blood as blight to your pure ways. I suspect also that being a moon priest you see us as prey. And prey is pathetic."

"So the abomination thinks he's so smart."

"I can also tell you are not the real Moonstalker Hunter. I know my brother's aura well and you do not have it. So what did you do to him?"

"The same I will do to you and your blight." The false Moonstalker grew in size and large claws slashed the air in front of Thirteen.

Thirteen barely acknowledged the attack. He lit his cigar and inhaled the medicine. He then blew out a purple smoke that obscured the false Moonstalker's vision. When the false Moonstalker could see, he looked around and felt a sharp pain in his abdomen. He looked down to see a bloodied blade sticking through his sternum. He spit up blood and fell, dissolving into ash which vanished back to its creator. Thirteen snuffed out his cigar and put it away. He shook his head and walked off.

***

Goroth sat looking at the two women before him. He raised his eyebrow. "So you two were born from my mother's friends' wombs. How interesting! May I request your names?"

The woman with fiery hair and wood-textured skin with sharp metal spikes on her shoulders spoke first, "I am Roanquake. My mother was Jinxi Bahamut. As you can see, I am bonded with the elements of fire, wood, and metal. Being a part dragon, I can take ona more imposing form, but I like this one the best."

The woman with ashy white skin and smoked black hair spoke next, "I am Margo Darkspeed. My mother was Vinyl Darkspeed. She was sterile and could not impregnate my mother, Octavia

Darkspeed, so your father volunteered his seed. I am the result."

"Yes, Silveran seed is quite potent and can get almost any species pregnant. I, on the other hand, am a fluke. Gilda Taka-doji, being th' follower of Oni Invictus, usually could not get pregnant by a Silveran. She fucked Bounty into submission when he was about to rampage due to the death of Feldspar and her sisters by Cherry's hand. The Oni god saw this violent display and allowed her to become pregnant. I like to think I've lived up to his expectations. But when you have a brother like Bounty Hunter 26, it's hard to measure up."

A silky, buttery voice spoke, "Oh, it must be my lucky day. Three abominations to consume. Which shall I eat first?"

Goroth spoke, "Do you wish to rethink that wight?"

A ghostly woman with a mouth full of fangs floated into view. She summoned black fire and threw it at the three. Goroth conjured his spiked shield, which reflected the fire back at the wight. She snarled and launched at them. Goroth pulled out the Blackguard Scythe and slew her mid-charge. Her body dissipated into ash and vanished.

"Bounty Hunter 26, we seem to have an issue. A wight just attacked me, Margo, and Roanquake."

"I am well aware, dear brother. Thirteen just notified me about a shapeshifter that tried to mimic Moonstalker. Moonstalker lies dead and father is nowhere to be found."

"Well, shit. Alright, I suggest we pull back to the main area. I have a feeling those Equus girls will need help."

"I'm a pinch busy right now, but Thirteen, Nightmare and Cherry are headed thatway."

A deep voice over their com spoke, "I am already here holding them back. Thankyou for bringing them out into the open."

***

Omega stood over six bodies, her blood dripping from some lacerations to her breasts. "I'd ask who you truly are, Lloda, after that demonic display, but I think I already know."

Lloda smiled, "I think you are wrong. I have always been Lloda. Ever since, an inexperienced summoner conjured me into this world. My body was permanently fused with Lloda Cacophony when she slipped and fell while I was mid-form. She became me and I became her."

"Who failed so hard to do that?"

Lucy whimpered and fell crying, "I was the one. I didn't mean to kill my sister, but..."

Lloda stroked Lucy. "Oh, sweetie, nothing could have prevented this. You barely survived the backfire. Honestly, I'm even surprised the domicile was destroyed and no one was hurt."

Omega started to fall but was caught by Li'l Boom's strong muscular arms. She lay her head against Li'l Boom's shoulder and passed out. Lude stood up while supporting the Olayazcan girl.

Jubilee spoke, "I think we need to get these two to the medical bay then see what we can do to assist our siblings. I just hope we're not too late."

***

Sin Seeker stood over the dissipating form of a giant stone beast. He clutched at the jagged gash that split through his side. "Everyone alright? Roll call!"

"Keiji reporting in don't quite think Tarot is going to be okay."

"Fang Ryofu reporting in. What the hell was that thing?"

"Bounty Hunter 26 reporting in. That was a stone-blood stalker, Ryofu. Shit, we had best get Arcanus and his girl to the med bay. How are you doing, Bubbles?"

"I'm fine, but I think Shimasake overdid it. She's burning up."

The Kitsune howled as her body burst into flame. When the fire vanished, she had another tail. She looked at it and wrapped her paws around it, giggling.

"Nevermind, she was just growing another tail. She's at seven now."

Bounty Hunter 26 smiled, "Alright, I'll get Arcanus and Tarot to the med bay. The rest of you pull back to the main area. This has the smell of Blood clan all over it."

"Will do, beast."

***

Dusk snarled and jumped back from the blood blade. "What the fuck do you want from us?"

The bald woman with blood-red tattoos all over her body spoke, "You killed our sister Bloodmare. You are a threat. I Bloodfey will drain you of your glorious blood."

The light blue Equus, Mint, staggered back from a whip made of blood. While Harpsichord, the teal Equus, tried to pull her mangled body back together.

"Pixie cannot hold it anymore. Pixie is sorry."

The dark blue Equus, Pixie, exploded and a deep red crystalline creature appeared. The others cried out as well and also exploded, revealing many different creatures. The only one still in her normal form was the Amber Equus. She sighed. That was when Thirteen, Nightmare, and Cherry arrived. Nightmare opened fire with his gun slaying the whip-wielding warrior.

The three others besides Bloodfey turned towards him. He smiled and pulled out a sword. "About time, I face a worthy opponent."

The deep voice they had heard over the com spoke, "Do be careful, Nightmare. Those three are Bloodcat, Bloodwolf, and Bloodstone. Bloodwolf is the most dangerous of them since he is the essence of The Dread Wolf of Norvcryog. The bastard who slaughtered millions of Silverans and even slew the Gods when they tried to retaliate. His mind, body, and spirit ceased to exist when Father killed him with the Blade of Vorpal. But he somehow managed to retain some essence which in turn joined with the Blood clan."

Nightmare spoke, "Do we have to be worried about any of the Shogun clan becoming Blood clan?"

Sin Seeker entered into the fray. "They are all dead and in the Havens. I doubt any of them would join with the Blood clan."

Bloodcat was skewered by Pixie and Mint. Bloodstone was quickly dispatched by Fang Ryofu and Keiji. Bloodwolf howled in fury. He leapt forward and took down the Equus girls except for the amber one, who was struggling against him. Sin Seeker and

Fang Ryofu charged him next. He slashed through Sin Seeker's throat and ripped open Fang Ryofu's stomach. The wounded were instantly teleported away. Bloodwolf let out another howl and skewered Nightmare and ripped through Cherry's chest. Both vanished, leaving Thirteen standing there alone. He had teleported Sin Seeker's familyout. Goroth and Bounty Hunter 26 entered the room. A blue-skinned fourth pure Silveran appeared from a cloaking device. He had a bloody trident ready. A final man entered; he was unknown to them, but the portal vanished behind him in a wave of butterflies.

Bloodfey moved to intercept them but fell in two as Bounty Hunter 26 warped through her. He pulled from his hammerspace a purple blade. Goroth brandished his scythe and Thirteen pulled four Void Forged blades from his hammerspace. The amber Equus summoned two fiery blades that looked to be made from the sun itself. Bounty Hunter 26 smiled and snapped his fingers.

A voice over the intercom spoke, "Uh Bounty, the med bay is locked down, Li'l Boom and I can't get out. Why are the others here?"

"Don't worry about it, Lude. Just help the computer with the injured."

Bloodwolf looked at the five and snarled. He leapt at the Equus girl, but she blocked his attack easily. She stabbed him in the chest with her second blade, which burst into flame, consuming Bloodwolf. His smouldering body stood back up and he leapt at the now defenceless Equus. The blue-skinned man stabbed Bloodwolf, who exploded in a shower of gore then reformed. As the blue-skinned man was caught off guard, Bloodwolf slashed at him. Thirteen intercepted him; he stabbed him with all four Void Forged blades. Bloodwolf choked up blood and tried to bite Thirteen. His head fell to the ground as Goroth cleaved through it with the Blackguard Scythe, which had now taken on an ax form. Bounty swung his sword and Bloodwolf ceased to exist in the past, present, and future.

"Lot of trouble he caused us. Where the hell is Father? He should have been here hours ago."

"I'm here. Unfortunately, those Blood clan bastards got the jump on me and dismembered me. Until my body parts are found and incinerated, I cannot rebuild my body. I can, however, make sure those that were critically injured in battle get healed. I'll be in the med bay."

"What do you want us to do about the Blood clan?"

"Bring the bodies outside. Sunspot uses your holy fire to burn the blood off the floor, walls, and whatever else it got on. Then I want you to prepare. The end of the Millenia is near. A large war will take place for the planet. We will be outnumbered. Oh and welcome back to the land of the living. I will notify Gilda you are alive. She will be incredibly happy."

Bounty Hunter 26 spoke, "Uh, before anything, who is the blue fellow?"

Bounty Hunter 13 smiled, "Bounty Hunter 26, meet your younger brother Bounty Hunter 1014. He was born from the ritual that allowed you to be free from the Haven of Dead Planets. Because he has the blood of all three Silveran species, that is, the Taur, the Oni, and the Silverans, he is a skilled and exemplary warrior and spy."

"I see. That does concern me, but I also know the Gods plot and scheme about anything. Very well, come siblings, let us get these bodies outside before their taint gets anywhere else."

The Equus girl nodded and her hands ignited. Bounty Hunter 26, Bounty Hunter 1014, Goroth, and Thirteen began hauling the bodies outside. After they had got the nine bodies outside, they began to hunt for their father's body parts. A large hawk-headed man stood watching the Hunter clan. He shook his head and vaporized his clan members' bodies.

"Lord Dragon, do you truly believe I can stand up to these men when my violent companion Bloodwolf couldn't?"

A greasy black and white-haired man with glowing purple eyes stepped forward. "I do believe you stand a chance. After all, you escaped the Haven Prisons and killed many Angelus and Daemus guards. Your clan members were unaccustomed to the Hunter clan style of combat. But you must also realize it took the Blade of Vorpal to kill Bloodwolf. He would have managed to kill them."

"Very well, but I still think you are putting too much faith in me."

"I am putting as much faith in you, Bloodhawk, as I did in Shogun Yu. He succeeded in annihilating the Hunter clan and sent their souls elsewhere. How they got free from the Haven of Dead planets is beyond me. So yes, I have quite a bit of faith in you."

As the two left, Devon stepped out of an orange portal with Reiga. Reiga went to assist Sunspot inside while she watched them go.

She spoke, "I hope you know what you are doing Dad. I really do."

A booming voice in her head spoke Behold the Chronicler the Most Ancient Z.

She looked as a portal opened and a blue-robed man stepped out. He muttered, "Thank you, Chekkers." then spoke to her directly as a red and black Cheshire Cat rubbed against her legs. "It's all good, sis. I have seen the future. And while Father thinks I am some lazy vagabond. I know many things. It all works out."

"Bounty Hunter 52? I see you are back from your foray into the pathways between realms."

"Yes, I am back. The groundwork has been done. All that is left is for the new goddess to build the remaining."

The Cheshire Cat jumped up onto his shoulder and grinned its menacing grin. She looked at him and shook her head. She walked into the Hunter Clan fortress to see what she could do to help. Bounty Hunter 52 chuckled and scratched the Cheshire's chin before following her.

The Arclands

Rino von Rhino walked out of his ship after it was forced to land. In front of him was a powerful woman in grey combat armour pointing an Infero Boom Boom spear at him. Her green eyes glittered with malice.

"You chaos creatures do not belong on the sacred grounds of Our Lady of War Jeann d'Arc."

Rino scoffed, "The lord of Magix, Merlin, requests our aid in defeating the Pale Elf Menace. Now will you allow us passage to where they are at or will you drain your energy trying to keep our ship here?"

"None may access the Arclands without Jeann d'Arc's permission."

"Very well, girl, you leave me no choice. Open fire."

A voice from his gauntlet spoke, "You sure about that, Rino? She is a possible ally in our quest."

"She refuses to move, so she will be moved."

"Er, let me try to speak with her before we do anything. Come back into the ship. If I fail, you may then open fire on her."

She watched the massive mechanical rhino man snort then walk off into his ship. She then saw a one-armed man in brown combat armour with a tattered half-cloak wrapped around his shoulders walk out. She gulped.

Captain Oneida Blacksin watched the girl survey him. He finally spoke, "So you are Jeann d'Arc's protege. Hmm… yes, you certainly do have some fight in you. If it would make you feel better, why not join us in fighting off the Pale Elf invaders that have already gained a foothold on this continent? We were about to head there when you stopped our ship."

"You are the deadly Oneida, the Blacksin. I thought you were a legend."

"That is new. Anyway, how about what I asked?"

"Yes, I will gladly follow you to hell and back."

"Close enough. Come along, girl. Welcome to the Blackheart Mercenary guild."

"Ohmygod yes!" She quickly and giddily followed Oneida onboard the ship.

They soon arrived at a large burned field. Merlin was standing there throwing barrages of elemental terror at the Pale Elf invaders. Next to him stood the knights of the round protecting their fallen lord. Flitting between infernal portals was a fiery-haired woman with thick hips, spiked forearms, orange-painted horns, and grey skin.

Merlin turned to them after sending up a massive wall of flame. He spoke sternly, "About time you got here. All the heroes who have gone against this Pale Elf horde have died. I came down to assist since all my warriors were dead. As you can see, even the Knights of the Round have come down to fight. Pity that Arthur got stabbed by a sneaky Elf. Nasty wound. I did not know they had tools that could take down a god."

Rino spoke, "Well, Oneida and I are here now. Lower your wall and get Arthur back to Avalon."

"Can't; as long as those creatures are in this realm, the path to Avalon is blocked. We cannot risk the eldritch gods learning the location of Avalon."

Oneida spoke, "Hanna be a dear and grab Braid the Deathseeker. We are going to need his assistance here."

The fiery-haired woman looked worried. "You sure that is a good idea? He's not exactly compassionate towards those that get defeated."

"How many summoned beasts are there?"

"Twenty."

"Twenty, so that means at least twenty groups of Pale ones in summoning circles. That, added to the army that is about to break through the firewall, puts us outnumbered seven thousand to one. Now Rino von Rhino and I may be able to handle one-fourth of that, but you gods are weak to their magic, so that puts Rino and I outnumbered."

A butch voice spoke, "You keep forgetting about me, old man. You going senile?"

Another spoke, "Don't forget I am here as well."

Oneida sighed, "Right. Pie can handle a decent amount and so can The BronzedTitan."

Pi smiled under her helmet and spoke, "We could still use The Deathseeker's help. Please bring him to us, Hanna."

"Your funeral." The fiery redhead then vanished and reappeared with a green-haired man with four arms and electric green eyes. He leaned on his pike emblazoned with the Hunter clan crest.

He spoke, "Why am I here? Have I not done enough for you?"

Oneida replied, "I do apologize for bringing you here. But as you can see, the Arclands have almost fallen. I could use your help in repelling the twenty Horrors that attack us. Then you are free to leave."

"Oh, very well. I will assist."

White fire engulfed the area as Braid charged the eldritch horrors. Pie opened fire with an autocannon that seemed to shoot pastries. As the pastries landed, they exploded into a sticky gel that caught fire easily. Ro-Jath charged into the first set of summoners he saw, swinging his axe, the glowing red blade cutting precisely where it was fatal. Oneida spoke into his communicator and the ship opened fire on the elves. The distraction allowed the gods to vanish through an orange portal made by Hannah. One of the Pale Elves tried to get to the portal but was incinerated by the white fire.

All the Pale Elves soon lay dead. Braid sighed and began walking off. He stopped when he saw a dark-skinned man with a skull painted on his face. The man wore a purple top hat and tailcoat.

"Samedi, why are you here?"

The man spoke in a deep and dark nasaly voice, "I am here to dig your grave. You are burned out."

Braid saw his scorched and smouldering body on the ground with many lacerations and wounds. "I see. Do you need help with any other grave? If I am dead, I may as well help you. After all, we don't want zombies."

"Yes, that would be acceptable."

Rino von Rhino and the others boarded their ship. He saw the armoured woman. "You may as well come with us. Felt a shift, almost as if your goddess bit off more than she could chew."

"She is no longer my goddess. I swore I would follow you until my death. I am your pawn."

"Oh, gods. Very well, girl. Come along, we have much work to do. But first, let me mark you as a Blackheart."

He burned a black sun with a horned skull and a sword sticking through the skull onto her armour. "You are now one of the Blackhearts. I accept your fealty. Let us hope you have the means to back up your words."

***

Noamaiza

A woman with long black hair, green eyes, and two horns that curved up from her temples stood near a woman wearing white and purple amazon combat armour. The woman was not happy.

"Why are you here, Xen-a? Shouldn't you be with Gabrial?"

"Your father allowed me to live as long as I helped out. This is my home as much as it is yours."

"But aren't you and Gabrial connected spiritually or some junk like that?"

"Yes, and it's not junk, we are bonded together no matter how many times we die. We always will find each other."

"Ugh! Regardless, do you know where our third member is?"

A woman in fur armour and green war paint on her face walked into the light. "I am right here, daughter of incest."

The woman sighed, "Hello, Beatrix Badger-Oda. Glad you could make it."

Beatrix smiled, "And I am glad to see you too, Jazzica Hunter. It is a pity your mother could not be here."

"Eris chose to go with her girlfriend to Cloud Cuckoo Land. You know, the flying island built by Chaos to contain his abominations."

"Well, now, not many abominations live there anymore. In fact, I see one in front of me."

"You know the Silveran culture, Beatrix, Incest is not taboo. Many families can tie their lineage back to an incestual couple. Well, not anymore now that only a handful of families remain on Eastern Silver."

"I am sorry, Jazzica. I sometimes forget that your people are being wiped out."

"No, I get it. Continent Silver has no allies. Diavonbre is tenuous allies and Organos only allies with them because of Olayazca. But we have bigger problems. Here come the Pale Elves. Seems they got through the rules or mayhaps Aphrodite Aria and her companions are no more."

"According to Goddess Silver, Aphrodite was slain by the lady of the pure world along with Jeann d'Arc and Old One-eye. The others have shifted their allegiance to Concubine Sylar and Sworn Brother Alexander the Holy Cathedral. That is not necessarily a good thing. But it seems because she is just regaining control that the rules of no man may touch foot on Noamaiza unless born here, is waning."

"Then let us show them the folly of attacking. It may cost us our lives, but we will wipe them out."

"I agree."

The three charged into the enemy slaughtering them. Beatrix whipped up a whirlwind that sucked many of the pale elves into it. She then released her second sword and leapt into the whirlwind. It became bloody. Jazzica threw all of her elemental abilities at the enemy. Some caught fire, others became stone, still more became ice, and the rest fell to the ground foaming at the mouth from her poison attacks. Still, they came. Wave after wave. Even Beatrix, who was the equal to Bounty Hunter 13, was beginning to falter. Jazzica was almost dead due to her using numerous high-level elemental attacks in a short period of time.

There was a thud. Beatrix, Jazzica, and Xen-a were thrown back. Jazzica looked at the massive mechanical Cathedral glowing with white energy. Beside this golem were a mechanical dragon, a mechanical giant, and five mechanical towers that quickly fused together to create a mechanical knight. A woman wearing only a grey duster appeared along with a prismatic maned taur. Finally, a woman wearing a forge master's smoke arrived.

The woman in the duster spoke, "My child, you have done enough. I am here to assist."

Beatrix gasped, "Goddess Silver! Then that must be Concubine Sylar and the Holy Cathedral, Alexander."

The golem chuckled deeply and attacked in unison with the other mechanical beings. Within minutes the Gods had wiped out the Pale Elf invaders before they could even summon an aspect of their dread god.

***

Olayazca

Devon Hunter stood garbed in her battle-kini with her green duster flapping in the wind. She was near a man wearing bone armour with feathers and scales. Next to them stood the heroine Wondra. A portal opened and an olive-skinned man walked out with a green-haired girl next to him.

He spoke, "I am here to assist on behalf of the Queen of the Rising Falls, Myssie Moth."

Devon smiled, "Glad to see you, Markus. I feel better knowing the Rising Falls has my back."

"Of course, you once ruled alongside your brother. Where is he, by the way?"

"Dead and lost to us. We do not know where he was sent. Though father fears it was the Havens of the Dead Planets."

"Eww, pity with what we saw on the way here. We could have used his help."

Devon gulped. "How many did you see?"

"Tens of Thousands. Plus five horrors."

Wondra gasped, "We are outnumbered. There is no way we can win this."

Devon placed her hand on Wondra's shoulder. "Then we die like warriors. We can't allow these blighted Elves to gain a foothold. If they do, then all of Continent Silver is theirs. They want to destroy everything."

"I... I... I understand. I don't know if I can do this. I'm sorry."

Wondra fled, leaving Devon behind. Devon shook her head and sighed, "Oh, Bounty, I wish you were here."

The massive army of Pale Elves soon breached the horizon. Devon gasped as she saw the horrors. Their amorphous yet tentacled shape sent shivers down her spine. Marcus opened fire with his auto turret while the green-haired girl covered herself in her hair and charged into the enemy like a hurricane. Devon raised her sword and a beam struck it, engulfing it in holy fire. The Bone Armored man pulled out a club covered in onyx spines. He chanted something in Olayazcan and he began to glow. A shape reminiscent of a feathered serpent rose behind him and he became a blur.

Even with Nemisio's help, Devon was being pushed back. Marcus was thrown into a tree by a horror and he went limp. This caused the green-haired girl to lose focus in worry and get a Pale Elf blade stabbed into her. She coughed up some blood and went limp. Nemisio suddenly cried out as three horrors converged on him. They tried to tear him apart.

The five horrors suddenly went rigid and exploded all over the Pale Elf army. Devon gasped as she saw Thirteen Hunter brandishing a black blade. Thirteen swung the blade sending a beam of energy that sliced through three-fourths of the army, causing them to be vaporized. He walked over and healed Nemisio, Marcus, and the green-haired girl. He smiled and vanished.

Devon stared down the last fourth of the army and raised her sword in preparation. Their general walked forward and lay his sword at her feet.

"You have bested us. We surrender. Please do not slay any more of my men."

"Why surrender now?"

"Not all of us wish to conquer Silver. Lord Dragon was the one who desired that. He killed our gods and forced us to worship his ally from beyond time and space. The Cult of the Horror are the ones that control and summon those things."

"I see. So the Cult of the Horror was forcing you to fight or else. I get it. Help my companions onto the ship that is coming down now. Then we will see what I want to do with you."

As the large ship bearing the mark of the Blackheart guild landed, it kicked up some dirt. As it landed, a glow emanated from the ground and the Magic Melody of the universe changed. Rino Von Rhino walked out. A beam shot out of the ground and disappeared over the horizon. Rino lit his cigar and blew the smoke from his nose.

Devon spoke, "Hold your blade. They have surrendered."

"Have they now? Very well. The prison is still mostly empty. I will escort themthere."

"First, though, let them do as I commanded."

Rino stepped aside as the Elves brought the injured warriors aboard. Rino thenled them to the hospital wing. When the three were placed in healing vats, he escorted them to the prison. He saw Pie sitting with the four previous prisoners.

The General of the Pale Elf army gasped, "Queen Schlaughter, you are alive?"

The woman smiled, "Yes, my friend, I am. When I saw my chance, I surrendered. I was afraid the Demon of Silver would strike me down anyway, but his hand was merciful."

***

Organos

A very tall woman with a scar down her forehead stood protectively over the body of another woman who looked exactly like her. Behind her, there was a man wearing organic armour. He held a blade that seemed to be made of some kind of energy. His face was skull-like, with glowing yellow eyes. Surrounding them was an army of Pale Elves and their horrors. She whimpered but stayed strong.

The man spoke, "Joe, what is taking so long?"

A skull rolled into the small clearing. Then an explosion happened, incinerating many of the horrors. From the smoke came a tall, slender man with no discernable features wearing a black tracksuit. His head was covered in nails. Next to him was a slightly less tall but still slender man made of bones. The bone man picked up his skull and placed it back on his neck. He bowed in a joker fashion and several more horrors exploded into nothing.

The woman gulped as the slender man slid over to her. He picked up the fallen woman and disappeared. Gunfire erupted from the sky. There was a thump as a large Rhino-headed cyborg touched down. As he landed, he set down a woman in grey combat armour. The Bronze armoured Dwarven Silveran next to them swung his red axe in an arc that cleaved many elves in twain. The ship that was with them sped away. The rhino man smiled and opened fire with his chain gun. Soon all but one platoon of Elves lay in pools of their own blood. He lit his cigar and exhaled the blue smoke.

The Dwarven Silveran spoke, "Ah, if it isn't little Arctos. You did well holding up. Where is Reiga?"

A whisper in the wind spoke, "I retrieved her, for she lay wounded and dying. In doing so, I saved her life."

"Ah, Slender Boogey. What is one of the lesser eternals doing here?"

"The same could be said of you Ro-Jath. Or should I call you by your true name?"

"Bup, bup, bup, let's just keep that unspoken."

"Yes, I thought so. My reasons are my own, just as yours are your own. So Bronze Titan, what is to be done with the final Elves?"

"Rino?"

The rhino man snorted then spoke, "Leader of the Pale Elven forces. Why do you hesitate? Make your mind up soon or I may finish the job."

The leader of the last platoon was a young woman with a severely scarred face. She lit her cigar and brushed her short hair back. "I was just debating with myself. I challenge you to a keg off."

"Now that is interesting. Let us up the stakes a bit. This is Tiamat's Tooth. It is the highest level of alcohol in the galaxy. Also a speciality of Casualty Station. Only three people have ever survived imbibing this drink. If you lose, you will likely be dead. But for some reason, if you win.

You may take this land."

The two sat down and Ro-jath placed the first two shots of Tiamat's Tooth in front of them. She drank it and placed her cup upside down. She grinned smugly. Rino drank his shot. The next one was placed down and she lifted it up only to fall on her face unconscious. Rino drank his shot and her shot, then smirked.

"I win. He shot up a flare and a Leviathan class ship appeared overhead. It beamed the elven army up into its prison cells, then disappeared. Rino nodded and poured himself another drink.

***

Diavonbre

Axel, the Fury of the Dancing Flames, dodged an attack by a slimy horror. He snorted and blew more fire from his mouth. "Burn, Baby Burn! Dance Flames Dance!"

The tall, imposing Brown Silveran next to him spoke, "Calm yourself, Axel. Don't burn them too fast. Focus on the horrors. My halberd will handle the Pale ones."

"I am doing the best I can, Lord Wulf. They just keep coming and your pals are out of commission."

Axel Wulf looked over to where a Gigas Silveran was tending to the wounds of a pack of Hyaenidae and two Serpenti. He shook his head. He blocked an attack by a rather brave Pale Elf who had opted to fight up close and personal instead of far away like the others. A shot went through his head and his body drastically changed. The smoke that billowed off of him became flames. And he took on the form of a bipedal winged wolf with tusks. His berserker rage exploded and he shot forward with the flames. He tore into the Pale Elf army. But there were still too many of them and he was quickly losing ground.

A large metallic pink dragon swooped from the sky alongside a massive Sphynx and a flock of Harpies armed with guns and landed. It swiped through one of the larger horrors causing the horror to vaporize. A woman with grey skin that looked to be made of metal, wood, stone, and flesh jumped off and went to the summoner Elves. She massacred them as the Harpies opened fire, raining steel from the sky. This forced the other Elves to back off a safe distance allowing some breathing room. The Pale Elves put up a barrier and seemed to begin debating with each other.

The dragon spoke, "There we go, Roanquake. That should buy us time. Get both Axel's to safety. You there, Belias, load up the injured onto the truck. I'll fly them out of here."

Belias rumbled, "Yes, lady Bahamut."

"Please call me Jinkxi."

"No, that would be disrespectful to your lineage."

"Whatever! You keep being you. Are they ready?"

"Yes."

"Then away I go." She flew off with the large medical truck leaving Roanquake and Belias behind. The Harpies followed soon after, but the Sphynx stayed. They watched as the Pale Elves quickly turned on each other. Belias sharpened his Baal Heth blade. Finally, the barrier went down and several Elves came towards them unarmed.

The tall, muscular Pale Elf with black hair and an unmistakable scent of a female spoke, "You have bested us. Please, we surrender. Can you come to heal our injured?"

Belias nodded his head. A hand held him back and he looked down at Roanquake. She spoke, "Please, uncle, be careful. It could be a trap."

"Do not worry yourself, little one. I can handle it. I survived the army that was sent after you as a baby. A small band of Elves is nothing."

"Just be careful. I don't trust these Elves."

He chuckled and walked over to the woman. "You take me to them, the rest of you stay here under the watchful eye of my niece."

The woman gulped as she stared up at him. "You looked smaller before."

"Hiding something, are we?"

"No! Just impressed with your stature."

He chuckled and followed her into the camp. He could see the bloodbath that took place. The wounded were all in a row lying down, with one Elf doing her best to heal them. She looked up at Belias and whimpered.

Belias spoke into his com, "Fury of the Dancing Flames, please signal for the Garuda Class Airship. We need the prison and medical facility."

"It's coming in now."

A large stingray-shaped ship landed and a large Shark Man walked out. He looked around and shook his head in bemusement. There was a Giant Crocodile Lizardman next to him holding a shotgun. Behind them was a behemoth of a robot. He had a pot belly and a large gear rotating on his back. One side of his rectangular body was painted red, the other side painted black. The shark looked curiously at Belias, then grinned.

The Crocodile man spoke, "Why are we here, Sting Ray? This is pointless."

The shark man smiled again. "We are here because I felt like it. Also, Argentorado and Talicon wish to assist Planet Silver."

Belias spoke, "You are not the airship I requested. Who are you?"

A large red knight walked out. Followed by another large man dressed in Mandelic power armour. The knight looked Belias over and then nodded.

He spoke in a heavy accent, "I am Jason Red. I am Bounty Hunter 13's sworn brother. We have been out of contact for some time. I came to check up on him. But itlooks as though you have injured warriors. Allow us to assist. Stinger one is equipped with a medical facility that can bring back the dead, so to speak."

"If you are his sworn sibling, you should know who I am."

"Yes, Belias, I know you. However, not because of Bounty Hunter 13. I know you from my stepbrother Leslie Torque."

"Then I trust you. I also trust you know what will happen if you betray me."

"Do not worry, Belias. I have no desire to test my luck. Now help us load these injured on the med carts coming out... now."

A large floating flatbed hovered out. It was being pushed by a pale man in all-black combat armour. His short black and grey hair spiked up. He had an eyepatch over his right eye. He was with an amber girl with three scars down her face. Her blond hair was a buzz cut and she was also dressed in black combat armour."

Belias rumbled, "Deathknight of Casualty Station. What are you doing here?"

The man looked up at Belias and then let out a hearty laugh. "Oi Belias, been a while, old man. So this is where you disappeared to. And I am no longer a Deathknight. Retired about a century ago and settled down with my partner. Call me Luke Darkfaith."

"Wait, you are one of the famous Darkfaith clan members?"

"Surprised? You shouldn't be. Most Deathknights can trace their lineage back to a Darkfaith, except for those pirates from the Blackheart fleet that ascended up the ranks to Deathknight. My son is already a Deathknight and he just turned two hundred."

The small group loaded the injured on the flatbed and then pushed it back into Stinger One. Belias rumbled, "Roanquake, you may escort the others back here. I have a prison ship ready for them."

His com chirped, "So they were not lying. Thank the gods. Come on, you jerks, follow me or perish."

"Be nice. They are no longer our enemy."

"Ugh, fine! Please follow me. I will make sure you get a good meal in your cells."

"Much better. Speaking of... thank you for your assistance, Goddess Cleopatra. Iam sorry you could not wet your claws."

The Sphinx smirked and flew off. She landed on a cliff overlooking the battlefield. Five women stood there.

The pink-armoured woman spoke, "I see that they managed to break the willpower of these pale ones."

The black-clothed woman spoke, "Yes, our brother's seed is certainly impressive. Roanquake is dangerous. I like her."

The woman with teal on spoke, "Of course you would, Lucina or should I call you Lucifer now?"

"I am Lucina Hunter, sister to the demon still. However, Lucifer Ankara is still my code name. So whatever makes you feel better, Rani."

The sphynx spoke, "What is the plan from here? The Gods are concerned and many are losing faith in Silver. I am still strong in my faith that he will somehow have a trick up his sleeve, but even I can't deny that the Pale Elves are almost ready to conquer the planet."

A blue-skinned woman with punk clothing spoke, "Fear not, Lady Cleopatra. We are the Daughters of Lord Bounty Hunter 12. His Plan B. We can assuredly hold back the Pale Elf horde."

"Can you, though? That remains to be seen. Regardless should you win the Alliance of the Sphinx, Efreet and Bahamut still standin' their faith in God Silver."

***

Irescotwel

Leslie Torque dodged a blade swipe from a Pale Elf warrior. Next to him were Arcanus Hunter and Gilda Taka-doji. Both were easily decimating the Pale Elf warriors that had opted to fight up close and personal with the three of them. Arcanus was using his Oni powers given to him by the Oni God for his hands in the massacre of the Xin clan and their Holy Order of Oni Hunters. Gilda was still sour that she had been overlooked by her god. But in a way, she was happy. Let someone else deal with the asshole who forsook the Oni and allowed the Oni Hunters to run rampant. She sidestepped a Pale Elf warrior and then stabbed him as he reeled from her dodge. The attack let up.

Gilda spoke in her gruff voice, "Wonder what they are planning. Are you okay, Arcanus?"

The man in blue bone armour next to her smirked, "I'm getting my workout in for the day, that's for sure."

"What about you, Leslie?"

"I am getting tired. I am not as spry as I once was."

"Why don't you back off for a bit and use the turret on Arcanus' ship."

"That sounds like a plan, lass."

The red and grey-haired man with a red and grey beard and red eyes jumped and landed on top of a turret seat. His amber-red face shined with sweat. He used the sleeve of his shirt to wipe some sweat from his vision. Then blinked.

"Ah, laddie, by any chance, do you have a contingency for an abomination from beyond space and time?"

Arcanus looked up and saw the slimy horror advance. "Well, that's new."

Gilda rasped, "So the answer, Leslie, is no."

"Then you best be saying your prayers."

That was when a large stingray-like ship opened fire from the sky, causing the horror to dissolve as the summoning circle was destroyed. Leslie blinked, then smiled. As the ship descended, the Pale Elf forces tried to destroy it. However, the hard light shields vaporized most of the incoming gunfire. The ones that got through fizzled out against the hull. The ship landed and a pale man in black combat armour jumped off along with an amber woman in black combat armour. He had an eyepatch on his right eye, while she had an eyepatch on her left where a claw mark-like scar was. The two lay down, covering fire while a large alligator lizard man lumbered out with a chain gun. Heopened fire with the gun, allowing a large shark-man to zip forward and begin cutting into the pale elf army. A red knight and a large golden gargoyle also walked out and beganto attack the enemy. Then a large rectangular robot with a potbelly and treads on wheels zoomed out. He put his body in front of the three of them and opened fire with his chaingun fingers. Blackheart one came into view and landed, allowing Rino von Rhino to get off. He shook his head sadly as he watched the massacre. Even I did not kill this many during the Chaos War. Oh, Volk and Harl, I miss you so much. This would be so much easier to do with you two by my side. The ship flew off. When the gunfire stopped, only nine Pale Elves remained. Two were cowering in terror while the restdropped their guns. Rino walked over to them and looked them over. Satisfied, he motioned the rest to follow him. They obeyed. He escorted them onto Stinger One.

***

Norvcryog

Moonstalker Hunter stood next to his elder sister Cherry. She was wrapped up in a heating suit since the poison in her system made her plant-like. The cold was wilting her. He looked in the distance. He could see the armies of the pale ones. They had already overcome Capital City. He could see the city burning. He could also see the Pale Elves slaughtering all the citizens. Once again, I fail in my duty to protect the people. Ugh. Am I forever going to be useless? He lifted Cherry up and walked away. The snow engulfed him. When it cleared, he saw a large ship waiting next to a crystal-clear dragon.

Her white scales were polished so as to reflect the snow making her near invisible. He saw his father talking with her. As he neared, he was startled to see a woman in a black and purple dress. Her eyes were covered by a band. Next to her stood a vicious-looking Dwarv Silveran.

She turned towards him and he could swear he felt his soul being judged. He did his best to maintain composure until his father spoke.

"Moonstalker. I am glad to see you still live. I was worried when I heard that the cities of Yggdrasil, Vanaheim, Alfheim, Muspell, and Niflheim fell."

He fell to his knees in front of his father and began weeping, "I was too weak to save any of them. I thought being a hero was some great thing."

Bounty knelt down and helped his son up and held him as best he could. Moonstalker was fifteen feet, while Bounty was only thirteen feet. "Being a hero is never easy. Especially now. The Pale Elves outnumber many armies thanks to their horrors. But I am proud of what you have accomplished, even if that is staying alive."

Cherry stirred and looked up at her father, seeing him seemed to invigorate her. Her leafy hair seemed to become livelier. He motioned her over and she wrapped her arms around him. He smiled and snapped his fingers, causing the two to vanish. He had sent them back to his home on Silver.

He looked at Karen. "So, Rokos, what do you think now?"

"You are still under scrutiny, Demon of Silver. But I can see some value in you. But now, how will you deal with the Pale Elves on this continent? They have made great headway."

"By letting someone else deal with it." "Who would that be?"

"Someone who, when revived, will likely be a big mistake."

"I am unsure about who you speak?"

"Behold my mistake!" Bounty pulled out his purple blade that could kill a soul. "You see, Karen, whoever this blade kills ceases to exist. It was once held by Bloodhawk, the destroyer. When I severed his arm in the havens, it fell to the locked sector. When I had killed the being his arm had become, the blade became one with me. But the alternative is true as well. Dark magics of the soul shorn, I summon you. Revive the Dread Wolf of Norvcryog."

There was a dark howl as a large Canis with an eyepatch and a large scar appeared. He looked at Bounty, then rasped, "Why did you bring me back to existence? Are you senile?"

"Hardly my wolfy enemy. You will be unable to slay me until you have completed your mission."

"Ugh! What, then is my mission?"

"Destroy the Pale Elf armies that have invaded Norvcryog. You will then be approached by a man known as Lord Dragon. From there, it is your choice what to do."

He scoffed, then let out an enraged howl and vanished. Karen stared at Bounty inshock.

She spoke, "He killed your people. He defeated the gods. Hells, he even slew you.Some of his essences became Bloodwolf, who slew your children. Why, then, did you bring him to this world?"

"I see great things for him. Once he is approached by Lord Dragon again, he will refuse him like the first time Lord Dragon approached him. This will cause Lord Dragon to get desperate. He will bring forth Zmatek. Then I will be able to destroy both of them. Plus, I revived him. His death and nonexistence will temper him. I see him becoming something else."

Ro-Jath spoke, "I see you still lack sensibility. I do not know how well this plan of yours will go."

"Says the man who hides from his past."

"Hmph."

The three left Norvcryog to the Dread Wolf. The Dread Wolf slaughtered the armies of the Pale Elves. Those that survived the first onslaught fled. His visage was so terrifying it caused him to become famous among the future generations of Pale Elves. He eviscerated the throat of the final Pale Elf general. He wiped the blood off of his claws on his fur.

"I see you still live, Dread Wolf. I come bringing you an offer you cannot refuse."

Dread Wolf turned to see the greasy man in green robes with his glowing purple eyes. "Hmph, Lord Dragon. What is this so-called un-refusable offer?"

"Join me and we can rule this world together."

"Ha! Only weaklings say that. You are not worth my time. Now begone before I decide to eviscerate you."

"Still a fool, I see. You lesser beasts will be wiped out all the same. I will see you on the chopping block."

"All talk! I grow tired of your presence."

Dread Wolf lunged at Lord Dragon. His claw slashed across Lord Dragon's face. Lord Dragon reeled from the attack. He snarled and vanished through a slimy green portal. Dread Wolf smirked and walked off. Leaving the remaining survivors to fend for themselves. Several hours later, he returned with some Nidavellir. The Nidavellir began rebuilding while Dread Wolf began training those willing to fight. He was the New Old One-Eye; his predecessor had been a naive moron and had suffered the consequences.

***

The Upper Depths

Bounty Hunter 13 stood leaning heavily on the cane of shadows. He had sweat running down his body. Dee Dee Hunter, his former brother now turned sister, stared down at her new body.

She spoke, "What did you do, little brother?"

"I made the world remember you, sister brother. Well, now, only sister. You were born a man but with feminine reproductive organs. Now you no longer have the masculine gene. Through a curse our father inadvertently put on you, the world forgot you existed. He was being petty. Very much like what happened to Braid. He deemed you worthless."

"I know. Because we didn't fit his version of the Hunter prophecy, he cast all of your older siblings aside."

"You are now whole or a version of whole."

"No, you were right the first time. I never felt like a man, thanks to my vagina. I always felt more like a woman. You have brought my mind and soul in balance with my body. Now if only my siblings were here."

A shadowy voice spoke, "Who's to say we aren't?"

Bounty smiled, "Chain, you old bastard, how did I overlook you?"

A man wrapped in bandages wearing a black cloak materialized out of the shadows. "My my, look at you, Bounty. You certainly grew up ugly."

"It's what happens when one's body can no longer keep up with their soul."

"Ah, Dee Dee, there you are. It is good to see you."

"Chain, what happened to you?'

"My body could no longer keep up. I am but a soul trapped in this outfit. More shadow than man."

Bounty smiled and tapped the Cane of Shadows on the ground, causing Chain to gasp. The shadows poured off his soul, cleansing it from their darkness. Bounty stood tall as the shadows struck him. They billowed off of him and were pulled into the Cane of Shadows. His blind grey eyes glittered almost malevolently. Rino von Rhino stood watching the reunion. He smiled.

Two Anubi walked over to them. One was female and the other male. Both radiated grey. The male suddenly went for Rino. His arms wrapped around him.

"Brother, it is you. Why did you take that form?"

Rino looked at the man hugging him and gently placed his arm around him. "Because Volk, it was the body my soul was placed in when I reincarnated. Then the lovely woman next to you must be Harl. I have been searching for you two for a long time."

Bounty raised his eyebrow. Then grinned, "Ah, you are my grandfather? Now that is interesting. But I also have a feeling of something else. Hmm. Ah, well, can't go down that path."

"I am sorry, Bounty, but this is where we part ways. My crew and I can no longer assist you or the dark woman. I hope you can forgive me."

"Ha! Don't worry about it, Rino. The Blackheart mercenaries will always have a place within Hunter Corporation. You have fulfilled your duty well. Come Pie, we have yet to finish this off."

The black-armoured Equus nodded. Karen spoke, "So if they are leaving us, how do we get to where we need to go?"

Ro-jath grimaced, "You just had to ask that question."

A large stingray-like ship descended. It opened up, revealing a red knight. "Bounty, it seems you need a lift."

Bounty looked up. "Argentorado? What in the thirteen hells are you doing here?"

"Come aboard and find out!"

Bounty hefted the three of his companions up and leapt. He landed on the top of the ship. "Oops, too high. Ah well. Here I'll lower you three down to the ramp."

As soon as the four got aboard, the ship flew off towards Continent Silver. Karen eyed the strange aliens. One was a massive shark man; one was a gigantic crocodile man, the other was wearing Mandela Power Armor from planet Metallic, one was an amber-skinned woman with a scar and eyepatch, while the man next to her was ashy white skinned with an eyepatch and black and grey camo armour, There was a cocky looking bronze-skinned man, a feather and fur clothed gunmetal grey-skinned man holding a black and silver sword, also a large rectangular robot with guns for fingers and a large gear rotating on his back, the final two scared her. One was the red knight who seemed to have a deep crimson aura and his red steel blade glittered with ancient energy. The last was large, his golden skin rippled with muscle. His two large bat wings were wrapped around him and he wielded a chain and sickle that was looped aroundhis waist like a belt. His face was very bat-like and his large ears twitched in annoyance.

He spoke, "Why is the reaper so scared?"

Bounty looked at her, then at them. "I do believe it is your presence she fears. She is but a mouse compared to us giants."

"Ah, I see! I understand her completely."

The knight spoke, "It also doesn't help that all of us are chosen by our patron god and therefore are strong and it may hurt her eyes to see us, especially if she relies on the PsyQi to see like our friend. Hi there, Argentorado Red 100 at your service."

Karen cleared her head then spoke, "I am not blind like Bounty Hunter 13 and can see you perfectly. I am just amazed that he has friends."

The Metallican spoke in his mechanically enhanced voice, "Yes, well, we have not been in contact for some time. Almost estranged, but our gods each told us that if Silver fell to the Pale Hordes that they may try to take the galaxy by force. We are the inner ring and, therefore, the main defensive line for the Star Vale. If we fall, the Star Vale can be pierced and then the first sector will fall. By the way, I am Talicon Metalcurse of the Metallic Osiris guard."

Bounty spoke, "Karen of Rokos, meet my allies. The shark is called Stingora Ray of the Ray clan of Stinalta. The big golden gargoyle is Bat Wing of Gold, the Lizard-man is Scarr, and the two that seem inseparable are Luke and Pain Darkfaith. The other two already gave their names. However, the last three are Azolas Dule of Bronze, Chief Coyote Black-fang of Gunmetal, and the Robot Robotechno 100 of planet Robotechnos He and his planet were once forgotten by the galaxy, but I reversed that. Robotchnos is a wholly robotic planet."

"I still can't fathom why you have friends. You are the most hated man in the galaxy."

"Ha! Like Talicon said, we have been estranged for quite some time. They are only here on orders from their gods. The Pale Elf menace is that severe."

The ship stopped above a small Island with a massive temple. Bounty looked down at it and then shrugged. He vanished along with Karen. They appeared near an all-grey Taur, which was strange since all Taur have different fur colours than their skin.

Bounty spoke, "Gunnar, what is wrong?"

"We have a small problem, Demon of Silver, look."

Bounty did and saw a formless mass that then shapeshifted into an ancient-looking man.

"Bloodsoul Invictus, why are you here?"

"I came to beg you for mercy."

"Oh?"

"Please, my son is rash, but he does not deserve what is coming. I know the Blood clan does not deserve mercy. That is why I was imprisoned by Coldharbour. You freed me."

"Yes, and you spread your taint to those who would seek ultimate power and revenge."

"They all lie dead now. Only my son Bloodhawk remains. Please, God Silver, please, I beg you to save him."

"Karen, judge the man."

"Don't tell me what to do, beast. But he has been judged. Goodbye, Bloodsoul. The haven prisons await you."

Bloodsoul bowed and a beam struck him, causing him to vanish.

Bounty spoke, "Well, Gunnar, that takes care of that. Will you be joining the final battle?"

"We will see. I still have many Taur here who desire to return to Coldharbour. I may still see you at the end of things."

Bounty nodded and vanished alongside Karen. She looked at him. "I judge you unworthy. You are a dangerous man. But death enjoys you. Damsel Death is my mistress. You are to be spared the culling. I leave you now, Burned Walker. Immortality is your fate."

***

Dragons Den Island

Elena Hunter stood with her shield sword, looking at the fleet of Pale Elf watercraft advancing on Dragons Den Island. Their Arial fleet had been wiped out by the Dragons. Now they looked to step on land. She was ready for them, along with the entire Scale folk army. There would be blood everywhere. The scale folk hated Elf kind with a passion. There was a large quake and a massive tidal wave engulfed the Pale Elf ships. A huge maelstrom whipped up. Elena could see inside that maelstrom was the Great Silver Dragon, the Husband of Planet Silver. What few ships that survived made landfall. The slaughter was swift and merciless. Elena grimaced and teleported off the island. She saw her brother Bounty's home and fell unconscious. Bounty picked her up.

"Whoops, sorry, Elena. Thought you were someone else."

Silver Destiny

Bounty Hunter 13 stood in a wide open plain. The trees had retreated for they had sensed impending danger. He looked back at his allies. His family members were led by Devon and Bounty Hunter 26. His friends were led by Argentorado 100, Rojath and Karen stood next to Elena and Gilda, only one of his siblings, Eris, chose to show up. In front of them, all was a massive horde of horrors and their summoners. He could see Lord Dragon in the back next to Bloodhawk, the destroyer and a being wearing the armour of chaos. He could also see five of his forgotten enemies.

Thirteen spoke, "So not only do we have to contest the Pale Elf horrors but also Zmatek, the first God Silver, then turned God Chaos. Also, a man from the past and Bloodhawk. This should be fun."

Bounty Hunter 13 spoke, "It's not going to be that fun. I am going to be facing Bloodhawk, Lord Dragon, and Zmatek. You and our allies will be facing the Pale Elf horrors and the Pale Elf army. You will also be facing my rivals Lord Slayerhammer, Lord Hellphayth, and Lord Slaughter."

Lord Dragon smiled as he looked upon the Gems from his original homeworld. It had taken him almost a millennium to find them all. With these, he was guaranteed to win. He looked down at his army.

"Go, my warriors. Destroy the last vestiges of this wretched planet. Then when this land falls, all others will follow."

There was a blinding flash of light and almost half of the Pale Elf army vanished. Lord Dragon blinked and looked down to see the Gems missing.

A silky voice spoke, "Hello, Fringe. I see your ambitions still are grandiose. I am sorry, but I can not allow you to succeed."

"Tannid, you... damn traitor. This is for our people to give us a new planet to call home."

"No, this is not for our people; otherwise, you would not have subjugated them and forced them to serve the ancient horror. This has always been about your ambition. Well, now fate has you by the balls just like your rival."

He turned to strike, but she was gone. A soft silky laughter hung in the air. He growled, then snorted. "It doesn't matter anymore. Now that I have weakened the barrier, the great horror from beyond time and space will be able to break through. Go, my army, destroy all who stand in your way."

His army charged forward. Bounty Hunter 26 pointed his sword up and his family charged forward and the two sides clashed. Bounty Hunter 13 snapped his fingers and he, Zmatek, Lord Dragon, and Bloodhawk appeared in empty space where a portal was forming. Zmatek scoffed. Then incinerated Bloodhawk. A bloody beam struck Bounty as he absorbed Bloodhawk into himself.

Lord Dragon yelled, "What was that for?"

Zmatek pointed at the portal, which suddenly burst open. A many tentacled monstrosity began to emerge. Lord Dragon grinned maniacally. He then grabbed Zmatek and absorbed his power, donning the chaos armour and stabbing the weakened Zmatek with a blade forged from his blood. Zmatek rasped, "Why?"

"You are no longer needed, old man. Behold Demon! Behold the great destroyer."

"Unimpressive. Sorry Lord Dragon, with what I have been through, a creature likethat is a drop in the bucket."

"It doesn't matter, he will consume you, then I will take down all the gods. And be supreme God of my new planet."

"You have gone completely mad."

A gruff voice spoke, "He's damn right."

Bounty smirked, "Hello, Shegor. Are the Others here as well?"

God Silver walked out of the stars. "Yes, we are, old man."

"See Lord Dragon. Your little apocalypse will be stopped by Bounty Hunter 13. All twelve of us."

"That is what you think, whelp! I am millions of years old. I have had time to plan. Do you truly think I would not plan for God Silver to intervene?"

"What part of Twelve Bounty Hunter 13's don't you understand?"

Ten more walked out of the stars. Lord Dragon looked sweaty. He panicked and summoned several thousand horrors. Bounty Hunter 13 and his godly counterparts charged into battle. Bounty Hunter 13 struck hard and fast at Lord Dragon. Lord Dragon screamed in rage and absorbed all of the Horrors and the great blasphemy from beyond time and space. His new monstrous visage was able to banish several of the gods, but Bounty Hunter 13 snorted. Lady Wyvern appeared and handed him a case which glowed and was absorbed by him. He roared in pain as four new arms burst from his torso. His burned side healed fully. No longer was it cracked and leaking. He still had a burn, but it was only a scar now.

He looked down at his visage and smiled. The other gods were startled and were quickly banished. Bounty Hunter 13 snapped his fingers and they all returned. He looked at Lord Dragon.

"I banish you to nothing, Lord Dragon. In doing so, I bring back Bloodhawk, the destroyer. You can keep Zmatek. Goodbye for eternity. May you suffer."

"I am all-powerful! You can't do that!"

"You used up all your power absorbing Athwntheziluxbthyvzsor. You have nothing left. Your cult lies dead and bloody. The Pale Elves that survived are now out of your reach. You are nothing."

The portal he had used to summon Athwntheziluxbthyvzsor yanked him in and sealed up. The mark of Bounty Hunter 13's Hunter clan appeared briefly, then vanished. The twelve other Bounty Hunter 13's returned to their roles in the Havens. Only Lady Wyvern remained.

"I am surprised at you, Bounty Hunter 3. At first, I believed you to be unworthy. Your power scared me. But I did not expect the remains of my home planet to bind with you."

"So I am bound with the Gems of the Dragon. Which effectively makes me immortal. Fate has come to pass. But what do you mean by Bounty Hunter 3? I am the thirteenth Hunter."

"The only Bounty Hunter 13 who was reincarnated from his ancestor. Here let me restore some of your memory."

"Ah, I see now. What of my children? Has my curse affected them?"

***

Bounty Hunter 26 stood triumphant over the bodies of his fallen foes. Thirteen Hunter leaned against a tree, panting while Devon treated the wounds of the others. Nightmare lit his cigar and inhaled the pain medication.

Gilda Taka-doji was also smoking one of the cigars. Her balefire burns glowed brightly from her exertion. Next to her were Axel Wulf and Gunnar Rhapsody. They were both drinking from their flasks. Vinyl Darkspeed was playing a tune on her turntable and she was breathing slowly.

Elena clung tightly to the body of Eris. She was weeping.

"Allow me to help. She is drained of her chaotic energy. She is barely alive."

Elena looked up at Rojath. He placed his palm on Eris and a large explosion happened.

Eris gasped for breath. "Fukking hell. What was that for?"

Elena gasped. "Oh gods, you live?"

Rojath smiled and walked away. "Oh no, you don't Grimm Chaosforge. You get back here."

"Sorry, Elena, I have duties to attend to. Especially with Karen of Rokos gone. I must administer last rights."

"Promise you won't disappear. We have a lot to go over."

"Ugh, fine. I will stay after my duties are performed."

As he began to perform the last rights on the Pale Elf horde that had been slain, several of the allied forces began to glow.

Gilda looked at her glowing aura. "So I become what I hate. Oh well. I will live up to the expectations placed on me."

Llude spoke, "Uh, Lunatic, what is going on?"

Lunatic looked down as her body began to change. "Oh no!"

Lodi gasped, "Lucy, what did you do?"

Lucy whimpered, "I didn't do anything to Lunatyc."

Lunatic sighed, "No, you did not, Lucy, at least not in this timeline. In an alternate timeline, We were members of the Hawthorn family. Like in this timeline, you desired the taboo. The succubus you summoned was bound to me. I was reincarnated in place of this timeline's Lunatyc. She desired to stay in the Havens and be with her family. But at the same time, she did not want to leave this family. So I took her place."

Lucy looked at Lodi and Lunatyc as both began to change drastically. Lodi took on her more demonic appearance with the spiky long hair and the horns visible. Her eyes became more teal and her body more voluptuous. Lunatic, on the other hand, became less voluptuous. Her skin turned electric blue and her hair became a neon blue that almost looked like fire. Her clothing became far more spikey.

Lica began to change, as well. Her brown hair became darker, two small spikes formed on her shoulders, and several tendrils burst forth from her back. The tendrils almost looked like electrical wires.

She grinned, "Ah, the exshperiment wash a shuccessh. I have been waiting for the effects to take place."

Loda Cacaphony also transformed into a succubus hybrid. Lucy whimpered. Loda stroked her. "It's alright, big sis. In an alternate timeline, I helped you summon the succubus, for in that timeline, I desired you. I still do. But when the succubus was summoned, she was far stronger than either of us could handle. I cast a spell that dragged her into me. In our permafusion you were hurt. I never left your side, even after you struck at me in anger. The succubus wanted me to consume you. I wrestled control at the cost of my soul binding with her. I took this Loda's place when she wanted to stay in the havens."

None of the others experienced much change. Devon, Bounty Hunter 26, Thirteen, and Nightmare all looked the same. However, Sin Seeker suddenly grew a tail and larger horns.

Sin Seeker looked at his tail and scoffed, "That's what I get for trusting the Monkey King. Ah, well."

Thirteen spoke, "Uh, what just happened?"

"You ascended to Godhood."

"Father?"

Bounty Hunter 13 appeared, "And it's your own damn fault. That is what you get for calling yourself the High Vizier of Silver. The same goes for you, Bounty. By calling yourself the Left Hand of the Demon, you ascended as well. I am unsure why Devon ascended, though, I have a strong theory. As she is literally of my blood, my curse affected her. So she is now a Goddess."

Reiga spoke, "And what of Arctos and myself?"

"As you are children of myself and Hannah, the master of the Dimensional knife, you were already demi-goddesses. So it is of no surprise that you ascended. But do not worry, my children, even if your family dies, you will still be able to be with them in the havens. You do not have Godly duties. I, on the other hand, do. I leave you but temporarily. Enjoy the peace. It is well deserved."

***

Carzoka

Strange is the night where black stars rise, And strange moons circle through the skies. Queen Schlaughter stood on a pyramid. She was looking out across the lands. She had been teleported here along with all of her brethren. Before she stood the dread gods of old. The Eternal Devastation, Seraphot, the one-winged Daeva, The White lord of Destruction Kuja, The Evil Priest Seemoor Delta, The Mad Jester of the Moon, and The Chancellor. But the one that terrified her the most was Lady Wyvern.

Then the sky split with lightning as the three moons turned aquamarine. A woman appeared with three others. An icy woman made of frost, a bird woman made of mercury and shadows, and a being who looked like an amalgamation of every beast folk of Planet Silver. They were led by a woman made of magma and onyx. Her six eyes glowed orange and her six arms pulsed with orange runes.

Lady Wyvern spoke, "Goddess Velris, you honour us with your presence."

Velris looked at Lady Wyvern then shook her head. "Why did you call me here, Lady Wyvern?"

"To help you become what is needed for this planet. You defeated God Silver in combat. But he has many strong chosen ones. You have nothing and no young Gabby does not count since she is of God Silver. I am here to teach you the essence of life. You will need someone who can match Bounty Hunter 13. But to do so, you must follow certain steps. Come forth, Queen Schlaughter. Come forth, General Kraxen. Your desire for each other is well known. Consummate that desire in the central temple."

The two gulped and walked into the temple. Lady Wyvern smiled, "Now that a seed is planted, you must imbue it. They consummate their desire under the three moons of Silver while they are full within one year's time. When the three moons are full and Aquamarine, a child will be born. This child will have the same curse as Bounty Hunter 13. She will be strong but hated. She will have five siblings aside from herself. One will be imbued with chaos, one will be imbued with the forest, one will be imbued with the sky, Shadows will love another, and the final will be like the light. She will be strong and will be your chosen."

One year later, The Magic Melody of the Universe echoed through the souls of the living. Tonight the melody would change. Whether for better or worse depends on who is speaking. Inside a large temple, Lady Wyvern stood with Goddess Velris. It smelled like blood, shit, and sulfur. In front of them was an elvish girl of the mountains, an elvish male wrapped in bandages, and Queen Schlaughter panting in agony as a small head was pushed out of her body. That was where the stink was wafting from. The head was followed by a body and was lifted into a bowl of water, where the elvish girl cleaned it.

The elvish girl spoke, "It's a boy. His eyes are like a Syrien's. What should his name be?"

The bandaged man looked at the child and saw it smile as a storm blew in. He nodded his head and spoke, "This looks like the one father wanted to be named Chiroptera. Which means that the girl that will be breached next is Tanya."

The next two came in quick succession. One male, the other female, a huge blast of thunder shook the room, causing the boy to scream and cry in terror. The bandaged man rolled his eyes. "Yep, figured that's why. He shall be named Myst for his cowardice. The girl is Enyo or, in common, Aerin."

The elf girl brought both over to the bowl and bathed them, soothing the boy until he fell asleep. She handed them over to the next servant girl, who soon found herself being sucked on by the girl.

Everyone in the room suddenly clutched their heads in pain as the woman screamed really loud. The storm outside suddenly became much worse than before. The sky was shredded by lightning and the house shook, trying to be torn apart. The only thing visible was the constellation of the Hunter. There was also a surprise as the Halberd of the Warrior appeared. No one saw the Prisoner's Chains appear as well. The moons took on a soothing aquamarine and the forest awoke. It would be a bloody night. Many huge sigils and runes suddenly lit up the home. Outside, numerous puffballs floated up the mountain, searching for the energy the runes blocked. Inside, the smell of gore was replaced by the smell of cinnamon.

"Whichever child is next is a powerful one. Svētais sūdi! Her psychic energy is tearing open the sky, causing a psychic storm. Good thing we're on a mountain with no living things outside or we'd be in trouble."

As the child was breached, the girl spoke, "By the gods, look at her eyes. They have no pupils. She is blind. Please tell me this isn't who I fear; it is?"

Lady Wyvern chuckled at her dramatics. "I am afraid so. Meet Bonnie Honetear 13, your most powerful and therefore cursed sister."

The one helping with the birth spoke, "If that's Bonnie Honetear 13, then... quick, get me the knives and anaesthetics. We're going to have to cut her open."

The two were suddenly drafted into surgery. Velris anaesthetised Queen Schlaughter while Lady Wyvern began brushing some strange-smelling liquid on her stomach. Then she pulled out a serrated knife. She used the sharp, not serrated, side to cut a small line across her womb.

Lady Wyvern tossed the knife behind her and it landed perfectly in the sink. She dug both hands into the cut she made and then tore open the womb pulling out two very small, very bloody children. She handed them to Velris, who waved her hands, causing three runes to appear. There was a sound not unlike the tearing of paper as the two were separated.

One quick surgery later and two children lay side by side on another operating table. Queen Schlaughter lay near dead from the energy she had expelled while giving birth. Lady Wyvern stroked her head.

"You did well, my child. I am proud of you. And now Goddess Velris, you now have a favoured."

Bounty Hunter 13 watched from the shadows. He smirked as he folded his four arms in prayer. *There you are, Vera. Welcome back to the land of the living. So this is godhood. How strange! After all these thousands of years fighting it. It feels natural.*

***

"There you are, old man!"

Gods and Politics part 3

Bounty looked up from his contemplation to see his children standing there. He chuckled. "I am still waiting on something. Go on, I'll be home shortly."

Bounty Hunter 26 spoke, "Not now, Old man. We have to learn what our new path will be now that we are gods. You're the only one who can teach us."

"No, he isn't. Hello nephew."

Bounty Hunter 26 looked over to where the voice came from to see a man dressed in a brown, white, and tan sleeveless robe with a horned badger mask covering his face. His shoulder spikes looked eerily like Bounty Hunter 13's; he even had the same body shape as Bounty Hunter 13.

"Who are you?"

Bounty Hunter 13 smiled, "Children, I'd like you to meet Lord Badger, my brother Mystic Hunter 4. The others will soon be here."

"Already are, bro."

A mismatched Kimera walked into the clearing along with a hot pink three-foot-tall cat creature with moth wings and a single horn on her head. Those two were followed by a weathered-looking man wearing a cloak of feathers and bone armour. His horns were spiral-shaped and his yellow eyes were like that of a bird.

"The Kimera is your aunt Eris Unicaterfly and her wife, Felicity Unicaterfly. The dark fellow is The Lord of the Woods and Nevermore's favoured, Corvus Hunter."

"Why did you never tell us you had siblings?"

"That is the first lesson. Before you are three of the dimensional protectors. I am Lord Shadow, Eris is Lord Chaos, and Mystic is Lord Badger. We are meant to be secretive and unknowable. I was never meant to have children who cared for me. You all were supposed to forget about me like I never existed in your life. But because you defied fate, you are ascended."

"What are our names now?"

"Devon, you are The Blade of the Demon's blood because you styled yourself as the blade of your brother. Bounty, because you call yourself the Left Hand of The Demon of Silver, that shall be your name. Your Ascension was not through fighting fate. You ascended to be with your wife, Lady Pegasus. You both died protecting Silver from Noamaiza and that allowed the first phase of ascension."

Bounty Hunter 26 nodded and smiled. "Of course. Why the hell not? Makes as much sense as any of this."

Bounty chuckled, "Thirteen since you style yourself as The High Vizier of Silver, that is your name now. Bounty Hunter 1014, you are the Infernal Sigil of Black Death, also known as the Slayer. Nightmare Hunter, since your soul has been through three gods, you have ascended to become Venomfire. Lodi, Loda, and Lunatyc, I am sorry that you are immortal. You will suffer seeing your siblings pass from this world. I am so sorry that that is your fate. Because you are part succubus, you are now like the gods, immortal."

Llodi smiled, "That's alright, Dad. I already suffered seeing them die thrice already. It is nothing new to me. And I will help Lunatyc and Loda through their grief."

"Sin Seeker, it looks as though you have become the second Monkey King. He must have imbued you with his power."

"He did but said there were no side effects. Eh, I always suspected I would ascend anyway. Since the Oni Shibata and Oichi Oda are bound to me."

Lodi spoke, "Wait, what of Lica? How did she become like us?"

Lica smiled, "I exshperimented on myshelf. I have been running the same exshperiment since our siblings were massacred by Cherry."

There was a booming voice, "Hated Hunter clan get off my land."

Bounty snorted derisively, "We were just leaving Lady Velris. I wish you the best of luck in your endeavours."

"You and your clan are a blight upon this land and I hope to see you all dead."

"Too late for that. Many of us have ascended to godhood."

"Then suffer."

She sent a wave against them. Bounty Hunter 13 absorbed the power as he teleported his children and siblings away. His burned side became blackened stone with silver scars cutting through it like lightning. She drew her sword. He drew him then scoffed. He sheathed his weapon and turned his back on Velris and walked off. She lunged for him. Her blade connected with his flesh and shattered. He looked back at her and then sighed. He reforged her blade and stabbed it into a black stone. That was when Gilda Taka-doji appeared with her blade drawn. A fiery explosion erupted from the ground and a Hyenidae and a winged boar-faced man walked from it. A grey bell appeared and chimed a dark reverberation and a Grey Taur walked out. A woman wearing a grey duster over tribal armour appeared as well. Then an Icy Howl shattered the air and the Dread Wolf appeared from a pool of Icy Blood. Bounty saw them and nodded.

Bounty spoke, "Work towards a better future, Velris. Don't be me and wallow in the past. Planet Silver is your garden now. God Silver is now the God of the Hunter clan. You have succeeded where no other god has. That should be enough. Come along my friends, we have much to accomplish."

Velris cried out, "I will spend eternity if I have to. I will wipe out your clan. You do not walk away. Face me so I may kill you."

Gilda was about to strike at her when the Dread Wolf stepped forward. "Lady Velris, I am the new Old One-Eye. We of the Triad against Silver seek to assist you. You succeeded in dispatching Silver. Something that we have been trying to do for many years. Come and meet us. Let us plot some more."

He led her off and Bounty placed his hand on Gilda. The two followed in the wake of Axel and Shenzi. Gunnar sighed and vanished back to his temple. The world as he knew it ended. A new one was to begin.

Printed in the USA
CPSIA information can be obtained
at www.ICGtesting.com
LVHW082245181023
761450LV00020B/1764